John Wilson

Homer and his translators, and the Greek drama

John Wilson

Homer and his translators, and the Greek drama

ISBN/EAN: 9783337304874

Printed in Europe, USA, Canada, Australia, Japan

Cover: Foto ©Andreas Hilbeck / pixelio.de

More available books at **www.hansebooks.com**

AND

THE GREEK DRAMA

BY

PROFESSOR WILSON

WILLIAM BLACKWOOD AND SONS
EDINBURGH AND LONDON
MDCCCLX

HOMER AND HIS TRANSLATORS.

PREFATORY NOTE.

In the Articles which compose this Volume, an unusually large amount of extract is embodied. This was rendered unavoidable by the aim which the Author had in view,—his object being not merely to discuss the poetry of Homer, but to present a critical estimate of the comparative merits of his translators. Superabundant, therefore, as the quotations may seem, the Editor has made no attempt at retrenchment, believing that, while the general reader will not object to the amount, the classical student will find in the specimens so fully placed before him, and so sagaciously commented on, the means of improving his scholarship, of cultivating his taste, and of sharpening his critical penetration. As fit accompaniments to the genial criticism of Professor Wilson, and as throwing much light on all that relates to the Homeric poems, the Editor may refer the studious reader to the erudite argumentation of Colonel Mure (*History of the Literature of Ancient Greece*, vol. i.), the vigorous summary of Professor Blackie (*Encyclopedia Britannica*, article " Homer,") and the able advocacy and fine analysis of Mr Gladstone (*Oxford Essays*, 1857).

The edition of Cowper's Homer which Professor Wilson made use of when writing these critiques was *the second*. Mr Southey has preferred to reprint *the first* edition in his collection of Cowper's Works. The two editions differ from each other very materially, and it is quite possible that Mr Southey may have been right in his opinion that the first is the better version of the two. In the present volume, however, it was of course necessary to reprint the extracts from the edition from which they were originally taken, as it is only to these that the reviewer's criticisms apply.

E S S A Y S

CRITICAL AND IMAGINATIVE.

HOMER AND HIS TRANSLATORS.[1]

CRITIQUE I.

[APRIL 1831.]

PATRIOTS as we are, as well as Cosmopolites, how relieving, how refreshing, how invigorating, and how elevating to our senses and our souls, to fly from politics to poetry—from the Honourable House to the Immortal Homer — from the vapid feuds of placemen and reformers, to the deadly wrath of nature's heroic sons—from the helpless limp of any middle-aged Smith, to the elastic lameness of old Vulcan—from O'Connell and Hunt, with their matchless blacking, to

"Atrides, king of men, and Thetis' godlike son!"

We are no great Greek scholars ; but we can force our way, *vi et armis*, through the Iliad. What we do not clearly, we dimly, understand, and are happy in the glorious glimpses ; in the full unbroken light, we bask like an eagle in the sunshine that emblazons his eyrie ; in the gloom that sometimes falls suddenly down on his inspired rhapsodies, as if from a tower of clouds, we are for a time eyeless as "blind Mæonides," while with him we enjoy "the darkness that may be felt ; " as the lightnings of his genius flash, lo ! before our wide imagination ascends " stately-structured Troy," expand

---

[1] *The Iliad of Homer.* Translated by WILLIAM SOTHEBY. 1831.

tented shore and masted sea ; and in that thunder we dream
of the nod that shuddered Olympus.

Some people believe in twenty Homers—we in one. Nature
is not so prodigal of her great poets. Heaven only knows the
number of her own stars—no astronomer may ever count them
—but the soul-stars of earth are but few ; and with this
Perryan pen could we name them all. Who ever heard of two
Miltons—of two Shakespeares ? That there should even have
been one of each, is a mystery, when we look at what are
called men. Who, then, after considering that argument,
will believe that Greece of old was glorified by a numerous
brotherhood of coeval genii of mortal birth, all " building up
the lofty rhyme," till beneath their harmonious hands, arose,
in its perfect proportions, immortal in its beauty and magnificence, " The Tale of Troy Divine ? "

Was Homer savage or civilised ? Both. So was Achilles.
Conceived by a goddess, and begotten by a hero, that half-
celestial child sat at the knees of a formidable Gamaliel—
Chiron the Centaur. Grown up to perfect stature, his was
the Beauty of the Passions — Apollo's self, in his loveliness,
not a more majestic minister of death. Paint him in two
words—STORMY SUNSHINE.

Was the breath of life ever in that shining savage—or was
he but a lustrous shadow in blind Homer's imagination ?
What matters it ? All *is* that we *think ;* no other existence ;
Homer *thought* Achilles ; clouds are transient, but Troy's
towers are eternal. Oh ! call not Greek a dead language, if
you have a soul to be saved ! The bard who created, and the
heroes who fought in the Iliad, are therein not entombed, but
enshrined ; and their spirits will continue to breathe and burn
there, till the stars are cast from the firmament, and there is
an end to what we here call Life.

Homer, you know, wrote in Greek, and in many dialects.
He has been translated into English, which, in heroic measures,
you know, admits but of one. All translation of the highest
poetry, we hold, must be, such is the mysterious incarnation of
thought and feeling in language, at best but a majestic mockery
—something ghostlike ; when supposed most substantial, suddenly seeming most a shadow — or change that image, why,
then, like a broken rainbow, or say, rather, like a rainbow re-
fracted, as well as reflected, from the sky-gazing sea. Glorious pieces of colour are lying here and there, reminding

us of what, a moment before, we beheld in a perfect arch on heaven.

But while the nations of the earth all speak in different tongues—they all feel with one heart, and they all think with one brain. Therefore, he who hath the gift of tongues, may, from an alien language, transfuse much of the meaning that inspirits it into his own ; although still we must always be inclined to say, listening to the " repeated strain,"

"Alike, but oh! how different."

All truly great or good poets desire that all mankind should, as far as it is possible, enjoy all that in the human is most divine ; and therefore while each has,

" Like Prometheus, stolen the fire from heaven,"

they have all exultingly availed themselves of the common privilege of stealing — whenever inspired so to do — and plagiarism is thus often the sign of a noble idolatry—of stealing from one another, that after hoarding them up in the sunny and windy air-lofts of their own imaginations, they may in times of dearth—or to make plenty more plenteous—diffuse and scatter those life-ennobling thefts—in furtherance of the desires of the dead—

" O'er lands and seas,
Whatever clime the sun's bright circle warms ! "

And thus, too, have the truly great and good poets sometimes —often — felt that it was dignified to become translators. What else—ay, ay, much else—was the divine Virgil ? Fools disparage him, for that he translated—stole from Homer. As well despise Shakespeare because he stole, not only from unwritten nature and her oral traditions, but from all the old Homeric war-chronicles people had got printed, that he could lay hands on ;

" For the thief of all thieves was the Warwickshire thief! "

Indeed, Shakespeare, who had " little Latin, and no Greek," contrived — heaven only knows how — to translate into English thousands of fine things from those languages. Marlow was an avowed and regular translator—so was Ben Jonson— and many others of that wonder-working age. But come down, without fear of breaking your neck by the fall—to Dryden and Pope at once ;—and then, sliding along a gentle

level, to Cowper—and, last of all, to Sotheby—all translators
—and who is good, who better, and who best, you sure will
find it hard to say—of the " myriad-minded " Homer.

Let it at once suffice for Mr Sotheby's satisfaction, that we
say he is entitled—and we do not know another person of
whom we could safely say as much — to deal with that well-
booted Grecian, even at this time of day, after all that has
been done to, in, with, and by " Him of the Iliad and the
Odyssey," by not a few of our prevailing poets.

Let us draw the best of them up in rank and file, and as
they march before us, try their height by a mental military
standard, declaring who are fit for admission into the grena-
diers, who into the light company, and who must go into the
battalion.

We shall confine ourselves to the First Book—itself a
poem—and let us try the volunteers by the test of the
Opening thereof—almost all educated persons being familiar
with that glorious Announcement in the original Greek.

CHAPMAN.

" Achilles' baneful wrath resound, O Goddess, that imposed
Infinite sorrows on the Greeks, and many brave souls loosed
From breasts heroic, sent them far to that invisible cave
That no light comforts, and their limbs to dogs and vultures gave ;
To all which Jove's will gave effect, from whom first strife begun
Betwixt Atrides, king of men, and Thetis' godlike son."

DRYDEN.

" The wrath of Peleus' son, O muse, resound,
Whose dire effects the Grecian army found,
And many a hero, king, and hardy knight,
Were sent in early youth to shades of night,
Their limbs a prey to dogs and vultures made.
So was the sovereign will of Jove obey'd ;
From that ill-omen'd hour, when strife begun
Betwixt Atrides great and Thetis' godlike son."

TICKEL.

" Achilles' fatal wrath, whence discord rose,   ◢
That brought the sons of Greece unnumber'd woes,
O Goddess ! sing. Full many a hero's ghost
Was driven untimely to th' infernal coast,
While in promiscuous heaps their bodies lay,
A feast for dogs and every bird of prey.

So did the sire of gods and men fulfil
His steadfast purpose and almighty will ;
What time the haughty chiefs their jars begun,
Atrides, king of men, and Peleus' godlike son."

POPE.

" Achilles' wrath, to Greece the direful spring
Of woes unnumber'd, heavenly goddess ! sing,
That wrath which hurl'd to Pluto's gloomy reign
The souls of mighty chiefs untimely slain ;
Whose limbs, unburied on the naked shore,
Devouring dogs and hungry vultures tore ;
Since great Achilles and Atrides strove,
Such was the sovereign doom, and such the will of Jove."

COWPER.

" Sing, Muse, the deadly wrath of Peleus' son,
Achilles, source of many thousand woes
To the Achaian host, which num'rous souls
Of heroes sent to Ades premature,
And left their bodies to devouring dogs
And birds of heaven (so Jove his will perform'd),
From that dread hour when discord first embroil'd
Achilles and Atrides, king of men."

SOTHEBY.

" Sing, Muse, Pelides' wrath, whence woes on woes
O'er the Acheans' gather'd host arose,
Her chiefs' brave souls untimely hurl'd from day,
And left their limbs to dogs and birds a prey ;
Since first 'gainst Atreus' son Achilles strove,
And their dire feuds fulfill'd the will of Jove."

What are the qualities that characterise the original?
Simplicity and stateliness. Each word in the first line is
great.

MHNIN ἄειδι, Θεὰ, Πηληϊάδιω 'Αχιλῆος.

Now, not one of all the translations makes an approach to the
grandeur of that magnificent line. It is then, we may conclude, unapproachable in the English—and consequently in
any other language. Dryden and Cowper, we think (please
always, if you have time and opportunity, to verify or falsify
our criticisms by reference to translation and original), succeed best ; Pope and Sotheby are about on an equality, though
Pope is the most musical; and Tickel is poor, though Johnson,

throughout that passage, waywardly prefers him to Pope.
Perhaps some will think old Chapman the best, after all, and
certainly his lines have the "long-resounding march," if not
the "energy divine." Pope says of Chapman sneeringly,
that he has "taken an advantage of an immeasurable length
of verse." The longer the better, say we, had he known how
to use it—which, though the above quotation be very good,
we say he generally did not, in spite of the Cockneys.

Observe with what a sonorous and significant, nay sublime,
word, Homer begins the second line, Οὐλομένην. The translators give "baneful," "dire effects," "fatal," "direful,"
"deadly," all right and good, but not one of them placed
where Homer placed his word in its power. Sotheby omits it.

The last line of the Announcement is full brother to the
first—only look at it.

Ἀτρείδης τε ἄναξ ἀνδρῶν καὶ δῖος Ἀχιλλεύς.

All the translators were bound by every tie, human and
divine, to have preserved—if that were possible—its sound,
and its sense, and its soul. Old Chapman has done so, and
praise be to him; Dryden had the gumption to steal old
Chapman's line, but even in an Alexandrine he could not
get a common title to Agamemnon's just title of "King of
Men," and had to cut it down to "great," thereby impairing
its majesty; Tickel also keeps to old Chapman, and wisely
drops out "betwixt;" Pope translates it poorly, and kills it
by transposition; Cowper keeps it in its right place, but has
dropped the noble and essential epithets; Sotheby almost
repeats Pope.

Let us go straight to the famous picture of the Descent of
the Plague-Apollo. We must really give the Greek.

Ὣς ἔφατ᾽ εὐχόμενος, τοῦ δ᾽ ἔκλυε Φοῖβος Ἀπόλλων,
Βῆ δὲ κατ᾽ Οὐλύμποιο καρήνων χωόμενος κῆρ,
Τόξ᾽ ὤμοισιν ἔχων ἀμφηρεφέα τε φαρέτρην·
Ἔκλαγξαν δ᾽ ἄρ᾽ ὀϊστοὶ ἐπ᾽ ὤμων χωομένοιο,
Αὐτοῦ κινηθέντος· ὁ δ᾽ ἤϊε νυκτὶ ἐοικώς.
Ἕζετ᾽ ἔπειτ᾽ ἀπάνευθε νεῶν, μετὰ δ᾽ ἰὸν ἕηκεν·
Δεινὴ δὲ κλαγγὴ γένετ᾽ ἀργυρέοιο βιοῖο.
Οὐρῆας μὲν πρῶτον ἐπώχετο καὶ κύνας ἀργούς,
Αὐτὰρ ἔπειτ᾽ αὐτοῖσι βέλος ἐχεπευκὲς ἐφιεὶς
Βάλλ᾽· αἰεὶ δὲ πυραὶ νεκύων καίοντο θαμειαί.

—I. 43-52.

This all men feel to be sublime. Yet, strange to say, we doubt if to two imaginations it presents anything like the same picture. The Sun-god, Phœbus Apollo, being incensed, slew mules, dogs, and Greeks. He is the Plague. Yet he is a Divinity too—and, at one and the same time, he plays to admiration the part of both, and we defy you to tell which is, in your mind, the predominant idea—of his Godship or his Plagueship. Down to the end of the line closing with βιοῖο, he is himself Φοῖϲος 'Απόλλων—Etty might paint him, Macdonald show him in sculpture. But henceforth he is entirely, or nearly, the Plague. True, he continues to shoot his arrows—but the Impersonation grows faint; and, finally, from before our eyes at least, fades utterly away. For how can the imagination, that was startled by the suddenness of the descent of the glorious Apparition from the summits of Olympus, figure to itself the same Sight sitting apart from the ships for nine nights and days of slaughter, and of blazing funeral piles! The bright Vision of Poetry gives place gradually to the dim vagueness of national Superstition. If this be true—and if it be possible to do it, then the translator should vary his version, in the same spirit as Homer saw and sung, and make us feel the strange transition from Divinity to Disease. How may he do so? By intensifying, as Homer did, the Personality of the Godhead, up to the highest pitch at Βιοῖο; and then letting it generalise itself away into the mere presence of the unweariable activity of death.

Competitors! right shoulders forward—wheel!

CHAPMAN.

"Thus he pray'd, and Phœbus heard him pray—
And, vex'd at heart, down from the tops of steep heaven stoop'd,
 his bow,
And quiver covered round, his hands did on his shoulders throw ;
And of the angry deity the arrows as he moved
Rattled about him. Like the night he ranged the host, and roved
(Apart the fleet set) terribly ; with his hard-loosing hand
His silver bow twang'd, and his shafts did first the mules command,
And swift hounds, then the Greeks themselves—his deadly arrows
 shot,
The fires of death went never out, nine days his shafts flew hot
About the army."

DRYDEN.

" He pray'd, and Phœbus hearing, urged his flight,
With fury kindled, from Olympus' height ;
His quiver o'er his ample shoulders threw ;
His bow twang'd, and his arrows rattled as they flew.
Black as a stormy night, he ranged around
The tents, and compass'd the devoted ground.
Then with full force his deadly bow he bent,
And feather'd fates among the mules and sumpters sent,
The essay of rage ; on faithful dogs the next ;
And last in human hearts his arrows fix'd.
The god nine days the Greeks at rovers kill'd,
Nine days the camp with funeral fires was fill'd."

TICKEL.

" Apollo heard his injured suppliant's cry ;
Down rush'd the vengeful warrior from the sky ;
Across his breast the glittering bow he flung,
And at his back the well-stored quiver hung
(His arrows rattled as he urged his flight).
In clouds he flew, conceal'd from mortal sight,
Then took his stand the well-aim'd shaft to throw ;
Fierce sprang the string, and twang'd the silver bow.
The dogs and mules his first keen arrows slew ;
Amid the ranks, the next more fatal flew,
A deathful dart.   The funeral piles around,
For ever blazed on the devoted ground."

POPE.

" Thus Chryses pray'd, the favouring power attends,
And from Olympus' lofty top descends.
Bent was his bow, the Grecian hearts to wound,
Fierce as he moved his silver shafts resound.
Breathing revenge, a sudden night he spread,
And gloomy darkness roll'd around his head.
The fleet in view, he twang'd his deadly bow,
And hissing, fly the feather'd fates below.
On mules and dogs, the infection first began,
And last, the vengeful arrows fix'd in man.
For nine long nights, through all the dusky air,
The pyres thick flaming, shot a dismal glare."

COWPER.

" Such pray'r he made, and it was heard.   The God,
Down from Olympus, with his radiant bow,

And his full quiver o'er his shoulder slung,
March'd in his anger ; shaken as he moved,
His rattling arrows told of his approach.
Like night he came, and seated with the ships
In view, despatch'd an arrow. Clang'd the cord,
Dread-sounding, bounding on the silver bow.
Mules first, and dogs, he struck, but aiming soon
Against the Greeks themselves, his bitter shafts
Smote them. The frequent piles blazed night and day."

SOTHEBY.

" Thus Chryses pray'd : his pray'r Apollo heard,
And heavenly vengeance kindled at the word.
He from Olympus' brow, in fury bore
His bow and quiver's death-denouncing store.
The arrows, rattling round his viewless flight,
Clang'd, as the god descended, dark as night.
Then Phœbus stay'd, and from the fleet apart,
Launch'd on the host the inevitable dart ;
And ever as he wing'd the shaft below,
Dire was the twanging of the silver bow.
Mules and swift dogs first fell, then far around
Man felt the god's immedicable wound.
Corse lay on corse, to fire succeeded fire,
As death unweary'd fed the funeral pyre."

Here again, old Chapman may be said, on the whole, to be
excellent. But Homer does not show us Apollo—that translator does—in the act of enduing himself with his bow and
quiver. We see from the first the " heavenly archer " (these
are Mr Milman's words) equipped for revenge. " His silver
bow twang'd," is indeed woefully inadequate ; and " hard-loosing hand," though rather expressive, and showing that old
Chapman may have been a toxopholite as well as Ascham,
nor yet un-Homeric, is not in the original, and therefore gives
offence to us who belong to the King's Body-Guard.

Dryden sadly mistakes and mars the majestic meaning of

"Εκλαγξαν δ' ἄρ' ὀϊστοὶ ἐπ' ὤμων χωομένοιο,
Αὐτοῦ κινηθέντος·

" His bow twang'd, and his arrows rattled as they flew ! "

This is an unlucky blunder—and it led him into another,—

" Then with *full force* his deadly bow he bent ! "

As much as to say, we presume, that though before his
" bow twang'd " it had not been bent with full force. " Glorious John " did not see that it had not before been bent at
all. Why should it, till he had taken his station apart from
the ships? " Feather'd fates " are fine things—but not in the
passage. " The Greeks *at rovers killed*," is a piece of pedantic
impertinence—which archers will understand—and for which,
could Homer have foreseen it, he would have longed even in
Hades to have broken Dryden's head.

Tickel's translation is nearly a total failure. Vengeful
" *warrior*," is somewhat impertinent.

> " The well-aim'd shafts to throw,"

suggests a suspicion that our friend was thinking of a " stone
bicker ; " yet, strange to say, the next line is more truly
Homeric than, perhaps, any other single line in any of the
other translations, and is almost perfect,—

> " Fierce sprung the string, and twaug'd the silver bow."

> " In clouds he flew, conceal'd from mortal sight,"

is an absolute and manifest lie ; for Homer saw him, and so do
we, and so did Tickel himself, unless he were bat-blind,
which he was not, but, on the contrary, had a couple of good
sharp eyes in his head.

On Pope's translation it is not possible to bestow much
praise.

> " Bent was his bow *the Grecian hearts to wound*,"

is false and feeble. " Resound " should have been " resounded," we suspect ; though such capricious change of tense is,
we know, a bad trick, common among the poets of Pope's
school.

> " And gloomy darkness roll'd around his head,"

is idle tautology. " Twang'd his deadly bow," not literal,
where literality was demanded; and " feather'd fates " may
be restored, without Pope being the poorer, to Dryden.

> " For nine long nights through all the dusky air,
> The pyres thick-flaming shot a dismal glare,"

are very noble lines ; but the pyres burned by day as well as
night—though by day they were doubtless not so visible.
Homer left us to see them of ourselves during both ; but since

Pope has grandly directed our eyes to the night-imagery, we owe him gratitude.

Cowper, on the whole, is good, forcible; but owing to some rather commonish words, we fear not sufficiently dignified— for Apollo. "March'd in his anger," is raw-recruitish; though raw recruits are often formidable fellows; and "told of his approach," is very prosaic. After it, only think of Milton's "far off his coming shone!" The attempt at imitative harmony or discord in the singular line about "dread-sounding, bounding," we confess we like—but liking is not loving, nor loving admiring, nor admiring astonishment, nor astonishment exultation.

Sotheby is excellent—but not all we hoped he might have been—with all these bell-rocks and beacon lights—to show him his path on the waters. "Kindled *at the word*," is sudden and sharp, but quaint and incorrect. "Then Phœbus stayed," has the same merit and the same demerit. We do not like the repetition of "dart" in "shaft." "Immedicable wound" and "inevitable dart," have a sameness of sound not satisfactory to our ears at the close of lines so near each other—nor is there anything answering to either epithet in Homer.

"Dire was the twanging of the silver bow,"

is admirable in its almost literal simplicity.

"Corse lay on corse, to fire succeeded fire,
And death unwearied fed the funeral pyre,"

are in themselves two strong lines—but are they both equal in power and glory, to

αἰεὶ δὲ πυραὶ νεκύων καίοντο θαμειαί;

No.

There is one half-line in the original of which we have yet said nothing—and which loses its identity in some of these translations, and scarcely preserves it in others. What effect does it produce on your imagination?

ὁ δ' ἤϊε νυκτὶ ἐοικώς·

Old Chapman renders it—rightly so far, for so far literally—

"Like the night he ranged the host."

Dryden—

"Black as a stormy night, he ranged around
The tents."

Pope—
> " Breathing revenge, a sudden night he spread,
> And gloomy darkness roll'd around his head,"

which last line wo have already abused. Tickel, idiotically as we said—

> " In clouds he flew, conceal'd from mortal sight."

Cowper, best of all, and perfectly—

> " Like night he came ; "

and Sotheby—

> " As the God descended, dark as night,"

—which is not so good as Cowper, only because not literally Homer.

We ask you again, what effect does it produce in your imagination ? Not surely that of night over the whole sky— not utter concealment of the God in a darkness not appertaining to himself, but in which he is merely enshrouded, as are the heavens and earth ? No, no, no, that cannot have been intended by Homer. But Homer, we think, in the inspiration of his religious awe, suddenly saw Apollo, the very God of Light, changing in the passion—the agony of rage—into an Apparition the reverse, the opposite, of his own lustrousness, —undergoing a dreadful Transfiguration. It was not as if Day became Night, but that the God of Day was wrath-changed into the Night God—almost as if Apollo had become Pluto. Milton must have understood the image so, for he has transferred it—not the change—but the image itself, to his most dreadful personage, " Black it stood as night,"—in the daylight you know, and therefore was that Foul Blotch so terrible. Try then each translation separately, by this the test of truth, and judge for yourself which is good, which bad, and which indifferent. We should like to hear your opinion.

Meanwhile, before we proceed to another passage, only hear old Hobbes, who, perhaps you may not know it, translated the Iliad and the Odyssey. " His poetry, as well as Ogilvie's " (which we have never chanced to see), says Pope truly, " is too mean for criticism."

> " His prayer was granted by the Deity ;
> Who with his silver bow and arrows keen,
> Descended from Olympus silently,
> In likeness of the sable Night unseen."

In this stealthiness there seems to us something meanly suspicious. True, that in Scripture we read of death coming like a thief in the night—but that was not said for the sake of sublimity, but to show us how we are, in our imagined deepest home-felt security, unsafe from that murderous wretch Death, or Williams.[1] But Homer, being a heathen, meant no uncivil scorn of Apollo, whereas Hobbes converts him into a cracksman.

> " His bow and quiver both behind him hung,
> The arrows chink as often as he jogs ! "

We come now to that immortal quarrel

> " Betwixt Atrides, king of men, and Thetis' godlike son ;"

and are thankful to learn that we ourselves have never felt tempted, by a rash ambition, to dare to try to translate it. Never did Wrath so naturally, we may say rightfully, — speaking of chiefs who were anything but Christian—flame up, from a single spark into a roaring flame, within magnanimous hearts. Ere yet he knew what Chryses was about to divulge as the cause of the Plague—unless, indeed, he had a sort of presaging forethought, that it somehow or other regarded the king—Achilles, by promising the priest immunity from all punishment, placed himself in the spirit and posture of a foe to Agamemnon. That Atrides should have been smitten with sudden rage against the suppliant Father, we cannot wonder ; for we soon have his own word for it, that Chryseïs[2] was now as dear, that is, dearer to him than ever had been Clytemnestra in her golden and virgin days. Kings, heroic and unheroic, are seldom subjects to right reason ; and, in his towering passion with the slow-footed Chryses, his looks could have been none of the sweetest towards the swift-footed Achilles. That fiercest of the fierce took him up at once, on his first tyrannical deviation from justice—thence instant revenge threatened not vainly by him whose will was law— the pride of unmatched power in one, conflicting with the more than pride of the invincible valour of the other—the indignation of habitual dignity on this side, watching the character of the rage of natural passionateness on that—till each seemed equally the fount of the stormy light that redly

---

[1] The perpetrator of several murders in London in 1812.

[2] Chryseïs—daughter of Chryses, the priest of Apollo. Agamemnon (Atrides) had refused the ransom which her father offered ; and hence Apollo had sent the plague upon the Greek camp.

discoloured the countenances of both heroes—and king and
prince shone and shook alike in the perturbation of their
savage spirits, the intolerant and untamed sons of headstrong
and headlong nature.

Is it not amazing to think of it, after we lay down this
dramatic scene, how Homer, without any apparent effort, has
kept up, throughout all the furious injustice of these heroes
to each other, such strong sympathy with both, that though
sometimes shaken, it is never broken ; and that, during the
course of the quarrel, though assuredly our hearts beat faster
and louder towards Achilles, they ever and anon go half over
to the side of Agamemnon ? *He* swore but to deprive his anta-
gonist of that blessing of which himself was about to be, as
he thought, robbed — the enjoyment of love and beauty.
What signifies right, or the observance or violation of right,
when disappointment, which in the soul of a king is equal to
a subject's despair, has darked conscience and corrupted will,
and seeks refuge in revenge ?   And what signifies blood-
thirsty heroism, that has been exulting in victorious fields of
death, to the soul in which it has burned, when its sweetest
meed is ravished out of its embrace, the light of woman's
eyes, and the fragrance of woman's bosom, that had capti-
vated the conqueror, and bound him within his night-tent, in
divinest thraldom, the slave of a slave ?   Patriotism, glory,
fealty, are all overpowered by pride raging in the sense of
degradation, injustice, and wrong, done to it, openly beneath
the sun, and before all eyes ; and down is flung the gold-
studded sceptre on the earth, that the clash may ratify the
oath sworn to Jove, that never more shall the hand that
swayed it draw the sword, though the hero-slaughtering
Hector should drive Greece to her ships, and Troy be triumphant over her flying sons.   Is not this a Quarrel indeed of
demigods, and who could have sung it but Homer ?

We cannot quote all the translations of the progress of this
Wrath up to the intervention of Minerva, and therefore we
shall quote none of them—but go to the passage in which
the goddess reveals herself to the goddess-born, and so far
calms the roar within his soul, as does a sudden lull for a
while that of the sea.   Agamemnon has just said—as Dryden
makes him say, " Briseïs shall be mine."[1]

<hr>

[1] Briseïs had been assigned to Achilles.

CHAPMAN.

" Thetis' son [1] at this stood vext, his heart
Bristled his bosom, and two ways drew his discursive part,
If from his thigh his sharp sword drawn, he should make room
  about
Atrides' person, slaughtering him, or sit his anger out,
And curb his spirit. While these thoughts strived in his blood
  and mind,
And he his sword drew, down from heaven Athenia stoop'd, and
  shined
About his temples, being sent by the ivory-wristed queen,
Saturnia, who out of her heart had ever loving been,
And careful of the good of both. She stood behind, and took
Achilles by the yellow curls, and only gave her look
To him appearance ; not a man of all the rest could see.
He turning back his eye, amaze shook every faculty ;
Yet straight he knew her by her eyes, so terrible they were
Sparkling with ardour "——

DRYDEN.

" At this the impatient hero sourly smiled ;
  His heart impetuous in his bosom boil'd,
  And, justled by two tides of equal sway,
  Stood for a while suspended in his way.
  Betwixt his reason and his rage untamed,
  One whisper'd soft, and one aloud reclaim'd ;
  That only counsell'd to the safer side,
  This to the sword his ready hand applied.
  Unpunish'd to support the affront was hard,
  Nor easy was the attempt to force the guard.
  But soon the thirst of vengeance fired his blood,
  Half-shone his falchion, and half-sheath'd it stood.
  In that nice moment, Pallas, from above,
  Commission'd by the imperial wife of Jove,
  Descended swift (the white-arm'd queen was loth
  The fight should follow, for she favour'd both) :
  Just as in act he stood, in clouds enshrined,
  Her hand she fasten'd on his hair behind :
  Then backward by his yellow curl she drew ;
  To him, and him alone, confess'd in view.
  Tamed by superior force, he turn'd his eyes
  Aghast at first, and stupid with surprise."

[1] Achilles.

POPE.

" Achilles heard, with grief and rage oppress'd,
His heart swell'd high, and labour'd in his breast.
Distracting thoughts by turns his bosom ruled,
Now fired by wrath, and now by reason cool'd :
That prompts his hand to draw the deadly sword,
Force through the Greeks, and pierce their haughty lord :
This whispers soft, his vengeance to control,
And calm the rising tempest of his soul.
Just as in anguish of suspense he stay'd,
While half-unsheath'd appear'd the glittering blade,
Minerva swift descended from above,
Sent by the sister and the wife of Jove ;
For both the princes claim'd her equal care.
Behind she stood, and by the golden hair
Achilles seized ; to him alone confess'd,
A sable cloud conceal'd her from the rest.
He sees, and sudden to the goddess cries,
Known by the flames that sparkle from her eyes."

COWPER.

" He ended, and Achilles' bosom swell'd
With indignation ; wracking doubts ensued,
And sore perplex'd him, whether forcing wide
A passage through them, with his blade unsheath'd,
To lay Atrides breathless at his foot,
Or to command his stormy spirit down.
So doubted he, and undecided yet
Stood drawing forth his falchion huge ; when, lo !
Down sent by Juno, to whom both alike
Were dear, and who alike watch'd over both,
Pallas descended. At his back she stood,
To none apparent, save himself alone,
And seized his golden locks. Startled, he turn'd,
And instant knew Minerva. Flash'd her eyes
Terrific, whom in haste he thus bespake."

SOUTHEY.

" He spake—Achilles flamed—wrath, deep disdain,
Swell'd his high heart, and thrill'd in every vein ;
In doubt, with sword unsheath'd to force his way,
Dash through the warriors, and the tyrant slay ;
Or, in stern mastery of his mind, control
Th' unsated vengeance of an outraged soul.

In this dread doubt, while now in act display'd,
His hand had half unsheath'd the avenging blade.
Pallas, at mandate of the wife of Jove,
Who watch'd the rival chiefs with equal love,
Unseen by all, behind Achilles stood,
Seized his gold locks, and curb'd his madd'ning mood.
He turn'd, and awe-struck, straight the goddess knew,
As from her eyes the living lightning flew."

Achilles has now lost all desire—all power to speak—and he late so insultingly, and scornfully, and savagely, and fiercely, and ferociously eloquent, is dumb. "Ὣς φάτο· Πηλείωνι δ' ἄχος γένετ'. Homer then in four lines says, that the heart of Achilles deliberated—to kill Atrides, or to subdue his own rage. The words he uses are strong as strong may be, and direct as his alternate purposes of slaughter or silence. Let them be so, therefore, in all translation. Old Chapman deserves to have his grave disturbed for having said " his heart bristled his bosom," which either means nothing, or that the hair thereon bristled, which is mean and miserable falsehood of the chest of the youth who excelled all living in heroic beauty. " Stood vext," is perhaps good—to them who remember Shakespeare's " still vexed Bermuthes." " This discursive part," no doubt, gives the right meaning, but is too formal and philosophical for the occasion. What follows on to the Apparition of Pallas, is forceful and rather grim—which is good—but there is a dignity in the original—in the verbs, especially—which has forsaken Chapman's eyesight. Minerva, sent by Juno, the protectress of both heroes alike, comes from heaven, and takes Achilles by his yellow hair, who, astounded, turns his head, and by her stern eyes recognises the Goddess. Now when Chapman says that Athenia " shined about his temples," he is manifestly thinking not of her Person, which was there, but of Wisdom, of which she was Goddess—and this open expression of Homer's hidden meaning is as bad as can be, and brings out marringly the lesson which the great moral bard doubted not all the world would read for itself.—Otherwise the translation has the merit of much vigour.

Dryden's version is, of course, also vigorous ; but it is not literal, but licentious ; and he wilfully violates throughout both the style and the spirit of Homer. The "hero sourly

smiled," is in itself good, but not in the original; and one
hates to see heightenings of the expression of any strong
passion beyond the aim of the mind that depicted it.

> "And, justly by two tides of equal sway,
> Stood for a while suspended in his way,"

is coldly conceived and inaccurately expressed, as are the two,
indeed the six lines, which follow—a sorry sort of declamation,
in which the plainest statement is perverted and falsified, and
fire made mere smoke. The rest is sweeping and sonorous ;
but thirteen lines of Greek into twenty-one of English, is a
dilution that must be severely condemned.

Pope's translation is very fine. It flows freely, and has few
faults, except that it is somewhat too figurative.

> "Now fired by wrath, and now by reason cool'd,"

is an antithesis not to be found—though there is something
like it—in Homer.

> "This whispers soft, his vengeance to control,
> And calm the rising tempest of his soul,"

sounds like commonplace to our ears now—though it is likewise common sense. "A soft whisper" did not suit the ear
of Achilles—at least not from cool reason, though assuredly
from warm Briseïs—and

> "A sable cloud conceal'd her from the rest,"

is not in Homer ; for Homer never spoke nonsense ; and nonsense it would have been to have said that a sable cloud was
present on this occasion.

Sotheby's translation, we may safely say, is admirable. It
has but one line more than the original—and loses little
either of the style or sense of Homer.

> "Swell'd his high heart, and thrill'd in every vein,"

is a line, the construction of which Pope was too fond of, and
its latter half is weak and futile ; and the last line of all,—

> "As from her eyes the living lightning flew,"

is a sorry substitute in its meretricious glitter, for

$$\delta\iota\nu\grave{\omega}\ \delta\acute{\epsilon}\ o\acute{\iota}\ \ddot{o}\sigma\sigma\epsilon\ \phi\acute{a}\alpha\nu\theta\epsilon\nu.$$

But with these blemishes—which to some people may not
seem blemishes at all, but beauties—the translation is such

as probably to surpass the power of any other of our living
Poets.

Even more admirable is the translation by Cowper. It is
almost as literal as translation can be; and we do not scruple
to say that it is faultless.

> "Stood drawing forth his falchion huge ; when lo !
> Down sent by Juno, to whom both alike
> Were dear, and who alike watched over both,
> Pallas descended"——

is perfectly Homeric. But were we to indulge ourselves in
criticism, we should find ourselves re-transcribing the whole
passage. Cowper is bald—Cowper is dull—Cowper is tame !
So drivel the dunces—but even at this time of day, few feel,
and fewer know, what is the power of blank verse—and of
blank verse Cowper was a great master.

Pallas has vanished away in the mansion of Ægis-armed
Jove, and Achilles is left again to struggle with his own great
heart. The awe of that sudden celestial visit yet lies upon
him, and his sword is chained in the scabbard. But though
he will obey the mandate, he feels free in his obedience still
to fling scorn and wrath into the face of the King. Enough
that he slays him not where he stands, but yet allows him
life. Juno herself, nor Jove either, shall wrong him out of
another—and a lasting revenge. Nay, Minerva's self—the
Goddess of Wisdom—had given him the privilege to shoot
through Agamemnon's heart the arrows of disdain—swift as
those of death—and foretold that the day is doomed, when
his great loss will be far greatlier repaid.

Such, we may believe, was his mood ; and Homer says, ere
the wrath of Achilles again bursts forth,

> Πηλείδης δ' ἐξαῦτις ἀταρτηροῖς ἐπέεσσιν
> Ἀτρείδην προσέειπε, καὶ οὔπω λῆγε χόλοιο.

This is introduction enough—and in the usual style of
Homer. But it does not satisfy Dryden ; and he chooses to
tell us how Achilles looked and felt, contrary to the positive
assertion of Homer.

> "At her departure, his disdain return'd ;
> The fire she fann'd with greater fury burn'd ;
> Rumbling within, till thus it found a vent."

Homer does not say that Minerva fanned the fire — that
would have indeed been a work of supererogation, and a Mile-

sian fulfilment of the mandate of Juno. " Rumbling within,"
is in the vein of old Chapman's " bristling his breast."
   Pope saw the simple words, and felt their power—and therefore says sufficiently well—

> " Nor yet the rage his boiling heart forsook,
> Which thus redoubling on Atrides broke."

Cowper writes,

> " But though from violence, yet not from words
> Abstain'd Achilles, but with bitter taunts
> Opprobrious, his antagonist reproach'd ; "

which is stiff and formal—as if written by a Quaker.
Sotheby says,

> " But Peleus' son again, with gather'd ire,
> Hurl'd on the monarch words of living fire."

He did so. His words were of " living fire." Just as
from Minerva's eyes " living lightning " flew. But why
should Mr Sotheby say what Homer did not—either in this
passage, or in any other in the Iliad or Odyssey? All the
translators—except Pope perhaps—have failed ; so difficult
must it be to do apparently a very easy thing. But Achilles
speaks—and we cry " Hear ! hear ! hear ! " though he is
sadly out of order — and others may cry " Chair ! chair !
chair ! " The son of Thetis excelled in a reply. Had Lord
Brougham " the accomplishment of verse," we think he would
give the closing speech of Achilles with characteristic power.

DRYDEN.

" Dastard and drunkard, mean and insolent,
   Tongue-valiant hero, vaunter of thy might,
   In threats the foremost, but the lag in fight ;
   When didst thou thrust amid the mingled preace,
   Content to bide the war aloof in peace ?
   Arms are the trade of each Plebeian soul ;
   'Tis death to fight ; but kingly to control.
   Lord-like at ease, with arbitrary power,
   To peel the chiefs, the people to devour.
   These, traitor, are thy talents ; safer far
   Than to contend in fields, and toils of war.
   Nor couldst thou thus have dared the common hate,
   Were not their souls as abject as their state.

But, by this sceptre, solemnly I swear
(Which never more green leaf or growing branch shall bear ;
Torn from the tree, and given by Jove to those
Who laws dispense, and mighty wrongs oppose),
That when the Grecians want my wonted aid,
No gift shall bribe it, and no prayer persuade.
When Hector comes, the homicide, to wield
His conquering arms, with corpse to strew the field,
·Then shalt thou mourn thy pride ; and late confess
My wrong repented, when 'tis past redress.
He said : and with disdain, in open view,
Against the ground his golden sceptre threw ;
Then sat : with boiling rage Atrides burn'd,
And foam betwixt his gnashing grinders churn'd."

POPE.

" O monster ! mix'd of insolence and fear,
Thou dog in forehead, but in heart a deer !
When wert thou known in ambush'd fights to dare,
Or nobly face the horrid front of war.
'Tis ours the chance of fighting fields to try,
Thine to look on, and bid the valiant die.
So much 'tis safer through the camp to go
And rob a subject, than despoil a foe.
Scourge of thy people, violent and base ;
Sent in Jove's anger on a slavish race,
Who, lost to sense of generous freedom past,
Are tamed to wrongs, or this had been thy last.
Now by this sacred sceptre hear me swear,
Which never more shall leaves or blossoms bear,
Which sever'd from the trunk (as I from thee),
On the bare mountains left its parent tree ;
This sceptre, form'd by temper'd steel to prove
An ensign of the delegates of Jove,
From which the power of laws and justice springs,
Tremendous oaths inviolate to kings ;
By this I swear, when bleeding Greece again
Shall call Achilles, she shall call in vain.
When, flush'd with slaughter, Hector comes to spread
The purpled shore with mountains of the dead,
Then shalt thou mourn th' affront thy madness gave,
Forced to deplore, when impotent to save ;
Then rage in bitterness of soul, to know
This act has made the bravest Greek thy foe."

COWPER.

"O charged with wine, in steadfastness of face,
Dog unabash'd, and yet at heart a deer !
Thou never, when the troops have taken arms,
Hast dared to take thine also ; never thou
Associate with Achaia's chiefs, to form
The secret ambush.   No : the sound of war
Is as the voice of destiny to thee.
Doubtless the course is safer far to range
Our num'rous host, and, if a man have dared
Dispute thy will, to rob him of his prize.
Tyrant ! the Greeks are women, else themselves
Would make this contumelious wrong thy last.
But hearken, I shall swear a solemn oath
By this my sceptre, which shall never bud,
Nor boughs bring forth as once, which, having left
Its parent on the mountain-top, what time
The woodman's axe lopp'd off its foliage green,
And stripp'd its bark, shall never grow again ;
Which now the judges of Achaia bear,
Who, under Jove, stand guardians of the laws,—
By this I swear (mark thou the sacred oath),
Time shall be, when Achilles shall be miss'd ;
When all shall want him, and thyself the power
To help the Achaians, whatsoe'er thy will ;
When Hector at your heels shall mow you down,
The hero-slaught'ring Hector ! Then thy soul,
Vexation-stung, shall tear thee with remorse
That thou hast scorn'd, as he were nothing worth,
A chief, the soul and bulwark of your cause."

SOTHEBY.

"Swoln drunkard ! dog in eye, but hind in heart,
Who ne'er in war sustain'st a warrior's part,
Nor join'st our ambush ; for alike thy fear
In war and ambush views destruction near.
More safe, 'mid Græcia's ranks th' inglorious toil,
To grasp some murmurer's unprotected spoil.
Plunderer of slaves—slaves void of soul as sense—
Or Greece had witness'd now thy last offence.
Yet—by this sceptre, which, untimely reft
From its bare trunk upon the mountain left,
Bark'd by the steel, and of its foliage shorn,
Nor bark nor foliage shall again adorn,

But borne by powerful chiefs of high command,
Guardians of law, and judges of the land :
Be witness thou, by this tremendous test
I ratify my word, and steel my breast,
The day shall come, when Greece, in dread alarm,
Shall lean for succour on Pelides' arm :
Then, while beneath fierce Hector's murderous blade
Thy warriors bleed, and claim in vain thy aid,
Rage shall consume thy heart, that madd'ning pride,
Dishonouring me, thy bravest chief defied."

Dryden has made some hits—but also many misses—
Achilles at once gives vent to a matchless burst of the concentrated essence of scorn.

Οἰνοβαρὲς, κυνὸς ὄμματ' ἔχων, κραδίην δ' ἐλάφοιο.

Drunkard, Dog-eye, Deer-heart !

We call this *multum in parvo*. Dryden leaves out both dog
and deer ! Incredible. And of one line makes three — a
commentary rather than a translation.

" Arms are the trade of each Plebeian soul "—

is a pure interpolation—and most unlike the direct charge
against the king by Achilles. Nothing can be worse.

"To peel the chiefs, the people to devour,"

is in itself good, and we suppose it impossible to translate
adequately the words " Δημοβόρος βασιλεύς." A fine flow of
versification perhaps redeems this version—but at its close we
feel how feeble, even in Dryden, is the proud prophecy of
Achilles, who in Homer concludes with calling himself what
all the world knew he was, ἄριστον 'Αχαιῶν, an avowal of the
consciousness of his own worth most suitable and sublime.

Pope almost entirely succeeds where Dryden utterly fails.
In the first burst, he ought not, however, to have let escape
him Οἰνοβαρὲς, which is ill supplied by the whole line, though
it be a strong one,

" O monster ! mixed of insolence and fear."

That strong line, indeed, does not contain within it Οἰνοβαρὲς
—but the dog and deer. The line naming these animals is
perfect.

Achilles becomes rather too much of the rhetorician in

Pope's hands ; but he declaims with great energy, and we shall not play the captious critic on his oration. We must object, however, to two lines, which, doubtless, Pope thought a mighty improvement on Homer,

"When flush'd with slaughter, Hector comes to spread
 The purpled shore with mountains of the dead."

It is not in such pompous terms that hero speaks of hero—especially when soul-enflamed; nor is it thus that Homer makes Achilles speak of Hector. No purple shores—no mountains of the dead—simply

εὖτ᾽ ἂν πολλοὶ ὑφ᾽ Ἑκτορος ἀνδροφόνοιο
Θνήσκοντις πίπτωσι·—

" When many dying fall beneath
  The hero-slaughtering Hector."

Cowper, as usual, keeps close to Homer. And, after all, of a Great Poet the most literal version must be the best. Better to lose something—than to get much that has no business there—which may be not only idle, but false to the truth—mingling styles and spirits that " own antipathy "—that will with difficulty be brought to coalesce, and that cannot be amalgamated.

" O, charged with wine " is not Οἰνοβαρὶς, for it restricts his accusation to that hour—but Achilles calls Agamemnon a drunkard — a wine-swiller — or beer-barrel. Had Achilles believed him drunk then, we scarcely think he would have honoured him by such prolonged and repeated Addresses to the Throne. With that exception, his abuse of Agamemnon is well rendered—and it is Homeric.

It is dangerous to Cowper to read his translation immediately after Dryden's and Pope's. There is a richness in their diction, and a profusion of harmonious sounds overflowing the page, which, along with the rhymes, fills the ear with a music that wafts on the mind, and makes reading something like flying—a pleasure accompanied with a sense, as it were, of our own easy-working power. Meanwhile, we too often feel and think vaguely and obscurely—or perhaps not at all ; and as for seeing, we can scarcely be said sometimes to see anything ; for we either trust to our ears, on which occasions people shut their eyes, or we behold men and things floating away by us, like clouds on the air, or bubbles on a stream.

But Cowper strives to set before us Homer's Iliad in its simplicity—and it is often most simple when it is most sublime,
—and under no delusion, or ignorance, regarding the Bard's
express and definite meaning, why, to enjoy his poetry, we
must see things as well as hear words; the imagination must
exert itself, or, let us say the truth at once, the gentle reader
will infallibly fall asleep. " How magnificent is Dryden's
Homer!" "How splendid is Pope's!" But be ordered to
sit down and mould a Hero from some of these magnificent or
splendid descriptions, or to stain one on the canvass, and you
will find, on comparing your statute or picture with the origi-
nals in Homer, that " Greek does not meet Greek," tough
as may be the tug of war; and that the wondering world, if
not admiring, must be left to conjecture in what forgotten
ancient bard or historian you can have found such and such
personages; and, above all, what it is that they are about—
" doing or suffering."

We have neither time nor room—nor indeed inclination—
to make many particular remarks on Cowper's translation of
this speech, wishing to come to Sotheby.

" When Hector at your heels shall mow you down,
The hero-slaughtering Hector."

Here, though the first line is not Homer, it is surely far better
in itself, and infinitely more characteristic of Achilles, than
Pope's " purpled shores and mountains of the dead,"—and
shows, that if at any time Cowper is forced to depart from the
original—and the structure of verse must often force every
translator so to do—he still writes in a kindred and congenial
spirit. In like manner, Cowper changes into a different form
of expression the final sentiment of Achilles, which he ought
not to have done, for 'twould have been easy to have kept
close to the Greek; but he adheres to the meaning of it, nay,
rather intensifies it; whereas Dryden " changes the drink
upon us," and for purple wine passes off pale negus, as you
may assure yourself by looking at the wishy-washy stuff of the
last two lines of Achilles' speech, than which nothing can be
wersher, except perhaps saltless parritch.

Now, read again Sotheby—after you have read the other
three—great names all, Dryden, Pope, Cowper—and read
again Achilles' last speech—but not like Sir Charles Wether-
ell's dying words—in Homer. You have done so. And do

you not think with us, that Sotheby's version is the foremost
of the four? It is—*longo intervallo.* From first to last, it
breathes insult and scorn, unweakened by one needless or
unnatural word of ornament,—a loftier indignation mixing
with them, as Achilles, swift of tongue as of foot, eyes his
own sceptre, which, after having sworn by, he intends to dash
on the ground,—and finally, insult, scorn, indignation, all,
themselves almost tamed in his heroic breast by the exultation
that fills it from the forethought, when he shall have aban-
doned the host, of his revenge on Agamemnon, coming too
from the very sword of Hector, his mighty foe, the hero-
slaughtering Hector, then unopposed by the man his king
had dishonoured—the best of all the Greeks—αριστος Αχαιων.

To have been able so effectually to rid himself of all remembrances of the words of Pope and Dryden (except in the first
lines, which he improves), shows how thoroughly imbued
Sotheby's mind is with the true feeling and knowledge of
Homer's genius—and this one passage alone proves him a
great translator.

A sudden thought strikes us—let us leave Achilles, and
see who of the ὁμοτιμοι are most successful in Jupiter's Nod—
when he was "a' nid noddin in his house at home."

Jove has been listening propitious to the prayer of Thetis
for her son, and he says,—

> Εἰ δ' ἄγι τοι κιφαλῇ κατανύσομαι, ὄφρα πιπθοίης.
> Τοῦτο γὰρ ἰξ ἐμίθιν γι μιτ' ἀθανάτοισι μίγιστον
> Τίκμωρ· οὐ γὰρ ἐμὸν παλινάγριτον, οὐδ' ἀπατηλὸν,
> Οὐδ' ἀτιλιύτητόν, ὅ τι κιν κιφαλῇ κατανιύσω.
> Ἦ, καὶ κυανίησιν ἐπ' ὀφρύσι νιῦσι Κρονίων·
> Ἀμβρόσιαι δ' ἄρα χαῖται ἐπιρρώσαντο ἄνακτος,
> Κρατὸς ἀπ' ἀθανάτοιο· μίγαν δ' ἰλίλιξιν "Ολυμπον.

—I. 524-530.

Even if you cannot read Greek, you will feel that something
sublime is going on there—depend upon it—by getting some
one who can (and to whom the gods have given to speak *ore
rotundo*), to recite that poetry. Should you be still rather at
a loss, let Dryden come to your assistance.

DRYDEN.

> "Go then, and on the faith of Jove rely,
>   When nodding to thy suit, he bows the sky—
>   This ratifies the irrevocable doom:
>   The sign ordain'd, that what I will, shall come.

The stamp of Heaven, and seal of fate,—he said,
And shook the sacred honours of his head.
With terror trembled Heaven's subsiding hill,
And from his shaken curls ambrosial dews distil."

POPE.

" But part in peace, secure thy prayer as sped,
Witness the sacred honours of our head,
The nod that ratifies the will divine,
The faithful, fix'd, irrevocable sign ;
This seals thy suit, and this fulfils thy vows—
He spoke, and awful bends his sable brows,
Shakes his ambrosial curls—AND GIVES THE NOD—
The stamp of fate and sanction of the god.
High heavens with trembling the dread sanction took,
And all Olympus to the centre shook."

COWPER.

" And to assure thee more, I give the sign
Indubitable, which all fear expels,
At once from heavenly minds. Nought so confirm'd,
May ever be reversed, or render'd vain.
He ceased ; and under his dark brows THE NOD
Vouchsafed of confirmation. All around
The sovereign's everlasting head his curls
Ambrosial shook, and the huge mountain reel'd."

SOTHEBY.

" Hence ! hence ! lest Juno now detect thee here—
Away ! Thy prayer is granted—disappear !
Go, firm in trust ; I pledge the brow of Jove,
The sign most sacred 'mid the gods above ;
This stamp of Fate, th' irrevocable sign,
That perfects all its promises, be thine !
He spake ; and fully to confirm his vow,
The sanction gave, and bow'd his awful brow ;
From his immortal head profusely flow'd
Th' ambrosial locks that waved around the god,
While all Olympus trembled at THE NOD."

Dryden is here not very good—nay, he is almost bad—bad
—very bad—though one quakes to say so of Glorious John,
as he was writing of Glorious Jove. True that these lines of

his have even a majestic flow—as is ever the case when he
wills it, with his versification ; but throughout there is, to our
mind, a manifest struggle to be strong, which nevertheless
fails to attain the effortless sublimity of Homer.   In this
version Jove tells Thetis that "he bows the sky," an expression which, the more you look at it, *here*, becomes the more
obscure.   Does it refer to

ἀθανάτοισι μίγιστον τίκμωρ ;

If it does, it could not easily be worse ; if it does not, there is
nothing equivalent to it in the original ; and if on any occasion Homer ought to have his own way entirely, it was on
this, for he is perfect.

" The *stamp* of heaven and *seal* of fate,"

is language fitter for the lips of a clerk in the Home-Office,
the Customs, or Excise, than the mouth of Jove.   Look at
the words in Homer !   Not one expression of artificial ap-
pliances.

" He shook the sacred honours of his head,"

is a shy line that rather shuns the original—

Κυανίησιν ἐπ' ὀφρύσι νεῦσι Κρονίων.

A "subsiding hill " may be something very impressive ; but
we should think a hill had little chance of subsiding while it
trembled with terror.   We speak, however, in the dark ; only
this we know, that Dryden was more than half-drunk when he
thought *that* a translation of

μίγαν δ' ἰλίλιξιν "Ολυμπον.

Nay, that he was whole drunk—(in a state of *civilation*)—is,
though an inadequate, still a humane excuse, for the enormity
of attempting to murder at one blow both Homer and Jupiter.
Far gone, indeed, must he have been, ere, after he had heard
Olympus tremble, he could yet hiccup out,

" And from his shaken curls ambrosial dews distil."

That is putting the horse behind the cart—the cause after the
effect—making the Nodder yield precedence to the noddee.

Pope is better—and he had probably been better still, had
he not been haunted by Dryden.   Witness

" The sacred honours of our head,"

and

" The nod that ratifies the will divine."

That last line is judiciously stolen or borrowed—of the first we have much pleasure in again expressing our dislike.

"The stamp of fate and sanction of the god,"

is another piece of plunder, of which we do not grudge Pope the possession—and so is "this seals thy suit," a style of talking less characteristic of Jupiter than of a Jew-clothesman. But the "sable brows," the "ambrosial curls," and even "all Olympus," &c., are excellent, and for their sake we praise the passage.

After these sonorous singers, Cowper's voice at first hearing sounds somewhat flat—but we soon perceive it is a fine tenor—he has the right tune, and knows and gives its true character. In Dryden and Pope, Jupiter is as proud as Punch ; in Cowper, he is every inch a King. He does not show off before Thetis, but gives her a solemn and sublime assurance of his benignant will—just as he did in Homer. No witnessing "the sacred honours of his head,"—no sealing —and no stamping. "Huge mountain reel'd " is magnificent, though we are loth to lose " Olympus." The passage reads like a version of Homer by Milton.

Sotheby far excels Dryden and Pope—does he equal Cowper ? Many will say yes—we reluctantly say no. Throughout the whole of his Translation of the Iliad, Cowper seems never to have—though he well knew them—cared what other translators had done. He might have said, like Anthony,

"I only speak right on."

From this wise forgetfulness arose utter fearlessness, and thence power. Sotheby, on the other hand, an accomplished and ambitious scholar, has come forward in order to excel, and he hopes to be the Prizeman. He is seen often striving to outshine; and sometimes, perhaps, he seems less desirous of honouring Homer than of triumphing over " his traducers." Jupiter, not wishing to awaken the jealousy of Juno, says to Thetis,

'Αλλὰ σὺ μὲν νῦν αὖτις ἀπόστιχε,

which, though decisive, is not discourteous—though peremptory, polite. That he was in no great quandary, and was very far from wishing Thetis to hurry herself, is manifest from the self-composure displayed in his preface to his celebrated Nop, no less than in his celebrated Nop itself, the beau-ideal of a Nop (as we believe it was remarked, without his being sensible of saying so, by our friend Charles Nodier), even in the Land of Nod. Why, then, should Sotheby have shown Jupiter in such flurried alarm of Juno? The terrified Thunderer orders Thetis off five times: 1. "Hence!" 2. "Hence!" 3. "Away!" 4. "Disappear." 5. "Go!" Such extreme repetition can be thought natural only on the ground of extreme trepidation—and gives one the idea, not of Jove the Cloud-compeller, but the Hen-pecked. Sotheby, too, must needs have the "stamp of fate," which, by the by, we should like to see fairly out of the hands of the distributor. "Firm in trust," for "ὄφρα πεποίθης" is simple and strong, and sufficient. "Pledge the brow of Jove" is very fine ; and its slight deviation from the original is on that account allowable. We do not see the beauty of the use of "sign" twice, and it probably had not been but for the rhyme. The five lines from "He spake" are noble—indeed, we cannot imagine them improved ; and therefore the judges—that is We—assign the prize to Cowper and Sotheby conjunct in brackets.

The feeling of the sublimity of this renowned passage of Homer is not, however, complete without what follows the Nod.

HOMER.

Τώ γ᾽ ὣς βουλεύσαντε διέτμαγεν· ἡ μὲν ἔπειτα
Εἰς ἅλα ἆλτο βαθεῖαν ἀπ᾽ αἰγλήεντος Ὀλύμπου,
Ζεὺς δὲ ἑὸν πρὸς δῶμα. Θεοὶ δ᾽ ἅμα πάντες ἀνέσταν
Ἐξ ἑδέων, σφοῦ πατρὸς ἐναντίον· οὐδέ τις ἔτλη
Μεῖναι ἐπερχόμενον, ἀλλ᾽ ἀντίοι ἔσταν ἅπαντες.
Ὣς ὁ μὲν ἔνθα καθίζετ᾽ ἐπὶ θρόνου.

—I. 531-536.

Let us compare here again the competitors for the Grecian Crown.

DRYDEN.

" The Goddess goes exulting from his sight,
 And seeks the seas profound, and leaves the realms of light.
He moves into his hall ; the Powers resort,
Each from his house, to fill the Sovereign's court.
Nor waiting summons—nor expecting stood—
But met with reverence, and received the God.
He mounts the throne," &c.

POPE.

" Swift to the seas profound the Goddess flies,
Jove to his starry mansion in the skies.
The shining synod of th' immortals wait
The coming God ; and from their thrones of state,

Arising silent, wrapt in holy fear,
Before the Majesty of Heaven appear.
Trembling they stand, while Jove assumes the throne," &c.

COWPER.

" Their conference closed, they went. She, down at once,
With headlong plunge into the briny deep,
And to his own ethereal mansion, Jove.
His dread approach perceived, uprose the Gods,
And all at once, to meet the sire of all.
He reach'd his throne and sat."

SOTHEBY.

" Their conference o'er, the Ocean Nymph again
Down from Olympus plunged beneath the main.
Jove sought his palace : as their sire appear'd,
The Gods his might and majesty revered ;
None dared regardless linger on his seat—
But on their king's advance arose to greet.
Jove on his throne reclined," &c.

Dryden may be called—should you happen to be in good
humour—spirited ; should you happen, " as is your custom of
an afternoon," to be in spirits yourself, then you probably will
call him splendid. But to us, who are scribbling away

" In the silence of midnight's contemplative hour,"

with no refreshment on the table but our snuff-box (filled, by
the by, with Incomparable, a kindly-taken present, at a pinch,
from our unforgetful friend in Wigmore street, No. 6), the
version is far from first-rate. In Homer, Thetis vanishes in a
moment — Εἰς ἅλα ἅλτο βαθεῖαν,—in Dryden, she is nominative to three verbs. She " goes," she " seeks," and she
" leaves." She lingers in that long lazy line — when she
should have been off like a shot—down to the deep like a
sea-eagle.

" The Powers resort,
Each from his house, to fill the sovereign's court,"

is good in itself, but bad, in so far as it is a misreading—for
the Powers were already at court, and Homer says they rose
up from their seats. But a mere mistake of ignorance is not
to us half so offensive, in a translator of Homer, as a wilful

error of arrogance, and therefore we are here gentle upon John.

Pope, here, is much inferior to his Master. In the first line, " flies " is not at all the right word ; neither is " starry mansion," in the second ; yet the suddenness of the parting is given, and the rapidity of the motion of the sea-diving and of the sky-soaring Immortal. " Rapt in holy fear" are words that, to our ears, seem not rightly applied to a Synod of Heathen Gods and Goddesses. They sound too Scriptural—we hope we are mistaken—but we are not mistaken, we fear, in objecting to " Trembling they stand." What, may we ask, were they so very much afraid of ? Still we pass Pope, by no means a pauper, with praise, to the next parish.

Cowper, again, beats both Dryden and Pope hollow. He was full of Homer then—when he saw Thetis

> " Down at once
> With headlong plunge into the briny deep ; "

and how calm the contrast of

> " And to his own ethereal mansion, Jove ! "

What can be better, too, than

> " Uprose the Gods,
> And all at once " ?

Nothing. Cowper, again, had Milton in his mind. He leans on the right arm of Homer, and on the left of Milton—and so doing, he is not likely to fall to the ground.

Sotheby is rather better, *perhaps*, than Pope—but very inferior to Cowper. " Ocean nymph " we do not relish—we hardly know why—applied here to Thetis. She was an Ocean nymph, but here we look on her as the mother of Achilles, and wish Sotheby had called her Goddess. Homer here calls her simply ἡ, and we prefer that monosyllable with its aspirate. " Again " is scarcely correct. She did not plunge "again." It was her first and only plunge—that day. " Linger on his seat " " is not the potato." " Reclined " is surely not " καθιζετ'." We believe he sat down on his throne, as straight as a pole or a pine. Stop—perhaps not. He leant a little back—like a glorious oak-tree—slightly off the perpendicular, yet with its golden crown steadfast in the sunshine.

Where is Tickel ?   Under a heap of slips.   Let us see how he and Addison—for Pope shrewdly suspected the Spectator had a finger in the pie—manage the matter.

> " Believe my nod, the great, the certain sign,
> When Jove propitious hears the powers divine,
> The sign that ratifies my high command,
> That thus I will ; and what I will shall stand.
> This said, his kingly brow the Sire inclined,
> The large black curls fell awful from behind,
> Thick shadowing the stern forehead of the God :
> Olympus trembled at the MIGHTY NOD.
> The Goddess smiled ; and with a sudden leap,
> From the high mountain plunged into the deep.
> But Jove repair'd to his celestial towers,
> And as he rose, uprose the immortal powers.
> In ranks on either side the assembly cast,
> Bow'd down, and did obeisance as he past,
> To him enthroned," &c.

'Pon our honour, Tickel, or Addison, or both, have acquitted themselves admirably.   They have deviated a little too much from the words, but they have preserved the spirit of Homer, and they need not shrink from comparison with the best of their competitors.

But where all this while has been sleeping old Chapman ? Why, we have been sitting on the flat folio.   Let us see.

> " To thy prayer my eminent head shall move,
> Which is the great sign of my will with all the immortal states ;
> Irrevocable ; never fails ; never without the rates
> Of all powers else ; when my head bows, all heads bow with it still,
> As their first mover, and gives power to any work I will.
> He said ; and his black eyebrows bent ; above his deathless head
> Th' ambrosian curls flow'd ; great heaven shook ; and both were
>   severèd,
> Their counsels broken. To the depth of Neptune's kingdom dived
> Thetis from Heaven's height ; Jove arose, and all the Gods received
> (All rising from their thrones) their Sire, attending to his court.
> None sat, when he rose ; none delay'd the furnishing his port,
> Till he came near—all met with him, and brought him to his
>   throne," &c.

The old boy had certainly a fiery spirit, and an energetic style.   Be satisfied to skip or slur over all his asperities and roughnesses; as you value your life, to steer clear of his jaw-breakers; and shut your eyes, if you can, against the bold blunders that he dashes into your face, and you may often be roused and elevated by his Iliad. He himself thought his translation a great work. He speaks of "the frontless detractions of some stupid ignorants that, no more knowing me *than their own beastly ends,* and I ever (to my knowledge) blest from their sight, whisper behind me—vilifying of my translation; out of the French affirming them," &c.; and afterwards saith of the judicious reader, "that he will easily see I understand the understandings of all other interpreters, and commenters, in places of his utmost depth, importance, rapture." And again, "For my other fresh fry, let them fry in their foolish galls; nothing so much weighed as the barking of puppies, or foisting-hounds; too vile to think of our sacred Homer, or set their profane feet within their lives' lengths of his threshold."

The old bouncing buck then tells us, that he has "not left behind him any of his (Homer's) sentence, elegance, height, intention, and invention;" and then to show his humility, he saith, "I know I cannot too much diminish and divest myself," which he does by elsewhere informing us that he translated the last twelve books in fifteen weeks! We must have an article on Chapman.

Mercy on us! here is that little thick, black, beast—Old Hobbes—We mean his Homer. Hark!

> " But go, lest she observe what you do here.
> I'll give a nod to all that you have spoken ;
> That you may safely trust to, and not fear—
> A nod from me is an unfailing token.
> This said, with his black brows he to her nodded,
> Wherewith displayed were his locks divine ;
> Olympus shook at stirring of his godhead,
> And Thetis from it jump'd into the brine.
> And Jupiter unto his house went down !
> The gods arose and waited on him thither ;
> But unto Juno it was not unknown
> That he and Thetis had conferr'd together," &c.

This is the unconscious grotesque, and burlesque of the sublime and beautiful, and will never, we venture to prophesy, be carried farther by any mortal Momus aping Apollo.

HOMER AND HIS TRANSLATORS.

CRITIQUE II.

[MAY 1831.]

READER, beautiful or brave! lend us your ears, while again we seek to hold with you converse high about old Homer and the Heroic Age. These are mechanical times in which we live; those knew no machinery but of the gods. Now, Science, the son of Intellect, is sole sovereign; then, the Muses, daughters of Memory, queenlike reigned on earth. Three thousand years ago, Rhapsodists roamed o'er continent and isle—all last summer we saw not so much as a poetical pedlar. Reason is our idol now—we bow down to it, and worship it; and Imagination, though she still have a dwelling-place in the world of Poetry, has been banished from life.

We, however, the Magicians, hold by another creed. We rejoice in being—we shall not say how far—behind the age in which, nevertheless, we flourish. The president of a mechanics' institution, in the suburbs of a hardware town, does not seem to us the beau-ideal of humanity. The schoolmaster who is now often abroad—when he ought to be at home—is less an object of our admiration than many an unlettered swain who lived before Cadmus. We can see much to rejoice in, throughout the ongoings even of that life,

"When wild in woods the noble savage ran;"

but then it is that our hearts burn within us, when that barbarian,

"The blind old man of Scio's rocky isle,"

brings before our eyes a whole host of barbarians, some of them "dark with excessive bright"—Agamemnon and Achilles —for specimen or example—who, glaring on that Devoted

City, had pitched their innumerous tents by the surrounding
sea. Yes—all the heroes of that age were but barbarians;
and so must have been the divinities they worshipped, and
from whose "shining loins" some of them had strongly
sprung. The high-browed Maid vainly imagined the Goddess of Wisdom was but a barbarian; though the delight of
heaven and earth—no better was Venus; nor Juno, when to
the smiles of Jove she

> " Roll'd the large orbs of her majestic eyes !"

And what else was Jove himself, with his knowing knack of
nodding, &c., but the barbarian king of a barbarian heaven?
Or Apollo, nathless his celestial beauty, the far-shooting god?
Barbarians like themselves, too, were all their messengers and
all their ministers. Witness, in particular, those two—Hebe,
the Morn-faced, and Iris, the Rainbow. Then their language!
Look at it in their own Αοιδος—singer, i. e. Homer—and
you pity alike the poor gods and men, when you think that
the best among them went gabbling to their graves, or, more
melancholy still, as they thought to all eternity — something they chose to call Greek! Yes, yes, yes, it is well
known now to the very braziers of Birmingham that they were
all barbarians. Vulcan could not have shown his face at
Sheffield—all the smiths would have smiled sardonically at
the Shield he fashioned for the Son of Thetis, and called it a
clumsy concern. What was Argive Helen at her Sidonian
loom, in the palace of Alexander the Fair in stately-structured
Troy, to a spinning-jenny in a manufactory at Salford? Still,
why! oh why! with all the scorn expressed by this civilised
age, of that age of barbarians, continue men inconsistently
still to talk of the "tale of Troy divine?" And how happens
it that on the shoulders of shifting Savoyards you see, among
a host of heads hoisted along through the streets of all the
cities, conspicuous in the very centre, the most awful of them
all, the head of old Homer?

  But no more prosing; let us come at once to our predestined
Selections from Sotheby and other worthies, who have striven
in spirit with the strength, stateliness, and solemnity, or in
spirit delivered themselves up to the softness, sweetness, sadness,—for in all these different delights is it indeed divine,—
of the Sixth Book of the Iliad. We have sat at the knees of
Professor Young, looking up to his kindling or shaded counte-

nance, while that " old man eloquent" gave life to every line,
till Hector and Andromache seemed to our imagination standing side by side beneath a radiant rainbow glorious on a show
cry heaven—such, during his inspiration, was the creative
power of the majesty and the beauty of their smiles and tears.
That was long, long ago, in the Greek class of the College of
Glasgow ; and though that bright scholar's Greek was Scotch
Greek, and in all its vowels and diphthongs, and some of its
consonants too, especially that glorious guttural that sounds
in loc*h*s,—all unlike the English Greek that soon afterwards,
beneath the shadow of Magdalen Tower, the fairest of all
Oxford's stately structures, was poured mellifluous on our
delighted ear from the lips of President Routh, the Erudite
and the Wise,—still hath the music of that " repeated strain"
a charm to our souls, remembering us of " life's morning march
when our spirits were young," and when we could see, even
as with our bodily eyes, things far away in space or time, and
Troy hung visibly before us, even as the sun-setting clouds.
Therefore till death shall we love the Sixth Book of the Iliad ;
and if we understand it not, then indeed has our whole life
been vainer than the shadow of a dream.

During Four Books earth and heaven have been tumulted
by battles. But now there is a pause in the Fight—a priest-
imposed pause—for Helenus, you know, is the chief Augur of
Troy, the metropolitan Bishop, Blomfield and Howley in one,
and he has commanded Hector to return to the city, in order
to appoint a solemn procession of the Queen and the Trojan
matrons to the Temple of Minerva, to entreat her to remove
from the field the dreadful Diomed. Hector obeys—leaps
from his car—vibrating his spears, slays the Greeks—and exhorting the Trojans, and their " far-called far-famed allies," to
stand firm till his return from Troy, as Homer and Sotheby
tell us—

> " Around him, passing from the battle-field,
> Cast the circumference of his bossy shield,
> Whose sable border, as he forward sprang,
> Clash'd on his neck, and on his ankles rang."

Behold, now, reader heroic or heroine, the two Battles lowering aloof, beneath the very walls, with but a short green
space between—a stately stage, is it not, for the representation of some high drama ? The whole house is thrown into
the pit, and both armies can see and hear to a man. Over-

head are the aerial galleries, filled with the gods. And should
Jove thunder, the flash and the crash of his electricity will
be something superior to either John Dennis's or Harry
Brougham's, though neither of them, in its way, is much
amiss; bear witness in a thousand bottles the sudden sour-
ness of much small-beer. No need for Jupiter, when he
brandishes his bolts, to cry, " that's my thunder!"

Who then shall dare, " insupportably their steps advance,"
to enact their swelling parts on such a stage ? Well-graced
actors must they be, whose prattle shall not be tedious ; and
lo ! Diomed, second only to Achilles, to represent the Greeks ;
and for the Trojans, Glaucus, no sorry substitute for Hector
—men of deeds both, as well as words ; with them 'tis a word
and a blow—the blow first, and sheer smite their swords, like
lightning the oak-splitter.   Diomed, fierce, fiery, and furious,
is like Edmund Kean—Glaucus, dignified in his dreadfulness,
reminds us of the late John Kemble.   Nor deem that these
similitudes sink the grandeur of the scene or of its actors ;
for Kean, had he fought at Troy, small as he is, would have
been a sweeping swordsman ; and Kemble, with a pair of
spears, would have been a fearful and an effulgent form.   This
is far from being their first appearance on any stage ; and
their parts have always been in deepest tragedy.   Stars are
they—and never have they acted to empty houses, save to
those themselves have thinned, making " lanes through
largest families," like hurricanes through corn or trees.   Silence ! The play is going to begin ; for hark ! a solitary
trumpet—blown by Sotheby—given to his hand by Homer.

" Now Glaucus' spirit, and Tydides' rage,
    Rush'd in the van infuriate to engage ;
    But ere they clash'd in arms, stroke threat'ning stroke,
    Foremost the son of Tydeus silence broke :
    ' Who art thou, bravest chief ? now first beheld —
    Thou by no son of mortal mould excell'd—
    Thou, whose stern confidence thus rashly shown,
    The vengeance of my spear confronts alone.
    Ill-fated are the sires whose offspring dare
    The measure of their force with mine compare.
    But if, descending from Jove's bright abode,
    Thou tread'st on earth, I strive not 'gainst a god.
    Lycurgus, Dryan's son, of mortal birth,
    Who warr'd against the gods, soon past from earth.

Madman ! who chased through Nyssa's sacred grove,
Those who o'er Bacchus hung with nurturing love.
They, all at once, each thyrsus on the ground
Cast, as Lycurgus' ox-goad dealt the wound ;
Nor less alarm'd, the god, with headlong leap,
Fled from his rage and plunged beneath the deep,
Where, in her bosom, Thetis shelter gave,
And hid his terror in her inmost cave.
But the dire hate of heav'n, and vengeful Jove,
Doom'd him in sightless wretchedness to rove—
Not long : so swift the stroke of vengeance burst
On his proud brow, by men and gods accurst.
If, then, a god thou art, I shun thy might ;
If mortal, now come forth to mortal fight.
Come—and if aught of earth sustain thy breath,
This arm now hurls thee to the gates of death.' "

Is not that noble ? Nor need you much lament, here, that
you cannot read the original, if so it be that, like Shakespeare,
you "have no Greek ; " for Sotheby is here of himself sufficient to raise your spirit to the height of noblest daring,
breathing deliberate valour, as you turn your wondering eyes
towards that other hero who, Diomed thought, might be a
god. So see and hear Glaucus.

HOMER.

Τὸν δ' αὖθ' Ἱππολόχοιο προσηύδα φαίδιμος υἱός·
Τυδείδη μεγάθυμε, τίη γενεὴν ἐρεείνεις ;
Οἵη περ φύλλων γενεὴ, τοίη δὲ καὶ ἀνδρῶν.
Φύλλα τὰ μὲν τ' ἄνεμος χαμάδις χέει, ἄλλα δέ θ' ὕλη
Τηλεθόωσα φύει, ἔαρος δ' ἐπιγίγνεται ὥρη·
Ὣς ἀνδρῶν γενεὴ ἡ μὲν φύει ἡ δ' ἀπολήγει.
Εἰ δ' ἐθέλεις καὶ ταῦτα δαήμεναι, ὄφρ' εὖ εἰδῆς
Ἡμετέρην γενεήν· πολλοὶ δέ μιν ἄνδρες ἴσασιν.

—VI. 144, 151.

POPE.

" ' What, or from whence I am, or who my sire,'
Replied the chief, ' can Tydeus' son require ?
Like leaves on trees, the race of man is found,
Now green in youth, now withering on the ground ;
Another race the following spring supplies ;
They fall successive, and successive rise :
So generations in their course decay ;
So flourish these, when those are past away.
But if thou still persist to reach my birth,
Then hear a tale that fills the spacious earth.' "

COWPER.

" To whom the illustrious Lycian chief replied,—
' Why asks the brave Tydides whence am I ?
For, as the leaves, so springs the race of man.
Chill blasts shake down the leaves, and warm'd anew
By vernal airs, the grove puts forth again ;
Age after age, so man is born and dies.
Yet if intelligence of my descent
Engage thy wish, a theme to many known,' " &c.

SOTHEBY.

" He spake, and Glaucus answered,—' Why inquire
Whence, from what race I sprung, and who my sire ?
Men, like the leaves, that flourish and decay,
Race after race come forth, and die away.
Autumnal gales here strew with leaves the plain,
There spring's soft breath new-robes the branch again.
Thus change the vital tides—wave follows wave ;
Here life, there death, the cradle and the grave !
But since thy wish, brave chief ! my lineage hear,
The far-famed race that distant realms revere.' "

Of these three fine translations of one of the most beautiful,
because Bible-like, passages in ancient poetry, Sotheby's is,
we think, on the whole, the finest ; yet is the original better
than them all—because more Bible-like. Pope felt the passage when he said, " There is a noble gravity in the beginning of this speech of Glaucus, according to the true style
of antiquity. ' Few and evil are our days.' This beautiful
thought of our author, whereby the race of man are compared
to the leaves of trees, is celebrated by Simonides, in a fine
fragment extant in Stobæus. The same thought may be found
in Ecclesiasticus, almost in the same words, ' As of the green
leaves on a thick tree, some fall and some grow, so in the
generations of flesh and blood, one cometh to an end, and
another is born.' " Pope then says, that the reader, who has
seen so many passages imitated from Homer by succeeding
poets, will no doubt be pleased to see one of an ancient poet
which Homer has here imitated ; this is a fragment of Musæus
preserved by Clemens Alexandrinus, in his *Stromata*,—

"Ὡς δ' αὔτως καὶ φύλλα φύει ζείδωρος ἄρουρα
"Ἄλλα μὲν ἐν μιλίχοισιν ἀποφθίνει, ἄλλα δὲ φύει,
"Ὡς δὲ καὶ ἀνθρώπου γενεὴ καὶ φύλλον ἑλίσσει.

Who, where, and when, was Musæus? All of him but his shining name, we fear, is in oblivion. He was not, as Pope thought, anterior to Homer. For while you read Homer, always remember, as Dr Blair and Mr Henry Nelson Coleridge have told us, that the Iliad is the oldest poetry save that of the Bible. But if it were not, nobody need steal leaves—or images of leaves. For we all see, hear, feel, and know, that they are our brethren. Life is a tree—and when all its sap is dry, and the last leaf, alias the last man, has dropt sere from its last withered branch, then will the old trunk itself be flung into the final fire.

It is pleasant to hear Pope speaking in such a true spirit of the Scriptural simplicity of the old poem. Nor has he here failed in imbuing with it his own sounding strain, although not to the degree one might have hoped and expected from the fine feeling of his illustrations. He makes another remark on this passage, which points out in it a peculiar beauty—a beauty appropriate to the person who utters it. Though the passage, he says, be justly admired for its beauty in this obvious application to the mortality and succession of human life, it seems, however, designed by the poet in this place as a proper emblem of the transitory state, not of man, but of families, which being, by their misfortunes or follies, fallen or decayed, do again, in a happier season, revive and flourish in the fame and virtues of their posterity. In this sense, it is a direct answer to what Diomed had asked, as well as a proper preface to what Glaucus relates of his own family, which, having been extinct in Corinth, had recovered new life in Lycia.

Cowper has attempted intense literalness—and has succeeded, perhaps, as far as success was possible. A slight tinge of beauty is all his version wants to be perfect.

Sotheby's verses have that tinge—not a slight one—of beauty; yet are they not perfect—because not intensely literal—like Cowper's. In Homer, the similitude of men to leaves is given in one line, and illustrated in three. The one line—as good a one as ever was written—is the text, the other three are the sermon; and 'tis a better sermon (independently of its shortness) than any (however long) that we have heard on the subject since Christmas, or indeed before it. But Sotheby confuses text and sermon—and that is a flaw in the integrity

of his translation.   Else, 'tis a sweet and solemn discourse of
most excellent music.   But how now?   What is this ?   Homer's
last line is, as it ought to be, a practical conclusion, almost in
the words of the text, introduced by an impressive "Ως.

Ὡς ἀνδρῶν γινεὴ ἡ μὶν φύει ἡ δ' ἀπολήγει.

But Sotheby, who hitherto has been as simply and severely
Scriptural almost as Homer or Solomon, changes suddenly,
and without warning, and without temptation — nay, in the
face of all temptation—into a Christian philosopher, which
the son of Seven[1] was not, nor yet the son of David, and
says—

> "Thus change the vital tides, wave follows wave,
> Here life, there death, the cradle and the grave !"

These are fine lines—not weeds, but flowers—yet they
"have no business there" on men's tombs.   Was the spirit
of Sotheby not satisfied with the image shown it by Homer ?
What alliance, in such inspired melancholy mood, between
the budding, blowing, fading, and falling of leaves, and the
change of vital tides, and the following of waves on waves ?
None.   Besides, in itself, the " change of vital tides " is not a
good expression.   It but faintly and obscurely tells of ebb
and flow.   While,

> " Here life, there death, the cradle and the grave !"

though fine in itself, is another new image still — or, rather,
two new images.   And we doubt if the latter, " cradle and
the grave," be Homeric, or indeed Greek at all.   A Christian
grave is, even in shape, like a Christian cradle, only it has no
rocking keel—it creaks not, and is still ; but a heathen, or
pagan cradle, we suspect, was most unlike a heathen or pagan
grave ; and indeed it may be asked, did a cradle ever swing
to and fro, or motionless contain the infant Diomed or Glaucus?
Or did they not lie in the same bed with the mother, or nurse,
sprawling and squalling to the disturbance of deep-breasted
dames who flourished long before the invention of those small
infantine dormitories, which even the very imps of the heroic
ages would have despised ?

---

[1] Seven cities claimed Homer as their son.

What does old Chapman make of this famous simile ? See,

> " ' Why dost thou so explore,'
> Said Glaucus, ' of what race I am ? When like the race of leaves
> The race of man is ; that deserves no question ; nor receives
> My being any other breath. The wind in autumn strowes
> Th' earth with old leaves ; then the spring the woods with new
>   endowes ;
> And so death scatters men on earth ; so life puts out again
> Man's leafy issue ;—but my race, if, like the course of men,
> Thou seek'st in more particular terms, is this,' " &c.

This is good in its own way — rough and racy — but it is hardly the way of Homer. Chapman here makes Glaucus somewhat sharp and satirical on Diomed—which, after the high but not undeserved compliment which Tydides had just paid him, in suspecting that he might be a god, was, to say the least of it, neither graceful nor gracious nor grateful in the Lycian Prince. " That deserves no question "—is very blunt indeed — boorish — and out of place, time, and character. " Thou seek'st in more particular terms," is also too toothy— and Diomed might have turned the tables on Glaucus, by hinting that, after so many generalities about leaves, a few particulars might not be amiss ;—but otherwise, the leafy part of the passage is well given—the umbrage and the bareness— in autumn the earth wind-strewn with old leaves—the woods by spring endowed with new — and " so life puts out again man's leafy issue," is sudden, short, and strong — and while very Chapmannish not un-Homeric.

We should like to see Travers' translation of the Iliad. Some quotations from it, in Wakefield's Pope's Homer, seem to us very good—but Gilbert improves upon most of them, at will, and we suspect his taste in poetics, though we respect himself as an able, respectable, and disagreeable man. " Travers," quoth Gibby, " is beautiful at this place," and he is so ;

> " But soon an infant race adorns the trees,
> A race succeeding with the vernal breeze ;
> Thus age with quick transition glides away,
> And the sons flourish as their sires decay."

We have just read and re-read, not only with undiminished, but with increased delight, on each perusal, the whole princely reply of Glaucus to Diomed—a speech worthy of Hamlet. It is nearly seventy lines long—narrative, biographical, and historical—and full of old traditions—of the wild and wonderful. Till you have read it, you can have no idea—or but a poor one — of the only genuine Chimæra, or of the bold Bellerophon,

> " He in whose favour'd birth the gods combined
> All grace of person, and all gifts of mind,"

the Joseph of the heroic ages, to whom Prœtus,

> ———— " to whose high command
> Jove gave the sceptre of the Argive land,"

was as Potiphar, and Antæa, who served fair Dione, when

> ———— " madden'd by his charms,
> Clasp'd the fair youth in her adulterous arms,"

as Potiphar's wife—the hero, who, when sent to Lydia to be slaughtered by the King, proved his innocence by his valour in killing the Chimæra, the Solymi, the Amazons, and an ambush of chosen warriors, then married the King's daughter, and swayed " half the sceptre of his wide domain," begetting sons and daughters, till he,

> ———— " for crimes unknown,
> Roam'd, scorn'd of Heaven, th' Aleian wastes, alone,
> And far from man, and friendship's kind relief,
> Consumed his heart in hopelessness of grief."

In such a grandsire rejoiced Glaucus—and therefore no wonder that he was like a god. And godlike he appears in Sotheby —almost as in Homer—for the translator of Oberon has transfused into his version the spirit of the strain so wonder-rife, and shown us in undimmed lustre the hero of that old Romance, and him too who exultingly relates the ancestral fame.

Passing over Diomed's short and spirited reply, full of the heart of heroic hospitality,—the virtue of an age when demigods passed to and fro over many lands, and there was no knowing who might be the great stranger seated at the hearth, —let us witness the famous Interchange of Armour.

Now, gentle and generous reader, we have a question to put to you—did Homer, think ye, mean to say that Jove enlarged the mind of Glaucus, or stupified it ? Pope you see, says, "enlarged," Cowper, " blinded," and Sotheby, " confused his

errant thought." What says that fine, fierce, generous old
fellow, Chapman? This,

CHAPMAN.

" From horse then both descend,
Join hands, give faith, and take ; and then did Jupiter elate
The mind of Glaucus, who, to show his reverence to the state
Of virtue in his grandsire's heart, and gratitude beside,
The offer of so great a friend, exchanged in that good pride,
Curets of gold for those of brass that did on Diomed shine,
One of a hundred oxen's price, the other but of nine."

POPE.

" Thus having said, the gallant chiefs alight,
Their hands they join, their mutual faith they plight ;
Brave Glaucus then each narrow thought resign'd
(Jove warm'd his bosom and enlarged his mind),
For Diomed's brass arms, of mean device,
For which nine oxen paid (a vulgar price),
He gave his own, of gold divinely wrought,
A hundred beeves the shining purchase bought."

COWPER.

" So they—and from their chariots to the ground
Descending, joined at once both hands and hearts.
Then Jove so blinded Glaucus, that for brass
He barter'd gold ; gave armour such as cost
A hundred oxen for the cost of nine."

SOTHEBY.

" They spake ; and from their cars down-springing joined
Hand pledged to hand, as heart to heart combined ;
Then as the barter'd gift the Lycian brought,
'Twas Jove himself confused his errant thought,
Made him, in blind exchange his arms resign,
His gold for brass, a hundred beeves for nine."

Did Jove enlarge the soul of Glaucus, think ye, or did he
take away his understanding? It is, you know—or now see
—a disputed point. Pope thus agrees with Chapman, who
is at pains to remove all ambiguity, and to explain at some
length the nature of the motives that inspired Glaucus to
make the exchange. Chapman, in a note, confesses that
the text of Homer is here against him,—"'Mentem ademit
Jupiter,' the text hath it—which onely I alter of all Homer's
original, since Plutarch, against the Stoics, excuses this sup-

posed folly in Glaucus. Spondanus likewise encouraging my
alterations, which I use for the loved and simple nobility of
the free exchange in Glaucus, contrarie to others that, for the
supposed folly in Glaucus, turned his change into a proverb,
χρυσία χαλκειων, 'gold for brass.'" Pope says, that "the words
in the original, ιξιλετο φρίνας, may be equally interpreted, 'he
took away his sense,' or ' he elevated his mind.' The former
being a reflection on Glaucus's prudence, for making so unequal an exchange ; the latter a praise of the magnanimity
and generosity which induced him to it. Porphyry contends
for its being understood in the last way, and Eustathius,
Monsieur and Madame Dacier, are of the same opinion. Not-
withstanding, it is certain that Homer uses the same word in
the contrary sense, in the 17th Iliad, ver. 470 of the original,
and in the 19th, ver. 137; and it is an obvious remark, that
the interpretation of Porphyry as much dishonours Diomed,
who proposed the exchange, as it does honour to Glaucus for
consenting to it. However, I have followed it, if not as the
juster, as the more heroic sense, and as it has the nobler air
in poetry." This is a good note of Pope's. But how does
the interpretation of Porphyry dishonour Diomed ? Can any
man of woman born believe, for one moment, that Diomed,
that Tydides—the son of that Tydeus who fought and fell at
Thebes—at the close of that glorious burst of confidence and
friendship leapt out of his chariot for the sole purpose of
cheating Glaucus out of his golden arms? An exchange of
arms was inevitable, according to the chivalrous courtesy of
the heroic age. It is not said which of the two first proposed it
—doubtless both at once. And was Diomed, seeing, like a
modern political economist that the exchangeable value of the
arms of his great compeer was greater than that of his own,
to have made a backward bow, and a refusing face, and exclaimed, " No—no—no, Glaucus, I must not swindle you out
of that shield, my honest fellow, lest χρυσία χαλκείων become a
proverb, and Diomed a convertible proper name with Jeremy
Diddler." Or, are we to suppose, on the other hand, that
Glaucus, seeing the comparative meanness and, in a money
or Galloway Stot view, worthlessness of Diomed's arms, hung
back with his golden shield on his shoulder, and, with certain
shrugs, said, " Beg pardon, Diomed, but I had rather be excused, my jewel, for I am not so simple as I seem ; with us
'tis diamond cut diamond ; so, very well, my sharp sir, ' I owe

you one;' but I am too good a grazier to swap a hundred oxen
for nine, and you may carry your pigs to another market."
Glaucus, remember, was a Greek, for his grandsire, Bellerophon, was the grandson of Sisyphus, who

—— " controll'd
In Argos' depths proud Ephyra of old ; "

and we cannot believe that he, who was thus sprung

" Of earth's first blood, had titles manifold,"

could have acted like that modern Greek patriot, Joseph
Hume, who flew off at a tangent, when he found that, in the
cause of liberty, he ran some risk of losing the "tottle of the
whole," of £44, 5s. 7¾d.[1] Is it credible that Glaucus could
have wished to propose a swap with Diomed, on the broad
basis of so many additional rounds of beef?—that he and
Tydides should have higgled and haggled about the " ex-
camby," as we say in Scotland, or " niffer," like two York-
shire horse-coupers ? No, no. We acquit Diomed of being a
kite, and Glaucus of being a pigeon. They were both eagles.
The one was no more a sharp than the other a flat—Diomed
was no Hookey Walker, nor was Glaucus a Yokel. In Homer's
day, as now, "a fair exchange was no robbery ; " and that,
say we, is a fair exchange which is made with your heart and
your eyes open, were it even a Number—Current and Double
and Nox-Ambrosial Number—of Maga for an old almanack.
Glaucus behaved like a man, a gentleman, a soldier, and a
prince, as he was; so did Diomed ; and if Jupiter thought he
had taken the Lycian's senses from him, then Jove was as
grievously mistaken as ever he was in all the days of his
life—even as when, on Mount Gargarus, he supposed he was
embracing Venus, when, in fact, it was but old Juno.

But, after all, can the expression in the original, ἐξέλετο
φρένας, bear a double sense? Gilbert Wakefield, alluding to
the liberal interpretation of Chapman, Ogilby, the Daciers,
Pope, Eustathius, Porphyry, and the "rest," says, "I wish
their attempts were more convincing." We have looked at
the two passages referred to by Pope—and in both the sense
is, as he says, adverse to the liberal view of the case ; yet
Heyne, we perceive, has not been deterred, by his knowledge
of these two passages, from saying, in a note on the words in
question, " Γλαύκῳ φρένας ἐξέλετο Ζεύς, antiquo sermone nihil

<hr/>

[1] See *Noctes Ambrosianæ,* i. 228.

amplius est, quam Glaucus de majore armorum pretio prorsus
non cogitavit; adeo incogitanter egit, ut decuplo cariora
paret Diomedi, quam ab eo acceperat."[1]   It turns out, then,
on the authority of Heyne himself, whose authority as to
the meaning of words and phrases no scholar disputes,
that "it is all right" — nay, that Chapman, in attribut-
ing intentional generosity to Glaucus, has not even done
that hero justice, for that he was neither vainglorious nor
prodigal overmuch ; but in pure forgetfulness of the relative
value of gold and brass, and in simple magnanimity of
mind, at the moment would have given Diomed his shield had
it been "one perfect chrysolite," nor known that he had received a flawed Scotch pebble in return.   In one word,
Glaucus was a Hero.   Just so, and in like manner, did Diomed
care nothing, know nothing, at the moment, of the difference
between brass and gold—but he took in the same spirit that
he gave—in the same spirit that his ancestor Æneas had
given to the ancestor of Glaucus, Bellerophon, when his guest
in Argos, "the belt whose purple broidery glowed"—in the
same spirit that Bellerophon had "a massive bowl all gold
bestow'd," each Hero mutually feeling that their gifts "were
twice blessed," blessing him that gave and him that received,
which is the case as well when princes give to each other in
their glory, as when in mercy they bestow a boon upon the
poorest of their subjects.

Many a supposed sharp witticism has been grinned by the
groundlings against the absurdity of this " celestial colloquy
divine " of Diomed and Glaucus, on the score of its untimeous-
ness, and of its being out of place—all of which have been
well answered even by Dacier (the husband), though he was
a Frenchman.   Consult him and others, if you be a doubting
or still dissatisfied boy, but first a few words more in your
ear from old Christopher.   The pause in the fight—and an
" awful pause " there was—though not "prophetic of its end"
—was most natural.   Did you ever fight for half a forenoon
in a stone or snow bicker?   Well then—were you not very
willing to have a " barley " (parley) for an hour, especially

---

[1] "Γλαύκω φρένας ἐξέλετο Ζεύς, means, in ancient speech, nothing more than that
Glaucus gave no thought at all to the higher value of his armour ; and acted
so unthinkingly as to present to Diomed a gift ten times more valuable than
that which he received in return."

when the bicker was likely to prove, at the best, a drawn battle, and the forces on both sides were drenched, if not in gore, in sweat? And if the dux of the rector's class in the High School, and the dux of ditto in the Academy, had met, by mutual attraction, in the clear space between the bickers, and had agreed to discuss their family histories, involving various high and heroic ancestral and hereditary feuds between Scotch and English, would you not have listened with all your ears and eyes, forgetful of the snow or stones at your feet? But what are men but children of a larger growth? What else were they even in the heroic ages of Greece and Troy?

But farther—our dear boy—know that Poetry possesses powers and privileges which it holds by the tenure of divine right direct from Jove. Homer was commander-in-chief of both armies that fought for Ilion. Yea—even Mars and Neptune and Apollo served under him—Juno, Venus, and Minerva—and Iris was his aide-de-camp. Therefore he did as he chose with day and night—and there was none to say that black was the white of his eye—though the whites of his eyes were large as stars in mist—for Homer, they say, was blind. The gods took away his sight, but they gave him in compensation the gift of song. Not that he was so blind, either, as not to see as far as the most lynx-eyed Lycian into a millstone. Then, so far was he from being deaf, that, like Fine-ear, he could hear the grass growing, and the dewdrop slipping from the blade. ˙ Well knew he the heavy tread of Ajax Tela-mon from the elastic spring of the instep of the swift-footed Achilles. A mile off could he distinguish the feet of Diomed,

" Brushing with hasty steps the dews away,"

from those of Ajax Oïleus, whose feet too were like feathers. Thus gifted with finest faculties of sense—though they say he was blind—so was he gifted with still finer faculties of soul —for it lived in the purple light of the World's earlier Morn.

Therefore in his own world—that is, the world of heroic poetry—Homer could not offend the gods, from whom all his gifts were derived; and if so, why should he offend men—or rather, why should they offend the gods by daring to find fault with the minstrelsy of him, their minister? Or to pick one diamond out of his jewelled crown that, for some thousand years, has been like a galaxy of stars—the Constellation Homer that will shine in heaven till time be no more?

But while Diomed and Glaucus have been speaking, or are speaking still, where has been — where is plume-waving Hector? Sotheby shall tell you—and, listening to him, you might here almost believe that you heard Homer.

"When Hector, now no more by war delay'd,
Had gain'd the Scæan gate and beechen shade,
Troy's wives, Troy's daughters, girt him, throng on throng,
Sire, husband, brother, trembling on their tongue.
He view'd, and pitying, bade them heaven implore
To ward the woe dark-gathering more and more.

But when the hero came—where, broadly-based,
Majestic porticoes the palace graced ;
Where fifty chambers, all of polish'd stone,
Each join'd to each, in beauteous order shone ;
Where the brave race that Priam's wedlock blest,
Each with his beauteous wife found peaceful rest ;
And 'neath the opposed roofs, one after one,
Twelve chambers of his daughters beam'd in stone ;
Where in the circuit of that court enclosed,
With their chaste wives, their wedded lords reposed ;
There his kind mother, passing on her way,
Where fair Laodice's bright chamber lay,
Met her brave son, and clasping to her breast,
Hung on his hand, and fondly thus addrest :—

' Why has my Hector left the field of fight ?
Has Greece around these walls worn down thy might ?
Or art thou come with wistful heart once more
Jove on Troy's sacred summit to adore ?
Stay till I bring thee here delightful wine,
To hail great Jove and all the powers divine ;
Wine, to war's wearied chief refreshing found,
Such as thou art—sole guard of all around.'

' Not now—thou most revered,'—the chief replied—
' Not now, for me, the nectar-bowl provide,
Lest my strength melt away, dissolved by wine,
And these uncleansed hands profane the shrine.
Not so the votaries to the gods repair,
And stretch their blood-stain'd arms to Jove in pray'r.
But thou call forth the matrons, lead the train,
And with rich incense greet Minerva's fane,
And spread the veil most prized of all thy store,
The finest, fullest web her knees before,

And vow twelve bulls, all yearlings, all unbroke,
Shall hallow'd victims on her altar smoke,
If the consenting goddess, at thy prayer,
Troy, and her wives, and speechless infants spare,
And from the walls of Ilion turn afar
The fury of Tydides, lord of war—
So hail the goddess : while my course I bend,
To learn if Paris at my call attend.
Oh, that now earth would cleave, and close his tomb !
So dreadful o'er us lowers the impending doom ;
So on his brow, to Troy, her king, and race,
Great Jove has graved a curse and deep disgrace.
Yet might I see him to the grave descend,
That sight would all my soul's deep woe suspend.'

He spake, the Queen return'd, and bade her train
Call forth the matrons of Minerva's fane,
Then to her fragrant wardrobe bent her way,
Where her rich veils in beauteous order lay :
Webs by Sidonian virgins finely wrought,
From Sidon's woofs, by youthful Paris brought,
When o'er the boundless main the adulterer led
Fair Helen from her home and nuptial bed.
From these she chose the fullest, fairest far,
With broidery bright, and blazing as a star,
Drew forth the radiant veil long hid from day,
Then led the matrons on their solemn way.

Now, when they came, where, based on Ilion's height,
Minerva's stately temple soar'd in sight,
The fair Theano, brave Antenor's bride,
O'er Pallas' fane selected to preside,
The portal to their entrance widely flung,
While to their cries the dome responsive rung :
Each hand was raised, each voice bade Pallas hail,
When fair Theano took the radiant veil,
Spread on Minerva's knees, devoutly pray'd,
And supplicating, thus implored her aid :—

'Supreme of goddesses ! Troy's guardian, hear !
Break into shivers, break Tydides' spear ;
Prone, strike him lifeless, let the slaughterer fall
Beneath our sight, before the Scæan wall.
Twelve yearling beeves, whose neck ne'er felt the yoke,
Now hallow'd victims on thy altar smoke,

So thou consent, and, at thy votary's prayer,
Troy and her wives, and helpless infants spare.'

But Pallas heard not, as Theano pray'd,
Nor listen'd to the vows the matrons made."

What elevation is thus given to the character of Hector!
and how are our hearts thus interested far more deeply than
ever in the fate of Troy! We must not say that every touch
of these pictures—for there is a beautiful succession of them
—shows the hand of the great master. We rather feel as if
they were all painted by Nature's own hand, and we wholly
forget Homer. Matrons and maids meet Hector just within
the Scæan gate—that is one picture. Hecuba and Laodice
come to him as he reaches Priam's stately courts—that is
another; and when we think of the colloquy, in such circumstances, between such a mother and such a son, no scene
was ever more affecting, or more solemn. Elevated, for a
time, by the high sense of his sacred mission, above the wants
and weaknesses of his ordinary humanity, Hector declines the
wine-cup, almost with disdain, even from the honoured hand
of Hecuba—nor would he even dare to pour it out, with those
horrid hands of his, in libation to the gods—a natural sentiment often expressed in ancient poetry, which at all times
doth breathe religion. Another picture is that of Hecuba
heading the long procession to the temple of Minerva on
Ilion;—the unfolding of the gates another;—and another, the
priestess, Antenor's consort, Theano, amid all those suppli-
cants, placing the veil

" With broidery bright, and blazing as a star,"

on the knees of the goddess. Ut pictura poesis, indeed; and
how instantaneously they brighten and fade!

We love Hector now, whom before we had admired, or
feared, in fight—and recognise him as loving and beloved of
the gods. Yet Minerva his piety may not appease, nor will
Jove save Troy from destruction though himself had said
(here we use Pope),—

" You know, of all the numerous towns that rise
  Beneath the rolling sun and starry skies,
  Which gods have raised, or earth-born men enjoy,
  None stands so dear to Jove as sacred Troy.

No mortals merit more distinguished grace
Than godlike Priam, or than Priam's race,
Still to our name their hecatombs expire,
And altars blaze with unextinguish'd fire."

Hector, having done the work of his mission, before going
into his own palace, where he believes is sitting Andromache,
seeks Paris to reanimate him to battle. What a picture of
the Seducer! His palace is the most superb of all.

" Plann'd by his taste, and by his wealth array'd,
Where all their art Troy's craftiest sons display'd.

. . . .

He found the youth, where, far from war's alarms,
He polish'd o'er and o'er his brilliant arms.
Gave his bright shield and breastplate brighter glow,
And smooth'd the graceful curve that shaped his bow ;
While Argive Helen her train'd handmaids taught
To weave the image by her fancy wrought.
Hector beheld, and by just anger moved,
With words of bitter taunt the chief reproved."

Pope, who himself, as Lady Mary tells us, was not un-
ambitious of the character of a gay deceiver, is partial to
Paris. " He has the ill fate," says the author of *The Rape of
the Lock*, " to have all his fine qualities swallowed up in his
blind passion. . . . But as to his parts and turn of
mind, I see nothing that is either weak or wicked, the general manners of those times considered. . . . So very
amorous a constitution, and so incomparable a beauty to provoke it, might be temptation enough even to a wise man, and
in some degree make him deserve compassion, if not pardon."
That is all very pretty, Master Pope ; but it was not according
to the general manners of the age for people to run away, like
Paris, with other men's wives, especially when, as strangers,
they had been loaded with honours by their husbands, and
their husbands kings. Hector would not have done so,
Master Pope ; rather would Achilles have bathed in fire his
" inaccessible hands." You say it " is *remarkable* that
Homer does not paint Paris and Helen like monsters, odious
to gods and men, but allows their characters such estimable
qualifications as could consist, *and in truth generally do*, with
tender frailties." Now, we say it is not remarkable that
Homer does this, for had he not, there would have been no

poem. The female dog would have been flung over the wall.
Neither do we hold with the author of the *Moral Essay on
Man*, that estimable qualifications generally do belong to
persons addicted to adultery. Nevertheless, it is true that
Paris had some imperfect virtues, and many perfect accomplishments; which last were his character. He had, as
Pope remarks, " a taste and addiction to curious works of all
sorts, which caused him to transport Sidonian artists to Troy,
and employ himself at home in adorning and furbishing his
armour; and now we are told, that he assembled the most
skilful builders from all parts of the country, to render his
palace a complete piece of architecture. This, together with
what Homer has said elsewhere of his skill on the harp,
which, in those days, included both music and poetry, may, I
think, establish him as a *bel-esprit* and a *fine genius.*" That a
furbisher and a fiddler is necessarily an established *bel-esprit*
and fine genius, we should be slow to admit, even were he
also a master mason; did we not know that, in Pope's day,
the addition of *bel* to *esprit*, and of fine to genius, was made
almost exclusively in cases of the weakest and most worthless
of mankind, provided they were but lords; and Paris was a
prince. Paris was not a coward; for, had he been, he might
peradventure have won, but he could not have retained, the
love of the sister of Castor and Pollux, and the wife of Menelaus. But brave he was not, if Hector was brave. His valour lay in his consciousness of surpassing beauty, and was
animated, at times, by the blood that galloped through his
veins in the rejoicing power of passion. Homer always paints
him as the object naturally endowed to charm Helen's eyes.
When first he comes before us, in the second book, what a
bright apparition !

> " Now front to front, as either army stood,
> Young Alexander,[1] beauteous as a god,
> Loose from whose shoulders flow'd the leopard's hide,
> And bow and falchion swung in graceful pride,
> Sprung forth, and challenged, as he waved each spear,
> The bravest chief to stand his fierce career.
> Him, Menelaus, him at once descried,
> On stalking in the madness of his pride :
> And as a famish'd lion, gladd'ning o'er
> A stag broad-antler'd, or huge mountain boar,

---

[1] Paris.

Gorges insatiate, nor forgoes his prey,
Though hunters threat, and circling blood-hounds bay :
Thus Menelaus' heart with transport swell'd,
When his keen eye th' advancing youth beheld :
Death, death, he deem'd, shall now deform those charms ;
Down leapt, and shook the earth with clang of arms.
Not Paris thus : his heart convulsed with fear,
Thrill'd, as he knew Atrides rushing near :
He dared not look on death, but back withdrew,
Shrunk 'mid his host, and past away from view.
As one, who, in a wood's entangled brake,
Views the roused terror of th' uncoiling snake,
Flies back, while all his limbs with horror start,
And the pale cheek betrays the bloodless heart ;
Thus Paris fled, and 'mid Troy's sheltering band
Shrunk from the vengeance of Atrides' hand.
Him Hector thus rebuked : ' Thou girl in heart,
Fair but in form, and foul with treacherous art,
Far better hadst thou ne'er the light survey'd,
Ne'er clasp'd a female, by thy guile betray'd,
Than live defamed, and die without a name—
A scornful spectacle, and public shame !
Hark ! how the Greeks deride—how shout in scorn !
Lo ! whom the Graces with their gifts adorn,
Sure—unto him a warrior's spirit given,
By valour to enhance the gift of heaven !
But—wert thou, dastard ! thus ignobly seen,—
So woe-begone, so spiritless thy mien,—
When to far Greece, with Troy's exultant train,
Thy streamers sweeping in their pride the main,
Thou sail'dst, a stranger's kindness to repay,
And steal the consort of the brave away ?
Curse to thy sire, thy kingdom, and thy race—
Derision to thy foes—thyself, disgrace—
Hadst thou withstood th' Atrides, thou hadst known
How brave the chief, whose bride thou call'st thy own.
Nor thee thy lute, nor beauty had avail'd,
Nor those fair locks, that death in dust had trail'd.
Troy too is vile, or thou, ere this unwept,
Hadst in thy stony shroud inglorious slept.' "

True, as others have said, that guilt made Paris quail before
Menelaus ; and that " conscience doth make cowards of us
all." Yet Homer had no moral lesson in view in the Seducer's
flight. For some seducers, even worse than Paris, would
have hewed down the Spartan king if they could, and not

turned tail so ingloriously in presence of both armies. But
Alexander the Fair was more of a woman's man than a man's
man, and therefore he took to his heels and fled. Had Menelaus been a slight-made man of middle age, and a silly
swordsman, think ye not that the Gay Cruel would have
killed him ? By and by, when he has recovered his breath,
his brother badgers him back into a blustering bravery, or
rather bravadoing ; and nothing will content him but to
challenge the Spartan to single combat with spear and sword.
Here Homer again shows the Seducer beautifying himself for
the fight ; but, in the tussle, he is little better than a great
girl.

> " Now the proud Lord of Helen's peerless charms,
> Young Paris, mail'd his limbs in radiant arms.
> First, on his legs his greaves the warrior bound
> With clasps of silver, brightly starr'd around.
> Next, with Lycaon's armour aptly graced,
> Firm on his breast his brother's corslet braced ;
> His silver-studded sword athwart him slung,
> Grasp'd the broad shield that far its shadow flung ;
> The helmet clasp'd, where awful o'er his head
> The crest's wide-waving horse-hair terror spread,
> And brandishing the lightning of his spear
> Eyed mail'd Atrides as the chief drew near."

Paris makes, as you know, but a poor fight of it, and when
Menelaus has thrown his lance, and his sword is shivered, and
the fear-chilled challenger has him at his mercy, why, instead
of going in, he hangs back, apparently with his hands in his
breeches' pockets, till the " Strength of the People "[1] grasps his
casque, and drags him towards the Greek side of the ring,
half-strangled,

> —— " by the lace that bound
> The helmet's clasp the *tender* neck around."

Venus, thou knowest, fair reader, mindful of Mount Ida and
the golden apple, cuts the string in twain, and wafts him to
his palace in a dense veil of darkness,

> " And gently laying on his peaceful bed,
> Sweet balms, distilling fragrance, round him shed."

Helen, " with sweet reluctant amorous delay," following

[1] Menelaus,

him from the ramparts, and half ashamed, yet "nothing loth,"
in daylight, to the dismay of the doubting Madame Dacier,
commits an additional sin against Menelaus—while we, in
spite of Sotheby, persist in dropping the curtain. Yet in spite
of all this discomfiture, the Seducer is soon as insolent as if
he had never been drubbed; and after the disgraceful truce-
break, when Antenor counsels the restoration of Helen to her
lord,

> "He spake, and Helen's youthful consort rose,
> And dared with scornful words the chief oppose :
> 'Ill suits my ear thy speech,'" &c. ;

while old Priam, "weak well-meaning man," like Eli of an
older day, gives in to the beautiful profligate. Wherever and
whenever Paris appears, he is always true to his character.
Who

> "Couch'd behind the stone, in darkness laid,
> That cast o'er Ilus' ancient tomb its shade ?"

who "arch'd the elastic horns," till the arrow pinned to earth
the foot of Diomed? Paris :

> "Then loudly laughing, with contemptuous pride,
> Leapt from his ambush, and exultant cried,
> 'Yes, thou art struck ; not vain my arrow sped,
> Would it had pierced thy heart, and left thee dead !
> Then had our host, now shuddering at thy might,
> As she-goats dread a lion, breathed from fight.'
> But Tydeus' dauntless son, thus scornful said,
> 'Vile bowman ! slanderer ! girl with glistening braid,
> Come front to front, in arms my force assail ;
> Then shall thy bow, nor shower of shafts avail.
> What! hast thou scratch'd my foot ? Is that thy joy ?
> So wounds a woman, or a feeble boy.
> Weak is the weapon in a hand like thine ;
> Far other, far, the wound that waits on mine,'" &c.

Such is the character, and such the exploits, of that "bel-
esprit and fine genius"—Pope's favourite and Helen's—Paris
—yet as well supported throughout as either that of Hector
or Achilles. He reminds one of that gay insect-image in the
Castle of Indolence,

> "As when a burnish'd fly in pride of May."

He is a beautiful serpent. We might apply to him Words-

worth's rich description of the Anglo-American soldier, Ruth's
seducer, who, in his civilisation, was yet a savage.

> "He was a lovely youth. I guess,
> The Panther in the wilderness
> Was not more fair than he ;
> And when he chose to sport and play,
> No Dolphin ever was so gay
> Upon the tropic sea."

The Panther in the wilderness Homer knew, and he paints,
as we have seen, Paris in a panther's hide ; nor do we doubt
that he also knew the dolphin—the very dolphin on whose
back Arion harped—the original of him whose image on the
bottom of that famous bowl, like a "spirit from the vasty deep,"
has so often bade cheer Christopher and the Shepherd, " and
they were cheered," at the Noctes Ambrosianæ. Homer,
however, likens not Paris to panther or dolphin, as Wordsworth has beautifully likened his poetic seducer, a kindred but
still brighter and far bolder sinner ; but he likens him, in his
pomp and pride, to a still nobler creature, the horse—τις στατὸς
ἵππος—no such steed as was bestridden of yore by that tailor
(one of the Place's mighty ancestors) thundering to Brent-
ford—or by that famous train-band captain knight-errant to
Ware—or by Mazeppa borne naked by living whirlwind to
the chiefdomship of the Cossacks,—but a shiny-sided snorter,

> " Far descended from the prophet line,"

—blood untainted through all his sires and dams, from him
whose neck was clothed with thunder, and who cried among
his enemies—Ha ! ha ! We wish we had room for the Greek.
But turn it up in your Homer.[1]

CHAPMAN.

> " And now was Paris come
> From his high towers, who made no stay, when once he had put on
> His richest armour, but flew forth, the flints he trode upon
> Sparkled with lustre of his arms ; his long-ebb'd spirits now flowed
> The higher for their lower ebb. And as a fair steed, proud
> With full-given mangers, long tied up, and now (his head-stall
>   broke)
> He breaks from stable, runs the field, and with an ample stroke,
> Measures the centre, neighs, and lifts aloft his wanton head ;
> About his shoulders shakes his crest, and where he hath been fed,

---

[1] VI. 506.

Or in some calm flood wash'd, or stung with his high flight, he flies
Amongst his females, strength put forth his beauty beautifies ;
And like life's mirror bears his gait ;—so Paris' son the Tower
Of lofty Pergamus came forth, he show'd a sunlike power
In carriage of his goodly parts, addrest now to the strife," &c.

SOTHEBY.

"Nor Paris linger'd ; but in mail array'd,
Whose brilliant light the warrior's pride display'd,
Rush'd through the streets—as when a stall-fed steed,
Swift, as he snaps the cord, from bondage freed
Strikes with resounding hoof the earth, and flies
Where spread before him the wide champaign lies ;
Seeks the remember'd haunts, on fire to lave
His glowing limbs, and dash amid the wave ;
High rears his crest, and tossing in disdain,
Wide o'er his shoulders spreads the stream of mane,
And fierce in beauty, graceful in his speed,
Flies, 'mid the steeds that wanton o'er the mead :
Not otherwise, from Troy's embattled height,
In pride of youth, in power of mailed might,
Exulting, on, impatient of delay,
Bright as the sun, young Paris sped his way," &c.

COWPER.

" Nor Paris now delay'd, but clad in arms
Of brightest lustre, wing'd his rapid course
Through the wide city right toward the field.
As when some courser, leaving far behind
His broken cord, on sounding hoofs escapes ;
To lave, as oft, in sliding waters smooth,
All joy he flies ; or with exalted neck,
Wide-floating mane, and pliant limbs, to seek
In well-known haunts his fellows lost so long ;
So clad in sun-bright arms, from Ilium's heights
Down flew the joyful Paris ; soon he came
Where, after sweetest colloquy. though sad,
With his Andromache, the godlike chief
His brother stood," &c.

Virgil, you know, in the Eleventh Book of the Æneid, has
borrowed Homer's Horse, misapplying the image from Paris
to Turnus, and also marring its majesty ; Tasso, too, has tried
his hand upon it, and chivalrously ; and so have so many other
ἱππόδαμοι, that were we to transcribe, in parallel passages, all

their descriptions, Maga would be neighing like a Sporting Filly. Suffice it to say, that Sotheby, as you may see, is superior to them all—that his copy is equal to the original picture. His version—do not stare, nor let that surprise you—is at once literal and free—at once metaphrase, paraphrase, and imitation—the three heads under which Dryden says all translation may be reduced—and here we have the " Tria juncta in uno," one of those " speciosa miracula" which genius only, guided by skill and scholarship, can perform.

But we must say farewell, or fare-ill, to Paris—remarking, as the glittering pageant disappears, that other bright but disastrous lights seem ever dazzling upon and around him, in the Iliad, coming uncertainly from afar, and not all evoked by Homer ; for we dream of his shepherd life on Mount Ida, before he voyaged fatally to Greece, or Troy was beleaguered —of his famous Judgment delivered amid the divine air breathed from the three naked goddesses—of his humbler rural loves by Ovid sung—witness Œnone and many a nameless weeping mother ere she was a wife—of his pugilistic exploits among the shepherd-swains, for example, Dares

"Solus qui Paridem solitus contendere contra ;"

and last of all, ere closed " his strange eventful history," we think we see him, while Apollo guides the shaft, sending Achilles himself to the shades. For we hear Ovid speaking through Dryden,—

" He said ; and show'd from far the blazing shield
And sword which but Achilles none could wield ;
And how he moved a god, and mow'd the standing field !
The Deity himself directs aright
The envenom'd shaft, and wings the fatal flight.
Thus fell the foremost of the Grecian name,
And he, the base adulterer, boasts the fame ;
A spectacle to glad the Trojan train,
And please old Priam, after Hector slain.
If by a female hand he had foreseen
He was to die, his wish had rather been
The lance and double axe of the Fair Warrior Queen."

Nor less dazzling than Paris is his Paramour. Her beauty, like that of Paris, was her fatal dower. 'Tis not so said by Homer, that we recollect ; but the fame was, that she was of

the seed of that Celestial Swan. Time touched her not; for
at the end of twenty years' residence in Troy—where she
was received but coldly at court—she was bright as on the
eve when, in Cranae's Isle, she first surrendered her charms
to the Royal Shepherd of Mount Ida. Beauty is felt intense-
liest when it is most pernicious. Sin, crime, and wickedness
set off its charms to their utmost witchcraft; witness Web-
ster's Vittoria, the White Devil of Corrombona. Now Helen
was the White Devil of Troy. She was so, though it is true,
at the same time, as Pope says, that Homer did not paint her
"like a monster, odious to gods and men." She was no
monster at all—but a miracle. She was not odious to gods and
men—better for them had she been—but she could move them
all with her little finger. She shone—a Sin. For sin is soft
and sweet, and bright and fair—and so is ushered into palaces
and temples, and sets them all on fire. Why, Helen still
loved her husband Menelaus, even when lying dissolved in
the arms of her seducer Paris. Was not that amiable? Soon
as she saw her Spartan, whom she had chosen, in her virginity inviolate by Theseus, from among a crowd of kings, to be
her θαλερὸς παρακοίτης, entering the lists against her Trojan,
why her poor, dear, weak, female heart flew again to the
broad bosom of her lawful wedded lord, and she yearned once
more to be an honest woman. Was not that amiable? We
defy you to hate her, whom even Hector and Homer loved,
and all the bright butterflies and grey grasshoppers on the
plain or in the town of Troy.

> "She walk'd in beauty like the night
> Of cloudless climes and starry skies;
> And all that's best of dark and bright
> Meet in her aspect and her eyes."

Yet was she plague, pestilence, and lingering death. But
try not to withhold from her your admiration—your love—for
'twill be all in vain—and should you say you do, you will
merely be a liar. For there is another Sin (nay blush not),
not like Homer's Helen, who haply, after all, was but a
shadow—but with a "brow of Egypt," "comely, though
black,"—a living, breathing, burning, flesh-and-blood Sin—
whom this very night you will visit, "though hell itself
should gape, and bid you hold your peace"—and who with

smiles and tears, and a showery something, shining deep
down and far out of her lustrous and troubled eyes, will, ere
sunrise, have sworn your soul to irremediable misery, beyond
the salvation of penitence or remorse, and for ever within the
damnation of despair.

But, meanwhile, turn your eyes on Homer's Helen. See
her at the hour when Iris, in disguise of Laodice, summons
her to behold the single combat between her Seducer and
her lawful Lord—

> " The goddess found beneath her palace-roof
> Fair Helen, weaving the refulgent woof,
> Charged with the fortunes of the changeful field,
> Where Greece and Troy commingled, shield with shield,
> And as she imaged forth the fate of arms,
> Join'd to destructive war her matchless charms." ·

See her attended by Clymene and Æthra, walking resplendent to the Scæan gate, where "in peaceful leisure sate"
those hoar chiefs Thymetes, and Panthous, and Clytius, and
Lampus, and Antenor, and Ucalegon, and Nicetaon, once all
great men of war, but now "garrulous as grasshoppers."

> " They seem'd like shrill Cicadæ that prolong
> In summer bowers their sweet and tender song ;
> And as they saw ascending to the tower,
> Fair Helen graced with beauty's winning power,
> Each to the other whisper'd, ' such, such charms
> Repay the toils of Greece and Troy in arms !
> Such are the beauties that, admired above,
> Lure by celestial grace the gods to love :
> Yet thus, so graced, let Helen sail afar,
> Nor leave to us and ours eternal war.' "

Or see her now—blushing and abashed—or rather pale and
piteous, " with heaving breast and soothing speech" confess-
ing to Hector, even in presence of her paramour, and in midst
of all her maids, that she is the "curse and scorn of Ilion!"

> " My brother ! hear me ! Ilion's curse and scorn !
> Oh ! that the hour which saw my natal morn
> Had seen me whirling in the tempest's blast,
> On the wide ocean, or bleak mountain cast ;
> That I had perish'd then without a name,
> Ere witness'd deeds that brand my front with shame !

> But—since the gods thus doom'd it—oh ! that heav'n
> Had to these arms a braver chieftain given,
> One who had heart to feel, and shame to bear
> The killing words that thrill his soul with fear.
> But Paris, now, and aye, to reason blind,
> Must reap the harvest of a wavering mind.
> Yet, here, my brother, on this couch repose,
> Here loose awhile the yoke of galling woes ;
> Woes that on thee the crime of Helen draws,
> And Paris, traitor to Jove's holiest laws ;
> We, whose recorded guilt all men among
> Shall pass from age to age in deathless song."

Ay—now she is all that is good—for she is standing by the side of Hector, and within the awful shadow of the virtue of " that godlike man." Yet another hour, and she shall burn to lie this very night in her Paris's bosom—as she did that forenoon she had wept o'er her faithlessness to her Menelaus. " Oh! that I never had been born ! " is now the passion that storms her soul. " Oh! that in thy arms I might lie for ever ! " will, ere midnight, " possess it wholly." Paris is a coward, she feels; for now she sees far above her head the waving crest of Ἕκτορος ἀνδροφόνοιο. But what will she care for the cowardice of the craven, when " the curled darling " of Venus again lays his head " insupportably " on the delight of her delighted heart? She seems to herself to scorn Paris, now " traitor to Jove's holiest laws." But even should the traitor visit not her couch this night, Dione shall send a dream that, unscared by the Thunderer, will " lap her soul in Elysium." See—through all her speech—sincere though she seems to herself to be—how she tampers with her conscience, and upbraids the heavens. " The gods have doomed it." And worse than foolish would it be—it would be impious—that the fair fatalist should struggle against Jove.

Are we too hard on Helen? Alas! we begin to feel " her conjurations and her mighty magic," and sorceress as we still know her to be in our wiser mind, our heart is almost willing to regard her with pity, even as a weeping Magdalene ! Grief, and shame, and remorse—if there be not repentance—bedim and bedew her pernicious beauty ; nor does illustrious Hector scowl now upon her on whom, fatal though she was, he had never scowled before, but utters for her relief those touching words—so beautifully given by Sotheby—

" the words of ancient date he thus translates "—and they are
at once light and music—" kind as thou art ! "

> " ' Kind as thou art,' illustrious Hector said,
> ' Urge not my stay—nor temptingly persuade.
> Onward I speed to front the desperate fight,
> And succour Troy, that claims her Hector's might.
> Thou Paris urge, let Paris rouse to fame,
> And join me, while those walls my presence claim.' "

Or see her—hear her—at the last Lament over the body of
Hector the Tamer of Horses—and methinks, gentle reader, that,
high-souled though thou be,

> " As Sidney's sister, Pembroke's mother,"

scarcely wilt thou withhold thy lingering reluctant forgiveness from one who, in goddess-doomed infatuation, set the
brand of her beauty to the towers of Troy.

> " ' Hector ! to Helen's soul more loved than all,
> Whom I in Ilion's halls dare brother call,
> Since Paris here to Troy his consort led,
> Who in the grave had found a happier bed.
> 'Tis now, since here I came, the twentieth year,
> Since left my land, and all I once held dear ;
> But never from that hour, has Helen heard
> From thee a harsh reproach or painful word ;
> But if thy kindred blamed me, if unkind
> The Queen e'er glanced at Helen's fickle mind,—
> For Priam, still benevolently mild,
> Look'd on me as a father views his child,—
> Thy gentle speech, thy gentleness of soul,
> Could by thine own their harsher minds control ;
> Hence, with a heart by torturing misery rent,
> Thee and my hapless self I thus lament ;
> For no kind eye in Troy on Helen rests,
> But who beholds me shudders and detests.' "

We have almost gone to the last of all the Iliad for this most
affecting speech.   How natural it is that such feelings should
flow from Helen's lips, when they are thus listened to in con-
junction with that soothing speech of Hector, addressed to her
a few weeks before !   Let the poor wretch have the benefit of
" the natural tears she shed," even though 'tis not unchari-
table to believe that " she wiped them soon."   Paris, in that
hour at least, had no place in her humbled heart—and as

Troy was soon to fall, and "the whole inhabiters perish," or be carried into captivity, what mattered it if they from whose beauty came that fatal overthrow, wandered about joylessly together in the disastrous twilight,

> " While peaceful slept the mighty Hector's shade ? "

But let us return to the living Hector of the Sixth Book. He has now fulfilled his mission, and done all his duty to the State, and his " mighty heart " is free now to turn towards his own house.

> " Home now I haste, revisiting in Troy,
> My wife, my household, and my infant boy,
> Whom—now foredoom'd to bleed on Phrygia's shore,
> Haply their Hector shall behold no more."

With swift foot he has gained his stately palace, but finds not her whom he seeks ; for,

> " She with her babe and nurse that mournful hour,
> Watch'd, steep'd in tears, on Ilion's topmost tower."
>
> .   .   .   .   .   .
>
> " For, when 'twas widely bruited Troy had fled,
> And Grecia to those walls the battle led,
> Thy wife, where Ilion's tower o'erlooks the fight,
> With her loved child and nurse flew wild with fright."

The meeting is well managed by all the translators; but we must confine ourselves to Sotheby.

> " Swift as the wind, impatient of delay,
> Through Troy's proud streets the chief retraced his way ;
> And now arrived, where to the battle-plain
> The Scæan gate recall'd his steps again ;
> His rich-dower'd consort from Eëtion sprung,
> Who erst held sway Cilicia's sons among ;
> And from far Thebes, and Hypoplacia's grove,
> Led the fair virgin to her Hector's love.
> Before him came—and with her came the maid,
> On whose fond breast their child was softly laid—
> Their only child, and lovelier in their sight,
> And fairer far than Hesper's golden light.
> From famed Scamander Hector named the boy,
> But proudly called Astyanax by Troy,
> In honour of his sire, whose single power
> So oft had turn'd the fight from Ilion's Tower.

And now the father, bending o'er his child,
Eyed him in silent joy, and sweetly smiled.
The while Andromache, dissolved in tears,
Hung on his hand, and pour'd forth all her fears."

What a distinction, with what a difference, feel we at once
and already between Helen and Andromache! No babe lies
on the bosom of the once Spartan Queen. Barren is the
adulterous bed, and never more shall she behold the face of
her far-off Hermione. Such mothers forget their children.
Not " wild with affright," but almost eager to behold the show,
had moved Helen in her transcendent beauty towards the
lists, where her paramour and her husband might be about to
die of mutual wounds—proudly conscious, no doubt, all the
while, of its power, even over those ancient " Grasshoppers,"
nor loth, after Paris had been rescued, to show her gratitude
to his guardian goddess by fullest oblations at her shrine.
But Andromache, had she seen Achilles in the remotest part
of the same field with Hector, would have sunk into the
earth. Yet that gentle Lady for Astyanax would have been
bold as a lion—and would have shielded him with her bosom,
without any shrieks. Look on her, the chosen of the Prince of
Troy — the loveliest, we ween — in her sorrow-shaded stateliness, of all the Trojan dames whose garments sweep the
ground—ere long, in the sack of the city, to be sadly soiled
with rueful dust. She shines not from afar like the resplendent Helen; but as she approaches, deeper settles down into
your heart the looks of the wife and mother, the loving,
lovely, and beloved! Homer says not one single word about
her being beautiful at all; for 'twas needless to tell future
ages that the Defender was to a " radiant angel linked."
They have all known well that Andromache was at that hour
fair as the Lily of the Field—ere fear fell on her, bright as the
Rose of the Royal Garden. Simple they have seen her as one
bearing water from the well—yet majestic as the daughter of
a Queen, which she was, the Queen of Cilician Thebè, whose
throne Achilles overthrew.

The above is Sotheby's—and it is beautiful. We have not
room to print, in comparison, the parallel passages, in full,
from all the other great or good translators. But we must do
so with a few of their most touching lines. And first, let us

look at the image of the star—and the two lines of the
original, in which it is enshrined,

Παῖδ' ἐπὶ κόλπῳ ἔχουσ' ἀταλάφρονα, νήπιον αὔτως,
'Εκτορίδην ἀγαπητὸν, ἀλίγκιον ἀστέρι καλῷ.
—VI. 400.

Chapman writes,

> "She ran to Hector, and with her
> Tender of heart and hand,
> Her son, borne in his nurse's arms,
> Where like a heavenly sign
> Compact of many golden stars
> The princely child did shine."

That is good—but the touching epithets, ἀταλάφρονα, νήπιον,
ἀγαπητὸν, are all left out—unless indeed "tender of heart
and hand" apply to the child—which seems doubtful—for
perhaps they apply to the mother. "Like a beautiful star,"
which is all that Homer says, Chapman has, in the intensity
of his sense of beauty, expanded into a lustrous line, which
we print here as if it were two—

> "Compact of many golden stars,
> The princely child did shine."

And he has our forgiveness.

Old Hobbes, whose bare and bald version is sometimes
strangely illuminated by sudden gleams of natural inspiration,
says,—

> "Now Hector met her with their little boy,
> That in their nurse's arms was carried;
> And like a star upon her bosom lay
> His beautiful and shining golden head."

He, too, omits the three epithets—though "little" is endearing; but the rest is exquisite. Hobbes' philosophic creed
was, of all frozen and freezing creeds, the most selfish; but

> "One touch of nature makes the whole world kin,"

and the old childless metaphysician — he was upwards of
eighty, we believe, when he translated Homer—is vivified
into a Man and a Father. Dryden says,

> "The royal babe upon her breast was laid,
> Who, like the morning star, his beams display'd."

He, too, leaves out the three endearments; but he alone of

all the translators, gives 'Εκτοςίδην, which is finely Englished,
"the royal babe." He is also good about the star.
Pope says,—

> " The nurse stood near, in whose embraces press'd,
> His only hope, hung smiling at her breast,
> Whom each soft charm, and early grace adorn,
> Fair as the new-born star that gilds the morn."

This, in itself, is not undelightful ; but far less delightful
than the lines in Homer.   " In whose embraces press'd,"
is a needless departure from the Scriptural simplicity of ἐπὶ
κόλπῳ ἔμψυς: " only hope," belongs not to the "antique speech."
" Each soft charm and early grace," is but pretty ; and
" gilds the morn," is an execrable libel on Homer—a lie—and
worse, pure nonsense.

Cowper says,—

> " The virgin-nurse, enfolding in her arms
> His yet unwean'd and helpless little one,
> Fair as the star of morn."

We love that, for the tendernesses are almost all there ; and
" virgin - nurse " lets us know that Andromache fed Astyanax from her own " fragrant bosom," for which we believe
she is praised by Tansillo.   Dryden, Pope, and Cowper,
all call the star " the star of morn ; " and, though Homer
does not say so, we believe it was,—for we think on the
morn of life.

Sotheby, as may be seen also above, says,—

> " Before him came—and with her came the maid,
> On whose fond breast their child was softly laid—
> Their only child, and lovelier in their sight,
> And fairer far than Hesper's golden light."

The second line is simple, but not so simple as the original,
which it might easily have been ; the next is very good.   By
the by, a spirited critic in the *Edinburgh Review* (in an article
in which he speaks justly of the " acuteness, vivacity, and
elegance " of Mr Henry Coleridge's " Introduction to the
Study of the Greek Classical Poets), says erroneously, speaking of Sotheby's translation of this passage, that there is
great poverty in the simple announcement, " Came with her
infant on the nurse's breast," as a version of the two Greek

lines we have quoted above. The ingenious critic must have been dreaming or nodding; for no such words are in Sotheby. The "only," "lovelier," and "fairer," must also be added to another simple announcement—the true one; and then, though the version hardly does justice to the exquisite beauty of the original, it is freed from the critic's objection. Stop— we find we are in the wrong. The critic in the *Edinburgh* may have taken the line from "Specimens of Translation," published by Sotheby, before the great work—the whole of the Iliad—and Sotheby may have improved the line objected to, perhaps at his suggestion. If so, we kindly beg our ingenious brother's pardon—but hating to blot out, we proceed to Andromache's address to Hector.

CHAPMAN.

——" O noblest in desire !
Thy mind inflamed with other's good, will set thyself on fire ;
Nor pitiest thou thy son, nor wife, who must thy widow be ;
If now thou issue—all the field will only run on thee.
Better my shoulders underwent the earth than thy decease ;
For then could earth bear joys no more, then come the black increase
Of griefs, like Greeks on Ilion ! Alas ! what one survives
To be my refuge ? One black day bereft seven brothers' lives
By stern Achilles. By his hand my father breathed his last ;
His high-wall'd rich Cilician Thebes sackt by him and laid waste,
The royal body yet he left unspoil'd—religion charm'd
That act of spoil, and all in fire he burn'd him complete arm'd,
Built over him a royal tomb, and to the monument
They left of him th' Oreades, that are the high descent
Of ægis-bearing Jupiter, another of their own
Did add to it, and set round with elms, by which is shown
In theirs the barrenness of death ; yet might it serve beside
To shelter the sad monument from all the ruffinous pride
Of storms and tempests used to hurt things of that noble kind.
The short life yet my mother lived he saved, and served his mind
With all the riches of the realm, which not enough esteem'd,
He kept her prisoner, whom small time but much more wealth redeem'd.
And she in sylvan Hypoplace Cilicia ruled again,
But soon was overruled by death. Diana's chaste disdain
Gave her a lance, and took her life ;—Yet all these gone from me,
Thou amply render'st all, thy life makes still my father's be,

My mother, brothers, and beside thou art my husband too,
Most loved, most worthy.   Pity then, dear love, and do not go ;
For thou gone, all these go again ; pity our common joy,
Lest of a father's patronage, the bulwark of all Troy,
Thou leavs't him a poor widow's charge—stay, stay then in this
tower,
And call up to the wild fig-tree all thy retired power,
For there the wall is easiest scaled, and fittest for surprise ;
And there th' Ajaces, Idomen, th' Atrides, Diomed, thrice
Have both survey'd and made attempt, I know not if induced
By some wise auguries, or the fact was naturally infused
Into their wits or courages."

DRYDEN.

" Thy dauntless heart, which I foresee too late,
Too daring man, will urge thee to thy fate.
Nor dost thou pity, with a parent's mind,
This helpless orphan, whom thou leav'st behind ;
Nor me, the unhappy partner of thy bed,
Who must in triumph by the Greeks be led.
They seek thy life ; and, in unequal fight
With many, will oppress thy single might.
Better it were for miserable me
To die, before the fate which I foresee ;
For, ah ! what comfort can the world bequeath
To Hector's widow, after Hector's death !
Eternal sorrow and perpetual tears
Began my youth, and will conclude my years :
I have no parents, friends, nor brothers left ;
By stern Achilles all of life bereft.
Then, when the walls of Thebes he overthrew,
His fatal hand my royal father slew ;
He slew Eëtion, but despoil'd him not,
Nor in his hate the funeral rites forgot ;
Arm'd as he was he sent him whole below,
And reverenced thus the manes of his foe.
A tomb he raised ; the mountain nymphs around
Enclosed, with planted elms, the holy ground.
My seven brave brothers, in one fatal day,
To death's dark mansions took the mournful way ;
Slain by the same Achilles, while they keep
The bellowing oxen and the bleating sheep.
My mother, who the royal sceptre sway'd,
Was captive to the cruel victor made,

And hither led ; but, hence redeem'd with gold,
Her native country did again behold,
And but beheld ; for soon Diana's dart,
In an unhappy chase, transfix'd her heart.
But thou, my Hector, art thyself alone,
My parents, brothers, and my lord, in one.
O, kill not all my kindred o'er again,
Nor tempt the dangers of the dusty plain,
But in this tower, for our defence remain.
Thy wife and son are in thy ruin lost ;
This is a husband's and a father's post.
The Scæan gate commands the plain below ;
Here marshal all thy soldiers as they go ;
And hence with other hands, repel the foe.
By yon wild fig-tree lies their chief ascent,
And thither all their powers are daily bent.
The two Ajaces have I often seen,
And the wrong'd husband of the Spartan queen ;
With him his greater brother ; and, with these,
Fierce Diomede, and bold Meriones ;
Uncertain if by augury, or chance,
But by this easy rise they all advance."

POPE.

" Too daring prince ! ah, whither dost thou run ?
Ah, too forgetful of thy wife and son !
And think'st thou not how wretched we shall be,
A widow I, a helpless orphan he !
For sure such courage length of life denies ;
And thou must fall, thy virtue's sacrifice.
Greece in her single heroes strove in vain,
Now hosts oppose thee, and thou must be slain !
Oh grant me, gods ! ere Hector meets his doom--
All I can ask of Heaven—an early tomb.
So shall my days in one sad tenor run,
And end with sorrows as they first begun.
No parent now remains my grief to share,
No father's aid, no mother's tender care—
The fierce Achilles wrapp'd our walls in fire,
Laid Thebe waste, and slew my warlike sire -
His fate compassion in the victor bred—
Stern as he was, he yet revered the dead ;
His radiant arms preserved from hostile spoil,
And laid him decent on the funeral pile ;

Then raised a mountain where his bones were burn'd :
The mountain nymphs the rural tomb adorn'd,
Jove's sylvan daughters bade their elms bestow
A barren shade, and in his honour grow.
By the same arm my seven brave brothers fell,
In one sad day beheld the gates of Hell,
While the fat herds and snowy flocks they fed,
Amid their fields the hapless heroes bled ;
My mother lived to bear the victor's bands,
The Queen of Hypoplacia's sylvan lands,
Redeem'd too late, she scarce beheld again
Her pleasing empire, and her native plain,
When, ah ! oppress'd by life-consuming woe,
She fell a victim to Diana's bow ;
Yet while my Hector still survives, I see   .
My father, mother, brethren, all in thee ;
Alas ! my parents, brothers, kindred, all
Once more will perish, if my Hector fall.
Thy wife, thy infant, in thy danger share—
Oh ! prove a husband's and a father's care.
That quarter most the skilful Greeks annoy,
Where yon wild fig-tree joins the wall of Troy,
Thou from this tower defend the important post ;
There Agamemnon points his dreadful host,
That pass Tydides, Ajax, strive to gain,
And there the vengeful Spartan fires his train.
Thrice our bold foes the fierce attack have given,
Or led by hopes, or dictated from Heaven ;
Let others in the field their arms employ—
But stay my Hector here, and guard his Troy."

COWPER.

"Ah ! doom'd ! Thyself the victim of thy own
Too daring courage ! Pity of thy boy
Thou feel'st not, nor of me, thy widow soon ;
For soon the whole united Grecian host
Will overwhelm thee, and thou must be slain.
Earth yield me, then, a tomb ! for refuge else
Or none so safe have I,—thenceforth forlorn
Of all defence, since father I have none,
Or mother's genial home to shelter me.
Achilles, when he sack'd Cilician Thebes,
And fired her lofty domes, my father slew ;

He slew Eëtion ; but a decent awe '
Forbidding him to bare a royal corse,
He burn'd him with his arms, heap'd high the soil
That hides the urn, and the Oreades,
Jove's daughters, circled it around with elms.
My seven brothers, feeding in the field
Their flocks and herds, all perished in a day,
For dread Achilles found and slew them all.
My mother, whom in all its green retreats
Hypoplacus obey'd, when, rich in spoils,
The Conqueror steer'd his gallant bark to Troy,
Came captive in the fleet, but, ransom'd hence
At countless cost, revisited her home,
And, by Diana pierced, at home expired.
All these are lost, but in thy wedded love,
My faithful Hector, I regain them all.
Come then—let pity plead ! to spare thy boy
An orphan's woes, and widowhood to me,
Defend this tower, and where the fig-tree spreads
Her branches, station thy collected force ;
For there Idomeneus, the King of Crete,
Tydides, either Ajax, and the sons
Of Atreus, thrice with their united powers
Have press'd to seize the city, whether taught
By some interpreter of signs from Heaven,
Or prompted by remark and self-advised."

SOTHEBY.

" Too rashly bold, thee, sole defence of Troy,
Thy brave right arm and fearlessness destroy—
Fails then thy child a father's heart to move ?
Fails then thy wife's unutterable love?
Thy wife !—no more—Greece arms 'gainst thee her force :
Thy wife ! a widow on thy blood-stain'd corse.
Ah ! reft of thee, be mine the wish'd-for doom
To hide my anguish in th' untimely tomb !
Ah ! reft of thee, no hope, no solace mine,
But grief slow wearing out life's long decline.
No mother waits me, no consoling sire,
The hapless victim of Achilles' ire.
Ere from the sack of Thebes the chief withdrew,
His ruthless rage my sire, Eëtion, slew,
Yet fear'd to spoil, but honouring, on the pyre,
Him, with his arms, consign'd to feed the fire ;

Then heap'd on high the earth, whose funeral mound
With planted elms the Jove-born Oreads crown'd.
They, too, in one fleet day all breathless laid,
Seven brothers sunk at once in Hades' shade.
These, 'mid their cattle on the pasturing mead,
Achilles' fury doom'd at once to bleed.
And here the conqueror, 'mid his plunder'd store,
From Hypoplacia's groves my mother bore ;
Then, richly ransom'd, back restored again,
Too soon to perish, by Diana slain.
Yet thou, my Hector ! thou art all, alone,
Sire, mother, brethren, husband, all in one.
In pity guard this tower, here shield thy life,
Leave not an orphan child, a widow'd wife.
There, by the fig-tree, plant thy war array,
Where, easiest of ascent, to Troy the way.
Thrice have the boldest chiefs that spot assail'd,
And thrice the efforts of the boldest fail'd :
Th' Atridæ, either Ajax, Tydeus' son,
And Crete's fierce king, there led their warriors on,
Whether by seer forewarn'd, or martial art
There mark'd out Ilion's vulnerable part."

Let us try old Chapman in this passage by the principles
by which he tells us he was guided throughout his translation, and we shall not withhold from him here our admiration.
He demands the right of " periphrasis or circumlocution ; " and
sayeth, "always conceiving how pedantical and absurd an
affectation it is, in the interpretation of any author (much more
of Homer) to turn him word for word; when (according to
Horace, and other best lawgivers to translators) it is the part
of every knowing and judicial interpreter not to follow the
number and order of words, but the material things themselves, and sentences to weigh diligently ; and to clothe and
adorn them with words, and such a style of oration as are
most apt for the language into which they are converted."
This and much more to the same purpose (which much
offendeth Pope) sayeth this fierce old Trojan—nor shall we
at present gainsay his creed. Let us therefore try his deeds
by his doctrine ; and, doing so, we declare at once that his
version is a noble one. The first words addressed by
Andromache to Hector are worthy of his wife : " O noblest
in desire ! " and here they may even be the true meaning,

for anything we know to the contrary, of Δαιμόνιε. The second line expresses, by a bold and bright periphrasis, the sense of Homer. "Nor pitiest thou thy son nor wife," is good as good may be; and so is "all the field will only run on thee." Deadly fear breathes in them, and they are Homeric. "Better my shoulders underwent the earth than thy decease," though quaint, smells strong of the Greek. "The black increase of griefs *like foes on Ilion*," is Chapman's own, and affects the imagination, though we cannot call it natural. Yet natural it may be, nevertheless—although it did not occur to the heart of Homer's and Hector's Andromache. Chapman, it will be observed, in the narrative, puts the death of her brothers before that of her father, contrary to the original. No great loss in that, perhaps—and as little gain. The funeral of Eëtion is grand; and we see what Chapman meant by the privileges he claimed as a translator in what he adds to the work of the Oreads. They planted elms round the tomb; but he adds, out of his own heart and brain, fiery and fertile,

——" by which is shown
In theirs the barrenness of death ; yet might it serve beside
To shelter the sad monument from all the ruffinous pride
Of storms and tempests used to hurt things of that noble kind."

Sentimental and stately—yea poetry—yet withal, methinks, more than Andromache was likely to have thought of saying to Hector. Yet, had Homer made her say it, we do not think we should have blamed him, and therefore we do not blame Chapman. The lines about Andromache's mother seem rather unintelligible, and rumble along like an old crazy cart. Then comes the TEST of translators—the two lines crowded with holy words:

"Εκτορ, ἀτὰρ σύ μοί ἰσσι σατηρ καὶ σότνια μήτηρ
'Ηδὶ κασίγνητος, σὺ δέ μοι θαλερὸς σαρακοίτης.
—VI. 429.

Chapman has certainly rendered them well—better, as we shall see, than Pope or Cowper. " Thou art my husband too," corresponds exactly with the Greek words, and the same their position at the close of the line—a beauty not found in any of the other translations. "Pity our common joy" is extremely tender—and so is " lest thou leave him a poor

widow's charge." Throughout the whole of Chapman's
English there is an earnestness—a beseeching and imploring
affectionateness, which is also, though otherwise, breathed
over all Homer's Greek—and therefore, without farther remark, we conclude as we began, with praise of the version—
and request you to admire it along with us, and not to be
offended by its oddnesses or additions, or " periphrases or
circumlocutions "—for, were you to do so, and Chapman's
ghost to overhear you, it would call you "a certain envious
windsucker."

Dryden's version, though in the simpler lines it loses not a
little of the simplicity of the original, does not depart far from
it; and throughout there is such an easy and musical flow,
that we are almost willing to accept it instead of that simplest
strain. " Better it were for miserable me," is extremely
touching; though Dryden had not much power over the
pathetic,

> " Eternal sorrow and perpetual tears
> Began my youth, and will conclude my years,"

have a truly tragic sound; and they have influenced Pope in
this part of his paraphrase. Eëtion's slaughter and funeral
are nobly given; and true to the picturesque of old Homer
are the verses,

> " A tomb he raised ; the mountain nymphs around
> Enclosed, with planted elms, the holy ground."

And how stands Dryden " THE TEST ?"

> " But thou, my Hector, art thyself alone,
> My parents, brothers, and my lord, in one."

Admirable—but of these lines a word or two hereafter.

> " O kill not all my kindred o'er again,"

seems to have been suggested by Chapman, and is afterwards
copied by Pope. It is not very good ; for not very natural in
feeling, and rather unnatural in expression. A few other flaws
in the diamond we see—but it is a diamond—and almost of
the first water. Let us do justice always to Glorious John—
though in his strength he is too often a wilful transgressor.

Had Homer's Andromache never spoken in the simple strain
in which, thank Heaven, she spake in the Sixth Book of the
Iliad, Pope's lovely lady of that name would have been

allowed by all to have uttered much natural pathos in the speech, which had then been not a paraphrastic translation from the Greek, but an absolute inspiration in English; and great had been the glory of the bard of Twickenham. For the lines are beautiful. But here, if anywhere, was Pope bound by the most sacred considerations to have adhered to the words of Homer, that all who might ever speak the English tongue might have known how, thousands of years ago, that high-priest of nature inspired, in the hour of trial, the lips of a Trojan princess pouring out the heart of a mother-wife to an heroic husband issuing to battle—the defender—if not the deliverer. In the first four lines Pope's Andromache utters three or four interjections, exclamations, or interrogations—Homer's Andromache but one—Δαιμόνιε. Pope's Andromache thinks first of herself and child—or chiefly so—for "whither dost thou run," is but faint; and worse, it is not "all one in the Greek." Homer's Andromache thinks first and solely of Hector—φθίσει σε τὸ σὸν μένος, thy courage will be thy death! Pope's Andromache is almost verbose— "Ah! too forgetful," &c.—"and think'st thou not," &c., words, however, which we condemn not; but Homer's Andromache piteously upbraids Hector that he will not have pity— οὐδ' ἐλεαίρεις. She asks him not, as her Shadow does in Pope —why? nor exclaimeth she ah! but passionately tells him, for she sees it, that he will not pity—for his courage she sees has killed pity, even for Παῖδα νηπίαχον, καὶ ἔμ' ἄμμορον —Hector's Andromache here putting their boy first, as was natural—but Pope's Andromache putting herself first—not unnatural either perhaps, in common cases, but assuredly so in that of the wife of Ἕκτορος ἀνδροφόνοιο and of the waving crest. The next four lines of Pope are glowing and fine; but in them he reverts to the strong words φθίσει σε τὸ σὸν μένος, which "shine well where they stand" in Homer, but come in here flat, comparatively, and are unnecessarily expanded into a sort of moral apothegm, or general reflection on the danger of too much courage, which is a sorry substitute for the Homeric—"Thy courage will be thy death." Homer's Andromache says to Hector, that "soon the Greeks will kill thee, all rushing upon thee at once." Pope's Andromache says, alas! what at length may be seen in lines seventh and eighth of the translation. Let us not, however, further compare the two Andromaches, lest the comparison should seem invidious; but merely complain of " O grant me Gods !" and "all I can ask of Heaven," as untrue to the simple pathos of the original—and the two lines which follow as untrue to the sense, though in themselves unobjectionable. " I have neither father nor mother," is all Homer makes Andromache say next ; and out of that scripture Pope makes her spin—

> " No parent now remains my grief to share,
> No father's aid, no mother's tender care."

The next fifteen lines are narrative—and Pope has, we think, on the whole, given them more than well—finely ; and throughout his translation, he has felt that Homer made Andromache speak with composure of " sorrows long ago," at least of sorrows that had been well-nigh forgotten in Hector's love, and that only now again came upon her in her dread of his death. That narrative over, Andromache turns to Hector in that most beautiful burst of affection, which has been for ever consecrated to tears, and which we have chosen, in our critical capacity, to call the TEST. Alas ! the Pope is not infallible ; for he fails where Homer and nature demanded that he should have been victorious over all hearts.

> " Yet while my Hector still survives, I see
> My father, mother, brethren, all in thee ;
> Alas ! my parents, brothers, kindred, all,
> Once more will perish, if my husband fall."

The first two lines are almost, but not quite perfect—for we miss in them the two endearing words that, to Hector's ear, must have been the most affecting of all—the words that conclude the two most comprehensive lines ever love breathed— Ɵαλερὸς παραχοίτης, " and thou art my blooming spouse !" While the last two lines—which contain the word desiderated in its proper place, "husband"—are too ingenious by far, and copied injudiciously from Chapman and Dryden, and, after all, liker Abraham Cowley than Dan Homer. The rest of Andromache's speech is, with the exception of the first two lines of it, well done ; and the two concluding lines, though not in Homer, make an affecting and a natural close, and may be more than forgiven.

Cowper at once seizes, grasps, and expresses the passion of Andromache. " Ah ! doom'd !" is the very word—the sound and sense—so seemeth it to us—of Δαιμόνιε. Or is it—Infatuate? Pope's "too daring Prince" is good—but this is far better—followed as it is by "victim of thy own too daring courage," which, though inferior to the Greek, is forcible. " Pity of thy boy thou feel'st not, nor of me thy widow soon," is all that could be desired—and is Homer's, Andromache's, and Nature's self. So—nearly—are the two lines that follow. By Homer all this is said in three lines and a half—by Pope in eight—and by Cowper in five. Having thus started in power—and with the true heart of tenderness—how does Cowper continue to fare? Well—though not so well. " Earth yield me then a tomb," is far better than Pope's " O grant me, gods," &c.; but "refuge else or none so safe have I," is, though simple, somewhat tame and cold ; nor is " Mother's genial home" entirely to our liking for πότνια μήτηρ. The history given by Andromache of her parents is exquisite—especially the lines describing Eëtion's funeral. They are indeed very noble in Cowper—equal to those in Homer. Not less so is the slaughter of the Seven Brothers. But how doth Cowper conquer the two immortal lines, and reduce them under the English yoke? How stands he the Test?

> " All these are lost—but in thy wedded love,
> My faithful Hector—I regain them all."

Here the meaning, the feeling, the passion is doubtless transfused into a comprehensive power of "English undefiled." The lines are good and great lines—and worthy of Cowper. But Homer's, though not greater—not so great—are better, for there is a tenderness in the words he puts into Andromache's lips, which surpasses all other merit. Cowper says " all these are lost ; " but Homer gives us " all these " themselves—over again—and in a heap—at once successive and clustering

> —— πατὴρ καὶ πότνια μήτηρ,
> 'Ηδὲ κασίγνητος, σὺ δί μοι θαλερὸς παρακοίτης.

No other words under the sun can make amends for the want of these—the eye must see, the ear must hear them, from Andromache's looks and lips—else neither her heart nor ours can be satisfied nor have any rest. "Come, then, let pity plead," is good—but too modern ; Homer does not say "let pity plead," but, " come now, take pity upon us," which

is infinitely fuller of prayer, and therefore more natural in
Andromache. All the rest is what it ought to be—except,
perhaps, the last line of all, which appears pedantic. As a
whole, however, the translation is, to our feelings, better than
Pope's.

Sotheby manifestly feels the force of the first words of Andromache's address to Hector, but he has not felicitously transfused them into his version, which is, indeed, awkward and
tautological. " Sole defence of Troy," is not in the original;
yet that here matters little or nothing, for such Hector was,
and therefore was " The Boy " called Astyanax. Still, Sotheby should not have said so here, because Andromache does
not ; and, as sure as Homer is now in heaven, did Andromache
say all, and no more, that was right. But " brave right arm
and fearlessness destroy," is positively bad speaking and bad
writing ; whereas Δαιμόνιε, ϛθίσει σε τὸ σὸν μένος, is positively
good speaking and good writing — we defy the tongue of
woman, or the pen of man, to speak or write better at such a
juncture. The four following lines are not much better—and
they cannot be much worse. The repetition of the word
"fails " is formal ; and "unutterable " is unnatural. The
repetition of the word " wife " is also formal ; and as no such
word at all is here in Homer, it is insufferable. " Blood-
stain'd corse " is a voluntary commonplace, to the use of which
we can conjecture no inducement. " Greece arms 'gainst
thee her force," is but tolerable. " Wish'd-for doom," is but
so-so ; and " to hide my anguish in th' untimely tomb," is
not excellent. In the Bible, it is said that sinners will call
" upon the rocks to cover them," that is, to hide them, from
the eye of God. But Andromache did not wish her anguish
to be hidden—for the sorrow of a widow is not shame. She
simply wished herself to be buried—to be insensate earth—
χθόνα δύμεναι—as Wordsworth's bereaved lover says, in equal
passion—

> " Rolled round in earth's diurnal course,
> With rocks, and stones, and trees ! "

What she said—so should have Sotheby. " Ah, reft of thee,"
is also unhomerically, if not anti-homerically repeated—repetition being, it would seem, in the eyes of Sotheby, a strong
secret—in ours a patent weakness.

> ———"No hope, no solace mine,
> But grief slow wearing out life's long decline."

is in itself good, because drearily expressive—but it wants the touching simplicity of Andromache's own words.

> "The hapless victim of Achilles' ire,"

seems superfluous—for we have in addition, with about one line intervening,

> "His ruthless rage my sire Eëtion slew."

The next twelve lines are as good as can be—as sonorous as Pope's, and as simple as Homer's. How beautiful the picture of a Hero's tomb!

> "Then heap'd on high the earth, whose funeral mound
> With planted elms the Jove-born Oreads crown'd!"

Look at Pope's lines—and you see they are too ambitious—Sotheby's are purely Homeric. Now for the—TEST. Yes! Sotheby has stood it with high aid—and is triumphant.

> "YET THOU! MY HECTOR! THOU ART ALL ALONE,
> SIRE, MOTHER, BRETHREN, HUSBAND, ALL IN ONE!"

Let ten thousand Translators try it—and not one will surpass —not one will equal—Sotheby. True, that he is indebted for these two exquisite lines almost entirely to Dryden. But how could he help that? John was before William. Therefore, all that William could do was to study John; and, if possible, to polish up John, with the fine feeling fingers of the soul, to uttermost perfection. Pope tried to do so, and failed. Cowper proudly shunned competition, and gave the difficulty the go-by. Sotheby, by simply changing "my parents" into "sire, mother," and "lord" into "husband," and leaving alone and out the two false lines that follow, has given us Homer—and nothing but Homer, the Bill, and nothing but the Bill, and it is a true Bill, unlike some others we could mention, and may well bid defiance to farther reform. The rest is all good—but not perfect. "In pity guard this tower," is nearly what it ought to be; but Andromache says,

> "Come now, have pity, and take your station on this tower,"

which is more tenderly beseeching; and she does not say, "here shield thy life," though we pardon Sotheby for making

her say so, as beyond doubt that thought was in her heart, as
indeed it betrays itself in her afflicted words. Yet terrified as
she was, Sotheby knows as well as we do that Andromache
would not, could not, have wounded Hector's ears with such
syllables as "shield thy life." They would have made his
crest shiver—and dimmed the shine of his golden helmet.

"Leave not an orphan child, a widow'd wife,"

is faultless—and thus have we a few lines almost sufficient of
themselves to redeem all sins either of omission or commission,
which in this version, we fear, are neither few nor feeble.

This speech of Andromache has been subjected to some
severe, and not very decorous criticisms by great authorities
—one of whom is Dryden. "Andromache," says he, "in the
midst of her concernment and fright for Hector, runs off her
bias to tell him a story of her pedigree, and of the lamentable
death of her father, her mother, and her seven brothers. *The
devil was in Hector* [we fear Christopher North sometimes falls
into imitation of John Dryden] *if he knew not all this matter,
for she had been his bedfellow for many years together ;* if he
knew it, it must then be confessed that Homer, in this long
digression, has rather given us his own character [what character is that ? of an old proser in his dotage ?] than that of
the fair lady whom he paints. His dear friends the commentators, who never fail him at a pinch, will needs excuse him,
by making the present sorrow of Andromache to occasion the
remembrance of the past; but others think that she had
enough to do with that grief which now oppressed her, without running for assistance to her family." This is sorry stuff;
Blackwood-Magazineish, and Edinburgh-Reviewish, in their
less happy hours. Homer's "dear friends, the commentators,"
were in the right. Yet was Homer at no pinch. Sorrow
evokes shadows of sorrow from the tomb, and they come
trooping like ghosts. Pope answers Dryden well, too, when
he says, "that nothing was more natural in Andromache than
to recollect her past calamities, in order to represent her present distress to Hector in a stronger light, and then her utter
desertion if he should perish." And we ask, what although
Andromache "had been Hector's bedfellow for many years?"
Never before had she been so inspired with those mournful
memories as now ; for they were standing together, husband

and wife, as it were, in the shadow of death. And then it is
that the soul re-sees the past, and prophesies the future—
both black. To borrow Dryden's bold phraseology—"*What
the devil* would *he* have made Andromache say?" Nothing
so persuasive, by a thousand degrees, to Hector's heart.
Devil take it, is it not natural for a wife, when in her misery
beseeching her husband not to go to death, to remind him of
what he has forgotten—the miseries she had already suffered,
ere she saw his dear face—miseries huge and wild — yet
though Ossa-and-Pelion-like in themselves, as mole-hills to his
slaughter under the spear of Achilles? Achilles! ay, that
was the dreadful vision ever before her eyes. She knew not
—how could she?—that he was sitting sullen at his ships.
Or if she did, might not the glaring lion come leaping from
his den upon Hector? We could say much more for Andromache; but, haply, this is sufficient from Christopher, the
Defender of the Faith.

Allow us to say shortly two other things : one from Pope—
one from ourselves. First, these dreadful stories of Andromache's again bring the absent Achilles before us—into the
heart of the poem. Second, they must have delighted the
listeners to the great Αοιδος, for who in the heroic age was
like Achilles? And they delight the listeners still, as they
see the golden helm of the Son of Thetis refulgent through
the mist of years.

Allow us to say shortly two other things — both from ourselves. First, we defy you to imagine human language,
simpler in style, more direct to the purpose of the passion,
more prose, and less poetry, than all that Andromache utters,
when Hector, and Hector alone, is in her quaking heart.
Look at the Greek words—in their strength—and you will
feel it to be so. Translate them into verses in prose, and they
will read just like some of the most pathetic verses in the old
Testament—or the New—say the story of Joseph and his
brethren—or David and Absalom—or the Prodigal Son, or
even some still more affecting narrative. All great poets, in
all ages, have always, on all great occasions of all great
passions, thus greatly written ; and Wordsworth—though, in
saying so, he said nothing new, yet something old that this
flowery age of ours had, when first he began to flourish,
foolishly forgotten — was therefore greatly right when he

called on all students in poetry to know that its language was
common to prose, in its foundations, and likewise in its super-
structures, except when — and then he told us, wisely and
well, what the exceptions are, and illustrated the principles
on which they occur to the inspired, in much of his own
life-ennobling and immortal song.   Second, see how Andromache adheres in her passion — it is the passion of fear
—to its two objects — Hector, Achilles.   Her soul for a
while undergoes absorption.   From that unendurable agony
it seeks escape into the memory of past miseries, in which
the Destroyer, slaying and slaughtering her kith and kin, is
yet far off—his image is far off—from her husband.   While
she indulges in the distress of that dismal dream, there is to
her relief in its worst horrors—for all the while Hector is held
alive to her side, and hopes come to her, out of the murders
she narrates, that he will shun the murderer.   These hopes
not only suffer, but persuade her to speak more freely—fully
—if you will poetically—about the persons, places, and things
that pass before her imagination : her Seven Brothers slaughtered while tending their flocks and herds ; her Father slain,
burned in all his arms, and buried beneath a mound, which
the Oreads, daughters of Ægis-bearing Jove—she calls them
so—crown with elms ; her Mother ransomed, and again reign-
ing, and by Diana smitten,—till Andromache being enabled at
last, by the truce afforded by fancy to the feelings that at first
were like to kill her, to indulge in the tenderness of affection,
then it is, and not till then could it have been, that her whole
love-charged heart effuses itself in one burst of divinest delight,
as from lips to which we may think we see the colour coming
back, and themselves quivering no more, is poured that
utterance,—

$$\text{Ἕκτορ, ἀτὰρ σύ μοι ἐσσι πατὴρ καὶ πότνια μήτηρ}$$
$$\text{ἠδὲ κασίγνητος, σὺ δέ μοι θαλερὸς παρακοίτης.}$$

What says majestic Hector to his Andromache ?   Thus :—

COWPER.

" Thy cares are all mine also. But I dread
   The matron's scorn, the brave man's just disdain,
   Should fear seduce me to desert the field.
   No ! my Andromache ! my fearless heart—
   Me rather urges into foremost fight,

Studious of Priam's glory and my own.
For my prophetic soul foresees a day,
When Ilium, Ilium's people, and himself
Her warlike king shall perish. But no grief
For Ilium ; for her people ; for the king,
My warlike sire ; nor even for the queen ;
Nor for the numerous and the valiant band,
My brothers, destined all to lick the ground,
So moves me, as my grief for thee alone !
Doom'd then to follow some imperious Greek,
A weeping captive, to the distant shores
Of Argos ; there to labour at the loom,
For a task-mistress, and with many a sigh,
But heaved in vain, to bear the ponderous urn
From Hypereia's, or Messëis' fount.
Fast flow thy tears the while, and as he eyes
That silent shower, some passing Greek will say,
' This was the wife of Hector, who excell'd
All Troy in fight, when Ilium was besieged.'
While thus he speaks, thy tears shall flow afresh,
The guardian of thy freedom, while he lived
For ever lost; but be my bones inhumed
A senseless store, or e'er thy parting cries
Shall pierce mine ear, and thou be dragg'd away!"

SOTHEBY.

" Hector replied—' These all, O wife beloved !
All that moves thee, my heart have deeply moved :
Yet more I dread each son of Trojan birth,
More Ilion's dames whose raiment trails on earth,
If like a slave, where chiefs with chiefs engage,
The warrior Hector fears the war to wage—
Not thus my heart inclines. Far, rather far,
First of Troy's sons, I lead the van of war
Firm fix'd, not Priam's dignity alone
And glory to uphold, but guard my own.
I know the day draws nigh when Troy shall fall,
When Priam and his nation perish all ;
Yet, less—forebodings of the fate of Troy,
Her king and Hecuba, my peace destroy ;
Less—that my brethren all, the heroic band,
Must with their blood imbrue their native land,—
Than thoughts of thee in tears, to Greece a prey,
Dragg'd by the grasp of war in chains away,—

Of thee in tears, beneath an Argive roof,
Labouring reluctant the allotted woof,
Or doom'd to draw from Hypereia's cave,
Or from Messëis fount, the measured wave:
A voice will then be heard that thou must hear
'See'st thou yon captive pouring tear on tear?
Lo, Hector's wife, the hero bravest far
When Troy and Greece round Ilion clash'd in war.'—
Then thou with keener anguish wilt deplore
Him whose cold arm can free his wife no more:
But first, may Earth o'er me her mound uprear,
Ere I behold thee slaved, or see thy tear!'"

We hesitate not to say that Cowper's version is perfect.
Unequalled it is at present; excelled it can be—never. It
is coloured not by the faintest hue of translation, but breathes
throughout the pure free air of a divine original. It is just as
good as Homer. The first six lines of Greek are given in six
of English, and their calm firm spirit is finely preserved. All
the others are exquisite.

We cannot say the same of Sotheby's. It is good—Pope's
(which look at) is better—for with more faults, it has greater
beauties—but Cowper's, we repeat, is best. For it alone is
" the tender and the true." In Sotheby the first six lines of
Greek become ten in English—and Hector seems to vaunt
himself rather too much. "My peace destroy," is neither
Homeric nor Hectorian; "yet less," and again "less," are
feeble and formal, cumbrous and clumsy. "The grasp of war"
is an unaffecting generality, compared with its definite original;
we do not admire here the alliteration of " labouring reluctant
the allotted woof," though others may ; " measured wave" are
two words not to our taste, especially the last, which is falsely
poetical for " water." " A voice will then be heard that
thou must hear," is not happy for καί ποτέ τις εἴπῃσιν. " Seest
thou yon captive pouring tear on tear," is a negligent miscon-
ception of ἰδὼν κατὰ δάκρυ χέουσαν, as Sotheby must in an instant
see. " When Troy and Greece *together clash'd in war*," is not
the natural language of a bystander, like ὅτε "Ιλιον ἀμφεμάχοντο.
The final line, " Ere I behold thee slave, or see thy tear," is a
poor impostor, detected at once in the attempt to pass itself
off for

Πρίν γ' ἔτι σῆς τι βοῆς σοῦ θ' ἑλκηθμοῖο πυθέσθαι.

Hector in Homer speaks twice of Andromache's weeping—

δακρυόεσσαν—κατὰ δάκρυ χέουσαν : in Sotheby four times — "thoughts of thee in tears"—"of thee in tears"—"pouring tear on tear"—"see thy tear." With more than double the effort, the translator produces less than half the effect.

Old Chapman felt Hector's address—and he labours to render it, if possible, still more dismal. He makes Hector say,

"And such a stormy day shall come, in mind and soul I know,
When sacred Troy shall shed her towers, for tears of overthrow."

Not in Homer, indeed, but dreadful—and afterwards,—

"As thy sad state when some rude Greek shall lead thee weeping
    hence,
Those free days clouded, and a night of captive violence,
Loading thy temples, out of which thine eyes must never see,
But spin the Greek wives' webs of task, and their fetch-water be."

Expansion and paraphrase all—but conceived and expressed in intensity of emotion, and full of ruth.

Who gives best the sense and feeling of

Καί ποτέ τις εἴπησιν,———   .
'"Εκτορος ἥδε γυνή, ὃς ἀριστεύεσκε μάχεσθαι
Τρώων ἱπποδάμων, ὅτε "Ιλιον ἀμφεμάχοντο.'
                                        —VI. 460.

Chapman says,

"This dame was Hector's wife,
A man that at the wars of Troy did breathe the worthiest life
Of all their army."

Dryden,

"While groaning under this laborious life,
They insolently call thee Hector's wife ;
Upbraid thy bondage with thy husband's name,
And from thy glory propagate thy shame."

Pope,

"There, while you groan beneath the load of life,
They cry, 'behold the mighty Hector's wife !'
Some haughty Greek, who loves thy tears to see,
Embitters all thy woes by naming me."

Cowper,

"This was the wife of Hector who excell'd
All Troy in fight when Ilium was besieged."

Sotheby, as you have seen,

> "Lo, Hector's wife, the hero bravest far,
> When Troy and Greece round Ilion clashed in war!"

Who, we ask again, is best? Cowper. Who next? Perhaps Pope—perhaps Chapman. Who next? Perhaps Sotheby. Dryden is the worst—inasmuch as he is the least Homeric—and his lines, though they have his usual copious flow, are failures; for "insolently" in the second is beyond and out of Hector's meaning; the third is superfluous, and the fourth absurdly and coarsely and vulgarly "propagated."

Dunces, with "hearts as dry as summer dust," have here found fault with Homer and Hector. Cold comfort this, they have said, from husband to wife. Hector is here chicken-hearted—cowed—crowed-down—cool in the pens—*fugy*, as cockers say; but he ought to have sung clear as unconquered chanticleer, dropt his wing, strutted crously, and sent his fair hen and chicken chuckling gaily to Troy. Such is the spirit of their fault-finding, though they were not up to the use of such appropriate terms of reprobation; for they are Fools. Hector speaks to Andromache, at first, like the heroic soldier—"jealous and quick of honour"—and conscious that in his arm lies the salvation of his country. But all at once, " O my prophetic soul!" He sees Troy taken—and Andromache captive. The vision asks not his leave—but embodies itself in words, leaving the choice of them to Love and Pity. Of that dismal day, " far off the coming shone" on his soul—and it will therefore speak as another great poet makes a sad seer say,

> " Though dark and despairing my sight I may seal,
> Yet man cannot cover what God would reveal."

But now for our concluding specimen of Sotheby, which completes the

> " Tale of tears, the mournful story."

> " He spoke, and stretch'd his arms, and onward prest
> To clasp his child, and fold him on his breast;
> The while the child, on whose o'er-dazzled sight
> The helm's bright splendour flash'd too fierce a light,
> And the thick horse-hair as it wavy play'd
> From the high helmet cast its sweeping shade,
> Scared at his father's sight, bent back distrest,
> And shrieking, sunk upon his nurse's breast.

The child's vain fear their bitter woe beguiled,
And o'er the boy each parent sweetly smiled.
And Hector now the glittering helm unbraced,
And gently on the ground its terror placed,
Then kiss'd, and dandling with his infant play'd,
And to the gods and Jove devoutly pray'd.
' Jove ! and ye gods, vouchsafe that Hector's boy,
Another Hector, all surpass in Troy,
Like me in strength pre-eminently tower,
And guard the nation with his father's power ;
Heard be a voice, whene'er the warrior bends,
Behold the chieftain who his sire transcends.
And grant that home returning, charged with spoil,
His mother's smile repay the hero's toil.'

He spake, and gave, now sooth'd from vain alarms,
The lovely infant to his mother's arms,
And the fond mother, as she laid to rest
The lovely infant on her fragrant breast,
Smiled in her tears, while Hector, as they fell,
Kiss'd her pale cheek, and sooth'd with fond farewell.
' Grieve not, my love, untimely ; ere the hour
My fate predestined dread no hostile power ;
But—at the time ordain'd, the base, the brave,
All pass alike within th' allotted grave.
Now home retire ; thy charge, beneath our roof,
To ply the distaff, and to weave the woof ;
To task thy maids, and guide their labour, thine ;
The charge of war is man's, and chiefly mine.' "

There is a screed—a sweep of Sotheby, gentlest reader ;
and as the parallel passage in Pope—who, you may depend
upon it, was a poet—is one of the most popular in poetry,
doubtless you have it by heart, and it comes in palpitations,
pat for comparison. But first of all, see the ebb and flow of
the tides of our sea-like passions. A while ago the waves of
sorrow came fast and loud, tumbling in, as

"Drumly and dark they roll'd on their way,"

and rueful was the plight of Hector's soul as a surf-beaten
ledge of rocks. It was drowning—drowned. But the overwhelming mass of foam all at once lulled, and wheeled back
into the sea, leaving bare the bright-shelled sands to the sunshine of Heaven. Let that image suffice in its insufficiency ;

and say simply that Hector again is, as the warful world goes,
happy, and so is Andromache.   Why not?   They know their
fate, and to it are now "deeply reconciled."   In such reconcilement there is often profound peace—sometimes still, yea,
even brightest joy;—and now the hour is blest, even

> "As when some field, when clouds roll thick and dun,
> Shines, in the distance, 'neath the showery sun ;   .
> Or as some isle the howl of ocean braves,
> And rises lovely 'mid the dash of waves."
>   (CHRISTOPHER NORTH, *MSS. penes me.*)

We said this moment "they know their fate, and to it are
now deeply reconciled."   Unsay the words—for they have
forgotten their fate, and in their blindness are blest.   Astyanax shall not be spun from the tower-top by Pyrrhus—Troy
shall not totter to its fall—still shall Ilion salute the sky.
For see ταιδ' ἐον, how he smiles, as Hector high in the air
holds up "his beautiful and shining golden head," starlike
even in mid-day, before the "weepingly smiling" eyes of
Andromache !   That is a vision "able to drive all sadness—
even despair."   That blood shall be a blossom—that blossom
a flower ; and that flower shall bear glorious fruit—fruit
worthy the scion of such a stem—deeds of deliverance, and
the fame that flames before the feet of the free.   Hector shall
be eclipsed by Hector's son—and by none but he ; and the
young warrior shall walk in the rescued city, among the
music of perpetual hymns.   Hector himself, ere then, may
have "undergone the earth," and the green mound over his
ashes be shaded with trees ; but Andromache will be surviv-
ing in her honoured and happy widowhood, and as her son
comes to her from battle, glorious in the arms of some van-
quished hero, χαρείη δὲ φρένα μήτηρ.   But why — oh why !
Sotheby ! Sotheby ! didst thou say that these three thrilling
words mean

> "His mother's smile repays the hero's toil"?

Hector, or his prophetic soul, had been glorying in the glory
of his Astyanax ; but just as he is about to shut his lips, he
thinks of what will then be the joy of his Andromache—and
that is his joy as he places his boy on her beloved breast.
This stroke of tenderness Sotheby does not seem to see ; and

sorry are we to say it, for here between a hit and a miss,
" Oh the difference to me ! "

Now, let us take things calmly, and criticise the execution
by the several translators, or engravers, of two of these celebrated pictures contained in this passage ; and first, that of
the Helmet.

"Ὡς εἰπὼν, οὗ παιδὸς ὀρέξατο φαίδιμος "Εκτωρ.

"Αψ δ' ὁ πάϊς πρὸς κόλπον ἐϋζώνοιο τιθήνης
'Εκλίνθη ἰάχων, πατρὸς φίλου ὄψιν ἀτυχθεὶς,
Ταρβήσας χαλκόν τε ἰδὲ λόφον ἱππιοχαίτην,
Δεινὸν ἀπ' ἀκροτάτης κόρυθος νεύοντα νοήσας·
'Εκ δ' ἐγίλασσε πατήρ τε φίλος καὶ πότνια μήτηρ.
Αὐτίκ' ἀπὸ κρατὸς κόρυθ' εἵλετο φαίδιμος "Εκτωρ,
Καὶ τὴν μὲν κατέθηκεν ἐπὶ χθονὶ παμφανόωσαν.
Αὐτὰρ ὅ γ' ὃν φίλον υἱὸν ἐπεὶ κύσε, πῆλέ τε χερσὶν,
Εῖπεν ἐπευξάμενος, Διί τ' ἄλλοισίν τε θεοῖσιν.

—VI. 466.

CHAPMAN.

" This said, he reach'd to take his son ; who, of his arms afraid,
And then the horse-hair plume with which he was so overlaid
Nodded so horribly, he cling'd back to his nurse and cried.
Laughter affected his great sire, who doff'd and laid aside
His fearful helm, that on the earth cast round about it light.
Then took and kiss'd his loving son, and balancing his weight
In dancing him, those loving vows to living Jove he used,
And all the other bench of gods."

DRYDEN.

" Then holding forth his arms, he took his boy,
The pledge of love, and other hope of Troy.
The fearful infant turn'd his head away,
And on his nurse's neck reclining lay,
His unknown father shunning with affright,
And looking back on so uncouth a sight ;
Daunted to see a face with steel o'erspread,
And his high plume that nodded o'er his head.
Then sire and mother smiled with silent joy,
And Hector hasten'd to relieve his boy ;
Dismiss'd his burnish'd helm that shone afar,
The pride of warriors, and the pomp of war.
The illustrious babe, thus reconciled, he took,
Hugg'd in his arms, and kiss'd, and thus he spoke."

POPE.

" Thus having spoke, the illustrious chief of Troy
Stretch'd his fond arms to clasp the lovely boy.
The babe clung crying to his nurse's breast,
Scared at the dazzling helm and nodding crest.
With secret pleasure each fond parent smiled,
And Hector hasted to relieve the child ;
The glittering terrors from his brows unbound,
And placed the beaming helmet on the ground,
Then kiss'd the child, and lifting high in air—
Thus to the gods preferr'd a father's prayer."

COWPER.

" The hero ended, and his arms put forth
To reach his boy ; but, with a scream, the child
Still closer to his mother's bosom clung,
Shunning his touch, for dreadful in his eyes
The brazen armour shone ; and dreadful more,
The shaggy crest that swept his father's brow.
Both parents smiled delighted ; and the chief
Let down the crested terror on the ground ;
Then kiss'd him, play'd away his infant fears,
And thus to Jove and all the powers above."

They are all " beautiful exceedingly." Chapman gives
strongliest of them all, the terror of the child—"then balancing his weight in dancing him," though it has not the con-
ciseness of σῆλέ τε χεροίν, is perhaps even more picturesque ;
" and laid aside his fearful helm, that on the earth cast round
about it light," for τὴν μὲν κατέθηκεν ἐπὶ χθονὶ παμφανόωσαν, is
very noble. In short, in Chapman's copy, you see the true
character of a divine original of the greatest of all the old
masters.

Dryden dashes off a somewhat too sketchy copy, but with
fine free-flowing lines.

" The pledge of love, and other hope of Troy,"

is a needless line—the first half of it weak, and the second a
repetition of what has been said before. " His unknown father,"
is a charming touch of Dryden's own, and flashes forth the
soul of the sense ; " dismiss'd his burnish'd helm," is a formality much inferior to the simple original, and he says
nothing of it "lying all ashine on the ground ;" " the pride of

warriors, and the pomp of war," is sad slavering; but the end, with the exception of " hugg'd," which is not the right word, is excellent. Faulty but not feeble, you still see in the sketch the hand of "glorious John," and therefore you may purchase it.

Pope's copy is almost as good as the original—to a common judge like Christopher or Nicodemus. The third and fourth lines seem to us perfect—" And Hector hasten'd to relieve his child," is, you will perceive, taken from Dryden. ' Glittering terrors," in line seventh, are the same thing as "beaming helmet" in line eighth, which ought not to have been ; and, indeed, Homer knew better than to have said " glittering terrors," a mode of speech the invention of a later day, when poets became impatient of speaking like other people, which Homer never was, nor even Apollo. Still, this copy from Homer by Pope, is a fine cabinet picture, and hangs in the Sanctum.

Perhaps you think Cowper's copy somewhat dim, and perhaps it is; but keep your gaze fixed steadfastly upon it, and the figures will come out upon you a bright and beauteous group. "With a scream," &c. for ἐκλίνθη ἰάχων, &c. is the truth most entirely ; so is the word " dreadful" for δεινὸν, which we see not in the other copies ; "shaggy " is fine ; but " crested terror," borrowed from Pope's " glittering terror," is but a poor plagiarism, unworthy of Cowper. "Play'd away his infant fears," may give the picture to the imagination, but not to the eye ; and Homer, you know, through the eye doth here appeal both to the imagination and the heart.

Sotheby's is far from a failure—but it might have been a more distinguished success. " Onward prest," &c. is minuter and more particular than Homer, who is here minute and particular just up to the proper point. " Bright *splendour* flash'd too fierce a *light*," is not the best of modern English, and has no resemblance to old Greek. " Cast its sweeping shade," is a picturesque particular, but though it might frighten a child, it is not so well adapted for that especial purpose as the circumstance Homer mentions ; the scaring, shrieking (both in themselves good), come in too late in Sotheby, for Homer, as was right, shows them the very first thing ; and we are sorry to see that Sotheby steals the " terror" from Pope, who had just pocketed it from Dryden, and we insist on both pilferers returning the property to the lawful owner—which they may

do without being the poorer, he the richer; for after all, it is
not better than a Bandana. Yet with these faults, real or
imaginary, the copy is a spirited—nay, a splendid one—and
speaks of Sotheby.

Look here, before we part, at another picture.

> "Ὡς εἰπὼν ἀλόχοιο φίλης ἐν χερσὶν ἔθηκεν
> Παῖδ' ἑόν· ἡ δ' ἄρα μιν κηώδεϊ δέξατο κόλπῳ
> Δακρυόεν γελάσασα. Πόσις δ' ἐλέησε νοήσας,
> Χειρί τέ μιν κατέρεξεν, ἔπος τ' ἔφατ', ἔκ τ' ὀνόμαζεν.
>   —VI. 482.

CHAPMAN.

>   " This said, the heroic sire
> Gave him his mother, whose fair eyes fresh streams of love's salt fire
> Billow'd on her soft cheeks, to hear the last of Hector's speech
> In her wish'd comfort. So she took into her odorous breast
> Her husband's gift, who, moved to see her heart so much oppress'd,
> He dried her tears, and thus desired," &c.

DRYDEN.

>   " Thus having said :
> He first with suppliant hands the gods adored ;
> Then to the mother's arms the child restored.
> With tears and smiles she took her son and press'd
> The illustrious infant to her fragrant breast.
> He, wiping her fair eyes, indulged her grief,
> And eased her sorrows with this last relief."

POPE.

> " He spoke, and fondly gazing on her charms,
> Restored the pleasing burden to her arms ;
> Soft on her fragrant breast the babe she laid,
> Hush'd to repose, and with a smile survey'd ;
> The troubled pleasure soon chastised by fear,
> She mingled with the smile a tender tear ;
> The soften'd chief with kind compassion view'd,
> And dried the falling drops, and thus pursued."

COWPER.

> " He spake, and to his lovely spouse consign'd
> The darling boy : with mingled smiles and tears,
> She wrapp'd him in her bosom's fragrant fold ;
> And Hector, pang'd with pity that she wept,
> Her dewy cheek stroked softly, and began."

" This said, he placed his infant in the arms
Of his loved wife ; she to her fragrant breast,
Smiling in tears, received it. Pity touch'd
His soul ; he fondly press'd her hand and spake."

Here, again, all the Seven are beautiful—from Homer to
Gilbert Wakefield, who in general was no great beauty.
Chapman, as usual, is intense ; and not satisfied with Homer,
he must needs translate δακρυόεν γελάσασα into " fresh streams
of love's salt fire billow'd on her soft cheeks," an atrocity deserving death.   Still the passage is passionate ; and Chapman
having chosen to add " dried her tears," which is not in Homer
(but afterwards in Milton), almost all the other translators
have followed him in this—and without blame, as there can
be no doubt that Hector did dry Andromache's tears with his
lips from which " not words alone pleased her," and that without those kisses her heart would have broken.

Dryden is not correct in saying that Hector first " with suppliant hands the gods adored," for Hector had done that
already ; but " wiping her fair eyes " is, if not in Homer,
Chapmannish and Miltonic, and mighty motherish ; and therefore, " dear child of nature, let them rail," the version is good.

Pope's translation is, in itself, so delightful, that we have
no heart to breathe a syllable in its depreciation, dispraise, or
disparagement.   Yet " fondly gazing on her charms" is not
so true to nature, as the simple ἀλόχοιο φίλης ἐν χερσὶν ἔθηκεν—
for Homer, though he knew that Hector felt how beautiful
was Andromache at that hour, likewise knew that all the world
would know it without being told so, in secula seculorum.
" Pleasing burden " is a pleasing expression, and always will
be, in spite of its being so very common a one ; but how much
better is παῖδ' ἑόν ?   " The troubled pleasure soon chastised by
fear" is very unhomeric—and though at first hearing it sounds
very fine, yet is it essentially faulty ; for observe that the
word " troubled " doth of itself necessarily imply in the pleasure the very " fear " which is said soon to chastise it !   Call
not this, we beseech you, O reader ! a verbal criticism, for it
strikes at the root of an error originating in the brain that at
the time was trying to do the business of the heart.

Cowper is very tender.   " Lovely spouse " is just ἀλόχοιο
φίλης, " darling boy " is just παῖδ' ἑόν, according to the corre-

sponding spirit of the Greek and English speech; with "mingled smiles and tears" comes as near to δακρυόεν γελάσασα as may be, without attempting to give the peculiarity of the expression; "panged with pity" is strongly true for ἐλέησε; "stroked softly" is right, and μιν is well changed into "cheek;" "wrapped in her bosom's fragrant folds" is very motherly, and very sweet. In short, though not perfect, the version in spirit is "tender and true."

Sotheby has much of the mellifluousness of Pope, with more of the delightful definiteness of the Homeric touch. He alone gives δακρυόεν γελάσασα aright—"smiled in her tears,"—literally, "weepingly smiling"—our version of the two well-matched words. "Kiss'd her pale cheek" we approve of—since it is written—and therefore the whole is good.

But after all, to give the demon his due, the most Homeric of them all is Gilbert Wakefield. Poor Gilbert! We have by heart one of his affecting confessions in one of his notes. On quoting that famous line αιεν αριστευειν και υπειροχον εμμεναι αλλων—he says, "a maxim imbibed by the writer of this note with such effect, even to the *marrow of his soul*, to use a bold expression of Euripides, that, could genius and fortune have conspired in his favour, he had owned no superior in literary accomplishment; but circumstances were unfavourable, and nature infused a large portion of *cold blood about his heart*."

None of the translations have missed Andromache's "fragrant breast," κηώδεϊ κόλπῳ; but we know not if any one of them knew why it was fragrant—the sole reason being, as Blackwall somewhere informs us in his rambling "Enquiry into the Life and Writings of Homer," that the Trojan ladies put certain odorous plants or preservatives into their clothes-baskets and chests to save them from the moths!

But we are at the end of our article—which, long as it is, may haply seem not too long, since it overflows with Homer —and ends with the parting of Hector and Andromache.

CHAPMAN.

"On went his helm, his princess home, half cold with kindly fears,
    When every fear turn'd back her looks, and every look shed tears;
    Foe-slaughtering Hector's house soon reach'd, her many women there
    Wept all to see her, in his life great Hector's funerals were;

Never look'd any eye of theirs to see their lord safe home,
'Scaped from the gripe and powers of Greece," &c.

DRYDEN.

" At this, for new replies he did not stay,
But laced his crested helm, and strode away :
His lovely consort to her house return'd,
And looking often back, in silence mourn'd ;
Home when she came, her secret woe she vents,
And fills the palace with her loud laments.
Those loud laments her echoing maids restore,
And Hector, yet alive, as dead deplore."

POPE.

" Thus having said, the glorious chief resumes
His tow'ring helmet, black with shading plumes.
His princess parts, with a prophetic sigh—
Unwilling parts, and oft reverts her eye,
That stream'd at every look, then moving slow,
Sought her own palace, and indulged her woe.
There, while her tears deplored the godlike man,
Through all the train the soft infection ran :
The pious maids their mingled sorrows shed,
And mourn the living Hector as the dead."

COWPER.

" So saying, the hero to his brows restored
The tufted helmet, and his lovely spouse,
Oft turning as she went, and show'ring tears
Of tenderest sorrow, left him, as he bade.
Arriving where, the terrible in arms,
Her Hector dwelt, with such afflictive moans,
She pierced their hearts, that all her numerous train
Mourn'd also ; mourning Hector, still alive,
In his own palace, as already slain,
For all hope fail'd them of his safe return."

SOTHEBY.

" He spake ; then raised from earth, and firmly press'd
On his brave brow the helmet's wavy crest.
She homeward went, and slow and sadly past,
Oft turn'd, and turning wept, with woe o'ercast.
And now beneath her Hector's proud abode,
Tears of deep grief from all around her flow'd,

> One woe in all, while all alike deplored
> In his own home as dead, their living lord,
> Who ne'er, they deem'd, escaped the battle-plain,
> Would look on his loved wife and home again."

Dryden says, that Homer is "much more capable of excit-
ing the *manly* passions than those of grief and pity." Are
grief and pity not manly passions? Ay, that they are, whether
in heroic or Christian hearts. Homer had power given to him
over them all ; and he knew when and where to touch them—
the proper place and the proper time—and the key to which
each heart-chord responded in terror or in tears. Mighty
masters of emotion as were in a later age the three tragedians,
neither Æschylus, Sophocles, nor Euripides in that power transcended Homer. But Homer seldom puts that power forth ;
for it is not the prime end of the epic, as it is of the tragic, to
purge the soul by pity and terror. "Homer," Dryden says
again falsely, "was *ambitious enough* of moving pity, for he has
attempted twice, on the same subject of Hector's death ; first,
when Priam and Hecuba beheld his corpse, which was dragged
after the chariot of Achilles ; and then in the lamentation
which was made over him, when his body was redeemed by
Priam ; and the same persons again bewail his death, with a
chorus of others to help the cry. But if this last excite compassion in you, as I doubt not but it will, you are more obliged
to the translator than the poet [he alludes here to Congreve!]
for Homer, as I have observed before, can move rage better
than he can pity." Dryden uttered this sad stuff, we suspect,
because he was the translator of Virgil. Now Virgil's pathos
is certainly more profuse than Homer's—but it is not so profound ; although, as certainly, it is more characteristic of his
delightful genius. Pope, too, in deference perhaps to Dryden,
has observed, "that pity and the softer passions are not of the
nature of the Iliad." Wood, the author of the *Descriptions
of Palmyra and Balbeck*, in his *Essay on the Original Genius
and Writings of Homer*, remarks well on this, that Pope might
have said that they "are not of the character of Homer's manners. Yet when they are introduced amidst the terrors of
death and slaughter, the contrast is irresistible ; and a tender
scene in the Iliad, like a cultivated spot in the Alps, derives
now beauties from the horrors which surround it." Well said,

Wood. But you say not so well, when you go on to say, " Should I presume to see a fault in this admired picture, it is one that falls not upon the poet, but his manners, and may help to explain my ideas on this matter. Andromache having raised our pity and compassion to the utmost stretch that tragedy can carry those passions—Hector answers—

'Ἦ καὶ ἐμοὶ τάδε πάντα μέλει, γύναι.'

and concludes 'Αλλ' εἰς οἶκον ἰοῦσα, &c. His meaning here was to divert Andromache's attention to other objects, and the expression was meant to convey the utmost tenderness ; but has it that effect upon us ? Is not the English reader offended at a certain indelicacy in those words which Homer puts into the mouth of an affectionate husband to his wife ?" A certain indelicacy forsooth ! No—the English reader is not offended— nor the Scotch reader either—nor yet the Irish ; for there is no indelicacy, but all is beautiful and Bible-like—which, dear reader, you will feel to-morrow—for it is the Sabbath—so farewell !

HOMER AND HIS TRANSLATORS.

[JULY 1831.]

WE have the highest respect for Blair's *Lectures on Rhetoric and Belles Lettres*. Dr Hugh had so much taste and talent, that his mind bordered on genius. It may be said to have lived in the debatable land between the two great kingdoms of Reason and Imagination. Not that we mean to say the Doctor was in any mood a poet; but in many a mood he loved poetry, and saw and felt its beauties. It spoke to something within him, which was not mere intelligence. In short, Nature had not gifted him with Imagination active, but of Imagination passive she had given Hugh a considerable share; and thus, though it was impossible for him to originate the poetical, it was easy for him to appreciate it when set before him by the makers. A pure delight seems to have touched his heart, in contemplating the creations of genius, in listening to the inspiration of those on whom heaven had bestowed " the vision and the faculty divine." The Professor doth sometimes prose, it must be confessed, " wearisome exceedingly;" but that in some measure was his vocation; and the heaviest of all vehicles is perhaps, in print, a Lecture. It was his bounden duty to be as plain as a pike-staff, perspicuous as an icicle; and rare would have been his felicity had he escaped the " timmer-tune" of the one, and the frigidity of the other, in his very elegant and useful prelections. Cowper, in one of his letters, commends Blair's good sense, but speaks most contemptuously of his utter destitution of all original power either of thought or feeling; but there the author of *The Task* was too severe, for compare him with the best critics going or gone, and he will appear far from barren. His manner is somewhat cold, but there is often much warmth in the matter—and let us say it at once, he had, in his way, enthusiasm. In private life Blair was a man of a constitution of character by no means unimpassioned; his human sensibilities were tender and acute; with finer moral, or higher religious emotions, no man was ever more familiar; and with these and other endowments, we take leave to think that he was entitled and qualified to expatiate, *ex cathedra*, nay, without offence, even now and then to prose and preach by the hour-glass, as if from the very pulpit, on epic poetry and poets, yea, even on Homer.

Mr Wordsworth has been pleased to say, that the soil of Scotland is peculiarly adapted by Nature for the growth of that weed called the Critic. He instances David Hume and Adam Smith. David certainly was somewhat spoiled by an over-addiction to French *liqueurs;* and he has indited some rare nonsense about Shakespeare. Adam, too, for poetry had a Parisian palate; and cared little for *Percy's Reliques.* It seems he once said that the author of the ballad of "Clym of the Cleugh" could not have been a gentleman. For this sentiment, he of *The Excursion* has called the author of the *Theory of Moral Sentiments* a weed. If he be, then, to use an expression which Wordsworth has borrowed from Spenser, 'tis "a weed of glorious feature." We agree with Adam Smith in believing that the ancient balladmonger was no gentleman. But we must not "cry mew" to him on that account; for ancient balladmongers are not expected to be gentlemen; and they may write admirably of deer-stalking, of deer-shooting, and deer-stealing, though in the rule of manners they have not anticipated Chesterfield. We found fault with Mr Wordsworth for having suffered his spite towards one of its productions, the *Edinburgh Review*, to vitiate his judgment of the whole soil of Scotland—and to commit himself before the whole world by declaring people to be worthless and ugly weeds, who are valuable and useful flowers. David and Adam are Perennials—or, "say rather," Immortals. Both the one and the other is

> ——"like a tree that grows
> Near planted by a river,
> Which in its season yields its fruit,
> And its leaf fadeth never."

So is William Wordsworth—and justifiably would he despise

the person who, pitying perhaps poor Alice Fell, without seeing anything particularly poetical or pathetic in her old or
new duffle cloak, should, forgetful of all his glories, call the
author of that feeble failure a weed. True enough, he is
there commonplace as a docken by the wayside ; but elsewhere rare as amaranth, which only grows in heaven.

The truth seems to be, that the soil of Scotland is most
happily adapted for the cultivation of philosophical criticism.
There was old Kames, though flawed and cracked, a diamond
almost of the first water. Hold up his *Elements* between
your eye and the firmament, and you see the blue and the
clouds. To speak sensibly, he was the very first person produced by this island of ours, entitled to the character of a
philosophical inquirer into the principles of poetical composition. He is the father of such criticism in this country—the
Scottish—not the Irish—Stagirite. He is ours—let the
English show their Aristotle. That his blunders are as
plentiful as blackberries, is most true ; but that they are so is
neither wonder nor pity— for so are Burke's ;—yet is his
treatise on the Sublime and Beautiful, juvenile as it is, full of
truth and wisdom. Change the image ; and fling Kames'
Elements of Criticism into the fanners of Wordsworth's wrath ;
and after the air has been darkened for a while with chaff, the
barn-floor will be like a granary rich in heaps of the finest
white wheat, which, baked into bolted bread, is tasteful and
nutritive sustenance even for a Lake poet.

By much criticism, sincerely or affectedly philosophical, has
the genius of Shakespeare been lately belaboured, by true
men and by pretenders—from Coleridge and Lamb, to Hazlitt
and Barry Cornwall. But, after all, with the exception of
some glorious things said by the Ancient Mariner and Elia,
little new has been added, of much worth, to the Essays of
Professor Richardson, a forgotten work, of which a few copies
have been saved by thieves from the moths. There, too, is
Alison's delightful book on Taste, in which the Doctrine of
Association is stated with the precision of the Philosopher,
and illustrated with the prodigality of the Poet. Compare
with it Payne Knight's *Analytical Enquiry*, and from feasting on the juicy heart of an orange, you are starving on its
shrivelled skin. Of the *Edinburgh Review*, and *Blackwood's
Magazine*,—mayhap the least said is soonest mended ; but

surely it may be permitted us to say this much for Francis Jeffrey, and Christopher North, that the one set agoing all the reviews, and the other all the magazines, which now periodically, that is, perpetually, illumine the world; and if the *Quarterly* and its train have eclipsed, or should eclipse, the Blue and Yellow, and the *Metropolitan* and its train take the shine out of Her of the Olive, let it be remembered with grateful admiration what those planets once were; and never for one moment be forgotten the illustrious fact, that Scotland has still to herself been true; for that certain new-risen Scottish stars have outshone certain old ones; that—again to change the image—the Tweed has lent its light and music to the Thames, and made it at once a radiant and a sonorous river.

As to German philosophical criticism, almost all that we know of it is in Lessing, Wieland, Goethe, and the Schlegels. We understand on good authority, that of Carlyle, Moir, and Weir, that there are at least seven wise men in that land of lumber, and we understand on still better, our own, that there are at least seventy sumphs, who, were the Thames or the Rhine set on fire by us, would speedily extinguish it. But of the above said heroes, the two first, like Hercules, conquer the bulls they take by the horns; of Wilhelm Meister on Shakespeare, our friends aforesaid have expressed their reverence; but that, we hope, need not hinder us from hinting our contempt; and as for the " bletherin brithers," as the Shepherd most characteristically called the Schlegels, they are indeed boys for darkening the daylight and extinguishing the moon and stars. So, let us return from these few modest remarks on the former schools of Philosophical Criticism to where we set out from, namely, the Chair of Rhetoric and Belles Lettres, with Dr Hugh Blair sitting in it decorously, and lecturing on Epic Poetry, particularly on Homer, and more particularly on the Iliad. The Doctor doth thus dissert on the opening of the Iliad.

" The opening of the Iliad possesses none of that sort of dignity which a modern looks for in an Epic Poem. It turns on no higher subject than the quarrel of two chieftains about a female slave. The priest of Apollo beseeches Agamemnon to restore his daughter, who, in the plunder of a city, had fallen to Agamemnon's share of booty. He refuses. Apollo, at the prayer of his priest, sends a plague into the Grecian

camp. The augur, when consulted, declares that there is no
way of appeasing Apollo but by restoring the daughter of
his priest. Agamemnon is enraged at the augur; professes
that he likes this slave better than his wife Clytemnestra; but
since he must restore her, in order to save the army, insists to
have another in her place; and pitches upon Briseïs, the slave
of Achilles. Achilles, as was to be expected, kindles into
rage at this demand; reproaches him for his rapacity and
insolence, and, after giving him many hard names, solemnly
swears that, if he is to be thus treated by the general, he
will withdraw his troops, and assist the Grecians no more
against the Trojans. He withdraws accordingly. His mother,
the goddess Thetis, interests Jupiter in his cause; who, to
avenge the wrong which Achilles had suffered, takes part
against the Greeks, and suffers them to fall into great and
long distress; until Achilles is pacified, and reconciliation
brought about between him and Agamemnon."

The Doctor has delivered his dictum that the opening of the
Iliad possesses none of that sort of dignity which a modern looks
for in an Epic poem. " It turns," quoth he, contemptuously,
"on no higher subject than the quarrel of two chieftains about
a female slave." Now, we wish the worthy Doctor had told us
what is the sort of dignity which a modern looks for in an
Epic poem—and that he had furnished us with a few specimens. The Doctor is not orthodox here—he is a heretic—
and were he to be brought to trial before the General Assembly of the Critical Kirk, his gown would, we fear, be taken
from his shoulders, and himself left to become the head of a
sect which assuredly, unlike some others, would not include
any considerable quern[1] of womenfolk. What higher subject
of quarrel between two chieftains would Dr Blair have suggested, than a beautiful woman ? That Briseïs was so—an
exquisite creature—is proved by the simple fact of her
having been the choice of Achilles. The City-Sacker, from
a gorgeous band, culled that one Flower, who filled his tent
with " the bloom of young desire, and purple light of love."
The son of Thetis tells us that he loved her as his own wife.
Nay, she was his wife—he had married her, just as if he had
been in Scotland, by declaring that they two were one flesh,
in presence of Patroclus, and then making a long honeymoon

[1] Quantity.

of it in the innermost heart of the tent. True, Briseïs was a
slave; but how could she help that circumstance, and was it
not the merest trifle in that age? For hundreds of miles
round, while Achilles Poliorcetes was before Troy, there was
not a king's daughter who in a day might not be a slave.
Ovid, we believe, or some other liar, says that Briseïs was a
widow, and that Achilles slew her husband when he ravaged
Lyrnessus. But she never was a widow in her life, till that
fatal flight of the arrow of Paris. Till Achilles made her his
own, she was a virgin princess.

But say that Briseïs was, in matter of fact, a "Female
Slave." She was not a maid of all work. Her arms were not
red, nor her hands horny; her ankles were not like bedposts;
huggers she wore not, nor yet bauchles. Her sandals so suited
her soles, and her soles her sandals, that her feet glided o'er
the ground like sunbeams, as bright and as silent, and the
greensward grew greener beneath the gentle pressure. Her
legs were like lilies. So were her arms and hands—her
shoulders, neck, and bosom; and had the Doctor but once
looked on her, he would have forgot his clerical dignity, and
in place of calling her "a female slave," have sworn, though
a divine, by some harmless oath, that she was an angel. "A
rose," Shakespeare says, "by any other name would smell as
sweet." True, men call her the Queen of Flowers. And she
is so. But were all the disloyal world to join in naming her
the Slave of Weeds, still would she be sole sovereign of her
own breathing and blushing floral kingdom. We defy
divine right, and holds, by a heavenly tenure, of the sun, on
humanity to discrown or dethrone her—for she is queen by
condition merely of presenting him with a few dewdrops every
dawn, during the months she loves best to illumine with her
regal lustre. Just so was it with her whom Dr Hugh Blair
chose to call "female slave." She was free as a fawn on the
hill, as a nightingale in the grove, as a dove in the air—a
bright bird of beauty, that loved to nestle in the storm-laid
bosom of the destroyer. Achilles was the slave. Briseïs
captived the invincible—hung chains round his neck, which
to strive to break would have been the vainest madness: the
arrow of Paris, it is fabled, smote the only vulnerable spot of
the hero—his heel, and slew him; but Briseïs assailed him with
the archery of her eyes, and the winged wounds went to the

very core of his heart, inflicting daily a thousand deaths, alter-
nating with life-fits that in their bliss alone deserved the name
of being. And what signifies it to Achilles, that Dr Blair
persists, like a Presbyterian as he is, in calling his Briseïs a
female slave? The Professor should have said a seraph.

The Doctor forgot that the loss of a mistress is sadly felt
by a general on foreign service. Had Agamemnon been at
Argos, he might not—though there is no saying—have been
so savage on the forced relinquishment of a Chryseïs. Had
Achilles been in Peleus' palace in Pthia, he might have better
borne the want of a Briseïs. In the piping times of peace,
people's passions are not so impetuous as in the trumpeting
times of war. Dr Blair admits that Agamemnon loved Chryseïs better than Clytemnestra; indeed, we have the king of
men's own word for it; and Achilles, who was the soul of
truth and honour, tells us that he adored his Briseïs, who,
though in childhood betrothed to one of her own princes, fell
into his arms a virgin, and that on his return to Pthia he
intended to make her his queen. Alas! such was not his
fate! He chose death with glory, rather than life with love.
And as for Agamemnon, he indeed returned to Argos; but if
those Tragic Tales be true that shook the stage with terror
under the genius of Æschylus, better for the king of men had
he too died before Troy; for the adulterous and murderous
matron slew him, even like a bull, with an axe before the
domestic altar. Oh! that bloody bath! As for his lovely
and delicious leman, the uncredited prophetess, the long-
haired Cassandra, Clytemnestra killed her too, smiting her on
the broad white forehead, with the same edge that had drank
the gore of Agamemnon. But ere long came the avenger—
and beneath the sacred sword of her own son, the murderess
" stooped her adulterous head as low as death." Then from
the infernal shades arose the Furies to dog the flying feet of
the distracted parricide. But at last the god of light and the
goddess of wisdom stretched the celestial shield of their pity
over Orestes, and at their divine bidding, the snaky sisters,
abandoning their victim restored to reason and peace, thenceforth Furies no more! all over Greece were called Eumenides!

But let us for a moment make the violent supposition that
Briseïs was a black—a downright and indisputable negro.
Jove, we shall suppose, made Achilles a present of her, on his

return from one of his twelve days' visits to the blameless
Ethiopians. What then? Although Thetis had white feet,
that is no reason in the world against her son's being partial to black ones; for surely a man is not bound to love
in his mistress what he admires in his mother. Neither is
there any accounting for taste—nobody dreams of denying
that apothegm. As for blubber-lips, we cannot say that we
ever felt any irresistible inclination to taste them; yet a
negress's lips are rosy, and her teeth lilies. And therefore,
had Briseïs been a negro, and Achilles so capricious as to
prefer her, black but comely, to paler beauties, the quarrel
consequent on her violent abreption from his arms, by the
mandate of Agamemnon, might not have given the opening
of the Iliad that sort of dignity which a modern—that is,
Dr Blair—looks for in a great epic poem; but still, as the act
would have been one of most insolent injustice, unstomach-
able by Achilles, who was not a person to play upon with
impunity, the quarrel would at least have been natural, and
so would the opening of the Iliad; in which case, perhaps, we
might have dispensed with the dignity, just as we do on seeing a delicate white Christian lady get married and murdered
by an immense monster of a Moor, the very pillow becoming
pathetic, and the bed-sheets full of ruth and pity as a shroud
prepared for the grave.

Well would it be for the world, lay and clerical, civil and
military, were kings and kingdoms to go together by the
ears, for no less dignified cause than that which produced the
quarrel between Achilles and Agamemnon. Indeed, we may
safely defy Dr Blair, or anybody else, to produce an instance
of an equally dignified cause of quarrel between crowned
heads with that which ennobles the opening of the Iliad.
Ambassadors keep hopping about at much expense from court
to court all over Europe, and Asia too at times, not to mention
America and Africa, maintaining the honour of their respective sovereigns, insulted, it would often seem, by such senile,
or rather anile, indefinable drivelling, as would have ashamed
the auld wife herself of Auchtermuchty; while state-papers,
as they are called, present such a gallemaufry of gossip as
was never equalled in the hostile correspondence of a broken-
up batch of veteran village tabbies, caterwauling in consequence of having all together set their caps at the new minister.

Not one war in twenty that originates in any more dignified dispute than, in a vegetable market, a squabble about a contested string of onions, or, in a fish one, about the price of some stinking haddies. What even is the right of search? But let us not disgust ourselves by the recollection of the sickening sillinesses that have so often drenched Europe in blood. We do not abhor a general war, for we despise it. The quarrels which cause general wars in our times, would indeed make pretty openings for great epic poems. They would possess, we presume, all that sort of dignity which a modern looks for in such noble compositions. Homer had no idea of dignity; Dr Blair had : Achilles and Agamemnon went almost to loggerheads about Briseïs; we could mention kings who deluged their lands in blood, tears, and taxation, about a beer-barrel.

The excellent Doctor talks with uncommon nonchalance about honest people's undignified daughters. The daughter of the Priest of Apollo, "in the plunder of a city, had fallen to Agamemnon's share of booty." She had ; and the old gentleman (as dignified as if he had been Moderator) not at all relishing it, complained to the god he served, who sent a plague into the Grecian camp. Now a plague, up to the time of Dr Hugh Blair, had uniformly been considered a very dignified visitation—and, begging the Doctor's pardon, it is considered so still—sufficiently so to satisfy the mind of any moderate modern meditating on what may be fit matter for the opening of a great epic poem. The plague Apollo sent was a very superior personage to Cholera Morbus, although even he is not to be sneezed at, even when, on his arrival at Leith from Riga, merely performing quarantine. Why, Apollo was himself the plague. He descended from heaven to earth νυκτὶ ἐοικώς. The sun became a shadow—day grew night —and life was death. Is not that dignity enough for the Doctor?

Throughout the whole passage you perceive the Doctor fumbling at the facetious. Having determined that the opening of the Iliad should be deemed deficient in dignity, he sketches it sneeringly and sarcastically, and yet it lours upon us, in spite of his idle derision, as something prodigious and portentous—black with pestilence and war, disunion, despair, and death.

But ere we dismiss Death and the Doctor, observe, that

while the latter somewhat pedantical personage is supposing himself to be criticising in this passage the opening of the Iliad, and pointing out how undignified it is, why, he is sketching, without being aware of it, the plan of the whole poem—beginning, middle, and end. Is it all undignified together? If not, at what point, pray, does the meanness merge into the dignified, and the march begin of the majestical? "Such is the basis of the whole action of the Iliad," he continues, meaning thereby to say, that it is all as insignificant in itself as the opening with the quarrel of two chieftains about a female slave. "Hence," he well says, "rose all those 'speciosa miracula,' as Horace terms them, which fill up that extraordinary poem; and which have had the power of interesting almost all the nations of Europe during every age since the days of Homer. The general admiration commanded by a poetical plan so very different from what any one would have formed in our times ought not, upon reflection, to be matter of surprise. For besides that a fertile genius can enrich and beautify any subject on which it is employed, it is to be observed that ancient manners, how much soever they contradict our present notions of dignity and refinement, afford, nevertheless, materials for poetry superior in some respects to those which are furnished by a more polished state of society. They discover human nature more open and undisguised, without any of those studied forms of behaviour which now conceal men from one another. They give free scope to the strongest and most impetuous motions of the mind, which make a better figure in description than calm and temperate feelings. They show us our native prejudices, appetites, and desires, exerting themselves without control. From this state of manners, joined with the advantage of that strong and expressive style which commonly distinguishes the composition of early ages, we have ground to look for more of the boldness, ease, and freedom of native genius, in compositions of such a period, than in those of more civilised times. And accordingly, the two great characters of the Homeric poetry are, Fire and Simplicity."

The one great original error of supposing that the subject-matter of the Iliad is in itself undignified, and that its poetical plan is, on that account, so very different from what any one would have formed in our times, runs through the whole

of the passage we have quoted from Blair, and vitiates the
philosophy of its criticism. Had any one in our times chosen
the subject for an epic poem in the heroic ages of Greece, he
would have been puzzled to find one different from that of the
Tale of Troy Divine, unless, perhaps, he had been at once a
Homer and a Shakespeare, and then there is no saying what
he might not have done ; and had any one in our times chosen
to choose a subject from our times, or from any other times
intermediate between that heroic and this unheroic age, he
might have stretched his brain till the crack of doom, ere he
had found one more dignified ; even though the Iliad begins
with the wrath of Achilles for sake of a female slave, Briseïs, is
conversant about the middle with his furious grief for loss of
a male friend, Patroclus, draws to a close with the lamentations of two old people, Hecuba and Priam, and ends with the
funeral rites of Hector the Tamer of Horses.

But making allowances for that first and fatal error, all
must admit that Blair speaks truly and finely towards the
close of the paragraph ; and that he says as much in a few
simple sentences, and more too, than both the Schlegels put
together, in their shadowy style, would have said in a whole
essay written in Cloudland. The good Doctor warms as he
walks—and finally escapes out of the ungenial gloom of heresy,
declaring, with an inconsistency that does him infinite credit,
" that the subject of the Iliad must unquestionably be admitted
to be in the main happily chosen."—" Homer has, with great
judgment, selected one part of the Trojan War, the Quarrel
betwixt Achilles and Agamemnon, and the events to which
that quarrel gave rise." In short, the Professor forgets all
his former folly about want of dignity and so forth, and expresses the admiration natural to so fine a mind, of the miracle
wrought by Homer.

We said that we should seize on Sotheby, as a subject for
six critiques—that is to say, on his translation of the Iliad, as
affording us fine opportunities of launching out upon Homer.
In the present utter dearth of poetry, caused by a drought—
" in the Albion air adust "—by the political dog-star which
not only looks so exceedingly Sirius, but foams at the mouth
like the Father of Hydrophobia, if not Hydrophobia himself,
we see nothing left for us but to take a flight of a few thousand years back into antiquity ; and being partial to the epic,

we propose prosing away thereupon—when wearied, taking a tift at Tragedy—and occasionally laying our lugs into a cup of Lyrics.

Having descanted on the First and Sixth Books of the Iliad, in a style not unsatisfactory to those who perused our articles, and inoffensive to those who, with a skip, gave them the go-by—both classes numerous—suppose, gruff or gentle reader, that we take a glimpse of what is going on in the Ninth. Some of the Books of the Iliad are, as you know, each in itself a poem. The Iliad is a river, that expands itself into Twenty-Four Lakes. Each Lake is a beautiful or magnificent watery world in itself, reflecting its own imagery all differently divine. The current is perceptible in each that flows through them all —so that you have always a river as well as a lake feeling; in the seclusion of any one are never forgetful of the rest; and though contented, were there neither inlet nor outlet to the circular sea on which you at the time may be voyaging, yet assured all the while that your course is progressive, and will cease at last, only when the waters on which you are wafted along by heavenly airs shall disappear underground among some Old Place of Tombs.

Now the Night-scene in the Ninth Book is bright with Achilles—an apparition, who vanished from our bodily eyes in the first, although he continued to move through the succeeding seven—and especially in the sixth—before those of our imagination. A night-scene in Homer, even without Achilles, is worth looking at—and therefore let us look at it without him. Lo, here it is!

Οἱ δὲ μέγα φρονέοντες ἀνὰ πτολέμοιο γεφύρας
Εἴατο παννύχιοι, πυρὰ δὲ σφίσι καίετο πολλά.
Ὡς δ' ὅτ' ἐν οὐρανῷ ἄστρα φαεινὴν ἀμφὶ σελήνην
Φαίνετ' ἀριπρεπία, ὅτε τ' ἔπλετο νήνεμος αἰθήρ,
[Ἐκ τ' ἔφανεν πᾶσαι σκοπιαὶ καὶ πρώονες ἄκροι
Καὶ νάπαι, οὐρανόθεν δ' ἄρ' ὑπερράγη ἄσπετος αἰθήρ,]
Πάντα δὲ τ' εἴδεται ἄστρα, γίγηθε δέ τι φρένα ποιμήν·
Τόσσα μισηγὺ νεῶν ἠδὲ Ξάνθοιο ῥοάων
Τρώων καιόντων πυρὰ φαίνετο Ἰλιόθι πρό.
Χίλι' ἄρ' ἐν πεδίῳ πυρὰ καίετο, πὰρ δὲ ἑκάστῳ
Εἴατο πεντήκοντα σέλᾳ πυρὸς αἰθομένοιο.
Ἵπποι δὲ κρῖ λευκὸν ἐρεπτόμενοι καὶ ὀλύρας,
Ἑσταότες παρ' ὄχεσφιν, εὔθρονον ἠῶ μίμνον.

—VIII. 553-565.

CHAPMAN.

"And spent all night in open fields ; fires round about them shined,
As when about the siluer moone, when aire is free from winde,
And stars shine clear, to whose sweet beams high prospects and the
    brows
Of all steepe hills and pinnacles thrust up themselves for showes ;
And even the lowly vallies joy, to glitter in their sight,
When the unmeasured firmament bursts to disclose her light,
And all the signes in heaven are seen, that glad the shepheard's harts :
So many fires disclosde their beames, made by the Troian part,
Before the face of Ilion ; and her bright turrets show'd.
A thousand courts of guard kept fires ; and every guard allow'd
Fiftie stout men, by whom their horse eate oates and hard white
    corne,
And all did wilfully expect the siluer-throned morne."

POPE.

" The troops exulting sat in order round,
  And beaming fires illumined all the ground,
  As when the moon, refulgent lamp of night,
  O'er heaven's clear azure spreads her sacred light,
  When not a breath disturbs the deep serene,
  And not a cloud o'ercasts the solemn scene ;
  Around her throne the vivid planets roll,
  And stars unnumber'd gild the glowing pole,
  O'er the dark trees a yellower verdure shed,
  And tip with silver every mountain's head ;
  Then shine the vales, the rocks in prospect rise,
  A flood of glory bursts from all the skies ;
  The conscious swains, rejoicing in the sight,
  Eye the blue vault, and bless the useful light.
  So many flames before proud Ilion blaze,
  And lighten glimmering Xanthus with their rays,
  The long reflections of the distant fires
  Gleam on the walls, and tremble on the spires.
  A thousand piles the dusky honours gild,
  And shoot a shady lustre o'er the field ;
  Full fifty guards each flaming pile attend,
  Whose umber'd arms by fits thick flashes send ;
  Loud neigh the coursers o'er their heaps of corn,
  And ardent warriors wait the rising morn."

COWPER.

" Big with great purposes and proud, they sat,
  Not disarray'd, but in fair form disposed

Of even ranks, and watch'd their numerous fires.
As when around the clear bright moon, the stars
Shine in full splendour, and the winds are hush'd,
The groves, the mountain-tops, the headland heights
Stand all apparent, not a vapour streaks
The boundless blue, and ether open'd wide ;
All glitters, and the shepherd's heart is cheer'd.
So numerous seem'd those fires, between the stream
Of Xanthus blazing, and the fleet of Greece,
In prospect all of Troy, a thousand fires,
Each watch'd by fifty warriors, seated near ;
The steeds beside the chariot stood, their corn
Chewing, and waiting till the golden-throned
Aurora should restore the light of day."

SOTHEBY.

" But Troy elate, in orderly array
All night around her numerous watch-fires lay.
As when the stars, at night's illumined noon,
Beam in their brightness round the full-orb'd moon,
When sleeps the wind, and every mountain height,
Rock, and hoar cliff, shine tow'ring up in light,
Then gleam the vales, and ether, widely riven,
Expands to other stars another heaven,
While the lone shepherd, watchful of his fold,
Looks wondering up, and gladdens to behold.
Not less the fires, that through the nightly hours
Spread war's whole scene before Troy's guarded towers,
Flung o'er the distant fleet a shadowy gleam,
And quivering play'd on Xanthus' silver stream.
A thousand fires ; and each with separate blaze
O'er fifty warriors cast the undying rays ;
Where their proud coursers, saturate with corn,
Stood at their cars, and snuff'd the coming morn."

There you see, most classical of readers, is the close of the
Eighth Book, in the original Greek—and there are four distinguished translations, by four of our true poets. The
Trojans, with Hector at their head, have, as you know, given
the Greeks a total—Agamemnon dreads a fatal—overthrow ;
and at sinking of the sun, the whole Trojan army, fifty thousand
strong, are lying on their arms beside their watch-fires, fifty
warriors round each ; so altogether, without aid of John
Cocker or Joseph Hume, there are, you perceive, a thousand
blazes.

Now this is, perhaps, the most celebrated simile in the Iliad. It has been lauded to the skies, of which it speaks, and from which it is sprung, by scholars who will here see no beauty but in the original Greek, and in it all beauty ; while, by the same scholars, the heaven reflected in Pope's translation is declared to be not only not Homer's heaven, but no heaven at all—a night-scene, say they, such as never was seen on this planet, and such as on this planet is impossible. People again, who are no scholars, admire Pope's picture as celestial, and without pretending to know that language, devoutly believe that it is all one in the Greek. Now, observe, most perspicacious of perusers of Maga's face, and of the face of heaven, that three separate questions are submitted to your decision—first, What is the meaning and the merit of the said simile, as it stands in Homer ? secondly, What is the merit or demerit of the said simile, as it stands in Pope ? and, thirdly, What is its character as it stands there, viewed in the light of a translation ?

As it is not impossible you may have forgot your Greek, or improbable that you may never have remembered it, allow us, with all humility, to present you with a literal prose translation.

NORTH.

" But they, greatly elated, upon the space between the two armies
Sat all the night ; and many fires were burning to them.
But as when the stars in heaven, around the shining moon,
Shine beautiful, when the air is windless,
And all the eminences appear, and pinnacles of the heights,
And groves ; and the immeasurable firmament bursts (or expands)
    from below,
And all the stars are seen : and the shepherd rejoices in his heart :—
So numerous, between the ships and the streams of Xanthus,
The fires of the Trojans burning their fires appeared before Troy.
For a thousand fires were burning on the plain ; and by each
Sat fifty (men) at the light of the blazing fire.
And the horses eating white barley and oats,
Standing by the chariots, awaited the beautiful-throned Aurora."

We are now all ready to proceed to form and deliver judgment. Taking, then, Homer's Greek and Christopher's English to be one and the same, what was the object of the old Ionian in conceiving this vision of the nocturnal heaven ? Why, aim and impulse were one. Under the imagination-moving mental perception of a thousand fires burning on the earth between the Grecian ships and the stream of Xanthus, Homer suddenly saw a similar, that is, for the time being, a kindred and congenial exhibition, up aloft in the heavens. That was the impulse. But the moment he saw the heavenly apparition, he felt it to be kindred and congenial with the one on earth ; and under the influence of that feeling he delighted to describe it, in order to glorify the one on earth—that was his aim—in four and a half hexameters, which have won the admiration of the world.

But the world often admires without knowing why, any better than the wiseacres who, in their pride, would correct the world. Why then has the world—meaning thereby that part of it that could or can read Greek—admired so prodigiously this passage ? Simply, because heaven and earth, the starry sky and the field with its thousand fires, appeared mutual reflections of each other ; for pleasant it is for us mortal creatures, high and low, rich and poor, to recognise a resemblance between our limited and evanescent scenery,—especially if the work of our own hands, which watch-fires are, the same being of wood we ourselves have gathered and heaped up into piles,—and the scenery of everlasting infinitude. Depend upon it, this emotion was in the very rudest minds when they kindled beal-fires. To the most beggarly bonfire it brings fuel. Homer felt this ; and he knew that all who should ever listen to his rhapsodies, either from his own lips, or from the lips of ἀοιδοί singing their way on continent or isle, would feel it ; for he had no forewarning given him of the invention of printing, or of Pope's or Sotheby's translation, or of this article in Maga.

So much for the spirit of the simile, almost identifying for the time the scenery of earth and heaven. If it does almost identify them, then it is successful, and the admiration of the world is legitimate. But when we come to analyse the passage, which is the self-same thing as to analyse our own perceptions, what do we find ? Difficulty and darkness in what we thought facility and light—and our faces are at the wall. We believe that we can see as far into either a mill or a milestone as ever Homer could ; but we doubt if we can see as far into heaven. For, simple as it seems to be, we do not believe that the man now lives who thoroughly understands that simile.

In the first place, take the line,—"As when the stars in heaven around the bright moon shine beautiful,"—with what object on earth does the "bright moon" correspond in heaven? With none. The thousand watch-fires are like the thousand stars. But no great central queen watch-fire, that we are told of, burned below—therefore the moon, wanting her counterpart, had perhaps no business on high. Would not a starry but a moonless sky have better imaged the thousand fire-encampments?

This natural, nay, inevitable feeling, has suggested the reading of ἄστρα φαει νῆν for φαεινήν—not a very violent change; and if we suppose the moon new, it will be the next thing to no moon at all; and as our present wish is, at all events, to get rid of the full moon, that reading is for that effect commendable. But then, alas! nothing less, we fear, will satisfy the shepherd—not the Ettrick Shepherd, but Homer's—than the full moon. She must be an ample shiner so to gladden his heart. The stars alone—though ἀριπρεπία—could not have done that sufficiently to justify Homer in mentioning his gladness on such an occasion. Was the moon then young or old, crescent or full—like Diana's bow when bent, or "round as my shield?"

It was round as my shield. The shepherd's delight is decisive. It is, then, a similitude of dissimilitude; and though haply not the less on that account Homeric—for Homer was a strange old star-gazer and moon-mouther, and would often absurdly yield to the temptation of a sudden glorious burst of beauty—it is so much less like that for resembling which all scholars have always admired it, except a few who, desirous to get rid of an unnecessary φαεινὴν σελήνην, have tried to prove her infancy by a violent or false reading. The truth is, that we can imagine Homer mentioning the full moon for the sake of her own transcendent beauty, though imaging nothing at the time seen below; but why he should have mentioned her at all if νῆν, that is, scarcely visible, and equally imaging nothing at the time below, surpasses, we fear, all reasonable conjecture. Be it then, we repeat, the full moon.

But in all this there is no real difficulty—and we have, as you will have perceived, been merely throwing about the waters, "like a whirling mop, or a wild goose at play." Now comes the pinch. Read the Greek on to νάται, line sixth—

our English on to " groves," ditto, and you have a picture in which the stars are conspicuous—they are beautiful—φαεινὴν ἀμφὶ σελήνην φαίνετ' ἀριπρεπέα. What, then, mean the mysterious words immediately following? " The immeasurable firmament bursts from below, and all the stars are seen." Or how do you translate ὑπερράγη? Another vision is seen by Homer—whence and how comes it? You are mute.

Perhaps it thus fared with Homer. At first there was no wind. He says so, and we must believe him, however suspicious may seem the assertion. There were some stars seen around the shining moon—not many—but such as were seen, were " beautiful exceedingly"— ἀριπρεπέα. By-and-by the wind, which was thought to be absent or dead, began to move in the region—the clouds falling into pieces, opened a new reach of heaven upwards—ὑπερράγη ἄσπετος αἰθὴρ—that is, to Homer's eyes looking from below—and he was not blind, not he indeed—there came a bursting, or breaking, or expanding, or unfolding, a gradual clarification of the immeasurable firmament, and then, indeed, all the stars were seen—not merely ἄστρα φαεινὴν ἀμφὶ σελήνην ἀριπρεπέα, but πάντα δέ τ' εἴδεται ἄστρα, or, in the more ornate, or rather gorgeous language of Milton,

" Then glow'd the firmament with living sapphires."

Observe, Homer does not again mention the moon. She was still there—shield or arc-like ; but even her orb ceased to be central to that vast " starry host ; " and though doubtless beheld by Homer and his shepherd, as their hearts gladdened, the gladness came from the universal face of the boundless heavens.

The picture then is, if such be the right interpretation of the words, of a glory that is progressive ; and if so, intended Homer, think ye, or did he so unintentionally, to depict, by the gradual illumination of the heaven, the gradual illumination of the earth—fires rising after fires, like stars after stars, till the lower and the upper regions were, respectively, all in a blaze, only the lower lights more flashful, the higher subdued by distance into a soft-burning beauty?

Remember, both regions were not brilliant at one and the same time—that was impossible in nature. The stars, in that clime so lustrous, would have bedimmed the fires ; the

fires, fed each by fifty warriors, would have extinguished
the stars. They would have neutralised each other, and
the scene would have been "dark with excessive bright."
But the earth-woke reality gave the heaven-born vision;
and both to this day are glorious—and sufficient, even when
separate, from dimness to redeem this article, and to shed
a splendour over our third critique on Sotheby.

Let us say, that such is the double soul—the twofold life
of Homer's Night-scene—and see if—bating all other objections—it has been transfused by Pope into his celebrated
version. No. According to our interpretation,

> "Around her throne the vivid planets roll,"

is so far right. "Vivid" may do for ἀριπρεπέα, but "roll" is
very bad for φαίνετ'. Roll perhaps they may ; indeed otherwise they would not be planets ; but certainly not round the
moon. Homer was perhaps no great astronomer—though he
knew well the Planetary Five. But Homer, who had the use
of his eyes, never, drunk or sober, thought, when looking at
the moon, that he saw "around her throne the vivid planets
roll." If by "her throne" Pope means the firmament, then
he forgets the Greek words ; but it is manifest he means the
moon herself, absurdly confusing with her throne the queen
who sits thereon, whom by the way he had chosen, injuriously
to Nature and to Homer, to call, a few lines before, "refulgent
lamp of night." However, we have said the line is so far
right ; but that which follows, if our interpretation of Homer's
heaven be true, is altogether wrong—

> "And stars unnumber'd gild the glowing pole ;"

for Homer yet has made no mention of stars unnumbered ; if
ἄστρα ἀριπρεπέα mean "vivid planets," which it may, Pope
had no right to surround them with "unnumber'd stars," for
it is afterwards, and when a great change has occurred to the
immeasurable firmament, that πάντα δέ τ' εἴδεται ἄστρα. Homer
speaks not of clouds—though we have suggested the probability of clouds being there, the disparting of which, and their
floating away into nothing, finally revealed this infinite starri-
ness ; but be that suggestion of ours right or wrong, Pope
had no right to assure us of what Homer did not, "that not
a cloud o'ercast the solemn scene." Homer says merely that

"the eminences and pinnacles of the heights appear, and the groves." Pope makes but sorry work of that, by needless elaboration of its picturesque simplicity; we do not know that he makes it unnatural, though he does make it confused; though there is far more light, there is far more darkness; and the landscape is no longer in aught Homeric. That much-admired line,

"A flood of glory bursts from all the skies,"

would almost seem to be intended for a version of οὐρανόθεν δ' ἄρ' ὑπερράγη ἄσπετος αἰθήρ, πάντα δὲ τ' εἴδεται ἄστρα—but then, unfortunately, Pope has given us before—"and stars un-number'd gild the glowing pole;" and really, after the refulgent lamp of night has been hung on high, and vivid planets roll round the throne of the moon, and stars unnumbered gild the glowing pole, while not a cloud o'ercasts the solemn scene, how any farther flood of glory can burst from all the skies, we are not astronomer enough, either scientific or empirical, to comprehend or conjecture—nor do we believe that Pope himself had any theory on the subject, but wrote away by candle-light, perhaps in his grotto, from memory somewhat dim, while the shining moon, it may have been, was herself in heaven, and the boundless firmament thick-strewn with stars. The scriptural simplicity of, "and the shepherd rejoices in his heart," how far more touching to every one who has walked over the hills by night, than Pope's philosophical paraphrase! As for the application of the sky-sight to the ground-scene, we have no room to remark upon it, farther than that while it departs equally from the original, and is laboured overmuch,—it possesses a certain shadowy magnificence, for sake of which its faithlessness, or departure from the faith, may, in some moods of mind, be forgiven.

We find that the three questions we wished you to decide for us, are running, or have run, into one; but no great matter; so, what think you, on the whole, of this famous passage in Pope's Homer? Three of our best descriptive poets, Wordsworth, Coleridge, and Southey, have, as you probably know, declared it infamous; and Wordsworth, especially, has not hesitated to hint, in his unceremonious style, that the many millions of his fellow-Christians who have fallen into

admiration of this moonlight scene, painted on transparent
paper, have been little better than blindfolded fools. The
entire description, he avers, in words we forget, but we quoted
them in our " Winter Rhapsody," is utter, contradictory, and
unintelligible nonsense.   It is no such thing.   We have seen
that it is not a translation of Homer's moonlight scene,
scarcely even a paraphrase.   And we have seen, too, that in
departing from Homer, Pope departed from nature ; but still
the picture is beautiful.   Forget that there is any such
passage in Homer as that of which it pretends to be a translation.   Read it by itself—try it by itself—and we are
willing to wager a crown with Wordsworth, that even he
will read with a benign aspect this very page of Maga.
What are its faults?   Why, we have told them already.
There is some vagueness where there should be none ; some
repetition, where Pope believed he was adding new touches ;
and perhaps objects are made to appear in light which must
have been in shadow ; but these defects, in no offensive degree, once admitted, there

> " Breathes not the man with soul so dead,
>   Who never to himself hath said,"

this is extremely beautiful.   In a description of external
nature, no doubt a poet is sworn at her shrine to speak the
truth—that is to say, to tell all manner of lies—provided
only they do so coalesce and hang together in their beauty,
that the poet believes them, and eke the whole world.   That
in poetry is true which, on sufficient grounds, and she is
often easily satisfied, Imagination conceives to be so ; and
Reason has no right to step insolently in upon Imagination in
her dream, and to dissipate all her dear delusions.   As long
as Imagination tells only white lies, her tongue should be
encouraged to wag night and day, that she may people the
air with pleasant fancies.   But what we were wishing to say
is this, that in the description of a moonlight scene, for
example, we must not exact from the poet, at every touch,
the utmost precision ; words, after all, do not paint to the
eye, but to the conceptive faculty ; and the conceptive faculty
delights at times in half-formed and hazy visionariness, which
it may be prompted to behold by the power resident in terms
collocated in an order that could not resist the onset of the
logician.   We do not mean to say that poets are not expected,

like other dishonest people, to speak sense ; but there are various sorts of sense ; some have very much the appearance of nonsense, and in that appearance lies their charm ;—let us but see that the supposed strange sweet specimen of some unsubstantial seeming, is nothing but absolute sense, and we commit suicide.

Chapman is good, for he adheres to Homer. He knew that Homer was not a man to bother people about the moon and stars, and that, except for illustration of life, he cared not a straw for such luminaries. Indeed, what great poet does or ever did? The human soul is, under God, the centre of the solar system. The sun seems to support it—but that is a vulgar scientific error—were we all dead, it would fly into flinders. " Living in the spirit of this creed," Homer eyed the heavens as part of his own being ; and so indeed did all those strong-souled mortals, who, age after age, kept continually constructing the Grecian Mythology. When constructed, what was it but an illuminated manuscript of biographies and autobiographies of men, women, and children, that had been conspicuous and famous on the terrene, and were thus immortalised in the celestial? True, that much of this spiritualisation was breathed over the skies before the invention of letters; but that mattered little or nothing, for natural and revealed religion was older far than Cadmus. But not to indulge in that reverie, suffice it now to say, that the ἄσπετος αἰθήρ was too magnificent in Homer's imagination to be played and dallied with, as a baby does with a doll, lisping, " Oh ! how pretty ! " He looked up—saw—and sung ; and his strong steady strain bespoke, in a few lines, the depth of his inspiration. The sky smote his soul with sudden perception and emotion of beauty and sublimity ; and he said, or could say, little more than that the sky was their source. Just as when a lovely lady smiles upon us, we exclaim, " Thou art beautiful ! " But to palaver away about the paleness or brightness of her countenance, belongs not to the poetry of beatified affection. " Grace was in all her steps, heaven in her eye : " he who said that of Eve said enough—volumes are in these words ; and they unfold themselves into millions of unwritten dreams—as a few seeds become an umbrageous and golden-fruited grove, filled with the warbling of nightingales.

Thus, in these few lines has Homer shown a moonlight and starry heaven, that continueth to shine over the whole world, and all the generations of its inhabitants. He did not set himself down to paint it, like an associate of the Royal Academy, as Pope did, bringing out the effect by long-considered and elaborate processes of art, touching and retouching, occasionally biting his nails, and sucking his pen ; but, as Shelley said, when

> " Some great painter dips
> His pencil in the gloom of thunder and eclipse ; "

so we say did Homer dip his pencil in moonlight, and, lo! his picture swam in lustre unbedimmable by the mist of years.

They who never before read Homer's fine Greek lines, or our fine English ones, and turn to them now from Pope's glittering paraphrase, may think them bald in their simplicity ; but study them in silence with your eyes shut, and you have a pure vision of the nocturnal heavens. Chapman saw the very night Homer did ; and all he wanted was adequate power of expression to make us see it too; but even in his lines it is serenely beautiful,—

> "And all the signs in heaven are seen that glad the shepherd's heart."

" Thrust up themselves for shows," are words not in Homer, but the feeling is in Homer ; for in his picture, the πᾶσαι σκοπιαί, καὶ πρώονες ἄκροι καὶ νάπαι seem indeed alive and conscious in the calm, and to look at us in their exaltation. Chapman says, " and even the lowly vallies joy to glitter in their sight,"—that is, the sight of the stars—a fine line, but rather Wordsworthian than Homeric. Homer mentions not " lowly valleys; " but Chapman seems so to have construed νάπαι, groves. For he omits groves; and it is not likely that the word νάπαι could have escaped his notice. It is not surprising that Pope, in this error, should have followed Chapman—he has, " then shine the vales ; " but it is surprising that such a scholar as Sotheby should—saying " then gleam the vales," a mere repetition of Pope's words, with " gleam " for " shine," which is a change for the worse, for no man of woman born, we suspect, ever saw a vale—unless there was in it a river or lake—gleam by moonlight. But that " the vales " should be seen gleaming by one and the same man—say Homer or Sotheby—at one and the same time —is manifestly impossible, according to the present laws of perspective, and in general of optics.

Cowper's translation is, as usual, admirable.   Of him, as truly as of any man that ever breathed, may we say, in that fine line of Campbell,

> " He mused on nature with a poet's eye."

He does not fear to say " the clear bright moon," despising the reading " φαει νῆν," and in love with "φαεινὴν."   Nor does he fear to say, that around the "clear bright moon," "the stars shine in full splendour."   Now, Coleridge asserted in one of his lectures in the Royal Institution, that in the immediate neighbourhood of a "refulgent" moon, the stars must look wan or dim ; and so, we understand, saith Wordsworth. 'Tis but a mere matter of moonshine, it is true; yet worth settling ; and we go along with Homer and Chapman and Cowper.   There cannot be two stronger words than φαεινὴν and ἀριπρεπεῖα ; moon and stars were alike lustrous.   "About the silver moon stars shine clear," are Chapman's words, and they are in the same spirit.   Cowper's you have before you, more radiant still.   Do not abuse Pope, then, O ye lakers, while you let Homer, Chapman, and Cowper go scot-free. Horace, too, speaks· of a lady bright as the moon among the lesser fires, meaning that they too were bright.   She shone with a larger and serener lustre, as if they from "her *silver* urn drew light."   In one line Cowper transcends all his competitors, and equals his divine original—

> " The groves, the mountain-tops, the headland heights,
> Stand all apparent."

Compare that with Pope, and " Oh ! the difference to me ! " But Pope's beautiful line,

> " And not a cloud o'ercasts the solemn scene,"

was in Cowper's memory when he said,

> " Not a vapour streaks the boundless blue ; "

for Homer says nothing of vapours, nor, had not Pope negatived the idea of clouds, had Cowper.   But seldom indeed it is that that most original writer owes even a word to anybody; here Pope was natural, and Cowper, in unconsciously remembering him, forgot Homer.   Neither does Homer speak of " blue " as Cowper does ; yet blue, beyond doubt or praise, is the firmament, and there can be no harm in saying so.

Cowper felt the meaning of that untranslatable word ὑπεϊμάγη, and his

> " Ether, open'd wide,
> All glitters,"

is magnificent—perhaps even finer than Homer, for it gives the effect in fewer and simpler words—it is indeed poetry. " And the shepherd's heart is cheer'd," is, like Homer—bible-like and divine.

And now for Sotheby. He must have come to the passage prepared for a high achievement. Has he succeeded? Not entirely to our heart's desire. " At night's illumined noon " is a fine expression, had it stood by itself—for it shows us at once the moon and stars in heaven. It proves Sotheby to be a poet. But it does not, like the town of Kilkenny, " shine well where it stands." That nothing resembling it is in Homer, is one fatal objection to it, on the score of fidelity, the first of virtues in a translator—herself the Queen, all others being her subjects, and brightening and extending her sway. But there is another. Why is there nothing resembling it in Homer? Because Homer is going to show us " night's illumined noon ; " and in what lies the illumination. Therefore he does not lay down that thesis, as Sotheby does, and then illustrate it by divine discourse. So pregnant is that thesis of Sotheby's, that it is in itself a shining sermon, and needed no preacher. Mr Sotheby will see at once that this objection is, like every objection of ours, insuperable. He has had the misfortune to paint a fine picture at one sweep ; and we are so perfectly satisfied with it, that we are dissatisfied with his future filling-up, and eager to snatch the pencil out of his hand. It may seem hard to punish a man for a flash of genius, but justice compels us to do so ; and Sotheby stands reproved before us, exalted, however, rather than humbled by the sentence of an incorruptible Rhadamanthus.

> " Beam in their brightness round the full-orb'd moon,'

is fine and bold ; and also in itself a picture. The next two lines are perfect ; " then gleam the vales," very imperfect, as we said before, and we do wish he had given us the woods. " Ether widely riven," comes perhaps as near as is possible to the difficult

> " ὑπεϊμάγη ἄσπιτος αἰθήρ,"

and there is great grandeur in the line,

> "Expands to other stars another heaven."

That, unquestionably, is the vision seen by Homer. Would not " for," in place of " to," perhaps be better ? The riving up from below of the boundless ether expands another heaven *for* (or *with*) other stars. In that expansion they have room for all their multitudes—then and there seems to be infinitude. With the concluding lines, fine as they are in themselves, we are not satisfied. Sotheby knows as well as any man wherein lies the power of Homer's immortal half-hexameter. Cowper caught it, and embodied it in equal bulk. Chapman likewise seized its spirit. Pope, unaffected apparently by that scripture, or betrayed into forgetfulness of its manifest character by the ruling passion in which he wrote, ambition to excel Homer, diluted the simple sentiment of the shepherd, which is indeed nothing else than natural religion, into feeble metaphysics and a cold philosophy. " Conscious swains," is silly ; and " bless the useful light," is absolutely the doctrine of the Utilitarians applied to the gratitude of the shepherd,

> " Where he doth summer high in bliss upon the hills of God !"

Our objections to Sotheby's lines, over and above the main one, amplification of simplicity, are different from those urged against Pope's, but nearly as strong. " Watchful of his fold," is an idea always interesting, but " watchful " is, to our ear, needlessly intense. In that beautiful chapter of the New Testament, the shepherds "were watching their flocks by night." " Watchful " could never have entered into that verse. On so serene a night as that Homer describes, when all was peace, the shepherd could have had no fears about his fold. He was sitting or lying beside them, but not " watchful ; " he merely felt that they were there ; for their sakes too, as well as his own, his heart was cheered by the heavens he looked on ; and happier even than he knew at that hour was the pastoral life.

This is but a slight matter; but slight matters affect the delight of the soul in poetry. Pope had said, " eyes the blue vault," and Sotheby, betrayed into imitation by admiration, says, " looks wondering up." That the shepherd looked up, there can be no doubt. Homer took it for granted that he did ; for the shepherd was not asleep. The truth is, that he had been looking up for a long time—had seen the moon rise,

and the stars—and perhaps had been composing a song on a
white-footed girl filling her urn at the fountain. To suppose
that he had been looking down, would be a libel, not only on
that anonymous shepherd, but on all Arcadia, and the golden
age. But we object more stoutly to the word, " wondering."
May this be the last line we shall ever write, if he did "look
wondering up." Shepherds from their infancy are star-gazers.
They are familiar with the skies—for on the hill-tops they
live, and move, and have their being, in the immediate neighbourhood of heaven. At a comet they would wonder—for he
is a wild stranger of a hundred years. But they do not
wonder even at meteors, for the air is full of them, and they
go skyring through the stars, and dropping down into disappearance, like the half-assured sights seen in dreams. But
the moon and the planets, and the fixed stars, are to the shepherd no more wonderful at one time than at another;—in one
sense, indeed, they are to him always wonderful — for he
wonders, and of his wondering finds no end, how and by whom
they were made ; or he wonders at them in their own beautiful eternity. But Sotheby's words do not imply this ; they
merely imply that the shepherd wonders to behold such a
night as that described by Homer. Why should he ? 'Twas
but one of thousands that had canopied his solitary grass-bed,
and its sole power was the peaceful power of accustomed gladness—still renewed, and never fading in his heart—γέγηθε δὲ
τε φρένα ποιμήν. The truth is, that three words of Sotheby's
two lines do of themselves produce the whole desired effect—
" gladdens to behold." All the rest are superfluous. That is
wholly nature, and almost wholly Homer. Sotheby, as an Athenian, knew what was right—he should have been a Lacede-
monian too—and practised it.

It is only with distinguished writers, like Sotheby, that such
criticism as this would be endurable ; with them, it is impera-
tive on us ; nor, unless we much mistake, is it without instruction. Poetry is indeed a Fine Art — fine as the pellucid air,
in which you may see a mote. The perusal of his composition,
generally so exquisite, sharpens all our inmost senses, and
makes us critical as eagles floating over a valley. And now
we pounce down on our prey — the poor word " lone " — and
swallow it. Let nobody pity it, for it " had no business
there." In Homer ποιμήν has no epithet. No need to tell us
he was alone. The one word of itself does that—that he was

all alone, is felt to be essential to that gush of gladness.
Homer, during that description, was not thinking of any shepherd. He had the heavens to himself; but no sooner was the
beauty of the scene consummate, than arose one image of
solitary life. He saw a being—and that his heart was glad;
and so dear a thing is human happiness, that sufficient for
Homer was the joy of one simple shepherd beneath the starry
cope of the ἄσπετος αἰθήρ. Another great poet knew, on an
occasion somewhat similar, but not the same, the proper use
of the word "alone." Thus, in "Rob Roy's Grave," Wordsworth, speaking of the remembrances or traditions of that out-
law, says,

> " Bear witness, many a pensive sigh
> Of thoughtful herdsman, when he strays
> Alone upon Loch Veol's heights,
> And by Loch Lomond's braes ;
> And, far and near, through vale and hill,
> Are faces that attest the same,
> The proud heart flashing through the eyes
> At sound of Rob Roy's name."

Here the bard had room to employ epithets—and he had likewise leisure—for he was quietly ruminating; "thoughtful,"
and "alone." "Loch Veol's heights," and "Loch Lomond's
braes," carry us along with the herdsman on his day-long
world of dreams; and descending from these solitary heights,
we find ourselves among "faces" in the vales, many faces far
and near, all kindling at "sound of Rob Roy's name," a name
there pronounced and heard,—but up among the mountains,
silent in the herdsman's heart, as he walks "thoughtful and
alone," in his uncommunicated memories.

By the way, we cannot help thinking, that all the translators we have looked at have mistaken the meaning of the
important words,—" ἀνὰ πτολέμοιο γεφύρας "—end of first line
of the quotation. From Chapman's translation it does not
clearly appear what he conceived to be the meaning of these
words—though perhaps " open field " answer to them, which
is indeed right, though vague. Pope writes,—" sat in order
round,"—which shows his understanding of the words—leaving
out πτολέμοιο. Cowper says,

> "They sat,
> Not disarray'd, but in fair forms disposed
> Of even ranks."

That is his interpretation of ἀνὰ πτολέμοιο γεφύρας. And Sotheby, by far the best Grecian of them all, translates them "in
orderly array." All this seems to us very odd, for what is
γεφύρα? Turning up Donnegan, we find — "a dam dyke
or mound — the space between hostile armies — a wall—
generally a bridge;" and he refers us to Pindar for πόντου
γεφύρα, an isthmus. But what does it usually mean in
Homer? In Iliad Δ 371: "Τί δ' ὀπιπτεύεις πολέμοιο γεφύρας,"
by Heyne translated, "quod prospicis intervallum inter utram-
que aciem." And he adds, "has enim esse γεφύρας, κελευθους,
ὁδους πολέμου, patet ex Θ 374. 549. Λ. 160. Υ.427. Τὸ μεταμιχαιον."
On referring to these passages, we find that τὸ μεταμιχαιον is
the meaning of ἀνὰ πτολέμοιο γεφύρας. The Greeks had been
beat back—and the Trojans kindled their fires on the space
lying between the two battles. We forget what annotator on
Milton it was that proposed reading for "on the rough edge
of battle ere it joined" "on the rough bridge of battle," an
emendation for which he got himself laughed at. We daresay
Milton wrote "edge;" but bridge is, we see, Homeric, and
therefore good. Ἀνὰ πτολέμοιο γιφύρας is "upon the bridge of
battle." Cowper and Sotheby seem, then, to have misunderstood the words here: as well as in such other places where
they occur, as we have had leisure to turn up. If we are mistaken—they will lay the blame partly at the door of Heyne.

But let us attend to the Greeks. Thus fared the Trojan
host; but "Flight, companion of soul-chilling Fear, despatched
from heaven"—so Cowper translates it; or "Grief, the feeble
consort of cold Fear, strangely infused from heaven"—so
chanteth Chapman; or "Fear, pale comrade of inglorious
flight, and heaven-bred horror"—so Pope hath it; or "Heaven-sent flight, chill Fear's ally"—so sings Sotheby—possessed the Grecians—and Agamemnon commands the heralds
to call by name each chief to council, but without the sound of
proclamation. Let us try the translators at the following four
lines :—

HOMER.

Ἷζον δ' εἰν ἀγορῇ τετιηότες· ἂν δ' Ἀγαμέμνων
Ἵστατο δακρυχέων, ὥς τε κρήνη μελάνυδρος,
Ἥ τε κατ' αἰγίλιπος πέτρης δνοφερὸν χέει ὕδωρ.
Ὡς ὁ βαρὺ στενάχων ἔπι' Ἀργείοισι μετηύδα.

—IX. 13-16.

NORTH (*literal prose*).

" They sat down therefore in the assembly, sad ; but Agamemnon
Stood up tears-shedding—as a fountain dark-water'd,
Which down a steep (goat-defying, or rather leaving) rock pours
  mist-emitting water :
Thus did he, heavily groaning out words—among the Greeks
  harangue."

CHAPMAN.

" They sadly sate ; the king arose and pour'd out tears as fast
As from a lofty rock a spring doth his black waters cast.
And deeply sighing, thus bespake the Argives.

POPE.

" These surround their chief
. In solemn sadness and majestic grief.
The king amidst the mournful circle rose ;
Down his wan cheek a living torrent flows :
So silent fountains, from a rock's tall head,
In sable streams soft-trickling waters shed.
With more than vulgar grief he stood oppress'd ;
Words, mix'd with sighs, thus bursting from his breast."

COWPER.

" The sad assembly sat ; when weeping fast,
As some deep fountain pours its rapid stream
Down from the summit of a lofty rock,
King Agamemnon in the midst arose,
And groaning, the Achaians thus address'd."

SOTHEBY.

" Bow'd by grief,
The summon'd leaders gather'd round their chief.
In tears Atrides stood ; thus ceaseless flow
The dark streams gushing from a rocky brow.
He spake and groan'd, ' Ye Argive leaders ! hear !' " &c.

A simpler, shorter, apter simile than this is nowhere to be
found ; let, then, all these qualities be preserved by the translator. Chapman, as he thinks, preserves them all—and he is
almost as good as Homer. In the original, we have μελάνυδρος
and δνοφερὸν ὕδωρ—both signifying, as many say, "black water"

—intensifying the gloomy aspect of Agamemnon. Perhaps in English such synonymes could not have been used—and Chapman confines himself to the one word "black."

But the truth is, that κρήνη μελάνυδρος means a fountain black-watered, because hidden from the light by overhanging rocks, or in some great depth. The water is not in itself black, or even drumly when smitten "by touch ethereal of heaven's fiery rod"—but pure as diamonds. In falling over the face of the inaccessible rock, it is not black, although the face of the rock may be, and probably is; indeed we do not remember ever to have seen black water when fairly poured out, unless you choose to call ink so—and we are sorry to say that the ink we are dribbling at this moment is light-blue; or unless you choose to call tea so—and we are still sorrier to say that the tea we are sipping at this moment is a faint green; while δνοφερόν, though misnamed in lexicons dusky, and so forth, assuredly is "spray-shedding," or "mist-emitting," or "vapoury," or something of that sort—for which if there be an English word, we cannot recollect its phiz. All the translators, therefore, are mistaken who call the falling water dark, or dusky, or sable, or black—confounding an accident of its source with the quality of the stream—and libelling Agamemnon's tears. The source from which they flowed may be said figuratively to have been "black"—his heart—and his face was gloomy; just as that other source and that other face in and of the rock—but his tears were clear, and glistened, just as the ὕδωρ to which Homer likened them; and, though the expression is strong, so were they mist-emitting, for his grief was very great.

It is not easy to read Pope's paraphrase without anger. Determined was he to improve upon Homer; and therefore will he spin out—beat out—his four lines into eight, not giving us one word in English exactly corresponding to one word in Greek. Τετιηότες—afflicted—*excruciantes se*, as Heyne gives it, he changes into—

" In solemn sadness and majestic grief."

Now, that is a downright lie. The Argive leaders were not in " solemn sadness," though we daresay their countenances were considerably elongated; and if they were "in majestic grief," it is more than Agamemnon himself was, for he wept and groaned, though we daresay that his presence was not without dignity. Here, then, is an absurd attempt to impose upon us, and to win from us that sympathy for a set of pompous magnificoes, which we give at once to men τετιηότες. "Mournful circle" is surely needless after "solemn sadness and majestic grief." Then Agamemnon's cheek is superfluously said to be "wan;" and "briny torrent" is unhappy, for though tears are salt, they are here likened to a fresh-water spring, and therefore we have no business with "brine." Why would not Pope say, shedding tears, or weeping, as Homer does? Is it not excessively childish to translate δαχρυχέων,

"Down his wan cheek a briny torrent flows"?

Proceed on that principle throughout, and the Iliad will reach from this to London.

"So silent fountains, from a rock's tall head,
In sable streams soft-trickling waters shed."

Why silent? Then observe how very awkward fountains, plural, and a rock's tall head, singular! Homer is not speaking of fountains in general, but of one "fountain blackwatered;" "soft-trickling" is not the right word, for χέει, stillat, means simply "sheds," and sheds by itself is sufficient.

"With more than vulgar grief he stood oppress'd,"

is a foolish interpolation. Who the deuce ever thought the king of men vulgar? But, after all, Pope has not been able by this line to put him on a par with his subordinates who surrounded him

"In solemn sadness and majestic grief."

Agamemnon among them looks like an old woman. "Words mixed with sighs" we must not complain of, for they are Milton's; but we want Homer's—and he gives us groans, and deep ones—ὁ βαρὺ στενάχων. However, that line will do. But is not the whole a wilful wickedness and a feeble failure?

Cowper is concise and vigorous. "The sad assembly sat" is so especially. There is much majesty in the rising of Agamemnon, "weeping fast;" and the lines about the fountain do finely show us the king. Cowper has chosen to sink the colour black. He calls the fountain "deep;" and as most

deep fountains look black, deep let it be ; but "rapid " we do
not like, for water falling down a rock must be rapid whether
it will or not—we defy it to help itself—and Cowper should
have given us ὀνοφερὸν, if he had even said "dismal." Homer's
ὀνοφερὸν is a strange word; and though we choose to believe
that it denotes spray, Cowper may have seen cause to call it
rapid. "Groaning" is good—for he who sighs deeply, groans.
The picture is in Cowper's hands Homeric.

Sotheby is strong—perhaps too concise ; but that in a
translator of Homer is a fine fault. "In tears Atrides stood"
is in itself excellent ; but it hardly comes up to the meaning
of ἵστατο δακρυχέων. That epithet implies an active, a profuse,
a prodigal pouring out of tears—and such pouring out there
must have been to suggest the simile of the dark-watered
fountain shedding its gloomy, or rapid, or sprayey stream,
down the cheek of a lofty rock. Homer's heroes, when they
weep, do so in right good earnest. At the same time, they
groan, or they roar, or they roll themselves on the ground.
So did Achilles. Andromache wept smilingly ; and her eyes,
we ween, looked lovelier through their tears—her whole face
—herself—Love, Grief, and Pity, in one. "Ceaseless" is not
the right word, for Agamemnon's tears did cease, while the
black-watered fountain Homer had in his eye may be flowing
down the face of the lofty rock at this very hour.

"The dark streams gushing from a rocky brow,"

strikes us as very fine. Perhaps they were dark after all—
and even the word "brow" has here a beauty not to be found
in the Greek. For it shows us Agamemnon's ; and it too was
rocky, for the broad bone above his eyes was rugged—we see
it now—as Sotheby did when he dropped that eloquent line on
paper. "He spake and groaned" ought to be transposed
thus—He groaned and spake. Judging by ourselves, a man
ceases to groan almost as soon as he begins to speak. 'Tis
well if his hearers do not then take up what he has laid aside;
though in this case, if the Argive leaders gave a groan accom-
paniment, 'twas in dismal sympathy with the sufferings of
their king.

Atrides then conducts the great chiefs of Greece to his
pavilion ; and after feasting them in kingly fashion, awaits
advice. Nestor rises, and thus harangues :—

" Ἀτρείδη κύδιστε, ἄναξ ἀνδρῶν Ἀγάμεμνον,
Ἐν σοὶ μὲν λήξω, σέο δ' ἄρξομαι, οὕνεκα πολλῶν
Λαῶν ἐσσὶ ἄναξ καί τοι Ζεὺς ἐγγυάλιξεν
Σκῆπτρόν τ' ἠδὲ θέμιστας, ἵνα σφίσι βουλεύῃσθα.
Τῷ σε χρὴ πέρι μὲν φάσθαι ἔπος ἠδ' ἐπακοῦσαι,
Κρηῆναι δὲ καὶ ἄλλῳ, ὅτ' ἄν τινα θυμὸς ἀνώγῃ
Εἰπεῖν εἰς ἀγαθόν· σέο δ' ἔξεται ὅ ττί κεν ἄρχῃ.
Αὐτὰρ ἐγὼν ἐρέω ὥς μοι δοκεῖ εἶναι ἄριστα.
Οὐ γάρ τις νόον ἄλλον ἀμείνονα τοῦδε νοήσει,
Οἷον ἐγὼ νοέω, ἠμὲν πάλαι ἠδ' ἔτι καὶ νῦν,
Ἐξ ἔτι τοῦ ὅτε, διογενὲς, Βρισηΐδα κούρην
Χωόμενος Ἀχιλῆος ἔβης κλισίηθεν ἀπούρας
Οὔ τι καθ' ἡμέτερόν γε νόον· μάλα γάρ τοι ἔγωγε
Πόλλ' ἀπεμυθεόμην· σὺ δὲ σῷ μεγαλήτορι θυμῷ
Εἶξας ἄνδρα φέριστον, ὃν ἀθάνατοί περ ἔτισαν,
Ἠτίμησας· ἑλὼν γὰρ ἔχεις γέρας. Ἀλλ' ἔτι καὶ νῦν
Φραζώμεσθ' ὥς κέν μιν ἀρεσσάμενοι πεπίθωμεν
Δώροισίν τ' ἀγανοῖσιν ἔπεσσί τε μειλιχίοισιν."
    Τὸν δ' αὖτε προσέειπεν ἄναξ ἀνδρῶν Ἀγαμέμνων·
" Ὦ γέρον, οὔ τι ψεῦδος ἐμὰς ἄτας κατέλεξας.
Ἀασάμην, οὐδ' αὐτὸς ἀναίνομαι. Ἀντί νυ πολλῶν
Λαῶν ἐστὶν ἀνὴρ ὅν τε Ζεὺς κῆρι φιλήσῃ,
Ὡς νῦν τοῦτον ἔτισε, δάμασσε δὲ λαὸν Ἀχαιῶν.
Ἀλλ' ἐπεὶ ἀασάμην φρεσὶ λευγαλέῃσι πιθήσας,
Ἂψ ἐθέλω ἀρέσαι, δόμεναί τ' ἀπερείσι' ἄποινα.
Ὑμῖν δ' ἐν πάντεσσι περικλυτὰ δῶρ' ὀνομήνω."

                                            —IX. 96-121.

NORTH (*literal prose*).

" ' Son of Atreus,—most illustrious,— king of men,—Agamemnon,
In thee will I end, from thee will I begin. Since of many
Nations thou art king, and Jupiter hath put into thy hands
Both the sceptre and the laws, that for them thou mightst
    deliberate,
Therefore thee it behoves, above all others, to speak your opinion,
    and to listen,
And to bring into effect another's (counsel), when his mind may
    move him
To speak for the (common) good ; for on thee will it depend
    whatever (counsel) may prevail ;
But I will speak whatever appears to me the best.
For no one shall find out better counsel than that
Which I find out, both formerly, and also now,
From the time when, oh, noble one ! the girl Briseïs
Thou didst go and take away from the tent of the enraged Achilles.
Not indeed according to my counsel ; for greatly indeed thee did
    I for my part

With many words dissuade ; but thou to thy mighty spirit
Giving way, the bravest man whom ever the Immortals have
    honour'd
Thou hast treated with disrespect ; for having taken, thou
    retainest his reward ; but even now
Let us deliberate how we may please and prevail on him, by
    soothing gifts, and honey'd words.'
Him on the other hand, address'd the king of men, Agamemnon.
'Oh, old man, not falsely my errors hast thou enumerated :
I have done unjustly, I deny it not ; equal, indeed, to a numerous
Host is the man whom Jupiter shall love in his heart ;
Him indeed hath he now honour'd, and hath humbled the nation
    of the Greeks.
But since I have err'd, by yielding to my wayward mind,
Again I wish to appease him, and to give him an immense
    recompense,
And, in the presence of you all, the splendid gifts will I enumerate.'"

POPE.

"'Monarch of nations ! whose superior sway
Assembled states, and lords of earth, obey,
The laws and sceptres to thy hand are given.
And millions own the care of thee and heaven.
O king, the counsels of my age attend,
With thee my cares begin, in thee must end.
Thee, prince ! it fits alike to speak and hear,
Pronounce with judgment, with regard give ear,
To see no wholesome motion be withstood,
And ratify the best for public good.
Nor, though a meaner give advice, repine,
But follow it, and make the wisdom thine.
Hear then a thought, not now conceived in haste,
At once my present judgment and my past ;
When from Pelides' tent you forced the maid,
I first opposed, and, faithful, durst dissuade ;
But, bold of soul, when headlong fury fired,
You wrong'd the man, by men and Gods admired ;
Now, seek some means his fatal wrath to end,
With prayers to move him, or with gifts to bend.'
To whom the king—' With justice hast thou shown
A prince's faults, and I with reason own
That happy man, whom Jove still honours most,
Is more than armies, and himself a host.
Blest in his love, this wondrous hero stands ;
Heaven fights his war, and humbles all our hands.

Fain would my heart, which err'd through frantic rage,
The wrathful chief and angry Gods assuage.
If gifts immense his mighty soul can bow,
Hear, all ye Greeks,—and witness what I vow.'"

COWPER.

"'Atrides! glorious monarch! king of men!
With thee shall I begin, with thee conclude,
For thou art sov'reign, and to thee are given
From Jove the sceptre and the laws in charge,
For the advancement of the general good.
Hence, in peculiar, both to speak and hear
Become thy duty, and the best advice,
By whomsoever offer'd, to adopt
And to perform, for thou art judge alone.
I will promulge the counsel which to me
⚫ Seems wisest; such, that other Grecian none
Shall give thee better; neither is it new,
But I have ever held it since the day
When, most illustrious! thou wast pleased to take
By force the maid Briseïs from the tent
Of the enraged Achilles; not, in truth,
By my advice, who did dissuade thee much;
But thou, complying with thy princely wrath,
Hast shamed a hero whom the gods themselves
Delight to honour, and his prize detain'st.
Yet even now conciliate him; perchance,
With soft persuasion and by gifts we may.'
    Then answer'd Agamemnon, king of men:
'Old chief, there is no falsehood in your charge;
I have offended, and confess the wrong.
The warrior is alone a host, whom Jove
Loves as he loves Achilles, for whose sake
He hath Achaia's thousands thus subdued.
But if, the impulse of a wayward mind
Obeying, I have err'd; behold me, now,
Prepared to soothe him with atonement large
Of gifts inestimable, which by name
I will propound in presence of you all.'"

SOTHEBY.

"'Atrides! king of kings, my word attend!
With thee my speech begins, with thee shall end;
For vast the sway by Jove to thee assign'd—
Power that controls, and laws that mend mankind.

Therefore, it thee behoves, beyond the rest,
To speak thy thoughts, and hear what ours suggest.
Then what may profit most the public state,
'Tis thine, O King! by act to consummate.
I speak what wisdom prompts, nor other word
More wise than Nestor's shall by thee be heard—
No sudden thoughts the words I speak create,
Long has my spirit labour'd with their weight,
From that dread hour, when thou by force of arms
From scorn'd Pelides reft'st Briseïs' charms.
In vain my warning voice thy rage withstood,
And strove to calm the torrent of thy blood,
When frantic passion bade thee proudly scorn
The bravest hero, whom the gods adorn,
Whose prize thou holdst.   Now all your counsel bend,
How best to soothe the chief thou daredst offend ;
How deprecate his wrath—how win his aid,
By gifts to gain him, and by prayer persuade.'
The King replied : ' O thou, for wisdom famed,
Whose words of truth my wrong has justly blamed,
I own the offence, and him whom favouring Jove
Holds in his heart, I rate a·host above.
Jove, to exalt his fame, our force subdues,
And Troy's wide plain with Hellas' blood imbrues,
But whom I wrong'd, let gifts unbounded gain,
And reunite fair friendship's broken chain.
Be witness all what now your king proclaims—
Hear, while his word each present singly names.' "

These speeches cannot be said to be remarkable in any
way, but they are very pleasant reading ; and our hearts warm
towards the speakers.   We confess that Nestor seldom rises
without causing us considerable alarm.   We are instantly
seized with the idea of a nightcap, and ere he sits down, we
are ready to sink into the arms of " tired nature's sweet re-
storer, balmy sleep."   Homer assuredly intended in him to
describe that mysterious phenomenon—dotage.   In his youth
he had been no mean warrior, but not much wiser, as far as we
have heard, than his neighbours.   But he probably always
had a turn for public-speaking ; and it is wonderful how
oratory grows upon a person, when it has happened to meet
with an idiosyncrasy open to its reception, and naturally disposed not only to imbibe but cherish the disease.   Such a
man was Nestor.   Eloquent overmuch he must have been

even in middle life; in old age his wisdom was still more
heavily overbalanced by the weight of words; but on tending
towards a hundred, and in the First Book of the Iliad it was
long since he had seen fourscore we shall swear, his most
reverential admirers must confess that it was well for Job that
he did not encounter the Pylian sage among the other trials
of his affliction. Yet was Nestor just the old man for an
oracle among those fiery Greeks. His disposition was mild,
without being milky; he laid claim chiefly to the wisdom of
experience; and he did not force his opinion upon any council.
He was no advice-monger. But when king or leader requested
the benefit of his time-instructed understanding, the sage—
say not he was superannuated—did then indeed pour out
" the treasures of experienced age," after the fashion of one of
those quiet floods that flow smoothly along a well-cultivated
level, which no doubt they help to fertilise; though without
manure, for our own parts, we have never hoped high of mere
irrigation. All noble nations reverence old age. 'Tis natural
for them to think

" That the sunset of life gives it mystical lore;"

and none felt that reverence more habitually than the Greeks.
A word from the wise, if the wise was aged, went far with
them, when fifty words far wiser from the warlike would not
have gone an inch; and thus " that old man eloquent," of
whom we speak—not North, but Nestor—" always fit audience
found, tho' few," a congregation assembled in council, of
Agamemnon and all his peerage.

Still we maintain that Nestor was in his dotage. Every
man, indeed, is so, after sixty, and most before it—with the
single exception perhaps of Homer himself—and old Parr.
But then ordinary dotage is but drivel; whereas there is a
kind of dotage that sometimes seems inspiration. The reason-
ing powers—if they ever were in any great force—are numb
or gone—but all conclusions that the mind had kept drawing
for many long and perhaps many-coloured years, remain un-
impaired, and in order, ready for use, and at any man's service,
who chooses to consult the sage. Full is he of " wise saws
and *ancient* instances;" and a strange case, indeed, will be
yours, if he cannot illustrate it by a parallel passage in the
life of some one buried before your father was born. After

all, what want we but a " few strong instincts, and a few plain
rules," for the conduct of the human understanding, even in
seasons of perplexity and peril? We fear to follow them, of
ourselves; but when an old grey-beard bids us do so, as if a
voice from Heaven did speak, we obey the oracle; and then
we wonder at the wisdom, which, after all, is but the self-same
knowledge which we fear to recognise as true, so long as we
thought it merely our own; while it proceeds from that principle, which we hesitated, in like manner, formerly to consider
paramount, but which now we admit to be so, under the
sanction of one whom we reverence,—and need we say that
that principle is—Conscience ?

In saying that Nestor was in his dotage, you perceive, then,
from this explanation, that we were desirous of recording our
most delicate testimony to his inappreciable worth. The
Greeks could never have done without him—and long ere
the opening of the Iliad must have raised the siege of Troy.
On the present occasion, in the royal pavilion, Agamemnon
knew, in his troubled conscience, that there was but one
course for him to pursue, in order to avert destruction from
the Grecian host—to confess the wrong he had done Achilles
—ask pardon—and request his return. No ghost needed to
come from the grave to tell him that—no Nestor. But many
emotions chained that thought in his heart, and shame upon
his lips

> " Then clapp'd the padlock on, and snapp'd the lock."

Nestor saw the inside of his soul through his eyes; and
said to him, as Nathan said unto David, " Thou art the
man." Verily the king heard, and was troubled; his heart
was sore afraid; and he must send, with large atonement, a
mission to the Monarch of the Myrmidons, the sole hope of
Greece.

One would think it not difficult to translate into good
English verse two such sensible speeches as these—and to
do justice to Nestor, here uncommonly concise—and to Agamemnon, who, in both thought and language, shows himself a
man and a king. Yet Pope's translation is far from being
what it ought to be—and of neither speech so characteristic
of the speaker, as the original. The purport and spirit of
Homer, says Gilbert Wakefield truly, " are but dimly seen

beneath the ornaments which Pope has thrown over them."
The following attempt is nearly literal:

"Most glorious son of Atreus! king of men!
With thee my words shall cease, with thee begin;
For thou art king of myriads; thine from Jove,
The laws and sceptres to direct mankind."

Gilbert's version is much the better; for Nestor was not
magniloquent. He loved many words, but he was not particularly partial to big ones. " Of many nations thou art king"
is all he says—and it is enough. Pope does not say more
—but he has a hubbub of sonorous words, which would have
sickened Agamemnon.

"Nor, though a meaner give advice, repine.
But follow it, and make the wisdom thine,"

is something very sententious, and so far Nestorian. But
not one word of all that does it please the good old man to
utter—and therefore Eustathius' comment upon it, praised by
Pope, in which he lectures on envy, is in the predicament
of a sermon without a text, nor would the world have lost
anything had there been no preacher. The well-deserved
compliment paid by Nestor to the excellence of his own
advice, Pope omits; and we suspect he did not see it.
" With prayers to move him or with gifts to bend," is a line
which must have been pleasant to Pope's ear, for he has a
thousand such in his works. But "move" and "bend" make
a poor antithesis, or rather no antithesis at all, nor has moving
any more to do with prayers than bending, nor bending any
more to do with gifts than moving; and what is unlucky,
Nestor does not mention prayers, but " soothing gifts and
honey'd words," applying equally to both "please and prevail"
—which is sound sense, and good language, such as always
distinguish the style of that raven-old moral philosopher.
Nor is the King's answer better off in Pope's hands. The
very first line of it loses its entire spirit. Agamemnon confesses his errors without hesitation or reservation. " Oh, old
man! not falsely my errors hast thou enumerated. I have
done unjustly—I deny it not." We love the king of men for
that he humbles himself before the princes. But in Pope,
Atrides tries to shirk the concern with the basest cunning—

to shift his own personality off his shoulders upon the imaginary back of some supposititious prince,—

> " With justice hast thou shown
> A prince's faults, and I with reason own."

The grammar is vile, too; and Agamemnon should have been
sent to school for a dult. The next is not so bad, but not one
line is exactly what it should be—which is a pity.

We will trouble you to point out a single fault in Cowper
—even to a word. You try, and cannot. Then we will. He
should not have put the word " Achilles " into Agamemnon's
mouth. Homer did not—and there were strong reasons for
Agamemnon to sing,

> " O, no, we never mention him,
> His name is never heard ;
> My lips are now forbid to speak
> That once-familiar word."

With this profound objection—not ours, but suggested by
Pope—Cowper's version is perfect.

Sotheby's ? About half-way between Pope's and Cowper's,
but somewhat nearer Cowper's. The character of Nestor is
well preserved, and the first eight lines could hardly be
better. " No sudden thoughts the words I speak create," is
a line in which thoughts and words struggle for the accusative ; and for a long time it threatens to end in a drawn
battle, but at last " words " has it, and vindicates his disputed
title to the accusative. Yet has he not much to boast of—for
he is in a very doubtful case. " By gifts to gain him and by
prayers persuade," is Popeish—and that is enough for us. " I
rate a host above," is constrained—but rhyme is a tyrant
—especially " Jove." " Reunite friendship's broken chain,"
is a mode of speech that Agamemnon would never have discovered had he lived a thousand years ; or if he had, he would
not have used it, till he had remodelled, not only his own
proper lingo, but the language of all Greece. There are other
minor faults. Mr Sotheby has unconsciously contracted a
constant habit of using the word " word." It ends, at least
a hundred lines in his Iliad, and becomes quite a " catch-
word." In this short passage we have,—" my word attend,"
—" nor other word,"—" the words I speak,"—" whose word
of truth,"—" while his word." We add, *verbum sapienti.* It
is odd enough that in the only two places where Homer uses

the word "words" in this passage, Mr Sotheby rejects it.
With the exception of "friendship's broken chain," which
must be flung away, the faults we have pointed out are superficial and accidental—and by an hour's labour of so skilful an
artist as Sotheby could be rubbed off, and the metal left without a stain on the silver polish.

A deputation is appointed by Nestor to go to Achilles—
consisting, as you know, of Phœnix, Ajax, and Ulysses—
attended by two heralds, Hodius and Eurybates—and the
Pylian sage having earnestly exhorted the son of Laertes to
exert his powers to the utmost to soothe Pelides' rage—the
embassy takes its departure from the pavilion.

Τὼ δὲ βάτην παρὰ θῖνα πολυφλοίσβοιο θαλάσσης,
Πολλὰ μάλ' εὐχομένω γαιηόχῳ 'Εννοσιγαίῳ
'Ρηΐδίως πεπιθεῖν μεγάλας φρένας Αἰακίδαο.
Μυρμιδόνων δ' ἐπί τε κλισίας καὶ νῆας ἱκέσθην,
Τὸν δ' εὗρον φρένα τερπόμενον φόρμιγγι λιγείῃ
Καλῇ δαιδαλέῃ, ἐπὶ δ' ἀργύρεον ζυγὸν ἦεν·
Τὴν ἄρετ' ἐξ ἐνάρων, πόλιν 'Ηετίωνος ὀλέσσας·
Τῇ ὅ γε θυμὸν ἔτερπεν, ἄειδε δ' ἄρα κλέα ἀνδρῶν.
Πάτροκλος δέ οἱ οἶος ἐναντίος ἧστο σιωπῇ,
Δέγμενος Αἰακίδην, ὁπότε λήξειεν ἀείδων.
Τὼ δὲ βάτην προτέρω, ἡγεῖτο δὲ δῖος 'Οδυσσεὺς,
Στὰν δὲ πρόσθ' αὐτοῖο. Ταφὼν δ' ἀνόρουσεν 'Αχιλλεὺς
Αὐτῇ σὺν φόρμιγγι, λιπὼν ἕδος ἔνθα θάασσεν.
'Ὡς δ' αὕτως Πάτροκλος, ἐπεὶ ἴδε φῶτας, ἀνέστη.
Τὼ καὶ δεικνύμενος προσέφη πόδας ὠκὺς 'Αχιλλεύς.

—IX. 182-196.

NORTH (literal prose).

" They two, therefore, went along the shore of the much-resound-
    ing sea,

Many things very much praying to the earth-encircling earth-
    shaker,

That he would easily bend the mighty mind of the grandson of
    Æacus.

And they came to the tents and the ships of the Myrmidons :

And there found him soothing his spirit by means of the sound-
    ing harp,

Beautiful, of exquisite workmanship, and it had a silver ζυγον,

Which he took from the spoils, when he destroy'd the city of
    Eëtion.

With it he was soothing his spirit, and was singing the glorious
    deeds of heroes.

But Patroclus alone sat opposite to him in silence,

Waiting till the grandson of Æacus should cease singing.

And they two went *farther* *ben* (*Scoticè*), and the illustrious
  Ulysses led the way,
And they stood before him. Amazed, Achilles started up,
Leaving his seat, along with his harp, where he was sitting.
In the same manner also Patroclus, when he saw the men, stood up:
Them both receiving kindly, address'd the swift-footed Achilles."

CHAPMAN.

" The quarter of the Myrmidons they reacht, and found him set,
Delighted with his solemn harpe, which curiously was fret
With works conceited, through the verge : the bawdricke that
    embrac't
His loftie neck, was silver twist : this (when his hand laid waste
Eëtion's citie) he did chuse, as his especiall prise,
And (louing sacred music well) made it his exercise :
To it he sung the glorious deeds of great heröes dead,
And his true mind, that practice fail'd, sweet contemplation fed.
With him alone, and opposite, all silent sat his friend
Attentive, and beholding him, who now his song did end.
Th' ambassadors did forward preasse, renown'd Ulysses led,
And stood in view : their sodaine sight his admiration bred,
Who with his harpe and all arose : so did Menetius' sonne
When he beheld them : their receipt, Achilles thus begun."

POPE.

" Through the still night they march, and hear the roar
Of murmuring billows on the sounding shore.
To Neptune, ruler of the seas profound,
Whose liquid arms the mighty globe surround,
They pour forth vows their embassy to bless,
And calm the rage of stern Æacides.
And now arrived, where on the sandy bay
The Myrmidonian tents and vessels lay,
Amused at ease, the godlike man they found,
Pleased with the solemn harp's harmonious sound.
(The well-wrought harp from conquer'd Thebæ came,
Of polish'd silver was its costly frame).
With this he soothes his angry soul, and sings
Th' immortal deeds of heroes and of kings.
Patroclus only, of the royal train,
Placed in his tent, attends the lofty strain :
Full opposite he sat, and listen'd long,
In silence waiting till he ceased the song.
Unseen the Grecian embassy proceeds
To his high tent ; the great Ulysses leads.

Achilles starting, as the chiefs he spied,
Leap'd from his seat, and laid the harp aside.
With like surprise arose Menœtius' son :
Pelides grasp'd their hands, and thus begun."

COWPER.

" Along the margin of the sounding deep
They pass'd, to Neptune, compasser of Earth,
Preferring numerous vows, with ardent prayers,
That they might sway with ease the mighty mind
Of fierce Æacides.   Arriving soon
Among the Myrmidons, their chief they found
Soothing his sorrow with his silver-framed
Harmonious lyre, spoil taken when he took
Eëtion's city : with that lyre his cares
He sooth'd, and glorious heroes was his theme.
Patroclus silent sat, and he alone,
Before him, on Æacides intent,
Expecting still when he should cease to sing.
The messengers advanced (Ulysses first)
Unto his presence ; at the sight, his harp
Still in his hand, Achilles from his seat
Started astonish'd ; nor with less amaze
Patroclus also, seeing them, arose.
Achilles seized their hands, and thus he spake."

SOTHEBY.

" On their high charge the delegated train
Pursued their way along the sounding main,
And to appease the Chief, devoutly pray'd,
And oft implored the Ocean monarch's aid.
But when they came, where, camp'd along the bay,
Pelides and his host in order lay,
They found him kindling his heroic fire
With high-toned strains, that shook the sounding lyre ;
That silver lyre that erst the victor bore
His chosen prize from sack'd Eëtion's store.
There, as the hero feats of heroes sung,
And o'er the glowing chords enraptured hung,
Alone Patroclus, list'ning to the lay,
Watch'd till the impassion'd rapture died away.
They forward march'd, Ulysses led them on ;
They came, and stood before famed Peleus' son.
Achilles, wondering, started from his seat,
Sped forth, his lyre in hand, the chiefs to greet :

Patroclus rose : and strait Achilles press'd
Their hands in his, and kindly thus address'd."

We have always thought this one of the most beautiful
pieces of poetry in the whole world. It seems to us indeed
to be perfect. How solemn the Mission moving along the
margin of the sounding deep, preferring prayers to Neptune
that its issue might be fortunate, for well they knew the
character of fierce Æacides! Not a word is said about the
night; and that shows that Homer never repeats himself,
except when he has some purpose to serve by the repetition.
A thousand Trojan watchfires were blazing ; but Phœnix,
Ulysses, and Ajax, all absorbed in their prayers to Neptune,
saw them not—and Homer himself had forgotten now the
vision of the moon and stars. No time is lost, and we see
them already among the Myrmidons. Had it been put before-
hand to any person of loftiest temper, who, knowing the character of Achilles, had yet no knowledge of this interview, how
he might imagine the goddess-born would be found employed, think ye that he could ever have made such a noble
guess as the truth ? Never. Homer alone could have thus
exalted his hero. Not many suns have yet gone down on his
wrath, and you remember how at its first outburst it flamed
like a volcano. It smoulders now in that mighty bosom—
but the son of Thetis is not sitting sullen in his tent—he has
forgotten the ungrateful, injurious, and insulting Agamemnon,
and all his slaves. His soul is with the heroes. Achilles is
a savage—a barbarian, forsooth—but half-civilised, though
Nereus himself was his grandsire ! There he sits, the bravest
and most beautiful of mortal men, a musician, perhaps a poet,
for Homer tells us not whether the Implacable is singing his
own songs, or those of the 'Λοίδοι. Yes, the Swift-footed is a
man of genius ; and among all the spoils he won when he
sacked the city of Eëtion, most he prized that harp on which
he is now playing—the harp with the silver cross-bar, and
beautiful in its workmanship, as if formed by Dædalus, and
fine-toned its strings, as if smitten by the Sun-god's hand.
His proud soul would disdain to harp even to Princes.
Patroclus alone, still and mute, is listening, hero to hero.

But how have our translators acquitted themselves here ?
—let us see. Chapman drops the epithet πολυφλοίσβοιο, and
merely says the shore, which was wrong, the noise of the

sea being essential to a maritime night. "The god that earth doth bind in brackish chains," are poor words—sorry substitutes for those two extraordinary ones γαιηόχῳ 'Εννοσιγαίῳ. Better have said simply, Neptune. All the rest is very nobly done. The two lines about Patroclus are perfect, except the words, "who now his song did end." He waited till the song should end. And he would have been willing to wait till midnight, had Achilles not started up on entrance of the ambassadors. "Who with his harp and all arose," is very majestic.

We have just been reading over Pope for the tenth time this evening, and though we might not unjustly find some faint fault with a few particular words, yet we should be ashamed of ourselves were we to do so; for he is Alexander the Great here,

> ——" and is attired
> With sudden brightness, like a man inspired."

The versification is most harmonious; and the lines might themselves be chanted to the harp. Pope, when happy, had a heroic genius; and though true it is that he too too often miserably misrepresents Homer, it is, as we have said, wilfully, and with malice aforethought—seldom in ignorance, and never in stupidity; but knowing that his strength lay in a style essentially different from the old bard's, it was not to be expected, perhaps not to be desired, that he should lay it aside, and endeavour to adopt Homer's, or imitate it, which, to a poet who had attained consummate excellence of another kind, would have been accompanied with the perpetual con-straint of difficulty, nay, impossible. We must take it, then, as it is, and be thankful for another Iliad.

Only a great master could safely come after Pope in this passage, and Cowper is a great master. How differently the two speak of the sea, yet both how finely! Pope brings the voice of the sea to our ears, by almost an accumulation of epithets—means legitimate, and dear to many delightful poets. We

> ——" hear the *roar*
> Of *murmuring* billows on the *sounding* shore."

Cowper fills our ear with the same voice at once,

> " Along the margin of the *sounding* deep."

Pope calls Neptune

> ——" Ruler of the seas profound,
> Whose liquid arms the mighty globe surround,"

which, though far from being intensely Homeric, is not without grandeur. Cowper calls him, more simply and Greek-
ishly, " compasser of earth," nor dreams of telling us that his
" arms are liquid," or his " chains brackish," liquidity and
brackishness being qualities lying so much on the surface,
as well as in the depths, that mention of them does not throw
much new or old light on the character of Neptune. All the
lines about the heroic Harper are very fine—the pauses
solemn—the repetition of the word " soothe," shows how
deeply Cowper felt for the sufferer ; the close is full of
elevation—" and glorious heroes were his theme." The
only line we do not entirely like, is,

> " Expecting still when he should cease to sing."

It seems to intimate that Patroclus was impatient of the
strain—a sad mistake. But perhaps Cowper uses the word
" expecting " for waiting ; and if so, it is all right.

> ——" At the sight,
> His harp still in his hand," &c.

is a picture. It is better than Pope's

> " Achilles, started as the chiefs he spied,
> Leapt from his seat, and laid the harp aside."

" Leapt " is undignified—Achilles " started," but Homer says
" leaving his seat." The start was momentary,—he walked
towards Ulysses with the calm air and stately step of the
Hero of Heroes.

Sotheby is not faultless—but his beauties are pre-eminent.
His versification, if inferior to Pope's, is flowing and sonorous
—and the diction glows like gold. Perhaps wisely, he for-
bears to touch the " earth-encircling earth-shaker," and calls
him the " ocean-monarch." Kindling his " heroic fire," is
fine and true. So is, " There, as the hero feats of heroes
sung." Equally excellent is, " Alone Patroclus listening to
the lay ; " and " Achilles, wondering, started from his seat."
But we said the version is not faultless. Perhaps nothing in
this world is—except a lily. " Delegated *train*," is not to

our mind. It is true, but formal. "Sounding strain" and
"sounding lyre" should not have been in one passage.
"Eëtion's *store*" smells of Boston. We are sorry for it,
but we cannot admire "Watch'd till the impassion'd rapture
died away." Impassioned rapture, if we are not much mistaken, is a very unhomeric form and spirit of speech. But
that is not our chief objection to the line. The impassioned
rapture did *not* die away. We do not believe it would, even
had Achilles not been interrupted. His lyrical poem and
music would have gone off in a tremendous burst—it would
have rolled away in very thunder. Such is our belief; but it
was interrupted—on the appearance of Ulysses, Achilles
stopt suddenly, even as we have seen an eagle do in the sky,
when flying at the rate of a hundred miles an hour. "Sped
forth," gives us the notion of covering more ground than
Achilles had to do ere he seized the hands of the chiefs.
That is a trifle—a speck; but the others are flaws. So rare
without them is " a gem of purest ray serene."

What a glorious volume of odes, elegies, and hymns would
be "The Lays of Achilles!" But who could write it? Let
all our poets form themselves into an association, to be called
the Achillean, and distribute among themselves the subjects
of song that bestrewed Greece, and the Isles of Greece, before
the Trojan War. To prevent all wrangling, let us who do not
belong to the Irritable, be appointed Perpetual Prose-Presi-
dent. The Achillean Association, at each celebration of the
anniversary of its own birth, shall put into our hands the
poetry of the preceding year, and we, like an old Grecian, *ore
rotundo*, shall chant the Lays of Achilles to the harp, an in-
strument on which the world acknowledges we excel. The
ladies in the gallery—our Festival being in Freemasons' Hall
—will "rain influence and dispense the prize." The prize-
poems shall all be engrossed in the Album of the Achillean
Association, and at the end of ten years, a period taken from
the Trojan War, the Album shall be printed by Ballantyne,
and published by Blackwood, under such auspices as never
before launched into light immortal songs.

From the Achillean Association, we prophesy the revival of
Lyrical Poetry. "The ancient spirit is not dead;" it but
sleepeth, and will awake as if startled by the sound of a
trumpet. Pindars will appear—and Coriunas too—for the

Hemans, and the Mitford, and the Landon must be members
—and the immortal Joanna. Sir Walter—more magnificent
than in *Marmion*—will invent moving minstrelsies for the
Mythic tales of Old Achaia; Wordsworth—nobler even than
in the "Song at the Feast of Brougham Castle"—will sanctify
in dim religious light the roamings of that sad Aleian field,
and awaken the whole world to ruth for fury-haunted Bellerophon ; Southey—in even loftier inspiration than that which
sang "Fill high the horn to Hirlas"—will celebrate Meleager
and the Boar of Caledon; Coleridge—wilder than in the
"Ancient Mariner"—will rave gloriously of Jason and the
Golden Fleece, and fling forth fiery fragments of argon-
autics ; Moore—eclipsing the light of his own "Loves of the
Angels," will breath Epithalamia for Venus and Juno, and
sigh-charged roundelays sung to his celestial Leman by
Endymion on Mount Latmos ; Crabbe—in vision more terrible
than the madness of Sir Eustace Grey—will paint Hercules
Furens, and call his picture-poem the Poison'd Shirt; Bowles
—pathetic more than on the "Grave of the Last Saxon"—will
murmur melody over Hyacinthus or Adonis ; Montgomery—
already familiar with the world before the flood—will darken
the despair of Deucalion ; and, illustrious above all, Campbell ;
but there is absolutely no end to the members of the Achillean Association !   To it, *eugete* and *valete*, all ye bright sons
of song, and starlike may you shine in the "high heaven of
vention ! "

Was the tent of Achilles, think ye, lighted with gas ? Unquestionably.   The ages of old were wonderful old ages.
Not in blind caves sat Thetis below the sea-depths. Lustrous were all her haunts in the groves of coral; and as she
could never have stooped to burn oil—indeed too well did she
love the phocæ—she must have lighted her marine palaces
with aerial fire ; nor can you doubt for a moment that she
provided her son with the unmetered radiance. As the ambassadors entered, the night-tent of Achilles was bright as
day, and he himself, harp in hand, rising from his seat, and
advancing towards them, stately as the beautiful Apollo.

How courteous that princely greeting ! No manners like
those of the heroic age.

" Χαίριτον· ἢ φίλοι ἄνδρες ἱκάνιτον· ἢ τι μάλα χριὼ,
Οἵ μοι σκυζομίνψ πιρ 'Αχαιῶν φίλτατοί ἰστον."

"Ὡς ἄρα φωνήσας προτέρω ἄγε δῖος Ἀχιλλεύς,
Εἷσεν δ' ἐν κλισμοῖσι, τάπησί τε πορφυρέοισιν.
Αἶψα δὲ Πάτροκλον προσεφώνεεν ἐγγὺς ἐόντα·
" Μείζονα δὴ κρητῆρα, Μενοιτίου υἱέ, κάθιστα,
Ζωρότερον δὲ κέραιε, δέπας δ' ἔντυνον ἑκάστω·
Οἱ γὰρ φίλτατοι ἄνδρες ἐμῷ ὑπέασι μιλάθρω."
                                    —IX. 197–204.

Achilles thus addresses the heroes. We adopt Heyne's
punctuation in the first line, which is different from others,
and best, because most in character with the "imperatoria
brevitas" of Achilles.

NORTH (literal prose).

" Hail : you are indeed friends who have come : verily some necessity
    strongly (presses on you).
Who to me, angry though I be, are of the Greeks the most beloved.
Thus indeed having spoken, the illustrious Achilles led them farther
    ben (Scoticè ut supra),
And made them sit down on reclining seats, on purple cushions :
And Patroclus, who was near him, he then quickly address'd.
' A larger goblet, oh son of Menætius, set down,
And more generous mix it : and for each provide a drinking-cup :
Since men, by me, the most beloved, are under my roof.' "

CHAPMAN.

"' Health to my lords ! right welcome men assure yourselves to be ;
Though some necessity I know doth make you visit me,
Incenst with just cause 'gainst the Greeks.' This said, a cover'd
    seat
With purple cushions he set forth, and did their ease entreat ;
And said—' Now, friend, our greatest bowle with wine unmixt, and
    meat,
Oppose the lords ; and of the depth let every man make proof ;
These are my best esteemed friends, and underneath my roof.' "

POPE.

"' Princes, all hail !· whatever brought you here,
Or strong necessity, or urgent fear ;
Welcome, though Greeks ! for not as foes ye came ;
To me more dear than all that bear the name.'
With that the chiefs beneath his roof he led,
And placed in seats, with purple carpets spread.
Then thus—' Patroclus, crown the larger bowl,
Mix purer wine, and open every soul.
Of all the warriors yonder host can send,
Thy friend most honours these, and these thy friend.' "

"'Hail friends! Ye are all welcome.   Urgent cause
Hath doubtless brought you, whom I dearest hold
(Though angry still) of all Achaia's host.'
So saying, he introduced and seated them
On thrones with purple arras overspread,
Then thus bespoke Patroclus standing nigh—·
'Son of Menœtius! bring a beaker more
Capacious, and replenish it with wine
Diluted less ; then give to each his cup ;
For dearer friends than those who now arrive
Beneath my roof, nor worthier, have I none.'"

" Whether a friendly visit lead your steps,
Or some necessity impels, all hail !
To me, though sad, most dear of all the Greeks."

" ' Hail friends ! ye come by strong compulsion moved ;
Though here I rage, I hail you most beloved.'
He spoke ; and to his tent the chieftains led,
And placed on seats, with purple arras spread.
· Now haste, Patroclus, to each guest assign
A larger beaker charged with stronger wine,
To greet the friends, whose presence I revere,
Guests who beneath my roof most loved appear.'"

That fine fiery fellow Chapman is seldom or never at fault,
when he has to deal with a burst of simple, natural emotion.
His spirit is strung to Homer's.   Like two harps tuned
together, when the one is struck the other responds—and 'tis
noble concert.   'Tis so in this passage.   A marginal note
says, "Achilles' *gentle receipt* of Ulysses, Ajax," &c. ; and it
is gentle—for Achilles, if ever there was one on this earth,
was a gentleman—not a finer one even Sir Philip Sidney—
whose *Life and Arcadia*, by Gray of Magdalen, we this morning perused with unfaded delight.   " Of the depth let every
man make proof," is perhaps going a *leetle* too far—though,
beyond doubt, Achilles did hope and trust that each hero
would drain it—not to the dregs—for dregs there were none—
but till he saw his face, a smiling oblong, at the bottom.   But
the warmth of welcome, and the simple style of it, and the

dignified sincerity of the noble host, are finely preserved—and Chapman is Homer.

It is provoking to see a man wilfully going wrong, who knows perfectly well how to go right—walking with his eyes open as if they were shut—and knocking himself against stools and chairs, like a blind blunderer in a room which he has himself set in order. So doth Pope. "This short speech," saith he, "is wonderfully proper to the occasion, and to the temper of the speaker. One is under a great expectation of what Achilles will say at the sight of these heroes, and I know nothing in nature that could satisfy it, but the very thing he here accosts them with." Admirable—but why, then, Pope! oh, Pope! didst thou perversely violate thine own true sense of the perfect fitness of the original, in thy translation? "Or strong necessity or urgent fear" is a bad line, for a stronger necessity than urgent fear we defy you to imagine—so "or" has no office, and no point the antithesis. "Welcome, *though* Greeks," is the very reverse of the feeling of Achilles at that moment; he rejoiced to see them *as* Greeks. "For not as foes ye *came*" is miserable, and its lame wretchedness is aggravated by its vile grammar. The change of tense destroys the intensity—pardon the pun. "And open every soul," is paying a poor compliment to his guests. Their souls were open; nor was Achilles the man to suspect that they were shut. Sincere as the sky himself, he saw no clouds on their brow, except of sadness, which the sunshine of his welcome would illumine or disperse. "Thy friend most honours these, and these thy friend," is very pretty, indeed; but Achilles "spoke right on," and not like the Master of Ceremonies at Bath. He was no Beau Nash. How impertinent, on such an occasion, and from such a man, a compliment to himself!—Pope has now dree'd his punishment. He winces—his back is red—he is about to faint—the army-surgeon looks at his watch, nods, "enough," and the culprit is released from the halberts.

Cowper is good—very good. "On thrones with purple arras overspread," gives great grace and dignity to the reception of the heroes. They were placed as in the days of chivalry, "under the dais." Chapman supposes each hero, time about, which is fair play, to lay his lugs in the same "great bolle," with an eye to view the bottom, like the Fellows of a

College, with their "cup," at the high table on day of Gau-
deamus. Cowper supposes one "beaker more capacious,"
replenished with wine diluted less, and then out of it Patroclus filling up each hero's own particular cup to the brim, till
no heel-tap was detectable, and a bumper brimmed with beads,
such as Ganymede gives to Jove when there is revelry in heaven. The terms in which he speaks of his visitors are full of
heart, such as a hero uses when speaking of heroes. Cowper!
we love thee well, and wish thou hadst not been so often and
so long so unhappy in this world. But now thou art in bliss,
which is more than we shall venture to say for old Newton.

Sotheby, as usual, is strong—and here strength was wanted;
but he is constrained—and his winged words should have
been free as sunbeams. " Strong compulsion moved" is liker
Dr Paley than Achilles. " Though here I rage" is not equal
to Cowper's "though angry still." Achilles " was angry
still "—yea, he was so, even when to his harp singing of
heroes. But he was not at that moment "raging ; " he knew
better than to " rage" in the unexpected presence of such
friends ; he was all kindness and courtesy ; sunshine and
music shone and murmured along his speech, which was like
a river-flash ; but all the while in the dark depths of his sullen
soul, nevertheless, growled wrath and indignation over the
drowned image of Agamemnon. Sotheby strove with Homer
—at line for line ; and though in the struggle he has shown
great muscle and skill, the champion has given him a fair
back-fall. " A larger beaker, charged with stronger wine," is
the best line we ever read, without the single shadow of an
exception. It would of itself atone for any sin in composition,
however flagrant; but Sotheby has committed no sins at all
in this passage—he is merely a little stiff or so—and his stiff-
ness was inevitable in the bold attempt to give eight lines of
Greek—and such lines, in eight of English—which, though
" by strong compulsion moved," are pregnant.

Before we can possibly understand anything of Homer, it
has been said, *ex-cathedralishly*, that we must study the manners of the heroic ages. And, pray, where are we to study
them ? Why, in Homer to be sure. Ho, ho ! So you merely
mean that we must read the Iliad? Such is the pompous impertinence of pedantry, pretending to rare erudition. Yet will
a German professor get you up a volume on the Manners of

the Heroic Ages, in which he will seem, for a while at first, to have had access to information in bards long anterior to Melesigines. Fling him into the fire, and let him make his escape, if he can, up the flue, and turn you to your Homer. Not a syllable, by any possibility, or impossibility, can be known of the Heroic ages, but from him—and him you must read along with the Bible. Yea! the Bible; and you will then know the meaning of the title of a book you may have never seen, any more than ourselves—*Homerus* 'Εξεαυζων.

Here is a specimen of the manners of the heroic age, how patriarchal! We quote Sotheby, who manages them, perhaps, better than any other translator:—

> "He spake; nor him Patroclus disobey'd—
> Then, nigh the fire his lord a basket laid,
> There cast a goat's and sheep's extended chine,
> And the huge carcass of a fatted swine.
> Served by Automedon, with dexterous art
> Achilles' self divided part from part,
> Fix'd on the spits the flesh, where brightly blazed
> The fire's pure splendour, by Patroclus raised.
> Patroclus next, when sank the flame subdued,
> O'er the raked embers placed the spitted food.
> Then raised it from the props, then salted o'er,
> And duly roasted, to the dresser bore:
> Next to each guest, along the table spread
> In beauteous baskets the allotted bread;
> Achilles' self distributed the meat,
> And placed against his own Ulysses' seat.
> And now Patroclus, at his lord's desire,
> The hallow'd offering cast amid the fire—
> The guests then feasted, and, the banquet o'er,
> When satiate thirst and hunger claim'd no more,
> And to hoar Phœnix Ajax gave the sign,
> Ulysses, mindful, crown'd his cup with wine,
> And to Achilles drank."

It is not easy to suppose a more savoury supper. We never read this steaming account of it, without lamenting that we did not assist at the feast. 'Tis, in truth, the model of the Noctes Ambrosianæ,—

> " There cast a goat's and sheep's extended chine,
> And the huge carcass of a fatted swine,—"

To the life! to the death! Nothing wanting but—oysters.

In nothing was the constitution of the heroes more enviable than its native power—of eating at all times, and without a moment's warning. Never does a meal to any distinguished individual come amiss. Their stomachs were as heroic as their hearts, their bowels magnanimous. It cannot have been forgotten by the reader, who hangs with a watering mouth over the description of this entertainment, that about two hours before, these three heroes, Ulysses, Ajax, and old Phœnix, had made an almost enormous supper in the pavilion of Agamemnon—   ·

> " There to the *sated* guests, the Pylian sage
> Unlock'd the treasures of experienced age."

Sated they might have been, a couple of hours ago, at the remotest, but their walk

> " Along the margin of the sounding deep,"

had reawakened their slumbering appetite. At the smell of the roasted goat, and the " huge carcass of the fatted swine" —a noble line—they feel themselves instantly sharp-set— *yawp* (*Scoticè*); and such another knife and fork—that is, finger and thumb—we have not, except perhaps in Picardy, seen played since the Heroic age. We allude more particularly to the performances of old Phœnix.

After all, there is nothing in this wicked and weary world like—good eating—" to which, if you please," whispers the pensive Public, " add good drinking," and then, with that yawn of hers—" sound sleeping"—in common terms, " Bed, board, and lodging." Good washing, too, is well ; but not vitally essential to national comfort—witness that worthy land lying north of the Tweed. Secret gluttons alone openly abuse gormandising—men of " steady, but not voracious appetites," alone publicly panegyrise it. We have known sallow sumphs scowl from a distance at Ambrose's suppers, as illegally and unnaturally enormous, who, after dinner on a fast-day, have been under the necessity of an emetic. Good must be the digestion of that Poet whose genius is divine. A bilious bard is abhorred of all the Muses ; nor will Apollo, physician though he be, prescribe for the Blue and Yellow. Homer himself thought nothing of a saddle of mutton or a sirloin of beef. In a twinkling vanished from his trencher a boar's head. Then washed he all well down with a glorious goblet.

There is something exceedingly satisfactory to our ear in the sound of the word—Rations. A rational repast. Mark the blind beggar devouring bread and cheese, or mouthfuls of cold rags of lean meat, by the wayside, and you see he is in heaven. He licks his shrivelled lips, folds his withered hands, turns up his sightless eyes, mutters something not unheard afar—and catching up his crutch, hobbles away with no unsuccessful attempt at a song. Lo! a whole army—nay, two whole armies—on the field of battle—*dining!* It requires much caution and dexterity to keep the biscuits from trundling into these pools of blood. What a ravenous set—three courses in one—a dreadful dinner! What tremendous thunder and lightning was that? Except our own little ship, are both fleets blown to atoms? Not at all. Merely the L'Orient. And now that the splash is over, let a double allowance of grog be served out to the merry crew of the Victory, for we are all dry as devils. If you desire to see indeed a dinner, under the delusive name of luncheon, endeavour to get access to a popular preacher between sermons. By that porter-jug he is a deep divine. Why, a man cannot be expected to make even a tolerable appearance on the scaffold, without a couple of rolls and of eggs to breakfast on the morning of execution. Let no man be so rash as to be hanged on an empty stomach. Then at Funerals, watched ye ever the chief mourners? How they do tuck in the cold ham, and the pigeon-pie, and the round! Sorrow is dry; and that fact, in the philosophy of the human mind, accounts for all these empty barrels. Never shall we forget the Funeral of the Chisholm!

To return to the Tent of Achilles. There sit Ulysses, and Ajax, and old Phœnix, hungry as hawks, though two hours ago we saw them preying in Agamemnon's Pavilion.

> " The guests then feasted, and the banquet o'er,
> When satiate, thirst and hunger claim'd no more," &c.

Thirst and hunger—observe—on a full stomach! And now, after that second most successful supper, when " their leathern sides are stretched almost to bursting," Ulysses has the face to say to Achilles,

> " But now we seek not feasts !"

Take the entertainment in the Tent—from first to last—and

it is a noble one. Where saw ye ever Three such Men-cooks as Achilles, Patroclus, and Automedon ? Lo ! the son of Thetis—the goddess-born—with the spit in his " inaccessible hands ! " Redder is his fine face in the kitchen-fire than it ever was flaming in the van of victorious battle. Is that an apron ? And now from Cooks the Three Princes become Waiters. Achilles is his own Butler.

How much more state in the simplicity of these natural manners than in the pomp of ours, where all is artificial ! A modern entertainment is made mean by menials. It cannot bear description—nothing more contemptible than a horse-shoe table, however august the guests, lined with flunkeys at a great city-feast. Compare with this repast of heroes, in the tent of Achilles, that given to four of the great European monarchs some dozen years ago in Guildhall, at which, if we mistake not, presided the Lord Mayor of London ! It is Blackwall, we think, who says, that we read with delight all Homer's most minute descriptions of the houses, tables, and way of living of the ancients ; but, on the contrary, that when we consider our own customs, we find that our first business, when we sit down to poetise in the higher strains, is to unlearn our daily way of life ; to forget our manner of sleeping, eating, and diversions; we are obliged to adopt a set of more natural manners, which, however, are foreign to us ; and must be like plants raised up in hotbeds or greenhouses in comparison with those which grow in soils fitted by nature for such productions. Nay, so far, he continues, are we from enriching poetry with new images drawn from nature, that we find it difficult to under-stand the old. We live within doors, covered from nature's face, and passing our days supinely, ignorant of her beauties. We are apt to think the similes taken from her low, and the ancient manners mean or absurd. But let us be ingenuous, and confess, that while the moderns admire nothing but pomp, and can think nothing great or beautiful but what is the pro-duce of wealth, they exclude themselves from the pleasantest and most natural images that adorn old poetry. State and form disguise men ; and wealth and luxury disguise nature. Their effects in writing are answerable ; a lord-mayor's show, or grand procession of any kind, is not very delicious reading, if described minutely, and at length ; and great ceremony is at least equally tiresome in a poem, as in ordinary conversation. So far Blackwall—and he writes like a philosophic gentleman.

But Ajax gives the sign to old Phœnix —and Ulysses, crowning his cup with wine, drinks to Achilles, and, on his legs, volunteers a speech. Let the wily orator stand there for another month or so—and then we shall listen to his eloquence, and give a fine specimen of it from Sotheby, and " the rest."

HOMER AND HIS TRANSLATORS.

[DECEMBER 1831.]

IT is to little purpose, we think, to attempt to enter into critical disquisitions on what does or does not fall under the description of beauty or of sublimity. Nor is it, in our opinion, of much avail, to go far into metaphysical enumeration of the different elements of which they may be constituted.

We should say, generally, that all the powers of our nature to which delight is annexed, are capable of a beauty of their own. Nor does more appear to be required to produce this perception, than the intimate blending of delight with the object presented; a blending so deep, that the object, when incapable of sense, shall appear to the mind invested with that power of emotion which the mind indeed brings forth from itself. In connection with the fact of this dependence of beauty on the capacity of delight in the soul, and on the power of the object to raise up such a sudden suffusion of that feeling as shall spread over itself, it may be observed, that our feeling to beauty is very variable; and that a state of greatly excited and joyous sensibility is capable of shedding the appearance of beauty over objects and scenes, like the sudden lighting up of sunshine, which do not at other times so recommend themselves to the imagination.

As delight is the source of beauty, so pain and fear, and power, which subdues pain and fear, are the sources of sublimity. There may be said, as possibly we may have somewhere else hinted, to be two classes of sublime objects; those which shake the soul and make it tremble in its strength, and those on the contemplation of which it feels itself elated and full of power. Or rather, it may be said, that both these kinds of emotion belong to sublimity; for both may perhaps be felt towards the same object in varying tempers of the mind.

In Burke's *Essay on the Sublime and Beautiful*, we believe the first attempt was made to establish terror as the source of sublimity; and assuredly it is one of its great elements. The error of the theory seems to have consisted in describing this as its sole constituent. Thunder, and the roar of ocean, and the roar of human battle, are sublime, because fear and power are there mingled into one. Mountains that lift up their eternal heads into the sky, that hang their loose rocks aloft, and pour the rage of cataracts down their riven cliffs, mingle power and fear together to the human soul that beholds them in its awe. Hence it is that the imagination of men, fearfully awakened in its superstitions, has gathered signs and voices, which to *our* apprehension are now sublime; because the fears of those who were terror-stricken, and the unknown powers which were the objects of their dread, are present to our mind together. How has Milton united power, and fear, and physical pangs, in vast and dread sublimity, when he has shown those mighty fallen angels, in their yet unvanquished and seemingly indestructible strength, arraying themselves to new war, in the midst of their dolorous regions of pain, in the dark and fiery dwelling-place of their eternal punishment! Over the whole earth, then, sublimity is spread, wherever fear and power meet together. The shadow of death is sublime, when it has fallen on a whole generation, and buried them in the sleep of sin. The power of decay is sublime, when

> " Oblivion swallows cities up,
> And mighty states characterless are grated
> To dusty nothing."

Every spirit of Power is sublime in itself; every spirit of Fear is sublime, when it has ceased to gripe and crush the heart,—when it can be surveyed in Imagination. Pain, which sickens the soul, and humbles it in the dust of mortality, can yet mix with sublimity when it is only half triumphant, and the spirit in its might yet wrestles with the pangs under which it is about to expire.

" I see before me the Gladiator lie,
He leans upon his hand—his manly brow
Consents to death, but conquers agony,
And his droop'd head sinks gradually low—
And through his side the last drops, ebbing slow
From the red gash, fall heavy, one by one,
Like the first of a thunder-shower ; and now
Th' arena swims around him—he is gone,
Ere ceased the inhuman shout that hail'd the wretch who won.

⸱   ⸱   ⸱   ⸱   ⸱   ⸱   ⸱   ⸱   ⸱

————Shall he expire,
And unavenged ? Arise ! ye Goths, and glut your ire."

Pain, endurance, and in death a prophetic dream of retalia-
tion and revenge! Such sublimity did Byron feel in that
Dying Gladiator, that, in the troubled light of his far-seeing
imagination suddenly inspired, he connected with his fall that
of the mightiest of empires, and from the arena's bloody dust
arose a vision of siege, storm, and sack—of Rome herself,
set on fire by the yet unborn brethren of that one barbarian,
" butcher'd to make a Roman holiday," fierce-flocking from
their forests to raze with the ground all the imperial palaces
of the city of the Cæsars.

Many other elements, no doubt, besides those we have
mentioned, may enter into sublimity. What we have wished
to indicate, is the region of the soul, where it is to be found.
It dwells in the regions of its power—whether that power be
made present to its consciousness in calmness ; or in the
uprisings of its might ; or in agitations that reach into its
depths.   In some of its forms it is totally disunited from
Beauty, which lives only in the capacity of Delight.   In
others it is intimately and indivisibly blended with it.   Who
will say in the great poems of Milton or of Homer, where the
quality begins or where it ceases?   Who will say among the
spirits of men, which are to be numbered with the Beautiful,
and which with the Sublime?

We commonly seek for examples in the physical world.
These offer themselves readily because they have hold upon
our senses.   But the passion of sublimity is as much moved,
and certainly may be more strongly excited, by the delineation of spiritual power. Prometheus! a mighty persecuted
spirit, subject to overruling power, and punished without

a crime—for is it crime to "steal the fire of heaven"? Lifting up his undaunted brow and voice to call on the earth and the winds and the seas to witness his unjust sufferings, maintaining in the prospect of his interminable punishment—for so he thought it, though Hercules set him free—all the calmness of his prophetic intelligence, and all the undisturbed fortitude of his indomitable heart—let the vulture gnaw his liver, as it seemed good to it and to Jupiter—and filling with the grandeur of his own being the solitary magnificence of nature! Satan—is not he sublime? What sayeth he to his mates? "Fallen cherubs! to be *weak* is miserable—doing or suffering!" "Better to *reign* in Hell than *serve* in Heaven!" And is not Achilles sublime—sovereign even over the King of Men, and slave but to his own passions, and in the wild world of the will, whence rise up from bright or black fountains all the bliss and all the bale that enrapture or agonise life.

That man is not ignorant of Homer who has read, even in translation, the First Book of the Iliad. He knows the grandeur of the character of Achilles—just as, if weather-wise, we may prophesy the nature of the whole day, from the lowering light of a tempestuous morning. It will be a day of storm, settling into a mild and magnificent sunset. What a gallery of pictures! Chryses, priest of Apollo, with the sacred symbols of his office, suppliant with richest ransoms for his captive daughter before the King of Men, in the midst of his assembled court. Apollo coming like night from heaven to earth, with the clang of his quiver, the angry godhead, the plague. Achilles rising in the council, to call on priest or prophet, or dream-expounder, to declare what crime had incensed the Heavenly archer, "what broken vow, what hecatomb unpaid." Calchas, the seer, afraid to awaken the wrath of kings, and asking the protection of Pelides, ere he reveal the truth hateful to Agamemnon. That immortal quarrel, full of fire and of thunder, from outburst to close, and sublimed by a celestial Apparition shedding a troubled calm over human passions. The mighty Myrmidon, gracious in his ire, receiving the heralds in his tent, come for his Briseïs—

"Hail, heralds, hail! draw nigh, your fears remove;
Hail, heralds! messengers of men and Jove!"

Her departure,—

> "Onward they went, while, lingering as she pass'd,
> On her loved lord her look Briseïs cast."

The son of Thetis supplicating his mother to hear him, "by the drear margin of the sea-beat shore." The goddess, ascending sudden like a mist, and hanging over him with these words, "why grieves my son?" Between mother and son, mournful all, "that celestial colloquy divine." Achilles again,—

> "There, nigh this naval host, in sullen ire,
> Achilles fed his soul-consuming fire,
> Nor join'd the council's honour'd seat, nor deign'd
> To mingle where the warriors glory gain'd,
> But idly pining from the field afar,
> Long'd but for battle, and the shout of war."

The Nod that heaven-quaked Olympus. And now there is mirth in heaven :—

> "Fair Juno smiled, and smiling sweetly, graced
> The nectar-cup her snowy arms embraced.
> And still as Vulcan's hand the goblet crown'd,
> And past from right to left the nectar round,
> Loud laugh'd the guests, while the officious god,
> Administ'ring the wine, unseemly trod.
> From morn till night, through that continued feast,
> The harping of Apollo never ceased :
> Nor ceased the voice that closed with song the day,
> The Muses warbling their alternate lay."

And, last picture of all—Repose in Heaven—

> "But when the sun had set, each blissful guest
> From the late banquet sought his couch of rest ;
> Each to his radiant palace went apart,
> Divinely wrought by Vulcan's matchless art—
> Jove past, where sleep had oft his eyelids closed,
> AND ON HER GOLDEN THRONE, NIGH JOVE, HIS QUEEN REPOSED."

All these are pictures in the First Book—and there are many more beautifully given by Sotheby, whose words we have now been quoting ; and then, as for bursts of passion, and illustrations of feeling, and fine traits, and bold aspects of character, where, within the same compass, may we find them, were we to search all the records of inspired song?

Achilles is now out of sight—but not out of mind. Out of his wrath arises the Iliad; and whether he be present or absent in the flesh, there he is in the spirit, from beginning to end — from the first great line that announces the subject of the Poem,

Μῆνιν ἄειδε, Θεὰ, Πηληϊάδεω Ἀχιλῆος,

to the simple last,

Ὣς οἵ γ᾽ ἀμφίεπον τάφον Ἕκτορος ἱπποδάμοιο.

To avenge his wrongs, Jove, at the intercession of Minerva, had sworn by THE NOD to send destruction among the Greeks— and destruction comes. Already has Agamemnon rued the wrong he did Achilles.

> "But Jove afflicts me. From Saturnian Jove
> My doom is altercation to no end ;
> Thence came, between Achilles and myself,
> That fiery clash of words, a girl the cause,
> *Myself aggressor !*"

He looks along his vast array—but blackness is on one part of the line—where Achilles lies encamped.

> " The warriors of Pelasgian Argos next,
> Of Alus, and of Alope, and who held
> Trechina, Phthia, and for woman fair
> Distinguish'd, Hellas, known by various names,
> Hellenes, Myrmidons, Achæans ; them
> In fifty ships embark'd, Achilles ruled.
> But these perforce, renounced the dreaded field,
> Since he who should have ranged them to the fight,
> Achilles, in his fleet resentful lay
> For fair Briseïs' sake ; her loss he mourn'd,
> Whom after many toils, and after sack
> Of Thebes and of Lyrnessus, where he smote
> Epistrophus and Mynes, valiant sons
> Of King Evenus, he had made his own.
> He, therefore, sullen in his tent abode,
> DEAD FOR HER SAKE, THOUGH SOON TO RISE AGAIN !"

The war rages—and mighty heroes are before our eyes— Agamemnon, Menelaus, either Ajax, and god-conquering Diomed. But still in all their lustre, they are all overshadowed by Achilles. The thought of his image dims them all—so said Juno, wafted by her steeds like doves on balanced wings

in among the host of Greece, where, in the form and with the
voice of Stentor, clear as the brazen trumpet, and loud as fifty
others, she sent her cry.

> "O splendid warriors! form'd to please the eye,
> And shame your country! while Achilles fought,
> That godlike chief, no Trojan stepp'd beyond
> The Dardan gates, through terror of his arm;
> But now they brave you even at the fleet!"

Does Hector seek the city by sacrifice to propitiate the gods,
and to take farewell of Andromache? Even there and then,
across our imagination comes the "dire Achilles." The image
haunts that royal lady in her waking and her sleeping dreams.
He it was who slew her father, and "burned him with all
his arms."

But Hector challenges all the Greek chieftains to single
combat. He dared not to have done so, had he not known
that his challenge could not be accepted by Achilles. What
says Pylian Nestor?—

> "Oh! day of dire calamity to Greece!
> Peleus, that noble counsellor and chief
> Of the brave Myrmidons, was wont to hear
> With rapture my recital, while I traced
> The blood of all our heroes to its source.
> But learning, as he must, that one and all
> They shrank from Hector, how will he lament,
> How supplicate, with lifted hands to Jove,
> A swift dismission to the shades below."

He thought of Achilles sitting sullen at the ships—but he
does not "name his name." Neither does any one — though
all thought of it—when to draw lots,

> "Nor fewer, when he ceased,
> Than nine arose—and, foremost of them all,
> King Agamemnon; after him, the brave
> Tydides; Oilean Ajax, next,
> And Telamonian, terrible in fight;
> Then King Idomeneus, and grim as Mars
> His friend Meriones; Eræmon's son,
> Eurypylus; Andræmon's, the renown'd
> Thoas; and Ithaca's Ulysses last.
> These nine arose"——

But what are they all Nine to One—to Achilles—who never drew lots, but rushed to battle with the Pelean spear, hewn on the hills by Chiron to be death to heroes.

Juno having spoken of Achilles, what says Jupiter?

> " To whom the storm-clad sovereign of the skies :
> Look forth ! and if thou wilt, at early dawn,
> See there exerted still the power of Jove,
> And more than ever thinn'd the ranks of Greece.
> For pause of Hector's fury shall be none,
> Till first he have provoked Achilles forth,
> And for Patroclus slain the crowded hosts
> In narrow space that at the ships contend.
> Such is the voice of Fate !"

Thus it is that through all those books of the Iliad (which we have now been skimming like an osprey the sea), from which Achilles " sits at his ships retired," glorious old Homer has, by a few grand intimations, kept him constantly before us—a dreadful Image. And lo ! in the Ninth—behold him, again, in his Tent, singing to his harp the deeds of heroes. Phœnix, Ulysses, Ajax, implore him, at the prayer of Agamemnon, to save the army. Hear Ulysses, how he aggrandises him whom he beseeches :—

> " O godlike chief ! tremendous are our themes
> Of contemplation, while in doubt we sit,
> If life or death, with loss of all our ships,
> Attend us—unless THOU put on thy might !"
>   *   *   *   *   " Hector glares revenge, with rage
> Infuriate, and, by Jove assisted, heeds
> Nor god nor man, but maniac-like, implores
> Incessantly the morn at once to rise,
> That he may hew away our vessel heads,
> Burn all our fleet with fire, and at their sides
> Slay the Achaians panting in the smoke.
> Dread overwhelms my spirit, lest the gods
> His threats accomplish, and it be our doom
> To perish here, from Argos far remote.
> Up ! therefore, if thou canst at last relent,
> O rise, and save Achaia's weary sons."

The heroic beauty of the interview in the Tent we expatiated on with delight in our last Critique ; but again the scene rises before us in its characteristic grandeur. Atrides sends, says Ulysses, princely gifts—seven tripods unsullied by fire—ten

talents of gold—twenty caldrons bright—twelve strong-limbed
steeds, victorious in the race—seven rich-born captives, expert in domestic arts, &c., Lesbians all (by Agamemnon received when " Thou didst conquer Lesbos ") in perfect loveliness of form and face, surpassing womankind—and Briseïs
self pure—so swears the king before all the gods—pure of his
embrace.

> " All these he gives thee now ! and if at length
> The blessed gods shall grant us to destroy
> Priam's great city, thou shalt heap thy ships
> With gold and brass, entering and choosing first,
> When we shall share the spoil, and shall beside
> Take twenty from among the maids of Troy,
> Except fair Helen, loveliest of their sex.
> And if once more we reach the milky land
> Of pleasant Argos, then shalt thou become
> His son-in-law, and shalt enjoy like state
> With him, whom he in all abundance rears,
> His only son Orestes."

And with his daughter—her whom thou shalt approve—Chry-
somethis, Laodice, or Iphianassa—such a dower will the king
bestow as " never father on his child before,"—seven strong,
well-peopled cities—

> " Cardamyle and Enope, and rich
> In herbage Hira ; Pheræ, stately built ;
> And, for her depth of pasturage renown'd,
> Antheia ; proud Opeia's lofty towers,
> And Pedasus, impurpled dark with vines.
> All these are maritime, and on the shores
> They stand of Pylos, by a race possess'd
> Most rich in flocks and herds, who, tribute large
> And gifts presenting to thy sceptred hand,
> Shall hold thee high in honour as a god.
> These will he give thee, if thy wrath subside ;
> But shouldst thou rather in thine heart the more
> Both Agamemnon and his gifts detest,
> Yet O compassionate the afflicted host
> Prepared to adore thee. Thou shalt win renown
> Among the Grecians, that shall never die."

Dr Jortin, in one of his Six Dissertations (half-a-dozen too
many), thus paints the portrait of Achilles—" a *boisterous,
rapacious, mercenary, cruel, unrelenting brute ;* and the reader

pities none of his calamities, and is pleased with none of his successes." Who "the reader" may have been, and where he now may be, we shall not too curiously inquire; but a word to the Doctor. Could you, Doctor (the Doctor has been long dead too, but that is no fault of ours) — could you, Doctor, have withstood, sulky as you may have been when at your sulkiest, the temptation to be sweet, and to coo even upon the bill, contained in an offer of seven silver tripods, ten talents of gold, twenty bright caldrons, twelve strong-limbed steeds, seven well-born maid-servants of all work, beautiful and handsome—your housekeeper, who had been forced or favoured from your service, returned as pure as before she left it—a wife with a tremendous tocher in lands, houses, and patronage—and to crown all, the metropolitan archbishopric, now worthily held by that enlightened and intrepid spiritual Peer, whom we knew many years ago as simple and wise Dr Howley?

How the evangelical Jortin would have acted, there can be no rational doubt; but Pelides, who was not evangelical, unseduced as unterrified, adhered to his principles in the worst of times, like a true Tory, and turned, not a deaf, but a determined ear, to the Bill of Reform, which was thrown out at the first reading—strangled by that glorious Unit. The persuasive eloquence of Ulysses was soft as snow; but his words that fell like flakes, all melted away in the fiery furnace of the wrath of Achilles. In the first sentence of his speech, what a lesson to the Peers!—

> "Laertes' noble son ! for wiles renown'd,
> I must with plainness speak my fix'd resolve
> Unalterable ; lest I hear from each
> The same long murmur'd melancholy tale.
> For as the gates of Hades I detest
> The man whose heart and language disagree.
> So shall not mine. My most approved resolve
> Is this ; that neither Agamemnon, me,
> Nor all the Greeks shall move ; for ceaseless toil
> Wins here no thanks ; one recompense awaits
> The sedentary and the most alert;
> The brave and base in equal honour stand,
> And drones and heroes fall unwept alike !"

The hero then with a noble modesty alludes to the sack of

twenty-four cities by himself overthrown ; yet such the man,
wronged, dishonoured, and insulted by the King ! He thinks
of Briseïs, and in the bitterness of his soul seems to discard
her from his love. " My bride, my soul's delight, is in his
hands, and let him couch with her." He disdains to receive
her back, even if unpolluted. " Let the tyrant have his will
of her—but let him not, hard and canine in aspect though he
be, dare to look me in the face—let him not—crazed as he is,
and, by the stroke of Jove, infatuate. What brought him to
Troy ? The fair Helen ? Of all mankind can none be found
who love their wives but the Atridae ? Ulysses, there is no
good man who loves not, guards not, provides not for his own
wife—and captive though she were in battle, a slave, in my
heart of hearts I loved my own beautiful Briseïs. He offers
me, forsooth, his daughter ! Agamemnon's daughter ! No
—her will I never wed—could she vie in charms with golden
Venus or with blue-eyed Pallas. Let him wed her to one
more her equal—to some Prince superior to Achilles. Yet
returning to my own country, if so it be that the gods preserve
my life, Peleus shall mate me with a bride, offering me my
choice of the loveliest daughters of the chiefs that guard the
cities of Phthia and of Hellas."

Such are some of his sentiments—and they are such as
would have done credit even to a Jortin. Unrelenting he
indeed is—but here neither " boisterous, rapacious, mercenary,
cruel, nor a brute ; " but every inch a man, and every yard a
king. Much they erred who thought that Achilles was fond
of war. " It hath ever been my dearest purpose, wedded to a
wife of suitable rank, to enjoy in peace, in my native kingdom, such wealth as may be bequeathed to me by my sire,
the ancient Peleus." He speaks like a Bishop. Not a spiritual on the bench could better expound the feelings of natural
religion. Hear him !

> " Me, as my silver-footed mother speaks
> Thetis, a twofold consummation waits.
> If still with battle I encompass Troy,
> I win immortal glory, but all hope
> Renounce of my return. If I return
> To my beloved country, I renounce
> The illustrious meed of glory, but obtain
> Secure and long immunity from death.

And truly I would recommend to all
To voyage homeward, since you shall not see
The downfall e'er of Ilium's lofty towers,
For that the Thunderer with uplifted arms
Protects her, and her courage hath revived."

Ulysses, Ajax, Phœnix, all silent sit—astonished at his tone—for it was vehement—and they are dumb. The old man beloved recovers his power of speech, and by all tenderest memories conjures his son to relent, for as a son he loved Achilles. But he conjures him too by the awful as well as the tender—by piety as well as by pity—not by men alone, but by the immortal gods. This conjuration and this mighty magic we give from Cowper's noble version.

"Achilles ! bid thy mighty spirit down,
Thou shouldst not be thus merciless ; the gods,
Although more honourable, and in power
And virtue thy superiors, are themselves
Yet placable ; and if a mortal man
Offend them by transgression of their laws,
Libation, incense, sacrifice, and prayer,
In meekness offer'd, turn their wrath away.
Prayers are Jove's daughters, wrinkled, lame, slant-eyed,
Which, though far distant, yet with constant pace
Follow offence. Offence, robust of limb,
And treading firm the ground, outstrips them all,
And over all the earth before them runs,
Hurtful to man. They, following, heal the hurt ;
Received respectfully when they approach,
They yield us aid, and listen when we pray.
But if we slight, and with obdurate heart
Resist them, to Saturnian Jove they cry
Against us, supplicating that Offence
May cleave to us for vengeance of the wrong.
Thou, therefore, O Achilles ! honour yield
To Jove's own daughters, vanquish'd as the brave
Have often been, by honour done to Thee ! "

Dr Jortin himself could not have preached such a soul-wringing sermon. Not a topic that is not touched on ; not a tale that is not told; not an illustration that is not used, to persuade the soul of Achilles from its resolve ; nor wanted these, you may be assured, the eloquence of voice, eye, and hand, nor yet the holy oratory of grey hairs. But the time

had not come for Achilles to relent—Patroclus was alive by
his side—alive to listen to his hymns when to his harp he
sung the deeds of heroes. The day was near when there
would be no need to rouse the lion from his den, when Antilochus had to utter but a few words that sent him to battle
in that celestial armour. " Patroclus is dead—they are now
fighting around his naked body—his arms are Hector's!"
But now Menetiades is blooming in beauty at the board—and
Achilles thus answers Phœnix :—

> " Phœnix ! my aged father ! dear to Jove !
> Me no such honours interest ; I expect
> My honours from the sovereign will alone
> Of Jove, which shall detain me at the ships
> While I have power to move, or breath to draw."

How gracious to the old man ! Yet somewhat sternly he
tells him to speak no more of Agamemnon, if he loves his
friend—and then rekindling into kindness, asks his aged
preceptor to rest all night in the tent.

What a coarse mercenary brute ! Demosthenes and Cicero
were great orators—so were Chatham and Burke—so was Canning—and so is Lord Brougham. But what were they all as
orators—to poor blind old Homer ! Demosthenes's famous in-
vocation to the shades of " those who had fought at Marathon ; "
or Cicero's " Quousque," &c. are spirited ejaculations and interrogations ; Chatham's vituperation of Sir Robert Walpole is
rather bitter, though it smells of the schoolmaster—that is,
Dr Johnson ; Burke spoke daggers, especially when he used
none ; Canning's words were rich when he " called a new
world into existence " to balance the old ; and Brougham's
celebrated Peroration, seventeen times written over, was
powerful when delivered in praise of her whose chastity was
pure as the unsunned snow—the icicle that hangs on Dian's
temple—but oh ! Lords and Commons ! what poor performances all, and how redolent of lamp-oil, compared with the
free full flow of the oratory of Ulysses, with the river, majestic
reach after reach, falling over precipices till all the green
woods are wet with the spray of the cataracts, of the oratory
of Achilles ! What old man or woman, either in House of
Lords or Commons, as now constituted, or even when re-
moulded and reformed, will ever be able to keep prosing away

for hours without wearying her auditors, like that famous old fellow Phœnix, who

> " Feeds on thoughts that voluntary move
> Harmonious numbers,"

and soothes the unslumbering listener into a wakefulness more delightful than any sleep! We have heard Phœnix abused for prosiness, and irreverently called an old dotard. True that he was so. We well remarked in our last Critique that all old men—that is to say, all men above forty—are more or less dotards. But, for all that, the Greeks never despised old age. They knew human nature and human life too well—better than we modern Athenians. We have heard that younkers have even laughed at Christopher North; but Achilles never laughed at Phœnix, even though that gentlemanly old Myrmidon was his private tutor. And now in the Tent he listens to him, not only without yawning (an asinine vice), but with manifest sympathy and delight, most grateful to mine ancient, and to his own immortal praise. The speech of Phœnix is not much short of two hundred lines, and much of it is characterised by the narrative propensity of " garrulous old age." Yet the son of Thetis kept his large bright-blue unwinking eyes affectionately upon him all the while; sometimes, we may suppose, bending his head towards the Sire, and accompanying the recital of the love—and war—adventures of the old man's youth with a heroic smile. And did not the aged warrior discourse of the Boar of Caledon, and of Meleager, who, at the intercession of his own Cleopatra, rose up from his ruinous wrath, and, alas! too late for his own happy fame, saved the Ætolians? " That hero, of old, was possessed by a demon—even as Thou art, O mine Achilles! But wiser Thou! dismiss thy demon to Hades, and, timeously for thy own fame, save! O save thy country! "

Such address, though long, was listened to, then, not impatiently by the fiery Achilles—by the wise Ulysses—by the blunt Ajax—by the mild Heralds—by the gentle Patroclus—and by the chariotcer-chamberlain, the Lord Automedon. And yet *you*—oh! shame to degeneracy of modern manners from those " of the great goodness of the knights of old "—*you* complain of prosiness—call for your nightcap, an absurdity

unknown to the heroic ages—and make an exposure of a
featureless face yet more unmeaning in a dreamless but not
unsnoring sleep!

The truth is, that no great, and but little good eloquence,
is to be anywhere found out of poetry. Passion must be at
once subdued and supported by verse, ere it can possess
divine power in words. Eloquence, music, and poetry, are
not three, but one. Prose never seems imbued with life till
upon the verge of blank verse. Be it granted that, even in
the high affairs of this life, blank verse is, and will be, unpermitted speech. What then? The high affairs of this life,
and all engaged in or affected by them, are therefore worthy
of our pity—almost of our contempt. For is it not pitiable,
is it not even nearly contemptible, to see and hear the mightiest matters spoken of in the meanest speech? In religious worship men use poetry—and we shall all speak it in heaven, *ad
libitum*, rhyme or blank verse. The soul, in its highest states,
always so speaks—witness Homer and Milton, Achilles and
Satan. Show us either Passion, or Imagination, or Reason in
prose (we exclude the abstract sciences—especially the pure
mathematics) as glorious as in poetry, and we cry *peccavi ;* but
till then we laugh at all eloquence, as it is called, out of
" numerous verse," and appeal to one who never spoke absolute prose in his life, the God of Eloquence, Music, and
Poetry, the unshorn Apollo.

But we are forgetting Achilles in his Tent. How kind,
how courteous, how affable, how princely, how heroic! A
Heathen that might almost be a model for a Christian! True,
that he has not yet forgiven Agamemnon—nor have you the
old lady who offended you so grievously by omitting to invite
your wife and daughters to her last week's rout. And you,
along with Dr Jortin, accuse Achilles of being an " unrelenting brute," though you know, or ought to know, that he for-
gave Agamemnon at last, from the very bottom of his distracted heart, and forgot, too, all his injuries and all his
insults, and lamented that even for Briseïs' sake he had
dashed on the ground his gold-studded sceptre, and consigned the tyrant and all his slaves to perdition.

The Tent-scene closes in a style suitable to its opening
and its continuance—heroic. The deputation, disappointed
perhaps, but unoffended, take their dignified departure—
Achilles praising Ajax for his sincerity, and calling him " my

noble Friend," though the son of Telamon has just told his host
that he is more relentless than all other men, none of whom
refuse to accept due compensation for a son or brother slain,
or to suffer the murderer to live secure at home, on his
pacifying their revenge by the payment of the price of blood.
The deputation gone—Patroclus bids the attendant youths
and women prepare a couch for Phœnix with fleeces, rich
arras, and flax of subtlest woof—and there lies the hoary
guest in expectation of the sacred dawn.

> "Meantime Achilles in the interior tent
> With Diomeda, Phorbus' daughter fair,
> Convey'd from Lesbos by himself, reposed.
> Patroclus rested opposite, with whom
> Slept charming Iphis ; her, when he had won
> The lofty towers of Scyros, the Divine
> Achilles took, and on his friend bestow'd."

So true is it, as Ovid says, that,

> "Ingenuas didicisse fideliter artes
> Emollit mores, nec sinit esse feros."

Achilles, we have seen, had learned faithfully the Fine
Arts—Music and Poetry—and thence, though at fitting time
and season his mind was fierce—never at fitting time and
season were his manners other than most mild ; and *now*
were they "beautiful exceedingly," even as the light of the
moon, not yet down, but hanging as if half-way between
heaven and sea, shining peacefully on both armies, and all
those Tents ; a world of Pyramids, as still as cones of snow,
or, should we rather say, green as shielings where the woods-
men sleep.

The Greeks, then, must try to take Troy without Achilles,
and Agamemnon grows before us up into the full stature of
a true warrior-king. Ulysses, Diomed, and Ajax, all tower
to a more heroic height—and glorious against them comes
κορυθαιόλος Ἐκτωρ. Machaon, the king's physician and sur-
geon, the Larrey of the Greek army, is himself wounded, and
carried from the fight in Nestor's chariot. Achilles, viewing
the battle from the poop of his ship, sends Patroclus to inquire
who has been smitten, suspecting that it is Machaon—the
highest honour ever paid to a professor of the healing art.
Nestor entertains him in his tent with an account of the incidents of the day, and a long recital of some former wars

which he remembered (for his memory is prodigious, and only
equalled by his power of speech), tending to put Patroclus
upon persuading Achilles to aid his countrymen, or at least
to permit him to do it clad in Achilles's armour.   After many
alternations of defeat and victory, the Trojans bear down all
before them, and are about to set fire to the fleet.   At this
crisis, Patroclus comes flying to Achilles, and pointing to
the ships, where the flames are already beginning to arise,
and bold in friendship, passionately beseeches him, with
many upbraidings, to avert the ruin.   All arguments seem to
be thrown away on the Inflexible and Unrelenting, and
pouring the tumbling torrent of his wrath upon Agamemnon,
he enjoys the deadly discomfiture, and seems determined to
deliver them all up—king and people—to death.

But suddenly, in the mid tempest of his fury, he sees a
burst of fire at the fleet, and that it is kindled by the hand of
Hector.   The hour is come when he may keep the promise
made to his pride, and yet yield to the prayers of Patroclus.
" Don, then, my glorious arms; and since the Greeks are
driven to the ships, lead forth my invincible Myrmidons.
The Trojans no more beholding my dazzling helmet, bolder
grown, all Ilium comes abroad.   But had it not been for Agamemnon, soon had they fled in panic, who now besiege us,
and their corpses choked the streams.   No longer, rescuing
the Greeks from death, rages the spear in the hand of
Diomed ; I hear not, issuing forth from his accursed throat,
the voice of Agamemnon ; but ' all around a shatter'd peal of
savage Hector's cries,'—encouraging and insulting — Then
go—go, my Patroclus !   Drive back the Trojans, and save the
fleet from fire.   But—mark well my words—for so shalt thou
glorify me in the eyes of all the Danai ; stay thy slaughtering
legions ere they reach the walls of Troy,

> ' Lest some Immortal Power on her behalf
> Descend. for much the archer of the skies
> Loves Ilium !'

Oh ! by all the powers of Heaven ! would that of all the
Greeks, and of all the Trojans, not one might escape alive !
That we—I and thou, Patroclus—might alone raze Troy's
sacred bulwarks to the dust."
So ceased he, frowning—and up gets that impudent French-

man, Mons. de la Motte, to prate his impertinence about the
absurdity of such a wish. Upon the supposition that Jupiter had granted it (Jupiter had too much good sense), if all
the Trojans and Greeks were destroyed, and only Achilles
and Patroclus left to conquer Troy, he asks what would be
the victory without any enemies, and the triumph without
any spectators? Pope reprehends the puppy well—answering that Homer intends to paint a man in a passion ; that the
wishes and schemes of such an one are seldom conformable
to reason ; and that the manners are preserved the better, the
less they are represented to be so. We beg to add, that a
victory without any enemies must be as gratifying as glorious
to the heroes who have, with their own hands, slain their
thousands and their tens of thousands—which feeling justifies
Achilles, in as far as he alluded to the Trojans ; and that he
hated and abhorred all that fought under Agamemnon, because
he hated and abhorred *him* as the gates of hell—which feeling
accounts for the wish, in as far as it regards the Greeks.
While, as to a triumph without spectators, though it might
not rejoice the soul of a vain frog-eater, it must have been
gingerbread nuts and Glenlivet to a hero hungry and thirsty
for revenge, and devouring and quaffing it, along with his
dearest friend, all by themselves, with not an eye to look at
them, up to the knees and elbows in blood, and dimly visible
to each other in smoke and dust.

Pope refers us well to that curse in Shakespeare, "where
that admirable master of nature makes Northumberland, in
the rage of his passion, wish for an universal destruction "—
" beyond the reaches of the soul " of Moshy Motte.

> " Now let not Nature's hand
> Keep the wild flood confined ! Let order die,
> And let the world no longer be a stage
> To feed contention in a lingering act ;
> But let one spirit of the first-born Cain
> Reign in all bosoms, that each heart being set
> On bloody courses, the rude scene may end,
> And darkness be the burier of the dead ! "

Even while he speaks, another burst of fire ! He smites
his thigh, and cries, " Patroclus—noble charioteer—arise !
arm, arm—this moment, arm !—I will call, myself, the band."
Patroclus is in the arms and armour of Achilles, and quick

as the word of command has Automedon yoked to his car
Xanthus and Balius, progeny of Podarge the harpy, the immortal chargers that despise not to snort by the side of mortal
Pegasus, once the pride of Eëtion, ere Achilles slew that king,
nor inferior in flight to the glorious get of the wind.   But, lo!
the Myrmidons !

NORTH.

———— " But they (the leaders of the Myrmidons),
Like raw-flesh-devouring wolves, in whose breasts is immeasurable
    strength,
And who, having slain a large-horn'd stag on the mountains,
Tear and swallow it ; the jaws of all are empurpled with blood :
And then in herds they troop—from a dark-water'd fountain
To lap up, with attenuated tongues, the dark-water
From the surface—belching up the clotted blood ; but the courage
In their breasts is untrembling, and distended are their stomachs :
Like (such) did the leaders and chiefs of the Myrmidons
Around the brave servant (friend) of the swift-footed grandson of
    Æacus
Rush vigorously on : and amid them stood the warlike Achilles,
Urging on the charioteers (horse) and the shielded heroes."

CHAPMAN.

" And now before his tents
Himself had seen his Myrmidons, in all habiliments
Of dreadful war.   And when you see, upon a mountain bred,
A den of wolves, about whose heart unmeasured strengths are fed,
New come from currie of a stag ; their jaws all blood-besmear'd ;
And when from some black-water fount they altogether herd ;
There having plentifully lapt with thin and thrust-out tongues,
The top and clearest of the spring, go belching from their lungs
The clotter'd gore, look dreadfully, and entertain no dread ;
Their bellies gaunt, all taken up, with being so rawly fed ;
Then say that such in strength and look were great Achilles' men,
Now order'd for the dreadful fight, and so with all these then
Their princes and their chiefs did show about their General's
    Friend."

POPE.

" Achilles speeds from tent to tent, and warms
His hardy Myrmidons to blood and arms.
All breathing death, around the chief they stand,
A grim, terrific, formidable band :
Grim as voracious wolves, that seek the springs,
When scalding thirst their burning bowels wrings.

When some tall stag, fresh-slaughter'd in the wood,
Has drench'd their wide insatiate throats with blood,
To the black fount they rush, a hideous throng,
With paunch distended, and with lolling tongue,
Fire fills their eye, their black jaws belch the gore,
And gorged with slaughter, still they thirst for more.
Like furies rush'd the Myrmidonian crew,
Such their dread strength, and such their deathful view,
High in the midst the great Achilles stands,
Directs their order, and the war commands."

COWPER.

" As wolves that gorge
Their prey yet panting, terrible in force,
When on the mountains wild they have devour'd
An antler'd stag new-slain, with bloody jaws
Troop all at once to some clear fountain ; there
To lap with slender tongues the brimming wave ;
No fear have they, but at their ease eject
From full maws flatulent the clotted gore.
Such seem'd the Myrmidon heroic chiefs
Assembling fast around the valiant friend
Of swift Eacides. Amid them stood
Warlike Achilles, the well-shielded ranks
Encouraging, and charioteers to war."

SOTHEBY.

" Meanwhile Achilles, breathing slaughter, went
Hailing the Myrmidons, from tent to tent.
As ravenous wolves that gorge their antler'd prey,
Drain his hot gore, and rend his limbs away ;
Then rushing down in troops, their jaws all blood,
Lap with their tongues the surface of the flood ;
And from their paunch, that labours with its load,
Belch the black gore and undigested food ;
Thus the fierce leaders of each gathering band
Rush'd round Patroclus, at their chief's command ;
In midst Pelides tower'd, their fury fired,
And his own spirit in each heart inspired."

Chapman is here almost as wolfish as Homer. "A den of
wolves" is savage. But savage as it is, not so savage as is
" raw-flesh-devouring wolves." "*Currie* of a stag" is excellent—and reminds us of our esteemed correspondent, the " old
Indian." It is needless to praise the other epithets, all in the

strongest style of Homer, Buffon, and Pidcock.   So ferociously
ought always to be translated the ferocities of the Iliad.
    It was not in Pope to be sufficiently savage for such a simile.
He spoils the simplicity of Homer at the very first, even before
coming to the wolves.   Homer says not a syllable about the
Myrmidons, except that Achilles went about ordering them to
arm—he lets loose upon us in a moment the wolves themselves,
and seeing them, we see the Myrmidons ; whereas Pope begins with a highly coloured description of the Myrmidons—
"all breathing death," "a grim, terrific, formidable band." This
is insufferable—but he will always be doing, and seldom lets
Homer take his own way.   "The principal design," he says
truly, in a note, " is to represent the stern looks and fierce
appearance of the Myrmidons, a gaunt and ghastly train of
raw-boned, bloody-minded fellows."   Just so.   Why, then,
begin by telling us so, as Pope does ; and not, as Homer
does, by likening them, at once, to wolves?   " Grim as voracious wolves," however, is good ; but then Pope had no business to introduce here the " springs," and their " scalding
thirst," and " burning bowels."   These come in again, afterwards, in his version—at the proper time and place—and
nothing so bad as needless repetition.   Who does not feel
how tame the slaughtering of the stag becomes, by the change
of the wolves into fed for feeding?   Homer says, " having
slain, they tear and swallow it ;" Pope says, that, "fresh-
slaughter'd, it has drench'd," &c.—all the difference in the
world.   " Has drench'd their wide insatiate throats with
blood," is a good line—but it does not give the picture—of
" the jaws of all are empurpled with blood ; " "and with lolling tongue," is poor and inadequate for "lap up with their
attenuated tongues" ; " fire fills their eye " is not in Homer ;
and " gorged with slaughter, still they thirst for more," is
the reverse of what Homer means, for he manifestly signifies
that they were satisfied with their " currie of a stag," their
bellies being distended to their hearts' content—or as old
Hobbes translates the line, as well as if he had done it at the
close of a Noctes—" With bellies full, and hearts encouraged."
Nevertheless, Pope's translation is neither to be coughed nor
sneezed at—and were we not in the comparative mood, might
even be pronounced excellent.
    Cowper is capital, and stands comparison with Chapman.

"That gorge the prey yet panting," is better even than our prose. "Mountains *wild*" is a fine touch; "with bloody jaws troop all at once" cannot be surpassed; "*slender* tongues" is just the word; and "eject from full maws flatulent the clotted gore," as the Shepherd would say, is "fearsome." The Myrmidons!

After such vigorous versions as those of Chapman and Cowper, we should have laid two to one, at least, against Sotheby. But he has, we think, beaten them both—by a head. No—'tis a dead heat. If in any particular point his version be inferior to theirs—and in one it is so ("antler'd prey" for "large antler'd stag")—that fault is fully compensated by the greater ease of his diction and versification, which, without any effort, move powerfully along—from first to last—while the passage, in his hands, ends finely, as it began, with Achilles.

There is not another such savage simile as this in all Homer. Whether is he or Thomson wildest on wolves? Ask Wombwell.

> "By wintry famine roused, from all the tract
> Of horrid mountains, where the shining Alps,
> And snowy Apennine, and Pyrenees,
> Branch out stupendous into distant lands;
> Cruel as death and hungry as the grave;
> Burning for blood, bony, and gaunt, and grim,
> Assembling wolves in raging troops descend;
> And, pouring o'er the country, bear along
> Keen as the north-wind sweeps the glossy snow.
> All is their prize. They fasten on the steed,
> Press him to earth, and pierce his mighty heart.
> Nor can the bull his awful front defend,
> Or shake the murderous savages away.
> Rapacious at the mother's throat they fly,
> And tear the screaming infant from her breast," &c.

Both bards are great. But Thomson expatiates more in his description—as was right—for he was at liberty to revel with the "raging troops," where'er they roamed, from repast to repast, insatiate with brutal or with human food. Homer seized on them as a simile; but his imagination was unwilling to let go its grasp—and holds fast the growling gluttons, as if he had momentarily forgotten what they imaged. But he had not forgotten it. The Myrmidons underwent transforma-

tion into wolves, and the wolves into Myrmidons. No man
of sense strives to see in a simile entire identity—as in a portrait. There are the wolves at their fiercest and their fellest
—and there too at theirs the Myrmidons. The wolves, raw-
flesh-gobblers all, are seen tearing and swallowing a large
antlered stag on the mountains—then with jaws all empurpled
in blood, trooping in herds to the fountain—then lapping up
the water with their thin tongues—then belching clotted
blood; and then, their bellies being full to distension, untrembling courage is at their hearts. But you surely do not
expect such behaviour in the Myrmidons. Homer was feasting his poetic eyes on the feasting wolves of the mountain
forest—on an image of rural active life. And what a delightful glimpse of the country! At the touch of his necromantic
wand, the monsters are all at once changed into Myrmidons—
who are monsters too—but not quite so hairy—nor with such
long tails—nor are their jaws so bloody—*as yet*—though
having had their rations—their bellies are distended—and
untrembling courage is at their hearts. Don't ye hear them
howling? "An Achilles! An Achilles!" for that is their
slogan, and it sounds terrible even in the ears of Hector.

Pray, who were those Myrmidonian chiefs, whom Homer
thus likened to wolves? Better born and better bred than
most of our readers, though we are eschewed by the Radicals.
Achilles was, of course, the colonel of his own regiment; and
under him were five captains: Menesthens, son of Polydora,
daughter of Peleus, by the ever-flowing Sperchius, that rampant river-god; Eudorus, whom Polymela, graceful in the
dance, daughter of Phylus, bore by stealth (he was called the
Bastard) to the Argicide who had wooed the nymph "while
worshipping the golden-shafted Queen Diana, in full choir,
with song and dance,"—ascending with her to an upper-room,
all-bounteous Mercury clandestine there "embraced her
who a noble son produced"; Pisander, offspring of Maimalus,
who far excelled in spear-fight every Myrmidon save Patroclus; "the hoary Phœnix, of equestrian fame, the fourth
band led to battle," (a grey old growler); and who the fifth
but Laerceus' offspring, bold Alcimedon, whom you may remember in the Tent waiting on Achilles, when the Royal
Commission entered, along with Lord Automedon, the celebrated charioteer. These were the wolves. Such liberties

does poetry take with the human face and form divine—
changing bipeds into quadrupeds "for the nonce," as our fat
friend would say—and sometimes not even leaving the brave
and beautiful the "likeness o' a dowg."

Let our living poets look here, and the best of them all
dare to say that he could equal—much more excel—*this*. We
quote from the incomparable Cowper.

> "So them he roused, and they, their leader's voice
> Hearing elate, to closest order drew.
> As when an architect some palace wall
> With shapely stones erects, cementing close
> A barrier against all the winds of Heaven,
> So wedged the helmets and boss'd bucklers stood :
> Shield, helmet, man, press'd helmet, man, and shield,
> And ev'ry bright-arm'd warrior's bushy crest
> Its fellow swept, so dense was their array.
> In front of all, two chiefs their station took,
> Patroclus and Automedon : one mind
> In both prevail'd, to combat in the van
> Of all the Myrmidons. Achilles, then,
> Retiring to his tent, displaced the lid
> That closed a curious chest by Thetis placed
> On board his bark, and fill'd with tunics, cloaks,
> And fleecy arras ; it contain'd beside
> A cup embellish'd with laborious art,
> From which no prince libation ever pour'd,
> Himself except, and he to Jove alone.
> That cup producing from the chest, he first
> With sulphur fumed it, rinsed it next with lymph
> Pellucid of the running stream, and, last
> (His hands clean laved), he charged it high with wine.
> And now, advancing to his middle court,
> He pour'd libation, and with eyes to Heav'n
> Uplifted pray'd, of Jove not unobserved :
> 'Pelasgian, Dodonæan Jove supreme,
> Dwelling remote, who on Dodona's heights
> Snow-clad reign'st sov'reign, compass'd by thy seers
> The Selli, prophets by their vow constrain'd
> To unwash'd feet and slumbers on the ground !
> I plainly see my former prayer perform'd,
> Myself exalted, and the Greeks abased.
> Now also this request vouchsafe me, Jove !
> Here, in my fleet, I shall myself abide,
> But lo! with all these Myrmidons I send

My friend to battle. Thunder-rolling Jove,
Send glory with him, make his courage firm !
That even Hector may himself be taught,
If my companion have a valiant heart
When he goes forth alone, or only then
The noble frenzy feel that Mars inspires,
When I rush also to the glorious field.
But soon as from the ships he shall have driven
The battle, grant him with his arms complete,
None lost, himself unhurt, and all my band
Of dauntless warriors with him, safe return ! '
    Such prayer Achilles offer'd, and his suit
Jove hearing, part confirm'd, and part refused ;
To chase the dreadful battle from the fleet
He gave him, but vouchsafed him no return.
Prayer and libation thus perform'd to Jove
The Sire of all, Achilles to his tent
Return'd, replaced the goblet in his chest,
And anxious still that conflict to behold
Between the hosts, stood forth before his tent.
    Then rush'd the bands, by brave Patroclus led,
Full on the Trojan host. As wasps forsake
Their home by the wayside, provoked by boys
Disturbing inconsid'rate their abode,
Not without nuisance sore to all who pass,
For if, thenceforth, some traveller unaware
Annoy them, issuing one and all they swarm
Around him fearless in their broods' defence,
With courage fierce as theirs forth rush'd a flood
Of Myrmidons all shouting to the skies,
Whom with loud voice Patroclus thus harangued :
' O Myrmidons, attendants in the field
On Peleus' son, now be ye men, my friends !
Call now to mind the fury of your might ;
That even from the courage of his train
The chief most excellent in all the camp
May glory reap, and that the king of men
Himself may learn his fault, when he denied
All honour to the prime of all his host.'
    So saying, he fired their hearts, and on the van
Of Troy at once they fell ; loud shouted all
The joyful Grecians, and the navy rang.
Soon as the Trojans then that sight beheld,
The brave Patroclus and his charioteer
Arm'd dazzling bright, fear seized on every mind,

And every phalanx quaked, believing sure,
That, wrath renounced, and terms of friendship chosen,
Achilles' self was there ; then every eye
Look'd round for refuge from impending fate."

But the bright Cheat is discovered :—

"Achilles' plume is stain'd with dust and gore,
That plume which never stoop'd to earth before ;
Long used untouch'd in fighting fields to shine,
And shade the temples of the man divine,
Jove dooms it now on Hector's helm to nod,
Not long—for fate pursues him, and the god."

And from the tumult of the disastrous battle, Antilochus flies
to Achilles, who, seeing his approach, instantly divines the
dreadful truth, and, ere the messenger has opened his lips,
exclaims, "Ah! woe is me ! I tremble lest the gods my fears
fulfil of the evil foretold by my mother—that during my lifetime
by Trojan hands is doomed to fall the bravest of the Myrmidons, and view the sun no more ! " Antilochus says—

HOMER.

" Ὦ μοι, Πηλέος υἱὲ δαΐφρονος, ἦ μάλα λυγρῆς
Πεύσεαι ἀγγελίης, ἣ μὴ ὤφελλε γενέσθαι.
Κεῖται Πάτροκλος, νέκυος ᾽ι δὴ ἀμφιμάχονται
Γυμνοῦ· ἀτὰρ τά γε τεύχε᾽ ἔχει κορυθαίολος Ἕκτωρ."

NORTH.

" Woe is me ! Oh son of the war-loving Peleus—verily, most
mournful
Tidings shalt thou hear (tidings) which ought not to have been.
Patroclus lies (dead), for his naked corse they fight :
Hector with the waving-plumed-helmet has his arms."

CHAPMAN.

                    " My lord, that must be heard,
Which would to heaven I might not tell ! Menœties' son lies
dead,
And for his naked corse (his arms already forfeited
And worn by Hector) the debate is now most vehement."

POPE.

" Sad tidings, son of Peleus ! thou must hear ;
And wretched I, th' unwilling messenger !

Dead is Patroclus !   For his corse they fight ;
His naked corse ; his arms are Hector's right."

COWPER.

" O brave Achilles ! charged with heaviest news
Of one who well deserved a gentler fate,
I seek thee.   Menœtiades is dead.
Between the warring hosts his body lies
In fierce dispute, and Hector hath his arms."

SOTHEBY.

" O son of Peleus ! thou must hear the word,
Such as I would had been by thee unheard.
Patroclus dies ; war flames his body o'er,
While Hector glories in the arms he wore."

We have quoted these few Greek lines and the translations,
that you might judge of the comparative skill of the Four (or
Five) in rendering into English what has been pointed out
by Quinctilian, and many other critics, as an instance of the
perfection of energetic brevity.[1]   Chapman has somewhat
altered the order of the words, and has erred thereby, as that
of Homer is perfect.   But the two first lines are all they
ought to be—reverential, but mortally plain—most sorrow-
fully uttering sorrow.   Far from bad are the others, and nothing is omitted ; but they sound quaint, at least to our ears
now, and should have ended with the word—Hector.   Pope is
very good.   Perhaps "right" is hardly the word there—
"has" or "wears" is better ; but rhyme is necessity with
law, so we are satisfied.   There is much tenderness in Cowper,
but " brave " is here a poor epithet; "of one who well deserved
a gentler fate" is pathetic, but not Homeric, nor do we think
it is the meaning of the original ; and " naked " is left out,
which it should not have been ; but "Menœtiades is dead," and
" Hector hath his arms," are just the very thing ; and therefore we love the version.   Sotheby, we are sorry to say it,
fails.   The second line is feeble and flat—nor do we altogether like the first.   " Patroclus dies," is bad ; he is dead—
dead—dead.   " War flames his body over " is " too bad ; "
and the fourth line, though well enough as a line taken per se,

[1] See Mr H. N. Coleridge's excellent Introduction to the Study of the Greek
Classical Poets.   Why has not this successful volume been followed by another ?

is not like the simple line and rueful, that leaves the lips of
Antilochus.

But let us look on Achilles.

NORTH.

"Thus he said : but him (Achilles) a dark cloud of grief enveloped.
And with both his hands lifting up dust and ashes,
He pour'd them on his head, and his comely countenance defiled ;
On his celestial tunic the black ashes everywhere alighted.
Large himself, and much-room-occupying, in the dust extended
He lay ; and with his own hands he pluck'd out and marr'd his
    locks.
But the maid-servants whom Achilles by plunder had obtain'd,
    and Patroclus,
Heart-sadden'd, lifted up their voices and wept, and from the
    doors
Out they rush'd around the warlike Achilles; and with their hands
    they all
Smote their breasts ; relax'd were the limbs of each :
On the other side mourn'd Antilochus, pouring out tears,—
Grasping the hands of Achilles ; his noble heart groan'd :
For he (Antilochus) fear'd lest he (Achilles) should cut his (Achilles')
    throat with the sword.[1]
Horribly he howl'd ; (him) heard his venerable mother
Sitting in the depths of the sea, beside her aged father,
And immediately wept aloud."

CHAPMAN.

"This said, Grief darken'd all his powers. With both his hands he
    rent
The black mould from the forced earth, and pour'd it on his head ;
Smear'd all his lovely face, his weeds (divinely fashioned)
All filde and mangled ; and himselfe he threw upon the shore,
Lay as laid out for funerall, then tumbled round, and tore
His gracious curls. His ecstacie he did so farre extend,
That all the ladies wonne by him, and his now slaughter'd friend,
(Afflicted strangely for his flight) came shrieking from the tents,
And fell about him ; beate their breasts, their tender lineaments
Dissolved with sorrow. And with them wept Nestor's warlike
    sonne,   .

_____

[1] Τίνις, ἐφοβεῖτο γὰρ 'Αχίλλιυς μὴ ἀποδυρομένεμεν 'Εκτωρ τοι Πάτροκλον—says the
scholiast, forgetting apparently that Patroclus had been Burked already, and
that it was now of little consequence whether the jugular should be Knoxed or
not.

Fell by him, holding his fair hands, in feare he would have done
His person violence ; his heart extremely (streightened) burn'd,
Beate, swell'd, and sigh'd, as it would burst ; so terribly he
    mourn'd,
That Thetis, sitting in the deepes of her old father's seas,
Heard and lamented.   To her plaints the bright Nereïdes
Flock'd all."

POPE.

" A sudden horror shot through all the chief,
    And wrapp'd his senses in the cloud of grief ;
    Cast on the ground, with furious hands he spread
    The scorching ashes o'er his graceful head ;
    His purple garments, and his golden hairs,
    Those he deforms with dust, and these he tears ;
    On the hard soil his groaning breast he threw,
    And roll'd and grovell'd, as to th' earth he grew.
    The virgin captives with disorder'd charms
    (Won by his own, or by Patroclus' arms),
    Rush'd from the tents with cries ; and, gathering round,
    Beat their white breasts, and fainted on the ground ;
    While Nestor's son sustains a manlier part,
    And mourns the warrior with a warrior's heart ;
    Hangs on his arms, amidst his frantic woe,
    And oft prevents the meditated blow.
    Far in the deep abysses of the main,
    With hoary Nereus, and the wat'ry train,
    The mother goddess from her crystal throne
    Heard his loud cries, and answer'd groan for groan :
    The circling Nereids with their mistress weep,
    And all the sea-green sisters of the deep."

COWPER.

" Then clouds of sorrow fell on Peleus' son,
    And, grasping with both hands the ashes, down
    He pour'd them on his head, his graceful brows
    Dishonouring, and thick the sooty shower
    Descending, settled on his fragrant vest.
    Then, stretch'd in ashes, at the vast extent
    Of his whole length he lay, disordering wild
    With his own hands, and rending off his hair.
    The maidens, captured by himself in war
    And by Patroclus, shrieking from the tent
    Ran forth, and hemm'd the glorious chief around.
    All smote their bosoms, and all, fainting, fell.

On the other side, Antilochus, dissolved
In tears, held fast Achilles' hands, and groan'd
Continually from his heart, through fear
Lest Peleus' son should perish self-destroy'd.
With dreadful cries he rent the air, whose voice
Within the gulfs of ocean, where she sat
Beside her ancient sire, his mother heard,
And, hearing, shriek'd ; around her, at the voice,
Assembled all the Nereids of the deep."

SOTHEBY.

" Grief at the word, and horror's gloomiest cloud,
Cast o'er Pelides their o'ershadowing shroud.
He grasp'd the ashes scatter'd on the strand,
And on his forehead shower'd with either hand,
Grimed his fair face, and o'er his raiment flung
The soil that on its splendour darkly hung,
His large limbs, prone in dust, at large outspread,
And pluck'd the hair from his dishonour'd head ;
While all the maidens whom his arm had won,
Or gain'd in battle with Menetius' son,
Left the still shelter of their peaceful tent,
And round Pelides mingled their lament,
Raised their clasp'd hands, and beat their breasts of snow,
And, swooning, sunk on earth, o'ercome with woe ;
While o'er him Nestor's son in horror stood,
And grasp'd his arm, half-raised to shed his blood.
Deep groan'd the desperate man, 'twas death to hear
Groans that in ocean pierced the sea-nymph's ear,
His mother's ear, where, deep beneath the tide,
Dwelt the sea-goddess by her father's side.
She heard, she shriek'd, while gathering swift around,
Came every Nereid from her cave profound."

There is agony, grief, despair, rage (alike against Hector,
heaven, and himself!) and, perhaps—who knows—a shuddering, too, of revenge! A cloud envelopes Achilles—he covers
himself with dust and ashes—down he falls all his huge
length extended, in convulsions; for see how he tears his
hair out in handfuls—the maniac looks like a suicide—and
hear how horribly he howls! And this is the — divine
Achilles! What would an American Indian say to such a
sight?

" The stoic of the woods, the man without a tear !"

Nothing. Nor do we — except that, though children of nature both, Achilles is not Outalissi—and that the moon is still the moon, though sometimes seen sailing clear and bright through a storm, and sometimes with a lowering light of blood.

Chapman feels the passion of the picture throughout, *intus et in cute*, and his copy may well content all amateurs who cannot see the original. Yet it is somewhat overcharged ; and, worst of all, it presents not to our sight the size of Achilles — " large himself, and much-room-occupying," as you behold him in our Greek-imitating English. This is an omission almost as fatal as would be that of " lay floating many a rood," from Milton's picture of Satan. " Lay as laid out for funeral " is a strong line, and presents a deadly image. But it is not Homer. Homer shows us Achilles, it is true, lying extended ; but not still—or, if still, only for a moment—and ere such a thought could cross us as that he was " laid out for funeral," " with his own hands he pluck'd out and marr'd his locks." These are two great crimes— of commission and omission—ay, capital crimes, for which we now order Chapman for execution. No—we respite him till next Wednesday—during pleasure—the royal clemency is extended to him—a free pardon—he walks out of prison, on his bold broad brows the unwithered laurel ! Yet why, old Chapman, did you change " lest he should cut his throat with his sword," for " in fear he would have done his person violence "? And why, seeing that Homer had already shown us Achilles in agony, should you have added, that " his heart, extremely straiten'd, burn'd, beat, swell'd, and sigh'd as it would burst" ? That is not only carrying coals to New- castle—but worse—telling us that there are fiery furnaces in the Carron Iron-works. It is not even for thee—to try to out-Homer Homer.

Pope, of course, commences operations with a paraphrase— but let it pass unpunished as unpraised. " Cast on the ground," in line third, applies either to Achilles or to the ashes. If to Achilles, it is false, for he was not yet cast on the ground—*he stooped* (Homer does not say so—but we see him), " with both his hands lifting up dust and ashes." If it apply to the ashes, then it is foolish as well as false—for the ashes were lying there of themselves, nobody being

suffered to cast ashes near the tent of Achilles. Neither were
the ashes " scorching," take our word for it; Homer would
not have let the hero set his hair on fire. *Those* he deforms
with dust, and *these* he tears," is an antithetical way of
writing, to which it is well known Homer had a mortal
aversion. " On the hard soil his groaning breast he threw,"
is entirely bad. It is, we believe, a repetition; neither
Homer nor Achilles were thinking of the hardness of the soil;
and " breast" is a poor *pars pro toto* indeed, as all men will
allow, for " large himself, and much-room-occupying, in the
dust extended he lay." " He rolled and grovell'd " is perhaps mean, and certainly gratuitous, and " as to the earth he
grew " makes it likewise ludicrous; for neither man nor tree
can hope to grow to the earth by rolling and grovelling—for
proof of which arboricultural remark, see Sir Henry Steuart,
passim. " The virgin captives with disorder'd charms," is a
line liable to two radical objections. They had ceased to be
virgins—and their charms had not begun to be disordered.
That their breasts were " white" is not to be doubted, and
therefore Homer does not say so—leaving the enunciation of
that discovery to Pope.

> " While Nestor's son sustain'd a manlier part,
> And mourn'd the warrior with a warrior's heart,"

is a pretty compliment to Antilochus; but it is paid him by
Pope, and not by Homer, who merely says he " pour'd out
tears," " that his noble heart groan'd," and " that he grasp'd
the hands of Achilles." " Prevents the meditated blow" is
not good, because not perfectly clear—but it may pass perhaps after Chapman's " have done his person violence."
Homer does not say that Achilles *oft* attempted to kill himself; nay, he does not say that he did so even *once;* but
simply that Antilochus feared he might, seeing that agony.
" Heard his loud cries " is not absolutely bad in itself—but
it is a poor expression in place of " horribly howl'd." Thetis
did not, as Pope says, " answer groan for groan." The duet
would have been sung out of all tune; " she immediately
wept aloud." Thetis had a " crystal throne;" but Homer
does not mention it on this occasion—having probably forgotten it. Still, 'tis a good passage, though a bad translation.

No such criticisms fall to be made on Cowper's version.
From all such faults it is free ; nor has it any other that we
can discern—it being, as usual, Homeric. "Lest Peleus' son
should perish self-destroy'd," gives the sense without the
shocking sound ; and perhaps it is better to our ears, so often
horrified by coroners' inquests. Let us say, then, that the
translation is perfect.

Sotheby cannot be allowed to escape scot-free, but must
with Pope share punishment.

> "Grief at the word, and horror's gloomiest cloud,
>   Cast o'er Pelides their o'ershadowing shroud,"

are not two good lines. "At the word," is a frequent offence
of his—and why "grief and and horror," when Homer has but
one ? How far better Cowper's "The clouds of sorrow fell on
Peleus' son !" They envelope him in a moment. No sooner done
than said—no sooner said than done. But rhyme has nothing
durius in itself than that it makes people drawl. "The soil
that on its splendour darkly hung" is picturesque, but somewhat too elaborate. Perhaps we say so from a sense of the
excellence of all this part of the version, which is indeed nearly
perfect." "Whom his arm *had won, or gain'd* in battle," seems
to express a distinction without a difference, and is cumbrous.
"Left the still shelter of their peaceful tent," is a beautiful line,
and introduced purposely, we presume—but needlessly, we
think—for sake of contrast. There is nothing like it in the
original. Neither is "raised their clasp'd hands" there,
though good ; and as we blamed Pope for telling us their
breasts were "white," so must we Sotheby for saying they
were "of snow." "O'er him Nestor's son in horror stood," is
not quite right—for Achilles was lying on the ground, and if
the posture of Antilochus was to be mentioned at all (Homer
does not mention it), it should have been "stooped." Nor is
that a hypercriticism ; for in a picture addressed to the eye—
the mind's eye—every word should be apt and unexchange-
able. "Half-raised to shed his blood" is not in Homer—but
it is vivid—so let it stand. "Deep groan'd the desperate
man, 'twas death to hear groans," &c., is not sufficiently
strong for the original, but it is stronger, with its adjuncts,
than Pope's. "Sea-nymph," and "sea-goddess," is an un-
pleasant repetition. "She heard—she shriek'd," is short,

and strong, and good; and the passage closes with a fine hurrying picture. On the whole, Sotheby is here superior far to Pope—but he is inferior, think we, to Cowper.

Bewailing for a while to the Nereids the woes of her " noble son magnanimous," the chief of heroes, whom she had seen shoot under her maternal care like a prosperous plant, " Thetis leaves her cave, with all her weeping nymphs attendant, where'er they pass the parting billows opening wide a way," and, arrived at Troy, climbs the beach, where, by his numerous barks encompassed, groaning lay Achilles. " Why weeps my son ?" and thus—(be gracious to the prose of Christopher!) —after much mutual suffering, during which Thetis, with streaming eyes, hath said to him, " Swift comes thy destiny, as thou hast said ; for after Hector's death thine next ensues,"—

NORTH.

" Her the swift-footed Achilles, greatly indignant, address'd :
' Let me die forthwith, since it was not to be—that I, my friend
While being slain, should assist ; he indeed far far from his father-
    land
Hath been cut off ; me had he need of to be a harm-averter.
But now, since never shall I return to my beloved fatherland,
Nor have I been a safeguard to Patroclus, nor to friends
Besides—who in numbers have been subdued by the valiant
    Hector—
Here sit I by the ships—a useless lump of sod, on the earth ;
Such as none other of the brass-clad Greeks
In war am I ; others there are better in council.
Oh, perish discord from among gods, and from among men,
And anger, which hath impell'd even the very wise to act madly ;
And which, sweeter far than honey dropping down,
Goes on gathering in the breasts of men like smoke ;
Thus angry now hath the king of men, Agamemnon, made me.
But pass we over these things as done before, vex'd though we be,
Our wrath in our breast keeping down by necessity.
But now I go,—of that beloved person that I may find out the
    destroyer
—Hector ;—death will I then receive whenever indeed
Jupiter shall *will* to accomplish *it*, and the other immortal gods ;
For not even did the might of Hercules avoid death,
Dearest though he was to Jupiter, the Saturnian king,
But him subdued Fate and Juno's stern resentment.
I, too, if a like fate is ordain'd for me,

Shall lie—when I shall have died ; but now bright renown let me
   gain,
And some one of the deep-bosom'd Trojan and Dardan dames,
With both her hands from her tender cheeks
The tears wiping away, will I compel to groan often ;
Let them feel that long have I been absent from the fight.
Though loving me, hinder me not from the fight ; persuade me
   thou canst not.'"

What says Thetis now? " Well hast thou said, my son !
No blame it is to save our suffering friends from threatened
death.   But thy magnificent and dazzling arms are now in
Trojan hands—the hands of Hector—exulting, but doomed to
exult not long in such habiliments.   His death is nigh.   But
with yon hosts contending mix not thou—till here again thou
seest thy mother—for with the rising sun I will return, and
bring thee all-glorious arms, forged by Vulcan's self, the King
of Fire."   And having so said, she soared to Olympus.

Then Iris, sent by Juno, flung herself from heaven to earth,
and bade him sally, all unarmed as he was, to the rescue of
the body whose head the Trojans were threatening to cut off,
that they might impale it on one of the towers of Troy.
" Issuing to the margin of the fosse, show thyself only—and,
panic-seized, the whole Trojan army will fly the field ! "

NORTH.

" The swift-footed Iris having thus spoken, departed :
But Achilles beloved of Jove upstarted : Minerva
Around his mighty shoulders threw her fringed ægis,
And the most august of goddesses crown'd his head with a cloud
Of gold, and from it she kindled a flame all-refulgent :
As when smoke arising from a city into the air ascends
At a distance from an island, around which enemies are fighting,
And who, during the whole of the day, are engaged in the tug of
   grim war,
(Making sallies) from their own city : but along with going down
   of the sun
Beacon-lights flare frequent, and aloft the gleam
Uprises, that their neighbours may observe it,
If so be that they may come in ships to ward off the war :
In like manner from Achilles' head the beaming light reach'd the
   firmament.
For having advanced to the fosse beyond the wall he stood : nor
   with the Greeks

Mingled he : for the prudent counsel of his mother he regarded.
There standing he shouted : and apart Pallas Minerva
Shouted : and among the Trojans immense confusion caused.
Shrill and clear as is the sound, when the trumpet clangs
On account of the life-destroying enemy encompassing a city :
So shrill and clear at that time was the voice of the grandson of
    Æacus.
And they, when they heard the brazen shout of Æacides,
Were all stirr'd up in courage : but the beautiful-maned horses
Wheel'd round the chariots,—for they divined the (coming) cala-
    mity in their hearts.
Astounded were the charioteers, when they saw the unwearied
    flame
Over the head of the magnanimous son of Peleus horribly
Gleaming,—which the blue-eyed Minerva had kindled.
Thrice on the trench loudly shouted the godlike Achilles :
And thrice were confounded the Trojans and the illustrious allies.
There then perish'd twelve most warlike men
Amid their own chariots and spears : but the Greeks
Having eagerly dragg'd Patroclus beyond the reach of weapons,
Deposited him on a couch ; and his loved companious surrounded
    him
Lamenting : then the swift-footed Achilles follow'd,
Shedding scalding tears, when he look'd upon his trusty friend
Lying on the bier—mangled by the sharp brass :
(Him) whom he had sent with horses and chariots
To war—and never again welcomed back returning."

CHAPMAN.

"She woo'd, and he was won,
And straite Minerva honour'd him ; who Jove's shield clapt upon
His mightie shoulders ; and his head, girt with a cloud of gold,
That cast beams round about his brows. And as when arms enfold
A citie in an isle ; from thence, a fume at first appears,
(Being in the day), but when the even her cloudie forehead rears,
Thicke show the fires, and up they cast their splendor, that men-
    nie,
Seing their distresse, perhaps may set ships out to their supply :
So (to show such aid) from his head, a light rose, scaling heaven.
And forth the wall he stept and stood ; nor brake the precept
    given
By his great mother (mixt in fight) but sent abroad his voice,
Which Pallas farre off ecchoed ; who did betwixt them hoise
Shrill tumult to a toplesse height. And as a voice is heard
With emulous affection, when any towne is sphered

With siege of such a foe, as kills men's minds ; and for the town
Makes sound his trumpet: so the voice, from Thetis' issue throwne,
Won emulously th' eares of all. His brazen voice once heard,
The minds of all were startled so, they yielded ; and so fear'd
The faire-maned horses, that they flew backe, and their chariots
    turn'd,
Presaging in their augurous hearts, the labours that they mourn'd
A little after ; and their guides, a repercussive dread
Tooke from the horrid radiance of his refulgent head,
Which Pallas set on fire with grace. Thrice great Achilles spake,
And thrice (in heate of all the charge) the Trojans started backe.
Twelve men, of greatest strength in Troy, left with their lives
    exhaled
Their chariots and their darts to death, with his three summons
    call'd ;
And then the Grecians spritefully draw from the darts the corse,
And hearst it, bearing it to flecte,—his friends, with all remorse,
Marching about it. His great friend, dissolving then in tears,
To see his truly-loved return'd, so horst upon a herse,
Whom with such horse and chariot he set out safe and whole ;
Now wounded with unpittying steele, now sent without a soule,
Never again to be restored, never received but so ;
He follow'd, mourning bitterly."

POPE.

" She spoke and pass'd in air. The hero rose,
  Her ægis Pallas o'er his shoulders throws ;
  Around his brows a golden cloud she spread,
  A stream of glory flamed above his head,
  As when from some beleaguer'd town arise
  The smokes, high-curling to the shaded skies
  (Seen from some island o'er the main afar,
  When men distress'd hang out the sign of war.)
  Soon as the sun in ocean hides his rays.
  Thick on the hills the flaming beacons blaze ;
  With long-projected beams the seas are bright,
  And heaven's high arch reflects the ruddy light ;
  So from Achilles' head the splendours rise,
  Reflecting blaze on blaze against the skies.
  Forth march'd the chief, and, distant from the crowd,
  High on the rampart raised his voice aloud.
  With her own shout Minerva swells the sound,
  Troy starts astonish'd, and the shores rebound.
  As the loud trumpet's brazen mouth from far,
  With shrilling clangour sounds th' alarm of war,

Struck from the walls, the echoes float on high,
And the round bulwarks and thick towers reply ;
So high his brazen voice the hero rear'd,
Hosts drop their arms, and trembled as they heard :
And back the chariots roll, and coursers bound,
And steeds and men lie mingled on the ground.
Aghast they see the living lightnings play,
And turn their eyeballs from the flashing ray.
Thrice from the trench his dreadful voice he raised,
And thrice they fled, confounded and amazed.
Twelve in the tumult wedged, untimely rush'd
On their own spears, by their own chariots crush'd ;
While, shielded from their darts, the Greeks obtain
The long-contended carcass of the slain.
A lofty bier the breathless warrior bears,
Around his sad companions melt in tears ;
But chief Achilles, bending down his head,
Pours unavailing sorrows o'er the dead,
Whom late triumphant with his steeds and car,
He sent refulgent to the field of war ;
(Unhappy change !) now senseless, pale, he found,
Stretch'd forth, and gash'd with many a gaping wound."

COWPER.

" So saying, the rapid Iris disappear'd.
Then rose at once Achilles dear to Jove,
Athwart whose shoulders broad Minerva cast
Her ægis fringed terrific, and his brows
Encircled with a golden cloud, that shot
Fires insupportable to sight abroad.
As when some island, situate afar
On the wide waves, invested all the day
By cruel foes from their own city pour'd,
Upsends a smoke to Heaven, and torches shows
On all her turrets at the close of eve,
Which flash against the clouds, kindled in hope
Of aid from neighbour maritime allies,
So from Achilles' head light flash'd to Heaven.
Without the rampart and beside the fosse
He stood, but mix'd not with Achaia's host,
Obedient to his mother's wise command.
He stood and shouted ; Pallas also raised
A dreadful shout, and tumult infinite
Excited throughout all the host of Troy.
As when fierce foes approach the city walls,

Shrill sounds the trumpet to alarm the town.
Such in that moment, and so shrill was heard
Thy voice, Æacides ! and tumult-toss'd
Was every bosom at the brazen tone.
With swift recoil the long-maned coursers thrust
The chariots back, all boding woe at hand ;
And ev'ry charioteer astonish'd saw
Fires, that fail'd not, illumining the brows
Of Peleus' son, by Pallas kindled there.
Thrice o'er the trench Achilles sent his voice
Sonorous, and confusion at the sound
Thrice seized the Trojans, and their famed allies.
Twelve, in that moment, of their nobles died
By their own spears and chariots, and with joy
The Grecians from beneath a hill of darts
Dragging Patroclus, placed him on his bier.
Around him throng'd his fellow-warriors bold,
All weeping ; after whom Achilles went
Fast-weeping also at the doleful sight
Of his true friend on his funereal bed
Extended, gash'd with many a mortal wound,
Whom he had sent into the fight with steeds
And chariot, but received him thence no more."

SOTHEBY.

" Then, as she waved her wing, and pass'd above,
Up rose Pelides, the beloved of Jove.
Swift on his breadth of shoulders Pallas spread
The ægis fringed with death's o'ershadowing dread,
Enwreath'd a cloud of gold his brow around,
And with wide dazzling flames its circle bound ;
As when the smoke's dark columns heaven ascend
From some far isle where hosts with hosts contend,
And through the city gates, in mail'd array,
The natives pour, and war the livelong day ;
But where, at sunset, through each nightly hour,
The watch-fires blaze, and crest with flame the tower,
And to the neighbour isles the sign repeat,
The beacon beckoning to some friendly fleet :
Thus from Pelides' brow a stream of light
Flow'd forth, and far illumed th' ethereal height.
The hero pass'd the wall, and, seen from far,
Tower'd o'er the fosse, but mix'd not with the war.
Forewarn'd of Thetis, there Achilles staid—
There shouted—and a sound that Troy dismay'd

Burst as Minerva's shout his outcry swell'd,
And with unearthly fear the host repell'd ;
Clear as the trumpet's voice, whose signal sound
Forewarns, ere gathering hosts the town surround,
Thus clear Pelides' voice ; from man to man,
Swift through the ranks appalling horror ran,
Started each war-steed, and with wild affright,
Foreboding slaughter, wheel'd the car for flight,
Cower'd every guide, who o'er that crest illumed,
Saw blazing forth, in brightness unconsumed,
The flames by Pallas fed. As thus his brow
Flash'd o'er the tumult in the fosse below,
Thrice burst his shout, and thrice, as doom'd to fall
On Troy, and Troy's allies, fear fell on all.
Then twelve, the noblest Trojans, bit the plain,
By their own darts and cars confusedly slain ;
And joyfully the Greeks withdrew the dead,
And laid Patroclus on a peaceful bed.
His warriors round him pour'd their loud lament,
But mute with woe behind Achilles went,
While o'er his ghastly death-wounds gush'd his tear,
Gush'd o'er his brother, bleeding on the bier,
Whom, sent by him, his car, his coursers bore,
Beaming with valour, but brought back no more."

Chapman shows throughout his translation of this sublime
passage, that the very Achilles stood before his imagination,
who had arisen before that of Homer. He makes, indeed,
Minerva throw over the hero's shoulders, not her own Ægis,
but the shield of Jove—a mistake, if it be one, of no moment,
for he was beloved by the King of Heaven. We believe it is
no mistake, for Jove gave Minerva her Ægis. His head is
then girt with a cloud of gold—and there he stands, worthy
of any simile from earth or sky. What is it? The beleaguered city sends up by daylight its signal smoke—and then
at night its beacon-fire. So—sayeth Chapman, well, "from
his head a light rose scaling heaven." Thus arrayed in saving terror, "forth the wall he stept and stood;" nor has Homer's
self better shown the sudden sally of the Apparition. "He
sent abroad his voice, which Pallas far off echoed" is great—
and "who did betwixt them hoise shrill tumult to a topless
height," though not in Homer, is yet Homeric, and sends the
shout into the skies, trumpet-tongued. But in the Greek the
clang is more dreadful; and the effect on the frightened horses

more instantaneously flashed upon us ; though Chapman says finely, "presaging in their augurous hearts ; " "and their guides a repercussive dread took from the horrid radiance of his refulgent head," is magnificent.   Towards the close, Chapman becomes cumbrous—and moves heavily under the weight of the images that seem to bear down the description. In Homer, the close is as majestic as it is mournful—as simple as it is sublime.

Pope felt the grandeur of the original, like a true poet ; but ambitious to excel it—*magnis tamen excidit ausis*—his performance is noble.   "*A stream of glory* flamed above his head," is one of those vague verses whose sonorous reign is over ; and how poor in comparison with "from it she kindled a flame all refulgent ! "   The smokes and beacons are on the whole good, but too elaborate.   Homer says, " Beacon-lights glare frequent, and aloft the gleam arises " — sudden and bright ; whereas Pope pursues the picturesque, forgets the poet in the painter, and gives us "*with long-projected beams the seas are bright*," and " heaven's high arch reflects the ruddy light,"— two fine lines undoubtedly, but the first implied to the imagination in the original, for the city is on an island.   " Reflecting blaze on blaze against the skies,"—is " doing into poetry " " in like manner from Achilles' head the beaming light reached the firmament."   We cannot think that " Troy starts astonished, and the shores rebound," is equally good for the occasion, as "among the Trojans immense confusion caused." But doctors differ.   " And the round bulwarks and thick towers reply," is a line that Darwin must have admired, and eke Mr Price on the Picturesque.   But Homer was not thinking of the roundness of bulwarks, or the thickness of towers— simply of a life-destroying-enemy-encompassed city startled by a forewarning trumpet.   What follows is spirited, but too much in the same style.   The concluding lines about Patroclus and Achilles, though not sufficiently infused with the scriptural simplicity of Homer, are however solemn and stately, and of powerful pathos.   With such exceptions and allowances, Pope's may be pronounced a very fine translation.

Cowper catches the soul of the simile just like Chapman. Nothing can be better than, "So from Achilles' head light flash'd to heaven ! "   " He stood and shouted," is equally good—and " tumult infinite excited," are three words more powerful than

Pope's pompous line, "Troy starts astonish'd, and the shores rebound." But criticise the passage for yourself, which, in our opinion, is excellent; but wants, we hardly know how, something of the spirit, and more of the sublimity of Homer. Read by itself, it is good; but along with the original, some-what tame. We desiderate the ἔπεα πτερόεντα of the rushing original.

Sotheby soars, here, above all his competitors. He has all the raciness and vigour of Chapman, without his roughness and his inversions—all the splendour of Pope, without his "false glitter"—the simplicity without the tameness, if tame-ness it be, of Cowper; and an ease and elegance all his own, we might almost say the majesty and magnificence of Homer. This is high praise; but the most critical examination will not prove it extravagant. As literal as prose or blank verse, no translation in rhyme can ever be; but here Homer is rendered into rhyme with the consummate skill of inspiration. All, down to the body of Patroclus. There Sotheby's wing flags—he falters in his flight, and falls. There is no studied contrast in Homer, as in Sotheby, between the grief of Achilles and the other warriors. He does not say that they poured their loud lament, but that Achilles was mute with woe. They surrounded him "lamenting"—he "shedding scalding tears." We believe he was mute—but on that so is Homer. "Gush'd his tear," is feeble; "bleeding on the bier," a poor repetition of "ghastly death-wounds;" "whom, sent by him," &c., very awkward; "beaming with valour," an interpolation far from felicitous; and "but brought back no more," how unaffecting, applied to the car and coursers, as it here is by Sotheby, in comparison with "never again welcomed back returning," applied to Achilles, as it is there by Homer!

All night long the Grecians weep o'er Patroclus, while, standing in the midst, Pelides leads the lamentation, on the bosom of his breathless friend imposing his homicidal hands —incensed as a grim lion, from whose lair among thick trees the hunter has carried off his whelps, and who, too late return-ing, growls over his loss, and then scours wood and glen, up and down on the footsteps of the robber, that he may rend him limb from limb, and drink his blood. In such mood Achilles addresses his Myrmidons—would we had room for his speech of tears and fire! All night long they stand around

him deploring his dead friend, whose body, bathed in water
from "the singing brass," and anointed with limpid oil, and
all its ruddy wounds filled with unguents mellowed by nine
years' keep, lies covered with a light linen texture from head
to feet. At morning thus is he found by Thetis, "bearer of
the gift of God," the Celestial Armour. "My son! however
reluctant, leave Patroclus' corse—for there it lies by doom of
Heaven; and receive thou these beauteous arms, 'such as no
mortal shoulders ever wore!'"

The SHIELD—the SHIELD! Vulcan's masterpiece—whereof
there was loud bruit in Heaven.

So has there been on earth. Thus my Lord Kames, a mis-
cellaneous man, whom we much admire, hath said, "the decorations of a dancing-room ought all of them to be gay. No
picture is proper for a church but what has religion for its
subject. Every ornament upon a shield should relate to war;
and Virgil, with great judgment, confines the carving upon
the shield of Æneas to the military history of the Romans.
That beauty is overlooked by Homer; for the bulk of the
sculpture on the shield of Achilles is of the arts of peace in
general, and of joy, and festivity in particular; the author of
Telemachus betrays the same inattention in describing the
shield of that young hero."

"Betrays the same inattention!" This, we presume, is
one of the occasions on which the good Homer was nodding;
and there was nobody by to give him a rap over the knuckles.
Yet let Lord Kames consider that this is no ordinary shield.
"None but itself can be its parallel," for 'tis the sole shield
made by Vulcan, at the order of Thetis, for Achilles. The
sea-goddess gave him no pattern to work by—'twas "all made
out of the forger's brain," and

> "Full twenty bellows working all at once,
> Breathed on the furnace, blowing easy and free
> The managed winds."

The artist allowed himself all latitude; and having formed
"a triple border beauteous, dazzling bright," with what filled
he the interior of the "broad circumference"? Why, with
the Earth, the Heaven, the Sea, the Moon full-orbed, and he
that wearieth not, the unresting Sun. Why not the Stars?
They too are there—

> " All the stars, which round about
> As with a radiant frontlet bind the skies—
> The Pleiads, and the Hyads, and the might
> Of huge Orion, hungry for the morn,"

and with him, " Ursa called, known also by his popular name, the Wain," the sole star that slakes not his beams in the briny baths of Ocean.

'Tis thus the good Homer nods.

But his lordship says, " that every ornament on a shield should relate to war." And was there never war in the skies? But here we have war, too, on the earth. Here men, as Milton says of devils,

> " Smote on *this sounding shield* the din of war,
> Hurling defiance towards the vault of heaven."

For lo, " such as men build, two splendid cities!" In one, rites matrimonial solemnised with pomp of sumptuous banquets. But not long that peace endures; for strife arises— and citizens contend for a mulct, the price of blood, and the people, as passion sways them, clamour loud, and heralds quell the tumult, and on polished stones the Elders in a ring, each with a sceptre in his hand, pronounce sentence—and then there is silence. The other (city) is invested by two glittering hosts—and they debate whether to divide the spoil, or burn and raze the city. " Here," says Pope, " in the space of thirty lines, a siege, a sally, an ambush, the surprise of a convoy, and a battle, with scarce a circumstance proper to any of these omitted"—and what would his lordship be at, in longing for more blood?

Surely mortal men are not *always* slaughtering over the whole world. Sometimes they sleep, work, eat, drink, dance, sing, and propagate their species. On the Shield, therefore, behold a fallow field, rich, spacious, and well-tilled—ploughers not a few—and oft as in their course they come to the bourne of the many-acred breadth of blackish but golden glebe, so oft meets them a man " who in their hands a goblet placed, charged with delicious wine."

But the green spring is over and gone, and so is the yellow summer, and lo! the likeness of a field crowded with corn, and the sharped-toothed sickles gleam among the jolly reapers! Boys binding the bundles, and among them, the master, staff

in hand, stands "enjoying mute the order of the field." Apart
beneath the shade of an oak his train prepare the banquet—
as if Ambrose' self were there—" a well-thriven ox new slain,
while for the hinds th' attendant maidens mix of whitest flour
large supper."

See—now—a vineyard all of gold. Purple did Vulcan make
the clusters, and the vines supported stood " by poles of silver
set in even rows." There, in frails of wicker, blithe youths
and maidens bear the luscious fruit; and in the midst, on his
shrill harp, a boy harmonious plays, and ever as he smites the
chords, he sings to it with a slender voice. Behind

> "Nodding their heads together go
> The merry minstrelsy,"

and how ancient the gallopade!

The pastoral age! Four golden herdsmen, by nine swift
dogs attended, drive the kine afield, forth to pasture by a
river-side, "rapid, sonorous, fringed with circling reeds."
From the brake outleaps a lion, the herdsmen fly, and as he
tears the hide of a huge bull, and laps his bloody entrails,
the dogs stand barking aloof, " for no tooth for lion's flesh
have they."

But see—with Sotheby (in whose hands the Shield is as
Dædalean as in Homer's), a scene of perfect peace. For, as
he beautifully says, in lines that shall be immortal,—

> " Now the god's changeful artifice display'd
> Fair flocks at pasture in a lovely glade ;
> And folds and shelt'ring stalls peep'd up between,
> And shepherds' huts diversified the scene."

" Last scene of all, to close this strange eventful history,"
a Choir,

> " Such as famed Dædalus on Gnossus' shore,
> For bright-hair'd Ariadne, form'd of yore."

The fair girls, all in white raiment, in light-flowing robes
of the linen fine, and the youths, in glossy tunics ; flower-
wreathed the paranymphs, and their heroic partners dancing
armed with

> " Swords that all gold
> From belts of silver swung."

Well done Vulcan, by Jupiter !

> " Last, with the might of ocean's boundless flood,
> He fill'd the border of the wondrous Shield."

The shade of Kames, then, must at this moment be blushing black and blue in Elysium. And now that we are about it, we may as well give his lordship another lecture. He is a stiff stickler for congruity. We have seen his objections to the inappropriate imagery of the Shield, of which all the ornaments should have been those of war. Having humbled Homer, he mounts his hobby and charges Milton. " In reading the description of the dismal waste, Book I. of ' Paradise Lost,' *we are sensible of a confused feeling* arising from dissimilar emotions forced into union, to wit, *the beauty of the description, and the horror of the object described,*—

> ' Seest thou yon dreary plain, forlorn and wild,
> The seat of desolation, void of light,
> Save what the glimmering of these livid flames
> Casts pale and dreadful ?'

With respect to this and many similar passages in ' Paradise Lost,' we are sensible, that *the emotions being obscured by each other*, make neither of them that figure they would make separately." *Euge !* What does the Paper-Lord mean, by saying that here dissimilar emotions are forced into union ? No such thing. The excellence of the description consists in its accuracy and vividness ; and therefore cannot be discordant, surely, with the horrors that it perfectly paints to the imagination. If, indeed, the description had *mingled images of beauty with images of horror*, then, according to Kames's theory of the matter, it might have been faulty, and the incongruity might have displeased or shocked ; but as it stands, no such objection can be urged against it, and the description is censured, *because it is good.* This we call the cant of criticism. His lordship has been mouthing away in a Scotch metaphysical mist. Such in those days, and it is but little better now, was the state in Scotland (yet Kames and Beattie were contemporaries, just like Maga and the Blue and Yellow) of the Philosophy of the *Belles Lettres.*

Lo ! Thetis the Sea-goddess ! Well might she say—for suitable to such a shield were the offensive arms she brought along with it from heaven—" My son ! receive, receive thou these beauteous arms, such as no mortal shoulders ever wore."

NORTH.

" Thus having spoken, the goddess laid down the arms
Before Achilles ; and they, Dædalean, all rung.
But trembling seized the Myrmidons all, nor durst any one
On them look—but were terrified ; Achilles,
When he beheld them, greater anger enter'd—and his eyes
From under his eyelids, like a flame, horribly out-gleam'd.
Delighted, however, was he, holding in his hands the splendid
        gifts of the god.
But when he had feasted his soul by gazing on the arms Dædalean,
Forthwith his mother, with these wing'd words, he address'd.
'Mother mine, these arms indeed hath a god bestow'd, such as it
        is beseeming
That the works of immortals should be ; and which no mortal
        man could have accomplish'd ;
Instantly then will I arm myself,' " &c.

CHAPMAN.

" Thus, setting down, the precious metal of the arms was such,
That all the room rung with the weight of every slenderest touch.
Cold tremblings took the Myrmidons ; none durst sustain, all
        fear'd
T'oppose their eyes ; Achilles yet, as soon as they appear'd,
Stern anger enter'd.   From his eyes, as if the dog-star rose,
A radiance terrifying men, did all the state enclose.
At length, he took into his hands the rich gift of the god ;
And, much pleased to behold the art that in the shield was show'd,
He brake forth into this applause," &c.

POPE.

" Then drops the radiant burden on the ground,
Clang the strong arms, and ring the shores around.
Back shrink the Myrmidons with dread surprise,
And from the broad effulgence turn their eyes.
Unmoved, the hero kindles at the show,
And feels with rage divine his bosom glow ;
From his fierce eyeballs living flames expire,
And flash incessant like a stream of fire ;
He turns the radiant gift, and feeds his mind
On all the immortal artist had design'd."

COWPER.

" So saying, she placed the armour on the ground
Before him, and the whole bright treasure rang.

Awe-struck, the Myrmidons all turn'd away
Their dazzled eyes, and, trembling, fled the place.
Not so Pelides. He no sooner saw
The gift divine, than in his heart he felt
Redoubled wrath ; a splendour, as of fire,
Flash'd from his eyes. Delighted, in his hand
He held the glorious bounty of the god,
And wondering at those shapes of art divine," &c.

SOTHEBY.

" She spake, and laid the arms his feet before,
And loud and long burst up the brazen roar.
Fear fell on all ; none, none, though bold in fight,
Dared on the gift celestial fix his sight.
But when Achilles saw them, flaming ire
Flash'd from his eyelids like a stream of fire.
Firmly he grasp'd them, and, with grim delight,
Felt, as he grasp'd, unconquerable might."

Chapman is grand, sir. The second line, though not perhaps exactly what you will see, by-and-by, we think the
hidden meaning, is most expressive of the subtile sound
sleeping and waking in the exquisite finish of the arms, and
the effect produced by what then happened on the Myrmidons and on Achilles, put with prodigious power—and how
finely! Pope's paraphrase is magnificent—always saving
and excepting "living flames," especially when said sillily
to be like " streams of fire." Cowper's version is close and
compact, and bright as the celestial armour. Sotheby's is
splendid as it should be—and the last two lines all that
could be desired ; but confound "flaming ire," like a " stream
of fire."

What was the nature of the noise, think ye, heard by Homer, when " τὰ δ' ἀνέϐραχε δαίδαλα πάντα." Pope says, " clang
and ring ; " Cowper, the " whole bright treasure rang ; "
Sotheby, " and loud and long burst up the brazen roar."
Pope and Cowper do not commit themselves by conjecture of
the imagination as to the nature of the noise, beyond the
revelation of the text. Sotheby does ; and, much as we admire him, as often a matchless translator, we here charge him
with gross exaggeration. There was no roar at all—much less
a long and loud one—and on that we lay our ears. The
noise was not like that of thunder—though thunder some-

times clangs and clatters alarmingly, as if something celestial, or rather infernal, were shivered, while it did shiver—
reperciussively broken back by gnarled oak, tower "cased in
the unfeeling armour of old time," or by the tinkling iron of a
precipice.   The noise was not like that of a cataract, though
sometimes a "grand water-privilege," as the Americans say,
through the rumbling hollowness of the howl intermingles a
metallic music that seems to come clangorous from the cliffs.
Neither was the noise like that of a bull in a china-shop,
which the calmest auditor pronounces decisive of the downfall of the whole Celestial Empire.   Nor was the noise like
that of the overturning of a huge waggon-ful of cast-iron
bars on the crown of a Scotch causeway of granite-pits, such
as endangered the limbs and lives of the natives of great
cities before the age of Macadam—a resistless species of
irony that drove the deafest dumb.   But it was more like
that than the long and loud bursting-up brazen roar of Sotheby.
Suppose, then, the sudden clash, clatter, and clang, of ever so
many cymbals savagely shattered and shivered, as if smitten
all at once together in the air by the cross currents of a brace
of whirlwinds.   The crash would be mighty, magnificent,
miraculous, and it would be *musical;* for they were all at-
tempered and attuned ; and all the time the noise continued to
endure—and that might not be inconsiderable—the earth
would *dirl*, and the air would quake ; but harmony, not discord,
would be prevailing over us, even while we clapt our hands to
our ears in fear and astonishment, absconded, swooned, or died.
No other noise can we imagine so near in its essential nature
to that of the armour of Achilles, as Thetis from her immortal
hands let it fall at the feet of the Hero of Heroes.   No wonder that the Myrmidons all took up a howling and fled, like
wolves on a wild night that in herds howl to the moon bursting out of the clouds, and in hideous hubbub away to the
woods.   No wonder that the soul of Achilles was glad within
him, even as the soul of the shepherd eyeing Homer's own
favourite nocturnal sky, when first a few beautiful stars appear round the shining moon, and then, as the clouds dispart
from below, is seen in ascension over the infinite altitude, all
the bright magnificence of heaven.

"These are no work of man!" exclaims the hero—"they
are the work of Vulcan, and worthy heaven.   Now will I

brace them on—but sore I fear lest worm-engendering flies,
piercing through his wounds, disgrace the body of my Patroclus."—"Peace—peace, my son; fresh—fresher than ever
here might it lie for a year!—But call all the heroes to
council—renounce thy rage against the king—and then,
girding thee in the glory of thy might, away—away to
battle!" Then with shouts Pelides passed along the strand,
the roused chiefs all flocking around him—and all those, too,
who used to tarry 'mid the fleet, and all who used to sit immovable at the helm—and all who ministered and doled the
food,—all once more behold—Achilles. Then came Ulysses
and Tydides, propt on their spears, and half forgotten their
wounds—and last to the council came the son of Atreus himself—the King. The reconciliation is complete—King and
Prince lay the blame of the quarrel on Jove—and the cry of
Achilles is for instant battle. Ulysses and Agamemnon both
counsel rest and food, that so with all the strength of soul
and body they may charge the Trojans. Atrides, too, is
eager to swear by all the heavenly powers that Briseïs is
intact—and to lay all the promised treasures at the feet of his
friend. The bearing of all is kingly—but Achilles is Achilles
still, his own will is his sole law, and he is subject but to his
passion.

NORTH.

"Him the swift-footed Achilles answering, address'd,
   Son of Atreus, most illustrious, King of men, Agamemnon,
   Hereafter, indeed, ought you rather to busy yourself about such
      things
   When some pause of war shall take place,
   And martial ardour is not so great in my breast:
   But now cut-in-pieces lie those, whom subdued
   Hath Hector, the son of Priam,—since to him hath Jupiter given
      renown:
   Do you, however, urge on (the soldiers) to take refreshments: I,
      for my part, would verily,
   Even now, exhort to the fight the sons of the Greeks
   Fasting, unfed: but along with the sun's going down
   To prepare a great supper, when we shall have revenged the
      affront.
   Until then, may never down my throat pass
   Or drink, or food,—while my friend lies dead,
   Who, in my tent, by sharp brass mangled

Lies (with his feet) turn'd to the vestibule :[1] and around him his
companions
Lament: in no respect, then, are these things (*food and drink*)
a care to my mind,
But slaughter, and blood, and the agonising groans of heroes."

The oath is sworn—and the gifts delivered—and Briseïs,
restored to the tent of her lawful lord, lovely as the light and
the golden Venus, clasps Patroclus in her arms, and in an immortal lay of lamentation, celebrates the gentle virtues of the
fallen hero.   At the close of all the *feminei ululatus*, the chiefs
again would press on him the proffered food—but Achilles
cries " Vex me no more—misery drinks my blood—and nor
food nor drink shall be mine till the close of day bring the
end of battle."

NORTH.

" Thus having said, one here, one there, the chiefs he dispersed ;
But there remain'd the two sons of Atreus, and the illustrious
Ulysses,
Nestor, and Idomeneus, and the aged charioteer Phœnix,
Trying-to-comfort him (while) sorrowing exceedingly : nor in his
mind
Would he be comforted, until he had rush'd into the mouth of
bloody war ;
Calling to mind (Patroclus), closely-pressing (groans) he heaved,
and spoke,
' Aye-unhappy one, thou most beloved of friends, even thou
for me
Wert, of thyself, wont to prepare a sweet banquet in the tent
Speedily and carefully, when the Greeks were hastening on
To carry much-weeping-causing war among the horse-subduing
Trojans :
But now mangled thou liest ; and my heart
Fasting from drink and food—(though these are within)—
(*On account of*) my longing for thee,—for no greater evil could I
endure,
No—not even were I to hear of my father's having been cut off,
Who perchance now drops a tender tear
For the bereavement of such a son : while I, among an alien
people,
For the sake of Helen the abhorr'd, am fighting against the
Trojans.

---

[1] The way in which the dead were laid out.

(*No — nor*) of his — who in Scyros is being rear'd — my son
beloved—
If indeed he still lives—the god-looking Neoptolemus.
Erst indeed was my soul in my breast wont to hope,
That I only should die far from the horse-rearing Argos,
Here at Troy, but that thou shouldst return to Phthia,
That my son, in a swift-sailing dark ship,
From Scyros thou mightst conduct—and show him everything—
My possessions, and my female slaves, and my lofty-roof'd spacious
mansion.
For Peleus, methinks, is by this time indeed
Dead, or scarcely still alive is sorrowing
In hateful old age, and of me expecting always
Doleful tidings, that he shall hear of me as dead.'
Thus spoke he weeping : the chiefs, too, groan'd—
As each call'd to mind what he had left at home."

Meantime Jove, moved by compassion for Achilles, commands
Minerva to go and instil ethereal substance into his heart.
And then comes such a burst of Poetry as nowhere else is to
be found out of Homer, except it be in Milton ; for all the world
has lifted up above all other poems " Paradise Lost " and the
Iliad.

NORTH.

" Thus having spoken, he stirr'd up Minerva, already anxious
(to obey his commands) :
But she, like a harpy, with wide-extended wings, shrill-voiced,
From heaven darted down through the air ; but the Greeks
Were then arming throughout the camp : in Achilles'
Breast nectar and pleasing ambrosia
She dropp'd, that painful hunger might not pervade his limbs.
She to the crowded mansion of her almighty father
Departed : while they from the swift-sailing ships were issuing.
As when dense snow-showers out-fly from Jove,
Cold from the impulse of the frosty-air-producing Boreas ;
So dense then were the bright gleaming helmets
Borne from the ships,—and emboss'd shields,
And strong cuirasses, and ashen spears :
The lustre heavenward ascended, and the earth all around laugh'd
With the lightning of brass : and a hollow sound started up from
under the trampling
Of heroes : in the midst was arm'd the godlike Achilles,
Grinding his teeth, and whose eyes
Roll'd glowing like a flash of fire, into whose heart

Enter'd intolerable pain : raving against the Trojans,
He donn'd the gifts divine which the artist Vulcan had made for
    him.
First around his thighs he placed the cuishes
Beautifully form'd, and fix'd with silver clasps.
Next the cuirass on his chest he placed.
Then around his shoulders he threw (the baldrick of) his sword
    studded with silver knobs
And brass : and then his shield, large and broad,
He took, whose refulgence spread far and wide like that of the
    moon.
As when from the sea, there shines to mariners a beam
Of flaming fire, which blazes aloft from the mountains,
In a shepherd's solitude : them reluctant, the tempests
Bear away far from their friends over the fishy sea :
In like manner the gleam mounted heavenward from Achilles'
    shield
Beautiful, Dædalean. His mighty helmet uplifting
On his head he placed ; like a star, shone
The horse-hair-crested helmet : there waved around him the hair
Of gold, with which in great abundance Vulcan had surrounded
    the crest.
The godlike Achilles essayed himself in his armour,
Whether it might fit him, and if his fair limbs should move
    easily :
To him it was like wings, and buoyed up the Shepherd of the
    people.
From the sheath his paternal spear he drew,
Ponderous, huge, strong : which none other of the Greeks was
    able
To brandish, and which Achilles alone knew how to rear,
—That ashen spear of Peleus which Chiron had hewed for his
    father
From the summit of Pelion,—to be death to heroes !"

CHAPMAN.

" This spurre he added to the free.
And like a harpye (with a voice that shriekes so dreadfully,
And feathers that like needles prickt) she stoopt through all the
    starres
Amongst the Grecians ; all whose tents were now fill'd for the
    warres.
Her seres strooke through Achilles' tent ; and closely she instill'd
Heaven's most-to-be-desired feast, to his great breast; and fill'd

His sinewes with that sweete supply, for feare vnsauorie fast
Should creepe into his knees. Her selfe the skies againe enchac't.
The host set forth, and pour'd his steele waues farre out of the
fleete ;
And as from aire the frostie northwind blows a colde thicke sleete
That dazzles eyes, flakes after flakes incessantly descending ;
So thicke helmes, curets, ashen darts, and round shields neuer
ending,
Flow'd from the nauie's hollow wombe ; their splendors gaue
Heauen's eye
His beames againe ; Earth laught to see her face so like the skie ;
Armes shined so hote, and she such clouds made with the dust she
cast ;
She thunder'd—feet of men and horse importuned her so fast.
In midst of all, diuine Achilles his faire person arm'd ;
His teeth gnasht as he stood—his eyes so full of fire, they warm'd ;
Vnsuffer'd griefe and auger at the Troians so combined ;
His greaues first vsde, his goodly curets on his bosome shined ;
His sword, his shield, that cast a brightnesse from it like the
moone.
And as from sea sailers discerne a harmfull fire, let runne
By herdsmen's faults, till all their stall flies vp in wrastling flame,
Which being on hils, is seene farre off ; but being alone, none came
To giue it quench, at shore no neighbors, and at sea their friends
Driuen off with tempests ; such a fire from his bright shield
extends
His ominous radiance, and in heauen imprest his feruent blaze.
His crested helmet, graue and high, had next triumphant place
On his curl'd head ; and like a starre, it cast a spurrie ray,
About which a bright thicken'd bush of golden haire did play,
Which Vulcan forged him for his plume. Thus compleate arm'd,
he tride
How fit they were, and if his motion could with ease abide
Their braue instruction ; and so farre they were from hindering it,
That to it they were nimble wings, and made so light his spirit,
That from the earth the princely captaine they took vp to aire.
    Then from his armoury he drew his lance, his father's speare,
Huge, weightie, firme, that not a Greeke but he himselfe alone
Knew how to shake. It grew vpon the mountaine Pelion,
From whose height Chiron hew'd it for his sire ; and fatall 'twas
To great-soul'd men."

POPE.

" He spoke ; and sudden at the word of Jove,
Shot the descending goddess from above.

So swift through ether the shrill harpy springs,
The wide air floating to her ample wings.
To Great Achilles she her flight addrest,
And pour'd divine ambrosia in his breast,
With nectar sweet (refection of the gods !)
Then, swift ascending, sought the bright abodes.
    Now issued from the ships the warrior train,
And like a deluge pour'd upon the plain.
As when the piercing blasts of Boreas blow,
And scatter o'er the fields the driving snow ;
From dusky clouds the fleecy winter flies,
Whose dazzling lustre whitens all the skies :
So helms succeeding helms, so shields from shields
Catch the quick beams, and brighten all the fields ;
Broad glittering breastplates, spears with pointed rays,
Mix in one stream, reflecting blaze on blaze :
Thick beats the centre as the coursers bound,
With splendour flame the skies, and laugh the fields around.
    Full in the midst, high-towering o'er the rest,
His limbs in arms divine Achilles drest ;
Arms which the Father of the Fire bestow'd,
Forged on the eternal anvils of the god.
Grief and revenge his furious heart inspire,
His glowing eyeballs roll with living fire ;
He grinds his teeth, and furious with delay
O'erlooks the embattled host, and hopes the bloody day.
    The silver cuishes first his thighs enfold :
Then o'er his breast was braced the hollow gold :
The brazen sword a various baldrick tied,
That, starr'd with gems, hung glittering at his side ;
And like the moon, the broad refulgent shield
Blazed with long rays, and gleam'd athwart the field.
    So to night-wand'ring sailors, pale with fears,
Wide o'er the watery waste a light appears,
Which on the far-seen mountain blazing high,
Streams from some lonely watch-tower to the sky :
With mournful eyes they gaze, and gaze again ;
Loud howls the storm, and drives them o'er the main.
Next his high head the helmet graced ; behind
The sweepy crest hung floating in the wind :
Like the red star, that from his flaming hair
Shakes down diseases, pestilence and war :
So stream'd the golden honours from his head,
Trembled the sparkling plumes, and the loose glories shed.

The chief beholds himself with wond'ring eyes ;
His arms he poises, and his motions tries ;
Buoy'd by some inward force, he seems to swim,
And feels a pinion lifting every limb.
  And now he shakes his great paternal spear,
Pond'rous and huge ! which not a Greek could rear.
From Pelion's cloudy top an ash entire
Old Chiron fell'd, and shaped it for his sire ;
A spear which stern Achilles only wields,
The death of heroes, and the dread of fields."

COWPER.

  " He urged Minerva prompt before.
In form a shrill-voiced harpy of broad wing
Through ether down she darted, while the Greeks
In all their camp for instant battle arm'd.
Ambrosial sweets and nectar she instill'd
Into his breast, lest he should suffer loss
Of strength through abstinence, then soar'd again
To her great Sire's unperishing abode.
And now the Grecians from their gallant fleet
All pour'd themselves abroad.   As when the snow,
Descending thick from Jove, is driven by gusts
Of the clear-blowing North, so smiled the field
With dazzling casques, boss'd bucklers, hauberks strong,
And polish'd weapons issuing from the fleet.
Upwent the flash to Heav'n ; wide all around
The champaign laugh'd with beamy brass illum'd,
And tramplings of the warriors on all sides
Resounded, amidst whom Achilles arm'd.
He gnash'd his teeth, fire glimmer'd in his eyes,
Anguish intolerable wrung his heart,
And fury against Troy, while he put on
His glorious arms, the labour of a God.
First, to his legs his polish'd greaves he clasp'd,
Studded with silver, then, his corslet bright
Braced to his bosom, his huge sword of brass
Athwart his shoulder slung, and his broad shield
Uplifted last, luminous as the moon—
Such as to mariners a fire appears,
Kindled by shepherds on the distant top
Of some lone hill ; they, driven by stormy winds,
Reluctant roam far off the fishy deep—
Such from Achilles' burning shield divine

A lustre struck the skies; his ponderous helm
He lifted to his brows ; starlike it shone,
And shook its curling crest of bushy gold,
Consummate work of Vulcan's glorious art.
So clad, the godlike hero trial made
If his arms fitted him, and gave free scope
To his proportion'd limbs ; they buoyant proved
As wings, and high upbore his airy tread.
Forth from its case he drew his father's spear,
Heavy, and huge, and long.   That spear, of all
Achaia's sons, none else had power to wield ;
Achilles only could the Pelian beam
Brandish, by Chiron for his father hewn
From Pelion's top for slaughter of the brave."

SOTHEBY.

" Each word Jove spake inflamed Minerva's mind,
By previous zeal to Grecia's aid inclined—
Like a shrill harpy, stretch'd on wing for flight,
The goddess darted through the ethereal light.
Greece stood in arms, when Jove's celestial maid
With willing zeal her sire's command obey'd,
And, lest their chief should fail beneath the strife,
Pour'd in his breast the nectar, stored with life ;
Then to Jove's starry realm return'd again,
While from the fleet Greece gather'd on the plain.
As flakes on flakes, thick falling, nature veil,
When the clear north-wind arms with ice the gale,
Thus dense, the dazzling helms, the hauberks blazed,
Boss'd shields, and lances to the sun upraised :
The flash beam'd up to heaven's illumined height,
And all the earth resplendent laugh'd in light,
And the wide plain with march of myriads reel'd,
While grim Pelides arm'd him for the field—
His teeth loud gnash'd, and through intense desire,
Stream'd from his eyes, like flame, the living fire,—
Grief gnaw'd his soul, that mad for vengeance glow'd,
While on his limbs he clasp'd the armour of the god.—
First round his legs the greaves Achilles braced,
With radiant clasps of silver ore enchased :
Then on his breadth of breast the hauberk hung,
Then his huge sword athwart his shoulders swung :
Last, seized the bulk and burden of his shield,
That like the full-orb'd moon illumed afar the field—

As when along the ocean streams a light,
Fed by lone shepherds on the mountain height,
Beheld of those, who cleave, where tempests sweep,
Far from their friends, unwillingly the deep :
Thus from that beauteous shield's celestial frame,
Shot up to heaven's high vault its dazzling flame.
Then, raising up its weight, Achilles placed
On his brave brow the casque by Vulcan graced.
The bushy helmet like a beauteous star
Shone, and a light around it stream'd afar,
That from the fulness of the golden hair
Waved, floating o'er the crest, and fired the air.
Then Peleus' glorying son his arms essay'd,
If fit, and free for battle-action made :
And as he tried them, moving in his might,
They lifted up his limbs, like wings on flight.
Then from the case, wherein its terror lay,
The chief brought forth his father's lance to-day,
Vast, weighty, strong, which, never warrior, none
Could vibrate, save the Achillean arm alone ;
The Pelian lance, the ash that Chiron gave,
From Pelion's summit hewn to slay the brave."

Let us try the Four great Translators by their respective success in grappling with, perhaps the most glorious passage in all poetry. What sees Homer ? The Grecians issuing from the ships. How ? " As when dense snow-showers outfly from Jove." Such their number, and such the motion of their number—dense, driving, and multitudinous. Such were they, and such were the snow-showers. But they were more than dense, driving, and multitudinous, which the snow-showers were not, for they were gleaming helmets, and embossed shields, and strong cuirasses, and ashen spears. Something very different from snow-showers even when "they outfly from Jove, cold from the impulse of the frosty-air-producing Boreas." The snow-showers, then, have done their duty, and are gone ; but "the lustre heavenward ascended, and the earth all around laughed with the lightning of brass." That is an image, not of the snow, but of the sun ; no, not of the sun, but of the sunlike earth laughing in brazen light, somewhat like the appearance Milton afterwards saw it assume, when "the field all iron cast a gleamy brown." Hitherto we have the dense, the driving, the multitudinous, the heaven-

ascending-lustrous, and the earth-laughing-brazen-lightning.
What more would ye have? Thunder. Hark! there it is!
"a hollow sound started up from under the trampling of
heroes." Of heroes? Ay, and in the midst of them—Achilles!
grinding his teeth, with eyes that rolled glowing like a flash
of fire—raving against the Trojans—"arming for battle."
He dons the gifts divine, which the artist Vulcan had made
for him, and Thetis had brought, flinging them down before
his feet, while the clash scared the heroes.

Well, stop here—draw your breath—and criticise Chapman.
He gives the snow-storm—for it was nothing less—as a snow-
storm should be given, and eke its counterpart.

"And as from air the frosty north-wind blows a cold thick sleet,
    That dazzles eyes, flakes after flakes incessantly descending,
    So thick helms, curets, ashen darts, and round shields never-
        ending,
    Flow'd from the navy's hollow womb."

Admirable! Then comes the lightning and then the thunder,
and then, "in midst of all, divine Achilles." Now, we call
this Homeric.

Look on Achilles "arming for battle"—armed. His act
is now to lift up his shield. Like what? "Its refulgence
spread far and wide like the moon." Like what else? "A
fire blazing aloft from the mountains in a shepherd's solitude
to mariners far at sea." Even so, if you believe Homer, "the
gleam mounted heavenward from Achilles' shield, beautiful,
Dædalean!" The shield is like the moon, and it is also like
a mountain-fire. Like what his helmet? "His mighty helmet uplifting on his head he placed—like a star. Like a star
shone the horse-hair-crested helmet ; for there waved around
him the hair with which, in great profusion, Vulcan had sur-
mounted the crest."

How then shines moon, mountain-fire, and star in an English
sky? Chapman says, "His shield, that cast a brightness
from it like the moon." Good. "Such a fire from his bright
shield extends *its ominous radiance.*" Better. "His crested
helmet, grave and high, had next triumphant place on his
curled head ; and like a star, it cast a spurry ray, about which
a bright thicken'd bush of golden hair did play, which Vulcan
forged him for his plume." Best. But good, better, and best,
are yet all inferior to Homer.

Thus armed for battle, how acts Achilles? Rushes he in among the routed ranks?—" The godlike Achilles essayed himself in his armour, whether it might fit him, and if his fair limbs should move easily ; to him it was like wings, and they buoyed up the shepherd of the people."

How does Chapman here manage the grace and the grandeur? Indifferently well, my lord ; but the last line is noble,—" That from the earth the princely captain they took up to air."

But Achilles unsheathed his paternal spear—and Chapman saw him do so—even as Homer, and " fatal 'twas to great-soul'd men "—" death to heroes."

Thou and we, gentle reader, and Chapman, are all full of the spirit of Homer. Pray, was Pope? Not he, indeed ;—the second line of the first simile shows he was shallow—" And like a deluge pour'd upon the plain." A deluge! with a snow-storm at the instant driving in his eyes. This is murder in cold blood, and deserves death. " And scatter o'er the fields the driving snow." No—no—no. That gives the idea of snow-drifts. In Homer, the heroes are flakes, as we have seen—dense, driving, multitudinous, as they outfly from Jove. " From dusky clouds the fleecy winter flies." Fleecy winter ! How like a sheep. " Whose dazzling lustre whitens all the skies." Nothing to the purpose. But cease criticism ; nor squander it in vain on such misery. All appearance of the original is lost ; and in its place nothing but contradiction and inconsistency, inconceivable by the imagination, and impossible in nature. Then, what wretched writing !—" Pour'd upon the plain,"—" scatter o'er the fields,"—" whitens all the skies,"—" brighten all the fields,"—" flame the skies,"—and " laugh the fields," all huddled and hubbubbed together into one chaotic sentence.

And how could a great poet, like Pope, write so poorly thus? Because he lived in a town—in a village—in a grotto —in a brown study—and never was in a snow-storm in his life—except perhaps in a close carriage. But Homer had been in the heart of a thousand, on the sea-shore and on the mountain-tops. So have we.

Having got the snow out of his eyes, Pope beholds Achilles, and he becomes himself again, though not Homer, in describing the hero. All goes on well till the moon rises, and then

ho again loses his eyesight, The moon does not "blaze with
long rays." Homer says, "the refulgence of the shield spread
far and wide, like that of the moon." So it did. The lines
that follow about the lonely watch-tower are beautiful; but
nobody, in reading them by themselves, could think they
were from the Iliad. It fares still worse with the star. It
makes one sick to look at it. 'Tis a patchwork star—and we
see in it a bit of a comet. "The chief beholds himself with
wondering eyes," is little short of ludicrous—and "feels a
pinion lifting every limb," excessively pretty. Yet, false and
feeble as is the whole passage, and laden with all kinds of
vices, splendid and mean, we must lay our account with being
abused for abusing it, and with being asked, "Could you, Christopher, write a better?"—a question which, as Dr Johnson
suggested, might be triumphantly put to the greatest of
kings on the subject of shoes, by the most contemptible of
cobblers.

It is seldom we have to find fault with Cowper—but ho
should not have said, "So smiled the fields." It destroys
the picture. "The champaign laughed with beaming brass
illumed," is Homeric and Miltonic. But it would seem as if
the fields first smiled and then laughed—a conceit alien from
the manner of Melesigenes. "Up went the flash to heaven,"
is glorious; but, "and tramplings of the warriors on all sides
resounded," is surely rather weak beside our "and a hollow
sound started up from under the trampling of heroes." "Luminous as the moon" is fine—so is the "distant top of some
lone hill"—so is "shook its curling crest of bushy gold"—
and so, especially so, is "they buoyant proved as wings, and
high upbore his airy tread." It almost transcends Homer.

Sotheby is almost on the same level with Cowper. Ho
commits the same error (as we think) in directing our eyes to
the "blaze of the hauberks," and "of the lances to the sun
upraised," when he should have had his own (like Homer's)
fixed—if not exclusively (that was impossible)—chiefly on
the density and driving of the snow-shower. Be that as it
may, assuredly "as flakes on flakes, thick-falling, nature
veil," is as tame as tame can be; whereas the line ought to
have been as wild as wild might be, as it is in Homer.
"Nature" is here used in a sense unknown to the Ionian.
"All the earth resplendent laugh'd with light" is admirable.

" And the wide plain with march of myriads reel'd" is too
good to be objected to, though not quite true to the original,
as you may see by glancing again over our prose. " Stream'd
from his eyes *like flame* the *living fire*" is not to our taste.
Fire is like flame, unquestionably; so very like, that we should
not think of saying so—unless put to it for a similitude.
" While on his limbs he clasp'd the armour of the god" is
sonorous, simple, and stately, and well prepares us for the
details of the Arming—all of which are given with great
power and truth. Nothing can excel the grace and grandeur
that Sotheby has given to the star-crested helmet. He is also
very successful in Achilles essaying himself in his new arms.
" They lifted up his limbs like wings on flight,"—how superior in its simplicity that line to Pope's—" And feels a pinion
lifting every limb."

> " Then from the case, wherein *its* terror lay,
> The chief *brought forth* his father's lance *to-day*,"

we cannot away with, as say the Cockneys. We prefer our
own, "from the sheath his paternal lance he drew." "Brought
forth " sounds slow and sluggish; and " to-day " seems to be
used for " that instant "—which is new to us in the northern
part of the island. But the whole sentence is unsatisfactory
in its clumsiness, running thus: " Then Achilles brought
forth his father's lance to-day, from the case wherein lay its
terror," so Sotheby. " From the sheath his paternal spear he
drew," so North. Ἐκ δ' ἄρα σύριγγος πατρώϊον ἐσπάσατ' ἔγχος, so
Homer. " The ash that Chiron gave." To whom? Peleus.
It would seem here to Achilles. These, and other flaws, or
rather specks, that might be mentioned, are slight—and, if
wiped off, Sotheby's version would, we verily believe, be the
best of the four.

But Achilles has not yet mounted to the meridian—not yet
complete is the climax. Automedon and Alcimus have prepared the car and the coursers—and armed complete Achilles
ascends, " as the orient sun all dazzling."

There he stands—and to whom does he speak? To Xanthus and Balius, of Podarge's strain, about to bear him like a
whirlwind " against the bosom of the Prince of Troy."
"Abandon not me—your master now—in battle, as you aban-
doned Patroclus." Low hanging his head, and sweeping

with his mane the ground, Xanthus, paragon of steeds, made
vocal by Juno, replies—"This day we shall bear thee, stormy
chief, safe from the battle ! But thy death-day is near, not
by fault of ours, but by Jove and fate. Not through our
slowness or sloth did the Trojans strip Patroclus of his arms ;
but He, of heavenly powers the most illustrious, offspring of
the bright-haired Latona, slew him in the van, and gave the
glory to Hector. Swiftest though he be of all the Winds, we
Zephyrus could equal in speed of flight—but doomed art
thou to fall, Achilles ! by mortal and by immortal hands."

> "Then ceased for ever, by the Furies tied
> His fateful voice—the intrepid Chief replied,
> With unabated rage—'So let it be !
> Portents and prodigies are lost on me.
> I know my fate ; to die—to see no more
> My much-loved parents and my native shore—
> Enough ; when heaven ordains I sink in night—
> Now perish Troy !' He said, and rush'd to fight."

These lines, you know, are Pope's, which we almost agree
with Beattie in thinking " equal, if not superior, to the original." They are wonderfully full of force and fire.

That Xanthus, a horse, should have not only spoken so well,
but at all, has set all the wide-mouthed critics agape, who,
on recovering their own powers of articulate utterance, have
argued that it is very unnatural. In answer to them, "Spondanus and Dacier," says Pope, "fail not to bring up Balaam's
ass," which is hardly a case in point. Livy makes mention
of two oxen that spoke on different occasions, and recites the
speech of one, which was " Roma, cave tibi ; " and Pliny tells
us, that these animals were particularly gifted that way—
" Est frequens in prodigiis priscorum bovem locutum." In
modern times we ourselves know a stot that has spoken, and
Leibnitz heard a dog soliloquise, somewhat after the style of
Coleridge, or Madame de Staël, we think at Amsterdam.
Bronte could do everything but speak—and therefore we
acquit Homer of any unphilosophical credulity in believing
that Xanthus was a powerful extemporaneous orator, and, like
a Fox, shone in a reply.

Farther, is there anything absurd, think ye, in Achilles
upbraiding his horses for having left the body of Patroclus ?
We may be assured, says Cowper, that it was customary for

the Greeks occasionally to harangue their horses, for Homer was a poet too attentive to nature to introduce speeches that would have appeared strange to his countrymen. Hector addresses his horses in the Eighth Book—and Antilochus, in the chariot-race, whose horses were not only of terrestrial origin, but the slowest in the camp of Greece. That Achilles, then, should have spoken to his steeds, is not surprising, seeing that they were of celestial seed.

Farther, there is no saying what a man will say or do, when in a state of extraordinary excitement—in a tremendous passion. He will even, in certain circumstances, "sing psalms to a dead horse." Achilles then stands acquitted of all folly —and his address was right. That being the case, on what principle of feeling, passion, discipline, or manners, were his horses to preserve silence, on such an appeal? Silence would have shown sulkiness—and sulkiness a cross in the breed—a taint in the blood—but they were twin-cast by Podarge, the famous Harpy mare, their Sire the Wind. Xanthus, therefore, "rose to reply," without waiting to "catch the speaker's eye;" he became "the gentleman on his legs;"—without "asking permission" "he explained;"—"our gallant friend—if he will allow us to call him so," has unjustly accused us of forsaking Patroclus;—and that the defence of Xanthus was most triumphant, the whole Greek army testified by a "Hear! hear! hear!" that startled Neptune, Juno, and Jupiter on their Thrones.

Xanthus—and Balius too—was not only one of the most eloquent, but most amiable of horses. What were their feelings on the death of Patroclus?

> "Meantime the horses of Eacides,
> From fight withdrawn, *when once they understood*
> Their charioteer outstretch'd in dust beneath
> The arm of homicidal Hector, *wept.*"

"It adds a great beauty," says Eustathius, "to the poem, when inanimate things act like animate. Thus the heavens tremble at Jupiter's nod, the sea parts itself to receive Neptune, the groves of Ida shake beneath Juno's feet. As also to find animate or brute creatures addressed as if rational. Here they weep for Patroclus, and stand fixed and immovable with grief—then is the hero universally mourn'd, and everything concurs to lament his loss." As to the particular fiction of

weeping (no fiction at all) Gilbert Wakefield rightly says, that
it is countenanced both by scholiasts and historians. Aristotle
and Pliny write that these animals often deplore their masters
lost in battle, and even shed tears for them—and Elian relates the same of elephants, who, like the Swiss, overcome
with the *maladie du pays*, weep in far-off captivity to think of
their native forests. Suetonius, in the *Life of Cæsar*, tells us
that several horses which, at the passage of the Rubicon, had
been consecrated to Mars, and turned loose on the banks, were
observed for some days after to abstain from feeding, and to
weep abundantly. Virgil knew all this—and could not, therefore, forbear copying this beautiful circumstance in these fine
lines on the Horse of Pallas :—

> " Post Bellator equus, positis insignibus Æthon
>   It lacrymans, guttisque humectat grandibus ora."

And Southey knew all this well—when he praised those
pathetic lines in the old ballad—at which cold critics could
not choose but laugh—speaking of a wretched worn-out
drudge-mare dying by the ditch-side—" tears were in her
eyes—she looked me in the face." And Scott knew all
this well, when he speaks of horses *shrieking* as well as weeping; and Bloomfield knew all this well, else he could not
have written his full and particular account of the miseries
of the Post-chaise hack; and the author of the *High-mettled
Racer* knew all this well, though he does not mention it—
else he could not have written that elegiac song; and Mr
Martin, the Member for Galway, knew all this well, else he
had not lugged up so many miscreants to Bow Street for
unmercifully abusing their cattle ; and we know all this well,
and much more, else had we not now into this episode run
off the course of our Critique. Let all merciful men, then,
be merciful to their beasts—horses and dogs, " and the
rest;" but let all men remember, that muscle and motion,
speed and strength, bone and bottom, are the characteristic
peculiarities of the " noblest of animals," and that the horse
is in his glory when in the fulness of his might he is running for the gold cup at Derby, or the brown brush at
Melton Mowbray, or crying among his enemies, Ha! Ha! in
a charge on the cuirassiers at Waterloo.

But look at the horses of Achilles in Homer, when Patroclus dies. What a picture!

> " Them oft with hasty lash Diores' son,
> Automedon, assail'd ; with gentle speech
> Address'd them oft ; oft threaten'd them aloud ;
> But neither homeward, to the ships that lined
> The sounding shore, nor to the Grecian host
> Would they return, *but motionless alike*
> *Stand both, as stands the column of a tomb,*
> *Some Chief's or Matron's ; bowing down their heads,*
> *They ceased not to deplore, with many a tear,*
> *Whom they had lost, and each his glossy mane,*
> *Dishevelled now, polluted in the dust."*

And would ye have such horses—*not to speak*, when upbraided by Achilles for having forsaken that Patroclus, for whom they had thus wept and mourned ?

What would all such people be at ? Is not the whole Iliad, in conception and execution, full of *speciosa miracula?* In reading it, we can believe anything, for we feel that all those fictions are truths. All those bold and bright beliefs burst in upon us—not through chinks—but the wide-flung open windows of our souls—and we know that this world of ours and this life, now so tame and terrorless, so chilled by civilisation, was once glorious in what we vainly call barbarism—and that it is yet " mightier than it seems," in the eyes and ears of all who have had their spiritual senses purged, and vivified, and invigorated by the divine power of Song.

But we fear that we are getting not a little extravagant— so let us calm our enthusiasm by a passage on this passage, from that beautiful *Essay on Poetry and Music*, by Beattie, the best critic (the present company excepted) that has yet been produced by Scotland.

" The incident is marvellous, no doubt, and has been generally condemned even by the admirers of Homer; yet to me, who am no believer in the infallibility of the great poet [We are, C. N.], seems not only allowable, but useful and important. That this miracle has probability enough to warrant its admission into Homer's poetry, is fully proved by——[in Beattie it is " Madame Dacier ;" but " oh no ! we never mention her."] But neither —— nor any other of the commentators (so far as I know), has taken notice of the propriety of introducing it in

this place, nor of its utility in raising our idea of the hero.
Patroclus was now slain ; and Achilles, forgetting the injury
he had received from Agamemnon, and frantic with revenge
and sorrow, was rushing to the battle, to satiate his fury upon
Hector and the Trojans.   This was the critical moment on
which his future destiny depended.   It was still in his power
to retire, and to go home in peace to his beloved father and
native land, with the certain prospect of a long and happy,
though inglorious life ; if he went forward to the battle, he
might avenge his friend's death upon the enemy, but his own
must inevitably happen soon after.   This was the decree of
fate concerning him, as he well knew ; but it would not be
wonderful if such an impetuous spirit should forget all this,
during the present paroxysm of his grief and rage.   His horse,
therefore, miraculously gifted by Juno for that purpose, after
expressing in dumb show the deepest concern for his lord,
opens his mouth, and in human speech announces his approaching fate.   The fear of death, and the fear of prodigies, are
different things ; and a brave man, though proof against the
one, may yet be overcome by the other.   'I have known a
soldier,' says Addison, 'that has entered a trench, affrighted
at his own shadow, and look pale upon a little scratching at
his door, who the day before had marched up against a battery of
cannon.'   But Achilles, of whom we already knew that he feared
nothing human, now shows, what we had not as yet been
informed of, and what must therefore heighten our idea of his
fortitude, that he is not so terrified or moved, by the view of
certain destruction, or even by the most alarming prodigies."

Now that we call criticism ; nor does it derogate from
Beattie's merit that he shares it with Pope, whose version, so
justly praised by the Minstrel, suggested the fine and profound remark.   In the original, we hear a prodigy ; but Homer
does not call it one : it is Pope who, feeling the power of the
inspiration, flings forth exultingly that fearless defiance from
the mouth of Achilles, " portents and prodigies are lost on me "
—and here Homer has found an impassioned translator and a
congenial critic.

Finally, that greatest of philosophical writers, Aristotle, in
his " Poetic," says that it is from Homer principally that other
poets have learned the art of *feigning well*.   The poet should
prefer *impossibilities* which *appear probable*, to such things as,

though possible, appear *improbable*. He profoundly observes, "that *supposing* a thing to be, it would certainly be followed by such effects—if we see those *effects*, we are disposed to infer the existence of that *cause*." And thus in poetry and all fiction, "this," says Twining, "is the *logic* of that temporary imposition on which depends our pleasure. Everything follows so naturally, and even, as it seems, so necessarily, that the probability and truth of nature, in the *consequences*, steals, in a manner, from our view, even in the *impossibility* of the *cause*, and flings an air of truth over the whole. With respect to *fact*, indeed, it is all equally ψεῦδος; for if the cause exist not, neither can the *effects*. But the *consequent lies* are so told as to impose on us, for a moment, the belief of the *antecedent*, or *fundamental lie*"—in this case the speech of a horse made vocal. Twining goes on to say, that of this art, almost all the *speciosa miracula* of Homer are instances—and even the wilder and more absurd miracles of Ariosto, whose poem is indeed a striking example of the most improbable, and in themselves revolting *lies*, to which, however, every poetical reader willingly throws open his imagination, principally from the easy charm of his language and versification, and the remarkable distinctness of his painting, but partly, too, from the truth of *nature*, which he has contrived to fling into the detail of his description. And he ends with pointing to the Caliban of Shakespeare.

Last of all, so enveloped in ominous glory is Achilles in that divine armour, on his chariot yoked to heaven-sprung steeds, "like the orient sun all dazzling;" and such the superhuman power of passion by which, heaven-inspired, he is possessed, that he is already before our imagination a prodigious being; and nothing he can say or do, and nothing he can cause be said or done—"all might being given him in that dreadful hour"—can surprise or astonish our belief, or even seem at the moment to be against the laws of nature, that bend and break before his will, and bring, like his ministering servants, fuel to the fire, that at once consumes and sublimes the transcendent hero.

And now that Achilles has taken the field, not idle must be the gods. And Jupiter commissions Themis to call the heavenly powers to council. "Why are we summoned?" asks Neptune; and Jove replies,—

" Myself shall, on Olympus' top reclined,
Well pleased, survey them ; but let all beside,
Descending to the field, then join and aid
As each shall choose, the Trojans, or the Greeks ;
For should Achilles, though alone, assail
The unassisted Trojans, he would drive
At once to flight their whole collected power.
His looks appall'd them ever, and I fear,
Lest, frantic for his loss, he even pass
The bounds of Fate, and desolate the town."

Juno, Pallas, the sovereign lord of Ocean, Hermes, and Vulcan, " rolling on all sides his eyes, but on limping feet and
legs unequal," seek the fleet ; Mars, and Phœbus never-shorn,
and Diana shaft-armed, and Xanthus (so called in heaven, on
earth Scamander), Latona and the Queen of Smiles, repair to
the Trojans, and all because of Achilles. The knees of all
the Trojans shook as they beheld him in the field again, till
Pallas from the trench beyond the wall, and Mars from the
lofty tower of Ilium, shouted to each other, and then both
armies burned for battle. Meanwhile Jove thundered—Neptune shook the earth and the high mountains—and upstarted
from his throne appalled the King of Erebus, and all because
of—Achilles.

He has no eyes but for Hector. But Phœbus Apollo in-
cites Æneas to engage him—the son he of Venus, daughter
of Jove,—Achilles, but of the daughter of the deep. But
Apollo forgot that Achilles had been the son of Jove himself,
had not the Thunderer paused in pursuit of Thetis, at the prophetic warning that the son of Thetis would be greater than
his sire. Æneas fight Achilles ! Whew !

" Thee have I chased already with my spear ;
Canst thou forget that, finding thee of late
Alone on Ida, with such hasty flight
I drove thee down, that, all thy cattle left,
Thou never dared'st once look me in the face
Till thou hadst reach'd Lyrnessus, with whose spoils
Enrich'd by Jove and Pallas, I return'd,
And led their women captive ? Thee, indeed, the gods
Preserved, but will not, as thou dream'st,
Now also. BACK INTO THY HOST—
HENCE I COMMAND THEE, nor oppose in fight
Achilles."

Æneas makes a long speech and a shortish battle; and then Neptune, lifting him high from the ground, "heaved him far remote." "Fight on, my friends," cried Achilles,

"With hands, with feet, with spirit, and with might,
All that I can I will; right through I go,
And not a Trojan who shall chance within
Spear's reach of me, shall, as a judge, rejoice."

Lo! Hector fronts the Destroyer! But Phœbus is at hand to admonish him, and he retires into the thick of the fight. Defrauded of him, Achilles slays and insults Iphition—and down with Demoleon. Miserably through Polydorus he drives his spear, and Hector again leaps out from the melée. Apollo snatches him away, wrapt round with thickest gloom, and,

"Thrice swift Achilles sprang to the assault,
Impetuous, thrice the pallid cloud he smote,
And at his fourth assault, godlike in act,
And terrible in utterance, thus exclaimed,
'Dog, thou art safe, and hast escaped again!'"

So saying, he pierced the neck of Dryops—turned on huge Demuchus, and piercing him with his spear, slew him with his sword. Laogonus and Dardanus then dismounting, the one he killed with his spear, "the other with his falchion at a blow." Then through ear to ear he thrusts the pointed brass through the occiput of Mulius, and drives his huge-hafted blade through the forehead of Echechlus, son of Agenor: but not till he had slaughtered Alastor, smiting the stripling through the side. Away at one blow went the head and casque of Deucalion. Rhigmus he put to death, pierced through the loins, with the beam fixed in his bowels; and right through the spine he struck Areïthoüs the flying charioteer, and then thus seemed the battle-field :—

CowPER.

"As a devouring fire within the glens
Of some dry mountain ravages the trees,
While, blown around, the flames roll to all sides,
So, on all sides, tremendous as a God,
Achilles drove the death-devoted host
Of Ilium, and the champaign ran with blood.
As when the peasant his yoked steers employs
To tread his barley, the broad-fronted pair

With wond'rous hoofs soon triturate the grain,
So bearing terrible Achilles on,
His coursers stamp'd together, as they pass'd
The bodies and the bucklers of the slain ;
Blood spatter'd all his axle, and with blood
From the horse-hoofs and from the fellied wheels
His chariot redden'd, while himself, athirst
For glory, his unconquerable hands
Defiled with mingled carnage, sweat, and dust."

And now, having separated the Trojans, he drives one part of
them to the city, and the other into the Scamander, all whose
sounding course is glutted with the mangled throng of horses
and warriors. Leaning his spear against a tamarisk tree,
sword in hand he plunges into the river, now redder and
redder, hewing them to pieces, while the terrified Trojans
secrete themselves, like the smaller fishes in the creeks and
secret hollows of a haven, flying the pursuit of some huge
dolphin. Wearied at length with slaughter, he selects twelve
death-doomed youths, in vengeance "for his loved Patroclus
slain," and driving them forth from the river stupified like
fawns, and manacling their hands fast behind them with their
own lance-strings, gives them in charge to his Myrmidons to
keep for the sacrifice. Suddenly he sees Lycaon, one of the
sons of Priam, whom he had surprised in the fields by night,
and sent in a ship to Lesbos. "Ha, ye gods! a miracle!
Talk not to me of ransoms." Then slaying him, he spins him
into the flood for food to fishes, who shall find "Lycaon's
pampered flesh delicious fare!" Asteropæus grazes his
hand with a spear, but dies.

"Lie there! The mightiest who from rivers spring,
Quell not with ease the mightier sons of Jove.
Thou thy descent from Axius made thy boast,
But Jove himself I boast the source of mine."

Then sent he to the shades the souls of Thersilochus, and
Mydon, and Thrasius, and Astypylus, and Ophelestes, and
Ænius, and Mnesus—nor had these sufficed, but in semblance
of a man stood before him the incensed river, Xanthus himself,
the Scamander, and they too, after angry parle, engage in
combat.

Would we could quote the combat! Achilles prevails, and
Scamander calls upon Simois.

" Thy channel fill with streams
From all thy fountains ; call thy torrents down ;
Lift high the waters ; mingle the hard stones
With uproar wild ; that the enormous force
Of this man, now triumphant, and who aims
To match the gods in might, may be subdued.
But vain shall be his strength ! his beauty nought
Shall profit him, or his resplendent arms ;
But I will bury him in slime and ooze.
And I will overwhelm himself with soil,
Sands heaping o'er him, and around him sands
Infinite, that no Greek shall find his bones
For ever, in my bottom deep-immersed.
There shall his tomb be piled, nor other earth,
At his last rites, his friends shall need for him."

But, at Juno's voice, comes Vulcan, burning up the dead,
willows, tamarisks, elms, lotus, rushes, reeds, and " all plants
and herbs that clothed profuse the margin of the flood," and
Xanthus' self is in dread of extinction. " I yield to thy consuming fires—cease—cease—I reck not if Achilles drive her
citizens this moment forth from Troy." " So spake he
scorch'd, and all his waters boil'd." And now all the gods
and goddesses engage in conflict,

" While the boundless earth
Quaked under them, and all around the Heavens
Sang them together with a trumpet's voice ;
Jove listening on the Olympian mountain sat,
Well pleased, and laughing in his heart for joy."

Another time, perhaps, we may poetise and philosophise
after our own fashion upon this wonderful Twenty-first Book
of the Iliad—the Combat of the Celestials. But again,

" Like a glory from afar,
Like a reappearing star,
First to head the flock of war."

Achilles ! Say with Homer—as when the columned smoke
reaches the wide sky, ascending from some city god-fired in
vengeance, " toil to all, to many misery." Priam beholds
from a sacred tower the giant driving the army, and mournful
cries,

" Hold wide the portals till the flying host
Re-enter—for Achilles is at hand,

And hunts the people home.   Now—woe to Troy !
But soon as safe within the city walls
They breathe again, shut fast the ponderous gates
At once, lest that destroyer too rush in."

Shooting back the bars, then wide open flung they the city
gates, and the opening was salvation—while Apollo sallied
to strike back ruin.   Right towards the city and the lofty
wall flew the whole host, " parched with drought, and
whiten'd all with dust," while Achilles, spear in hand, " on
their shoulders rode," for rabid was his heart, and he raged
in the lust of glory.   Then, but for Agenor, by Apollo roused
to face that fury, and by Apollo saved from death, had fallen
haughty Ilium.   But Phœbus, from the chase of Ilium's host,
by art has seduced Achilles away in far pursuit of the semblance of Antenor's son.

NORTH.

" Meanwhile the other Trojans through-terror-fleeing came in a body
Eagerly to the city ; but the city was-being-fill'd with those who
     had rush'd towards (it).
Nor truly durst they (while) beyond the city and the wall
Remain there for one another, and to ascertain who might have
     escaped
And who had died in the fight : but eagerly crowded they
Into the city (each), whomsoever his feet and his knees had saved."

CHAPMAN.

          " In mean time, the other frighted powers
Came to the city, comforted, when Troy and all her towers
Strootted with fillers ; none would stand, to see who staid without,
Who 'scaped and who came short ; the ports cleft to receive the rout,
That pour'd itself in.   Every man was for himself ; most fleet
Most fortunate ; whoever 'scapt—*his head might thank his feet.*"

POPE.

" While all the flying troops their speed employ,
And pour on heaps into the walls of Troy ;
No stop, no stay ; no thought to ask or tell
Who 'scaped by flight, or who by battle fell.
'Twas tumult all, and violence of flight ;
And sudden joy confused, and mix'd affright.
Pale Troy against Achilles shut her gate,
And nations breathed, deliver'd from their fate."

COWPER.

"The Trojan host
Meantime, impatient to regain the town,
Tumultuous fled, and entering, closed the gates.
None halted to descry, without the walls
Who yet survived, or had in battle fallen ;
But all, whom flight had saved, with eager haste
Pour'd through the pass, and crowded into Troy."

SOTHEBY.

"Meantime the rest,
Crowd urging crowd, through Troy's throng'd portals press'd ;
None paused to ask who 'scaped, or swell'd the slain,
But all, whoe'er had strength, in fearful joy
Rush'd like a flood, once more to breathe in Troy."

Homer means merely to give the liveliest picture of rout, confusion, and fear; and of fear—the blind and utter selfishness. All alike regardless of each other, and, for the time, cowards all, into the town they rush *helter-skelter, pell-mell.* He had no thought of making the picture a grand one ; and though the words are strong as strong can be, and go hurrying and staggering along, there is no magniloquence. Chapman saw and felt this ; and in his heart arose such scorn and contempt for the fugitives, that he gave expression to the bitterness, and closes purposely with a line almost ludicrous. We cannot find much fault with him for doing so ; though we suspect he supposed—mistakenly—that something of the same sort was intended by Homer in " ὅν τινα τῶν γε πόδες καὶ γοῦνα σάωσαι." He seems to have thought these words almost equivalent with "as fast as their legs could carry them." And if Homer had said so, we really should not have objected to it. " The ports cleft to receive the rout that pour'd itself in," is a picturesque and powerful paraphrase, and it is Homeric.

The first four lines of Pope are admirable. The next two are in themselves good, but they are unnecessary, and had been better away—all but the "sudden joy confused," which is, though free, yet not an untrue version of ἀσπασίω. The last two lines are exceedingly sonorous, and mighty magnificent, no doubt, but they are needless supernumeraries, and, especially the concluding one, unlike Homer's usual style,

and most alien from the spirit of this particular passage—and
that nobody can deny.

Neither is Cowper's version—though vigorous—all right.
"Impatient" is a poor tame word for ἀσπάσιοι; and "entering closed the gates," poorer and tamer still for ·πόλις δ'
ἔμπλητο ἀλέντων — which is indeed "the perfection of energetic brevity." "With eager haste" has the same fault—
tameness ; but all the rest is good—though the whole description, thus weakened, wants tumult and terror. It is not
forceful.

Sotheby, perhaps, is the most successful. But what word
in his version is equal to περςοβημένοι? "Pause" is not,
to our ears, good for μεῖαι ; and "who swell'd the slain,"
to our ears—they may be fastidious--is bad for "who had
fallen in battle." The last two lines are good ; yet "fearful
joy" we doubt being Homeric ; and ἐσίχυιτο, "are pour'd in,"
is better than "rush'd like a flood," for it implies the flood,
and saves a simile, which Homer in the hurry had no leisure
for ; he writes as if he himself had narrowly escaped being
trampled to death, or jammed up flat against post or pillar.

But Achilles has one more fight before him, ere he be at
"the top of the tree," and wear the baldrick of the
Champion :

"In somnis ecce ante oculos mœstissimus Hector
Visus adesse mihi ! "

But on that combat, and on the character of Achilles—
when he shall stand before us a full-length portrait—as yet
he is but kit-cat—we shall ere long enter into colloquy with
thee, heroic reader ; till then farewell to Homer, and
his four illustrious friends—Chapman, Pope, Cowper, and
Sotheby.

HOMER AND HIS TRANSLATORS.

[FEBRUARY 1832.]

ONE man has put to rout a whole army, and filled a city with fugitives—and is not that Bombast? No ; it is sublimity—for that one man is Achilles—that city is Troy ; and the poet of the Fear and Flight is Homer. Not in all poetry is there such another continuous blaze of inspiration as that which wraps the Iliad from the hour when Achilles is told of the death of Patroclus to that when he falls asleep,—"revenge and all ferocious thoughts," dead within him, in the bosom of Briseïs. We have been in the very heart of that blaze—we are in it still—and we shall abide in it, till, with the ransomed corpse of his beloved son, we behold Priam returning in his car to Troy from the Tent of the Destroyer.

The city gates are shut—and within, reclining against the battlements, the Trojans, who had "been driven like hunted fawns into the town," are slaking their fiery thirst with drink; while you may behold the Grecians, "beneath one roof of well-compacted shields," advancing towards the walls. But you forget all within and all without the walls—your eyes overlook them as things of no worth—for, lo! standing exposed before the Scæan gate—Hector! and in the immediate neighbourhood of—Achilles!

And why tarry the feet of the son of Thetis? Why kills he not, at that moment, the murderer of his Menœtiades? Because he is parleying with Apollo. "Achilles! mortal thyself, why pursuest thou me immortal?" "Of all the Supernals! to me most adverse, Archer of the skies! Thou hast defrauded me of great renown—and would that on thee —sun-god as thou art—I might have my revenge!"

"Thus saying (Achilles), with haughty thoughts, went towards the city,
Rushing like a prize-winning horse along with the chariot,
Which (the horse) outstretched runs swiftly over the plain :
So nimbly did Achilles move his feet and his knees.
Him the aged Priam with his eyes first perceived,
Rushing over the plain,—all resplendent, like the star
Which comes forth between the rising of the day-star and Arcturus,
   i. e. (at the departure of summer) : but most brilliant do its beams
Shine amid the multitudinous stars at the milking-time[1] of night,
And which by name they call the Dog of Orion :
Most brilliant it is, but of evil omen,
And much fiery-fever brings to miserable mortals."

CHAPMAN.

      " Thus with elated spirits,
Steed-like, that at Olympus' games wears garlands for his merits,
And rattles home his chariot, extending all his pride,
Achilles so parts with the God.   When aged Priam spied
The great Greek come, sphered round with beams, and showing as
   if the star,
Surnamed Orion's Hound, that springs in autumn, and sends far
His radiance through a world of stars, of all whose beams his own
Cast greatest splendour, the midnight, that renders them most
   shown,
Then being their foil, and in their points cure-passing fevers then
Come shaking down into the joints of miserable men :
As this were fallen to earth, and shot along the field his rays,
Now towards Priam, when he saw in great Eacides,
Out-flew his tender voice in shrieks," &c.

POPE.

" Then to the city, terrible and strong,
  With high and haughty steps he tower'd along.
So the proud courser, victor of the prize,
To the near goal with double ardour flies.
Him, as he blazing shot across the field,
The careful eyes of Priam first beheld.
Not half so dreadful rises to the sight,
Through the thick gloom of some tempestuous night,

---

[1] 'Ἀμολγῷ, milking-time, morning and evening.

Orion's Dog (the year when Autumn weighs),
And o'er the feebler stars exerts his rays ;
Terrific glory ! for his burning breath
Taints the red air with fevers, plagues, and death.
So glow'd his fiery mail."

COWPER.

" So saying, incensed he turn'd towards the town
His rapid course, like some victorious steed,
That whirls, at stretch, a chariot to the goal.
So flew Achilles lightly o'er the field.
Him first the ancient King of Troy perceived,
Scouring the plain, resplendent as the star
Autumnal, of all stars at dead of night
Conspicuous most, and named Orion's Dog.
Brightest it shines, but ominous, and dire
Disease portends to miserable man ;
So beam'd Achilles' armour as he flew."

SOTHEBY.

" Then rush'd to Troy, in fury of his speed :
Thus rushes with his car a conquering steed,
Who, at full stretch, as conscious of his prize,
To the near goal along the level flies :
Thus flew Pelides—him the king perceived,
Him flashing on, first saw, and sorely grieved—
Saw him resplendent, like Orion's star,
Whose beams at autumn, radiant from afar,
'Mid heaven's innumerous host, at dead of night,
Pales all their lustre with surpassing light :
Terrific sign ! whose unremitted blaze
Pours in the fever'd blood its fiery rays :
Thus as th' Avenger rush'd, a dazzling light
Flash'd from Pelides' arms on Priam's sight."

All good. But no time this for criticism. See ! hark !
loud wailing on the battlements the hoary king. What
heart-and-soul-rending beseechings and supplications on his
Hector to shun death ! Hecuba, too, bares before her son,
in sight of all the people, the bosom that gave him nourish-
ment, and implores her hero to cope not with that dreadful
adversary !

" So they with prayers importuned and with tears
Their son, but him sway'd not ; unmoved he stood,
Expecting vast Achilles, now at hand."

For Achilles had seen him, as soon as Apollo disappeared, the
Trojan's guardian-god—and on the instant, like car-whirling
steed victorious near the goal, had shot to the slaughter.
Achilles was like the star Orion.   How looked Hector?

NORTH.

" Nor prevail'd they over the spirit of Hector,
But he awaited the vast (πελώριον) Achilles approaching nearer,
As when a mountainous [1] (*i. e.* savage) serpent at its haunt a man
    awaits,
Fed on baneful poisons, and dread fury enters it,
And hideously it looks, coiling itself around its haunt ;
In like manner, Hector, having confidence unquenchable, with-
    drew not,
But, placing his bright shield against a projecting turret,
His own mighty spirit he address'd."

CHAPMAN.

" And now drew deadly near
Mighty Achilles ; yet he still kept deadly station there.
Look how a dragon, when she sees a traveller bent upon
Her breeding den, her bosom fed with fell contagion,
Gathers her forces, sits him firm, and at his nearest pace
Wraps all her cavern in her folds, and thrusts a horrid face
Out at his entry ; Hector so, with unextinguish'd spirit,
Stood great Achilles, stirr'd no foot, but at the prominent turret
Bent to his bright shield, and resolved to bear fall'n heaven
    upon it."

POPE.

" Resolved he stands, and with a fiery glance
Expects the hero's terrible advance.
So, roll'd up in his den, the swelling snake
Beholds the traveller approach the brake ;
When, fed with noxious herbs, his turgid veins
Have gather'd half the poison of the plains ;
He burns, he stiffens with collected ire,
And his red eyeballs glow with living fire.
Beneath a turret on his shield reclined
He stood, and question'd thus his mighty mind."

COWPER.

" Unmoved he stood,
Expecting vast Achilles now at hand.
As some huge serpent in a cave, that feeds

---

[1] 'Ορέστιος nunc ἄγριος, Heyne.

On baneful drugs, and swells with deadliest ire,
A traveller approaching, coils himself
Around his den, and hideous looks abroad,
So Hector, fill'd with confidence untamed,
Fled not, but placing his bright shield against
A buttress, with his noble heart conferr'd."

SOTHEBY.

" Confiding in his strength, their dauntless son
Survey'd the mighty man, and staid his coming on.
As in his cavern, nigh the wanderer's way,
Gorged with rank herbs, a dragon waits his prey,
And rolling in his wrath the den around,
Eyes when to strike, and watches where to wound ;
Thus, fill'd with unextinguishable fire,
Brave Hector stood, disdaining to retire ;
Against a buttress his bright shield reclined,
And inly communed with his noble mind."

All good. But no time for criticism. For we, too—as if he
were our brother—tremble for Hector ! We feel that his hour
is come. Well may Priam and Hecuba tear their grey locks !
But where is Andromache ? Buried in her palace—that the
thick walls may deaden the horror breathed from the field
where her husband fights. Too sacred a thing was such
sorrow as hers to Homer's soul, to suffer the Bard of Nature
to smite it with such affliction as the sight of *him* alive, and
about to die, under the hands of that inexorable homicide.
He mentions her not ; but all the people thought of her then—
and how many million eyes have since wept for her, unnamed
at that catastrophe ! We remember the parting between her
and her hero—her hopes and her fears—her tears and her
smiles—as their Astyanax hung back alarmed from the
waving crest of his father. At this moment her once prophetic soul has lost its gifted vision—and she is dreaming of
his return !

But how fares it now with the noble Hector ? Not unheard
had been the outcries of his parents—for Hector to them was
pious, as he was to the gods. For their sakes he desired to live
—and think ye that, at that moment, though he names not her
name, that the image of his Andromache came not across him
with Astyanax on her " fragrant bosom" ? But Polydamas
would reproach him, if now he shunned the combat—Poly-

damas, who bade him lead the Trojans back that last calamitous night

"In which Achilles rose to arms again !",

Man and matron—base and brave alike—will dishonour Hector as the cause of all that slaughter—if he slay not or be slain by Achilles. Shall he then seek to parley with the king of the Myrmidons, and offer to restore Helen to the sons of Atreus, and all the treasures Paris brought with her in his fleet to Troy? Perish all such thoughts — let them meet at once in mortal combat, and leave the victory in the hands of Jove! So communed Hector with his own heart; nor can we imagine words more affecting than are Homer's in this place—in the divine skill of Genius, instructed by the nobility of nature. He shows us a hero struggling against fear, and at last overcome—taking to flight, and yet still a hero. Should any one deny it—he may depend upon it that he is himself a coward—and what is worse, a blockhead.

Not so thought Homer — not so thought the immortal gods. They saw Hector flying before Achilles — as flies a dove before a hawk — a fawn before a hound, " as trembling she skulks among the shrubs " — and yet they despised him not — but they pitied the hero. The sire of gods exclaimed,—

> " Ah ! I behold a warrior dear to me
> Around the walls of Ilium driven, and grieve
> For Hector ! who the thighs of fatted bulls
> On yonder heights of Ida many-valed
> Burn'd oft to me, and in the heights of Troy.
> But him Achilles, glorious chief, around
> The city walls of Priam now pursues.
> Think then, ye gods, delay not to decide ;
> Shall we preserve, or leave him now to fall,
> Brave as he is, by Peleus' mighty son ?"

But we are hurried away by our scorn of hypocrisy ;—look at Achilles ere Hector flies, and then at the Flight and the Pursuit, all of which you must be contented with in our prose— for we have not room always to quote all the great translators.

NORTH.

"These (thoughts) he revolved while tarrying: but near to him
  came Achilles,
Equal to the helm-shaking warrior Mars,
Over his right shoulder brandishing the Pelian spear
Terrible : and around him shone the brass like to the flash
Of blazing fire, or of the rising sun.
Hector, therefore, when he saw (him), trembling seized, nor
  dared he
There remain, but left the gates, and flying went.
The son of Peleus, to his swift feet trusting, rushed after,
Like as a falcon on the mountains, the swiftest of birds,
Darts easily on a trembling dove :
But it flies aslant ; and he near-at-hand shrill screaming,
Rushes frequently, and his appetite impels him to take her :
Thus eagerly indeed did he (Achilles) flee on him directly :
  trembling, fled Hector
Under the walls of the Trojans, and plied his agile limbs.
But they pass'd the prospect-mount and the wind-exposed fig-
  tree,
Out-from-beneath the wall along the chariot road rush'd on :
To the beautiful-flowing fountains they came, where springs
Two (in number) up-rise from the gyrating Scamander.
The one with tepid waters flows, and around a smoke
Arises from it, as from flaming fire.
But the other in summer even out-rushes, like to hail
Or cold snow, or crystallised water (Κρυστάλλῳ.)
There near-by them are broad washing tanks,
Beautiful, of stone, where their gorgeous robes,
The Trojan dames, and their daughters fair, were-wont-to-wash
Erst in time of peace, ere the sons of the Greeks had come."

The moment Homer's imagination recreates Achilles, he
reappears terrible, and more terrible, his figure and his
aspect sublimed by more transcendent imagery, borrowed
from the great phenomena of earth and heaven. Stars,
comets, moon, and sun—and no objects less glorious—are
made to aggrandise the hero of the Iliad ; and yet the same
images are always, in something mighty, when applied to
him *new;* as, indeed, to the eye of a poet, they are always
new, even in themselves—no two sunrises, or sunsets, being
identical to the vision of a "Maker." The Apparition that
puts Hector to flight is the most insupportable of all ; and,
though seen from afar, felt, on its close approach, sudden as

supernatural. More deadly is he, thus opposed, Mars to
mortal, than when the whole army fled before him ;—there is
intenser concentration of terror in his armour, "like lightning,
or like flame, or like the sun ascending." Had Hector not
fled, Homer had nodded when broad awake. The Prince of
Troy would not have fled from Ajax, the son of Telamon,
nor from Diomede, who, when Achilles lay in his wrath among
his ships, was thought equal to Achilles, nor from Agamemnon, king of men. But there was one, in presence of whose
spear no hero might abide—before whom the river-gods themselves quailed, " and hid themselves among their reedy
banks ; " and at close of that combat, in which he shone
brightest even in the midst of the celestials, it was inevitable
in nature, that even the defender of his country should be
appalled. For he was not goddess-born ; bright indeed
were the arms he wore—once worn by Achilles—but what
were they to the Vulcanian panoply, at whose sound, as
Thetis let them fall at her son's feet, fear "bowed the astonished souls " of the Myrmidons? It would have been most
unnatural for man of woman born not to fly. Then, how absorbed is all that might have been in any way degrading in
the emotion inspired by the Destroyer ! Most mournful but
magnificent picture ! King and queen shrieking in their old
age, about to be utterly desolate, from the doomed city walls
that quake to the dreadful voice of that Invincible ! All the
power within silent ; and the gods themselves looking down,
and descending to decide the final issue of the ten years'
strife—for Troy was to fall with Hector, and Ilion to be shorn
of her towery diadem. As for Achilles, he saw not—heard
not Priam and Hecuba—he cared not in his passion even for
the gods. His eyes were all on Hector.

> " The son of Peleus, as he ran, his brows
> Shaking, forbade the Grecians to dismiss
> A dart at Hector, lest a meaner hand
> Should pierce him, and USURP THE FOREMOST PRAISE."

So blent into one in his fiery spirit were Revenge and the Love
of Glory.

Apollo still strove to save his beloved prince ; but now,
balancing his golden scales, Jove placed in each a lot—one
Achilles, and one consigning Hector to the shades.

"Seized by the central hold, he poised the beam ;
Down went the fatal day of Hector, down
To Hades, and Apollo left his side."

The blue-eyed Pallas exultingly cried to Achilles that he should return, "crown'd with great glory, to the fleet of Greece," for that not even could the King of radiant shafts himself now save the life of Hector, not even were Apollo to roll himself in supplication at the feet of the Thunderer. By her deceived, Hector turns and faces Achilles. The heroes seem to our ears to speak well—thus—in our Greek-resembling English,—

" 'Thee no more, son of Peleus, shall I fly as before :
Thrice around Priam's mighty city have I fled, nor ever durst I
Await thy onset ;—but now doth my spirit impel me
To withstand thee—slay I, or be slain.
But come now, call we the gods to testify, for they the best
Witnesses and guardians of covenants shall be.
Not savagely will I dishonour thee, if to me Jupiter
Vouchsafe a steady-fought-victory (καμμονίην), and I shall take
    away thy life :
But when I shall have despoil'd thee of thy illustrious arms,
    Achilles,
Thy corse to the Greeks will I restore : do thou so likewise.'
Him eyeing sternly, the swift-footed Achilles address'd—
'Hector, thou never-to-be-forgotten one, speak not to me of cove-
    nants.
As between lions and men there are no faithful covenants,—
Nor have wolves and lambs a same-thinking disposition,
But perpetually are plotting evil to each other ;
In like manner it cannot be that I and thou can have friendship,
    nor between us
Can covenants exist, until one of us prostrate
Shall satisfy with his blood Mars, the indefatigable warrior.
Call to mind (thy) every-kind of valour : much now it behoves
    thee
To be a combatant, and a doughty warrior.
There is no escape for thee more ; thee forthwith Pallas Minerva
By my spear subdues : now at once shalt thou expiate all
The agonies of my companions—whom with the spear in thy fury
    thou didst slay.' "

The combat—though we *know* it must be fatal to Hector—
is not *felt* to be altogether hopeless on his part, because of the

uplifting of our spirits by the return of his heroism to its
former high pitch, and because of the love and admiration
with which we regard his character, that has sustained no
loss from his god-driven flight thrice round the towers of the
city which his valour was unavailing to save.   There is now
glory accumulated on glory around each illustrious crest.
Hector's has not been " shorn of its beams " by any disgrace.
His flight is more than forgiven ; and we admire him more
now than when he set fire to the fleet.   It has been said that
Homer was partial to Hector.   So are all men.   But believe
us when we say, that his favourite was Achilles.   He in all
things was the greater spirit.   From whom would he have fled ?
Not from Mars and Bellona.   One qualm of fear would have
destroyed that transcendent ideal of unconquerable will.   But
he was invulnerable.   Would that in our boyhood we had
never been confounded by that lie !   He was of all the heroes
who fought before Troy the sole Doom'd Man, yet never knew
he fear within the perpetual shadows of death.   But again
behold Achilles!

NORTH.

" Achilles too rush'd forward, and his soul he fill'd with anger
  Savage, and his breast his shield o'erspread,
  Beautiful, Dædaleau : with his shining helm he nodded
  Four-coned, waved were the beautiful hairs
  Of-gold, which in profusion Vulcan around the crest had placed.
  Such as when among the stars at the milking·time of night comes
      forth the star
  Hesperus,[1] which is placed in the firmament the brightest star ;
  In like manner beam'd (the light) from the well-pointed spear
      which Achilles
  Brandish'd in his right-hand, planning evil to the noble Hector,
  Looking-into his beautiful body, where it might yield (to the spear-
      point) most easily."

CHAPMAN.

" So fell in Hector ; and at him Achilles ; his mind's fare
  Was fierce and mighty ; his shield cast a sunlike radiance ;
  Helm nodded ; and his four plumes shook ; and when he raised
      his lance,
  Up Hesperus rose 'mongst th' evening stars! His bright and
      sparkling eyes
  Look'd through the body of his foe," &c.

---

[1] *Vide* Milton—" Hesperus, that led the starry host," &c.

POPE.

" Nor less Achilles his fierce soul prepares ;
Before his breast the flaming shield he bears,
Refulgent orb ! Above his fourfold cone
The gilded horse-hair sparkled in the sun,
Nodding at every step (Vulcanian frame !)
And as he moved his figure seem'd on flame.
As radiant Hesper shines with keener light,
Far-beaming o'er the silver host of night,
When all the starry train enblaze the sphere :
So shone the point of great Achilles' spear.
In his right hand he waves the weapon round,
Eyes the whole man, and meditates the wound."

COWPER.

" Achilles opposite, with fellest ire,
Full-fraught came on ; his shield, with various art
Divine portray'd, o'erspread his ample chest,
And on his radiant crest terrific waved,
By Vulcan spun, his crest of bushy gold.
Bright as, among the stars, the star of all
Most splendid, Hesperus, at midnight moves,
So in the right hand of Achilles beam'd
His brandish'd spear, while, meditating woe
To Hector, he explored his noble form,.
Seeking where he was vulnerable most."

SOTHEBY.

" Thus Hector rush'd, and as he onward flew,
The Son of Peleus gloried at the view :
Before his breast, with outstretch'd arm upraised,
The shield that brightly in its horror blazed :
And, while his heart boil'd with o'erflowing ire,
Rush'd like the fierceness of consuming fire.
On as th' avenger in his terror trod,
His casque, four-coned, the wonder of the god,
In restless motion round about him roll'd
The fulness of its hairs that blazed with gold.
As Hesper's star, the brightest of the bright,
Outshines heaven's radiant host at dead of night :
Thus, vibrated aloft, the Pelian lance
Shot from its sharpen'd point the lightning glance,
While stern Achilles keenly eyed the foe,
And paused upon the meditated blow."

All the versions are very noble—Chapman's the most so —then perhaps Sotheby's, which is more liberal than usual, but splendid; but take your choice of the four, heroic reader of Homer. Such combat soon comes to a close. The "ashen beam" is driven through his throat—but it takes not from Hector—now lying in the dust—the power of utterance. You must be contented with the colloquy in prose—perhaps it may be felt more touching so than in " numerous verse."

NORTH.

" In the dust, therefore, he fell, and over him gloried the illustrious
    Achilles,—

' Once wert thou wont to think, Hector, when despoiling-the-slain
    Patroclus,

That thou shouldst be safe, and nought stood'st in awe of me when
    absent.

Fool ! I, his avenger, mightier far (than thou) apart,

At the hollow ships was left behind—

And have unnerved thy limbs : *thee*, indeed, the dogs and birds of
    prey

Shall tear unseemly, *him* shall the Greeks bury-with-due-funeral
    rites.'

Him, the waving-plume-helm'd Hector exhausted, address'd,—

' By thy life, by thy knees, and by thy parents—thee I supplicate ;

Let not the dogs of the Greeks at the hollow ships tear-and-devour
    me ;

Brass in abundance, and gold, do thou receive

As gifts, which my father and my venerable mother will give thee ;

But send home my body,—that of a funeral pyre, me,

When dead, the Trojans and Trojan matrons may make a partaker.'

Him, eyeing sternly, the swift-footed Achilles address'd,—

' Dog, me supplicate-not-embracing-my-knees, by my knees, nor by
    my parents.

Would that my rage and fury would by any means permit me

To chop and devour thy raw flesh, for what thou hast done to me.

No—not even if ten or twenty-fold-equally-great ransoms

Were they to bring hither and place (in the balance), and promise
    others besides :

No, were *he* even to counterpoise thy body with gold,

Priam, the son of Dardanus ; not even thus should thy venerable
    mother,

Having placed thee on thy bier, lament him whom she bore ;

But dogs, and birds of prey, shall thoroughly devour thee.'

Him, the waving-plume-helm'd Hector dying, address'd,—

'Knowing thee well, I foresaw, indeed, that never should I
Persuade thee ; assuredly within thee is a spirit of steel.
Beware now, lest towards thee I become the subject-of-anger to
    the gods
On that day, when Paris and Phœbus Apollo, thee,
Brave though thou be, shall destroy in the Scæan gate.'
Him, while thus speaking, the completion of death veil'd ;
And his spirit flying from his limbs to Ades descended,—
Its fate bewailing in having left the robustness and vigour of youth.
Him also, when dead, the illustrious Achilles address'd,—
'Die ! fate will I then receive whenever
Jove may wish to bring it about, and the other immortal gods.'
He said, and from the corpse he drew the brazen spear,
And placed it apart ; and from his (Hector's) shoulders forced
    away his armour,
Blood-stain'd ; around him hasten'd the other sons of the Greeks,
Who gazed-with-wonder on the size and the grand form
Of Hector : nor did any approach without-inflicting-a-wound (on
    the corpse) ;
And each, as he look'd to his neighbour, thus spoke,—
'Ha ! ha ! assuredly much more gentle in being handled
Is Hector, than when he fired the fleet with glowing flames.'
Thus, indeed, spoke each ; and standing near, inflicted wounds."

This is tragical—for it is surcharged with pity and terror.
We weep for the dying Hero, whose last words betray the
anguish of nature, for his own miserable fate even beyond the
sable flood,—for the wretchedness of his father and mother, in
vain longing for his corpse, which is out of the reach of
ransom. There is no savage spirit of revenge in the prophecy
that expires on his lips ; it is almost a passionless predic-
tion of death to one who feared not death—an enunciation of
the will of Heaven about to be executed by a god. It adds to
the greatness of Achilles ; for he was not to fall by the un-
aided arrow of such a person as Paris, but to receive the
winged fate from Phœbus Apollo ; and what moral sublimity
in the answer of " the dreadless angel ! "

"Die Thou the first ! when Jove and Heaven ordain—
    I follow thee, he said, and stripp'd the slain."

And what must we say of the behaviour of the common
soldiers ? Eustathius tells us that Homer introduces them
wounding the dead body of Hector, in order to mitigate the
cruelties which Achilles exercises upon it ; for if every com-

mon soldier takes a pride in giving him a wound, what insults may we not expect from the inexorable inflamed Achilles? Pope, whose notes are almost all good, confesses himself unable to vindicate Homer in giving us such an idea of his countrymen; for what they say over Hector's body is a mean insult, and the stabs they give it are cowardly and barbarous. We cannot deny the truth of Pope's remark. But vulgar souls—and there were many such, doubtless, who fought at Troy as well as at Waterloo—are subject to strange fits of vulgar passion; and their own mean nature will at times suddenly ooze out, repressed, for the most part, by the glorious deeds, looks, and words of the Heroes. They misunderstood the character and conduct of Achilles. They beheld him triumphing, exulting, insulting, over Hector. But they knew not, neither could they conceive, the trouble of his soul—to them the flashings of his eyes were a mystery—they comprehended not, even in his agonies, his own sublime submission to the decrees of heaven. Seeing how, " with visage all inflamed," Achilles " incensed stood," they caught the contagion of his ire—but the fever falling into baser blood, it boiled up in unworthy outrage; they grew sarcastic, and they stabbed; and lo! Hector lies beneath their brutalities,

" Smear'd with gore, and ghastly pale ! "

From the height of glory, he has fallen into the depth of degradation; and the contrast of the two conditions is to the utmost degree affecting—the breast on which Andromache was wont to lay her head, mangled by ignoble hands—the Prince of the people, a naked corpse insulted by slaves ! Had Shakespeare some thought of this sort in his mind, when he makes Falstaff stab the dead body of " Hotspur, coldspur ; " and shows us the glorious corpse of a hero hanging across the shameful shoulders of a buffoon?

But what matter all these indignities that idly seek to dishonour the corpse ? It is but a lump of clay. The soul of the Defender is beyond and above insult, alike from the base and the brave. The ensuing speech of Achilles reinvests the corpse with grandeur. " Let us return to the hollow ships, and carry Hector along with us ! Great glory have we won ; we have slain the illustrious Hector ! to whom the Trojans, throughout the city, as to a God, were wont to offer prayers."

Nobler eulogium never graced the head of fallen hero. Achilles alone could kill—the meanest Myrmidons might insult Hector when dead, who had all shunned his path when he was hewing it to set the ships on fire. Hector is conquered ; but the sacred cause for which he died survives ; the glory of his character is immortal. " Tell me not," he once said, " tell me not of auguries ! Let your birds fly to the east or the west—I care not in this cause : we obey the will of Jupiter, who rules over all, and—

> Εἷς οἰωνὸς ἄριστος ἀμύνισθαι πιρι πάτρης.

" The one best omen is our country's cause."

Therefore, in spite of defeat and death, Hector is victorious still in our imagination ; his waving crest may be dragged in the dust, but the patriot spirit sees it high in air, not only un-extinguished, but uneclipsed, even by the god-wrought golden helm of Achilles.

But let us look at the Speech of the Destroyer in the five translators.

NORTH.

" Him when the powerful-footed, illustrious Achilles, had despoil'd,
Standing among the Greeks (these) wing'd words he utter'd,—
' Friends, chiefs of the Greeks, and counsellors,
Since this man, the gods have permitted (us) to subdue,
(*Him*) who hath done more evil than all the rest beside,
Let us on—and essay the city with arms,
That we may know the intention of the Trojans, what it may be,
Whether they are to abandon the Acropolis, since he has fall'n ;
Or whether they dare remain, when Hector is no more.
But why does my mind revolve these things ?
(*He*) lies at the ships a corpse unwept, unburied ;—
(*My*) Patroclus ! him will I not forget, while I
Shall be among the living, and my knees move.
And though (the living) forget the dead in Ades,
I, for my part, will remember my friend, even though there.
Come now, ye youths of the Greeks, chanting pæans,
Let us return to the hollow ships, and carry him (Hector) along
    with us.
Great glory have we won ; we have slain the illustrious Hector
To whom the Trojans throughout the city, as to a god, were-wont-
    to-offer prayers.' "

POPE.

" High o'er the slain the great Achilles stands,
Begirt with heroes, and surrounding bands,
And thus aloud, while all the host attends,—
' Princes and leaders ! countrymen and friends !
Since now at length the powerful will of Heaven
The dire destroyer to our arms has given,
Is not Troy fallen already ?   Haste, ye powers !
See, if already their deserted towers
Are left unmann'd ; or if they yet retain
The souls of heroes, their great Hector slain !
But what is Troy, or glory what to me ?
Or why reflects my mind on aught but thee,
Divine Patroclus !   Death has seal'd his eyes ;
Unwept, unhonour'd, uninterr'd he lies !
Can his dear image from my soul depart,
Long as the vital spirit moves my heart ?
If, in the melancholy shades below,
The flames of friends and lovers cease to glow,
Yet mine shall sacred last ; mine undecay'd,
Borne on through death, and animate my shade
Meanwhile, ye sons of Greece, in triumph bring
The corpse of Hector, and your pæans sing.
Be this the song, slow-moving toward the shore
" Hector is dead ! and Ilion is no more ! " ' "

COWPER.

" And now, the body stripp'd, their noble chief,
The swift Achilles, standing in the midst,
The Grecians in wing'd accents thus address'd,—
' Friends, chiefs, and senators of Argos' host !
Since, by the will of Heaven, this man is slain,
Who harm'd us more than all our foes beside,
Essay we next the city ; so to learn
The Trojan purpose, if, this hero slain,
They will forsake the citadel, or still
Defend it, although Hector be no more.
But wherefore speak I thus ? still undeplored
Unburied in my fleet Patroclus lies ;
Him never, while, alive myself. I move
And mix with living men, will I forget.
In Ades, haply, they forget the dead,
Yet will not I Patroclus, even there.
Now chanting pæans, ye Achaian youths !

Return we to the fleet with this our prize ;
We have achieved great glory, we have slain
Illustrious Hector, him whom Ilium praised
In all her gates, and as a god revered.' "

SOTHEBY.

" Princes, and leaders, since, by favouring Heaven,
To us o'er such a foe this victory given,
This mighty man, whose force, surpassing all,
Long injured Greece, and guarded Ilion's wall,
Come, with our battle gird in arms their towers,
So learn the purpose of their hostile powers,—
If they abandon Troy, its guardian slain,
Or, the great Hector perish'd, dare remain ?
But why thus commune ? still Patroclus lies
Unwept, ungraced with solemn obsequies.
Ne'er, while I breathe, he sleeps by me forgot,
Ne'er, while remembrance mine, remember'd not.
E'en in the dark oblivion of the grave,
My soul with thine, sweet friend, shall commune have.
Now, youths ! your pæans raise, now swell the song,
Lead to the navy, lead the corse along.
Great is our glory ; Hector breathes no more,
Whom Ilion hail'd, and wont as god adore."

Chapman fails, and therefore we do not quote him. He is
harsh, inverted, and elaborate overmuch ; nor has his version
the majestic march of the original. But, " dead, undeplored,
unsepulchred, he lies at fleet unthought on," is passionate—
and reminds one of " unhousel'd, disappointed, unanneal'd ;"
and there is a melancholy grandeur in what he says of Oblivion
and of Memory in Hell. We say he fails ; because, in such
noble passages, he in general nobly succeeds. Pope is magnificent. Cowper is somewhat tame in a few lines ; and perhaps his version is throughout wanting in passion ; but the
close is simple and stately—so it seems to us—as in Homer.
The last three lines sound to our ears like a song of triumph
in the Old Testament. They are heroic as if in the Book of
Kings. Sotheby, in the first part of his version, is not so felicitous as usual ; but the lines about Patroclus are more tender
than in any of the other translations, though we do not think
" the dark oblivion of the grave " Homeric, and the conclusion
breathes of the true Achillean spirit. There is not in all the

Iliad one finer touch—one bolder stroke of nature—than the
sudden revulsion of feeling that tears the heart-strings of the
exulting victor, and " checks his thunder in mid-volley," when,
about to storm the city, he is struck, as it were, with palsy by
the cold air from the corpse of Patroclus.

But rage rises again out of grief.   Sorely mangled had been
the body of Patroclus—Achilles sees it in all its ghastliness—
and shall it fare better with the body of Hector?   No—let
there be horrid retribution.

NORTH.

" He said, and purposed unseemly deeds against the illustrious
    Hector ;
Of both feet he pierced the tendons behind
From heel to ankle, and inserted thongs of ox's hide,
And bound them behind the chariot ; but allowed the head to be
    dragg'd.
Having ascended the chariot, and the renown'd arms uplifted,
He lash'd (the horses) onward ; and they not unwilling flew ;
From (the corpse) thus dragged rose dust ; on both sides, his
    hair
Of-a-dark-hue was scatter'd, and his head in the dust completely
Lay, so graceful once ; then, indeed, had Jupiter to foes
Given him to be dishonour'd, in his own native land."

CHAPMAN.

" This said ; a work not worthy him, he set to ; of both feet
He bored the nerves through, from the heel to th' ankle ; and
    then knit
Both to the chariot, with a thong of whitleather ; his head
Trailing the centre.   Up he got to chariot, where he laid
The arms repurchas't and scourged on his horse that freely flew,
A whirlwind made of startled dust drave with them as they drew ;
With which were all his black-brown curls, knotted in heaps, and
    filed.
And there lay Troy's late Gracious, by Jupiter exiled
To all disgrace, in his own land, and by his parents' care," &c.

POPE.

" Then his fell soul a thought of vengeance bred,
    Unworthy of himself and of the dead.
The nervous ankles bored, his feet he bound
    With thongs inserted through the double wound ;

There fix'd up high behind the rolling wain,
His graceful head was trail'd along the plain.
Proud on the car th' insulting victor stood,
And bore aloft his arms distilling blood.
He smites the steeds ; the rapid chariot flies ;
The sudden clouds of circling dust arise.
Now lost is all that formidable air ;
The face divine and long-descending hair
Purple the ground, and streak the sable sand ;
Deform'd, dishonour'd in his native land !
Given to the rage of an insulting throng,
And in his parents' sight now dragg'd along !"

COWPER.

" He said ; then purposing dishonour vile
To noble Hector, both his feet he bored
From heel to ankle, and inserting thongs,
Them tied behind his chariot, but his head
Left unsustain'd to trail along the ground.
Ascending next, the armour at his side
He placed, then lash'd the steeds ; they willing flew.
Thick rose the dust, as with his sable locks
He swept the ground ; his head, so graceful once,
Plough'd deep the dust ; to such dishonour Jove
That day consign'd him on his native plain."

SOTHEBY.

" Then with unmanly gash, dishonouring gored
The feet of Hector, and their tendons bored ;
With leathern thongs behind his chariot bound,
And left the head to trail along the ground ;
Sprung in his seat, the arms in order placed,
And lash'd the willing steeds that swiftly raced :
From the dragg'd corse the dust in clouds upflew,
The dark clay grim'd his locks of sable hue ;
And that once beauteous head, half hid in earth,
Tore, as it trail'd, that soil which gave him birth.
So Jove, who oft had o'er him stretch'd his hand,
Dishonour'd Hector in his native land."

Ay—this was indeed " purposing unseemly deeds against
the illustrious Hector," and horridly carrying them into execution. But one single moment before, and Achilles was
commanding his Myrmidons to lift along the body of Hector
to the hollow ships, himself leading the song of triumph.

"Great glory have we won—we have slain the illustrious Hector—to whom the Trojans, throughout the city, as to a god were wont to offer prayers!" Now whelmed in dust, the corpse is dragged at his chariot wheels — while the mother-queen, standing on the battlements, fills the air with shrieks, and casting far aside her lucid veil, flings her hairs by hand-fuls from the roots, and his father weeps aloud, and all around, long, long lamentations are heard through the streets of Troy,

"Not fewer, or less piercing, than if flames
Had wrapt all Ilium to her topmost towers!"

And Andromache, who, in her chamber at the palace-top, was framing a splendid texture, on either side with flowers of vari-ous hues all dazzling bright, and had given command to her maidens to encompass an ample vase with fire, that a bath might be prepared for Hector on his return from battle, hears the voice of the queen-mother! so piercing-shrill it was, in her agony the shuttle falls from her fingers, and she knows of a truth that her Hector is dead. She crests the tower — and then indeed she sees him in front of Ilium, whirled in such shameful guise, away towards the Grecian fleet. But what cared Achilles for all that mortal misery? He knew it not. Deaf in his own distraction, he heard not theirs; his passion was concentrated on two dead bodies—Patroclus and Hector; love and hate, ruth and rage, pity and ferocity, each with its scalding tears; unforgiving was he, without mercy and with-out remorse; and as the axle of his chariot glowed, and unim-peded were the wheels by the accursed corse, so burned his spirit in the terrible turmoil of its insatiate revenge.

Let us take relief from all this misery in a small bit of what is called Philosophical Criticism. Aristotle, the best of critics —and Eustathius, not one of the worst — have made each a remark on this combat, which seem to us scarcely worthy such philosophers. Aristotle says, according to Pope, "the wonder-ful ought to have place in Tragedy, but still more in Epic Poetry, *which proceeds in this point even to the unreasonable; for as in Epic Poems one sees not the persons acting, so whatever passes the bounds of reason is proper to produce the admirable and the marvellous.* For example, what Homer says of Hector pursued by Achilles, would appear ridiculous on the stage; for the spectators could not forbear laughing to see on one side the Greeks standing without any motion, and, on the other, Achilles pursuing Hector, and making signs to the troops not to dart at him. But all this does not appear when we read the poem ; for what is wonderful is always agreeable, and as a proof of it, we find that they who relate anything usually add something to the truth, that it may the better please those who hear it." This is miserable murder of Aristotle—especially the barbarity in italics—and we quote it as an example of the style of treatment it has been his fate to receive alike from friends and foes. Take Twining's version—which is sense. " *The surprising is necessary in Tragedy; but the Epic Poem goes farther, and admits even the improbable and incredible, from which the highest degree of the surprising results, because there the action is not seen.*" What follows it is needless to quote, as Pope's translation gives, generally, the sense of the original, with considerable confusion. But the question is, would the Flight and Pursuit appear ridiculous on the stage ? Twining thinks " the idea of stopping a whole army by a nod or shake of the head" (a circumstance, he says, distinctly mentioned by Homer, but sunk in Mr Pope's version), " was perhaps the absurdity here principally meant; and that, if this whole Homeric scene were represented on our stage, in the best manner possible, there can be no doubt that the effect would justify Aristotle's observation. It would certainly set the audience in a roar." Pye again, who is in general empty, and on Twining extremely crusty, says sensibly enough here, that he " cannot possibly conceive that the idea of stopping an army by the nod of a head, could be the absurdity meant by Aristotle, or that there could have been anything more absurd in an army stopping at a nod of the head in the theatre, than by the single word *halt* in Hyde Park." Pope seems to have entirely missed the meaning of Aristotle, whatever that may have been—who, he says, " was so far from looking on this passage as ridiculous or blamable, that he esteemed it admirable and marvellous." True, he did so esteem it, occurring as it does in the Epopee ; but had it happened in Tragedy, then, he says, it would have been ridiculous ; and the question is, why ? The answer seems to be, " it would have been ridiculous to see on the stage the army standing still ;" and so it would, thinks Twining—so it would not, thinks Pye—and so it would not, thinks North.

Pye gives the *rationale*. "The defect mentioned by Aristotle lies deeper; for he, in the next chapter, mentions this identical circumstance as a general error against probability, excusable only as it renders the scene more interesting. To us, who are used to the point of honour in military affairs, this improbability does not appear. But the ancients made war on a different plan. . . . . . The ancients looked on this action of Achilles as censurable on the ground of rashness—which appears from a remark on it in Plutarch's Life of Pompey, where, speaking of a rash action of Pompey, in assisting the Cretan pirates merely to deprive Metellus of a triumph, he compares this action—which he calls rather the exploit of a mad boy, intoxicated with the love of fame, than of a brave man." Pye adds, "In deference to the opinion of Plutarch, it does not appear that Achilles was actuated by the love of fame, but the wish to monopolise the revenge of his friend's death." And we, in deference to the opinion of Pye, say that Pye is mistaken, for we have seen that Achilles is inspired by both passions, which Homer makes him tell us in the clearest and boldest words. Therefore, Aristotle, Plutarch, Pope, Twining, and Pye, are all wrong—Homer and North, as usual, all right; for, though it is true that it was not exactly a pitched single combat, in which case any assistance from the army would have been wicked, and not ridiculous, yet it was very like one indeed, and therefore, again begging Aristotle's pardon, we really cannot yet see how the non-interference of the army would have been ridiculous on the stage, any more than on the field.

Eustathius, who, if we mistake not, was a bit of a bishop, says that this is not a single combat of Achilles against Hector, but a rencontre in a battle; and so Achilles might and ought to take all advantage to rid himself, the readiest and surest way, of an enemy whose death would procure an entire victory to his party. Wherefore does he leave the victory to chance? Why expose himself to the hazard of losing it? Why does he prefer his private glory to the public weal, and the safety of all the Greeks, which he puts to the venture by delaying to conquer, and endangering his own person? We grant it is a fault, but it must be owned to be the fault of a hero.

All the above is given us by Pope, through Dacier, from

Eustathius. And is it not pretty considerable stuff? Achilles ought to have killed Hector by hook or crook—by the spears and swords of the soldiers! (Loud cries of oh! oh! oh!) The Greeks, it has been observed, were no favourites with the feudal writers on the Trojan war, and to depreciate the character of Achilles, they have made him in that way murder Hector. See Shakespeare's "Troilus and Cressida," where Achilles is at once a sumph and a savage. As to his leaving the victory to chance, and exposing himself to the hazard of losing it, the answer is, that the Greek army would have laughed in your face, had you hinted such a suggestion, and taken you for Thersites.

Stop—we all at once see the meaning of Aristotle. He alludes neither to the shaking of the brows of Achilles (which was almost equal to the nod of Jupiter), nor to his rashness in exposing himself to be killed by Hector in single combat (a stupid charge, worthy of that Bœotian, Plutarch), but to the circumstance of the whole army standing stock-still during the flight thrice round the walls, instead of intercepting the fugitive (which fifty thousand men could surely have done, without putting themselves into a sweat), and thereby enabling Achilles to get to in-fighting. Now, in the Epopee, this absurdity—and it is one—escapes notice, because the scene is not submitted to our sight. And Homer is eulogised by Aristotle for his genius in so narrating it, that there is produced by it on our minds a sense of the wonderful. Had the scene been exhibited before our eyes on the stage, it would, for the reason assigned, have been ridiculous;—and thus, after all, Aristotle is right, and so is North, while Plutarch, and Eustathius, and Twining, and Pye, are wrong, though each in his degree no contemptible philosophic critic.

But let us return to the agonies of Achilles. He has reached the ships, with Hector at his chariot wheels, all the power of passion within his mighty heart more savagely inflamed by the motion of that horrid race. Let there be due pomp in the celebration of the ritual of revenge; and let Thetis' self, who brought him the armour in which he conquered, come again from the sea to inspire all their hearts with the rage of grief. The Myrmidons shall fiercely partake of the funeral banquet—and the body of Hector shall be given to the dogs, that they may tear to pieces and devour

it. Agamemnon may send the chiefs to bring Achilles to the
royal tent, and he will go; but not to sit down with the king
of men, not to cleanse from his homicidal hands the clotted
gore—not to purify his person—if such blood be pollution—
" in the large three-footed caldron," but to demand that the
old trees may be hewn on the mountain for the funeral pyre
of his Patroclus.   It is a dreadful picture.

NORTH.

" Thus were they groaning throughout the city ; but the Greeks,
  When they had come to the ships and the Hellespont,
  Went-dismiss'd each to his own ship ;
  But Achilles permitted not the Myrmidons to go dispersed ;
  But among his war-loving companions (*thus*) spoke :—
  ' Ye swift-riding Myrmidons, my beloved companions,
  Let us not yet from the chariots unyoke the solid-hoof'd horses,
  But with the horses themselves, and the chariots nearer ap-
      proaching,
  Let us weep for Patroclus ; for this is an honorary-tribute to the dead.
  But when we-have-had-our-full of sorrowing lamentation,
  Having unyoked our steeds, we shall sup here altogether.'
  Thus he spoke; together-brought, they lifted-up-their-lamentation,
      and Achilles took the lead.
  ¹ Thrice around the corpse drove they their beautiful-maned
      horses,
  The Myrmidons, and among them did Thetis stir up the longing-
      love of lamentation ;
  Moisten'd were the sands, moisten'd was the armour of heroes,
  With tears, such a panic-causing hero did they desiderate.
  Among them did the son of Peleus take the lead in the closely-
      thronging wailings,
  Placing his homicidal hands on the breast of his friend.
  ' Rejoice with me, Patroclus, even in the mansions of Ades ;
  For everything shall I now fulfil, which I formerly promised,
  That having dragged Hector hither, I would give him to dogs to
      be torn raw ;
  That at the pyre I would decollate² twelve

---

¹ This passage is borrowed by Virgil, in *Æneid*, lib. xi. 186.   Imitated by
Chaucer in the " Knight's Tale."—

" Ne how the Greeks with an huge rout,
Thrice did riden all the fire about,
Upon the left hand, with a loud shouting,
And thrice on the right, with their speares clattering."

² Comes nearer the etymological meaning of ἀποδειροτομήειν, than "behead."

Illustrious sons of the Trojans, being enraged for thy having been
slain.'
Thus he said, and against the illustrious Hector unseemly deeds
he purposed,
Beside the bier of the son of Menœtius having stretch'd him prone
In the dust ; and each put-off-his-arms and accoutrements,
Brazen (and) bright ; and unloosed the shrill-neighing horses.
Down sat they by the ship of the swift-footed grandson of Æacus
In great numbers (lit. ten thousand) ; but he laid out for them a
desire-gratifying funeral-feast.
Many a slow¹ moving ox was extended on the iron (spits)
Slaughter'd, many a sheep and bleating she-goat,
Many a bright-tusk'd boar, blooming with fat,
Were extended to be roasted over the flame of Vulcan.
Meanwhile, on all sides around the corpse flowed the blood, as-if-
from-vessels-outpour'd, (κοτυλήρυτον.)
But the Prince, the swift-footed son of Peleus,
To the illustrious Agamemnon, were the chiefs of the Greeks con-
ducting,
With urgency, artfully-persuading him, enraged at heart on ac-
count of his friend.
When they then had in their course come to the tent of Agamemnon,
Forthwith the shrill-sounding heralds he commanded
To surround with fire a large three-footed caldron,² might they
persuade
The son of Peleus to wash away the clotted gore.
But he stubbornly refused, and moreover swore an oath,
' No—not, by Jupiter ! who of gods is the loftiest and best,
Until I shall have placed on the pyre Patroclus, and thrown up a
sepulchral mound,
And shorn off my locks ; since never again a second time thus
Shall grief pervade my heart, whilst I shall be among the living.
But yet let us now obey (celebrate) the hateful repast.
At-to-morrow's-dawn, king of men, Agamemnon, urgently-com-
mand

---

¹ It is difficult to determine whether the epithet ἀργοὶ should here be translated "white," or "swift," or "slow" (in the sense in which Homer often
uses εἰλίποδες βόες—trailing-footed, an epithet very descriptive of the way in
which they drag after them their hind-legs)—or "idle"—quasi ἀεργὸς.
² To prepare a bath.
It is argued by some that white animals were never sacrificed to the dead ;
but perhaps the living had no objection to the colour of the animal—provided
the flesh were good—and Homer is here describing the περίδειπνον—or funeral
repast given to the living. Another critic is determined to have the oxen
white, even at the expense of their skins. "After they are flayed," says he,
"they are white from their fatness,"

Wood to be collected and piled up, as is beseeming
For a corpse having (*these honours*) to go down to the gloomy
    darkness ;
That the unwearied fire may burn it up
Quickly away from my eyes, and the soldiers turn themselves to
    their labours.'
Thus said he ; and they to him earnestly listen'd and obey'd him,
And each and all having eagerly girded themselves to prepare supper,
Feasted, nor lack'd their hearts an equal repast."

And what shall still for a while the storm in the destroyer's
soul ? No power on earth or in heaven. It keeps feeding on the
black atmosphere—the grim clouds come sailing along incessantly in tempestuous procession—broken but by flashes of
lightning ; never was there seen such a dreadful mental sky.
But the soul is the slave of the body, and over-wearied nature
yields to the access of sleep. Like a calm that enchains the
fluctuating sea, sleep seizes on Achilles, and his huge frame
is stretched motionless along the shore. Then is he visited
by a dream.

                                NORTH.

" But Pelides, on the shore of the much-resounding ocean,
Lay heavily-groaning amid a multitude of Myrmidons,
In a purified[1] place, where the billows were dashing[2] on the shore,
When sleep, unbinding the cares of the mind, seized him,
(*Sleep*) sweetly pour'd around (him)—(for wearied much were his
    beautiful limbs
By rushing after Hector at wind-exposed Troy).
(Then) the spectre of the hapless Patroclus approach'd,
In all respects resembling him in stature, in beautiful eyes,
And voice, and similar garments clothed its body ;
O'er his head it stood, and in these words address'd him,—
' Sleepest thou, and forgetful of *me* art thou, Achilles ?
Of me when living, not neglectful ; but now, when dead,
Bury me with all speed, that I may pass the gates of Ades.
The spectres, the shadows of the slain, keep me afar,
Nor allow me to mingle with them beyond the river ;
To-no-purpose wander I about the wide-gated mansion of Orcus.
Give me thine hand, with-tears-I-implore thee, for never again
    hereafter

_____

[1] Καθαρῷ may here mean a place not usually frequented.
[2] Κλύζεσκον, some interpret, " were sounding ;" others, " washing." Perhaps
Homer means that the dashing of the waves washed away the blood, and consequently purified the place.

Shall I return from Ades, after you shall-have-given-me-my-por-
tion of the pyre.
Never again apart from our beloved companions, shall we alive,
Sitting, hold counsel together ; but me, hath Destiny,
The hideous, and ordain'd to me at my birth, yawning wide,
devour'd.
And even of thee thyself, oh godlike Achilles, the fate is
To perish under the walls of the nobly-born Trojans.
This other (*request*) will I communicate and enjoin, if perchance
you will grant it ;
Place not my bones apart from thine, Achilles,
But together ; that as we were brought up together at your
house—
(Since me then young Menœtius from Opöeis
To your (house) had conducted, on account of a mournful man-
slaughter,
On that day, when I slew the son of Amphidamas,
Unwittingly, unwillingly, being angry about dice :
Me, did the equestrian Peleus, having then received me into his
house,
Nurture zealously, and name your attendant :)
So also let the same urn enclose your bones,—
That golden vase, which thy venerable mother gave thee.'
Him, the swift-footed Achilles answering, address'd,—
'Why, beloved one, hast thou come hither,
And on me enjoin'd all these things ? To thee, will I
Faithfully perform them all, and grant as thou orderest.
But stand nearer me, that having embraced for a little while
One another, we may-take-our-full of sorrowing grief.'
Thus having said, he stretch'd himself out with his hands,
But grasp'd not; for the spectre, down under the earth, like smoke,
Pass'd shrill-wailing ; amazed, Achilles started up,
Made-a-clattering-noise with his hands struck together, and spoke
these sorrowful words,—
'Ha ! ye gods, verily there are in the mansions of Orcus
The spirit and the semblance, but nothing substantial[1] is there
there at all ;
For of my hapless Patroclus, all-the-night has
The spirit, moaning and wailing, hover'd o'er me,
And has given me orders about everything ; wonderfully like
was it to himself.' "

Most beautiful example of the power of the deepest passion
of sorrow which men know—the sorrow for the dead—to awaken

---

[1] Θίσκιλον, may also be translated " god-like."

creative imagination ! Nothing will satisfy it here but the
ghost of Patroclus. From the lips of the phantom falls but
the expression of those ideas and feelings which the heart of
the living hero has indeed brought forth in the visions of its
own grief. And how profound the hush breathed over all that
distracting passion from the tender interview of sleep! Achilles
awakes with a spirit tranquillised for the funeral. So passed
the night—and " rosy-palm'd Aurora found them all mourning
afresh the pitiable dead." Then up rose Meriones, friend of
the virtuous chief Idomeneus, and led the mules and mule-
driver to the groves of Ida fountain-fed ; and down fell the
towering oaks with crash sonorous ; and ere long they were
cast on the beach in order, where Achilles had designed a
tomb of ample size for Patroclus and for himself—for in death
he desired that they should not be divided. Round the pile
of fuel sat down all the warlike throng ; till Achilles issued
orders that his warriors should gird on their armour, and yoke
their steeds to their chariots. On a sudden all in bright arms
stood arrayed ; mounted the combatants and charioteers ;
first moved the chariots, and then came the foot, dense as a
cloud. In the midst, between his companions in arms, was
borne the body of Patroclus. But behold the funeral-rites
in Sotheby's exquisite translation :—

" Behind, Achilles held the hero's head,
    And groan'd amid the pomp that graced the dead—
    The mourners, where he bade, deposed the bier,
    And urged their toil the enormous pile to rear.
    Then Peleus' son, alone, from all apart,
    Mused on the solemn vow that swell'd his heart,
    And severing from his head the golden hair,
    That, to Sperchius vow'd, flow'd full and fair,
    Deep-groaning on the world of waters gazed,
    And thus his voice of lamentation raised :
    ' Peleus to thee, Sperchius, vow'd in vain
    This offering, if his son return'd again,
    This consecrated hair, when hail'd my home,
    And with this gift his votive hecatomb,
    And fifty rams that at thy fount should bleed,
    And in thy sacred wood the altar feed—
    Thus Peleus pray'd ; but thou hast scorn'd his pray'r ;
    Not thine, Sperchius, this devoted hair.
    Ne'er shall the son of Peleus greet his sire,
    And this shorn lock falls on Patroclus' pyre.'

He spake : and bowing down, the corse embraced,
And in Patroclus' hands the offering placed.
All grieved : and thus the daylight had declined,
Had not Achilles then reveal'd his mind :
'Atrides ! thee all willingly obey ; —
Grief has its season ; now send these away :
Dismiss them from the pyre, the feast prepare,
Rites yet unpaid be my appropriate care.
I, and my host, the last sad charge sustain,
Yet let with us the leaders here remain.'
Atrides heard, and utter'd his command,
And to their ships dispersed each separate band.
The assistants there remained : the pile prepared,
And paced on every side the structure squared,
An hundred feet : then, on his funeral bed,
On that high summit, weeping, placed the dead.
There many a sheep and bullock slew and flay'd,
And, heap'd before the pyre, each carcass laid :
From all alike the fat Achilles drew,
Spread o'er the corse, and wholly hid from view :
Then piled their limbs, and hung, with many a tear,
Jars of rich oil and honey round the bier.
Then Peleus' son cast quickly on the pyre,
Four steeds, proud-crested, foaming in their ire ;
And from nine household dogs, his hand had fed,
Cast two, that on the pile, fresh slaughter'd, bled :
Then twelve brave youths of Troy, in sternest mood,
Slew with revengeful blade that drain'd their blood.
Last, on the structure hurl'd the force of flame,
And deeply groaning, named Patroclus' name :
'Patroclus ! hail ! Oh hear, though dead, my voice !
All that I vow'd is perfected. —Rejoice !
Twelve high-born sons of Troy, in youthful bloom,
The fire at once shall with thy corse consume,
But ne'er shall fire on Hector feed, the hound
Shall, fattening on his carcass, search each wound.'
He, threat'ning spoke : but by high heaven o'erpower'd,
No ravenous hound the Hectorean corse devour'd,
By Jove's fair child, by Venus, driven away,
Who watch'd the corse, and guarded night and day :
With roseate oil ambrosial bathed him o'er,
That smooth'd, when dragg'd, each lacerated pore.
And a dense cloud from heaven Apollo drew,
And where the corse reposed deep darkness threw,
That not the fierceness of the solar ray,
The tendons bare, and dry the flesh away."

What is wanting to the magnificence of such a funeral?
Nothing is wanting—our imaginations are satisfied, and we
feel it to be sublime. But the imagination of Homer was not
satisfied; greater grandeur still was due to the funeral rites
performed to his friend by Achilles; and the elements must
be called to give the finishing glory to the work.   No fire
kindled on the pile.   It remained, without a spark, sullen in
its mighty mass.   It seemed unwilling to be consumed.
Therefore, Peleus' son withdrew a short distance in prayer,
and, vowing to each large sacrifice, invoked Boreas and
Zephyrus, pouring out libation from a golden cup, and thus
imploring their coming, that the flames, kindling, might instantly consume the dead.   Iris heard his supplication—and
the Rainbow—"she that wears the thousand-colour'd hair"
—flung herself from heaven into the hall of the heavy-blow-
ing West, where all the Winds sat feasting; and the moment
she alighted on the threshold, they all starting rose at once,
and each invited Iris to his side.   " Borne over ocean's stream
again, I go to Ethiopia, where with 'the rest' I wish to share
in hecatombs offered to the gods.   But Achilles sues for the
aid of Boreas and Zephyrus, vowing to you large sacrifice, if
ye will fan the pile on which now lies his Patroclus, by all
Achaia wept."   Even in our prose, the description bears
perusal well ; in Sotheby it is superb.

" Thus having spoken, she (Iris) departed ; but they (the winds) rush'd
    With magnificent sound,—driving the clouds before them !
Instantly to the sea they came to blow ; uprose the billows
By the shrill-sounding blast.   To rich-glebed Troy they came,
Upon the pyre they fell, and the magnificently-burning flame
    crackled aloud.
All-night verily indeed did they, at one and the same time, uplift
    the blaze around the pyre,—
Blowing shrilly : and all-the-night did the swift Achilles,
From a golden goblet, having a double-handled cup,
Draw the wine, pour it on the ground, and moisten the earth,
Invoking the spirit of the hapless Patroclus.
As a father bewails (when) burning the bones of his son
Betrothed, who, by his death, hath render'd wretched his miserable
    parents,
    In like manner bewail'd Achilles when burning the bones of his
        friend,

Gliding along by the burning-pyre—*groaning chokingly ;*[1]
But when the morning-star arose—the harbinger of light upon the
earth,
After which the saffron-robed Aurora is diffused over the sea,
Then did the pyre-blaze languish, and the flame ceased.
Back went the winds again to return homeward,
Athwart the Thracian deep : but it groan'd, boiling with its swell-
ing (waves).
But Pelides, turning away to the other side, apart from the pyre-
blaze,
Lay down, worn-out ; and upon him sweet sleep came.
But Atrides and his followers in numbers were assembled,
Of whom passing to and fro the noise and disturbance awoke
(Achilles) ;
Upright therefore he sat, and these words address'd to them,—
' Atrides, and ye others, ye nobles of all the Greeks,
First extinguish down with dark wine the pyre-blaze
Wholly, as far as the fury of the fire hath seized it ; and
next
The bones of Patroclus Menœtiades let us gather together,
Distinguishing them carefully ; for easily recognised they are,
Since they lay in the midst of the pyre, but the others apart,
On the outermost verge, were burn'd, horses and men promiscu-
ously :
Those in a golden urn, and in twice-folded fat [2]
Let us deposit,—till I myself be conceal'd in Ades.
I wish not now to elaborate a very large tomb,
But of moderate and befitting dimensions — thus : *it* hereafter,
ye Greeks,
Both broad and high you may make, you who after me
Shall be left behind in the many-bench'd ships.'
Thus spoke he : and they obey'd the swift-footed son of Peleus.
First then did they extinguish down with dark wine the pyre-
blaze,
As far as the flame had come, down-fell the deep ashes :
The white bones of their gentle companion, with tears,
They collected into a golden vase, and twice-folded fat :
In the tent having placed it, they veil'd it with delicately-woven,
fine linen :
The circumference of the mound they form'd, and laid the founda-
tion

---

[1] Ἀδνά, closely pressed—from ἀδην, to satiety.
[2] "Notabile inventum ad excludendum aërem et cum eo putorem."—
Heyne.

Around the funeral pile : ¹ and raised the heap'd-up earth.
Having raised the mound, they return'd.   But Achilles
Detain'd the people there, and made-to-sit-down a wide-encircling
   assembly.
From the ships prizes he brought, caldrons and tripods,
Horses and mules, and the vigorous heads of oxen,
And women with-lovely-waists, and grey iron."

                              SOTHEBY.

" Swift at the word, the winds with mighty roar
   Flew, and far drove the gather'd clouds before,
Swept o'er the sea, while far and wide the deep
   With all its billows swell'd beneath their sweep :
Then Iliou reach'd, there rushing on the pyre,
   Heard at their blast loud roar the blaze of fire.
The pyre, in every part, throughout the night,
   Spread, as they shrilly blew, large flakes of light :
And, all that night, Pelides, the divine,
   Held with pure hand a bowl of votive wine,
And fill'd it from a beaker framed of gold,
   Then pour'd the offering on the hallow'd mould ;
And ever as he pour'd it from the bowl,
   With solemn voice invoked Patroclus' soul.
As when a father, lone, with grief half-wild,
   Consumes the bones of his beloved child,
A youth just plighted, whose untimely death
   Dooms to unsolaced woe his closing breath :
Thus as Achilles burnt Patroclus' bones,
   Slow pacing nigh the pile, groans burst on groans.
Thus pass'd the night ; but when with dawning ray
   Rose the fair morn-star, harbinger of day,
And saffron-robed Aurora onward came,
   Sank on the wasted pile the dying flame—
Home rush'd the winds, and with returning blast
   Swell'd up the Thracian billows, as they past :
Then worn Pelides from the pile withdrew,
   And sleep her soothing mantle o'er him threw.
But when the host, a still increasing throng,
   Tumultuous, to Achilles flock'd along,
Their din aroused him from refreshing rest :
   He rose, and thus assembled Greece addrest :

─────────────────────

" Si recto assequor, tumulus in ipso rogi loco exstruitur," *ut sup.* II. 336.—
Heyne.

'Atrides ! and ye chiefs, my voice attend !
First, to Patroclus' pile your footsteps bend,
And there extinguish, far as spread the fire,
With copious wine the yet half-smouldering pyre.
Next, let us gather up each hallow'd bone
Of Menœtiades, distinctly known :
In the mid pyre he lay ; but, round his bed,
Far off the steeds and men confus'dly spread.
In a gold vase, with double cauls enclosed,
Place we his bones, till mine are there deposed.
I will not now a mighty mound upraise ;
Yours be that hallow'd charge in after days ;
Ye, the survivors of our hapless doom :
There the large mound extend, and pile a loftier tomb.'
  He spake : the host Pelides' word obey'd,
Pour'd the dark wine, and all the flame allay'd,
Far as the fire had spread its strength around,
And the heap'd ashes sank, and strew'd the ground ;—
Then tearful gathering up, the bones reposed
In the gold vase, with double cauls enclosed :
Bore to the tent, and hiding it from view,
O'er all a veil of finest linen drew.
Then, circling round the place, mark'd out the mound,
And there the broad foundation firmly bound,
Earth heap'd on earth, to raise the structure, laid,
And back return'd, that last sad duty paid.
Achilles then the multitude detain'd ;
And all spectators of the sports remain'd.—
Forth from his ships, along the crowded shore,
His train the great rewards of contest bore :
Caldrons and tripods, and the proud-neck'd steed,
Mules, and large bodies of the bovine breed,
And lovely girls, that richest vesture wore,
And the bright splendour of his iron ore."

In this way has imagination at all times blended itself with the passion of sorrow. The strong feeling in which the mind begins to work is the wound of its own loss. But immediately its wider feelings are opened up, and from all its stores of thought, from all its sources of passion, images and desires begin to crowd in, which belong not to that particular affliction, but to the universal constitution of our nature, and to its common lot. Such has been the origin of the funeral honours and consecration of the dead. The soul in its sorrow was not satisfied to mourn. But awakened by its own anguish to the

vivid realisation of all those conceptions which the living
spirit has gathered upon the name of death, it went down into
the regions to which the ghost was gone, and found it shiver-
ing on the shores of the unnavigable river, till its funeral rites
were paid. It found the departed soul yet troubled with the
passions it had left on earth, and still communicating, by its
mysterious sensibility, with the affections and the acts of the
living. Hence stately obsequies were made, to solace with
the last tribute of love that shadowy being ; warriors circled
thrice with inverted arms the figure of the warrior slain ; wine
was shed on the flame ; and blood was poured from human
bosoms to gladden the immortal spirit with earthly revenge.
Wailings and shrieks were raised around the pile, to thrill for
the last time unhearing ears ; and the farewell of the living to
the dead was duly spoken, as if he were but then departing
from the coasts of life.

> " Salve æternum, mihi, maxime Palla !
> Æternumque vale ! "

Delightful is it thus to recall to memory a parallel passage
from Virgil the divine—the Funeral of Pallas. The same passionate spirit breathes over that beautiful picture—coloured
by a gentler and more pensive genius. From Homer's
" Golden Urn " Virgil " drew light ; " and poets there have
been, who, at the farthing rushlight of some poetaster, have
kindled their own huge pine-torch, that far and wide has
illuminated the horizon. What is the use of making compari-
sons between Homer and Virgil? Of each it may be said, in
the mystic language of Wordsworth—

> " Thou—thou art not a child of Time,
> But offspring of the Eternal Prime."

Virgil, according to " the whisper of a faction," is an
imitator. So is every great poet. Shakespeare was a thief,
and Homer was a robber. Sympathy is one of the strengths
of a poet's soul ; and sympathy, at its height and depth, works
into imitation. Imitation, therefore, is proof, power, test, trial,
growth and result, cause and effect, of original genius. " The
same ! but oh ! how different ! " What a fund of philosophy
in these few words ! Æneas is not Achilles—Pallas is not
Patroclus. But each illustrious pair were Knights-Commanders

of the Order of the Stainless Shield—and theirs were immortal friendships. Achilles and Patroclus were nearly of an age. But Æneas was like the elder brother of Pallas, who had been committed to his care by old Evander, that his princely boy might learn the last lessons of chivalry from the great Trojan. When Pallas fell, Æneas mourned with a twofold passion of grief. Nor had he the fiery spirit of Achilles. Therefore there is the most touching tenderness, but no startling intensity, in his sorrows. The anguish—and the agony—these are reserved for Evander; and our bosoms are rended by his lamentations as sorely as by those of Priam. Nothing can be more affecting —more pathetic—than the following Virgilian strain sounded through the fire-touched lips of Dryden.

" Thus, weeping while he spoke, he took his way,
Where, now in death, lamented Pallas lay :
Acœtes watch'd the corpse ; whose youth deserved
The father's trust, and now the son he served
With equal faith, but less auspicious care :
The attendants of the slain his sorrow share.
A troop of Trojans mix'd with these appear,
And mourning matrons with dishevell'd hair.
Soon as the prince appears, they raise a cry ;
All beat their breasts, and echoes rend the sky.
They rear his drooping forehead from the ground ;
But when Æneas view'd the grisly wound
Which Pallas in his manly bosom bore,
And the fair flesh distain'd with purple gore :
First, melting into tears, the pious man
Deplored so sad a sight, then thus began.

Thus having mourn'd, he gave the word around,
To raise the breathless body from the ground ;
And chose a thousand horse, the flower of all
His warlike troops, to wait the funeral :
To bear him back, and share Evander's grief
(A well-becoming, but a weak relief).
Of oaken twigs they twist an easy bier ;
Then on their shoulders the sad burthen rear.
The body on this rural hearse is borne,
Strew'd leaves and funeral greens the bier adorn.
All pale he lies, and looks a lovely flower.
New cropt by virgin hands, to dress the bower :

Unfaded yet, but yet unfed below,
No more to mother earth or the green stem shall owe.
Then two fair vests, of wondrous work and cost,
Of purple woven, and with gold embost,
For ornament the Trojan hero brought,
Which with her hands Sidonian Dido wrought.
One vest array'd the corpse, and one they spread
O'er his closed eyes, and wrapp'd around his head :
That when the yellow hair in flame should fall,
The catching fire might burn the golden caul.
Besides the spoils of foes in battle slain,
When he descended on the Latian plain :
Arms, trappings, horses, by the hearse he led
In long array (the achievements of the dead).
Then, pinion'd with their hands behind, appear
The unhappy captives, marching in the rear :
Appointed offerings in the victor's name,
To sprinkle with their blood the funeral flame.
Inferior trophies by the chiefs are borne ;
Gauntlets and helms, their loaded hands adorn ;
And fair inscriptions fix'd, and titles read,
Of Latian leaders conquer'd by the dead.
Acœtes on his pupil's corpse attends,
With feeble steps ; supported by his friends :
Pausing at every pace, in sorrow drown'd,
Betwixt their arms he sinks upon the ground.
Where grovelling, while he lies in deep despair,
He beats his breast, and rends his hoary hair.
The champion's chariot next is seen to roll,
Besmear'd with hostile blood, and honourably foul.
To close the pomp, Æthon, the steed of state,
Is led, the funeral of his lord to wait.
Stripp'd of his trappings, with a sullen pace
He walks, and the big tears run rolling down his face :
The lance of Pallas, and the crimson crest,
Are borne behind ; the victor seized the rest.
The march begins : the trumpets hoarsely sound,
The pikes and lances trail along the ground.
Thus, while the Trojan and Arcadian horse
To Pallantean towers direct their course,
In long procession rank'd ; the pious chief
Stopp'd in the rear, and gave a vent to grief.
'The public care,' he said, ' which war attends,
Diverts our present woes, at least suspends ;
Peace with the manes of great Pallas dwell ;
Hail, holy relics, and a last farewell ! ' "

Æneas did not act well towards Dido. We do not mean in leaving her, for his departure was inevitable, it being doomed; and had he stayed at Carthage, what had become of the Æneid? but in allowing her to indulge in "loving not wisely, but too well;" especially in that cave. Electricity is always perilous; and hence knight and lady fair have seldom escaped scathless from such seclusion during a thunderstorm. We forgive them both. But Æneas redeems his character from the charge of selfishness, by his whole conduct towards Pallas and Evander. He had a good heart. He remorsefully reproaches himself for having suffered the young hero to encounter danger and death in *his* war. He fears to look again on the face of the good old king, whom he has made sonless.

"And what a friend hast thou, Ascanius, lost!"

That is the last line of his heroic elegy over the corpse; and afterwards, on the decisive day, what are his words to Turnus?

"Pallas te hoc vulnere, Pallas
Immolat!"

Yes! Æneas was a hero.

Say not that Virgil is often pathetic, but never sublime. For believe thou with us that the pathetic is the sublime, as it comes pouring purely forth from the ether of a poet's soul. Thus,—

"The morn had now dispell'd the shades of night :
Restoring toils, when she restored the light ;
The Trojan king, and Tuscan chief, command
To raise the piles along the winding strand :
Their friends convey the dead to funeral fires ;
Black smould'ring smoke from the green wood expires ;
The light of heaven is choked, and the new day retires.
Then thrice around the kindled piles they go
(For ancient custom had ordain'd it so).
Thrice horse and foot about the fires are led,
And thrice with loud laments they hail the dead.
Tears trickling down their breasts bedew the ground ;
And drums and trumpets mix their mournful sound.
Amid the blaze, their pious brethren throw
The spoils, in battle taken from the foe ;
Helms, bits embost, and swords of shining steel,
One casts a target, one a chariot-wheel :

Some to their fellows their own arms restore :
The falchions which in luckless fight they bore :
Their bucklers pierced, their darts bestow'd in vain,
And shiver'd lances gather'd from the plain :
Whole herds of offer'd bulls about the fire,
And bristled boars, and woolly sheep, expire.
Around the piles a careful troop attends,
To watch the wasting flames, and weep their burning friends.
Lingering along the shore, till dewy night
New decks the face of heaven with starry light."

The ancients—Hebrews, Greeks, Romans—had all noble
ideas and feelings in their friendships.   David and Jonathan
—Achilles and Patroclus—Pylades and Orestes—Damon and
Pythias—Nisus and Euryalus—and many others—real or
phantoms—of the sages or the heroes.   What is such friendship, when flowering on the battle-field, but peace-in-war!
Profoundest repose of all the heart's best affections in the
midst of its most tempestuous passions!   A *lown* hour in
midst of a day of storms!

Virgil pours his entire heart into the episode of Nisus and
Euryalus—Homer all his into that loftier brotherhood.   Both
alike, under such inspiration, must have felt confident of
immortality.   The consciousness in the soul of genius of its
own imperishable greatness, meets our perfect sympathy,
when that genius exercises itself in the finest and most
famous arts.   We are easily able, for example, to imagine
that the sculptor or the painter, while he looks with delight
himself on the beautiful forms that are rising into life under
his hand, feels rejoicingly that other men, formed by nature
with souls like his own, will look with the same emotion on
the same forms, and thank him to whose genius they owe
their delight.   We can conceive, without difficulty, the consciousness which Virgil felt of the delight which his verse
would inspire, when, having celebrated, in that perhaps the
most beautiful passage in all his poetry, the perilous and
fatal adventure of those two youthful warriors, and closed
their eyes in death, he adds, rejoicingly,—

" Fortunati ambo ! si quid mea carmina possunt,
    Nulla dies unquam memori vos eximet ævo,
    Dum domus Æneæ Capitoli immobile saxum
    Accolet, imperiumque Pater Romanus habebit !"

He prophesied falsely of the duration of the Roman greatness; but he committed no error in prophesying his own fame; and the delight which he felt himself in the tender and beautiful picture he had drawn, is felt, as he believed it would be, by numberless spirits. He was not deceived, then, in the assurance he felt of an undying sympathy among men with his own emotions; in his certainty that he should touch their hearts with a pensive pleasure, and win from them, along with love for his fallen heroes, some fond and grateful affection to him who had sung so well the story of their fortunes.

And think ye not that Homer, too, exulted in the consciousness that he had won himself an immortal fame, when he was conceiving for Achilles the tender desire that his body should lie in the same tomb with that of his Patroclus? " The time may come," said the hero, " when Greece may decree us a vaster monument." There spake Homer's own heart, in the fulness of the pride of inspiration. Millions yet unborn would visit that mound, because of the glorifying song that illuminated its verdure with immortal light. Achilles was either to return home, and live and die obscurely happy, or to " fall in the blaze of his fame " before Troy. And the bard, in his prescience, knew that congenial spirits, in the after-time, would think it happiness enough for Achilles that he had been sung by Homer. Not else had Alexander the Great sought the tomb of the hero whom he admired and resembled —though Homer's Achilles never saw the light of our day, but was in the air-world of imagination an ideal phantom, glorified by genius into the life that never dies.

From this unintended digression we now hasten back to the close of the funeral rites of Patroclus.

Those magnificent rites are followed duly by the funeral games—and who should preside over them—but Achilles? Agamemnon himself is there—and all the chiefs. But Achilles is king to-day; and he has received his sceptre from the hand of sorrow. How heroic his bearing from first to last!

COWPER.

" Atrides, and ye other valiant Greeks!
These prizes, in the circus placed, attend
The charioteers. Held we the present games

In honour of some other Grecian dead,
I would myself bear hence the foremost prize ;
For well ye know my steeds, that they surpass
All else, and are immortal ; Neptune's gift
To my own father, and his gift to me.
But neither I this contest share myself,
Nor shall my steeds ; for they would miss the force
And guidance of a charioteer so kind
As they have lost, who many a time hath cleansed
Their manes with water of the crystal brook,
And made them sleek, himself, with limpid oil.
Him, therefore, mourning, motionless they stand,
With hair dishevell'd, streaming to the ground.
But ye, whoever of the host profess
Superior skill, and glory in your steeds
And well-built chariots, for the strife prepare !"

So spake Pelides, and arose the charioteers for speed renowned : Eumelus, accomplished in equestrian arts ; Diomede,
the son of Tydeus—he yoked the coursers won by himself in
battle from Æneas, what time Apollo saved their master ; the
son of Atreus with the golden locks, Menelaus, who joined to
his chariot the mare of Agamemnon, swift Æthe, and his own
Podargus ; and Antilochus, son of Nestor, his bright-maned
steeds prepared, of Pylian breed.   At the sight, grief for the
dead fades before the glory of the living—yet with what noble
pathos does Achilles here remember his friend !

Tydides is victor ; and the prizes are delivered in order ;
the last of all to—Nestor, by Achilles himself, the Flower of
Chivalry and Courtesy, in honour and reverence of Old Age.
" Take thou, my Father ! and for ever keep this in store, that
thou mayst never forget the funeral of my friend ! accept it as
a free gift : for, fallen as thou art into the wane of life, thou
must wield the cestus, wrestle, at the spear contend, or in the
foot-race, henceforth no more ! "—" My son ! I accept thy gift
with joy ;—glad is my heart that thou art evermore mindful
of one who loves thee, and that now thou yieldest me such
honour as is due to my years, in sight of all the Greeks.   So
may the gods immortalise thy name ! "   Such the princely
bearing of Achilles on the first contest ; and look on him now
at the proposal of the last.   In the circus he places a ponderous spear and caldron yet unfired, and around embossed with
flowers—and uprise at once the spearmen, Agamemnon and

Meriones, when Achilles thus addresses the king of men—nor is Sotheby's English inferior to Homer's Greek:

> " Achilles spake—'.King ! thy surpassing art
> All know, far far o'er all to hurl the dart,
> And—if thy will, Atrides !—such is mine—
> The lance be that brave chief's—the caldron thine.'
> He spake : and Atreus' son, with joyful mind,
> The lance to brave Meriones resign'd :
> And bade Talthybius to his tent convey
> The beauteous caldron, to record the day."

Old Homer was indeed a perfect gentleman. In the noblest of all warlike arts, that of the spear, he makes Agamemnon's self rise to contend, in honour of Patroclus—the brother of him he had so outrageously wronged—but whom he has now gloriously righted in the presence of all Greece. The mutual forgiveness is now complete—complete the reconciliation. Both heroes stand now in each other's estimation as they did before that fatal quarrel. Achilles, indeed, needed no vindication ; but Agamemnon did ; and in that incident, closing the games with such dignity, we feel that he was indeed the King of Men,—such a king as even Socrates himself—in that divine dialogue of Plato which Cicero asked who could read without tears—hoped,

> " When he had shuffled off this mortal coil,"

to converse with in Elysium.

The games are over—the army is broken up—and to repast and sleep have gone all the people. Night and silence once more invest the camp ; and again begins the passion of Achilles. His thoughts are like the rage *Leonum vincula recusantum.*

> " The assembly broke up, and to the swift-sailing ships the people all
> Dispersed went : for mindful were they of repast,
> And of sweet sleep to have their full : but Achilles
> Wept, calling to mind his beloved friend ; nor him did sleep,
> The all-subduing, seize, but now here, now there he toss'd,
> Desiderating the manhood and the vigorous might of Patroclus ;
> What toilsome labours he had terminated along with him, what
> distresses he had endured,

> While passing through the battles of heroes, and dangerous
>   waves :
> Remembering all this—he let fall abundant tears.
> One while reclining on his sides,—at another
> Supine, and now on his face, then, standing up aright,
> He saunter'd about sorrowing, along the shore of the sea : him
>   not the morn,
> When dawning on the sea and on the shore, missed :
> But he, when he had yoked the swiftest horses to the chariot,
> Bound Hector, to be dragg'd behind his chariot :
> Thrice having dragg'd him around the mound of the dead Menœ-
>   tiades,
> Again he paused in his tent, him (Hector) he left
> Extended prone in the dust : but Apollo from his
> Body warded off all unseemliness[1] (putrefaction), pitying the man
> Even though dead : all around he veil'd him with his Ægis
> Of gold, that when dragging him along he might not lacerate
>   him."

The Fury will not leave his heart; she still glares in his
bloodshot eyes—and through that ghastly light, discolouring
and disfiguring, Achilles still sees the character and the
corpse of Hector. Would that his rage suffered him to chop
the slayer of Patroclus into pieces, and devour him raw!
That savage desire is dead, but it gave way but to another,
satiated—if his hate be not insatiable—by thus dragging the
body at his chariot round the mound of Menœtiades. ·He
sees not in that body the son of Priam, the Prince of the
people, the defender of his country, the worshipper of the
gods, but a wretch accursed—a hound abhorred—trampled
on, stabbed, mutilated, but not yet enough insulted, and
punished, and excommunicated from humanity ; as is its
ghost from all other ghosts in the world of shadows. 'Tis
thus that in his insanity he has looked on Hector, living or
dead—thus that he has thought on him, ever since Patroclus'
death. And thus it is that rage, and hate, and revenge,
kindled in war, or haply in peace, separate the souls of us
mortal beings in bitterest enmity, whom nature graciously
framed to live in the bonds of brotherhood. Had Helen and
Paris never sinned, how heroic might have been the friendship of Achilles and Hector ! The heir-apparent of the throne

---

[1] 'Αικίην, " ne corpus fœdaretur nec ulceribus et livoribus, nec putresceret,"
says Heyne.

of Troy might have visited the son of Peleus in his father's court of Phthia, and bards immortalised the mutual affection of the heroes. For prodigally endowed were they both by the gods with the noblest gifts of nature, and to Achilles Hector might have been Patroclus. Such is the mystery of this life; but in the Elysian Fields they may repose together in immortal love on the meads of Asphodel.

While thus Achilles in his wrath disgraced his noble foe, looking down from heaven the Immortals pitied him; all but Juno and Pallas—remembering how Paris in his rural home had disdained them, and preferred to theirs the charms of Venus—and the sovereign power of Ocean, the earth-encircling Earth-shaker. Apollo pleads with Jove for the restoration of the body of his beloved Hector to Priam; and Iris summons Thetis to heaven from her lamentations for her noble son, ordained to die at Troy far distant from his home. She is commissioned by the Thunderer to tell the Implacable that it is the will of heaven he should now relent, and receive the ransom.

COWPER.

" So spake the God, nor Thetis not complied :
Descending swift from the Olympian heights
She reach'd Achilles' tent. Him there she found
Groaning disconsolate, while others ran
To and fro, occupied around a sheep
New-slaughter'd large, and of exuberant fleece.
She, sitting close beside him, softly stroked
His cheek, and thus, affectionate, began :
'How long, my son ! sorrowing and mourning here,
Wilt thou consume thy soul, nor give one thought
Either to food or love ? Yet love is good,
And woman grief's best cure ; for length of days
Is not thy doom, but, even now, thy death
And ruthless destiny are on the wing.
Mark me—I come ambassadress from Jove.
The gods, he saith, resent it, but himself
More deeply than the rest, that thou retain'st
Amid thy fleet, through fury of revenge,
Unransom'd Hector. Be advised, accept
Ransom, and to his friends resign the dead.'
To whom Achilles, swiftest of the swift :
' Come then the ransomer, and take him hence ;
So be it, if such be the desire of Jove.'"

And now Iris, " who to her feet ties whirlwinds," is despatched to Troy, to enjoin Priam to repair unto Achaia's fleet
with such gifts as may assuage Achilles.   The old king sets
out on his journey, and, under the guidance of Hermes, who
meets him in shape of a " princely boy, now clothing first
his ruddy cheek with down, which is youth's loveliest season,"
reaches in his car, with the glorious ransom-price of Hector,
the tent of the Destroyer.   See it in Sotheby, who has a fine
eye for the picturesque :—

> " Then to the tent of great Achilles came,
> Whose wider amplitude, and loftier frame,
> To grace their king his Myrmidons had made,
> With trunks of pine on pine in order laid,
> And, from the marshes, for the shelt'ring roof,
> Mow'd many a reed, and firmly rear'd aloof,
> And compassing the court's wide spreading bound,
> Girt it with fence of thickest stakes around.
> One bar, a pine, immense in size and weight,
> From free intrusion fenced the guarded gate ;
> Three Greeks alone, with all their strength amain,
> Could draw it back, or forward force again ;
> Achilles singly heaved it.—There the god
> Gave Priam entrance to the chief's abode."

And will the wretched old man indeed venture into such a
presence ?   Yes—and without fear.   For he has yet a kingly
spirit—though, for his dear Hector's sake, willing with his
hoary locks to sweep the dust.   Hermes had told Priam from
Jove not to dread Achilles.

> " The Argicide shall guide, shall onward lead,
> Till to Achilles' presence thou proceed :
> There boldly enter, nor Pelides dread,
> That hero will not wound, but guard thy head.
> For Peleus' son, not senseless, rash, unjust,
> But prompt to raise the suppliant from the dust."

So Hermes spoke to Priam in his own palace ; and now that
they have reached the tent of the Terrible, before reascending
the Olympian heights, he comforts him with the same assurance, bidding him enter, and seize fast the knees of Achilles,
and adjure the hero to compassionate him, by his aged sire,
by his beauteous mother, and his darling son.

We shall venture to give in our literal prose, from beginning to end, the whole of this immortal scene. It is manifestly impossible for us to quote the poetical versions of the Four. Suffice it to say, that Sotheby, in this severest trial of skill and power, sustains his high character, and is inferior to none of his rivals.

NORTH.

" Right on to the tent march'd the old man
In which Achilles was sitting, beloved of Jove : in it himself
He found : but his companions were seated apart : these two alone,
The hero Automedon, and Alcimus—a shoot of Mars,
Minister'd, standing near : for he had newly ceased from food,
Having eaten and drank : and the table still stood near :
The huge Priam having enter'd, escaped the notice of these, and standing near,
With his hands Achilles' knees he grasp'd, and kiss'd (those) hands
Terrible, homicidal, which had slain so many of his sons.
As when an overwhelming calamity hath taken hold of a man, who, in his own country,
Having slain a human being, hath come among another people,
To a rich man's (house), amazement seizes those looking upon him !
In like manner stood Achilles aghast, when beholding the godlike Priam :
Aghast, too, stood the others,—gazing on each other.
But him Priam, supplicating, address'd :
' Think on thy father, oh, Achilles, like to the gods !
Who is of the same years as I, on the mournful threshold of old age :
Him, peradventure, some neighbouring (rivals) dwelling around him,
Are oppressing, nor is there one to avert evil and destruction :
Yet he, indeed, hearing that thou art alive,
Rejoices in his soul, and every day hopes
To see his beloved son return'd from Troy :
But I (am) thoroughly ill-fated, for I begat most valiant sons
In wide Troy—of them not one can I say to have been left.
Fifty they were to me, when the sons of the Greeks arrived :
Nineteen were from one womb,
But all the rest (my) concubines brought forth to me in the palaces.
Of many of these did impetuous Mars unnerve the knees ;
But him who was my alone one, and defended my city and them,

Him hast thou lately slain, while defending his native land,
—Hector: on his account now come I to the ships of the
    Greeks,
To redeem him of thee, and bring an unbounded ransom.
But, oh! Achilles, reverence the gods, and pity me,
Calling to mind your own father! truly still more pitiable am I,
For I have endured what never did any other earth-inhabiting
    mortal,
—To draw to my mouth the hand of the man that-slew-my-
    children.'
Thus spoke he: and in him he stirr'd up the longing of grief
    for his father,
And, having taken him by the hand, he gently push'd away the
    old man.
Both call'd to remembrance (the past); the one, Hector the
    manslayer
Lamented incessantly, prostrate at the feet of Achilles:
But Achilles bewail'd his own father, and, by turns,
Patroclus; and their groans rose up throughout the house.
But after Achilles had had his full of bewailing,
And the longing for it had departed from his mind and from his
    body,
Forthwith from his seat started he, and by the hand upraised the
    old man,
Taking pity on his hoary head, and hoary beard;
And, addressing him, spoke (these) wing'd words,—
'Ah, wretched one! many evils hast thou endured in thy mind.
How didst thou dare to come alone to the ships of the Greeks,
Into the presence of a man who thy many and brave
Sons slew? Surely thou hast a heart of steel!
But come, sit down beside me on the seat; and our sorrows alto-
    gether
Let us allow to lie down in our minds—grieved though we be;
For there is no profit in freezing lamentation.
Thus, then, have the gods spun the destiny of miserable mortals
To live mourning; but they themselves are without cares.
In the threshold of Jove lie two casks
Of gifts which he gives, the one of evils, but the other of
    blessings;
(He) on whom Jupiter, who delights in thunder, having mingled
    (them), shall bestow (both),
At one time is in evil, at another in good:
(But) to whom he shall give of the bad, him hath he made subject
    to reproach;
Him ravenous misery persecutes on the gracious earth,

And he goes about, neither honour'd by gods nor mortals.
So, indeed, on Peleus did the gods bestow splendid gifts
From his birth : for he was distinguish'd among all men
For plenty and wealth, and ruled over the Myrmidons ;
And to him, though a mortal, they gave a goddess to wife :
Yet even on him hath God inflicted an evil, in that no
Offspring of sons has been born in his house, to rule after him,
But an only son hath he begot, destined-to-perish-untimely ; nor
   him indeed
Do I cherish in his old age, since very far from my native land
Do I sit before Troy, saddening thee and thy children.
Thee, too, old man, have we heard, as once abounding in as much
   riches
As Lesbos southward, the seat of Macar, contains within itself,
And Phrygia eastward, and the far-extended Hellespont—
All these, old man, they say, didst thou surpass in riches and in
   sons.
But from the time when the celestials have inflicted on thee this
   calamity,
Battles and man-slayings have continually beset thy city.
Endure, nor unceasingly mourn in thine heart,
For nothing will it profit thee to be sad for thy son,
For thou shalt not raise him up again, before some new evil shalt
   thou suffer.'
Him then answer'd the old man, the godlike Priam,—
' Do not at all make-me-to-sit-down on a seat, Jove-nourish'd one,
   in so long as Hector
Lies uncared for (unburied) in the tents, but quick as possible
Ransom'd-restore him, that with (these) eyes I may behold him ;
   and do thou receive the ransom
Magnificent, which we bring to thee : and mayst thou enjoy it,
   and return
To thy fatherland, since thou hast first permitted me,
Myself, both to live and to look upon the light of the sun.'
Him the swift-footed Achilles, sternly-eyeing, address'd,—
' Provoke me no more, old man ; I myself purpose,
Ransom'd-to-restore Hector : from Jove to me came as a mes-
   senger
The mother who bore me, the daughter of the sea-dwelling old
   man ;
But, Priam, I know thee in my mind, nor deceivest thou me,
In that some god hath conducted thee to the swift ships of the
   Greeks ;
For no mortal might dare to enter, not even though very youth-
   vigorous,

The camp; since neither could-he-escape-the-notice-of the guards, nor the bars
Of our gates easily unbolt.
Therefore, no more rouse thou my soul in (its) sorrows,
Lest thee, old man, even thee I endure not in the camp,
Suppliant though thou be, and offend against the behests of Jove.'
    Thus spoke he : the old man fear'd, and obey'd the command.
But the son of Peleus from the house like a lion sprang forth ;
Not alone : along with him two attendants follow'd,
The hero Automedon, and Alcimus, whom chiefly indeed
Of his companions Achilles honour'd, since Patroclus was now dead,—
They then from the yoke unloosed the horses and mules,
And introduced the summoning herald[1] of the old man,
And placed him on a seat : from the beautifully-polish'd car
They took the unbounded ransom of Hector's head.
But two robes they left, and a fine-woven tunic,
That covering the corpse, he (Priam) might give it to be carried home.
Calling to him his maid-servants, he order'd them to wash, and to anoint all around
(The corpse)—taking it apart, so that Priam might not behold his son,
Lest he should not in his sorrowing heart restrain his anger
When looking on his son, and rouse up the heart (wrath) of Achilles
To slay him, and violate the behests of Jove.
It, when the hand-maidens had wash'd, and anointed with oil,
Around it they cast the beautiful mantle and the tunic,
And Achilles himself having lifted up, placed it in the couch,
And along with him his attendants raised it up into the beautifully-polished car.
    Then groan'd he, calling-by-name on his beloved friend,—
' Be not angry with me, Patroclus, if perchance thou mayst hear,
Even in Ades, that ransom'd-I-have-restored the illustrious Hector
To his father ; since no unbeseeming ransom hath he given,
Of which I verily on thee will bestow as much as is befitting.'
    He said, and to his tent return'd the illustrious Achilles,
And sat down on his splendidly-Dædalian reclining-chair, from which he had uprisen,
From the opposite wall, and to Priam these words address'd,—

---

[1] " Κήρυκα καλήτορα." Ἐπιθιτικῶς τον κήρυκα, ἀπὸ του βοᾷν και συγκαλεῖν ὄχλον.—Schol.

'Ransom-restored hath been thy son to thee, old man, as thou didst
   wish ;
Iu the couch he lies, and, along with the day-spring,
Thou thyself shalt behold and carry him away ; but now let us be
   mindful of supper.
For even the beautiful-hair'd Niobe was mindful of food,
Although even her twelve children were cut off in the house,
Six daughters truly, and six blooming sons ;
Them Apollo slew from (by means of) his silver bow,
Being enraged at Niobe ; the former, Diana that-delights-in-arrows
   (slew),
Because she (Niobe) had compared herself with the beautiful-
   cheek'd Latona,
For she said that *she* had brought forth two, while she herself had
   produced many.
But they (Apollo and Diana), though two destroy'd them all,
For-nine-days lay they in their slaughter (blood), nor was there
   one
To bury them ; for Jove had made the people stone.
Them, however, on the tenth day did the gods of heaven bury :
Yet even she was mindful of food, when weary of weeping.
And now somewhere among the rocks, among the sheep-frequented
   (solitary) mountains,
In Sipylus, where they say is the cradle of the goddess—
Nymphs, who move-vigorously (dance) around (on the banks) of
   the Achelous,
There, although of stone, does she digest[1] her sorrows, from (in-
   flicted by) the gods.
But come, illustrious old man, let us concern ourselves
About food, and afterwards mayst thou weep for thy beloved
   son,
When you have carried him to Troy ; much-wept-for shall he be
   by thee.'
   He said, and starting up, a sheep, white-fleeced, the swift
   Achilles
Slew, (which) his companions flay'd, and prepared skilfully and
   gracefully,
And into small-portions-cut it attentively, and spits pass'd through
   it,
And roasted it circumspectly, and drew all off (the spits).
But Automedon having taken bread, portion'd it out on the table
In beautiful baskets, and Achilles portion'd out the flesh.

---

[1] Κήδεα πέσσει — Shakespeare's "chewing the cud of sweet and bitter
memory."

They stretch'd forth their hands to the good cheer[1] (now) ready
and served up.
After they had removed the desire of food and drink,
Then indeed did the Dardanian Priam gaze-with-admiration on
Achilles,
How large, and what kind he was (his stature and beauty); for he
seem'd in presence like the gods :
And Achilles gazed with admiration on the Dardanian Priam,
Contemplating his benevolent countenance, and listening to his
words !
But when they were satisfied with beholding one another,
The godlike aged Priam first address'd him,—
'Send-me-to-repose, Jove-nourish'd-one, that now
Lull'd in sweet sleep we may be recruited ;
For never have my eyes under my eyelids closed,
From the time when, under thy hands, my son lost his life,
But ever I groan, and ten thousand woes digest,
In the enclosures of my court, rolling myself in the dust :
But now have I fed upon food, and the dark wine
Have I sent (pour'd) down my throat : for never before had I fed.'
He said : but Achilles gave orders to his companions and bonds-
women
To prepare a bed beneath the portico, and beautiful bedclothes
Of purple to onlay, and thereupon coverlets to place,
And soft fleeces to put on, to be drawn over from above.
They went forth from the house, having in their hands each a
torch,
And immediately they made up two couches-with-sedulous haste,
When the swift-footed Achilles, false-fear-infusing[2] into him, thus
address'd him,—
'Sleep thou without, beloved old man, lest any one of the Greeks
As a consulter should come here, for such continually
Are sitting by me deliberating in council, as the manner is :
Of these, if any one should see thee through the swift dark night,
Forthwith will he tell it to Agamemnon, the shepherd of the people,
And peradventure a procrastination of the ransoming of the corse
may take place.
But come now, tell me this, and truly tell me,
How many-days art-thou-anxious-for to bury the illustrious Hector,

---

[1] 'Ονιαθ, lit. profitable things.

[2] 'Επιχετευιων—*wounding by sarcastic raillery*—must here mean, falsum timo-
rem incutere cupiens—τὸ κιρτουίν ὁν τραχότητα ἰχον ὑβριστικὴν, ἤ ὀνιδιστικὴν, 'ἀλλ'
ἰσσήγησιν φόβου ψευδοῦς—not a contumelious or sarcastic roughness, but an exhibition of pretended fear, says Eustathius on this passage. Heyne, however,
translates it, "*Subridendo et quasi leniter jocando.*"

Since *so* long will I myself be at rest, and restrain the people.'
Him the venerable godlike Priam then address'd,—
' If me thou wish to celebrate funeral rites to the illustrious Hector,
By so doing, a grateful-favour wilt thou confer on me, Achilles.
Thou knowest that we are shut up in the city, and from afar must
    wood
Be brought from the city, and much panic-struck are the Trojans
For nine days him shall we bewail in the house,
But on the tenth day would we bury him, and let the people have
    the funeral banquet :
On the eleventh day would we erect a mound upon him,
And on the twelfth will we renew the war, if it must needs be so.'
Him then address'd the swift-footed, godlike Achilles,—
' It shall be so, venerable Priam, since thus thou wishest it :
The war, for as long as thou orderest, will I restrain.'
Thus having spoken, the old man's right hand at the wrist
He grasp'd, that he might not in any respect be alarm'd in mind,
And in the vestibule of the abode *there*, there went to sleep
The herald and Priam, having prudent counsels in their breast ;
But Achilles slept in a corner of the well-compacted tent,
And beside him lay the beautiful-cheek'd Briseïs."

This was, perhaps, the boldest attempt ever undertaken
and achieved in one single scene by any poet. We do not
except even the wonderful works of Shakespeare, who " exhausted worlds, and then imagined new ; " or of Milton, who
not only brought together angels and us conversing in Paradise, but ventured even on more transcendent strains. The
heart of Homer could not rest till he had reconciled the
Destroyer and the Bereaved. Such was the nobility of his
nature, and such the congenial grandeur of his genius, that
he felt a high and holy duty imposed on him by the Muse, of
which he was the Voice, to conquer and overcome all mortal
horror, repulsion, and repugnance in the hearts of his heroes,
and to vindicate in them the laws that bind together the
brotherhood of the human race. His triumph is perfect in
that reconciliation. Throughout the whole interview the flow
of feeling is strong " as a mountain river " that issues in
power from its very source ; with many magnificent breaks
and many majestic flows it pursues its way ; and ends tran-
quilly in the wide wide sea, under the hush of night, " when
all the stars of heaven are on its breast."

We beheld a stormy morning—and a day of storms—nor

knew how to hope for termination of the tempest. But we
find ourselves "at dewy to-fall of the night" in the midst of
profoundest peace. All passion has raved itself away; no
sound is heard in the Tent but the murmurs of the midnight
sea; and Achilles and Priam, like princes at peace, are asleep
beneath the reed-roof of the pine-pillared edifice, while their
tutelary gods inspire into their souls undisturbed dreams.
Out in the open air, before the porch, and beneath the pity of
the stars, laid thereon by the heroic hands that slew the hero,
and decently composed his limbs at last, and covered with
fair vesture, lies on the car of Priam the ransomed body of
Hector. From all disfigurement and decay Apollo had saved
it with his golden shield; nor will Hecuba and Andromache
need to regard with horror in their grief the face of the Defender.

ΜΗΝΙΝ ἄειδε, Θεὰ, Πηληϊάδεω 'Αχιλῆος.

That great line has been developed—out of it has grown
the Iliad.

"Like some tall palm the stately fabric rose."

Yet have there been critics, and those, too, of some "mark
and likelihood," who have been unable to construe Μηνιν—to
understand the meaning of WRATH. They forget, too, that it
was the wrath of Achilles. They have complained of Homer,
that he has inspired his hero with two Wraths—one, of
which Agamemnon was the object—of the other, Hector. O
the blind breasts of mortals! There was but one Wrath—but
it was "wide and general as the casing air;" in its atmosphere Achilles breathed—it was the plague—and Apollo sent
it; it broke not out in boils, and blains, and blotches on the
face of Achilles—for nothing could change the beautiful but
into the terrible—but it bathed his eyes in fire, and discoloured to them all the green earth with blood. Wrath is a
demon—and its name is Legion—for there are many; and
the devils are like gods. The passion of Achilles—who was
the Incarnation of the Will—hewed down, on all the high
places, woods for fuel to burn on its own altar, a perpetual
oblation and sacrifice, flaming day and night, to Revenge.
Achilles had a noble understanding—no Greek among them
all had larger Discourse of Reason. But he appealed to
another power in his being, on his mighty wrong; and a

response came to him, more sacred even than of conscience,
" Relent not till Greece is trodden in the dust by Troy."

MHNIN ἄειδι, Θεὰ, Πηληϊάδεω 'Αχιλῆος.

It is a miserable mistake to think that Achilles was at any
time, except just at the very first burst on sustaining that
injurious insult, wrathful with Agamemnon. The King of
Men was the cause—but the effect flashed over his whole
life. Never before had his heart conceived the possibility of
insult to him the goddess-born. He had " taken the start of
this majestic world," and allegiance in all eyes looked acknow-
ledgment of the divine right of him whom nature had made
and crowned a monarch of her own. In his superior presence
the wisdom of Ulysses was mute—the strength of Ajax lost
all its praise—dim was the fire of Diomede—and the grey head
of Nestor shone with joy when he did it reverence. Thersites'
self dared no scurrile jest within hearing of the son of Thetis.
At the uplifting of his peaceful hand, the Myrmidons were
meek as lambs—another wave, and away went the herd of
wolves to lap the blood of battle. And then, had he not
sacked a score of cities, slain their kings, and led captive the
daughters of kings, gladly to live in the delights of love—
lemans all of the man who had extinguished their kindred,
but who still cherished closest to his great heart his affianced
bride, Briseïs ? *She* was—*not torn*—for Agamemnon dared
not violence to the Invincible—but taken from his Tent by
the heralds—holy men even as the priests were holy—and
Achilles in his wrath respected the servants of the laws, because
the laws, he knew, are from Jove. His great soul enjoyed a
religious pride (remember he was a pagan) in obedience—on
that trial—to the Sire of the Gods.

MHNIN ἄειδι, Θεὰ, Πηληϊάδεω 'Αχιλῆος.

The Wrath, you know, was just. And what is Revenge,
but what one of the wisest of men has called it, a wild kind
of Justice ? Achilles sat not at the ships " nursing his Wrath
to keep it warm." " No fear lest dinner cool." It was a repast
of one dish, hot as if it had been baked in Erebus. It streamed
up in his nostrils a bitter-sweet savour, while they dilated
with the lust of that infernal food. To greatness of character
is essential inflexibility of purpose ; and he sat there, out of

the battling in which, till then, had been his delight, a martyr
to his own fury. His Wrath embraced now all the Greek
army—all Greece—and especially himself—wroth was he exceedingly with Achilles. "Man pleased not him, nor woman
either"—except Patroclus—and now and then, in dreadful
dalliance of disappointed passion for another,

> "Diomeda, Phœbus' daughter fair;"

yet he had delight still in Music and Poetry. Nor did the
Harper smite the strings like a madman. They yielded
solemn sounds and high, for the chords were struck to odes
chanted by the hero's voice, to the praise of the heroes. That
voice was like a bell chiming among groves. It was of miraculous reach—but his contr'alto that soared skywards, was no
falsetto—and his basso was like the sound of the hollow sea
when the flowing tide is musical on the yellow sands in the
night-silence. Beautiful 'twas felt to be by Ulysses, and
Ajax, and Phœnix, when, on their hopeless mission, they
paused at the door of the state-room of his Tent, to listen to
Achilles, as if he had been Apollo. His very courtesy awed
them ; and they left him unmoved in his majesty, within even
higher ideas of his heroic character, because that he was inexorable to all their prayers—while

> "The war wide-wasted, and the people fell."

From within—if at all—must be moved the soul of Achilles.
The more terrible the passion, the more entire its joy. And
never is joy so deep, "as when drumly and dark it rolls on its
way"—the main flood swollen by a thousand tributary
streams, each, as it joins, lost in one general grim discolora-
tion. And the soul of Achilles was moved—at last—from
within, by his love for Patroclus. The first relenting of his
Wrath—the first "change that came o'er the spirit of his
dream," vindicated his character at once from all that might
have seemed questionable in his passion. The hero felt that
Hector was too near the ships—in the remonstrance of the
man dearest to his heart; and while other voices might as
well have spoken to the winds, that of his brother began to
move the hero. Like two trees had they grown up together
in front of the palace of Peleus—they were as the pillars of
his state. "Go then to battle— my Patroclus—and in the

armour of thy Achilles!" He went—and died; and was his death, think ye, an anodyne to lull asleep the Wrath of him who sent his brother to destruction? But it became—say the philosophers—another Wrath; it continued the same Wrath, say we; but, like lightning glancing from tree to tree, or if lightning act not so, like an arrow which does, it glanced from Agamemnon, and stopped not till it smote Hector.

ΜΗΝΙΝ ἄειδι, Θεά, Πηληϊάδιω 'Αχιλῆος.

But that Wrath, as yet, kindles not against the killer of Patroclus. It turns and fastens on his own heart. Dismally streaked is it now with the bloodshot agonies of grief. He rages against all that breathes—stirs—lives—dies. He is angry with gods and men—with Agamemnon, king of men— with himself—most of all with Hector, though he names him not—and with the doom of death, since it has fallen on Patroclus. What fierce embracement of the corpse! What fury in the aim meditated against that vein-swollen throat of his, choking in convulsive agonies heaved from his bursting heart! The Invincible about to be a suicide! But his hand is withheld—not by the warrior who kneels beside him, but by the same Familiar who had been with him ever since the insult—by Revenge. Then it is that the insult is forgotten —and Agamemnon too—and that one phantom establishes itself before his eyes, never more to leave them till it be laid in blood—the image of Hector stripping Patroclus, and daring now to wear the armour Achilles wore. That now is the wrong—that now is the insult—let the living Briseïs warm with love and delight the couch of Agamemnon, and none disturb their embraces; the dead body of Patroclus is now all his thought, and all his desire—and he will pursue his murderer till he has "torn the bloody reckoning from his heart."

ΜΗΝΙΝ ἄειδι, Θεά, Πηληϊάδιω 'Αχιλῆος.

But who was it that rescued the body of Patroclus? Not Meriones and the Ajaces, from Hector's self, and restored his dead brother to Achilles? Achilles, unarmed—naked—but for the burning light with which Minerva halo'd his head— beyond the fosse stood and shouted. That portentous apparition is the most sublime sight in poetry, and in nature; if, as we have said, sublimity be the union, as of cause and effect,

of power and terror. Such is the union of the two, in thunder,
lightning, and the sea, and the roar of battle when hosts com-
mingle ; and such then was their union in the figure, face, and
voice of one then invested by heaven with supernatural attributes, to astound and scatter a whole warlike host.

His goddess-mother alone knew how to lay the agonies of
his wrathful woe. It was by elevating his whole spirit to a
still loftier pitch of heroism by those heavenly Arms and
Armour, to forge which roared all the furnaces in the celestial
smithy. She knew the sight of that Shield, engraven with
the glories of earth and heaven, would pacify her hero. From
the dread music of the bright trembling and quivering beaten
silver and gold, as Thetis dropt it, arms and armour, at the
feet of her son, all the Myrmidons fled howling ; but in that
music Achilles heard the death-doom of Hector. He armed,
he mounted, and, like the sun-god—unappalled by portents
and prodigies, when his war-steeds spake—he drove to battle,
in a whirlwind of wrath, as when the orb of day looks angry
in heaven, and seems to move through the storm.

ΜΗΝΙΝ ἄειδε, Θεὰ, Πηληϊάδεω ᾽Αχιλῆος.

Patroclus is with him all over the battle-field. For his sake
he slaughters. Each foe that falls is a victim to his shade.
So much dearer the sacrifice, if of the same blood—like Poly-
dore and Lycaon—as Hector. Yet he scorns not even to take
captives. Twelve Trojan princes he binds like slaves, reserved
for the funeral pile of Patroclus, for a moment prefigured in a
dream. Nor is the grandeur of Achilles abated by the sight
of " the gods descending mixed in fight." The mortal sustains
compare with the immortals. His fury has brought them all
from heaven. And now he rages alone before the walls of
Troy—and as Hector stands at the Scæan gate, we hear again
Homer's voice, saying in a low mournful tone,—" If Hector
perish, then Ilium falls ; " and perish he will, we well know,
for his lot, in the eternal balance, kicks the beam held in the
hand of Jove. The wrath of Achilles enkindles the burning
light of his celestial armour. Kindled from within and from
without, he is a figure of fire, or he is the lightning, the flame,
the sun, the moon, the star Orion, or like him " that leads the
starry host, and shines brightest," Hesperus,—all that is most
beautiful, most dreadful, most deathful in the skies.

He pursues—grasps—kills Hector, as a bird of prey a bird of peace. Yet Hector, too, was an eagle. Is the Wrath then assuaged at last? No doubt Achilles for a moment imagined that it was assuaged, and therefore he cried aloud, "great glory have we achieved; we have slain the illustrious Hector." But he knew not the full power of his own passions of grief and revenge. What is glory now to him the lover of glory? What though Pergamus totter with all its towers? Patroclus is dead; and at that thought all is forgotten but the carcass of the dog that killed him; which shall have no burial but in the bowels of dogs and of the fowls of the air. Not sufficient to satiate his Wrath the wounds the soldiers gave. Achilles perhaps saw them not while they were stabbing; nor heeded the crows picking at the fallen quarry. But he was himself the lion to drag away into his lair the infatuated hunter that dared to turn upon him on the edge of the forest.

Then a sudden thought smote him—and away he drove in his chariot, amid clouds of dust, the hero's hated head, with its long black-brown curls, dashing, and leaping, and bounding, the whole naked body bloodily begrimed, and distorted all its once fair proportions; and thus doth the noble Hector now approach the fleet he so lately fired, while the city shrieks to see the flight, and there is the silence of consternation among them who have their dwelling in heaven.

MHNIN ἄειδι, Θιά, Πηληϊάδιω Ἀχιλῆος.

It—the Wrath—heaves so broad and high the funeral pyre of Patroclus. Sullen as the soul of Achilles, that pyre smoulders, but will not burst into devouring flames. But the hero calls upon the Winds—they obey the spell of his passion, and the sudden conflagration is in a roar. A mingled immolation of hounds, horses, and princes, sacrificed in horrid mixture of brute and human life, expiring in the same pangs in the same expiatory fire! But the bones of the beloved, they are apart—and, gathered out of the reach of contamination, remain in their own hallowed mould for the consecration of Achilles' tears. And now let the heroes contend in the games, and every heart be joyful—while he decides the victory, and bestows the prize—in honour of the shade that once animated that dearest dust. The pomp fades away; and then comes the final transport of passion—its last agony

—truculent as its first—just as in external nature we see the tumult of the elements collecting all its violence for the explosion in which it dies. Achilles having tossed, till midnight on his sleepless couch, rushes off to the lonely sea-beach, and raves there, " till the ruddy morning rises o'er the waves." Into his savage spirit no pity is breathed by "the innocent brightness of the new-born day." Its rising glory but aggravates his gloom; the general joy embitters his own peculiar loss ; and his wrath flames up to a fiercer height, now that its object is again exposed before his eyes in the blaze of light. There stands the monument of Patroclus—suddenly heaved aloft by the Grecian army ; and there lies his murderer. Thrice round it he drives the corpse—and then the Avenger, having exhausted his heart, sinks down into sleep. Patroclus had already visited him in a dream—all the prayers of the phantom had been religiously fulfilled; and we can believe that the sleep of Achilles was passionless as that of death.

But he awakes from that oblivion—and again we hear

"the voice of loud lament,
And echoing groans that shake the lofty tent."

His companions in arms are preparing the unheeded repast ; Achilles is " feeding on his own heart." That such unrelenting wrath should longer abide in such heroic bosom, is now displeasing to the gods. Nature has had its dreadful indulgence, and must be restored to sanity ; nor will Heaven suffer a dead son to lie longer out of the reach of his parent's tears. Throughout all the Iliad, the Immortals have been coming and going before our eyes ; and now they appear, like " blessed angels pitying human cares." The silver-footed mother, Jove-sent, beseeches her son to vent no more his vengeance on senseless earth. Achilles becomes, in one moment, merciful ; a divine calm is instantly inspired into his being, and not merely without reluctance, but in a movement of his whole soul, as if it met the benign command with the joy of deliverance from evil, he utters but these few words,

" Be the ransom given—
And we submit—since such the will of heaven."

Simple—and sublime ! and now we feel more than ever the grandeur of the opening line of the Iliad.

ΜΗΝΙΝ ἄειδι, θεὰ, Πηληϊάδιω 'Αχιλῆος.

We are prepared now for the Interview between Achilles and Priam. He, who abhorred as the gates of hell the man who said one thing and did another, has pledged his word to his immortal Parent that he will accept the ransom—and we know that he will do so in a manner worthy of himself; that all the beauty of his character will again break forth as bright as the day. The being whom, for some time past, we have been shuddering at with fear, we shall ere long regard with love—and then be conscious of the perfect admiration due to the noblest of heroes.

Yet Homer, reverent of humanity, is afraid, even in the mightiness of his power, that he may offer violence to nature. And therefore, with what holy skill does her High Priest prepare the way to his ministrations at her altar! Achilles is gentle as a child; but Priam rages in the impotence of grief. The wretched old man plays the tyrant in his palace, more imperious in his misery than he ever had been in his joy; more self-willed, now that they are all dead, and wrested from his sway, than when surrounded by his princely sons, and his tributary princedoms. How unlike his wrath to that of Achilles! But the heavens look down with pity on his grey and almost discrowned head, and under their guidance he takes his way, with good omens, to the Tent of the Destroyer. It is the Will of Jove that all those agonies of the old and young—the weak and the mighty—should cease; that for a while there should be a truce to sorrow—and that the peace of heaven, with healing under its wings, should descend on earth.

" Right on to the Tent marched the old man." Achilles was not now singing to the harp old heroic songs; for the ear was cold that used to listen to his music and his poetry. Patroclus was dead—and therefore mute was Achilles. Automedon and Alcimus still ministered near; and in midst of all that silence, like a night-vision, entered the figure of Priam. Achilles' self stood aghast at sight of the Apparition. For a moment he recognised not the kingly supplicant embracing his knees, as some homicide driven from his native land; but soon knew he that it was even very Priam himself, kissing those hands, terrible, homicidal, which had slain so many of his sons. Those lips had already done their work, even before one word had found its way through them from that broken

heart.   Still—but not stern—stood Achilles, like a statue.
He feared to stir hand, foot, or figure, lest he should disturb or dismay the old King, whom his wrath had thus
prostrated into the posture of a slave.   Yet — think not
that he felt any remorse—for he was the prince of "souls
made of fire, and children of the sun, with whom revenge is
virtue."

"Think on thy father, O Achilles! like to the gods!"
Words that like arrows pierced his heart!   For the Destroyer
knew that never more was he to see the face of Peleus.   He
thought of far-off Phthia, and Pity "her soul-subduing voice
applied" to his mournful and melancholy spirit.   The plead-
ing of Priam was indeed most pathetic—but we cannot believe
that more than a low indistinct murmur from his lips was
heard by Achilles.   There was a confusion before his eyes—
and in his spirit—of Priam and of Peleus—one image—one
phantom mysteriously combined of two fathers left utterly
desolate.   But the last words of the kneeler he did hear,—" I
have endured to draw to my mouth the hand of the man that
slew my children."   And then, Achilles took Priam by the
hand, as tenderly almost as if it had been the hand of his own
father, and "gently pushed away the old man," that he might
not abide another moment in that attitude of abasement; but
even, in worst affliction, might rise up to the bearing proper
to a king, "taking pity on his hoary head and hoary beard!"
How consolatory that address to the royal supplicant! and
how dignified!   Admiration of the fearlessness of the old man
mingled with pity of his sufferings; and what a princely expression of profoundest sympathy,—" Come, sit down beside
me on this seat!"   Priam is again about to be enthroned.
The momentary abjectness of misery gives way to a kingly
comfort; and the shades of Patroclus and of Hector would
have rejoiced in Hades to behold such a spectacle.   The
great soul of Achilles speaks in the heroic homily with which
he soothes the sorrows of the King.   A high moralist he
becomes, in the midst of their common misfortunes—common
not to them alone, but to all the human race.   "Thus, then,
have the gods spun the destiny of miserable mortals!"   He
reconciles his illustrious guest, as well as himself, to all that
has befallen, and to all that is about to befall them, by re-

ligion; and he ennobles their reconcilement by the sublimity
of the fiction in which the "truth severe" is expressed, and
shadowed forth the moral providence of Heaven.

But, elevated as is the mood in which Achilles converses
with the father of Hector, they both feel as men; and the
peculiar character and passion of each breaks out suddenly in
the midst of that divine dialogue. Priam, though calmed by
the pouring out of his own sorrow, and by the sympathy of
the "Lord of Fears," is all at once seized on by a longing to
see, and to receive, and to embrace the dead body of his son.
" Do not at all make-me-to-sit-down on a seat, Jove-nourished
one! in so long as Hector lies uncared-for-in the tent; but
quick as possible ransomed-restore-him, that with these eyes
I may behold him; and do thou receive the ransom magnificent, which we bring to thee; and mayst thou enjoy it, and
return to thy fatherland!" "Him, the swift-footed Achilles,
sternly eyeing, addressed,—'Provoke me no more, old man!
I myself purpose ransomed-to-restore Hector!'"

And yet this finest touch and trait of nature has been found
fault with by the critics! "I believe every reader," says
Wakefield, "must be surprised, as I confess I was, to see
Achilles *fly out into so sudden a passion*, without any apparent
reason for it." He then explains the proper meaning of the
passage. "Priam, perceiving that his address had mollified
the heart of Achilles, takes this opportunity to persuade him
to give over the war, and return home, especially since his
anger was sufficiently satisfied by the fate of Hector. Immediately Achilles took fire at this proposal, and answers:
'Is it not enough that I have restored thy son? Ask no
more, lest I retract that resolution!' In this view we see a
natural reason for the sudden passion of Achilles." This is
very bad. It represents Priam as cunning and crafty even in
his distraction; and why should he have desired a cessation
of the war? All his sons were dead—Hector and all—and
yet so fond was he of life, so tenacious of his throne, that
he took this favourable opportunity of eliciting a promise
from Achilles to spare Troy!

Achilles did not "*fly into a sudden passion*." But as Cowper,
on the whole, well says, he was "mortified to see his generosity, after so much kindness shown to Priam, still distrusted,

and that the impatience of the old king threatened to deprive
him of all opportunity of doing gracefully what *he could not
be expected to do willingly.*" He was about to do it willingly ;
for Thetis had told him, that such was the will of Jove. But
a sudden flash of memory came across him—and he said,
" No more arouse thou my soul in its sorrows." Achilles, all
his life long—at least all through the Iliad—*took his own way
in all things ;* and he could not bear to be baffled in his own
mode of mercy, even by the unhappy father of the prince
whose body he was about—ransomed—to restore.

MHNIN ἄειδι, Θεὰ, Πηληϊάδεω ᾿Αχιλῆος.

But an end to all criticism—alike of others and our own—
on the immortal interview. That was the last cloud that
passed across the countenance of Achilles. " The son of
Peleus from the house (tent) like a lion sprung forth." Yes,
like a lion—though it was to order in the herald—" to take
from the beautifully-polished car the unbounded ransom of
Hector's head"—to enjoin the women to wash the corpse apart
from Priam, that the passionate old man might not, by giving
sudden vent to his agony, provoke him (Achilles, who knew well
his own WRATH) " to slay the king, and violate the behests of
Jove"—and to lift it with his own hands up upon the bier on
the car that was to convey it to Troy. In the tenderest offices
of humanity to the living and to the dead, aware of the danger
of his own fiery spirit ! In self-knowledge, if not in self-con-
trol—a philosopher—and a hero.

MHNIN ἄειδι, Θεὰ, Πηληϊάδεω ᾿Αχιλῆος.

That Wrath has now blazed its last, yet " even in its ashes
live its wonted fires ;" and he asks forgiveness of Patroclus,
that even now, and thus, has been quenched his Revenge.
" But large, O beloved Shade ! hath been the ransom—nor
shalt thou not receive thereof thy due even in Hades." Now
all in the Tent shall be perfect peace. Priam must partake
of the repast. Famished is the Woe-begone, but he must eat
and drink—even as Niobe did in the midst of all her dead
children. " Then indeed did the Dardanian chief gaze-with-
admiration on Achilles, how large, and what kind he was
(his stature and beauty) ; for he seemed in presence like the
gods : And Achilles gazed with admiration on the Dardanian

Priam, contemplating his benevolent countenance, and listening to his words!" They retire to sleep—Priam on a couch
graciously provided for him by the "great lord" in a place
safe from all intrusion of the Greeks, that he may take his
departure—without an eye to see him—early in the morning,
with the body of his son, to Troy; Achilles in the bosom of
Briseïs, wherein not often will the hero lay his head,—for we
remember the dying words of Hector,

> " Phœbus and Paris shall avenge my fate,
> And stretch thee here, before the Scæan gate."

HOMER AND HIS TRANSLATORS.

CRITIQUE VI.—THE ODYSSEY.

[JANUARY 1831]

THE Iliad was written by Homer. Will Wolf and Knight tell us how it happened that all the heroic strains about the war before Troy, poured forth, as they opine, by many bards, regarded but one period of the siege? By what divine felicity was it that all those sons of song, though apart in time and place, united in chanting the wrath of Achilles? The poem is one—like a great wood, whose simultaneous growth overspreads a mountain. Indeed, one mighty poem, in process of time, moulded into form out of separate fragments, composed by a brotherhood of bards—not even coeval —may be safely pronounced an impossibility in nature.

Achilles was not the son of many sires; nor was the part he played written for him by a succession of "eminent hands," all striving to find fit work for their common hero. He is not a creature of collected traditions. He stands there —a single conception—in character and in achievement; his absence is felt like that of a thunder-cloud withdrawn behind a hill, leaving the air still sultry; his presence is as the lightning in sudden illumination glorifying the whole field of battle. Kill, bury, and forget him, and the Iliad is no more an Epic.

No two men at the same time ever yet saw a ghost; because a ghost is an Eidolon begotten by the imagination on the air of night, or some night-like day, and is visible but to his own frightened father. Now, Achilles was an Apparition; and his seer was a blind old man, with a front like Jove's, and a forehead like Olympus. "All power was given him in that dreadful trance;" and Beauty and Terror accompanied the

Destroyer. He haunted Homer, who no longer knew that he had himself created the sublimest of all Phantoms. But the Muse gave the maker command over his creature ; and, at the waving of his hand, the imaginary Goddess-born came and went obedient, more magnificent than any shadowy form that at the bidding of sunlight stalks along mountains into an abysm of clouds.

The Odyssey—also and likewise—was written by Homer, and the proof lies all in one word—Ulysses. There he is —the self-same being as in the Iliad, and the birth of one brain. Had Homer died the day he said, " And thus they celebrated the obsequies of Hector the Tamer-of-Horses," before no mortal eye would have stood on the threshold of his own hall, pouring out from his quiver all the arrows at his feet, that vision of a ragged beggar, suddenly transfigured into an Avenger more glorious far than Apollo's self transfixing the Python,—for Lartiades stretched along his ancestral floor the whole serpent brood.

The opening of the Iliad is very simple—and so is the opening of the Odyssey ; and both openings are, you will agree with us in thinking, sublime. In the one you are brought in a moment into the midst of heaven-sent death threatening the annihilation of a whole host ; and, in pacifying Apollo, Agamemnon incenses Achilles, whose wrath lowers calamity almost as fatal as the visitation of the Plague. Men's minds are troubled—there is debate of doom in Heaven—nation is enraged against nation—and each trusts to its auxiliar gods. In the other there is no din below—the earth is silent—and you hear not the sea. Corn grows where Troy-Town stood—and you feel that Achilles is dust. All the chiefs who fought there and fell not, as Sotheby solemnly says—

> " At home once more
> Dwell free from battle and the ocean roar "—

and there is an almost melancholy peace. There is mysterious mention of shipwreck on account of sin—and one guiltless and great Survivor is spoken of and then named—who is to take the place in our imaginations of all the other heroes living or dead—affectingly named—for he has been and is to be a Sufferer—" All but Ulysses ! " And shall the Celestial Synod care for that One Man ! Ay, Minerva says to Jove,

" With bosom anguish-rent I view
    Ulysses, hapless chief ! who from his friends
    Remote, affliction hath long time endured
    In yonder woodland isle, the central boss
    Of ocean. That retreat a Goddess holds,
    Daughter of sapient Atlas, who the abyss
    Knows to its bottom, and the pillars high
    Himself upbears which separate Earth from Heaven.
    His daughter there the sorrowing chief reclaims,
    And ever with smooth spirit, insidious seeks
    To wean his heart from Ithaca, meantime
    Ulysses, happy might he but behold
    The smoke ascending from his native land,
    Death covets. Canst thou not, Olympian Jove,
    At last relent ? Hath not Ulysses oft
    With victims slain amid Achaia's fleet
    Thee gratified, while yet at Troy he fought ?
    How, therefore, hath he thus incensed thee, Jove ? "

At once we love the Man of whom the Muse is to sing—
longing for his home, his wife, and his son—and pitied at
last by Jove, at the intercession of Minerva, because of his
piety. That she should fly to Ithaca, and that Hermes should
wing his way to the Isle of Secresy—on behalf of Ulysses—
seems demanded of the justice of heaven. And simple as
all this is—we said it was sublime—for our sympathies are
already awakened for

" A good man struggling with the storms of fate."

Ulysses longs for Ithaca—but knows not what may have
passed, or may be passing there—if Penelope and Telemachus
be alive or dead. All we are told is, that year after year he
has been lamenting for his native Isle—sighing for a sight of
its ascending smoke, ere he dies—unforgetful of Ithaca even
in Calypso's arms.

How finely Sotheby has given Minerva's " alighting," and
the sudden showing of the scene—the first sight of which
reveals to us all the lawless life of the Suitors, and the evils
to which the kingless Island has been so long a prey ! We
are at once in the heart of it all—and the thought comes
across us in the midst of the revelry, " if Ulysses were
here ! "

" Then on her feet her golden sandals laced,
        With bright ambrosial wings divinely graced,

Wings that o'er earth and sea the Goddess bear
And challenge in their speed the viewless air—
Then grasp'd her brass-edged lance, of matchless strength,
Vast, massive, ponderous, whose far-shadowing length,
When the mail'd Goddess in her fury burns,
Rank after rank heroic chiefs o'erturns.
Then downward flew from steep Olympus' height,
And on Ulysses' island deign'd alight,
And at the threshold of his portal staid
Beneath the vestibule's protecting shade:
Held in her grasp the spear, and took her stand
Like Mentes, leader of the Taphian band:
There found the suitors festively array'd,
Who, gay, at dice before the palace play'd,
Their seats on hides of many a numerous herd,
Slain at the dictates of their haughty word:
Heralds, and minist'ring menials stood around,
Some who with temper'd wine their goblets crown'd.
With many a porous sponge some cleansed the board,
And with carved meat their proffer'd chargers stored.
Her first the young Telemachus perceived,
Who 'mid the wooers sat, and inly grieved,
Bright picturing in his mind, how, home again,
His sire would put to flight the wassail train,
Resume his honours, and ancestral right,
And, musing thus, the Goddess caught his sight.
Forward he sprung, in wrath, that nigh their feast
A stranger stood, an uninvited guest:
Then clasp'd her hand, received the brazen spear,
And pour'd his welcome in her gladden'd ear:
    'Hail! stranger—welcome—now the banquet share,
Then, feasted, wherefore here—thy wish declare.'
    He spake—and at the word, the blue-eyed Maid
Where the prince led the way not loth obey'd.
Now, 'neath his dome, within the channel'd height
Of a vast column, towering on the sight,
He fix'd the lance, where, ranged in order, stood
Ulysses' war-spears, like an iron wood:
Then, on a stately seat the Goddess placed,
With linen spread, and with a footstool graced,
And near it drew his own resplendent throne,
At distance from the suitors placed alone,
Lest the contemptuous rioters molest,
And vex with noise and insolence the guest,
Nor yield him peaceful leisure to inquire,
And hold free commune of his long-lost sire.

From a gold ewer, a maid, their hands to lave,
Pour'd in a silver bowl the cleansing wave,
And a bright table brought, where, largely spread,
The sage dispenseress heap'd the food and bread.
The sewer with flesh, all kinds, the plates supplied,
And golden goblets placed each guest beside,
Which oft with wine the busy herald crown'd ;
Then, rushing in, the suitors gather'd round,
And on their separate seats and thrones of state,
Where heralds wash'd their hands, in order sate :
The attendant maids in baskets piled their bread,
On the carved dainties as the feasters fed ;
And youths oft crown'd their goblets o'er and o'er,
Till thirst and hunger, satiate, sought no more ;
Then other joys inflamed their keen desire,
The song and dance, that charm the festive choir.
The herald gave to the reluctant hand
Of Phemius, leader of the minstrel band,
A silver lyre. By force the bard obey'd,
And, preluding the song, the measure play'd."

Telemachus is no favourite with many critics. But we
hope you admire and love the Princely Boy—for he was
assuredly a great favourite with Homer. So well did Homer
know his worth, that he is at no great pains to describe his
character. He puts him, however, into some situations that
serve to show what is in him—and he behaves, we think, like
heir-apparent to the throne. Here he allows the dicers to
shake their elbows undisturbed—in their pastimes perhaps
playing for the Queen. But he is picturing in his mind
another kind of game—in which his father will play the Lion,
and he the Lion's Whelp. Mentes, the leader of the Taphian
Band, though no vulgar stranger, is disregarded by the
Suitors, heralds, and menials — but how courteous is the
Prince ! "Manners maketh the man," and Telemachus, we
feel, will be a hero. He takes not his guest into some nook
or corner, to question him of his Sire—but places him on a
stately seat, with a footstool, "and near it drew his own resplendent throne." Let all the Suitors behold them two in
converse—nor dare to intrude upon their privacy—apart but
open — and confidential during the measure preluding the
Poet-Laureate's song. Minerva must have been pleased with
such graceful and dignified reception—and how wisely does

she insinuate into his heart, by half-truth and half-fable, hopes even of his sire's return! True that Telemachus speaks like one that will not be comforted; but his looks belie his words, for we see his face brightening as he listens to the stranger's counsel. Who does not see that he believes his father will return, as Minerva, after foretelling that return, says,

> "But this I urge—now truly this declare,
> Art thou, for such thou seem'st, Ulysses' heir?
> Thy features such, thy eyes so beaming bright,
> Such as the chief oft tower'd before my sight,
> Ere with their bravest heroes, Argos' boast,
> The Warrior moor'd his fleet on Phrygia's coast."

Pallas was not a goddess addicted to the complimentary— and she loved Ulysses too well to be easily satisfied with his son. But she was satisfied with his beaming eyes—nor at all dissatisfied with his answer about his mother, though it has given serious offence in certain quarters, not in the contemplation of Telemachus. The Prince said, "my mother assures me that I am the son of Ulysses—but I know it not." In this, says Pope, "there seems something very shocking;" but as Minerva approved of it, and said cheeringly, "heaven shall one day grace thee, not nameless, nor of a nameless race, sprung from Penelope," there can be no doubt that it was the answer usually returned to such a question, in that simple age, a sort of apothegm, that conveyed no imputation on any mother's fidelity to her husband, but, on the contrary, entire reliance on every mother's truth. That Telemachus in this conversation expresses no tenderness for his mother, has been foolishly said to show a want of due filial affection. But he knew she was pretty well, up-stairs—while he feared his father was dead or in misery—and that was the thought that wrung his heart. It would have been exceedingly silly to begin puling about Penelope to a person who was not much troubling his head about her—but who had paid her, nevertheless, a high and just compliment. There can be no doubt that he loved and honoured her—but he was now in his twentieth year—and at that age sons are shy of seeming before strangers too fond of their mothers—nay even before their mothers themselves—especially when surrounded by suitors. But hear him on his father :—

" Once I had hope while here my sire remain'd,
That wealth and virtue had our house sustain'd ;
But heaven, devising ill, not this design'd,
And left his fate obscurest, 'mid mankind ;
Nor could his death so sharply have impress'd
The sting of sorrow in my filial breast,
If, with his brave compeers, in Phrygia slain,
Or, 'mid his friends from Troy return'd again.
Then all the Greeks had raised his funeral mound,
And by his father's fame the son renown'd.
But him the Harpies from the light of day
Unknown, unseen, unheard, have swept away."

The noble boy listens with delight to the recital of his
Father's prowess, and the eagerness with which he embraces
the advice of Mentes to sail to Pylos, and travel thence to
Lacedemon, to inquire if Nestor or Menelaus can give him
any tidings of his lot, gives assurance not only of a confiding
and an affectionate, but of an adventurous and heroic spirit.
He weeps to emulate Orestes, who had so nobly avenged his
murdered Sire ; and on the stranger suddenly vanishing, in
awe and wonder he feels that his guest was a god, while
heroic fire is more strongly kindled in his heart. Is not this
a picture—in a few bold bright strokes—of the characteristic
virtues of youth ? What is wanting here that should have
been seen in the son of Ulysses ?

But where is Penelope ? Guess. Walking with her maids
of honour on the beach, eyeing the sea for a sail, or blindly
listening to the idle dash of waves ? No—guess again. Sitting among the rocks, in some small secret glen, where twenty
years ago she used to take an evening walk with Ulysses ?
No. Wandering sad and slow in the woods once wont to
echo to that hunter's horn—while she, fair as Diana,

" A sylvan huntress by his side,
Pursued the flying deer " ?

Not now. In her chamber weaving that famous web? That
artifice has been detected, and the shuttle is still. Sunk in
stupor there, or aimlessly employing her hands on embroidery in the listlessness of a long despair? Not far off the
truth—yet hardly are you Homer. She is in her chamber—
but not in stupor nor despair—her senses are all wide-awake—
her ear has caught the measure wild of the aged harper—into

her soul sinks the strain that sings of the return of the chiefs
on the downfall of Troy! That mournful inspiration is more
than she can bear; the music is but an insupportable memory
of her husband—a dirge for the dead. She fears not the face
of the Suitors in their feasting—and appears before us in all
the tenderness, the affection, and the dignity of a wife, a
mother, and a queen.

"The Prince the wooers sought, who, seated, hung
In silent rapture as the minstrel sung,
Sung the chiefs' sad return, when to and fro,
By Pallas' will, they sail'd from Troy's o'erthrow.
While thus he sung, Icarius' daughter heard,
Lone in her upper room, his chanted word :
Down stepp'd, and where she moved, attendant came
Two faithful damsels, on their royal dame.
Onward she went, and nigh the revel throng,
Now hush'd to silence by the minstrel's song,
Beneath her lofty palace porch reclined,
Hid her fair brow the fine-wove veil behind,
And, as on either side a maiden stood,
Wept, and the bard address'd in mournful mood :
'Bard, thy sweet touch can temper to the lyre
All deeds of men or gods that bards inspire.
Sing thou of these, and so enchant the ear,
That e'en these feasters may in silence hear.
But cease that strain which bids my sorrow flow,
Which searches every spring that feeds my woe,
And racks keen memory for that godlike chief
Whose fame through Greece but echoes back my grief.'
'My mother! why displeased?' the Prince rejoin'd,
'Leave to the bard free mastery of his mind.
'Tis not the minstrel, 'tis the will of Jove
That breathes the inspiration from above—
Then blame not Phemius, whose recording lay
Mourns their sad fate who steer'd from Troy their way.
More grateful far their song which all admire
When novelty attunes the awaken'd lyre.
Brace thou thy mind to hear : for not alone
Ulysses strays to Ithaca unknown,
But many a Grecian strews the Trojan plain,
And many a chief ne'er hails his hearth again.
But thou return, thy household cares resume,
Look to thy maids, the spindle, and the loom :
To men, as fit, discourse with men resign,
And—where I rule—that office chiefly mine.'

> Penelope, astonish'd, back return'd.
> Nor his wise counsel negligently spurn'd,
> Went with her maids, her loved Ulysses wept,
> Till the tired mourner, soothed by Pallas, slept."

Music—poetry—love—grief—comfort—repose of passion
—and to the afflicted heaven-sent sleep not unvisited, let us
hope, by soothing dreams ! The song sung to the harp did
of itself still the souls of the Suitors ; for though fit for murders, stratagems, and plots, they were high-born men—and
had they fought at Ilium, not a few of them would have been
heroes. A lawless and despotic life had not wholly quenched
their hereditary fire—and the Ithacenes were by nature a noble
race. Laertes had been a warrior in his youth—in his prime
of manhood a king. But old age had subdued the regal spirit
—and where and what is he now ? In the palace, 'tis affectingly said,

> " he now resides,
> But in his fields afar his misery hides,
> With one who serves his board, an aged dame,
> While sore fatigue comes o'er his toil-worn frame,
> When, from slow-creeping through his vineyard rows,
> The old man seeks his dwelling's still repose."

His wife, too, had died of " love and longings infinite," and
the suitors had long had their sway. Dulichium, Samos, and
Zacinthus sent their princes—accomplished men many of
them—nor unworthy altogether of a widow's love. Fierce as
fire, and as bright, is Antinous—and Eurymachus, with passion not less strong but more controllable, is a chief that might
prevail on one less tender and true than Penelope to change
the garments of grief for the saffron robe of joy. The de-
vourers of that widow's house were not dancing bears, but
leaping leopards—they knew how to fawn—and hoped to
" hold her with their glittering eyes " till she became a prey.
Descending in stately sorrow the flight of steps leading down
to the great hall, in hushed admiration they beheld the Queen.
No interruption is attempted of her pathetic address to the
Bard—no insult, while she is present, to her Son. Their
bad nature is rebuked and abashed by the Matron still
beautiful in her fidelity to her godlike Lord—their better
nature feels how " awful goodness is," " Virtue in her own

shape how lovely,"—conjugal, maternal, and filial love have their hour of triumph—and on the check of old Phemius bending over his silent harp, may be seen the heart-sprung tear.

And is there any harshness—as has been often said—in the behaviour of Telemachus? None. His soul was elate. He had sought the Suitors, the moment after having held converse with a Divinity—and his Hope hushed, impatiently, but not unkindly, his mother's fears. Now he felt himself a man, commissioned by heaven for a holy quest. He would fain that the Bard had prolonged his Lay—for his inspiration too was from the will of Jove. Ulysses is not dead, he is but a wanderer—and that harp shall ring through all its chords congratulation on the King's return. His looks and his tones reconciled his mother's heart to all his words—astonished, she obeyed the child whom till that hour she had commanded; and if her high heart was satisfied, who, after the lapse of three thousand years, shall be offended with her noble progeny for the first expansion of his pride in the consciousness of being about to enter on a destiny that, ere another moon had waned, was to be gloriously fulfilled in a shower of blood!

See and hear him among the Suitors now—passive no more, but flashing far-sighted scorn. Their outrages break out again on the disappearance of Penelope—but he beards them all. "Banquet in peace—cease your brawls, listen to Phemius, 'this gifted minstrel's heaven-attemper'd song.' To-morrow meet me in council—and I will dismiss you to your own homes. If thither you go not at my command, I warn you that vengeance is preparing against you in heaven, and that no hand will be outstretched to save you when its hour is come. You are all doomed to die!" They too are astonished —gnaw their mute lips, and are sore afraid. But there is not a coward among them—and they recover courage to gibe and jeer—yet are they tamed—and their eloquence wants fire. Antinous himself, even in the war of words, is now no match for Telemachus. The fearless Youth, in the joy of hope, *lies* to his insulter. He believes his father will return—for he trusts to the "veiled divinity," but he calls her by the feigned name of the feigned Taphian chief, and inly exulting, says, "My sire will return no more." The close of the scene is as perfect as its opening and its progress; and how delightful to us of these artificial and civilised days is the picture of the domestic life of the simple heroic age!—

> " Now in sweet interchange of song and dance,
> The suitors revell'd till eve's swift advance,
> Then, tired with song and dance, at daylight's close
> Each in his separate mansion sought repose.
> The Prince departing, went, where tower'd in sight
> Of that vast hall, his roof's conspicuous height,
> And Euryclea, child of Ops, upbore
> In either hand a torch his step before.
> Her, erst Laertes bought, a blooming slave,
> And for her purchase twenty oxen gave :
> Like his chaste wife revered her, but suppress'd
> Each wish that might his household peace molest.
> She lit his way, she watch'd his lightest word,
> And more than all his females loved her lord ;
> Loved like a son, and more and more endear'd,
> Hung o'er the youth by her from childhood rear'd.
> The Prince the door unclosed, and sought his rest,
> And loosed the fine-wove tunic from his breast,
> And gave it to his nurse, whose careful hand
> Hung nigh his couch its nicely-folded band.
> She onward passing where the youth reposed,
> Drawn by a silver ring, the portal closed,
> With bolt and brace secured :—the Prince, there laid
> On the smooth couch with finest wool array'd,
> Throughout the night with deep-revolving mind
> Ponder'd the course that Pallas had enjoin'd."

One great purpose nobly conceived changes the whole character, by showing the whole of life under a new aspect. Say, rather, it brings out the character, and makes the man feel and know what he is, as he firmly plants his foot on the threshold of his own house, which a high destiny calls on him to leave, and to go forth in power on a career that must have a glorious end. Look on the Telemachus of the Morn of Hope. Is he not
> '' attired
> With sudden brightness like a morn inspired"?

Homer rejoices to look on him—he lavishes beauty on his head ; but not from his own hands—the glory there is shed by Pallas. It is an emanation from the young hero's own awakened heart. So Ulysses looked, when, but a few years older, he set sail for Troy. How his nurse must have gazed on him going forth in the morning sun—Euryclea, whom his grandfather purchased when a virgin for twenty oxen, but respected her virginity from fear of his wife. She nursed, too, Ulysses ; yet never loved she him so dearly as Telemachus, —for love descends, and settles on its latest, its last object— soft as snow and sweet as light—accumulated and accumulating there till the eyes wax dim and the heart scarcely beats —at the last gasp of life. His nurse loved him more than did even his own mother ; for his own mother was a Queen, and his nurse was a slave. Penelope had been lamenting for twenty years her absent, or her lost lord—and the stream of sorrow kept flowing on from the fountain of love, that needed not to be fed—inexhaustible in a woman's heart as the sea. There was an affection, holiest of the holy, which she could not transfer but to the assured place of his lifeless rest. It had imagined a hundred graves for her Ulysses—it had been haunted far oftener by his ghost. But his ship too had often sailed through her dreams—and often had sleep laid her in her hero's bosom. The face, the form of her son, had a thousand times troubled her—so like those of him who was not— or was somewhere, known but to the Ruler of the Skies. By fits and starts to her must her Telemachus have been all in all. But she had dignities to guard, and indignities to endure, and duties to perform, and suits to repel, and temptations to resist, and fears to banish, and hopes to bring from afar— and all because she was faithful to the husband of her youth —to him for whose sake she had covered her face with her veil, and to whom she had said in a sweet low voice, when her father Icarius asked her would she go or stay—" I go to Ithaca, Ulysses, with Thee ! " But Euryclea was, as you know, a mere aged slave. She may have had some swineherd groom for a husband, half a century ago, and a swarm of children ; but we hear nothing of them—only of two sons of hers do we hear—and they are, Ulysses and Telemachus. Perhaps she once loved Laertes, when they were in their prime— she in the bloom of purchase—and from fear an unenjoyed handmaid that decked the nuptial couch. Both old now, and weak, and miserable—but she the happier far, because repining not now very painfully even for Ulysses, and having no care—no love—nothing to live for—but that bright Boy

climbing up to manhood, and now standing majestically as on
a hill-top between her and the sky. She the slave belonged
to him, Prince Telemachus; but he belonged to her, Nurse
Euryclea; and now that he is about to sail in search of his
Father, it is to her he confides the secret—for in that still,
simple, sworn heart of hers he knows it will lie buried beneath
a weight of wishes for his safe return, nor be confided even to
the air, that might repeat the whisper, if one word of it were
joined with the name of her Telemachus even in her prayers.
Twelve days is a long time to keep a secret—in fear and
trembling too; but Euryclea kept it, and would have kept
it against all instruments of torture angrily seeking to tug it
out of her heart. Her trustful silence was proof alike against
fear and joy. Think for a moment—but no more now—of her
discovery of the scar, and whose feet they were that it was
at last given her in that bath to embrace!

But here is Telemachus walking to the Council in the light,
as we said, of the Morn of Hope :—

> " Ulysses' son, when first Aurora spread
> O'er earth her roseate splendour, left his bed :
> Athwart his shoulders his sharp falchion braced,
> On his fair feet his radiant sandals laced ;
> And like a god from his ancestral hall
> Went forth, and bade the herald's loud-voiced call
> Summon the chiefs to council : they obey'd,
> Nor the long summons of the Prince delay'd.
> The Prince, when all were met at his command,
> Went with a brazen spear that arm'd his hand,
> And two fleet faithful dogs : as on he pass'd
> Round him celestial glory Pallas cast.
> Awed to mute wonder through the admiring throng
> The youth divinely graced thus stepp'd along,
> Then 'mid the yielding elders pass'd alone,
> And sat unquestion'd on his father's throne."

Nothing can be more finely illustrative of the character in
the first book shown to belong to Telemachus, than his whole
conduct during the council that is held in the second ; yet
his speeches, as they are reported by Homer, have not
escaped criticism. It was, certainly, an admirable first
appearance. Till now, no council had been called in Ithaca
since the departure of Ulysses. It must have been rather

a formidable thing for so young a person to rise up and arraign the Suitors before the peers. Telemachus does not rise till old Ægyptius asks by whom the council had been summoned; and then he indeed does rise, and majestically, and answers—"Behold him who convened the council—I am he!" We have heard it said by an apostate Tory, now fallen from Whig into Radical, that his speech has no bones. But no speech had ever a more pithy spine. Only its spine is straight, and the speech itself clothed with flesh-and-blood life. Bones are only observable in distortion or the rickets—but deformity is seldom strength—abrupt, awkward, angular osseous projections do not constitute a speech, but a skeleton. What had he to prove? Nothing. They knew all it was possible he could have to say; but he was desirous to ascertain if they, the peers, were insensible to shame—tongue-and-hand-tied—that is, gagged and manacled by fear. Was the house swamped? Or basely waiting to see who should be at the Head of Affairs? He, in a few touching words, reminds them of his noble father, who once governed them all, even as a father his children; he speaks of the imminent ruin of his house, and of his mother's persecution by the Suitors, which he calls "a more alarming ill" than the loss of his father; for were the palace freed, and the island under law, he might, without offence to nature, weep for Ulysses no more, and be indeed happy as a king. We say so—not Telemachus. But there has been a conspiracy among critics to accuse and convict the young prince of selfishness, and want or weakness of natural affection; and as a painful proof of their charge, they point to this passage, of which the good sense, say we, is as conspicuous as the right feeling—and altogether worthy the heir-apparent. There is no exaggeration of any grief or grievance, and he speaks fervently the simple truth. He had never seen his father. His feelings were those of love, and honour, and reverence, and awe, towards a being whom his heart and imagination created and called Father—created, if we may say so, of attributes furnished to fancy by all the voices of the Isle that sighed for Ulysses. Yet him fain would he seek over land and sea—and for his sake was he now sounding the souls of the Peers in Council to ascertain if any generous sentiments slept there, that might be awakened by his return, and rise up to

the rescue.   Cowper here is very Homeric—far more so than
Sotheby.

> "'Resent, yourselves, this outrage ; dread the blame
> Which else ye must incur from every state
> Around us, and the anger of the gods,
> Lest they impute these impious deeds to you.
> I next adjure you by Olympic Jove,
> By Themis, who convenes and who dissolves
> All councils, that ye interpose, my friends !
> To check them, and afford to my distress
> A solitary and a silent home.
> But if Ulysses, my illustrious sire,
> Hath injured any noble Grecian here,
> Whose wrongs ye purpose to avenge on me,
> Then aid them openly ; for better far,
> Were my condition, if yourselves consumed
> My revenue ; ye should compensate soon
> My sufferings at your hands ; for my complaints
> Should rouse all Ithaca to my redress,
> Nor cease till I were satisfied for all ;
> But now, conniving at the wrong, ye pierce
> My soul with anguish not to be endured !'
> He spoke impassion'd, and to earth cast down
> His sceptre weeping."

His tears were tears of disappointment, shame, indignation
and rage. He had shown he did not fear the suitors — while
he bitterly confessed he had not power to rid his house of
them, or put them all to death. But he called on the Council
to raise up all Ithaca to redress his wrongs—they sat mute—
and therefore he dashed down his sceptre, and wept. And
what ensued ? "Pity at that sight seized all the people."
But what is the use of pity ? To dry a maiden's tears. And
who were the people ? Not knowing, we cannot say ; but we
suppose the Suitors, natives and aliens, had their adherents
in that assemblage : a course of connivance generates falsehood
and fear—kills loyalty and patriotism—deadens, if it does not
destroy, all sense of justice—bends the necks of nobles as if
they were serfs or villains—and

> "Slips the slave's collar on, and snaps the lock."

Up starts Antinous to answer him whom he scornfully calls
"high-sounding orator," and we admire his speech. In it he

narrates the pious fraud of Penelope in weaving and unweaving the famous web, a funeral robe—so feigned she—for the ancient Laertes—and we can imagine that Telemachus listened with a smile. Nor displeased could he have been to hear even from such lips such a character of his mother.

> "Studious alone to merit praise for arts
> By Pallas given her largely ; matchless skill
> To weave the splendid web ; sagacious thought ;
> And shrewdness such as never fame ascribed
> To any beauteous Greek of ancient days,
> Tyro, Mycene, or Alcmena loved
> By Jove himself, all whom the accomplish'd Queen
> Transcends in knowledge, ignorant alone,
> That, woo'd long time, she should at last be won ! "

Noble English of noble Greek, dear Cowper; and it must have been difficult for Telemachus, hearing such eulogium, to hate Antinous with all his heart—so filial was it as well as heroic—nor yet implacable, had the Suitors ceased to devour his house. He would have forgiven them even at the eleventh hour ; but there was one—Penelope's own dear Dread—inaccessible to forgiveness ; and though he was now far-off—not long the time till he was to be near—and then—but now the Prince hears Antinous tell him, that either his mother must be dismissed from the palace and forced to wed, or that they will all continue to banquet at his cost; and if you are not satisfied with the burst of filial affection that glows through his righteous rage, and makes it more withering in its intensity, you must look for nature and the truth of nature where you choose, but can never hope to find them in Homer.

The reply of Telemachus electrified even that abject assembly, and astounded the profligates who had made it base. But it did more than move the timid and the tyrannical—it stirred the sky and was heard by Jove. We know not how the passage may look in prose, but in the Greek it is as portentous poetry as ever flashed luridly from a gloomy shrine.

CHRISTOPHER NORTH.

(Literally, and line for line with the Original.)

" Thus spoke Telemachus : but to him, the far-seeing Jupiter two eagles
Sent-on from aloft, to fly from the summit of a mountain.

They for a while skimm'd along with the blast of the wind,
Abreast of each other, outstretch'd on wing :
But when they indeed came to the midst of the many-voiced
(πολύφημον) assembly,
There sweeping round they shook their numerous plumes,
And gazed on the heads of all, and look'd destruction :
And with their talons having lacerated-their-own jaws, and their
necks around,
They rush'd to the right through (*over*) their (*the people of Ithaca's*)
houses and city.
They (*the people*) were-stunn'd-with-amazement at the birds, as
they gazed with their eyes,
And they ponder'd in their hearts, what this was to bring-about.
Them, however, address'd the venerable hero Halitherses
Mastorides, who alone excell'd his years-mates
In the knowledge of birds (*auguries*), and in interpreting porten-
tous omens,
He, judging wisely, harangued and thus address'd them :
' Listen to me verily, ye people-of-Ithaca, in what I shall say :
The wooers above-all I single-out in this my speech,
Since for them great destruction is revolving : Ulysses not
Long apart from his friends shall be, but even now somewhere
Near at hand he is, and for these very men is he planning
(φυτείει, planting) slaughter and destiny,
(*Yes*) for-all-of-them : and evil shall come on many more of us
Who inhabit Ithaca favourably-situated-towards-the-west (or *con-
spicuous*) ; but long before
Let us deliberate how we shall put a stop to this, and let them (*the
wooers*) too
Cease (*from their doings*), forstraightway this will be better for them.
Not inexperienced (*in omens*) I prophesy, but from full knowledge :
For on that man (*Ulysses*), I say, has everything been brought
about—
Just as I declared to him, when for Ilium embark'd
The Greeks, and along with them went Ulysses fertile-in-ex-
pedients,
I declared that (*after*) having suffered many evils, (after) having
lost all his associates,
Unknown to all, in the twentieth year,
Home should he come ;—and now truly is all this being-brought
about.' "

Eustathius — as we find him in Pope — for we have not himself at hand—says well, " This prodigy is ushered in very
magnificently, and the verses are lofty and sonorous. The

Eagles are Ulysses and Telemachus: by Jove's command they fly from a mountain's height: this denotes that the two heroes are inspired by Jupiter, and come from the country to the destruction of the suitors.   The eagles fly with wing to wing conjoined; this shows that they act in concert and unity of councils : at first they float upon the wind ; this implies the calmness and secresy of the approach of those heroes : at last they clang their wings, and hovering beat the skies ; this shows the violence of the assault : with ardent eyes the rival train they threat.   This, as the poet himself interprets it, denotes the approaching fate of the suitors.   Then sailing over the domes and towers, they fly full towards the East ; this signifies that the suitors alone are not doomed to destruction, but that the men of Ithaca are involved in danger, as Hali- therses interprets it." Good.   But why did the Bishop—if he wrote this at all, which we doubt, our faith beingsm all in the notes furnished to Pope by Brome—omit mention of their tearing one another's necks? Because, perhaps, he did not understand it.   Why did the Royal Birds, imaging Father and Son, take a turn up in the sky ? Was it because they saw no other mode of letting the wretches beneath see that there was to be a fight in the Palace? Or was it merely in mirth and glee that the Eagles, full of might and fight, joined combat in the air, by way of a spree ? Or was it to show the Suitors how Eagles fought ? Everything in Homer, and in every other Great Poet, has a meaning ; and you may adopt whichever of our conjectures you will—but as you love us, do not slur the tussle over as a mere tissue of words. Halitherses, as an augur, said enough to frighten all but the infatuated ; but he was not bound to explain all the omen— enough that he predicted dismay, disaster, and death.

How do the translators handle the two Eagles? Let us see.   Brome did Beta for Pope—and here is Brome :

BROME.

" With that the Eagles from a mountain's height,
By Jove's command, direct their rapid flight ;
Swift they descend, with wing to wing conjoin'd,
Stretch their broad plumes, and float upon the wind ;
Above the assembled Peers they wheel on high,
And clang their wings, and hovering beat the sky ;

With ardent eyes the rival train they threat,
And, shrieking loud, denounce approaching fate.
They cuff, they tear, their cheeks and necks they rend,
And from their plumes huge drops of blood descend :
Then sailing o'er the domes and towers, they fly
Full toward the East, and mount into the sky."

COWPER.

" So spake Telemachus, and while he spake,
The Thunderer from a lofty mountain-top
Turn'd off two Eagles ; on the winds awhile,
With outspread pinions ample, side by side
They floated ; but, ere long, hovering aloft,
Right o'er the midst of the assembled Chiefs
They wheel'd around, clang'd all their numerous plumes,
And eycing with a downward look the throng,
Death boded, ominous ; then rending each
The other's face and neck, they sprang at once
Toward the right, and darted through the town."

SOTHEBY.

" Thus spake Telemachus ; and thundering Jove
Sent earthward down two Eagles from above.
They, side by side, on level pinions flew,
And floated with the wind that smoothly blew.
But o'er the Forum, when to all reveal'd,
Fierce clanging their dense plumes, in circles wheel'd,
Eyed all beneath, and glaring death around,
Rent each the other's neck with many a wound ;
Then upward soar'd, and wheeling to the right,
Wing'd through the city their portentous flight."

M. J. CHAPMAN.   (TRINITY COLLEGE, CAMBRIDGE.)

" And lo ! far-seeing Jove two Eagles sent,
Which from a mountain-brow far and aloft
Came flying down ; whiles with th' impulsive wind
They flew, flapping their outstretch'd mighty wings,
One near the other ; but the midway space
Over the crowded Session once attain'd,
They wheel'd, and their thick-feather'd pinions shook,
And look'd upon the heads of all, and voiced
A boding death ; then with their talons tore
Their jaws and necks, and with a right-hand flight
Over their houses and their city rush'd."

Which is best? Brome is bad. Dr Johnson said no man could distinguish Brome or Fenton from Pope. All men may —most women, and some children. A wishy-washy imitation of the style of Pope cannot be very like Homer. Our belief is, that though Pope may have brushed and burnished up a bit his coadjutors' versions, he was pleased to let them remain in their manifest inferiority to his own. They were two good foils. "Rapid" and "swift"—to say nothing of the tautology—are wretched epithets, applied here to eagles—and of course not in Homer. Nothing is said in the Greek about "descending." That they did descend, we see. "Stretch their broad wings," seems to imply that they had not stretched them from the first. "Float on the wind" is not quite right. "Wheel on *high*" is very poor indeed : nobody supposes they were very low—and yet they were lower than they had been, by some thousand feet at least — for the people saw the sparkles of their eyes. "And clang their wings, and hovering beat the sky," is no great improvement on our truthful prose— which, by the way, we perceive, is a verse, and a good one— "There sweeping round, they shook their numerous plumes." The line that follows is a mean version of the magnificent. Not a syllable in Homer about "shrieking"—they yelled not. "They cuff—they tear"—Brome must have thought very fine—so fine that he must like a fool say something still finer. "And from their plumes huge drops of blood descend," which does not happen even when a tercel gentle strikes a heron-shew into what seems a fortuitous congregation of atoms. The concluding lines are sonorous—but ambitious over-much— and the whole the failure of a man who never saw even a buzzard. Cowper is almost as good as possible—and shows that a poet may keep tame hares, and yet admire wild eagles. In Sotheby we are sorry to miss the mountain ; and there seems a "they" wanting for grammatical construction ; but the flight coming and going is finely given, and so is the threatening and the portent. Sotheby has seen many eagles. Chapman (not old, but young Chapman) is admirably Homeric. But "Voiced a boding death," we promise a crown to any man who shall explain. Cowper and Chapman are "both best." Of the rest of the passage, Brome makes very weak work—Cowper rather heavy work—and Sotheby rather imperfect work—so let their versions sleep. At present there really seems to be nothing in English so like the Greek as our own prose. No merit that of ours—'tis all Homer's. A few words, with your leave, about this Portent.

To know Fear, you must either live, or imagine you live, in an age of soothsaying and superstition. Prognostications of a direful event are sublime, seen shadowy on a strange-clouded sky—typical of retribution, in all ghastliest shapes—shifting to and fro, and of a bloody colour. Seers stand staring there, till they shudder to pronounce the doom declared by the troubled heavens, and wander, wild-eyed, up and down a mountainous country, mad and miserable, and wishing they were dead. You can think with what Fear they may inspire a lone Highland glen by a few woeful words—of old withered maniacs, almost naked, cowing chieftains, even when " plaided and plumed in their tartan array." In the ancient world, seers, and soothsayers, and prophets (surely they were not all deceivers), for the revelation of the Fates were under obligations, which it was impossible they could ever repay, to birds. Yet they were no great ornithologists. The science of augury was high, but not apparently very complicated; and the flight-inspired man had in truth but to know his left hand from his right. Yet the people, with a firm faith in his inspiration, awfully heard his interpretation of the omen, to common sense seemingly as simple as sublime—as in those two eagles. Halitherses gave utterance but to the thoughts of the people, gazing on the birds—for amazement and fear had fallen on them—and they all felt that the rushing of wings and the glaring of eyes were ominous of death. But he, they believed, was " endowed with clear credentials from above "—and that utterance was to them not merely confirmation, but revelation. In his prophetic exultation he became unconsciously a Liar of the first magnitude, yet spoke Jove's truth. That Ulysses and Telemachus were to come flying wing to wing like eagles, he saw and said, as he heard aloft the whistling plumes ; but that twenty years ago he had told Ulysses of his fated return to Ithaca, we no more believe than that he told Us, at the era of the French Revolution, that Christopher North was to be the Editor of Maga yet unconceived in the womb of Fate. But he held that strange tale devoutly true, and so did all who heard him ; for he threw his feelings of the present on his feelings of the past, and they all so bandied

themselves back and forward, that by collision they kindled
into a new birth—the feeling of the Future. No wonder
there were awe and amazement,—nor can there be a doubt
that all felt Fear. But as a heroic character, in Burns's "Hal-
loween," under the influence of superstitious fear, "whistled
up ' Lord Lennox' March,' to keep his courage cheery," so now
did the bold Eurymachus burst out into abuse of Halitherses,
and, with a quaking heart, resumed his countenance and
speech—pale and faltering—for the nonce, to simulate scorn.
Cowper felt that well—

> " Hence, dotard ! hence
> To thy own house ; there, prophesying, warn
> Thy children of calamities to come.
> Birds, numerous, flutter in the beams of day,
> Not all predictive. Death, far hence remote,
> Hath found Ulysses ; and I would to Heaven,
> That, when he died, thyself had perish'd too.
> Then hadst thou not with these prophetic strains
> O'erwhelm'd us, nor Telemachus impell'd,
> Already thus incensed," &c.

His mind is ill at ease—he is not self-consistent—and he
must have felt the weakness of his own logic. " Go, dotard,
and prophesy to children ; for thou hast o'erwhelmed us, and
compelled the mind of Telemachus." That showed Halitherses was a prophet fit to speak before men. The whole
harangue is fierce and furious, but Eurymachus keeps harping
on one string, and the discordant twanging disturbs not the
spirit of the young hero. He demands a twenty-oared bark,
that he may seek sandy Pylos, and thence hasten to Lacedemon, to obtain tidings of his sire. " If I hear he lives, one
year I shall be patient for his return. If I hear he is dead, I
will perform his funeral rites with such pomp as his great
name demands, and raise at home his tomb, and then give my
mother to—whom I choose." Then rose Mentor, illustrious
Ulysses' friend, to whom, on his departure, he had consigned
the care of his household, and speaks like a wise man.

> " Hear me, ye Ithacans, be never King,
> From this time forth, benevolent, humane,
> Or righteous ; but let every sceptred hand
> Rule merciless, and deal in wrong alone,
> Since none of all his people, whom he sway'd

With such paternal gentleness and love
Remembers the divine Ulysses more.
That the imperious suitors thus should weave
The web of mischief and atrocious wrong,
I grudge not ; since, at hazard of their heads,
They make Ulysses' property a prey,
Persuaded that the hero comes no more.
But much the people move me ; how ye sit
All mute, and though a crowd opposed to few,
Check not the suitors with a single word."

Alas ! all was rotten in the State of Ithaca. Twenty years
is a long minority—and misrule, during half that time, can
sadly change the character of a people.

" Injurious Mentor ! headlong orator !
How darest thou move the populace against
The Suitors ? "

So asks Liocritus ; but the populace are palsied—dead is the
quickening spirit of love and loyalty—and so utterly have
they forgotten Ulysses that they see nothing of him in his
blooming son. 'Tis this that makes Telemachus feel his
weakness; his native modesty induces him to think and
speak humbly of his own immature powers ; his native heroism inspires him with resolution to face all dangers ; but the
sight of his own people's degradation forces him to confess
that in Ithaca he must succumb to the crew whom, were
Ithaca what once it was, the Land of the Leal, he could
mow and swathe like grass. Where was this assemblage
held ? In a building, or in the open air ? If in a building,
the council-hall had no roof, for the eagles were seen coming
and going in the sky. It was, therefore, no Hole-and-Corner
Meeting—and the sun saw the sin and shame of all the people,
and of all the peers.

The council—a pretty council indeed—breaks up—and
where goes Telemachus ? To lave his hands in the surf of
the grey deep. They have refused to give him a twenty-oared
bark—and shall they thwart the designs of Minerva ? He
calls upon the goddess, and she appears in the form of Mentor.
There, by the sounding sea, commune the seeming old man
and the young—and ere nightfall they will embark. The
Suitors' renewed showers of scorn now glance off the Prince's

mind like hail from sunbright armour; and Pallas fools that
drunken multitude, dashing the goblets from their hands,
drenching their eyes in drowsiness, and driving them, blind
and deaf, staggering through the streets. Meanwhile the sun
had set, and twilight dimmed all the ways—the bark was in
the bay impatient for the Prince.

M. J. CHAPMAN. (TRIN. COL. CAM.)

" This said, he led the way : they follow'd him,
 And placed the sea-stores in the well-bench'd ship,
 As bade Ulysses' son.   On ship-board went
 Telemachus, Athene going first ;
 She sat down at the stern ; he near to her.
 The mariners, meanwhile, the shore-ropes loosed,
 And on the benches went and took their seats.
 Grey-eyed Athene sent a favouring breeze,
 A full strong west-wind with a rushing sound
 Ruffling the dark sea ; then Telemachus
 Bade them handle their tackle, cheering them ;
 They cheerful heard ; and in the socket first
 They fix'd the fir-mast, and secured it well
 With the fore-braces ; then with twisted thongs
 They raised the white-sails, and the mid-sail full
 Bellied the wind ; and as the ship went on,
 Around the keel loud roar'd the purple wave.
 Along the wave she ran, making her way.
 Then having made all fast in the dark ship,
 Goblets they brimful crown'd with wine, and pour'd
 Libations to the ever-living gods,
 And first of all to Jove's own grey-eyed child.
 All night and through the following dawn she ran."

We perceive, from Pope, that Rapin is very severe on
Minerva and Jupiter, who contrive the action of the Odyssey.
That action, it seems, is very imperfect; because it begins
with the voyages of Telemachus, and ends with those of
Ulysses. Why, surely a son stands in a pretty close relation
to his own father. A son voyaging to find his father, and
even if possible bring him home, appears to us to be helping
the action as much as can be reasonably expected of him,
especially when the action is being helped on still more
effectually by the father himself, whose whole soul is set on
getting home to find his son. But of the two divinities, the
old gentleman is most crusty on Pallas. She knew that

Ulysses was in Ogygia—and that Jove had promised to let him return to Ithaca. True—but what did that amount to? To much less than the old gentleman seems to suppose—for Pallas did not know that Neptune was to dash him, after ever so many miseries on a raft, on Phæacia—that Nausicaa was to fall in love with him—that he was to hear Demodocus harping and singing in the gardens of Alcinous—and that he was to be landed sound asleep on his own beloved shore. All she did know was, that Jove had promised he should return. Calypso, for aught Minerva knew, might send him to Pylos; or Neptune, on his return from Ethiopia, might drive the slayer of his son Polyphemus to the Hyperboreans. What if Ulysses had been sitting with old Nestor at a sea-shore feast? Rapin might have been dumbfoundered, and Minerva somewhat surprised; but nothing is impossible in poetry of which the machinery is not spinning-jennies but Gods.

Old Rap likewise thought honour, duty, and nature ought to have moved Telemachus to seek tidings of his Father, without the instigation or guidance of a goddess. That acute remark cuts in pieces the whole poetry of Homer, and makes shreds and patches of the whole Greek religion. But it would be well if all youths would act like Telemachus, even at the bidding of a superior power, human or divine.

Minerva takes him, quoth Rap, to all the most improbable places;—to the houses of Nestor and Menelaus! Would he have had her to take him to Ogygia? But we must be contented with Homer's Odyssey—however much we may regret that it was not rewritten by Rapin.

We know and love Telemachus as well as if we had been for years with him in Ithaca. What he may end in, no man who has studied human nature may pretend to say—but now his character is as transparent as the purest well he ever stooped to drink at, with a dead deer, or boar, or wolf, lying at the young hunter's feet on the greensward among the rocks. Never, we may venture to say, will he be so fertile in ex-pedients as his Father—nor so eloquent nor so wise—for in genius Ulysses was the greatest of all the Greeks; but as brave, as affectionate, and as faithful to all old loves, will be the son as the sire—and one day as good a king.

How delightful to land with him on the shore in sight of

the old city of Peleus, and witness his delight on beholding
—so Sotheby finely calls what we dully construed seats—the
Nine Green Theatres! In each, five hundred men feasting on
nine bulls. Four thousand five hundred men, good and true,
in the act of devouring eighty-one bulls. All the fourscore
and one bulls had been coal-black, without one single ashy
spot, when alive in their hides, and now are all done brown
on the sacrificial fire. All the thighs—one hundred and
sixty-two—are laid on the altar of Neptune; all the other
flesh, not sinking offal—for the entrails are especially mentioned — consumed, we are willing to believe, by his wor-
shippers. On the approach of the strangers, "all arose" to
welcome them—not all the four thousand five hundred men—
but all the ὃι πέρι, a noble band, conspicuous among them all
the young Pisistratus, who has already embraced the Prince
of Ithaca, and welcomed him—his birth and name unknown—
to Pylos. And old Nestor is not only alive still, but as fresh-
looking and hale as he was some ten years back before Troy!
What a trump for a Tontine! and as garru—— as eloquent as
ever! Pisistratus sure must be his great-grandson. By no
means. And in the palace perhaps there is a rocking-cradle.
Remember we are now flourishing in the heroic age, and in the
presence of a Patriarch. In good time Telemachus tells his
name and purpose—but Nestor, alas! knows nothing of
Ulysses whom he loved, and pronounces matchless. Then,
with what a fine sense of propriety does Telemachus, instead
of mourning for the darkness that shroud's his father's fate,
modestly put such questions to the Old in Days as may lead
him to narrate events in his own history, and in that of other
heroes —his friends—after the fall of Troy. The young
Prince's own sentiments and sympathies suggested indeed
the theme—and the aged king had by a few words awakened
his desire to hear again the oft-repeated tale,—

> " Ye, too, far off have heard Atrides' death,
> By fell Ægisthus' will, how closed his breath ;
> But rightly has the base adulterer paid
> Dire vengeance due to Agamemnon's shade :
> 'Tis glorious when heroic sons remain
> The great avengers of their fathers slain ;
> Such as Atrides' heir, whose righteous ire
> Slew the base murderer of his far-famed sire ;

> Such thou ; so match by deeds thy stately frame,
> That ages yet to come extol thy name."

The example of Orestes had been set before him by
Minerva's self, ere they left Ithaca ; and Menelaus—brother
of the murdered King of Men—again tells him the dreadful
tale in the words of the ever-changing Proteus of the sea.
Not a word anywhere (are we mistaken ?) about Orestes killing his mother.   Telemachus resembled the son of Agamemnon only in being called on by earth and heaven to avenge
his parent's wrongs ; but his father was blessed with a faithful wife—so said the shade of Atrides to Laërtiades beside
the trench of blood in that doleful region where he had
not forgot the fatal bath—and called Ulysses happy in all his
woes,—for the Phantom thought of Penelope and then of
Clytemnestra.

Friendship is like love in young hearts—it rises at first
sight and endures for ever.   Echephron, Stratius, Perseus,
Thrasymedes, Aretus—Nestor's sons—are all kind to the
son of Ulysses ; but Pisistratus is at once his brother.   All
the rest are married men—these two noble youths have room in
their hearts to receive each other, for as yet they have known
not love.   Each is chaste as Hippolytus ; and their bosoms
glow with less selfish passions.   Their life breathes a heroic
innocence.   On a carved couch, beneath the resounding porch,
Telemachus lies down to sleep—and near him Pisistratus.
They keep conversing till midnight, and we could—though
Homer has not recorded it—make a poem of their talk about
heroes.

The rosy-fingered morn sees Nestor sitting alone (probably
in Monologue, for his tongue never tired) on the Seat of
Justice before his gates—of white polished, oil-glistening
stone (marble ?), with his sceptre in his hand, and the finest
beard in all Greece.   Minerva had revealed herself the evening before, in the shape of an eagle—and to her he commands
a solemn sacrifice.   For hours his sons are busy in preparations, nor idle, we may well believe, nor far apart—those
two illustrious boys.   In the evening they are to set out in
their chariot for Pheræ—Diocleus' Dome—one-third of the
way perhaps to Lacedemon.   But not till

> " Nestor's youngest daughter deign'd to lave
> Ulysses' offspring in the tepid wave,

> With oil anointed, and the tunic bound,
> And the resplendent robe his limbs around—
> Fresh from the bath, the prince, a God in grace
> Stepped forth, and sat by Nestor's honour'd place."

'Tis thus old Homer sings to boys and virgins. The bluest bend of heaven that ever hung the Ionian Isles, and all their shadows among the soft confusion of water and of air—one grovey wilderness of upward-and-downward-growing trees, and miraculous temples—never was purer,

> " With its white families of happy clouds,"

than was the lofty arch of his spirit letting fall gentle light on the heads of the brave and beautiful—the mild and the lovely—and all the bright world—vision-like in its reality— in which youth breathes empyrean air, and human life is invested with a grandeur of joy breathed from the heart of uncorrupted nature.

Behold the Twain in " Lacedemon's hollow vale " before the gates of Menelaus' palace. How fortunate their arrival during the celebration of a double marriage! And such nuptials! Why, Hermione, "graced with Aphrodite's charms," leaves Lacedemon for " Phthia's glorious city," with chariots and with horses, to bless the bed of Neoptolemus, a son whose fame had transcended that of the most glorious sire, had not that sire been Achilles. And to Megapenthes, his son by a handmaid—for Helen had but one child, almost as bright as herself, now the Phthian Queen—Menelaus was now giving for wife Alector's beauteous child, the flower of Sparta. The Twain draw up their smoking steeds in the palace porch ; but read the scene in Sotheby, almost as alive as in Homer :—

> " While in his palace porch, great Nestor's son,
> And the Prince staid the steeds, their journey done,
> Them, Eteoneus, issuing forth, survey'd,
> And backward speeding, to Atrides said :
> ' Lo ! Jove-born Menelaus, at thy gate
> Two strangers, likest gods, thy word await :
> Shall we here loose their steeds, and claim their stay,
> Or to some roof more willing send away ?'
> ' Thou wert not once,' the indignant king replied,
> ' Devoid of sense, untaught thy words to guide.
> Thou babblest like a child—from dome to dome
> We, hospitably feasted, reach'd our home :

So Jove may henceforth guard us : loose the steed,
And to our banquet, haste, the strangers lead.'
 He spake : nor Eteoneus disobey'd,
But, summoning the menials, urged their aid,
Loosed the hot yoke, and where the steeds reposed,
Within the monarch's spacious stalls enclosed,
Oats and fine barley in their manger threw,
And to the radiant wall the chariot drew :
Then usher'd in the guests, who, wondering, gazed,
As the proud palace of Atrides blazed,
Which like the lunar orb, or solar light
With strange magnificence amazed their sight.
But, when their wonder paused, they went to lave
Their bodies in the bath's refreshing wave ;
Then, when the females with anointing oil
And the warm flood had freed their limbs from toil,
And the bright vest and mantle round them cast,
They, nigh the king, partook the rich repast.
In a bright vase of burnish'd silver wrought
On a gold stand, a maid pure water brought.
Spread for the feast, with dainties largely stored,
A matron placed the tables' polish'd board :
The sewer with varied flesh their food supplied,
And served with golden cups of royal pride.
Then, with kind warmth their hands Atrides press'd,
And welcoming the strangers, thus address'd :
 'Feast, and rejoice—when satiate keen desire,
I, who my guests, and whence you came, inquire.
Not yet, I deem, has pass'd away from earth
The memory of the men who boast your birth.
In yours, the form of Jove-born kings I trace,
For ne'er vile fathers bred such godlike race.'
 Then deign'd himself their portion'd feast assign,
The monarch's share, the bullock's roasted chine.
 They richly feasted, and, the banquet o'er,
When thirst and satiate hunger sought no more,
Then, bow'd o'er Nestor's son, that none might hear,
The Prince thus whisper'd in his listening ear :
 'Round this refulgent dome, my friend ! behold
What blaze of amber, ivory, silver, gold :
Such Jove's Olympian hall 'mid realms of light,
The infinity of splendour awes my sight.'
 His whisper'd wonder Menelaus heard,
And to the admiring guests thus spake the word :

' No—let not mortal man contend with Jove,
'Tis immortality stamps all above.
Man may with me hold contest, or decline,
Whate'er my wealth, toil, suffering made it mine,
Brought from far wandering, by my restless sail,
Ere the eighth year, I bade my country hail.
To Cyprus, Ægypt, to Phœnicia's shore,
To Æthiopia me, my vessel bore,
The Erembi, Sidon, Libya, where the horn
Crowns the fair forehead of the lamb new-born,
Where sheep thrice yearly breed, nor lord nor swain
For dearth of cheese, or flesh, or milk complain,
Nor ere throughout the year the udder fails
To tempt the hand that fills the milking-pails.
While thus I stray'd, and with incessant toil
Vast wealth amass'd from many a distant soil,
By a vile wife's dark guile, the sudden blow
Smote unawares, and laid a brother low.
Thus rich, I joyless reign—yet, ye have heard
Whate'er your race, your sires have spread the word,
How sore I suffer'd, and to ruin brought
A hospitable home with luxury fraught ;
With half its wealth, I would contented dwell,
Were they but living who at Ilion fell.
How oft beneath my roof I lone deplore
The loss of those who here return no more :
Now feed my soul with grief, and now at peace
Rest, when, worn out with plaint, afflictions cease ;
Yet less I weep them all, though sore I weep,
Than one whose loss embitters food and sleep,
Mindful of him whose ardour unrepress'd
Sustain'd the weight of woe that bow'd the rest,
Thee, loved Ulysses, bound by fate to grief,
And to my soul by woe without relief—
Where the long-absent hero ? whither sped ?
Strays he alive, or slumbers with the dead ?
His loss bows down to earth his aged sire,
Penelope consumes with vain desire,
And whom he left, the babe just sprung to day,
Telemachus, deplores his long delay.' "

We always liked, but now we love Menelaus. That Helen
should have left such a man for Paris ! Brave as his own
sword—bright in honour as his own shield—hospitable as his

own board—strong as the tree at his own palace-gate—tender
withal, as well as true—with a heart in his manly bosom
overflowing with all kind affections—love, friendship, grief,
pity—and yearning not towards kith and kin alone, but, as
now, towards the sons of his old companions in arms, Nestor
and Ulysses. For Nestor wore arms—but Menelaus knows
not who the youths may be—he loves them for their own
noble sakes—and well one of them will ever after love the
Great Spartan King, for having mourned so for Ulysses, and
Laertes, and Penelope—and for him who now with both hands
upholds before his face his purple robe, that it may hide his
gushing tears. But where is Helen ?

CHRISTOPHER NORTH.

(Literally, and line for line with the Original.)

" Whilst he was revolving these things in his mind and heart,
Helen from her odoriferous, lofty-roof'd chamber out-
Came, like to Diana with-the-golden-arrows :
For her then did Adrasta place a beautifully-fabricated couch,
And Alcippe bore a carpet of soft wool :
Phylo carried a silver basket, which to her (Helen) gave
Alcandra, the wife of Polybus, who dwelt in Thebes
Of Ægypt, where most-numerous possessions lie in-the-houses.
Who to Menelaus gave two silver baths,
And two tripods, and ten talents of gold.
Apart (from these) did his wife besides bestow on Helen beautiful
    gifts,—
A golden spindle, and added a basket rimmed-beneath
Of silver, but its lips were perfected of-gold.
This then did the attendant Phylo bear and place before her,
Completely-filled with elaborately-wrought thread ; and over it
Was extended the spindle having wool of-a-deep-violet-hue.
(Helen) on her reclining-couch sat down, and under her feet was a
    footstool,
And forthwith she questioned her husband on all."

SOTHEBY.

" While thus the Monarch paused with doubt o'ercast,
Forth from her fragant chamber Helen past,
Like gold-bow'd Dian ; and Adraste came,
The bearer of her throne's majestic frame ;
Her carpet's fine-wrought fleece Alcippe bore,
Phylo her basket bright with silver ore,

Gift of the wife of Polybus, who sway'd
Where Thebes, the Ægyptian Thebes, vast wealth display'd ;
There too the monarch's hospitable hand
To Atreus' son, departing from his land,
Gave ten weigh'd talents, all of purest gold,
Two tripods and two baths of silver mould.
His wife, Alcandra, from her treasured store
A golden spindle to fair Helen bore,
And a bright silver basket, on whose round
A rim of burnish'd gold was closely bound ;
Before her sovereign placed, this Phylo brought
And charged with wool elaborately wrought ;
There the bright spindle lay, whence Helen drew
The fleece that richly flow'd with purple hue—
Thus on her footstool'd throne the Queen reclined,
And to her lord unbosom'd all her mind."

M. J. CHAPMAN. (TRIN. COL. CAM.)

" From her high-roof'd and fragrant chamber came,
Like to Diana of the golden shaft,
Helen : her following, Adraste placed
A well-made couch for her ; Alcippe brought
A carpet of soft wool ; Phylo, the gift
(A silver basket) which Alcandra made
To the bright Queen,—the wife of Polybus,
Who in Ægyptian Thebes his dwelling had,
Where in his palace lie treasures immense ;
He gave to Menelaus tripods twain,
Two silver baths, and talents ten of gold ;
His wife, besides, made Helen gifts of price
And beautiful,—a distaff all of gold,
And silver basket, silvery circling round,
But tipp'd with gold ; which stuff'd with threads made fit
To spin withal, Phylo her handmaid brought ;
The distaff was upon it, wrapt with wool
Of violet colour. On her couch she sat,
And on a cushion placed her dainty feet."

GEORGE DRAKE. (KIRKTHORPE.)

" While thus his thoughts in doubtful current flow,
Like the bright Goddess of the golden bow,
Forth from her lofty chamber the fair dame—
Her chamber rich in perfumes—Helen came.
For her a well-wrought couch Adraste bare :
A carpet of soft wool Alcippe's care :

Phylo a silver basket brought :—her load
Alcandra, wife of Polybus, bestow'd,
With divers treasures on their Spartan guest,
When they in Thebes of Egypt wealth possess'd ;
Two golden lavers, two of tripod mould,
And ten pure talents were annex'd of gold :
Besides his spouse rich works of rare device
To Helen gave, and gems of costly price ;
A golden distaff, and a sculptured vase,
She gave, of silver on a rounded base,
Whose upper rims with burnish'd gold were wrought :
The same now Phylo for her mistress brought,
Fill'd with spun thread : and on the pile she threw
A distaff charged with wool of purple hue.
A footstool underneath, a couch above
Received the queenly form of beauteous love."

'Tis impossible to hate the traitress. Homer himself loved
her—and so did Hector. In Troy we could not forgive her
—for the tears of the Fair Penitent were shed on the bosom
of Paris. Alas! and alack-a-day! what could she do? For
wicked Venus would show her gratitude for the golden apple
after her own wicked way; but Helen is again an honest woman—nay, start not at the homely words—for we have seen
honest women beautiful as angels. Menelaus suspected from
his weeping, at mention of Ulysses, that it was Telemachus ;
but Helen—whose beautiful eyes were always wide-awake—
knew that it must be the son of the great-hearted Ulysses—
from his wondrous likeness to the hero. Then the King—but
not before—sees the likeness too, in feet, hands, head, hair,
and eyes! Helen can still make him see—or not see—anything; but for our parts, we now see nothing but her own
radiant self, and since she is yet alive, what matters it that
Troy has ceased to be even a heap of ashes ?
Pisistratus declares it is no other than Telemachus.

CHRISTOPHER NORTH.

(Literally, and line for line with the Original.)

" Him the auburn-(haired) Menelaus answering address'd :
' Ye Gods ! of a truth indeed hath the son of a most friendly man
     to my house
Come, who for my sake hath toil'd in many combats :
And him when he came, I said, that I would welcome conspicuously
     above all

The Greeks, if to us a return over the sea, should grant
The Olympian, far-seeing Jupiter,—to take place in (*our*) swift ships.
And I-should-have-caused-to-be-inhabited for him a city in Argos, and a palace should have built,
Bringing him from Ithaca with his possessions and his son,
And all his people, removing-the-inhabitants from one city,
(*Of those*) which are-dwell'd-in-around (*me*), and are-ruled-over by myself.
And having much intercourse here we should have mingled together, nor us two,
Loving and pleased (*with each other*), should anything have separated,
Until the dark cloud of death had veil'd-us-around.
But-it-was-to-be that a God himself should-be-jealous-of these things,
Who, him alone, the-wretched-one, hath destined not-to-return.'
   Thus he spoke ; and among them all stirred-up a longing for lamentation.
The Argive Helen born of Jove on the one hand wept,
And on the other wept Telemachus, and Menelaus the-son-of Atreus.
Nor verily had Nestor's son tearless eyes :
For he-called-to-mind, in his heart, the amiable Antilochus,
Whom the illustrious son of the brilliant Aurora slew.''

But weeping soon becomes cold comfort—and '' they to the good things lying before them ready their hands outstretch'd.'' Hungry and thirsty as they are after their long travel—scarcely can they either eat or drink for gazing upon Helen. Homer does not say so—but it was so—for there she sits, spinning like an enchantress—her white hands so lovely among the violet-coloured wool — and her arms gracefully twirling the distaff till their eyes are dazzled with the light of lilies, and closed of their own accord, that they may better endure the softened beauty mellowing away in the mist of a momentary dream.

Yes—Helen is an Enchantress. She is going to drug their wine. Down she drops spindle and distaff—and will herself be cupbearer. Or glides she on a sandal of swan-down close behind the youths, and interposing between them the gleam of her right arm, imposes a charm more divine than Hermes' Moly into the liquid ruby that sends its perfume into the joyous brain. Hear Homer :—

(*Literally, and line for line with the Original.*)

" Then truly did Helen born of Jove devise another (*plan*),
For forthwith she mix'd a drug in the wine of which they were
    drinking,
(A drug) grief-assuaging and anger-dispelling, inducing-forgetful-
    ness of all evils.
He who shall-have-swallow'd-it-down, when-it-shall-have-been
    mix'd in the goblet,
Shall not during-the-whole-day be pouring down his cheeks the
    tear,
Not even if his father and mother should have died,
Not even if before him, his brother. or his beloved son,
One should have cut off with the sword, and he looking on with
    his eyes.
Such a drug skilfully-prepared had the daughter of Jove (*Helen*),
Efficacious, which Polydamna the wife of Thôn gave her
(*Polydamna*) the Ægyptian : in which (*country*) the all-beautiful
    soil produces most-numerous
Drugs, many of good when mix'd, and many destructive,
And (*there*) every physician is skill'd beyond all
Men : for their descent is from Pæon."

What was it ?   Some say music, history, and philosophy ;
and there indeed is in them—especially in music—a charm,
which you may call Nepenthes.   Plutarch, in a Symposiac,
says it was discourse well suiting the present passions and
conditions of the hearers ; and it was very pretty in Plutarch
to say so in a Symposiac.   Macrobius (we are using one of
Pope's notes) says, " Delinimentum illud quod Helena vino
miscuit, non herba fuit, non ex India succus, sed narrandi
opportunitas, quæ hospitem mœroris oblitum flexit ad gau-
dium."   We know Plutarch well—Macrobius not at all—nor
the other moralisers ; but wishing to be wise, they are foolish
—and so thought Milton.   You remember the unforgetable
lines in " Comus "—

> " Behold this cordial julep here
> That flames and dances in his crystal bounds !
> Not that Nepenthes which the wife of Thone
> In Ægypt gave to Jove-born Helena,
> Is of such power as this to stir up joy.
> To life so friendly, or so cool to thirst."

Egypt was the land of wonders, and that drug did an Egyptian to bright Helen give. " What drugs, what charms, what conjurations, and what mighty magic," had not the daughter of Leda ! Some in boxes, but many more in her bosom. And,

> " Oh, father ! what a hell of witchcraft lay
> In the small orb of each particular tear ! "

Now she used the best of all—smiles, tears, sighs, " thoughts that breathed and words that burned ; " these soothed the souls of the young heroes—and then she dropped in the drug —they drank and were in Elysium.

Was it opium ? Perhaps. For the youths soon grow drowsy ; and Helen and Menelaus have all the conversation to themselves about Ulysses and the wooden horse. Telemachus, at the close of Menelaus' tale of Helen's mimicry of the voices of the wives of the Greek heroes enclosed in that Hobby, abruptly exclaims,

> " But haste, and with dismission to repose,
> Now needful, gratify my friend and me."

It must have been opium. And poor Helen had need of " some sweet oblivious antidote " for the troubles of her brain —for Paris died for her sake—and she it was that laid low Achilles. Yet she was on the whole happy—and why not— since she made Menelaus perfectly so—and had now seen their Hermione married to Neoptolemus. She knew, too, that they were to enjoy an immortal life of love in the Elysian fields. For Proteus (what a wild and wondrous tale !) had said,—

> " But Jove-loved Menelaus ! not thy doom
> To die at Argos, and there have thy tomb.
> Thee, where the earth's extremest bounds extend,
> The powers immortal to Elysium send,
> Where gold-hair'd Rhadamanthus ever dwells,
> And blissful life, all bliss of man excels.
> There hail nor snow earth's beauteous face deform,
> Nor winter's bitter blast, nor pelting storm,
> But, in sweet murmurs heard, the western wind
> Breathes o'er the ocean, to refresh mankind ;
> There shalt thou, blissful as the Gods above,
> Live, Helen's husband, and the son of Jove."

A beautiful belief—(pardon the expression)—almost as beauti-

ful in Sotheby as in Homer!   Yet must Helen drink the drug of
forgetfulness, that she may not walk up and down the palace
in her sleep, with fixed eyes wringing her hands—such in
the sinful is the indestructible power of Conscience.

Telemachus might have gone to the continent in search of
his father—without Minerva—said Rapin; and why, asked
the same sapient sir, go for information to Menelaus ?   There
he is without Minerva—and Menelaus tells him that Proteus
said Ulysses was detained in an island by a Goddess.   True,
that was long ago ; but he may be there still; and Telemachus is prepared to believe it by his trust in his heavenly
guide, who disappeared in an Eagle.   But was his visit to
"Lacedemon's hollow vale" thrown away upon him by Homer?
He is finishing his education.   His whole soul is kindled by
tales of the heroes—" tales of tears and tragic stories ; " but
pity and terror instruct the heart—and he feels that he too,
like Orestes, will be an Avenger.   Were some God to divulge
to Ulysses weeping on the sea-shore, that his Telemachus is
now listening to the Tale of the " Returns " from the lips of
the Hero with the auburn hair, and that no name falls so
honoured from those lips as that of him the Castaway—the
joy in his heart would diffuse over all Calypso's Isle a brighter
light and a sweeter fragrance than are now burning and
breathing there from that enchanted cedar-fire.

Menelaus and Helen will not let Telemachus go—yet he is
impatient to be gone to-morrow!   " Twelve days you must
stay ; " but hear Homer.   Our literal line-by-line prose will
not do here—and Sotheby here beats Fenton black and blue,
and takes the shine even out of Cowper.

> " ' But thou, beneath my roof, thrice welcome, stay,
>   Till o'er thee glide the twelfth returning day.
>   Then graced with splendid gifts, thee, forth I send,
>   A car, and three brave steeds, thy course attend :
>   And I with these the golden goblet join,
>   That, henceforth, when thou pour'st to heaven the wine,
>   A thought on me may dwell.'
>   The Prince replied,
>   ' Bid me no longer here with thee abide :
>   Yet, the whole year, full gladly could I rest,
>   Thoughts of my home, my parents still repress'd,
>   Charm'd by thy words.   But my sad friends the while
>   Urge me to Pylos, and my native isle.

Whate'er thou givest in hospitable proof
Of thy kind heart, be treasured 'neath my roof:
But not thy coursers to my realm I lead,
For thy own glory, king! reserve the steed:
Thine, spelt, thine, lotus, and thy spread of plain
Teems with rich wheat, and barley's floury grain.
But not in Ithaca broad glades, or meads:
Yet dear the cliff whereon the wild-goat feeds:
No sea-girt islands, pasturing fields expand:
Yet most beloved by me, my rocky land.'
 He spake: his hand the admiring monarch press'd,
And smiling, thus with kindest speech address'd:
'Thee, born of noble blood, thy words declare,
And I for thee will fitter gifts prepare:
Of all my treasured stores—whatever mine
The prime—the most renown'd—most costly—thine.
A bowl, all silver, exquisitely chased,
Its rim, all gold, by art celestial graced,
The work of Vulcan: this, when hast'ning home
I left the monarch's hospitable dome,
The king of Sidon deign'd to me consign—
This bowl, the prime of all my treasures, thine.'
 Thus they: and while the menials served the feast,
Brought in the luscious wine, and chosen beast,
Their wives bright-filleted, with plenteous bread
The tables furnish'd as the revellers fed."

But how the while fares Penelope? Had the old nurse kept her secret? Close as a toad in a stone. But when the twelfth morn comes, Noëmon tells the Suitors that the bird— the young eagle—had flown; and Medon tells Penelope. They swear to lie in ambush for him on his return—She—but now that we have given so many fine specimens of Sotheby, let us see if we can touch your hearts—as we have done ere now—by our prose.

"Thus he spoke: and there her knees and heart were relax'd,
And long did a speechlessness of words hold her; her eyes
With tears were fill'd, and her blooming (clear, ϑαλερή) voice was
 restrain'd:
At length, however, answering in words, she address'd him:
'Herald, why went-forth my son? no need was there that he
Should go-on-board swift-passing ships, which sea-horses
Are to men, and pass over the vast moist (deep).
Is it that not even his name should be left among men?'

Her then answer'd Medon, inspired with wisdom :
'I know not if any god hath stirr'd-him-up, or if his own
Mind hath instigated him to go to Pylos, that he may ascertain
Either the return of his father, or what fate he hath under-
    gone.'
    Thus having spoken, he passed-on through the house of
    Ulysses.
But a soul-wasting grief was-pour'd-around her, nor any longer
    could she venture
To sit on a seat, although there were many in the house.
But she sat down on the threshold of her elaborately-built
    chamber,
Piteously wailing-aloud, and around her her maidens moan'd
All,—all throughout the house, young and old,
Whom Penelope, incessantly groaning, address'd :
    'Listen to me, my friends, for the gods have given sorrows
    to me
Above all who were born and brought up with me :
Who first lost my brave, lion-hearted husband,
Adorned with every kind of virtue among the Greeks,
(*My*) brave (*lord*)—whose glory was wide throughout Hellas, and
    the midst of Argos.
And now again have the tempests hurried away my beloved son
Ingloriously from his home, nor heard I of his-hastening-away.
Cruel ones, ye thought not,—no one (thought)
Of rousing me from my couch, although he knew it well,
When he went on board the hollow, dark ship :
For had I learn'd that he was hurrying-away on such a journey,
Yea, truly he would have remain'd, how great soever his haste to
    go away :
Or had left me dead in the house.
But let some trusty one summon the aged Dolius,
(My slave, whom my father gave to me when setting-out hither,
And who tends my many-tree'd garden)—that with the utmost
    speed
He may sit by Laërtes, and tell him all these things,
If peradventure he may devise any plan in his mind,
And going out among the people may wail (*the crime of those*) who
    long
To cut-off his and the offspring of the godlike Ulysses.'
    Her loved nurse Euryclea in turn address'd her :
'Lady beloved, slay me indeed with the merciless sword,
Or leave me in the house : but I will not conceal from thee a
    single (*thing :*)
I knew it all : and I supplied him with whatever he order'd,

Bread and luscious wine ; and he exacted from me a great oath,
Not to tell thee until the twelfth day had come,
Or (till) thou thyself shouldst desire it, and hadst heard of his
    hastening-away,
In order that thou mightest not by weeping mar the beauty of thy
    person.
But do thou, having bathed thyself, put on clean vestments on thy
    body,
Having-gone-up to the upper-chamber with thy attendant women,
Pray to Minerva, the daughter of the Ægis-bearing Jove :
For she may be inclined to save him from death.
Nor evilly-afflict an old man evilly-afflicted ; for methinks not
That the race of Arcisius to the blessed gods are altogether
Hateful,—but that somewhere shall survive, who may possess
The lofty-roof'd palaces, and far-lying rich lands.'
    Thus she spoke, and lulled her lamentation, and restrain'd her
    from weeping.
And having wash'd-herself, and taken clean vestments for her
    person,
She went up to an upper-room with her attendant women ;
And in a basket placed a bread-offering, and pray'd Minerva,
    ' Hear me, invincible one,—daughter of Ægis-bearing Jove,
If at any time Ulysses fertile-in-expedients has in the palace to
    thee
Burn'd the fat thighs either of ox or sheep,
Call to mind these things for me, and save my beloved son,
And repel the wooers (*who are*) wickedly overbearing.'
    Thus speaking, she wail'd-aloud, and the goddess heard her
    prayer."

He shall elude the ambush. But what if he were to fall into
it ? Antinous is fierce and strong—but hand to hand, Telemachus would hew him down, cleaving the head of the beautiful Scorner. Antinous takes with him twenty men—and
Telemachus has twenty; but are they armed? Most likely
—but if not, they can use their oars. Telemachus has two
spears in his hand—as Flaxman shows him landing on the
Pylian shore—and he was not his father's son if he left behind
him his sword. "Follow me, my lads—our cry is Ulysses;"
and leading the boarders, in three minutes he would have
taken the ambuscade. Not so willed Jove and the blue-eyed
daughter of Jove.

In her upper room lies the mourner. Food or wine she
will have none—her waking-dreams are of murder. To what

does Homer liken her? To a lion wounded by the hunters? No. But he likens her thoughts to the thoughts of a lion wounded by the hunters; and no other man that ever lived would have done so, excepting Shakespeare.

> " Numerous as are the lion's thoughts who sees,
>   Not without fear, a multitude of toils
>   Encircling him around."

People always sleep sound for some hours the night before they are hanged—dreaming either not at all, or of a reprieve, or of themselves on the scaffold asking for water. Penelope was doomed to die—of grief for Telemachus. The sorrow of twenty years may be a profound, but it is a still sorrow. One's life may not unpainfully float down it as on a gloomy but not roaring river—and there are gleams of beauty on its banks. So felt Penelope, sorrowing for Ulysses. But all at once she missed " my son—my son." She then knew what is *anguish;* yet, her body, her senses—not her spirit, not herself—slept. Minerva saw her, the childless widow—for so Penelope was in her mind, soul, heart—and sent a comforter.

" There then did the blue-eyed Minerva devise another plan :
  She form'd a representation, (*which*) in person resembled the
      lady
  Iphthime—daughter of the great-hearted Icarius .
  Her Eumelus, dwelling in a house in Pheræ, had married.
  Her did (*Minerva*) send to the house of the godlike Ulysses,
  If by any means Penelope, wailing and lamenting,
  She might restrain from weeping, and tearful mourning.
  And she enter'd her chamber by the bolt of the lock,
  And stood over her head, and address'd her in these words :
  ' Sleepest thou, Penelope, vex'd in thy heart ?
  The gods who live in ease permit thee not
  To weep, nor to be sorrowful,—since about to return is
  Your son : for to the gods he is sinless.'
  Her then answer'd the discreet Penelope,
  Most sweetly slumbering in the gates of dreams !
  ' Why, sister, comest thou hither ? by no means formerly indeed
  Wert-thou-wont-to-come, since thou dwellest in a house very
      remote :
  And thou orderest me to stop from sorrowing and lamentations
  Numerous, which provoke me throughout my mind and my heart:
  (*Me*) who first lost my brave, lion-hearted husband,

Adorned with every kind of virtue among the Greeks,
(*My*) brave (*lord*) whose glory was wide throughout Hellas, and
the midst of Argos.
And now again hath my beloved son gone in a hollow ship,
A child, neither acquainted with labours, nor commerce.
On his account I the more lament, than on his (*the father's*) :
For him I tremble and fear, lest anything suffer
Should he among the people among whom he hath gone, or on the
sea :
For many enraged foes plot against him,
Longing to slay him, before he come to his fatherland.'
    Her the pale shade answering address'd :
'Be of-good-cheer, and not at all fear too much in thy mind :
For such an attendant goes along with (*him*), as other
Men would choose to go alone with (*them*)—for powerful (*is she*)
(*Namely*) Pallas Minerva : thee she pities in thy lamentations :
And me hath she sent forward to tell thee so.'
    Her address'd the discreet Penelope :
'If thou art indeed a goddess, and hast heard the voice of a
goddess,
If so, come, tell to me with respect to that hapless one,
If anywhere he live, and look on the light of the sun,
Or if he be dead, and in the dwellings of Ades.'
    Her the pale shade answering address'd :
'With respect to him I will not answer thee directly
Whether he be alive, or dead : for it is a bad thing to answer the
things that may-be-borne-away-by-the-wind.'
(*The shade*), thus having spoken through the lock of the door, with-
drew
Into a breath of wind : but from sleep roused-herself-up
The daughter of Icarius, and her heart was delighted
That a manifest dream had come upon her in the hours of mid-
night."

Is this an IDEA of the First Four Books of the Odyssey?
And would you wish them all away? If you would, then it
would surely be by gently disengaging them from the Twenty,
and giving them an asylum in some secret and sacred cell in
your heart. But what to you would be the Twenty, were
these four buried in dust! They would be much; for a deep
human interest overflows one and all, among the wonderful
and wild that seem to belong but to imagination's sphere.
You would sympathise with Ulysses longing for rugged Ithaca
even in Ogygia's enchanted isle; for home-sickness is the

malady of a noble heart, and conjugal affection its most endearing virtue. But on the first sight you *now* have of Ulysses
weeping to the waves, you know, better far than he does, a
thousand reasons in nature for his tears. The Muse has told
you far more than Minerva told him—and all your love and
admiration of his Penelope and his Telemachus, insensibly
changed into a profound pity, are poured on the majestic
mourner's head. Your heart burns within you to think that
he will return *to that home*, to redress, to vindicate, to avenge,
and to enjoy. Here is "the sea-mark of his utmost sail."
Happiness enough here—by his presence made to emerge from
misery—to compensate all the woes of the much-enduring
man, and leave him deep in debt to Heaven.

And do you grudge Telemachus his visit to Nestor and to
Menelaus,

"In life's morning march, when his spirit is young"?

Joy tempers his grief, till it smiles—as sunshine will seek out
and not suffer a flower to be sad in mists and storms. And
how pure those courts of kings! The manners there how
virtuous in their simplicity—the morning air how bright—and
the evening air how still, in religious service duly done to
the Gods! The whole life we see—the whole life of which we
hear—heroic; and Poetry shedding over it, generally, a gentle
lustre—sometimes, as in the narration of the adventures of
Menelaus by himself, a gloomy light that seems strangely to
darken and illumine a hardly human world.

You have been made to feel that Penelope is worthy of the
love of Ulysses—and you long for the REALISATION OF HER
DREAM.

HOMER AND HIS TRANSLATORS.

[FEBRUARY 1834]

WERE not the first Four Books of the Odyssey felt to be in themselves a Poem? Perhaps you might liken them to the porch of a palace. We would rather liken them to the arms of a tree. Part only of the green umbrage is visible, but sufficient to show that it belongs to a noble bole; and ere long we shall behold the whole Wonder, proportioned in the perfect symmetry of nature, with broad crown familiar with storms, yet a pavilion for the sunshine, and in its magnificence rooted among rocks.

A tender and profound interest has been breathed into our hearts in all that concerns Ithaca; it is invested with the hallowed charm of Home; we love the rocky yet not unfruitful isle as if it were our own birthplace, and the smoke seems to ascend from our own hearth. In the midst of all that trouble, we are conscious of a coming calm. 'Tis a stormy day, but not a cloud, we are assured, will disturb the serenity of sunset. We believe the Seer and the Eagles. Penelope is no object of pity now—not even when seen sitting on the stairs, stupified into stone by the voice telling her that her Telemachus has left her alone in her widowhood among all those lawless men. For that doleful and delusive trance is succeeded by a delightful and faithful Dream; her Ulysses is not dead—her Ulysses will return; and what matters transient misery to any mortal, when it purchases steadfast bliss?

Homer is fond of Dreams. And not one of them all is more apparently heart-born than the Dream that appears to Penelope in the shape of her sister. Iphthime tells her that the Gods will restore her son. "But what canst thou tell me of Ulysses?" Of his fate the phantom will make no revelation.

Eustathius says that if she had, the poem would have been at
an end. But that was not the reason of her silence. Iphthime
was Penelope. Telemachus had left her, and her soul was
troubled; but she had seen the young hero in his pride,
unappalled by the Suitors, and knew that he had gone on a
holy quest to Pylos and Lacedemon—to Nestor and Menelaus.
Her heart, cheered by the thought in sleep, felt her brave boy
would escape the ambush. But Ulysses! he had been away
from her for twenty years. Hope was almost dead in her
waking—as now in her sleeping dreams. Her heart asked
her heart, " Oh ! tell me of my lord?" But in her despair
there was no response—and she awoke. But she awoke to
joy, and in that joy no doubt the wife was comforted as well
as the mother; nor could she believe, as she did, in the return
of her son, without some hope stealing with the morning
light of the return of her husband! The Philosophy of Dreams
in Homer's poetry is the Religion of Nature.

That Dream made the widow's heart sing aloud for joy.
There is light in her eyes, though still broken and dashed
with tears. Her son's heroic piety comforts her—the seer's
prophecy comforts her—and comforts her beyond all else her
own faithful heart. Yet how blind, though visited by
glimpses, are the eyes of sorrow! How idle often all our
holiest tears ! What if Penelope could see Ulysses sitting on
an enchanted shore, and, forgetful of heavenly charms, weeping
for her sake ! For her sake struggling with the tempest that
drives him—homewards! Swimming towards an unknown
shore—day and night—all for her sake—and saved from sinking by a talisman given him by a compassionate Spirit of the
Sea ! What if she could see the Falcon of Alcinous wafting
to her embrace her lord the King? But love knows not—
either in its joy or its grief—what a day may bring forth ;
and beautiful is the poetry that sings of the uncertainties of
human life heaving like the world of waves—all settling down
into peace at last—a gracious lull descending from Heaven at
the command of Providence.

There is much to mourn over in the Greek Mythology ; but
now we see but Love and Mercy ; and the Deities assembled
on Olympus are like

" Blessed angels pitying human cares."

At one council Minerva had permission from Jove to carry comfort to Ithaca; and now at another Mercury is sent to Ogygia—a messenger bolder if not so bright as Iris; and at the word of Jove, we behold him in Homer, as in an after vision we behold him in Shakespeare, "the herald Mercury, new-lighted on a heaven-kissing hill."

"Thus he spake: nor did the messenger (*of the gods*), the Argicide, disobey
And then forthwith he bound on his feet beautiful sandals,—
Ambrosial, golden :—which were-wont-to-bear him, whether over the deep,
Or over the unlimited earth, along with the blast of the wind.
He took also his rod, by which he lulls the eyes of men,
Whomsoever he wills, and when sleeping rouses them up again.
With this in his hands the brave Argicide flew :
And having lighted on Pieria, from the ether he fell into the sea :
And over the waves hasten'd, like the bird the sea-mew,
Which, along the mighty bosom of the immeasurable ocean,
As it hunts after fishes, oft moists its wings with spray.
Like to it (*the sea-mew*) was Hermes wafted over the multitudinous waves.
But when indeed he came to the island placed at a distance,
From the violet-colour'd ocean ascending to the mainland
He came-on, till he reach'd a spacious cave, in which the nymph
With-beautiful-ringlets dwelt : her he found within.
A great fire was blazing on the hearth, and far the odour
Of easily-cleft cedar-wood, and of incense, spread-fragrance throughout the island
As they were burning : while she (the nymph), warbling with her beautiful voice,
And plying the loom, was weaving with a golden shuttle.
A wood in-full-luxuriance had-grown-around the cave,
The alder, and the poplar, and the sweet-smelling cypress.
There, too, the wing-widely-expanded birds nestled,
Owls, and cormorants, and long-tongued divers (*sea-birds*)
Of-the-sea, to which (*birds*) sea employments are a concernment.
There also around the hollow cave was extended
A young-luxuriant vine which flourish'd in clusters.
Four fountains in-order flow'd with limpid water,
Near to each other,—being turn'd one, in one direction, and another, in another.

Around soft meadows of violets, and of parsley,
Were blooming : thither even an Immortal, had he come,
Would have admired (*it*) as he gazed, and had been delighted in
    his spirit.
And there standing, the messenger, the Argicide, gazed.
But when he had admired the whole in his heart,
Forthwith into the spacious cavern he entered : nor him in her
    presence
Did Calypso, the divine one among goddesses, when she saw him,
    not recognise.
(For gods are not unknown to each other,
The immortals,—not even if one dwell-in mansions remote.)
But the great-hearted Ulysses he found not within,
For he sitting on the shore was weeping : where formerly indeed
    (*it was his wont to do so*),
Torturing his heart with tears, and groans, and griefs,
Pouring out tears (*while*) he looked on the immeasurable ocean.
Calypso the divine one among goddesses question'd Hermes,
Having seated him on a brilliant shining throne.
' Why, oh ! golden-rodded Hermes, hast thou come to me,
Thou venerable, and loved (*one*) ?—for erst thou camest not often.
Speak whatever thou hast-in-thy-mind : my heart impels me to
    bring-it-about,
If I can indeed bring it about, and if it be practicable.
But follow (*me*) further-on, that I may place before thee the rites-
    of-hospitality.'
    Thus having spoken, the goddess placed before him a table,
Having fill'd it with ambrosia, and mingled the ruddy nectar.
But the messenger (*of gods*), the Argicide, drank and eat.
And when he had regaled and refresh'd his heart by eating,
Then indeed did he answering thus address her."

                                                    —V. 43-96.

This is the most elaborate description of natural scenery in
all Homer. In the Iliad, the bard but illumines the visual
sense by a few sunny strokes, that make start out tree, glade,
or rock. Here we have a picture. Say rather a creation. In
a moment the poet evokes the enchanted isle out of the violet-
coloured ocean. There it is hanging in air. But all we know
is, that it is beautiful—for we are Mercury, and see nothing
distinctly till we find ourselves standing at the mouth of a
spacious cave. The light of a magical fire—the odour of
sacred incense—the music of an immortal voice—Calypso
herself plying the golden shuttle as she sings ! All felt at

once, yet in loveliest language evolved in a series of words
expanding like a flower with all its bright and balmy leaves
—an instantaneous birth. We must not disturb the daughter
of Atlas—but gaze and listen—till by degrees the congenial
beauty of the place withdraws our soul and our senses from
the tones and tresses of the Divine among Goddesses, and,
still conscious of her living enchantments, we are won by delight to survey the scene in which she enjoys her immortal
being, yet about to be disturbed by visitings like our own
mortal grief! The scene is sylvan. " A wood in full luxuri-
ance had grown around the Cave !" One line gives the
whole wood, another its composing trees, another their inhabitants—and all together breathe of the sea. Look again
at the Cave. The entrance is draperied with green and
purple—for in such sunny shelter luxuriates the vine ! The
beauty of nature is nowhere perfect without the pure element
of water wimpling in peace. And there it is—flowing fresh
as flower-dews—in mazy error—through blooming meadows
—its " sweet courses not hindered"—and happy to blend its
murmurs with the diapason of the deep. True it is that
earth is as beautiful as heaven. So felt now the Argicide—
" standing there till he had admired the whole in his heart."
Beauty begets love—and love admiration—and admiration
hushes the heart of Gods and men till they are still as statues ;
and not till the passionate trance subsides can Mercury
himself move a footstep—though his sandals are golden and
ambrosial, and bear him over earth and sea like the breath of
the wind.

Whereabouts—in what latitude lies Calypso's Isle ? To
what bright neighbourhood of stars is it dear with its yellow
woods ? Of what constellation beholds it, during calm nights,
the image trembling in the sky-seeming sea? The flight of
Mercury betrays not the secret of its birthplace—from Pieria's
top he falls plumb-down upon the sea—and away like a wild
gull he scours—but whether towards the rising or the setting
sun, not a whisper from Homer—only we afterwards hear from
the messenger himself that he had " measured a breadth enormous of the salt expanse"—and something very vague of its
position on the watery wilderness may be gathered from
Calypso's Seaman's Guide, orally delivered on his departure
to Ulysses. 'Tis all a beautiful mystery—imagination dreams

a dream—the understanding surrenders its privilege of ques-
tioning, and the heart delighted believes that all is truth.
Ogygia! A glimpse of the spiritual world of old that still
fluctuated waveringly between sense and soul, and was constructed by poetry of idealised realities, that may cease to be
seen on troubling of the ether, but can never cease to be, if
mind be immortal. Ogygia! it is felt to be "self-withdrawn
into a wondrous depth" of seclusion! Though "light the
soil and pure the air," and the scenery composed of all
familiar objects, yet is the region felt to be almost as preternatural as if it were submarine—and Calypso's cave as wondrous as a Mermaid's grotto.

How very still! No screen to the mouth of the cave, but a
few vine-festoons—so, blow as it may on the main, and all
around the isle (and a storm brought hither Ulysses), on the
land *all is lown*—merely breath enough to keep the pure air
for ever pure, and to enable the leaves to take a dance now
and then upon the tree-tops, to some Æolian harp capriciously
playing in the shade. Calypso is a queen—but she has no
subjects, only her attendant nymphs—and of them we see,
hear nothing—only once are they mentioned—they are to us
but mere momentary shadows passing unheeded along the
walls of the cave. There is no building made with hands
anywhere on all the isle—not a vestige of antiquity in the
shape of a rudely sculptured stone. No roads, no pathways,
no flocks, no herds, no four - footed creatures, either wild
or tame—not even—we are sorry for it—a dog. Food and
drink are set before Ulysses, such as are eaten and drunk
by mortal men—but we know not whence they come—they
seem served by invisible hands—and of kitchen or cellar there
is no *sugh*. A charm is over all—yet 'twould be hard to say
by what spell it has been wrought. 'Tis all the doing of the
finest possible spirit of poetry, that works wonders without
appearing to be at work at all; of genius instinctively knowing how far fiction may be interfused with truth, and within
the domain of wildest imagination be brought all the home-
liest, and therefore holiest, sympathies of nature. Is it not
so in Ogygia?

But whose English is likest the Greek? Perhaps, after all,
our own prose—faithful to the meanings, if false to the measures of the words; yet not false even to the measures—for

we have them in our heart—as we hope you have in yours;
nor can there be ever more now than a faint echo of such
music from even the highest harp—humble the highest when
struck in rivalry with Homer's—and powerless to imitate the
gold and silver of those heaven-tempered strings.

POPE.

" He spoke. The God who mounts the winged winds
Fast to his feet the golden pinions binds,
That high through fields of air his flight sustain
O'er the wide earth, and o'er the boundless main.
He grasps the wand that causes sleep to fly,
Or in soft slumber seals the wakeful eye :
Then shoots from heaven to high Pieria's steep,
And stoops incumbent on the rolling deep.
So watery fowl, that seek their fishy food,
With wings expanded o'er the foaming flood,
Now sailing smooth the level.surface sweep,
Now dip their pinions in the briny deep.
Thus o'er the world of waters Hermes flew,
Till now the distant island rose in view ;
Then, swift ascending from the azure wave,
He took the path that winded to the cave.
Large was the grot, in which the nymph he found
(The fair-hair'd nymph with every beauty crown'd ;)
She sate and sung : the rocks resound her lays ;
The cave was brighten'd with a rising blaze :
Cedar and frankincense, an odorous pile,
Flamed on the hearth, and wide perfumed the isle ;
While she with work and song the time divides,
And through the loom the golden shuttle guides.
Without the grot a various sylvan scene
Appear'd around, and groves of living green ;
Poplars and alders ever quivering play'd,
And nodding cypress form'd a fragrant shade ;
On whose high branches, waving with the storm,
The birds of broadest wing their mansion form,
The chough, the sea-mew, the loquacious crow,
And scream aloft, and skim the deeps below.
Depending vines the shelving cavern screen,
With purple clusters blushing through the green.
Four limpid fountains from the clefts distil ;
And every fountain pours a several rill,
In mazy windings wandering down the hill :

Where bloomy meads with vivid greens were crown'd,
And glowing violets threw odours round.
A scene, where if a god should cast his sight,
A god might gaze, and wonder with delight !
Joy touch'd the messenger of heaven ; he stay'd
Entranced, and all the blissful haunt survey'd.
Him, entering in the cave, Calypso knew ;
For Powers celestial to each other's view
Stand still confest, though distant far they lie
To habitants of earth, or sea, or sky.
But sad Ulysses, by himself apart,
Pour'd the big sorrows of his swelling heart ;
All on the lonely shore he sate to weep,
And roll'd his eyes around the restless deep ;—
Tow'rd his loved coast he roll'd his eyes in vain,
Till, dimm'd with rising grief, they stream'd again."

COWPER.

" He ended, nor the Argicide refused,
Messenger of the skies ; his sandals fair,
Ambrosial, golden, to his feet he bound,
Which o'er the moist wave, rapid as the wind,
Bear him, and o'er th' illimitable Earth ;
Then took his rod, with which, at will, all eyes
He softly shuts, or opens them again.
So arm'd, forth flew the valiant Argicide.
Alighting on Pieria, down he stoop'd
To Ocean, and the billows lightly skimm'd
In form a sea-mew, such as, in the bays
Tremendous of the barren Deep her food
Seeking, dips oft in brine her ample wing.
In such disguise o'er many a wave he rode,
But reaching now that isle remote, forsook
The azure Deep ; and, at the spacious grot,
Where dwelt the amber-tressèd nymph, arrived,
Found her within.   A fire on all the hearth
Blazed sprightly, and, afar-diffused, the scent
Of smooth-split cedar and of cypress-wood
Odorous, burning, cheer'd the happy isle.
She, busied at the loom, and plying fast
Her golden shuttle, with melodious voice
Sat chanting there ; a grove on either side,
Alder and poplar, and the redolent branch
Of cypress hemm'd the dark retreat around.

There many a bird of broadest pinion built
Secure her nest, the owl, the kite, and daw,
Long-tongued, frequenter of the sandy shores.
A garden-vine, luxuriant on all sides,
Mantled the spacious cavern, cluster-hung
Profuse ; four fountains of serenest lymph,
Their sinuous course pursuing side by side,
Stray'd all around, and ev'rywhere appear'd
Meadows of softest verdure, purpled o'er
With violets ; it was a scene to fill
A god from heaven with wonder and delight.
Hermes, Heaven's messenger, admiring stood
That sight, and having all survey'd, at length
Enter'd the grotto ; nor the lovely nymph
Him knew not soon as seen, for not unknown
Each to the other the Immortals are,
How far soever sep'rate their abodes.
Yet found he not within the mighty chief,
Ulysses ; he sat weeping on the shore,
Forlorn ; for there his custom was with groans
Of sad regret t' afflict his breaking heart,
Looking continual o'er the barren Deep."

SOTHEBY.

"Nor Hermes disobey'd, but swiftly bound
The ambrosial sandals his fair feet around.
The golden sandals that his flight upbear
O'er earth and ocean, fleet as fleetest air :
Then, took his wand, of power at will to close,
Or raise the lid of mortals from repose.
Thus graced, the god to high Pieria pass'd,
Thence downward 'mid the main his body cast,
Swift as the sea-mew, whose voracious sweep
Catches on flight the fish that cleaves the deep,
And dips his wing in brine : thus Hermes sped,
Light-ruffling as he skimm'd the ocean bed.
But now, when reach'd the island's distant strand,
The god ascending fix'd his foot on land,
Pass'd on, and found within her spacious cave
The fair-hair'd nymph, the goddess of the wave :
The fire wide-blazed, and o'er the isle outspread
Cedar and incense fragrant odours shed.
Bent o'er her web the goddess sweetly sung,
While through the threads the golden shuttle rung,

Groves round her grot, the poplar, alder wreathed,
And as the cypress waved fresh odours breathed :
Birds of broad pennons there their plumage dress'd,
The owl, the hawk, couch'd peaceful in their nest,
And thin-tongued daws, that from their airy flight
On the low margin of the sea alight.
Round the dim cave the vine's lithe tendrils flow'd,
And the ripe grape in purple clusters glow'd ;
Four fountains, nigh each other, to and fro
Wreathed their pure streams, and gush'd with gurgling flow :
'Mid the soft meads the undying parsley bloom'd,
And the grass gleam'd with violets illumed.
'Twas there, where gods might feast the ravish'd sight,
Stood Hermes, wrapt in wonder and delight.
But when the god there long had tranced his view,
Him, as he sought her grot, the sea-nymph knew ;
For not unknown, though distant their abode,
A god at once acknowledges a god.
He found not there Ulysses : far apart
Lone on the beach he fed with grief his heart,
Sore groan'd, and gazing on the boundless deep
Where oft the wretch had wept, return'd to weep."

LEIGH HUNT.   (FROM "FOLIAGE.")

" He said ; and straight the herald Argicide
Beneath his feet the feathery sandals tied,
Immortal, golden, that his flight could bear
O'er seas and lands, like waftage of the air ;
His rod too, that can close the eyes of men
In balmy sleep, and open them again,
He took, and holding it in hand, went flying ;
Till from Pieria's top the sea descrying,
Down to it sheer he dropp'd, and scour'd away
Like the wild gull, that fishing o'er the bay
Flaps on, with pinions dipping in the brine ;
So went on the far sea the shape divine.
And now arriving at the isle, he springs
Oblique, and landing with subsided wings,
Walks to the cavern 'twixt the tall green rocks,
Where dwelt the goddess with the lovely locks.
He paused ; and there came on him, as he stood,
A smell of citron and of cedar wood,
That threw a perfume all about the isle ;
And she within sat spinning all the while,
And sang a lovely song, that made him hark and smile.

A sylvan nook it was, grown round with trees,
Poplars, and elms, and odorous cypresses,
In which all birds of ample wing, the owl
And hawk, had nests, and broad-tongued waterfowl.
The cave in front was spread with a green vine,
Whose dark round bunches almost burst with wine ;
And from four springs, running a sprightly race
Four fountains, clear and crisp, refresh'd the place ;
While all about, a meadowy ground was seen,
Of violets mingling with the parsley green :
So that a stranger, though a god were he,
Might well admire it, and stand there to see ;
And so admiring, there stood Mercury."

M. J. CHAPMAN.   (TRIN. COLL., CAM.)

" He said ; nor disobey'd the messenger,
Slayer of Argus ; to his feet he bound
Sandals, ambrosial, beautiful, of gold,
Which ferry him over the flood, and o'er
The vast round earth, quick as the wind-breath goes ;
And took his wand, with which he charms men's eyes,
Whom he would lull to sleep, or else at will
Wakens the sleeping ; having which he flew.
Standing on the Pierian-top, he shot
From ether on the sea, and skimm'd the wave
Quick as a sea-gull ; which in the deep folds
Of the untill'd salt sea-surge hunts for fish,
Dipping his feathers in the briny foam ;
Not less quick o'er the white wave Hermes rode.
But when he reach'd the island far apart,
Forth from the violet-colour'd deep he went
On dry land ; where dwelt in her cavern'd home
Well-tress'd Calypso ; her he found within.
Blazed on the hearth a mighty fragrant fire
Of fissile cedar and of incense wood,
Far through the island odorous as they burn'd ;
And her sweet voice kept murmuring into song,
As she with golden shuttle plied the web.
All round the cavern grew a verdant grove ;
Alder and poplar, cypress sweet of smell :
And there the long-wing'd birds would couch themselves ;
Owls, sea-hawks, choughs, and far-voiced cormorants,
Whose farms are on the deep. And there the vine
With lively tendrils twined around the cave,
Heavy with clust'ring grapes. Forth issued thence

Four fountains flowing with a limpid stream,
Their water-courses in sweet neighbourhood ;
Soft meadows bloom'd around, with violets
And parsley purfled.   There well-pleased might gaze,
Should one arrive, an Immortality ;
There stood and gazed Hermes the messenger.
He gazed his fill ; then went into the cave.
Nor knew him not, seeing him face to face,
Calypso, the divine of goddesses,
(For to Immortals not at sight unknown
Immortals are, though one may dwell apart).
High-heart Ulysses found he not within,
For he upon the sea-shore sat and wept ;
Where was his wont, with tears and groans and griefs,
To look upon the sea, dropping down tears."

WRANGHAM.

" He said : the Argicide obey'd ;
Fast to his feet his sandals made,
Celestial, golden—through the skies
With these o'er lands and seas he hies,
Fleet as the wind—his rod then takes,
With which he or the slumberer wakes,
Or at his will with slumber seals
The wakeful.   So prepared, he wheels
On pinion strong his airy flight,
Descends upon Pieria's height ;
Thence towering, o'er the billows sweeps :
As sea-bird in vast ocean's deeps
Dips oft its wing in quest of prey—
So skimm'd the god the salt sea-spray.
   Soon as he reach'd the distant isle,
Lighting he paced the beach awhile ;
Till to a spacious cave he came,
Where sate within a bright-tress'd dame :
Blazed on the hearth a cedar pile,
And woods high-scented, o'er the isle
Diffusing odours far and wide :
She still her golden shuttle plied,
And sang the while a witching lay,
As 'mid the threads her fingers play.
Around, thick groves their summer-dress
Wore in luxuriant loveliness—
Alder and poplar quiver'd there,
And fragrant cypress tower'd in air.

And there broad-pinion'd birds were seen,
Nesting amid the foliage green ;
Birds, which the marge of ocean haunt—
Gull, prating daw, and cormorant ;
And there, the deep mouth of the cave
Fringing, the cluster'd vine-boughs wave.
Sprung from near sources, bright and gay
Four limpid fountains urge their way,
Divergent, o'er the parsley'd mead,
Where the sweet violet droops its head—
A scene, should gods survey the sight,
E'en gods might gaze on with delight !
Raptured stood Hermes and amazed,
And long and fondly round him gazed ;
The cave then enter'd. Straight her guest
Calypso knew—for Gods confest
Are known of Gods, though sunder'd wide
In distant mansions they abide.
       But no Ulysses was within—
On the lone shore, his sorrow's scene,
His longing eyes he frequent threw
O'er the wild ocean tossing blue,
With many a tear and deep-drawn sigh
Heaved to the thought of days gone by !"

GEORGE DRAKE. (KIRKTHORPE.)

" Hermes obey'd : then bound the herald fleet
The ambrosial golden sandals on his feet ;
With these he rushes like a blast of wind,
And leaves the ocean—leaves the land behind.
He grasp'd the wand—with which in slumber deep
Of whom he will, he bids the troubles sleep ;
Again the potent rod if he should wave,
Dispels the slumber which before it gave.
Bold Argiphontes, brandishing this wand,
Pursued his easy flight o'er sea and land.
At length he gain'd Pieria's rugged steep,
Then stoop'd his headlong passage to the deep :
Lightly he skimm'd—as when the wild sea-mew,
Dipping his lusty wing in briny dew,
Pursues his fishy prey with rapid glance
O'er the rough bosom of the vast expanse :
Like him his wings in ocean Hermes laves,
And rides like him in triumph o'er the waves.

But where the lonely isle its shore extends,
From the blue waters he the path ascends :
He came to where the spacious grotto show'd
The fair-hair'd goddess' beautiful abode.
Within she sat—before her clear and bright
The blazing cedar pour'd its fragrant light ;
And as the slender fagots cheer'd the gloom,
Rich incense rose, and delicate perfume ;
The golden shuttle ran the weft along ;
She cheer'd the labour with her sweet-toned song.
In verdant harmony around the cave
Poplar, and alder, and sweet cypress wave ;
Here broad-wing'd birds erect their airy nest,
Owls, and sea-hawks, and croaking ravens rest ;
All of that strong-plumed tribe here safely sleep
Who hunt their prey across the stormy deep.
Thick o'er the front was spread a shady vine,
Rich in rife clusters of the promised wine.
Four founts in order gush'd with crystal clear,
Turn'd to each other, and each other near ;
Meadows enamell'd with sweet flowers of spring
Eternal verdure o'er the landscape fling.
A deity might bend his downward flight,
View the rich scene—and view it with delight.
The herald-god in admiration stay'd
His hasty course : till all its charm survey'd,
The grot he enters :—him at earliest view,
Fairest of goddesses, Calypso, knew ;
For should their dwelling e'en be far and lone,
To each Immortal are the Immortals known.
But there was not Ulysses :—on the strand
He mourns in solitude his native land ;
With sighs and groans and choking griefs his heart
Pants from this sweet imprisonment to part.
O'er the wide sea his longing gaze he threw,
Till rising tears bedim the hopeless view."

WILLIAM HAY.

" The messenger of gods, the Argicide,
Obey'd, and on his feet the sandals tied,
Sandals of gold, ambrosial, useful these
To waft him swiftly as the winged breeze
Across the boundless earth, or the far-rolling seas.
That rod, wherewith he lulls the eyes of men,
And as he lists, from sleep can rouse again—

Great Hermes seized :—down to Pieria's steep,
Thence, sheer through air, he plunged upon the deep,
Whose waves he skimm'd along,—(like the sea-mew
That doth o'er ocean's lap the fish pursue,
And dips his closely-feather'd wings in spray)—
Thus o'er the numerous waves, great Hermes sped his way.
The violet-colour'd sea he leaves for land,
Since the sequester'd isle is now at hand,
Straight to the mainland, and the cavern borne
Where dwells the nymph whom lovely locks adorn.
Within the cave a blazing hearth he found,
Diffusing heat and fragrance all around,
By fissile cedar, and rich incense fed,
Which o'er the isle refreshing odours shed.
Plying the loom she trills her warbling song,
While the gold shuttle swiftly shoots along.
With thicket overgrown the cavern stood,
Embower'd in verdure of the stateliest wood :
The alder and the poplar spread their leaves,
And cypress there its spicy umbrage weaves.
Thither the long-tongued cormorants repair,
And wide-wing'd birds delight to nestle there :
There, too, the owl and hawk their revels keep,
And every bird that loves the stormy deep.
And there a young, luxuriant vine outspreads
Its mantling shade, and glowing clusters sheds.
Four neighbouring fountains, each the gurgling source
Of limpid waters, roll their separate course.
And all around the downy meads are seen
The soft blue violet and the parsley green.
Oh ! had a god but only lighted there,
Enraptured had he view'd a scene so fair !
There Hermes gazed upon the wondrous sight,
Feasting his soul on beauty and delight,—
Then sought the cave ;—which not unknown he trode,
Divine Calypso saw, and knew the god :
For not unknown, though far apart they dwell,
Are gods to gods, they know each other well.
Ulysses, the great-hearted, was not there ;
For to the beach he would full oft repair,
There seated would he gaze, with streaming eyes,
Wasting away his soul in groans and sighs.
' Why, Hermes,' said Calypso the divine,
While on a seat she bade the god recline ;

' Why, Hermes, famous for the golden rod,
Thou much beloved, thou much respected god,
Why this unwonted visit ? Speak thy mind,
If mine the power,—to that am I inclined ;
But first our hospitable rites be shared.'
Thus spoke the goddess, and the feast prepared ;
Ambrosia, food of gods, was now served up,
And blushing nectar sparkled in the cup,
Of which he eat and drank till satisfied,—-
The messenger of gods,—the Argicide."

Pope's version is on the whole a fine one—and perhaps
may please you more than any of, or all the others—and if so,
we shall not find fault with your taste. But why should he be
perpetually improving on Homer ? He substitutes " pinions "
for " sandals "—omits "ambrosial "—calls Mercury, which Homer does not, " the god who mounts the winged winds,"—
and says, without authority from Homer, that the pinions "*high
through fields of air his flight sustain* "—the very flight described being chiefly along the level of the sea. The next four
lines are good in themselves, but not Homeric ; and the four following them bad, and most unhomeric—the change of " a sea-
fowl " into " watery fowl," in the plural, destroying the indivi-
duality of the image—to say nothing of the needless epithets
and the verbiage that deaden the apt simile so lively in the
rapid original. He spoils, by confusion, the cave. He had
no right all at once to say that Calypso " sate and sung "—no
right to say " the rocks resound her lays ; " for Homer merely
says, " her he found within," and mentions the fire and the
incense, before he speaks of her song and her golden shuttle
—while Pope tells us over again that the nymph sang—and
in words all unlike the simple Greek. His mind could not
have been possessed by the passage ; if it had, he could not
have helped giving it in the order of Homer—which is that of
nature. " Without the grot a *various* sylvan scene " is a good
line, but Homer does not say *at first* that it was " various "—
he tell us *that* immediately afterwards, as the wood brightens
before his eyes ; nor does Homer say that the alders and
poplars " ever quivering play'd ; " but Pope wished to show
his knowledge—not very recondite—of the habits of those
trees. Neither does Homer say the cypresses " nodded "—
nor that their high branches were " waving to the storm."
All was then still—nor was it possible for Mercury to think of a

storm in such perfect peace. Pope is here most impertinent. " Their mansion form " is absurdly pompous ; and he would fain be more picturesque with his " scream aloft " than the Prince of Painters. What immediately follows is better—but in nothing very felicitous ; and the translator entirely mistakes the meaning of the line about the gods always knowing one another ; yet so pleasant to the ear is something sonorous, and to the eye something splendid, that we cannot help more than liking—absolutely loving this version—with its manifold defects and vices, and hope that all good critics will pardon our bad taste for sake of our excellent judgment. " Pope is always so correct—so elegant—so polished ! " quoth a gentleman of the old school. Elegant and polished he may be—for these are epithets we do not pretend precisely to understand—but here he is very incorrect, whether you look to the passage as a translation or as a description. He had not a steady vision of the scene, and dealt with words rather than things—as have done almost all his admirers, proud as they have ever been of their knowledge and love of reality and truth.

In Cowper we see so little to object to that we give his version our unqualified praise. How could such a passage be translated in aught amiss by the author of *The Task ?* He wanted nor force nor fire ; but here nor force nor fire were needed ; only a fine sense of beauty, and a command of fitting words, and both are here conspicuous—to our eyes and those of Allan Cunningham.

Sotheby's version, with much of the musical flow of Pope's, has much of the vivid precision of Cowper's ; yet cannot be said to unite the beauties of both, for it wants ease, and some sacrifices are made to rhyme. The repetition of the word " sandals " is heavy, where all should have been light as air ; " his fair feet around " is positively bad ; " the lid of mortals" not good ; " voracious sweep " we do not like ; and it is a strange nominative to " dip his wing in brine." Calypso was not a " goddess of the wave." " O'er the isle outspread " is awkwardly placed, and does not clearly apply to the odours. Sotheby makes the cypress " wave," as Pope made it " nod." "Feast the ravish'd sight" is all unlike Homer ; and "tranced his view " is not English. The lines move languidly in couplets ; and the whole wants fusion. Sotheby manifestly had the scene more steadily and distinctly before his eyes

than Pope ; but he seems not to have been sufficiently inspired
with an emotion of beauty, and therefore failed fully to
express the spirit of the scene—though, where there are so
many fine touches, it would be wrong to call his version a
failure.

Leigh Hunt's version is far superior to Pope's and Sotheby's ; and we feel inclined to prefer it even to Cowper's. It
is so very vivid. The putting on of the sandals is admirable ;
and nothing can be happier than "like waftage of the air."
The power of Mercury's rod is expressed quite in the spirit of
Homer ; and "holding it in hand, went flying " is itself a
picture. Every word he uses about the sea-bird is as good as
can be ; and the imagination is delighted, as the simile has
done its duty, with the sudden restoration of the Godhead—

" So went on the far sea the shape divine."

" Springs oblique," though not in the original, is more than
pardonable, it is so very picturesque ; so is "landing with
subsided wings ; " and so is the walking "'twixt the tall
green rocks." Mr Hunt has a vision given him by Homer,
and so delighted is he with it that he does not hesitate to express more than the magician did in words, not more than the
scene contained of various enchantment. " He paused " is
deeply felt, and the effect on the Godhead of all he saw, and
breathed, and heard—only we miss the Fire. The Goddess,
too, is spinning, instead of weaving—so there is no golden
shuttle—yet to spin is the work of an enchantress. " That
made him hark and smile " is good in itself ; but, though
simple, it is rather quaint—and hardly the simplicity of Homer,
" A sylvan nook it was, grown round with trees," is nearly
equal to our own prose—and we like much the mention of the
trees and the birds. " Almost burst with wine" is, we think,
rather too much intensified ; and we were going to say that
Calypso never drank wine—only nectar ; but then she gave
wine to Ulysses—so we shall not quarrel with Mr Hunt about
a bunch of grapes, which were certainly as purple as purple
could be—and perhaps their colour would not have looked so
beautiful, but for the thought of "wine, generous wine "—
sorrow-soother and joy-brightener — and, therefore, let it
bedew the cheeks of Calypso's cave. Begin well—and you
are almost sure to end well ; and in none of the other versions

do we feel so pleasantly, as in this one, the contrast between the motion of Mercury and his rest—between the haste with which he ties on his sandals, is off and away, and the stillness of admiration in which he stands—for a while forgetful of his mission—ere he can break away from all that beauty, and enter the cave.

Wrangham, who has translated so many of the finest things of antiquity into so many measures, has chosen to try here the octosyllabic—and we feel as if we were reading one of the most picturesque passages in *The Lady of the Lake*. Not a single touch in the original has he omitted—not a single additional touch has he dreamt of giving; the diction is simple, yet rich—and how that may be, you know right well, if ever you saw Calypso's hair; and though on the first reading we confess the music in lines of such narrow compass came somewhat monotonously on our ear after that of the Greek hexameters, yet there was on a second and third recitation a sweetness in it entirely accordant with the serenity of the scene described, and the charming ease of the style gives it perhaps more than any of the other versions—except Mr Hunt's—the look and air of an original composition.

Compare Drake with Sotheby, and Drake shines. But then our esteemed contributor had his choice, though we suggested it to him, of his own passage, while Sotheby has accomplished both epics. Compare him with Pope, and bating the true dazzle and the false glitter of that most melodious master, he shines no less ; and in good truth his version is at once vigorous and graceful as the best among them all.

Mr Chapman's style is a bold one ; he grapples fearlessly with Homer—and when Greek meets Greek, tough is the tug of peace. We are thinking now of his versions of some other passages in the Odyssey, remarkable for their strength and strictness, and for which we are truly sorrow we have not room ; but we are much mistaken if this specimen of his blank verse, though it might have been more harmonious, be not equal to Cowper. But we—perhaps you too—are getting weary of our criticisms, and therefore leave you all, classical readers, to compare the various versions for yourselves, not overlooking Hay's. Indeed, it will not suffer itself to be overlooked; and we have placed it last, because perhaps on the whole best of all ; for while inferior to none of them in

particular touches—except perhaps Mr Hunt's—and to none in
case, except perhaps Wrangham's—the spirit of the original
is, we think, more uniformly sustained than in any one of the
others, and fewer expressions to be found in it that are not
equivalent with the Greek, and as far as English can be so
—without violence done to its genius—Homeric.

Alas for poor Calypso! Her eight years' dream of love is
broken by that cruel rod, and she must part for evermore with
her Ulysses. The Argicide delivers the command of Jove,
and " at the sound she shudder'd." How tender—how passionate her complaints of the injustice of the heavenly gods!
So when the rosy-palmed Aurora chose a mortal husband—
Orion—they could find no rest, even in their blest abodes, till
pierced by Diana's shafts in Ortygia he died! So when Ceres
enfolded young Iasion in her arms " in a thrice-laboured fallow," yielding to soft desires, Jove slew with his bolts her
paramour that dared aspire to that divine embrace. And now
ye envy Calypso her husband, whom she saved from the sea.
"But no ship—no sailors—have I wherewith to send him home
—yet yield must I to the sovereign will of Jove." Hermes
counsels instant submission, for fear of the fiery wrath of
Heaven, and vanishes. Alas for poor Calypso! Penelope
herself might well forgive, and almost pity her now, for the
Divine among Goddesses is about to be deserted—the immortal
nymph of the lovely locks has all this while been but Ulysses'
paramour, imposed upon him by shipwreck; but the daughter
of Icarius, she, twenty years ago, was his bride, and is still
his wife—and she is the mother of his Telemachus, and she
will yet clasp him to her faithful bosom—and when she dies,
she will be buried where his body may be laid by her side, in
that still inland region fated to be their final resting-place,
beyond reach of the murmur of his old enemy the Sea!

The God is gone—and Calypso will seek Ulysses sole-
sitting on the shore. The God is gone—but how changed
now to her is all the isle! But her extreme passion of grief
dies away—for such cannot abide against the known will of
Jove, " in mortal or immortal minds." She no longer deludes
herself with the vain belief that she it was who saved the
shipwrecked; that sophistry of love will not avail her now;
and now that she has been commanded to let him go, she
behaves with the dignity of a divine nature, and her face

begins to wear its wonted serenity of smiles. She had loved the Sea Eagle, and cherished him in her bosom as if he had been a soft-plumed Bird of Calm—but long has the ungrateful been aweary even of that spicy nest. She had nothing to reproach herself with in loving Ulysses. The unconquered in war—the matchless in wisdom—the fertile in genius—the poet who could rehearse so eloquently all the disastrous chances that his youth had suffered—the man who could patiently endure all that Heaven could inflict, except endless separation from home and kindred, wife and son, and, longing for them far away, loathed the proffered boon of immortal life! And can it be that Ulysses never loved her—that he had never been happy in her arms? Ay, he had loved Calypso, he loves her still, and will for ever love her —for no vile cup of enchantments had she like Circe—and though her songs were most sweet, no malice was in their music as in the singing of the Sirens. But in the core of his human heart lay a whole world of sweet remembrances that could never die—that could not be charmed into oblivious sleep even if a lullaby were sung by a voice divine. The love of glory may leave his great heart, and Ulysses care not though he die without his fame. The love of pleasure charms no more—and passion palls now, pure as it ever breathed from that celestial bosom. But the love of home is the concentrated love of life—and were he to bleed to death, the rocks of Ithaca would reel before his dying eyes, and the last image that seemed steadfast before their last dim gaze, would be the faded or unfaded face of his Penelope bent down to kiss him—the sound sweetest to him in death, the Spartan accent still hanging on her lips as she bade an everlasting farewell to her Ulysses!

"Thus having spoken, the mighty Argicide departed.
But the venerable Nymph to the great-hearted Ulysses
Went, when she had heard the behests of Jove.
Him she found sitting on the shore ; and never were his eyes
Wiped-dry from tears : and his sweet life was melting-down
While-he-wept for his return (home) ;—for no longer did the
    Nymph delight him.
During the night indeed he slept from necessity
In the hollow cave,—he unwilling, with her willing :
But during the day sitting on the rocks and the shore.
In tears and groans and griefs wasting-away his own soul,

He gazed-upon the immeasurable deep,—dropping tears.
Standing near him the divine one among goddesses address'd him :
' Ill-fated one, no longer weep here, nor let thy life
Be-wasted-away : for now most willingly will-I-send-thee forth.
But come, having cut long planks, fit with the steel
A broad skiff : but make on it a close-compacted deck
(Rising) high, so that it may carry thee through the gloomy sea.
Moreover, corn, and water, and ruddy wine
That-gladdens-the-soul, will-I-put-on-board,—which may-ward-off
     hunger from thee :
And with vestments will I clothe thee : and wind will I send thee
     on the stern (*of thy ship*),'
That in perfect safety thou mayst reach thy fatherland,
If indeed the gods will it so—who dwell in the wide heavens,
Who are more powerful than I am both in devising and judging.'
     Thus she spake : but the much-enduring godlike Ulysses shud-
         der'd,
And addressing her, utter'd these wing'd words.
' Something different from a dismissing art thou plotting, oh !
     goddess,
In exhorting me to cross the great abyss of the sea in a skiff,
(*An abyss*) tremendous and difficult,—which not the ships, equally-
     flank'd,
(*And*) swift-sailing, can pass, (*though*) exulting in the blasts of Jove.
Nor would I, unpermitted by thee, go-on-board a skiff,
Unless thou dare indeed, goddess, to swear a mighty oath,
Not to plot against me any evil affliction.'
     Thus he spake : and Calypso, the divine one among goddesses,
         laugh'd,
And with her hand stroked him, and spoke and address'd him :
     ' Thou art indeed an incorrigible one, and art knowing not un-
         instructedly :
٠ What a speech is this which thou hast presumed to premise !
Be conscious of this Earth, and wide lofty Heaven,
And the water of Styx gliding below,—(and this the greatest,
And most solemn oath is to the blessed gods),—
That I will not plot against thee any evil affliction.
But what I think, and what I advise, *that* for my-
Self would I counsel—if such a necessity should beset me.
My purpose is honourable, nor in me
Is there a heart of-steel in my breast, but (*one*) of compassion.'
     Thus having spoken, the divine one among goddesses led the
         way
Swiftly : and he then follow'd the footsteps of the goddess.
They came to the hollow cave—the goddess and the man :

And there he seated-himself on the seat from which had arisen
Hermes : and before him the nymph placed every kind of food
Fit-for-eating and drinking,—such as mortal men eat.
And she sat over-against the godlike Ulysses,
And to her her maidens served-up ambrosia and nectar.
And they stretch'd-forth their hands to the good-things lying
    ready.
But when they were satisfied with food and drink,
With these words Calypso, the divine one among goddesses, began :
  ' God-born son-of Laertes, fertile-in-expedients, Ulysses,
Is it thus that homeward to thy fatherland
Forthwith thou wishest to go ? nevertheless mayst thou be happy.
If indeed thou knewest in thy mind, how many it is thy fate
To go-through of calamities, before thou canst reach thy father-
    land,
Here wouldst thou remain and keep to this home,
And immortal shouldst thou be : how much soever longing to see
Thy wife,—for whom thou yearnest daily.
Assuredly not inferior to her I boast in being,
Nor in person, nor in disposition ;- -since by no means is it be-
    seeming
That mortal-women should vie with immortal, either in person or
    beauty.'
  Her Ulysses, fertile-in-expedients, answering address'd :
  ' Venerable goddess, be not angry with me in this matter, for I
    myself know
All this well, that the discreet Penelope
Is inferior (to thee) in appearance, and stature, and to look upon :
But if any one of the gods should destroy me on the wine-faced
    sea,
I will endure it,—having in my breast a grief-suffering heart.
For much already have I borne, and much have I endured,
From the waves and war ; and to those evils let this too be added.'
  Thus he spake : and down went the sun, and darkness came.
And they two having come to a retired-part of the hollow'd cave
Were entranced in love."

Homer has placed before us his two greatest heroes consuming their hearts, in uncompanioned passion on the solitary
sea-shore—and we know not which of the pictures is the more
affecting to the imagination and the heart. Achilles is possessed with wrath, Ulysses with sorrow ; and both alike feed
their sufferings on the hollow-sounding deep. The son of
Peleus desires that the sea shall sympathise with his rage in
gloomy heavings and fierce dashings congenial with the

tumult of his own insulted and scornful spirit. He loves the
breakers on the rocks—the din and the foam—and his thoughts,
like winds let loose, " tempest the ocean." He flings himself
upon the beach, and writhes in convulsions that transfigure
the most beautiful of the sons of men into a terrible demon.
In that dreadful trance he would fain see the whole Grecian
host strewed along the plain,

" Like ocean-weeds heap'd on the surf-beaten shore,"

trodden like sand and shells under the feet of Hector at the
head of a victorious sally from Ilion of all the Trojan Power.
Ulysses—he rushes not in madness to the lonesome shore—
there long has it been his wont to sit motionless as the stones
that surround him—quiet at times even as the sea-bird afloat
in the sunny calm. But " never were his eyes wiped dry
from tears." " In tears, and groans, and griefs wasting away
his own soul! " And this is the much-enduring hero—
ashamed not to weep like a woman or a child—all his patience,
all his fortitude, all his pride utterly overcome—humiliated
into an abject wretch by the weary weight of endless expatria-
tion ! He heeds not whether the sea be hushed or howling ;
the calm to him is as impassable as the storm ; the ripplings
on the yellow sand to him are all one with the billows broken
on the black rocks—for he feels in them alike his perpetual
imprisonment—and as he " gazes on the immeasurable deep,"
he knows that Fate has commanded Nature to destroy all
hope—because all possibility of his ever seeing Ithaca any
more ! He does not ascend a watch-tower on the cliffs to look
from morn to night for some glancing sail. For he knows
that that sea is shipless—that the echoes of that isle shall
never be awakened by the clank of oars. The Isle of Secresy
—untrodden since the birth of Time by any human foot but
his own—undiscoverable—and incommunicable to all that
die. From his dungeon of stone the prisoner may be brought
into the blinding light of day, and again guess that the trouble
on his brain is shot from the sun ; but from these beautiful
groves, and violet-covered meadows, and rills of amber, never
shall Ulysses be rescued—nor from the nightly pressure of
that loveliest but most cruel breast.

All this, and a million times more, is contained in a few
lines of Homer. But when was ever misery just? Calypso

is not the cruel one he thinks—and at this moment is at his side—" Ill-fated one ! no longer weep ! " Was it unnatural for her—Goddess though she were—to desire his stay as passionately through all her being as he desired his return? Never had she loved mortal or immortal but Ulysses—and in him was all the bliss of the undying one. Of her own free will she will let him go ! Not a word does she say of Mercury or of Jove. From her own exceeding love she will make the sacrifice—send him away for ever and ever far beyond the seas—and, left all to herself and her immortality, to her golden shuttle never will she sing again.

Ulysses is still Ulysses, and suspects some love-wile—but the oath by the Awful River opens his heart to the truth, and following the gracious Goddess to the Cave, behold him sitting on the seat from which Mercury had arisen—more beautiful in Calypso's eyes than the messenger of heaven. No transports agitate him—he falls into no ecstasy—in thanksgiving he embraces not her feet—he is unable as yet to comprehend the extent of his own happiness ; the burden he had borne for so many years is taken off—and yet he bounds not up into the air of joy—he eats and drinks like a man to whom nothing of great good or great evil had befallen ; he calmly confesses that his Penelope is in nothing to be compared with Calypso—that much he has yet to suffer, he doubts not, ere he see home—if ever indeed home he shall see ; if death be his doom, he will accept death—and now that " the sun has gone down and darkness come," he accompanies Calypso to their inner chamber—and there,

> " side by side
> Reposed, they took their amorous delight."

And five farewell nights have they to pass together in that Cave. Four days, from sunrise to sunset, must Ulysses—girding his loins, and baring his arms—restored to all their majestic muscular masses of indomitable power—be at work in the woods. Calypso does not by incantation or wave of hand bring a boat, with oars and sails, to the beach, that Ulysses may step in ; the hero " fertile in expedients " must construct his own vessel—and she only furnishes him with implements, whence brought or wrought by whom he asks not, as he receives them from her beautiful hands—for wondrous were the powers of the daughter of Atlas.

M. J. CHAPMAN.   (TRIN. COLL., CAM.)

" But when the rosy-finger'd Queen uprose,
Light-flower'd Aurora, mother of the dawn,
His tunic and his vest Ulysses donn'd ;
Her full white-tissue robe the Nymph put on,
Of texture thin, and rich embroidery,
And fasten'd round her glittering golden zone,
Then set her head-dress on.   Now to dismiss
High-heart Ulysses she address'd herself.
A brazen axe, well-fitting to the hand,
And double-edged (of the wild-olive made
Its handle), gave she him ; also an adze
Well-polish'd ; to the green end of the Isle
Then led the way, where grew the tallest trees ;
Alder and poplar, and heaven-kissing fir
There grew, close-grain'd, and of a hard dry core,
Which would swim lightly for him on the wave :
But when she show'd him where the tall trees grew,
Back to her home Calypso went her way."

" Back to her home Calypso went her way."   How full of
nature that one line !   She could not bear to see him at work—
felling the very trees under whose shade they two had so often
sat—that they might bear him away for ever !   She did not,
like Miranda with her Ferdinand, assist in carrying the logs ;
for this was no romantic love-toil, the mere mimicry of a worky-
day, and to be succeeded by life-long happiness ; the sound
of every stroke that cut into the heart of the tottering tree,
smote her heart too till it ached ; and dismal to her was each
crash among the brushwood, as alder, poplar, or fir, " went to
the earth."   It would have looked very pretty, had she brought
her web in its frame to the forest, and all the while kept plying her golden shuttle and singing a low sweet song.   Had
Ulysses been her husband she would have done so—she would
have been with him at his work, just like the wife of a forester
in the woods of our own world—for in the boat then growing
into shape, the wedded might go out by themselves to sea
with their fishing-nets, or to take their pastime on the waves.
As it was, they were better apart—yet Calypso came to him
again as soon as she knew twenty trees had fallen—but how
often she came and went, and how long at each time she
stayed during those four trying days, is not written in Homer.
But it is written in Homer how the King of Ithaca, like the

Czar of Muscovy, was a master shipwright—and the building of the Float is described with the spirit of a Symonds. Homer would have made an excellent Surveyor of the Navy. Ulysses is himself again—and we can hardly credit that he is the same weeping, groaning, despairing, and wasting-away wretch whom but yesterday we saw sitting on the shore. He has not only built, but launched, ballasted, masted and rigged the Calypso ; and though she might have looked a little queer at Cowes, a craft less crank never glanced with her clean-cut spritsail along the moonlit Mediterranean sea.

There is no description of the parting of Ulysses and Calypso. If you wish for a parting, read that of Hector and Andromache. What pathos is flung back on that beautiful scene of love and sorrow by the shrieks from the city-walls, when the wife falls down as one dead at sight of her husband's body in that gory whirlwind, and again by the lamentations of all Troy going forth to meet the hero lying in the composure of his glory in his old father's chariot. But here there is no occasion for any big grief. If " some natural tears she shed," Calypso " wiped them soon;" and high-heart Ulysses was not the man to behave at that hour with insincerity—with hypocrisy—to her who had admitted him to a celestial bed.

> " He finish'd all his work on the fourth day ;
> And on the fifth, Calypso, nymph divine,
> Dismiss'd him from her Isle, but laved him first,
> And clothed him in sweet-scented garments new.
> Two skins the goddess also placed on board,
> One charged with crimson wine, and ampler one
> With water ; nor a bag with food replete
> Forgot, nutritious, grateful to the taste ;
> And yet, her latest gift, a gentle gale,
> And manageable, which Ulysses spread,
> Exulting, all his canvass to receive."

Ogygia, with all its woods, soon sinks into the sea; but as he sits at the helm, think not that Ulysses forgets Calypso. Homer it was who made her immortal—for true it is that such heavenly sweetness, gentleness, tenderness, and loveliness, shall never die. Strange had been that seclusion ; and though we cannot reveal it all, profound is its meaning in this moral song. Eight years out of the ten since Troy was fired had the hero been lost to all the duties of life. All that long term

passive—worst trial of all to such a man endowed with
powers of mind so transcendent—the active, restless, ingenious,
energetic, sagacious, life-studying, world-knowing, eloquent
and wise Ulysses, doomed so long to pine away, for ever idly
gazing on the barren deep. The nobility of his nature had
been there his curse. Human life, with all its woes and all
its troubles, is made dearer to us who read, seeing how far
dearer it was to him than the love-soothed stillness of promised immortality, hearing him sighing for sickness, decay,
death, and burial in the bosom of his own native earth—for
what else sighed he for? — not for joy, not for bliss,
not for transport; but for return to Ithaca — if it were
but to see his wife and son — and then to lay him down and
die! For seventeen days and nights sleep never sealed his
eyes—and still he steered obedient to the advice of the wise
daughter of Atlas. Intent he watched the watery Pleiades—
Bootes slow to set—the Bear, called else the Wain, which,
circling ever there, looks towards Orion, and of all these
luminaries alone never partakes of the ocean-baths. That
constellation the Goddess bade him keep for ever on his left;
and on the eighteenth day,—as it is finely said in Mr Chapman's MS.,—

———"in the distance loom'd
The skyey-cloud-like mountains of the land
Of the Phæacians, where it nearest was,
And like a bull's hide look'd on the dark sea."

The good Homer—it has been said by high authority—sometimes nods—*dormitat;* that is, grows drowsy, forgets himself,
and maunders in his doze. We say, never. Not Horace,
we hope, but critics who thought themselves Horatian,
have instanced this eighteen days' uninterrupted wakefulness
of Ulysses as a proof that the Bard himself had been taking a
pretty long nap. Ulysses kept the Calypso full by a touch of
his little finger—for the wind was on her quarter, and blew
steady as between the tropics. He had plenty to eat and
drink—and as Helen drugged the bowl to Telemachus and
Pisistratus, that no feverish dreams might disturb their sleep
beneath the porch of the palace, so mayhap did Calypso
infuse into that wine-skin a few wakeful drops that kept the
large eyes of her mariner, as he sat in the stern-sheets, unwinking as the stars. We knew a girl, eight years old, who

lived for eighteen days without shelter or sustenance, but from bushes and berries—on a Highland moor, in the wet, and wild, and chill month of September. That is more than Homer says of Ulysses. As to sleep—a man with the ophthalmia will lie broad awake with his large scarlet eyes sticking out of his head, *experto crede*, all spring. Ulysses was in a burning fever, in Nostalgia, and all the world knows that Nostalgia murders sleep. Well for him that he escaped calenture—for then the waves would have seemed the green hills of Ithaca, and he would have leaped overboard to kiss his imaginary fatherland. But perhaps, after all, he did sometimes sleep, without himself knowing he did so any more than Homer. A strange dim slumbrous influence—sleep-and-no-sleep—yet neither feverish nor unrefreshing, comes and goes over the brain of the solitary student, whether in a close cell poring on his books, or in an open boat perusing the stars. At sea, 'tis as if a mist for a few minutes or moments shrouded the Bear, or as if the wing of some bird kept wavering between the eyes of the watcher and the Wain. In such slumber —if it indeed invaded the dragon eyes of Laërtiades—never did the Calypso either fall off or run up into the wind—for if a man can walk, and ride, and play the fiddle sleeping, so can he steer—unless he be a great hulking landlubber, or a horse-marine.

But Neptune, "traversing, on his return from Ethiopia's sons, the mountain heights of Solyme," espies the Calypso "as she were dancing home !" and shaking his brows at the slayer of Polyphemus, he

——"call'd
Storms from all quarters, covering earth and sea
With blackest clouds, and night rush'd down from heaven."

She is driven wild about the deep, as Boreas drives over the autumnal plain a mass of matted thorns. As if in sport, the South gives her to the North, and the West receives her like a plaything from the East ; and then all at once—as when the tempest falling on a heap of stubble disperses every way the arid straws — asunder fly all her timbers ! — And lo ! Ulysses, bestriding a plank, " oars it onward with his feet as he had urged a horse." Then, binding on the girdle he had given him a few minutes ago in his jeopardy by the merciful sea-nymph Leucothea—once a mortal—and who assured him

that long as he wore it he should not perish—he " prone into
the sea, with widespread palms prepared for swimming,
fell."

We have ourselves been shipwrecked in a small way on
salt-water, and boat-wrecked in a smaller on fresh water,
and we know of no description of a struggle of the sort at all
comparable in power and truth to this in the Odyssey. The
escape is prodigious—but surely not therefore incredible—and
the swimmer Ulysses.

> " Two nights of terror and two dreadful days
> Bewilder'd in the deep ! "

To have made that nothing miraculous—though it would still
have been wonderful—all that was wanting was—a plank or
an oar. In a cork-jacket a man may float till he dies of inani-
tion. Ulysses had Leucothea's life-preserver, the most poetical
ever worn—and Minerva bade the billows subside before him
—and Boreas blew him drifting on towards the Phæacian land.
He was saved by his own vast strength and magnanimous
spirit, encouraged and assisted by sea-nymph, and heavenly
Goddess, and the will of Jove. If such a struggle and such
an escape be not within the rightful use of imagination in " a
wild and wondrous tale," then let poets write of ponds and pits,
and not of the Sea. Nay, they had better keep to land-
carriage, and take care not to exaggerate the speed of a Comet
on a railway, or its burden of cotton bales. The desperate and
often-baffled attempts of Ulysses to effect a landing are all so
naturally and variously and minutely described—with absolutely no exaggeration at all—that we forget the supernatural
aid that had hitherto borne him up — and now see merely an
able-bodied seaman, sole survivor of a wreck. saving himself
in the last extremity by great presence of mind, strength, and
skill, in spite of surf and rock — and soon as he crawls
ashore laying himself down — as does Ulysses—on some
rushes growing by, and passionately, and gratefully, and
piously " kissing the life-giving Earth."

Numb and naked—lying on ooze among rushes—perhaps
in the haunts of wild beasts—on an unknown coast—what a
contrast is his condition to what it was within that quiet cave
on Calypso's bosom ! But he rues not the hour he left that
repose—he was prepared to suffer—and seeks the shelter of

a wood near the river, up whose mouth he had swum—and creeps into a close covert formed by two olive-trees.

> " A covert which nor rough winds blowing moist
> Could penetrate, nor could the noonday sun
> Smite through it, or unceasing showers pervade,
> So thick a roof the ample branches form'd,
> Close interwoven ; under these the chief
> Retiring, with industrious hands amass'd
> An ample couch, for fallen leaves he found
> Abundant there, such store as had sufficed
> Two travellers or three for covering warm,
> Though winter's roughest blast had raged the while.
> That bed with joy the suffering chief renown'd
> Contemplated, and occupying soon
> The middle space, heap'd higher still the leaves.
> As when some swain hath hidden deep his torch
> Beneath the embers, at the verge extreme
> Of all his farm, where, having neighbours none,
> He saves a seed or two of future flame
> Alive, doom'd else to fetch it from afar—
> So with dry leaves Ulysses overspread
> His body, on whose eyes Minerva pour'd
> The balm of sleep, and eager to restore
> His wasted strength soon closed their weary lids."

And there, coiled up like some animal of the wood, beneath a huge heap of leaves, lies Ulysses—chief of all the chiefs of Ithaca—of old chosen companion of the King of Men—and in front of Troy, with his wiles and his valour, in power of destruction second but to Achilles !

There let the magnanimous sleep, while we with Minerva glide into the sumptuous chamber of the Princess Royal, in the palace where King Alcinous[1] reigns—the divine Nausicaa. She is smiling in her sleep, for she is dreaming of her nuptials. Her dearest companion seems to say, " Awake! awake! Nausicaa! Oh! wherefore hath thy mother born a child so negligent ! Up, up, and away with us all to the fountains, where, midst of merry-making, we shall cleanse thy robes and garments all, for the days of thy virginity are numbered. Awake! awake! the prime of the land have long been wooing Nausicaa to become a bride !" Apparelled is she, quickly as a rose-tree

---

[1] King of Phæacia, on whose shore Ulysses had been cast.

seems apparelled by the dawn; and meeting her father on his
way to council, asks if he will lend her for a day the use of
mules and a carriage to convey *his* wardrobe, and that of her
brothers, to the sea-side Fountains? " Welcome art thou to
mules and carriage, or to aught else thou choosest to ask,"
replies her father, who sees through the lids of his Nausicaa's
eyes, too transparent to hide the truth that comes in innocent
revelation from her heart. As is the king of a land, so are
his people, and these few words dispose us kindly towards the
Phæacians. The tempest-tost, we now know, has fallen
neither among savages nor barbarians; and his sleep next
night will not, we are assured, be among withered leaves,
between two olive-trees, in a wood, but perhaps among soft
folds of purple, on a sculptured couch, beneath the portico of
a palace.

" Thus having spoken, he gave orders to the slaves, and they obey'd,
They, on the one hand, the well-wheel'd mule-drawn car outside
Were-preparing, and they brought out the mules, and yoked them
    to the vehicle.
But the virgin, on the other, from her chamber was bringing
    beautiful vestments,
And placed them on the well-polish'd car :
And her mother put-up in a chest desire-gratifying eatables
Of-every-kind, and in (*it*) she placed *kitchen* (ὄψα), and wine she
    pour'd
In a bottle of-goat-skin ; and the maiden mounted the car.
(*The mother*) also gave, in a golden cruet, moist oil,
In order that she (*the maiden*) might-anoint-herself together with
    her attendant women.
She seized the lash and the shining reins,
And lash'd (*the mules*) to hurry (*them on*) ; and there was a creak-
    ing sound from the mules,
For unceasingly they were straining-onward ; and carrying-for-
    ward the vestments, and (*the maiden*) herself,
Not alone, for along with her verily went her other attendants.
    But when they came to the very-limpid current of the river,
Where there were perennial washing-tanks, and much water
Beautiful from-under-onward-flowed, excellently (*adapted*) to
    purify what-is-foul,
There they indeed from the car the mules first unyoked,[1]

---

[1] ὑπεκπροέλυσαν. How comprehensive and expressive this combination of pre-
positions ! ὑπο from under the yoke, ἐκ out of the harness, προ before proceeding
to wash.

And drove them near the eddying stream
To eat honey-sweet couch-grass: while they (*the maidens*) from
the car
With their hands took the vestments, and bore them into the dark
water.
And forthwith challenging to a contest, they *tramp'd* them in
tanks.
But when they had wash'd them, and purified them from all filth,
Forthwith they spread-them-out by the shore of the sea, where
especially
The ocean laved the pebbles on the mainland.
And having bathed and anointed themselves with rich oil,
They then took dinner by the banks of the river.
And they waited while their clothes were-being-dried by the
brightness of the sun.
—But when the maid-servants, and herself (*the princess*), were
satisfied with food,
They fell-a-playing at ball, having laid-aside their head-gear.
And to them the beautiful-arm'd Nausicaa began a song:
As when Diana delighting-in-arrows bounds along a mountain,
Or along the extremely-steep Taygetus, or Erymanthus,
Gladdening-herself with (*in the pursuit of*) boars, and swift stags,
And along with her the Nymphs, the daughters of the Ægis-
bearing Jove,
The rural (*goddesses*) sport,—and Latona exults in her soul:
And above them all bears her head and front,
And is easily distinguish'd-beyond (*all*), and all are beautiful,
In like manner was the unsubdued (*unmarried*) virgin (*Nausicaa*)
pre-eminent among her attendant maidens."

Beautiful was the Isle of Secresy—and beautiful, singing at
her web among the incense of the cedar-fire, its immortal
Queen. But more touching far to our human heart, the sight
of those virgins at their playful employment among the silver
springs; nor, wild as it was, had Calypso's voice such perfect
sweetness as hers who now leads in their sport the choral song.
A Princess—the daughter of a King!

Borne back are we, as we gaze and listen, thousands of
years, into the blest simplicities of the primeval time. Simplicities! Yet accordant all with rank's distinctions—then
drawn by a fine spirit, separating not the innocent hearts that
felt and obeyed its gentle sway—and leaving the manners,
then loveliest far, to the gracious guidance of nature.

What a Scotch picture! Perhaps to us therefore is it so

pleasant to look upon; for change that virgin into one of
humbler rank and with a homelier name, and let the place be

> " A flowrie howm between twa verdant braes,
> Where lasses use to wash and spread their claes,"

and lo! we are in the heart of our own Pentland hills, and
see a gentle shepherdess not less lovely than Nausicaa, though
she be but a cottar's child, and the Scherian[1] damsel the
daughter of a king.

But why shriek the maidens in their glee? The Princess
casting the ball at one of them misses her mark, and it falls
into the river. That shriek has awakened a sleeping lion.
The monster shows himself at the edge of the wood, and the
sportive train are dispersed in terror—all but Nausicaa. A
lion? Ay, a lion. For everything, for the time being, is
what it seems—and a lion seems Ulysses.

> " Like a huge mountain lion forth he went,
> Whom winds have vex'd and rains ; fire fills his eyes,
> And whether flocks or herds, or woodland deer
> He find, he rends them, and athirst for blood,
> Abstains not even from the guarded fold.
> Such sure to seem in virgin's eyes the chief,
> All naked as he was !"

Nausicaa alone fled not, for Minerva quelled the fear quaking
at her heart, and from her fine limbs took away all tremors—
in other words, she behaved like a king's daughter. Lion-
like as was Ulysses, her attendants probably after all saw he
was a man, a mother-naked man—and while they fled knew
that he was not going to devour them ; but Nausicaa, con-
stitutionally brave—a great happiness, having never yet
once in all her life met with evil—having been brought up
by a sensible mother, Arete, her sex's pride—and seeing, at
the hasty glance she had ventured to take, wretchedness but
not wrath in the countenance of the man and not monster,
waited his approach, unappalled—should he approach ; but
Ulysses, with a spreading bough held between him and the
virgin, kept aloof in suppliant posture—and the noble virgin
after her short fright, became calm as a dove.

Genius, some one said, is of no sex—neither is Mercy,
here willing to minister in the shape of Innocence. Homer

---

[1] *Scherian*—another name for *Phæacian*.

does not say Nausicaa blushed, nor did she blush; she was, we daresay, "something more pale than wonted"—the fine flush of exercise was blanched on her checks—and her eyes fell without seeing them on the wild-flowers at her feet. But the wretch before her was not an object from which modesty was now to avert her sight, but humanity to look at and to relieve. And a hard trial this for Ulysses the Leonine! In such guise to stand before and accost a virgin whom he must have known could be no other than a Princess. But he knew, yet all in honour, the way of womankind—he who had woo'd and won Penelope from all Sparta—he who had been admired by Helen, nor by her yet forgotten, as she showed by her Tale of the Wooden Horse to Telemachus—he who had ascended the bed of Circe, and had yet, in spite of all the sea-brine, the fragrance of Calypso's kisses lingering on his lips—he accosted well the high-born nymph, whom, in his magnanimous heart, he felt was as pure as her own zone; and the fine-souled sculptors of Greece, working in the spirit of Homer, fixed them, as at that moment they stood there, in the Parian marble.

"Suppliantly-embrace-I-thy-knees, oh! princess: art thou a god-
    dess, or a mortal?
If thou art one of (those) goddesses who dwell in the wide
    heavens,
Thee, do I, to Diana the daughter of great Jove,
Both in appearance, and stature, and disposition, most nearly
    liken:
But if thou art one of those mortals who inhabit earth,
Thrice-bless'd in thee truly (are) thy father and venerable
    mother,
Thrice-bless'd are thy blood-relations: much truly must their
    hearts
Be always exulting with delight on thy account—
When they look-upon such an shoot entering-upon the dance.
But bless'd beyond all in heart, conspicuously above all (is) he
    (bless'd)
Who prevailing (over his rivals) by bridal-presents may lead thee
    to his home.
For never such a mortal (as thou art) saw I with these eyes,
Neither man nor woman: veneration fixes me gazing.
Once indeed, by the altar of Apollo in Delos, such
A young shoot of a palm-tree starting-up observed I.
(Thither also went I, and much people follow'd me

On that journey,—which verily was about to be (*the source*) of
many vexing sorrows) :
Gazing on it, just as (*on thee now I gaze*), amazed-was-I in soul
For-a-long time : for never from the earth such wood upsprang ;
Thus, lady, thee do-I-admire, and struck with admiration, fear
exceedingly
To clasp thy knees : deep grief pervades me all :
Yesterday on the twentieth day, I escaped the wine-faced sea :
For so long did the waves continually, and the rapid storms
carry me
From the island Ogygia : and now hither hath a god driven me,
That still, perchance, here also I may suffer evils : for never, me-
thinks,
Will the gods cease (*from afflicting me*), but much (*evil*) have they
to inflict before (*they cease*).
But, oh ! princess, have pity, for having laboured-through many
evils, with thee
First I met : none know I of other
Human-beings who inhabit this city and country.
Point-out to me the city, and give me a rag to-throw-around-me,
If perchance with any folds of clothing thou camest hither.
And may the gods grant thee whatever thou longest for in thy
soul,
May they bestow (*on thee*) a husband, and a family, and same-
ness-of sentiment
Gracious ; for than this nothing is better or more excellent,
Than that being-of-the-same-mind in their counsels, their house
should manage
A husband and wife ; for many evils have the ill-assorted (*pair*),
And joys, the well-disposed : and above all do they hear the report
of themselves."

How persuasive to pity in that fair breast to take the place
of fear ! And with pity for the suppliant, how natural that
the Princess should at such winning words feel pride in herself—thus likened to Diana ! Nowhere in poetry is there a
more appropriate image than here that of the palm-tree. It
shows Nausicaa motionless, serene, and stately—while something of a holy beauty, breathed from religion, hovers
around her head. The petition for himself is enveloped in
love and admiration, and all prayers for the felicity of her
of whom he begs a boon—and his closing benediction how
comprehensive ! " Home—husband—concord ! "

" Stranger, thou seem'st not worthless or unwise. I am

daughter of the king, the brave Alcinous." Forthwith she
orders her attendants to bring him garments, and wine and
food—and oil for the bath. " For a wretched wanderer is he,
and the poor and stranger are from Jove. To them such
gifts are great." Ulysses bids the maidens stand apart, saying that he is ashamed to appear uncovered in a woman's
sight. The critics cannot understand this — thinking of
Telemachus bathed by Nestor's youngest daughter. But
Telemachus was a mere youth—and the virgin was in the
house of her parents—and the chamber was hallowed—and
the Prince was not naked—but folds of drapery hung wet
around him—and delicate was the touch of the hand that from
the cruise let fall the oil on the limbs and body of the son of
her father's friend. But here was an utter stranger whom the
sea had vomited—begrimed with ooze and mud, squalid from
his bed of withered leaves—and in presence of a Princess, and
her bevy of well-robed maidens—naked as drowned death.
Time, place, person, circumstances — all are different, and
therefore a different feeling and another law. Pity and ruth
prevailed with Nausicaa, but Ulysses felt shame—and therefore, retiring apart,

> " the hero in the stream
> His shoulders laved and loins encrusted rough
> With the salt spray ; and with his hands the scum
> Of the wild ocean from his locks express'd.
> Then Pallas, progeny of Jove, his form
> Dilated more, and from his head diffused
> His curling locks of hyacinthine flowers.
> As when some artist, by Minerva made,
> And Vulcan wise to execute all tasks
> Ingenious, binding with a golden verge
> Bright silver, finishes a graceful work,
> Such grace the goddess o'er his ample chest
> Copious diffused, and o'er his manly brows.
> Retiring, on the beach he sat, with grace
> And dignity illumed."

The Princess is amazed by his majestic beauty—but here
is the whole passage in prose ; for though Cowper and Sotheby have given it well, each in his own way, it has still to be
done in verse—and after many trials we laid down our own
pen in despair.

" ' Listen to me, my maidens, ye white-arm'd ones, that I may speak
to you a word,
Not against the will of all the gods who inhabit Olympus
Is this man to mingle with the godlike Phæacians.
Formerly indeed he appear'd to me an unseemly (*person*),
But now is he like the gods who dwell in the wide heavens.
Oh ! would that such an one were to be called my husband,
To dwell here, and that it might please him to abide here.
But, my maidens, give to the stranger food and drink.'
   Thus she spake : and they earnestly listen'd to her and obey'd
her :
And before Ulysses they placed food and drink.
And Ulysses indeed, the much-enduring godlike one, eat and
drank
Rapaciously ; for long had he been fasting from food.
   But Nausicaa the fair-arm'd devised another (*plan*).
Having folded up the clothes, she placed them on the handsome car,
And yoked the powerful-hoof'd mules, and herself mounted,
And roused-up Ulysses, and spoke and address'd him :
   ' Rise up now, (*our*) guest, to go city-ward, that I may send
thee
To the house of my valiant father, where methinks thou
Shalt see of all the Phæacians as many as are the noblest.
But strictly thus must thou act,—(for thou seemest not one that-
lacks-understanding :)
Whilst we are travelling through the fields and the labours of men,
So long with the maidens, behind the mules and the car,
Step-on quickly, and I will guide you on the way.
But when we shall-be-approaching near the city, around which (*is*)
a fortification
(*That is*) lofty, and on-both-sides of the city (*is*) a beautiful harbour,
But narrow the inlet : and ships on-both-sides-(*by oars*)-impelled,
by this way
Are hauled, and to each of all of them is there a mooring-place.
There too have they a forum, and around it (*is*) the beautiful
sanctuary-of-Neptune
Rear'd of drawn quarried stones.
There too they attend to the tackle of the dark ships,
Ropes, and cables, and (*there*) they smooth the oars.
For neither the bow nor quiver is the concernment of the Phæa-
cians,
But masts, and oars of vessels, and equal-sided ships,
In which exultingly they bound over the hoary deep.
Their (*the people's*) bitter tattle I avoid, lest any one behind (*my
back*)

Should scoff: for there are very-overbearing persons among the people.
And perchance some of-the-baser-sort meeting us might thus speak,
'Who is it that follows Nausicaa—that handsome, tall
Stranger?—where met she with him ?—assuredly he is to be her husband :
Some wanderer hath she taken from his ship.
Some (*one*) of those from foreign regions :—for none such (*as he*) are near.
Or some god earnestly-supplicated hath come to her supplicating,
From heaven come-down : she will have him for all (*her*) days.
Better (*had it been*), had she gone and found a husband
Elsewhere : for assuredly she disdains those among the people
—The Phæacians—who numerous and noble court her.'
Thus will they speak ; and such things were a reproach to me :
I should be indignant at any other (*female*), who should do such things,
Who, indeed, against the will of her beloved father and mother,
Should hold intercourse with men, before marriage should come openly.
Stranger, do thou thus understand my words, that as soon as possible
Thou mayst obtain from my father the power-of-departing, and returning (*home*).
We shall-meet-with a magnificent grove of Minerva, by the way-side,
Of-poplars : and in it flows a fountain, and around it (*is*) a meadow.
There are my father's separate grounds, and blooming orchard,
(*Distant*) so far from the city, as one is who has to shout aloud :
(i. e. to be heard by another at a distance.)
There seating-thyself-down, tarry for a time, till we
Come to the city, and reach the mansion of my father.
Then mayst thou wend thy way to the city of the Phæacians, and inquire for
The mansion of my father, the great-hearted Alcinous,
For very well-known it is, and a child even could conduct thee,
—A mere infant (*to it*) ;—for not the least like to it are
The houses of the Phæacians,—(no) house like that of Alcinous
The hero : but when the mansion and hall shall have received thee,
Quickly further on go into the palace, that thou mayst come to
My mother : for she sits by the hearth in (before) the brightness of fire,
Twirling the sea-purple spindle,—a miracle to look upon,—
Leaning-back on a pillar : and her maidens sit behind her.

And there towards-her-inclines the throne of my father,
Seated on which he quaffs-the-wind,—like an Immortal.
Having pass'd him, thy hands to the knees of mother
Mine stretch forth, that the day of-thy-return thou mayst behold
Rejoicing, and soon,—even though very far from hence thou mayst
  be.
Verily indeed if she counsel friendly (*counsels*) for thee in her
  heart,
Then is there hope for thee of seeing thy friends, and of coming
To thy well-built house, and to thy fatherland.'
  Thus having spoken,—with the shining lash, she lash'd
The mules: and they speedily left the current of the river,
And well ran-they-onward, and well lifted-they-foot-after-foot,
And earnestly managed-she-the-reins, that those-on-foot might
  follow together—
The maidens, and Ulysses: and with judgment she applied the
  lash.
The sun was setting (when) they reach'd the illustrious grove,
Sacred to Minerva, where forthwith sat down the divine Ulysses,
And immediately he supplicated the daughter of mighty Jove:
  'Hear me, indefatigable daughter of Ægis-bearing Jove,
Now truly indeed hear me, since never erst hast thou heard me
When dash'd-about,—when the illustrious Earth-shaker (Neptune)
  toss'd me,
Grant me to come among the Phæacians,—an acceptable and a
  pitied (*guest*).'
  Thus spoke he, praying, and Pallas Minerva heard him.
But she appear'd not before him: for she fear'd indeed
Her uncle (*Neptune*): for he raged furiously against Ulysses."

If ye do not delight to read that, you cannot delight to
read the Old Testament. Has Nausicaa fallen in love with
Ulysses? No—though it be sworn to by all the critics; she is
in love with nobody; and that washing of garments was for
no man's individual sake. Pure of all thoughts of man is she
as Jephtha's own daughter, who nevertheless wept her virginity on the mountains. It was time she should be wedded—
though no time had been lost—and all Phæacia was beginning
to get impatient for her nuptials. She knew that, and was
happy to know it; and therefore she dreamt of the silver
fountains, and gladly obeyed the dream. She was a rose in
June—for a rose in June is as young as a violet in March,
and she felt, though she had never read Shakespeare, that
" Earthlier sweeter is the rose distill'd,"—and that was all she

as yet knew of love. Love in those days shone like sudden sunshine at withdrawal of a cloud ; the virgin gave her heart with her hand to the chosen at her parents' bidding ; and Alcinous and Arete had but to select for her a husband from the flower of the Phæacian youth, and their Nausicaa, the most dutiful of daughters, would have been happy beneath the bridal veil. Observe it is to her attendants that the simple creature says, "Would that such an one were to be called my husband ! " She was familiar with them as if they had been her sisters ; and that gentle wish was as natural as could be, born as it was of admiration and wonder at the majestic beauty of the stranger, from a hideous outcast transfigured into a god. " Formerly, indeed, he appeared to me unseemly, but now is he like the gods that dwell in the wide heavens ! " Now his words—then not unwelcome—come back upon her heart with gratitude and pride. " By this godlike being was I likened to the sacred palm-tree, the stateliest in all the world, that grows in Delos, by Apollo's altar!" Songs had been breathed in her praise by princes, but not one among them all had ever thought of such an image—never till then had she heard eloquence ; and what a musical voice had he—his words, so Homer elsewhere says, falling like snow ! She saw a hero far excelling in form and features all the nobility of the Isle— king, no doubt, of some far-away land—she was herself the Princess-Royal—to him she had been kind in his destitution, to her his eyes looked thanks in admiration, and in the gladness of her spirit she expressed—without suspicion of their tenderness, for they were more deeply touched than she thought—all the feelings that kept rising there, like fair birds of calm floating or flying on a sunny sea. No design had she to let him understand what was passing in her heart, by telling him what the people would say were they to see them two together—she said but the simple truth ; and had her bosom been disquieted, she would have held her peace. But she keeps prattling away prettily and gracefully, with the most perfect ease of mind and manner ; her injunctions are altogether proper, and equally free from prudery and coquetry —words indeed that are felt, soon as they are pronounced, even to scout them—almost an offence to the high-born and fine-souled child of nature, for she is sincere as the fountain that reflects the skies. How filial the proud delight with

which she describes her father and her mother in their palace!
To them she wishes the illustrious stranger may endear himself, that they may incline their ear favourably to his prayers,
and send him in safety to his fatherland—" though very far
from hence thou mayst dwell;" and so saying, happy as a bird,
she glides beneath a sky beautiful in sunset into her car, and
so regulates the pace of her strong-hoofed mules, that the
stranger and her attendants, at double-quick time, are just
able to keep close to the whirl of the wheels till he, as she
bade, dropped behind, and sat down in the grove sacred to
Minerva. This may be what *we now* call Love ; but it is not
what men called Love in the earnest ages before the rising of
Homer.

A great poet painted the isle and the island-life ; but where
is the philosopher who comprehends the entire nature of this
bright creation ? Primitive manners in the midst of magnificence of power and state—virtue uncorrupted by wealth—and
all the richest and rarest splendours of art shining undisturb-
ingly among the simplicities of nature. On her arrival at her
father's palace, her five brothers, " all godlike youths," assemble quickly around Nausicaa, unyoke the mules, and bear
in the raiment ; she goes to her chamber, and her nurse lights
a fire ; yet almost might we say

> " Not Babylon
> Nor great Alcairo such magnificence
> Equall'd in all their glories,"

as we read the description of the Palace. Sotheby has given
nobly the entrance there, and the reception of Ulysses.

> " On stepp'd the chief, but with deep thought o'ercast,
> Paused, ere his foot the brazen threshold pass'd.
> Resplendent as the moon, or solar light,
> Alcinous' palace awed the o'erdazzled sight.
> On to its last recess, a brazen wall
> That from the threshold stretch'd, illumined all,
> Round it of azure steel a cornice roll'd,
> And every gate, that closed the palace, gold.
> The brazen threshold golden pillars bore,
> A golden ringlet glitter'd on the door,
> The lintel silver, and to guard his gate,
> Dogs in a row, each side, were seen to wait,
> In gold and silver wrought, by Vulcan made,
> Immortal as the god, and undecay'd.

From the far threshold, to its last retreat,
Ranged round the wall, rose many a lofty seat,
With fine-spun carpets strew'd, by virgins wrought,
Where, as each newborn day new pleasures brought,
Phæacia's chiefs from thought and care released,
Sat throned, and lengthen'd the perpetual feast.
Stood on bright altars golden youths, whose hands
Lit through the night, the guests, with flaming brands :
And fifty maids administering around,
Some, the ripe grain, beneath the millstone ground,
Some whirl'd the distaff, and the fleeces wove
Swift as the leaves, that shake the poplar grove :
And ever as they plied their radiant toil,
The glossy web shone like transparent oil.
Nor less expert their course the seamen kept,
Than through the loom the female shuttle swept,
The gift of Pallas, who had there combined
The skilful hand with the inventive mind—
Without the court, yet nigh the city's bound,
A garden bloom'd, four-acred, wall'd around ;
Tall trees there grew, the red pomegranate there,
Each glossy apple, and each juicy pear,
Sweet figs, and living olives : none decay'd
Or in the summer blaze, or winter shade ;
While western winds unfolding every flower,
Here gemm'd with buds the branch, there fill'd with fruits
    the bower.
Pears ripen pears, the apples apples breed,
Figs follow figs, to grapes the grapes succeed :
The fruitful vineyard there, where, spread to-day
The raisin dries beneath the solar ray :
Here jocund labour gathers in the fruit,
There the stamp'd clusters gush beneath the foot,
And while the grape here blossoms on the spray,
The swelling orbs there blacken day by day.
There at its confine many a cultured bed
And flowers, all kind, undying fragrance shed.
Two fountains there, this in perpetual play
Through all the garden winds its order'd way ;
That glides beneath the threshold of the king,
And fills each urn from its o'erflowing spring ;
Such were the gifts that they whose realm is heaven
Had to that favour'd man profusely given.
    Long stood the chief, with awe each wonder view'd,
Then to the palace swift his way pursued,

And found the chiefs, who, mindful of their bed,
To Hermes now their last libation shed.
Onward he pass'd unseen, in mists obscured
That still around his path Minerva pour'd,
Till reach'd the royal thrones, where bending low
He clasp'd Arete's knees, and breathed his woe :
The goddess then at once the night dispell'd,
And all in silent awe the chief beheld :
' O deign,' the suppliant said, ' Arete, hear,
Born of divine Rhexenor, bow thine ear !
Queen ! at thy knees I bend, with woe oppress'd,
And sue thy lord, and each high-honour'd guest :
So may the gods in bliss their lives extend,
And all their honours to their heirs descend :
But deign convey to his paternal soil
A wanderer worn with unrelaxing toil.'
    Then, in the ashes, on the hearth reclined,
While the chiefs gazed to silent awe resign'd—
At last Echeneus, on whose reverend head
Time had the snow of many a winter shed,
A man for eloquence and wisdom famed,
Thus, kindly counselling the king, exclaimed :
' Ill suits, Alcinous, that a stranger guest
Should. seated at thy hearth, in ashes rest—
We wait thy word—king ! raise him, though unknown,
And seat him on the silver-studded throne :
Bid crown the goblet, and 'mid rites divine
Pour to the thundering God the votive wine :
Be Jove, who hears the suppliant's prayer, adored,
And feed the stranger from thy present board.'
    The monarch clasp'd Ulysses' hand, and raised
The suppliant from the hearth that brightly blazed,
Displacing for the stranger from his throne
The young Laodamas his favourite son.
From a gold chalice on a silver stand
A maid shower'd water on Ulysses' hand,
And a smooth table fix'd the guest before,
Where the house-guardian heap'd his ready store ;
And when the chief sat satiate at the board,
Thus to the herald spake Phæacia's lord :
' Pontonoüs ! mix the wine, and pass around
From guest to guest the cup with nectar crown'd,
Then pour it forth, and to the Thunderer pray,
The God who guards the wanderer on his way."

No fear now of Ulysses. The power of such an Apparition would have subdued a tyrant on his barbarous throne; but Alcinous is a gracious king, and Queen Areto a gracious Queen — an Adelaide to all the loyal island dear, and an example to all matrons.

"Onwards he pass'd unseen, in mists obscured."

But when the veil of concealment was withdrawn, what a shiver and what a hush must have stirred and stilled the Presence Chamber! The Apparition must have been remembered by Milton—till out of the remembrance rose a still sublimer imagination—while he, telling of Satan's return to Pandemonium from the ruin of our race, said,—

> " He through the midst, unmark'd,
> In show plebeian angel militant
> Of lowest order, pass'd, and from the door
> Of that Plutonian hall, invisible,
> Ascended his high throne, which, under state
> Of richest texture spread, at th' upper end
> Was placed in regal lustre. Down a while
> He sat, and round about him saw, unseen.
> At last, as from a cloud, his fulgent head
> And shape, star-bright, appear'd, or brighter, clad
> With what permissive glory since his fall
> Was left him. or false glitter. All amazed
> At that so sudden blaze, the Stygian throng
> Bent their aspect, and whom they hoped beheld,
> Their mighty chief return'd."

'Tis thus one great Poet inspires another—all of them from one another's golden urns drawing light—till burns the firmament more gloriously with the large lustre of unsetting stars. Lucifer suddenly revealed " star-bright or brighter " on his throne—Ulysses, soon as beheld in his majesty, sitting down in the ashes of the hearth !

In an hour and less he has gained a conquest over King, Queen, and Court. For they at first thought—perhaps he may be a god.

But soon is Alcinous so won by the hero's recital of his abode on Calypso's Isle, and of his perils by shipwreck, that he offers him Nausicaa in marriage, if he will settle among them, and become for the rest of his life a Phæacian ! Nausicaa

is with her nurse, sitting by the fire; and 'tis as well for her
peace, perhaps, that she did not hear the proposal; and
Ulysses contrives delicately to elude it, and to avail himself
of a turn in the King's discourse to repeat his desire for far-
off home.   The subject is dropped for ever — and he is conducted to his couch, leaving all in the palace in admiration
and awe of the mighty stranger-guest.

Next day all the island is astir to see the hero of whom
such bruit has gone abroad; and in full senate it is decided
in his presence, that a fifty-oared barge shall convey him home
wherever may be his fatherland, across the sacred deep.
A mighty feast is prepared in the palace for multitudes of
young and old; and when two beeves, twelve sheep, and
eight fatted brawns, have been devoured,—no doubt with
bread and vegetables in proportion—awakes to the Harp the
Song.

F. T. PRICE. (BRIGHTON.)

> " A herald came, and with him led along
> A noble bard, whom well the Muses loved ;
> But from the cup of good and evil too
> Had given him to drink—for he was blind—
> Yet was his heart by inspiration warm'd.
> For him a seat with silver studs adorn'd,
> Upon a lofty column high upraised
> Amid th' assembled guests, Protonoüs placed ;
> And from a peg above his head a lyre
> The herald hung, and placed it in his hands ;
> And on a beauteous table near at hand
> He laid a basket with a cup of wine,
> So at his will the bard might freely drink.
> Meanwhile the guests, upon the sumptuous fare
> Stretch'd forth their hands ; but when the feast was o'er
> The muse inspired the bard of noble deeds
> To sing an hymn, whose glory reach'd the sky :
> He sang Ulysses' and Achilles' strife.
> How at the godlike banquet once they strove
> With words of fearful import, and the heart
> Of Agamemnon king of men was glad
> Because the bravest of the Greeks were wroth.
> For that to him Apollo had foretold,
> When he the Pythian threshold cross'd, to seek
> The oracle ; then burst the fount of woe

On Greece and Troy, by Jove's almighty will.
So sang the bard.   But great Ulysses then
With stalwart hand his purple mantle seized,
Drew o'er his head, and hid his manly face,
Lest the Phæacian chiefs should see him weep.
But when the godlike bard gave o'er his song,
The hero dried the fountain of his tears,
And from his head withdrew the mantle's shade :
Then, having raised a double-handled cup,
He pour'd a rich libation to the gods :
But when again the bard took up his song,
For the Phæacian nobles loved the strain,
Again Ulysses veil'd his head and wept.
And now the weeping hero none observed,
Except Alcinous, who, sitting near,
Heard from his bosom burst the deep-drawn sigh,
And straight the chiefs around him, thus address'd :—
  ' Rulers, and lords of proud Phæacia, hear !
Now from the finish'd banquet let us rise—
Still'd be the voice of music and of mirth,
To the gymnasium let us bend our way,
And strive in friendly conflict for the prize.' "

Alcinous is proud of his people, and desirous that the great
unknown may carry to his own land a high report of their
prowess in leaping, boxing, wrestling, and running — and his
guest looks on with well-feigned admiration of all their exploits.
They knew not he had thrown Ajax Telamon, and assisted at
the games that glorified the obsequies of Achilles.   Yet
Laodamas, the king's favourite son, graciously asks him to
show a specimen of what he can do " with feet or hands ; "
and, on his declining to enter into any contest,

> " Then arose,
> In aspect dread as homicidal Mars,
> Euryalus,"

and insultingly tells him that he suspects he is but the skipper
of some trading craft,—

> " well learn'd
> In steerage, pilotage, and wealth acquired
> By rapine, but of no gymnastic powers."

Ulysses had a fearful habit of frowning when in aught annoyed, and now his frown cast a gloom over the forum like a thunder-cloud.   But the speech in which he reproves Euryalus is full of wisdom and majesty, being meant not for him alone, but for all in the Forum.

"Heaven, it seems,
Imparts not, all to one. the various gifts
And ornaments of body, mind, and speech.
This man in figure less excels, yet Jove
Crowns him with eloquence ; his hearers charm'd
Behold him, while with unassuming tone
He bears the prize of fluent speech from all ;
And when he walks the city, as they pass,
All turn and gaze as they had pass'd a god.
Another, form'd with symmetry divine,
Yet wants the grace that twines itself around
The listening hearers' hearts.   Such deem I thee :
Thy form is excellent—not Jove himself
Could mend it—but the mind is nothing worth."

So saying, he seized a huge stone, and swiftly swinging it, sent it while it sang far beyond the farthest mark of a heavy three-pound Phæacian quoit !   The natives were astonished ; and then with another frown, bent chiefly on Euryalus, he stepped into the middle of the ring, and cried,

"Then come the man, whose courage prompts him forth,
To box, to wrestle with me, or to run ;
For ye have chafed me much, and I decline
No strife with any here—I CHALLENGE ALL
PHÆACIA, save Laodamas alone.
He is mine host."

You might have heard a mouse stirring ; and though he was no boaster, looking around on the silent sea of heads all fear-frozen, he exclaimed,—

"There is no game athletic in the use
Of all mankind too difficult for me."

He soon lets out that he was at the siege of Troy, and acknowledges no superior among mortal men—in the use of the bow—save Philoctetes.   To a few of ancient times he yields the palm—to Hercules—to Œchalion Eurytus, who dared defy to archery the gods themselves, and whom there-

fore Apollo slew. Alcinous applauds his speech, and confines now his praises of his people's feats to light-footed-
ness in the race, skill in navigation, feasting, harping,
singing, changing of garments, dancing, the tepid bath,
and the delights of love. And Demodocus adapts his tune-
ful chords to a sprightly strain—singing the loves of Mars
and Venus enveloped in that invisible web by Vulcan, among
the gibes and jeers of all the gods and goddesses—a voluptuous lay, and all unfit for the ears of Nausicaa; but she is
in her chamber, pensively thinking perhaps of him with the
locks of hyacinth.

> " Such was the theme of the illustrious Bard."

And Ulysses heard the song with delight—for, as all the
world knows, he was no woman-hater, and no remiss worshipper of Venus, who soon recovered from the shame of that
exposure in her Paphian home,

> " Where deep in myrtle groves
> Her incense-breathing altar stands embower'd."

By this time the temper of Ulysses had become quite amiable—and there is something very pleasant in the sly humour
of his panegyric on the astonishing dancing-feats of the agile
and ball-catching Phæacians.

> "' ILLUSTRIOUS ABOVE ALL PHÆACIA'S SONS !
> INCOMPARABLE ARE YE IN THE DANCE,
> EVEN AS THOU SAIDST. ASTONISH'D I BEHOLD
> FEATS UNPERFORM'D BUT BY YOURSELVES ALONE.'
> HIS PRAISE THE KING ALCINOUS WITH DELIGHT RECEIVED."

All hearts are opened, and all hands. The King and his
Twelve Peers make splendid presents of gold and garments
to Ulysses; and Euryalus generously makes friends with him
by the gift of a steel-bladed, silver-hilted, ivory-sheathed
sword, which the hero slings athwart his shoulders. It is
now near sunset, and they all return to the palace, where
golden gifts are heaped on golden gifts—and above all, " one
splendid cup elaborate," that what time he pours libation to
Jove and all the gods in his own house at home, the stranger
may remember the giver, and bless the roof-tree of Alcinous.

Not one word, it would appear, had Ulysses interchanged

with Nausicaa since they parted at Minerva's grove ! She
had kept her chamber all evening on her return from the Silver
Fountains, and all next day ; and why she did so, must have
been better known to herself than to us—though even to herself not very distinctly ; but now, when all are doing honour
to the stranger, and loading him with gifts, and that all preparations have been made for his departure on the morrow,
she too must join the congratulating throng : she who was so
communicative ere she mounted her car by the river-side,
cannot surely refuse to say a few words of farewell—and a
few she does say to him, as standing beside the portal of the
hall, with admiring eyes, she beholds him entering bold,
bright, and beautiful from the bath,—

> "Hail, stranger ! at thy native home arrived
> Remember me ! thy first deliverer here."

These are all her last words—and he answers his preserver
in as few—solemnly assuring her, that while he lives, he will
adore her as he adores the gods !

But the night is all before them, and Demodocus must
resume his harp, and sing them another lay. He sings, and
the song is again of Troy and Ulysses ! Again the hero
weeps—and now Alcinous feels he is entitled to ask the name
of the mysterious stranger. The time is come for that revelation, and for the recital of the tale of all the exploits and
adventures of the much-enduring man, since he and the Peers
laid Ilion in the dust. Not at once does he answer the
question of Alcinous ; but in language the most beautiful
gives utterance to sentiments the most amiable, all laudatory
of the gracious and noble reception he had met with from the
King and Queen, and their delightful Court. How charmingly
it reads in Cowper ! But in the Greek !

> "Alcinous ! o'er Phæacia's sons supreme !
> Pleasant it is to listen, while a bard
> Like this, melodious as Apollo, sings.
> The world, in my account, no sight affords
> More gratifying than a people blest
> With cheerfulness and peace, a palace throng'd
> With guests in order seated, and regaled
> With harp and song, while plenteous viands steam
> On every table, and the cups, with wine

From brimming beakers fill'd, pass brisk around.
No lovelier sight I know. But thou, it seems,
Thy thoughts has turn'd to ask me whence my groans
And tears, that I may sorrow still the more.
                    I AM ULYSSES ! "

What sensation must have been created by that announcement ! Or had they begun—the more thoughtful among them
—to conjecture which of the heroes this might be who had
fought before Troy ? " Famed o'er all the earth for noblest
wisdom, and renowned to heaven," could it be that Ulysses
himself had been storm-blown to Phæacia ? And Demodocus
the divine, rushed on by Apollo in all his power, has he filled
the great hero's eyes with tears, by a song recording his own
triumphs, during the night of that great conflagration,

" Through the aid
Of glorious Pallas, conqueror over all ! "

GREEK DRAMA.

THE AGAMEMNON OF ÆSCHYLUS.[1]

[AUGUST 1831]

PHILOSOPHICAL critics—from Aristotle to North—have often
been pleased to institute inquiries into the grounds of the
comparative difficulty, importance, and grandeur of the different kinds of poetical composition.   But, in our humble
opinion, they might have far better employed their time and
talents in elucidation of the principles common to all depart-
ments of the Art sacred to "the Vision and the Faculty Divine."
The same genius, in our humble opinion, shines in them all—
the Genius of the Soul.   Sometimes we see it lustrous in
Epic, sometimes in Dramatic, sometimes in Lyrical Poetry.
Observing some mysterious law of heaven, it assumes now the
shape of a Homer, or a Dante, or a Milton—now of an Æschylus, a Shakespeare, or a Baillie—now of a Pindar, a Chiabrera,
or a Wordsworth.   It sleepeth perhaps for a long time, but is
never dead ; it effulges by eras ; the same spirit, believe us,
but in different manifestations ; while "far off its coming
shone," clothed, in divers climes and ages, in various raiment
—yet ever and everywhere but one glorious apparition.
    The truth of this assertion—at first perhaps startling—is so
clear the moment you consider it calmly, that it needs neither
proof nor attestation.   Two sentences will show it in the light
of day.   Homer was the Father of Epic Poetry—because in
him the Genius of the Soul, obeying heavenly instinct and instruction, chose to be Epic.   But how dramatic, too, and how
lyric likewise, is the blind Melesegines !   Had it not been his

[1] Family Library—Dramatic Series, No. IV., Potter's Æschylus.
The *Agamemnon* of Æschylus, translated by John Symmons, A.M., late
Student of Christ Church.

doom to pour forth Epics—had the Iliad and Odyssey "slumbered yet in uncreated dust"—what had hindered him from bequeathing to his kind Tragedies and Odes ? Milton walked in his blindness up and down the whole of Paradise—Lost and Regained. But is "Samson Agonistes" not a tragedy? If it be not, neither will the Last Day. Is his "Christmas Hymn" not an ode ? Then never by human hand become angelical, shall harp-string be smote in heaven. In these 'Αοιδοι you perceive the Genius of the Soul, though essentially epic, sometimes changed before our eyes, the colours continuing celestial, into dramatic and lyric forms. Oftener, perhaps, it abides in one and the same form, in one and the same breast—as in the Southern or the Northern Ariosto—where we behold it raging in the irregular epic. Or as in Collins, the pensive chorister —or in Wordsworth, the high-priest of Nature's joy—immortal lyrists both—and coeval with all future time. And thus we designate the Singers by the strongest manifestation and most permanent in their being, of the Genius of the Soul ; we class them accordingly, and we set them—not order above order, for we are speaking of the highest—but in radiant rows, in dazzling files, on parallel levels, within holy regions which on earth are heaven—and these are the Hierarchies.

So fareth it with all favoured mortals, in whose breasts abide, temporarily or always, the Genius of the Soul. True to their high calling, and dedicated to its duties, they

"Walk the impalpable and burning sky ;"

and all good people below devoutly exclaim, "Lo ! the Poets," All but the many whose eyes are with their feet, and their feet among the weeds ; all but the few who with evil eyes look even upon the stars. The ground-grovellers know not of the existence of the luminaries who shine in the cerulean ; the heaven-haters look up "and curse their light."

But it has been, is, and ever will be, with Poetry as with Religion. They suffer scathe and scorn from heretics and unbelievers. The Primal Creed, natural and revealed, becomes obscured to the eyes of the half-initiated, and they cease to read aright the lines of light—the letters of gold—in which it is written, by a hand, on the walls of the house we inhabit. The uninitiated deny that the characters are there at all, for they have scribbled them all over with their own worthless or

unhallowed alphabet. To them the few syllables still visible
seem to belong to a dead language—all that is alive is but
their own jargon. Just as if on the leaves of a Bible, rain-
washed and weather-stained, some wretched person were to
scrawl blasphemy or pollution.

It behoves all who love the Beautiful, which is the Immortal, to guard from profanation or oblivion all holy relics. Such
are words—the words of the wise—and beyond and above all
others in power and glory—of the Great Poets. They must
be guarded in sanctuaries, when no longer breathed from
living lips in intercommunion of spirit with spirit enshrined in
mortal mould. Dead languages in one sense they are—for
dead are all, or worse than dead, of whom they were, or are,
the native speech. But living languages in another sense are
they, for from the silent page they still breathe inspiration.
Spoken are they no more in their power and purity—or spoken
not, perhaps, at all, any more than the Sanscrit, which they
say never was spoken ; but what music begins to play as soon
as we open the leaves of the book !

> " And now 'tis like all instruments—
> Now like a lonely flute ;
> And now 'tis like an angel's song,
> That bids the heavens be mute."

Is it not so with the relics of Grecian Poetry ? Is Homer
dead ? No more dead than that star,—

> " The star of Jove so beautiful and large."

They who can read Greek see him as he is in the sky—
they who cannot, see him in reflection, as if they were in a lake
or the sea. Or say, rather, in the " pure well of English undefiled "—of Chapman, or Pope, or Cowper, or Sotheby. He
has been translated *from* the skies, and sometimes we
scarcely know whether we be gazing on the orb or its image.

Are Æschylus, and Sophocles, and Euripides dead ? No ;
the Wondrous Three are still in constellation. Bright are they
as when first they shone, thousands of years ago, in the
heavenly sky. But which are they ? In what quarter of the
region hang their golden lamps ? Yonder. You see the
glorious gems, enclosing as in a triangle a deep-blue portion
of stainless ether. The apex-star is Æschylus—to the east is
Sophocles—to the west, Euripides !

Now think we of Milton's praise of the "Attic Tragedies of stateliest and most regal argument." Now we remember and murmur to ourselves—from the *Paradise Regained*—

> "Thence what the lofty, grave Tragedians taught
> In chorus or Iambic, teachers best
> Of moral wisdom, with delight received
> In brief sententious precepts, while they teach
> *Of fate, and chance, and change in human life,*
> *High actions and high passions best describing!*"

These last two lines how pregnant! They involve the whole Philosophy of the Grecian stage. What are all lectures on that drama—if good for anything—in French, English, or German—but discourses on that Text! And like the texts in the Bible—how it teaches us all that can be known, without the useless assistance of Sermons! Schlegel, for example, is a good preacher—an orthodox divine. But what light throws he over the Greek Tragedy, but scatterings from that Urn?

But you are turning your eyes away from the Three Luminaries, and now you are fixing them upon One—on a single star, all by itself, so it seems—although in the midst of thousands. It shines so softly and so sweetly in its transcendent brightness, that it seeks neither to repel nor to extinguish, nor to dim the lower and the lesser lights—but rather to render them all lovelier and happier in the heavens. Ay—that is Shakespeare.

In him, far and high beyond all other manifestation, shone in dramatic form the Genius of the Soul. The earthen O became before his eyes the wooden O—and the wooden O became the earthen.

> "All the world's a stage,
> And all the men and women merely players!"

The Rules of the Drama!—do not speak of them, we beseech you; for with him they were the Rules of Life. What cared he for Farce, or Comedy, or Tragedy, but as he saw them laughing, weeping, going mad, and dying—in Man? Broad grins and deep groans were all alike food to Shakespeare; the fool with his cap and bells; the Imperial Eye, whose "bend did awe the world;" "the rump-fed ronyon," wife to the Master of the Tiger; the "Gentle Lady married to the Moor;"

Dame Quickly with Falstaff, the fat buck, in a clothes-basket beneath a foul load of linen; and—CORDELIA !

It is the fashion, we perceive, to sneer at Samuel Johnson. But he had a soul that saw into Shakespeare's. How else could he have written these words ?—

> " Each change of many-colour'd life he drew—
> Exhausted worlds, and then imagined new.
> Existence saw him spurn her bounded reign ;
> And panting Time toil'd after him in vain ! "

Many-coloured life ! That is fine. Change ! Good. Shift its position but an inch, and it shifts its hues, like the neck of a bird. So did Shakespeare in all his pictures. Then he was a scientific painter. For he was taught by Apollo. He knew whence came the lights and the shadows. He was the weather-wisest of all mortal men. On rising of a morning, he had but to take one look at the Lift of Life—he saw how the wind blew, from what airt, the main current, and by intuition was given him the knowledge of the character of all the clouds. Therefore he foresaw and prophesied meridan, noon, eve, and night, and whether still or stormy the " witching hour." That, or something like it, is what Samuel the Sage meant by saying of Shakespeare,

> " Each change of many-colour'd life he drew."

And what difficulty can there be in knowing what he meant by saying,

> " Exhausted worlds, and then imagined new " ?

There is no exaggeration in the expression "exhausted worlds." It is a noble hyperbole. He did not exhaust them as a chemist exhausts air below a glass, leaving there, perhaps, a mouse to die, because it can no longer expire. Neither did he exhaust them as you exhaust an orange by sucking it—not perhaps in the most elegant style supposable—and then throwing the peel to a schoolboy, who, being fond of fruit, despiseth not the dessert. But he exhausted worlds, as you exhaust the face of the maiden you love, by drinking all its beauty—a drink divine—till you are transported out of yourself, as by the inspiration of the Gas of Paradise. The face continues to overflow with beauty ; but you have put it into poetry, and should any other bard attempt

to do so after you, he finds that you have exhausted the
subject ;—that brow of Egypt is still bright as ever—but he
must seek for another Cleopatra. Every soul of passion and
genius thus exhausts worlds, thereby making them his own ;
but Shakespeare reduced more worlds than any other man that
ever breathed to a state of exhaustion ; and that is all, and
enough too, that Sam of Lichfield meant to say of Will of Strat-
ford. But unfortunately for most men, after they have exhausted worlds, they cannot imagine new ; they are under the
necessity of allowing them to recover from the state of exhaustion, and so to live on upon them till they die. Shakespeare, again, has no sooner done with all the worlds that lie
about us, round our feet or over our heads, in the atmosphere
and on the ground of reality, than he " imagines new," nor
could anything satisfy him but to exhaust them likewise ; so
that had he not died at the age of fifty-seven, we believe he
would, there is but too much reason to fear, have exhausted
all the worlds lying in the universe of Imagination, and there
would have been no more Poetry—no more Poets !

> " Existence saw him spurn her *bounded reign.*"

And so she did. Observe, you must lay the emphasis on the
word bounded. Johnson has already said that Shakespeare
" exhausted worlds." Now, he speaks of the style in which
Shakespeare spurned—not exhausted, mind you—but spurned
existence. He lost all patience with existence, because her
reign was *bounded.* Bounded by what? Why, you ninny,
by space ! One kingdom lies here, another there ; two poles
there are at the least, though Parry never touched one. The
magnetic poles are *four.* Europe is one continent, Africa a
second, Asia a third, and America is very generally supposed
to be a fourth. Now, all this is what Johnson meant by
" bounded reign ; " and this is what Shakespeare could not
endure—therefore " existence saw him spurn " it—and he
absolutely went so far as to create an existence of his own
with an *unbounded* reign—making *his* Bohemia a maritime
kingdom, famous for the multitude of its seaport towns, while
it continued all the time to be just as conspicuous as ever
among inland communities, pretty well in towards the centre
of its own continent.

> " Panting Time toil'd after him in vain,"

is a line that by no means caricatures the " lame and impotent
conclusions" of Saturn, when absurdly attempting to keep up
with Shakespeare. Saturn sometimes contrived to keep pretty
close to him in the daytime—but in the night Shakespeare
always shot so far ahead, that the betting in all the circles
was all on one side—all givers and no takers; all against
Time, who, on many occasions, came panting up at the end
of the play—weeks, months, years after the spectators had left
the ground, and when there was no more appearance of a race
than if it had been a Sunday between sermons in Scotland.

This may seem a light way of speaking of the Swan of
Avon. But, after all the solemn stuff that has been uttered
about the Unities, perhaps we shall be excused for our
philosophical frivolities. The Unities of Time and Place in
the Drama of Real Life we must observe, whether we will or
no—because we are then obliged to obey our bodies. We
shall not be able to get over them even by railroads. But
in the Drama of Fictitious Life, what have we to do with our
bodies? Nothing but to sit upon them—still and civil. We
are but the spectators and the audience. And what cares the
Mind about Time and Place? Not one brass farthing. As to
the actors, we do not expect more of them than to pretend
plausibly being one hour at Thebes, and the next at Athens.
'Tis all smooth sliding and plain sailing over land and sea in
shandrydan or ship of Imagination. " Here away, Jack—
there away, John !" Hero and heroine are both off at the
nail as quickly and naturally as bits of wet paper—and back
again as dry as whistles.

It would appear, however, that though all mankind, rude
and civilised, have recognised this power of the Mind to go
where and when it would, all over the fields of space and time,
in the seven-league boots of Fancy, yet that they have all
always had some confused notion that the mind could only
exercise that power with satisfaction to itself, when its eyes
were shut; and that though it rejoiced in the divine right of
flying in thought, and making others fly in thought along
with it, to the uttermost parts of the earth in the space of a
couple of minutes, it has been slow to assure itself that it
possessed an almost equal and entirely the same kind of
power over those comparatively hulking concerns, things, as
over thoughts, over bodies as well as souls, over the " very

guts in a man's brain," as well as the thinking principle.
Accordingly, in all theatres of which we ever read, there has
been respect shown to Time and Space—an attempt to compress Time into such a period as might be thought to pass
while the people were staring, and to compress Space within
that part of "bounded existence," at the door of which tickets
had been taken and money paid, whether Temple or Barn.

Distrustful of her power of self-delusion, thus has always
acted the Mind with theatrical representations. Nor can we
either blame her, or think that she did much amiss. Her object was a good one—to preserve in a Fiction of Life the
Unities that reign in the Reality, and thus to have a true
resemblance.

All dramas we ever heard of began thus—and all dramas,
but the English, have stuck to this scheme—some closer,
and others more laxly; but on no stage but the English have
we ever heard of a young lady wooed in the first act, married
in the second, seen *enceinte* in the third, brought to bed in the
fourth, and in the fifth leaning upon the arm of her son, who
has just succeeded, on the death of his father, to a fine landed
property, and come to pay a visit in the jointure-house to his
Lady-mother, who looks so charmingly in weeds, that no
doubt she will get another husband in the Afterpiece.

With respect, again, to Unity of Action—that seemeth to
be a higher and a profounder Thought. The soul seeks it in
all Fiction and in all Truth. But it often knows not when it
has got it, and when it has not got it—in either; and when it
does know, its knowledge comes by feeling, and the feeling is
the sole assurance of the Unity. It needs little reflection to
see, that the preservation of the Unities of Time and Place
may destroy or prevent the Unity of Action. But it would
seem, that generally they are an assistance, in skilful hands;
and that extreme license and latitude, or rather the allowed
disregard or violation of the Unities of Time and Place, while
often a great help to genius in its endeavour to attain Unity
of Action, furnish strong temptation, and do of themselves
almost necessarily lead to the destruction of that Unity in
dramatists of inferior endowment. Being at liberty to do as
they will with place and time, they submit reluctantly to the
restrictions of severe science on the other—and thus are
dramas conceived and executed, which are but a series of

fallings-out in Time and Place—not Ones, Wholes, Cycles
—but Parts, Fragments, and Fictions. And this is bad.

Now, we cannot but come to this conclusion at last—that
the law of the Unities is death to weak dramatists. Claims
such as they impose, strong genius alone can bear. Inferior
powers " drag at each remove a lengthened chain," till they
get lame, halt, and at last sink down as if they were dead.
They give up the ghost—when they find how difficult it is to
introduce him—that place and time make him a most un-
manageable spectre. But inferior powers may contrive to
construct a very passable drama, when free from all such
fetters and drawbacks on their onward movements towards a
catastrophe. " Time and the hour run through the *roughest
play*"—and the piece is given out for repetition amidst great
applause; whereas, had the author been obliged to work upon
another model, it is questionable if his work had not been
" unanimously damned with a great majority."

Of this we are convinced as of our own existence, that had
the law of the three Unities prevailed in this country, we
should not have had such a multitude of dramatic compositions which, while they display genius, and much power over
the passions, are so crude, so imperfect, and so barbarous, as
to be utterly unworthy the name of works of art. They have
poetry in them—but they are not poems. They are tragic
—but they are not tragedies. Sayings and Doings they are
—but neither regular nor irregular Dramas.

Why, with all our admiration, high and just, of the elder
English dramatists—great you may call them if you choose—
how few of their plays can we bear to see acted—how few of
them can we read without a frequent, or perpetual feeling
of dissatisfaction accompanying the awkwardness of their
plots, of the evolution of their incidents and events, and the
imperfect developments of their characters! Few indeed.
Shakespeare alone triumphs over our souls—his tragedies
alone fulfil their destinies—his catastrophes, and few else,
satisfy our entire capacities of passion. He alone " exhausts
worlds" of woe—he alone preserves the Unities in his utter
forgetfulness of their existence. For we see through the
magic power of tears; and in that mist Time stops or flies
unheeded; Space is expanded or contracted; and we are
sensible but to our own mortal miseries, which have all their

source and their termination in the spiritual kingdom—of which Space and Time are not then known even to be so much as accidents. There often is " Satan's invisible kingdom displayed"—and there we sometimes behold the beauty of the soul almost as if it were fair and fresh from the hand of God.

This brings us close upon our more immediate subject—the Greek Drama. In it the Unities seem to reign with sovereign power, whereas they are subjects all of a kingly genius. As works of art and science, those tragedies are perfect. Are they lifeless? No—instinct with spirit. Are they cold? No—they burn with fire. Are they stiff? As Apollo when he slew the serpent. Are they natural? Ay, and what is more, likewise preternatural, and supernatural—for the actors are men, and demigods, and gods—and earth is shown, as it is, in intercommunion with heaven.

We feel assured that all who know those tragedies, will agree with us in thinking them far nobler works of the Genius of the Soul than any others except Shakespeare's. And perhaps they may agree, too, with us, in thinking, that the reason why they are so is, that what the Greek tragedians attempted and performed was an achievement fairly within the reach of a high intellect and imagination, inspired as those were which created the "Attic Tragedies of stateliest and most regal argument," by as many and as strong causes of inspiration as ever bore upon man's spiritual being; whereas, what Shakespeare attempted and performed seems to be beyond the reach, and far beyond the reach, of any other mortal creature that ever appeared on this planet in the flesh.

For what did they attempt—and what did they perform? Milton has told us—and we are afraid to say another word. But they did this—they illustrated some high ancestral story, or fable, in all its grand outlines and proportions familiar to the whole of Greece. They illustrated it by poetry, and dance, and music. Heroes and heroines of the olden time restored to life—stood on a magnificent stage in all their majesty —in a glorious theatre—before all the illustrious People of Athens. All that was mean and low—and even in the ancient Athens there was much—even in the age of Pericles—ceased to be ; the solemnities alone were seen of the heroic ages—and coming and going the celestial Sanctities. Wound up to that

highest pitch, the soul was still sustained by the scene far
above this common world, of which it yet beheld a glorified
shadow ; or rather the light which shone of old, and which
had "languished, grown dim, and died," on earth, descended
again upon it, and in all the splendid pomp and august cere-
monial of an imaginative religion. Dresses, decorations,
language, music—all partook of "the consecration and the
Poet's dream"—all were august, all congenial with the
"stateliest and most regal argument"—more august in that
representation in which Genius reigned, than ever had been
the Tragedies themselves, acted in life to the pouring out of
richest blood, by the heroes that fought at Troy, or by their
sires' sires, whose dooms darkened or brightened the fabulous
histories of most remote antiquity. All that the soul ever
imagined was shown to the senses ; and that mighty Theatre
became a world, in which elated and ennobled Imagination
believed the wonders it saw to be very realities. There shone
Agamemnon before his palace-gates at Argos, glorious from
the Fall of Troy—there the Furies shook their unextinguished
torches and their snaky locks—there Minerva and Apollo stood,
with the light of heaven on their heads—and the eye of Greece
beheld the presence of her tutelary Deities. Such was the
Drama—and it was felt, indeed, to be Divine.

The accomplished Editor of Potter, in the Family Dramatic
Library, has some beautiful paragraphs on the character of
the Greek Drama. And we wish we had left ourselves room
to quote some of them ; but we are too much addicted to the
habit of writing to leave ourselves opportunities of profiting so
often as we might do, by the talents of our friends. One fine
passage, however, we must quote.

" To those who have the power of reading these noble productions of antiquity in the original language, and to those
who possess the still rarer faculty of being able to abstract
themselves from modern usages and feelings, and of throwing
themselves back into the times from which these intellectual
banquets were derived, Milton's high commendation of its
uses and delights will seem little, if at all, overcharged. Such
persons find themselves at once thrown back upon a state of
things, for which modern compositions can furnish no equivalent. Lofty figures stalk before their eyes ; visions of heroic
greatness and superhuman dignity become familiar to their

thoughts; they hold converse with majestic minds, which the storms of fate might shake but could not subdue; and if they come out of this intercourse without experiencing those feverish excitements and gusts of passion, by which the modern drama at once delights and enervates the mind, they feel in themselves that calm repose or chastened emotion which were the legitimate and wiser aims of the ancient drama, and of which the one will be found the best relief against the cares, as the other will be the surest preservative against the pains of life."

Mr Campbell—as fine and as true a critic as he is an original and imaginative poet—has some admirable observations on Lillo, "the tragic poet of middle and familiar life," which bear strongly on our present subject. He has been speaking of Lillo's *Arden of Feversham*, in which there is a scene of intended murder so true to nature, that the audience, it is said, with one accord rose up and interrupted it. Mr Campbell admits that this was a proof of the *power* of the dreadful semblance of reality; but what we want is the "magic illusion of poetry." He continues — "Undoubtedly the genuine delineation of the human heart will please us, from whatever station or circumstances of life it is derived. In the simple pathos of Tragedy, probably very little difference will be felt, from the choice of characters being pitched above or below the line of mediocrity in station. But something more than pathos is required in Tragedy; and the very pain that attends our sympathy, requires agreeable and romantic associations of the fancy to be blended with its poignancy. Whatever attaches ideas of importance, publicity, and elevation, to the objects of pity, forms a brightening and alluring medium to the imagination. Athens herself, with all her simplicity and democracy, delighted on the stage to

———'let gorgeous Tragedy
In sceptred pall come sweeping by.'

"Even situations far depressed beneath the familiar mediocrity of life, are more picturesque and poetical than its ordinary level. It is certainly in the virtues of the middle ranks of life that the strength and comforts of society chiefly depend, in the same manner as we look for the harvest not on cliffs and precipices, but on the easy slope and the uniform plain. But

the painter does not in general fix on level situations for the
subjects of his noblest landscapes. There is an analogy, I
conceive, to this, in the moral painting of Tragedy. Dispari-
ties of station give it boldness of outline. The commanding
situations of life are its mountain scenery, the region where
its storm and sunshine may be portrayed in their strongest
contrast and colouring."

In such a Drama, we hope you will agree with us in thinking that the Unities were Cardinal Virtues. The scheme
was severe as it was stately—truth idealised. Therefore
violence must be done, if possible, to nothing in nature—else
had art been stained with imperfection. As things were, so
let them be—only lifted up into greater majesty, but obedient
still, as the meanest, to the sovereign laws.

But remember that this wonderful people—the poets of this
wonderful people, which is the same thing—had an invention by
which they gave the Unities a far-extended reign. We allude
to the Trilogy. Three plays were written on one subject,
each a perfect whole in itself—but the three also a whole—so
that comprehensively each play was an act, and of three acts
consisted the Triune Drama. Was not this great ? Shakespeare has something like it in the first and second part of his
historical plays. For Shakespeare has everything ; but his
first and second parts have neither separately nor conjointly
the power and glory of the Grecian Trilogy. They have not
indeed—you must not be angry, for we speak the truth.

Now, whether or not Trilogies were acted in succession, all on
one day, to the same audience, we do not know ; nor do we
well see how we should, any more than Augustus W. Schlegel,
who was a far more learned man than Christopher North, and
a far more unprincipled and hypocritical plagiary. But this
we do know, that there was nothing to prevent it—and that if
they were, then we lament that we were not born a few thousand years ago, that we might have sat out a Trilogy. The
Trilogy of *Agamemnon*, the *Choephoræ*, and the *Eumenides*,
might have been performed, we should think, all within the
fifteen hours—certainly within the twenty-four ; and would it
not have been easier to look and listen for that time to such an
exhibition—opera and tragedy all in one—dance, music, and
poetry—to say nothing of the scenery and the assemblage—
than to sit for six hours—no uncommon occurrence—in the pit

of Covent Garden or Drury Lane, under the infliction of the most dismal of all imaginable trash—or in St Stephen's Chapel, twice that length of time, to trash, dismal far beyond imagination, and incredible even to those who ultimately died under it?

. But besides the audience or spectators, and the actors and their stage, there was that sublime idealism—the Chorus—the ideal representative of Human Nature in its character of sympathetic witness, and judge, we had almost said, the Shadow of the Man within the Breast—the Conscience. " The Chorus," as Mr Symmons finely says, " was the original and substantive part of the representation. The *getting it up* was a matter of state, and the frequent contention of the Tribes, who vied with each other in the exhibition of their respective Choruses. The first persons in each Tribe were appointed Choragi, and rivalled each other in the splendour and apparatus of their Choruses, who were chosen, taught, and practised for some time before the grand Lenœan and Dionysian Festivals. It was a grand national exhibition of music and dancing ; and the poets, properly speaking, tacked on the dialogue to heighten the pleasure and diversify the amusement. From the splendour of the representation, and the beauty of the dresses, the dancing and the music, associated with the finest flights of poetry, the Chorus was probably the most attractive part of the representation ; though to us, stripped of all its adjuncts, it is the least interesting, and considered, in a modern play, as a useless encumbrance. Rousseau, in his remarks on the opera of *Alcestis*, has some very pertinent remarks both on the dramas and language of Greece ; contending that the former were operas, and that the latter was of so musical a nature, that its mere pronunciation, when in verse, constituted music ; whereas, he says, in all modern languages the association of music with words is unnatural, and hardly tolerable. Hence with us in operas, where music prevails, sense, poetry, and dramatic interest vanish ; very differently in Greece, where one heightened the pleasure of the other." But its true character will best appear when we come to the Tragedy of *Agamemnon*, in which the Chorus is perhaps the grandest in the Greek Drama.

Suppose Tragedies with such an aim, and on such a model, composed by genius of the highest order, working under inspiration, and yet obedient to the severest laws—and see you not at once that they must be most glorious works!

Turn we then again, for a moment, to Shakespeare. His dramas were written for a mean theatre, and a miserable stage. Orchestra? Why, yes—a couple of fiddlers. Chorus? None, except in a couple of instances or so—a prologue. Ancestral tales of heroic ages? Sometimes—for our civil wars were wars of heroes. But all ages, all characters, all occupations, all ranks, were almost alike to him; what he wanted were—men and women.

"Creation's heir! the world! the world is thine!"

All passions, all emotions, all affections, all sentiments, all opinions, all fears, all hopes, all desires—whatever constitutes the heart, the soul, and the mind—were the subject-matter of Shakespeare's plays. Majesty, magnificence, dignity, splendour, state, pomp—why, he beheld them all " in the light of common day "—his genius was " wide and general as the casing air " —and all the world of " man and nature, and of human life," swam before his eyes as God made it, and as sin and trouble changed it from the day of the Fall. Heroes! hide all your diminished heads before—Hamlet the Dane! Heroines! fade away in presence of Desdemona! But we must positively say not one single word more, at present, about Shakespeare, or we shall never get at Æschylus. We shall have said enough—and all we wished to say—if we have succeeded, even imperfectly, in proving that the Greek Drama is in idea —and the execution nobody denies is nearly perfect—great and glorious; but that the idea of the English Drama is greater and more glorious far, only that Shakespeare alone has realised it, and that in all other hands so many imperfections have clouded it, and marred its majesty, that he being placed aloof and " left alone in his glory," all other Trage- dians, though often Shakespearean too, must veil their faces though bright, and stoop their heads though anointed, when brought for comparison into the presence of Æschylus, So- phocles, and Euripides. In greatest attempts it is indeed glorious even to fail, but not so glorious sure, as in attempts only not the greatest, to be crowned with consummate success and perfect triumph.

Of the three, Æschylus is the greatest, for his genius is the

most original, and it has the most power. The soul of Sophocles possessed in perfection the sense of grace and beauty;
that of Euripides breathed in a perpetual atmosphere of tenderness and pathos; the whole being of Æschylus was imbued
with the sublime. So, speaking generally and of course
vaguely, may we along with all others characterise with truth
the respective genius of these illustrious poets. But we shall
speak falsely, if we mean for a moment to deny to any one of
the Three the possession of any one gift which may have been
bestowed more bountifully on one or other of his compeers.
For Æschylus, while his thoughts are vast and stupendous,
and his region the Sublime, is often visited with the loveliest
imagery. "Beauty pitches her tents before him;" and he
holds in his hands the golden key that opens the door of the
"sacred source of sympathetic tears." So too, though Sophocles loves to range through all the richest realms of Beauty,
his images being all exquisite—(*far-sought-and-brought-from-
the-foreign-climes-of-by-others'-untouched footsteps ;*) and though
he wantons in the profusion of the flowers of fancy that sometimes obstruct his path through the meads of asphodel, or
among the olive-groves filled with the songs of nightingales,
yet Sophocles is sometimes—not seldom—sublime ; and perhaps his sublimity is the noblest of all sublimities, for it
seems to be but Beauty changing its character as it ascends
the sky—even as one might think a Dove high up in the
sunshine, and soaring so loftily that eye can no more discern
her silver plumage—an Eagle ; nor in such heavenward
flight would the Bird of Venus be not as sublime as the Bird
of Jove. Euripides, again, is the Poet of the Pathetic. But
the wrath of Medea, and the madness of Orestes, are excelled
in sublimity by no poetry alive ; and though he affected, or
let us say rather, with the boldness of a great master (for
Euripides was a Wordsworth, and Wordsworth is a Euripides),
bore with him into highest tragedy a style simpler and less
ornate, humbler than had belonged to it before, for which
Aristophanes lashed him without ruffling his skin, yet are
many of his Choruses the perfection of poetical language, as
well as of feeling, fancy, and thought, and thousands of his
Iambics such as thrill the soul within you—if you have such
a thing within you—with that shiver and shudder that shows
the presence — the access of the Sublime. Schlegel and

Mitchell, following Aristophanes, have been very hard on poor
Euripides. But Socrates and Milton loved him—and so doth
North ; and you shall see, before Christmas perhaps (Euripides was sprung from the people—Aristophanes was a noble-
man), what wisdom there may be in the sneer at—"the son of
the old herb-woman."

Mr Symmons, when speaking of the extreme difficulty of
doing anything like justice in translation to the Greek tragedians, says beautifully : "Those languages also admitted of a
greater variety of tropes and figures and metaphors, (some of
which—such, for instance, as hypallage—though so frequent in
the Greek tragedians, are yet unknown to modern languages),
which gave a spring and soar to the wings of the poets. From
its infinite variety and richness, its plastic nature, and the
capacity of its compounds, the language accommodated itself
to all varieties of natural talent, supplying compound epithets
for the dithyrambics and metaphors for the tragedians ; and
equally answered to the buskined magnificence of Æschylus,
the forensic subtlety of Euripides, and the soft and voluptuous
colouring of Chæremon. The style of each great master kept
aloof from that of another, and afforded to the public an infinite
variety of amusement. Of the contrast of styles, the Frogs of
Aristophanes presents us with a most delightful and entertaining specimen in the ludicrous contention between Æschylus and Euripides, between the *high-crested cavalier* diction of the one, and the *slender filings and scrapings* of the
tongue of the other. In short, no two nearly contemporary
poets of our own country could afford so striking a contrast,
which must be ascribed, not merely to the difference of their
geniuses, but also to the great scope and versatility of their
language. The most unskilful auditor of Athens might safely
pronounce from which of the two poets it proceeded."

This is admirable ; it is finely philosophical. So, indeed,
are all the observations and reflections of this scholar. He
brings to his work all the accomplishments of a first-rate translator, and he knows the difficulties he has to encounter and to
overcome. For he tells us that times, customs, religion, and
manners, are all changed : words which vibrated on the ear,
and went straight to the heart of an Athenian, causing a thrill
through their crowded Theatres, are known to us only by the
dim light of lexicons, context, and glossaries ; and even when

understood, we search in vain for corresponding expressions in our own language. Words consecrated to religious uses, long since forgotten, have become untranslatable. An immeasurable distance, therefore, must there always be between an ancient original (especially a Tragedy or an Ode) and a modern translation; that is, not only the difference between the genius of the writers, but the still greater difference between the genius of languages and ages. The Greek Poetry pleased, and was imposing in its simplicity and nakedness; it has a charm perfectly impossible to be conveyed to those who have not read it in the original; whereas an attempt at the same simplicity in an uncongenial and less powerful language, or a less poetical age and country, would produce only a displeasing effect; " pretty nearly," adds Mr Symmons, though we confess we do not see the propriety or applicability of the image—" pretty nearly what would be produced by the exhibition of a modern *beau*, stript of his clothes, by the side of the naked beauties of Antinous, Adonis, or Apollo ! " Why, if the Modern Beau were, which he most likely would turn out to be, a poor misshapen rickety Cockney, he would look extremely absurd naked, even standing by himself on the banks of the Serpentine ; but if he were a young Life-guardsman of a noble family, we believe he might stand comparison with any statue that ever breathed in marble.

Mr Symmons says truly, that while the two great Epics of antiquity have been rendered in our own language by some of the greatest geniuses of earlier and more modern times, the Gawin Douglases, the Chapmans, the Popes, and the Drydens, the few remains (alas! how few !) of the no less celebrated Greek Tragedians have not been equally fortunate ; and with the exception of Gascoyne, whose *Phœnissæ* is partly an original composition, and partly a close and very spirited translation, these master-pieces have never been attempted except merely in our own times ; and of those who have attempted them, general opinion is disposed to think but indifferently of Franklin and Woodhall *in toto* (Mr Symmons wrote, we believe, or should suppose, before the publication of Mr Dale's very beautiful translation of Sophocles), and of Potter in his versions of Sophocles and Euripides, though inclined to make an exception in favour of his Æschylus. This exception appeared to Mr Symmons as unfounded, or as arising rather out of the

nature of the original, the beauties of which were of too transcendent a nature to be wholly obscured, than from any great
merit in the translator, and therefore he was emboldened to attempt the *Agamemnon*.   He speaks, however, with a manly
modesty, of his own translation.   The only advantage which
he hopes his own attempt may boast over Potter's, is that it is
a more faithful transcript, and that the numerous errors, totally
subversive of the sense, to be met with in Potter, are avoided.
He has striven to be as literal as possible ; though he fears
that in endeavouring to give the sense of Æschylus, when
sometimes that sense was untranslatable *literally*, in para-
phrases, he may have fallen into languor and diffuseness.

With Mr Symmons's judgment on Potter, mildly as it is delivered, we cannot altogether agree—from his judgment on
himself, modestly as it is delivered, we wholly dissent.   Potter
is sadly inaccurate—and no wonder ; for he engaged with the
most difficult perhaps of all the Greek Poets (Lycophron is
not difficult, he is *impossible*), and he was no great Greek
scholar.   He goes right in the teeth of the sense a hundred
times ; and many thousand times he slurs it over in such a.
strange style that we defy you to tell whether he understood
it or not ; while often and often his verses flow on sonorously,
with about as much meaning as the Thames or the Tweed,
when, laying your ear to the bank, you entreat him—not to
speak up, for he is loud enough—but for heaven's sake not to
keep murmuring on in that unintelligible strain which is not
even so much as oracular, but mere sound—music if you will ;
while ever as you fondly imagine that the river is about to
make a confidential communication, he passes you off with the
liquid lapse of a superficial shallow, or confounds you utterly
with the thunder of a waterfall.   Still, Potter is often excellent ;
and though it would be going too far to call him a Poet, he
had poetry in his soul.   He certainly exhibits at times a lofty
enthusiasm ; and his version of Æschylus, though about as fit
to be compared with the original " as *I* to Hercules," may be
read with high satisfaction—just as *I*, that is—to speak less
egotistically—WE, may on our own account be looked at, not
only without much displeasure, but with no inconsiderable delight.   We recommend, therefore, the Fourth Volume of the
Dramatic Series of the Family Library to all families desirous
of acquiring the best knowledge within their power of the

Greek stage; and we hope that the editor will give us, after like fashion, Sophocles and Euripides. This volume is edited by an elegant and accomplished scholar, who has enriched it with several short but pithy dissertations. The translations of the Dramas are not given entire; but he has judiciously selected the finest parts of Potter, preserving the order of each Drama, and filling up the *lacunæ* with prose sketches of the matter left out—so that you are carried along the main current of song; and these óccasional breaks may be compared to little pleasant green islands, to which you float away into moods of repose and of meditation on the wondrous scenery through which you have been descending in a visionary dream.

The *Agamemnon*, by itself, is as noble a tragedy as ever " went sweeping by " along the floor of a stage. But it is but One of Three; and the Three together are one Tragedy —called, as you know, a Trilogy ;—and that Trilogy of all Trilogies extant is the grandest and the most sublime. Of the *Choephoræ* and the *Eumenides* you shall hear and see all the most glorious features by-and-by; but now for the *Agamemnon*, who was, as you know, King of Men.

Schlegel gives an analysis of this play in his eloquent *Lectures on Dramatic Literature ;* but we shall give no formal analysis, we shall let evolve before your eyes the whole bright consummate Flower—bright with a dreadful purple and crimson, for every leaf is streaked with blood.   .

The drama opens with the soliloquy of a watchman on the top of a lonely tower of Atreus' palace in Argos, placed there " like a night-dog," to bark as soon as he shall

> " See the appointed signal,
> The fire in the horizon, whose red dawn
> Shall spread the downfall of proud Ilion's towers,
> Swifter than noisy fame, or murmuring tongues."

For ten years has he kept his watch,

> "Sprinkled with views, unvisited by dreams."

The picture reminds one of our own Great Minstrel. The watchman says,

> "Meanwhile it pleases me by fits to pipe,
> Or sing some roundelay ; for song has charms
> To pass dull time, and wheedle drowsy sleep."

Schlegel says, that it was of importance to Clytemnestra
that she should be aware of Agamemnon's approach (for you
know she had designed to murder him), and that therefore
"the night-dog" was placed on the Tower to bark at the
coming king. But this is one of Schlegel's many mistakes,
though he has not to answer for all the errors and ignorance
in Black's Translation—for example, not for that learned person's assertion that Agamemnon was "*strangled* in the bath,"
as Homer says, "like an ox at the stall." He was *not* strangled
in the bath, nor was Homer's ox strangled at the stall; in
both cases the business was done by the axe. The agreement
that beacon-fires should declare the Fall of Troy, was made
between Agamemnon and Clytemnestra before the army left
Argos, before the fleet left Aulis, and at that time she had not
sold her soul to Pluto and Ægisthus. Philosophical critics
should read the poets they lecture on, and so should their
translators.

All at once the beacon blaze bursts upon the night, and the
watchman exclaims,—

> " O hail, thou lamp of darkness ! in the night
> Shedding a splendour of diurnal beams,
> Bringing to Argos jubilee and joy,
> And many a choir with thy eventful light."

He then, after some fine poetry (and why should he not be
poetical, who has watched the stars for ten years from the top
of a lonely tower ?) in which he gives dark hints that all has
not been going on well in the palace, descends to communicate the intelligence to the queen.

The Chorus then enter, composed of old men and wise—
the senators of Argos—and sing their lofty strains in front of
the palace. It is indeed an Ode. The Chorus begins to sing
of the sailing of the Fleet to Troy, in poetry worthy of the
magnificent array, when suddenly he exclaims,—

> " See ! all the altars of our city gods,
> The Powers of Heaven above and Hell below,
> With heap'd oblations blazing glow !"

Clytemnestra, on the watchman's words, has thus kindled the
city, which is now alive with the " solemn stir of sacrifice."
The Chorus knows not, though he conjectures, the reason of

all the joyful and religious fires—but, kindled into higher enthusiasm by the hundred blazes, continues to sing of the expedition to Troy. It is a song of triumph ; and yet melancholy breathes over it all, as if inspired by the presaging fear of some mighty misfortune. With wonderful skill Æschylus has scattered and sprinkled sadness and misgivings and forebodings over the whole ode, which is one of gloomy exultation. The Chorus alludes to that fatal sacrifice at Aulis, to free the wind-bound Fleet—the sacrifice of Iphigenia. Fatal, not only because that Innocent died to expiate some mysterious wrong done by her sire Agamemnon to Diana, (mysterious it is in Æschylus—in Sophocles 'tis said to have been his slaying a White Doe sacred to the goddess), but fatal because Wrath for that cruel wrong done to her child is one of the real or pretended reasons of Clytemnestra's murderous hatred of Agamemnon. We shall quote the celebrated passage descriptive of the sacrifice, in the original—in a literal prose translation—in Potter—and in Symmons.

Λιτὰς δὲ καὶ κληδόνας πατρώους
Παρ' οὐδὲν αἰῶνα παρθένιόν τ'
Ἔθεντο φιλόμαχοι βραβῆς,
Φράσεν δ' ἀόζοις πατὴρ μετ' εὐχὰν,
Δίκαν χιμαίρας ὕπερθε βωμοῦ
Πέπλοισι περιπετῆ,
Παντὶ θυμῷ προνωπῆ
Λαβεῖν ἀέρδην, στόματός τε καλλιπρώρου φυλακὰν κατασχεῖν,
Φθόγγον ἀραῖον οἴκοις,
Βίᾳ χαλινῶν τ' ἀναύδῳ μένει.
Κρόκου βαφὰς δ' ἐς πέδον χέουσα
Ἔβαλλ' ἕκαστον θυτήρων ἀπ' ὄμματος βέλει φιλοίκτῳ,
Πρέπουσά θ' ὡς ἐν γραφαῖς, προσεννέπειν
Θέλους', ἐπεὶ πολλάκις
Πατρὸς κατ' ἀνδεῶνας εὐτραπέζους
Ἐμέλψιν, ἀγνὰ δ' ἀταύρωτος αὐδᾷ πατρὸς
Φίλου τριτόσπονδον εὔποτμον τ'
Αἰῶνα φίλως ἐτίμα.

—V. 228-246.

NORTH.

" But her prayers, and her callings upon her father,
And her virgin life, of no value
Held the battle-loving chiefs.
And her father order'd the fagot-burners (priests), after the prayer,
(Her) on the altar, after the manner of a she-goat.
Fallen and involved in her robes,

Fallen (on the ground) in a swoon,
To lift up, and to set a guard on her beautiful-faced mouth,
(And) on her voice cursing the house,
By means of violence and the dumb force of muzzles.
And pouring out on the ground the dye of the saffron (*i. e.* dropping
    her saffron-colour'd veil),
She kept wounding each of the sacrificers with a pity-loving dart
    from her eyes,
Beauteous as though in a picture, to address them
Wishing, since often in the hospitable banquet-halls of her father
She had sung : for the chaste unmarried one, with her voice, of
    her father
Beloved, the pious (*lit.* often-pouring out libations), well-fated
Life, was lovingly in the habit of honouring."

POTTER.

    " Arm'd in a woman's cause, around
    Fierce for the war the princes rose ;
    No place affrighted pity found.
    In vain the virgin's streaming tear,
    Her cries in vain, her pleading prayer,
      Her agonising woes.
    Could the fond father hear unmoved ?
    The Fates decreed : the king approved :
    Then to the attendants gave command
      Decent her flowing robes to bind ;
    Prone on the altar with strong hand
      To place her, like a spotless hind ;
    And check her sweet voice, that no sound
    Unhallow'd might the rites confound.
EPODE. Rent on the earth her maiden veil she throws
      That emulates the rose ;
    And on the sad attendants rolling
    The trembling lustre of her dewy eyes,
      Their grief-impassion'd souls controlling,
      That ennobled, modest grace,
      Which the mimic pencil tries
      In the imaged form to trace,
      The breathing picture shows :
    And as, amidst his festal pleasures,
    Her father oft rejoiced to hear
    Her voice in soft mellifluous measures
      Warble the sprightly-fancied air—
    So now in act to speak the virgin stands ;
    But when, the third libation paid,

She heard her father's dread commands
Enjoining silence, she obey'd ;
 And for her country's good,
With patient, meek, submissive mind
 To her hard fate resign'd,
Pour'd out the rich stream of her blood."

SYMMONS.

" Mailed chiefs, whose bosoms burn
 For battle, heard in silence stern
 Cries that call'd a father's name,
And set at naught prayers, cries, and tears,
And her sweet virgin life and blooming years.
 Now when the solemn prayer was said,
 The father gave the dire command
  To the priestly band,
Men with strong hands and ruthless force,
To lift from earth that maiden fair,
Where she had sunk in dumb despair,
And lay with robes all cover'd round,
Hush'd in a swoon upon the ground,
And bear her to the altar dread,
Like a young fawn, or mountain kid :
Then round her beauteous mouth to tie
Dumb sullen bands to stop her cry,
Lest aught of an unholy sound
Be heard to breathe those altars round,
Which on the monarch's house might hang a deadly spell.
Now as she stood, and her descending veil,
Let down in clouds of saffron, touch'd the ground,
The priests, and all the sacrificers round,
All felt the melting beams that came,
With softest pity wing'd, shot from her lovely eyes.
Like some imagined pictured maid she stood,
So beauteous look'd she, seeming as she would
Speak, yet still mute : though oft her father's halls
 Magnificent among,
 She, now so mute, had sung
 Full many a lovely air,
 In maiden beauty fresh and fair ;
And with the warbled music of her voice
Made all his joyous bowers still more rejoice ;
While feast, and sacrifice, and choral song,
Led the glad hours of lengthen'd day along."

Our literal prose translation we give merely for the use of
the English reader, that he may have some notion of the simple, but rich and grand style in which Æschylus at all times
delights, even in the pathetic, which with him is always also
the picturesque. Potter's verses are *pretty*—and we are sorry
for it. They have little or nothing about them—Greekish.
Yet Potter felt the beauty of the passage, though he could not
transfuse it into his own words. He says in a note, " The behaviour of Iphigenia is described with inimitable beauty;
there is a pathos in her actions, in her eyes, in her attitude,
beyond the power of words." No ; not beyond the power of
words. For do not words give them all? The words of
Æschylus, however—not the words of Potter. Words are
wonderful magicians, and almost nothing is beyond their power.
Besides, in wise men's lips they know their power, and never
use it but when it is sure to tell—else they are mute. Potter
adds well, " As she has been admitted to her father's feasts,
and accustomed to entertain him with her songs, she presumed
on his fondness, and, throwing off her maiden veil—as its colour
signifies—[which colour Æschylus calls saffron, Potter rose]
—stood in the act to speak to him ; but hearing his voice commanding silence, she obeyed with meek submission. This is
the painting of a great master." It is.

Symmons is far superior to Potter, and is very fine. 'Tis a
noble paraphrase in the spirit of the original. All the *intense*
words he strives to keep ; but some of them tear themselves
out of his grasp, and will not be translated. Throughout the
whole, however, you see the Greek scholar, and enough, too,
to convince you that Mr Symmons is himself a Poet.

This Chorus is complicated—for there is an ode within an
ode. Calchas it is—the Prophet, of whom Agamemnon, at the
opening of the Iliad, says, that from his lips he never heard
but evil—that wails a wild and melancholy and woeful strain
respecting the sacrifice of Iphigenia, and the wrath of Clytemnestra. And that strain is given by the Chorus. Thus in
Symmons—

> " Ha! from the dropping blood arises rife,
>   Discord and consanguineous strife,
>   And woman's deadly rage with blackening face behind.
>   Homeward returning see her go,
>   And sit alone in sullen woe ;

And child-avenging Anger waits,
Guileful and horrid, at the Palace gates ! "

With the sound of these prophetic strains yet in their cars, the Chorus sees the approach of—Clytemnestra. Their strain has prepared us for something dreadful in the face and figure of the avenging Queen,—

" For ne'er was mortal sound so full of woe."

She comes—and then we have such a description as makes the glow-worm light of modern poetry

" Pale its ineffectual fires."

She comes rejoicingly, exultingly—floating on stately and beautiful in her revenge—of which the passion, about to be satiated and appeased, breaks out into a glorious burst, that shows how sin and wickedness can make a Poetess of the Highest Order.

She tells the Chorus that Troy has been taken, and they ask, " How long ago ? When was the city sacked ? " She replies, " 'Twas in the night that bore this rising light." The Chorus, incredulous, asks again, " But how? What messenger could come so fast ? " And this is her glorious reply—in the Greek of Æschylus—in the literal prose English of North—in the poetical versions of Potter and Symmons.

ΚΛΤΤΑΙΜΝΗΣΤΡΑ.

"Ηφαιστος "Ιδης λαμπρὸν ἰκπίμπων σίλας.
Φρυκτὸς δὶ φρυκτὸν διυρ' ἀπ' ἀγγάρου πυρὸς
Ἐπεμπιν. "Ιδη μὶν πρὸς Ἑρμαῖον λίπας
Λήμνου· μίγαν δὶ πανὸν ἐκ νήσου τρίτον
Ἄθωον αἶπος Ζηνὸς ἰξιδίξατο,
Ὑπιρτιλής τι, πόντον ὥστι νωτίσαι,
Ἰσχὺς πορευτοῦ λαμπάδος πρὸς ἡδονὴν
Πιύκη τό χρυσοφιγγὶς ὡς τις ἥλιος
Σίλας παραγγιίλασα Μακίστου σκοπαῖς·
Ὁ δ' οὖτι μίλλων οὐδ' ἀφρασμόνως ὕπνῳ
Νικώμινος παρῆκιν ἀγγίλου μίρος·
Ἑκὰς δὶ φρυκτοῦ φῶς ἱπ' Εὐρίπου ῥοὰς
Μισσαπίου φύλαξι σημαίνι μολόν.
Οἱ δ' ἀντίλαμψαν καὶ παρήγγιιλαν πρόσω
Γραίας ἰρίκης θωμὸν ἄψαντις πυρί.
Σθίνουσα λαμπὰς δ' οὐδίπω μαυρουμίνη,
Ὑπιρθορῦσα πιδίον Ἀσωποῦ, δίκην
Φαιδρᾶς σιλήνης, πρὸς Κιθαιρῶνος λίπας

"Ἥγιιρον ἄλλην ἰκδοχὴν πομποῦ πυρός.
Φάος δὲ τηλίπομπον οὐκ ἠναίνιτο
Φρουρά, πλίον καίουσα τῶν ιἰρημίνων·
Λίμνην δ' ὑπὶρ Γοργῶπιν ἴσκηψιν φάος·
"Ορος τ' ἰπ' Αἰγίπλαγκτον ἰξικνούμινον
"Ωτρυνε θισμὸν μὴ χατίζισθαι πυρός.
Πίμπουσι δ' ἀνδαίοντις ἀφθόνῳ μίνιι
Φλογὸς μίγαν πώγωνα, καὶ Σαρωνικοῦ
Πορθμοῦ κάτοπτον πρῶν' ὑπιρβάλλιιν πρόσω
Φλίγουσαν· ιἶτ' ἴσκηψιν, ἴς τ' ἀφίκιτο
'Αραχναῖον αἶπος, ἀστυγιίτονας σκοπάς·
Κἄπιιτ' 'Ατριιδῶν ἰς τόδι σκήπτιι στίγος
Φάος τόδ' οὐκ ἄπαππον 'Ιδαίου πυρός.
Τοιοίδι τοί μοι λαμπαδηφόρων νόμοι,
Ἀλλος παρ' ἄλλου διαδοχαῖς πληρούμινοι·
Νικᾷ δ' ὁ πρῶτος καὶ τιλιυταῖος δραμών.
Τίκμαρ τοιοῦτο ξίμβολόν τι σοὶ λίγω,
'Ανδρὸς παραγγιίλαντος ἐκ Τροίας ἐμοί.

                                        —V. 281-316.

CHORUS.—And who of messengers could have come with such
expedition ?

NORTH.

" CLY.—Vulcan from Ida out-sending a brilliant blaze ;
But (one) beacon (another) beacon of *Courier* fire despatched.
Ida first to the Hermæan promontory of Lemnos ;
Then a third large torch from the island
Did Jove's pinnacle of Athos receive,
And the pine torch flared aloft, so that (there) skimmed along on
    the surface of the sea
The strength of the posting light, for our gratification,
The golden-gleaming splendour, like a sun,
Announcing to the watch-towers of Macistus.
And it neither lingering, nor laggardly by sleep
Subdued, omitted not its office of messenger ;
But at a distance the beacon-light to Euripus' streams coming,
Gives the signal to the warders of Messapius.
And they in their turn kindled up, and heralded onward the blaze,
Touching with fire a heap of aged heather ;
But the vigorous torch, in no respects bedimm'd,
Leaping over the plain of Asopus—like
A resplendent moon—to the promontory of Cithæron,
Roused up another relay of onward-sped fire.
And the far-sent light, rejected not
The warders,—who kindled up more than those mention'd ;
And the blaze skimmed over the lake Gorgopis ;

And having reach'd the mountain Ægiplanctus,
Stirred up (the warders) that the order of the fire might not fail—
And kindling up, they send on, with ungrudging fury,
A mighty beard of flame, and gleaming (so as)
Onward to overleap the summit looking down on the Saronic
    gulf;
Then impetuous it rush'd, and arrived at
Arachne's height watch-towers near the city ;
And then to this house of the sons of Atreus rush'd
This light—not unrelated to the fire of Ida.
Such indeed to me are the laws of the torch-bearers,
Accomplish'd one after another in mutual succession ;
But the first and the last runner has the victory.
Such a signal and watchword tell I to you ;
My husband having announced it to me from Troy."

POTTER.

" The fire, that from the height of Ida sent
    Its streaming light, as from the announcing flame
    Torch blazed to torch.   First Ida to the steep
    Of Lemnos ; Athos' sacred height received
    The mighty splendour ; from the surging back
    Of Hellespont the vigorous blaze held on
    Its smiling way, and like the orient sun
    Illumes with golden-gleaming rays the head
    Of rocky Macetas ; nor lingers there,
    Nor winks unheedful, but its warning flames
    Darts to Euripus' fitful stream, and gives
    Its glittering signal to the guards that hold
    Their high watch on Mesapius.   These enkindle
    The joy-announcing fires, that spread the blaze
    To where Erica hoar its shaggy brow
    Waves rudely.   Unimpair'd the active flame
    Bounds o'er the level of Asopus, like
    The jocund Moon, and on Cithæron's steep
    Wakes a successive flame ; the distant watch
    Discern its gleam, and raise a brighter fire,
    That o'er the lake Gorgopis streaming holds
    Its rapid course, and on the mountainous heights
    Of Ægiplanctus huge, swift-shooting spreads
    The lengthen'd line of light.   Thence onwards waves
    Its fiery tresses, eager to ascend
    The crags of Prone, frowning in their pride
    O'er the Saronic gulf: it leaps, it mounts

The summit of Arachne, whose high head
Looks down on Argos : to this royal seat
Thence darts the light that from th' Idæan fire
Derives its birth.   Rightly in order thus
Each to the next consigns the torch, that fills
The bright succession, whilst the first in speed
Vies with the last : the promised signal this
Given by my lord t' announce the fall of Troy."

SYMMONS.

" Twas Vulcan : sending forth the blazing light
From Ida's grove, and thence along the way
Hither the estafette of fire ran quick :
Fire kindled fire, and beacon spoke to beacon,
Ida to Lemnos, and the Hermæan ridge :
Next Athos, craggy mountain, Jove's own steep,
Took the great torch held out by Vulcan's isle.
Standing sublime, the seas to overcast,
Shone the great strength of the transmitted lamp ;
And the bright heraldry of burning pines
Shone with a light all golden like the sun
Rising at midnight on Macistus' watch-tower :
Nor did Macistus not bestir him soon,
Oppress'd with sleep, regardless of his watch ;
But kindled fires, and sent the beacon-blaze
To distance far beyond Euripus' flood,
To watchmen mounted on Messapian hills ;
They answer'd blazing, and pass'd on the news,
The grey heath burning on the mountain-top.
And now the fiery, unobscurèd lamp,
At distance far shot o'er Asopus' plain ;
And up the steep soft rising, like the moon,
Stood spangling bright upon Cithæron's hill.
There rose, to give it conduct on the road,
Another meeting fire ; nor did the watch
Sleep at the coming of the stranger light,
But burnt a greater blaze than those before :
Thence o'er the lake Gorgopis stoop'd the light,
And to the mount of Ægiplancton came,
And bade the watch shine forth, nor scant the blaze.
They burning high with might unquenchable,
Send up the waving beard of fire aloft,
Mighty and huge, so as to cast its blaze

Beyond the glaring promontory steep
Athwart the gulf Saronic all on fire ;
Thence stoop'd the light, and reach'd our neighbour watch-
tower,
Arachne's summit ; and from thence, derived
Here to the Atridæ's palace, comes this light
From the long lineage of the Idæan fire.
Such is the course of the lamp-bearing games,
When torches run in solemn festivals
One from another, in succession fill'd,
And the last runner and the first is victor.
Such are my proofs, and such the signal news,
Sent by my consort from the plains of Troy." [1]

Potter is excellent. He makes a mistake or two, but of no very great moment, for he has caught the spirit of the passage, and gives it with great animation. It would not be easy to do it better, or so well. Following a faulty reading, he introduces the Hellespont; whereas the word which he understood as Hellespont signifies the rising of the beacon over the sea. And he has ignorantly and absurdly made the word "Erica," which signifies heath (heather *Scoticè*, *ac multo melius*), a proper name, and made it a mountain with a "shaggy brow," thereby improperly adding another station. But let these mistakes pass, and let us repeat our praise of his most spirited translation.

[1] Mr Macaulay's admirable imitation of this celebrated passage is too well known to be quoted. The following description of "The Beacon Telegraph" by Mr Blew, in his elaborate translation of the *Agamemnon*, is animated and picturesque : –

"Hephæstus, from the hill of Ide, a brilliant blaze he cast,
And beacon unto beacon call'd, and on the bale-fire pass'd.
First Ida unto Lemnos' isle—then from the Hermæan crag
The peak of Jove, tall Athos, took the mighty meteor-flag ;
And onward still, with lightning track that bridged the broad sea's length,
The jocund lamp came travelling in the greatness of its strength ;
Till lifting, like the sun at noon, its flame of golden flake,
Unto Macistus' tower the pine its sparkling summons spake.
Nor slack was he, nor sluggishly forbore due watch to keep ;
Nor fail'd of his allotted charge, o'ercome by drowsy sleep :
But fast and far that beacon-star o'erstept Euripus' stream,
And to Messapius' watchers gave the greeting of its gleam.
By fire they answer'd—and forthwith the sign went on in turn,
High kindling, on its rocky stance, a pile of wither'd fern :
And onward still, with ray undimm'd, and strength that never slept,
Across Asopus' lowland plain the hurrying cresset leapt,

But Symmons has far excelled—outshone Potter—nor is he one whit inferior to Æschylus. It may look as if his description were elaborated into even greater splendour; but that effect is produced by the language in which he writes; he had to find equivalents—equipollents for the luminous and leaping Greek words; and if they were nowhere to be found, because they do not exist, he was forced by necessity to fix upon others that might do the business—and he has done so with the eye and imagination of a true poet.

" The Bard of the North," says Mr Symmons, " has several spirited descriptions of the burning of beacons, which glow with all the splendour of his vivid imagination.' Here is one of them, which has this moment been pointed out to us by our ingenious friend, Mr James Ballantyne, who every month *presses* Maga to his bosom till she leaves his embrace blushing like the rosy morn. It is delightful to compare the pictures of the Great and Kindred Poets, when their imaginations have been kindled by the same fires—in this instance, beacons.

> " Is yon the star, o'er Penchryst Pen,
> That rises slowly to her ken,
> And, spreading broad its wavering light,
> Shakes its loose tresses on the night ?
> Is yon red glare the western star ?—
> O, 'tis the beacon-blaze of war !
>
> .   .   .   .

Then rising, like a merry moon, upon Cithæron's height,
It waken'd, for the courier flame, a fresh relay of light.
Nor blind the watch, nor heedless of the far-transmitted flame ;
But trimm'd afresh, and forward sent, yet brighter than it came,
It flash'd along Gorgopis' marsh, up Ægiplanctos shot,
With stirring challenge that for lack of food it tarry not.
Nor call'd in vain ; with might and main, upon the heap they toss
Fresh fagots, and the mighty beard of flame send forth, to cross
The foreland cliff that beetleth o'er the deep Saronic sound,
Broad blazing ; then Arachne's steep it climb'd, and with a bound,
Along the watch-tower summits ran, that gird the city round :
Lit thence, o'er this, the royal roof of Atreus' sons, it plays,—
The beam, in right succession borne from Ida's parent blaze.
Thus snatching each from each their brand, the ready torchmen run,
When, by the first, and by the last, the fiery race is won :
And thus to thee aright I read yon signal-fire of joy—
The token from mine absent lord : the gage of conquer'd Troy."

The ready page, with hurried hand,
Awaked the need-fire's slumbering brand,
  And ruddy blush'd the heaven ;
For a sheet of flame, from the turret high,
Waved like a blood-flag on the sky,
  All flaring and uneven.
And soon a score of fires, I ween,
From height, and hill, and cliff, were seen ;
Each with warlike tidings fraught ;
Each from each the signal caught ;
Each after each they glanced to sight,
As stars arise upon the night.
They gleam'd on many a dusky tarn,
Haunted by the lonely earn ;
On many a cairn's grey pyramid,
Where urns of mighty chiefs lie hid ;
Till high Dunedin the blazes saw,
From Soltra and Dumpender Law ;
And Lothian heard the Regent's order,
That all should bowne them for the Border."

At the conclusion of Clytemnestra's description, the Chorus says,—

  " Hereafter to the gods, O Queen ! I'll pray.
  But now, in wondering pleasure at thy words
  I fain would stand, and hear them o'er again."

So say we of Sir Walter's.

Clytemnestra having thus gloriously gloated over the beacon-lights announcing that her husband would soon be at hand for her to murder him—though of that dreadful design as yet the Chorus knew not—she goes on uttering her dark sentences, and Potter felt the meanings of her speech well, and well does he comment on it : " It was observed in the preface to this tragedy, that the character of Clytemnestra was that of a high-spirited, close, determined, dangerous woman. This character now begins to unfold itself. She had, with deep premeditation, planned the murder of her husband; he was now returning; her soul must of course be full at this time of her horrid design, and all her thoughts intent upon the execution of it. We have in the speech (the one that follows) a strong proof this ; she is dark, sententious,

and even religious, so the Chorus understands her words, and
so she intends they should; but the very expressions by
which she wishes to conceal her purpose, by being ambiguous,
and by conveying a double meaning, so far mark the working
of her mind, *as to give us a hint what she is revolving there.*"
Read—with this intimation—is there not a fearful grandeur in
these dark lines? She has been speaking of the destruction
of Troy, sullenly and fiercely, and not with that bright exultation that would *otherwise* have been natural to the wife of the
Destroyer.

> ——— " If they (the victors) show
> Due reverence and homage to the gods
> Of that forsaken city and their fanes,
> They may chance 'scape such sad vicissitude,
> Nor feel themselves what they inflict on others ;
> But let no inferior lust, no thirst of gold,
> Light on their longing for disastrous spoils,
> Mad passion for those things 'tis sin to love !
> Let them beware ; they still want Heaven's high favour
> To bring them back unhurt ; they still have left
> The whole side of the Stadium's length to run.
> But should they come, their forfeits on their heads,
> With Heaven's high wrath benighted, then indeed
> The curse of blood might follow at their heels,
> And Troy's ensanguined sepulchres yield up
> Their charnell'd dead to cry aloud for vengeance,
> E'en should not Fortune blow them other ills.
> These are but woman's words ; but O prevail
> Our better destinies ; nor let the balance
> Hang in suspense ; *of many an offer'd blessing,*
> *I would have fix'd my heart and chosen this.*"

Clytemnestra re-enters her palace, and the Chorus again
uplifts its lugubrious strain, singing dolefully of the destruction
of Troy, and along with it that of many of the Grecian heroes.
Agamemnon, they know, is about to return; but still their
song is sad, and strewed with melancholy images. That
strange air of aimless fear still hangs over it, and we listen to
it with that indefinite apprehension which these two celebrated lines in " Lochiel's Warning " inspire,—

> " Though dim and despairing my sight I may seal,
> Yet man cannot hide what Heaven would reveal."

Thus, in place of hymning the living heroes, and at their happy head the King of Men—they chant the dirges of the dead.

> " Instead of man, to each man's home
> Urns and ashes only come,
> And the armour which they wore ;
> Sad relics to their native shore.
> For Mars, the barterer of the lifeless clay,
> Who sells for gold the slain,
> And holds the scale, in battle's doubtful day,
> High balanced o'er the plain,
> From Ilium's walls for men returns
> Ashes and sepulchral urns ;
> Ashes wet with many a tear,
> Sad relics of the fiery bier.
> Round the full urns the general groan
> Goes, as each their kindred own.
> One they mourn in battle strong,
> And one, that 'mid the arm'd throng
> He sunk in glory's slaughtering tide,
> And for another's consort died—
> Such the sounds that, mix'd with wail,
> In secret whispers round prevail :
> And Envy, join'd with silent griefs,
> Spreads 'gainst the two Atridæ chiefs,
> Who began the public fray,
> And to vengeance led the way.
>
> .   .   .   .   .   .
>
> My soul stands tiptoe with affright ;
> I stand like one with listening ear,
> Ready to catch the sound of fear ;
> And lift my eyes to see some sight
> Coming from the pall of night.
> For gods behold not unconcern'd from high,
> When smoking slaughter mounts the sky,
> The mighty murderers of the direful plain,
> For then the black Eriunyes rise,
> With Time their helper, and with Fate reversed,
> And make the mighty justice-slighting man
> Pale in the midst of Glory's proud career," &c.

Clytemnestra, who, we may suppose, has been inspecting within the palace all the preparations and instruments for murder—trying the fatal tunic with which her heroic husband's

arms are to be inextricably involved—feeling the edge of the
axe with her delicate but firm finger, all the while giving *such
a smile* to her paramour—Clytemnestra now reappears, and
hails the approach of a herald fast approaching from the beach
with his olive-boughs—using this singular but strong expression,

> " Lo ! Mud's brother,
> The parching, thirsty dust, proclaims his speed."

She then says to the Chorus—no doubt with a savage scowl
of a smile,—

> " Now we have got, my lords, one who will speak,
> Speak to your doubtings—not with treacherous flames
> Of mountain wood and ruddy smoke, but one
> Who, face to face, will swell our joy more high ;
> *Oh, but my tongue abhors ill-boding words—*
> *All looks well now—God grant it so may end."*

The Watchman spoke well—the Herald, who is a higher
character, speaks still better—and we have chosen his fine
speech as another test of the comparative merits of Potter and
Symmons.

ΚΗΡΥΞ.

Ἰὼ πατρῷον οὖδας ᾿Αργείας χθονὸς,
Δεκάτῳ σε φέγγει τῷδ᾽ ἀφικόμην ἔτους,
Πολλῶν ῥαγεισῶν ἐλπίδων μιᾶς τυχών.
Οὐ γάρ ποτ᾽ ηὔχουν τῇδ᾽ ἐν ᾿Αργεία χθονι
Θα:ὼν μεθέξειν φιλτάτου τάφου μέρος.
Νῦν χαῖρε μὲν χθών, χαῖρε δ᾽ ἡλίου φάος,
῞Υπατός τι χώρας Ζεὺς, ὁ Πύθιός τ᾽ ἄναξ,
Τόξοις ἰάπτων μηκέτ᾽ εἰς ἡμᾶς βέλη·
Ἅλις παρὰ Σκάμανδρον ἦλθες ἀνάρσιος·
Νῦν δ᾽ αὖτε σωτὴρ ἴσθι κἀπαγώνιος,
Ἄναξ Ἄπολλον. τούς τ᾽ ἀγωνίους θεοὺς
Πάντας προσαυδῶ, τόν τ᾽ ἐμὸν τιμάορον
῾Ερμῆν, φίλον κήρυκα, κηρύκων σέβας,
῞Ηρως τε τοὺς πέμψαντας, εὐμενεῖς πάλιν
Στρατὸν δέχεσθαι τὸν λελειμμένον δορός
Ἰὼ μέλαθρα βασιλίων, φίλαι στέγαι,
Σεμνοί τε θᾶκοι, δαίμονές τ᾽ ἀντήλιοι,
Εἴ που πάλαι, φαιδροῖσι τοισίδ᾽ ὄμμασι,
Δέξασθε κόσμῳ βασιλέα πολλῷ χρόνῳ.
Ἥκει γὰρ ὑμῖν φῶς ἐν εὐφρόνῃ φέρων
Καὶ τοῖσδ᾽ ἅπασι κοινὸν ᾿Αγαμέμνων ἄναξ.
᾿Αλλ᾽ εὖ νιν ἀσπάσασθε, καὶ γὰρ οὖν πρέπει,

Τροίαν καταπκάψαντα τοῦ δικηφόρου
Διὸς μακίλλῃ, τῇ κατιίργασται πίδον.
Βωμοὶ δ᾽ ἄἴστοι κὶ Θιῶν ἰδρύματα,
Καὶ σπίρμα πάσης ἰξαπόλλυται χθονός.
Τοιόνδι Τροία πιριζαλὼν ζιυκτήριον
"Αναξ 'Ατρείδης πρίσζυς ιὐδαίμων ἀνὴρ
"Ηκιι, τίισθαι δ᾽ ἀξιψτατος βροτῶν
Τῶν νῦν· Πάρις γὰρ οὔτι συντιλὴς πόλις
'Εξιύχιται τὸ δρᾶμα τοῦ πάθους πλίον.
Οφλὼν γὰρ ἁρπαγῆς τι καὶ κλοπῆς δίκην
Τοῦ ῥυσίου Θ᾽ ἥμαρτι καὶ πανώλιθρον
Αὐτόχθονον πατρῷον ἔθρισιν δόμον.
Διπλᾶ δ᾽ ἴτισαν Πριαμίδαι Θαμάρτια.

—V. 503-537.

NORTII.

" Oh paternal soil of the Grecian land !
In this tenth light of the year [1] have I reach'd thee,
Of many broken hopes having realised but one.
For never could I have confidently hoped that in this land of
  Argos
I should, when dead, be a sharer in a much-wish'd-for tomb :
Hail now, O Earth, and hail, thou light of the sun,
And Jupiter supreme over the country, and the Pythian king,
From thy bow no longer discharging weapons against us :
Implacable enough at Scamander wert thou to us ;
But now on the other hand be thou a saviour, and a deliverer of
  us from our struggles,
O King Apollo. The gods-that-preside-over-games also
All I invoke, and my protector
Mercury, the herald beloved, of heralds the divinity,
And the heroes (demigods) sending us forth (and) gracious again
To receive the army spared by the spear.
Hail, ye palaces of kings, abodes beloved,
Venerable seats, and sun-exposed deities,
If erst you ever (did),—do you now with these eyes serene
Receive becomingly the king, after a long time.
For he hath come—a light in the night—bringing to you,
And to all these in common King Agamemnon.
Propitiously then salute *him*—for this is becoming—
Who dug up Troy with the spade of justice-bearing
Jupiter, whereby the foundation hath been upturn'd.
And the altars are *nameless* [2] (things whereof nothing can be
  known) and the gods' seats,

---

[1] For—this light of the tenth year.

[2] "Αἶστοι, from α *priv.* and ἴσημι, to know ; that whereof nothing can be
known.

And the seed of all the land is utterly destroy'd.
Having imposed on Troy such a yoke,
The king, the son of Atreus the Elder, a prosperous man,
Has come, of being honour'd the most worthy of mortals
That now are : for neither Paris nor his associate city
Boasts that the deed done was greater than the suffering ;
For having incurr'd the penalty of rapine and of theft
He had forfeited his pledge of security ; and his utterly-ruin'd,
Aboriginal, paternal house hath he mow'd down.
Doubly then have the children of Priam render'd back the price
    of their offences."   ·

POTTER.

" Hail, thou paternal soil of Argive earth !
In the fair light of the tenth year to thee
Return'd, from the sad wreck of many hopes
This one I save ; saved from despair e'en this ;
For never thought I in this honour'd earth
To share in death the portion of a tomb.
Hail then, loved earth ; hail, thou bright sun ; and thou,
Great guardian of my country, Jove supreme ;
Thou, Pythian king, thy shafts no longer wing'd
For our destruction ; on Scamander's banks
Enough we mourn'd thy wrath ; propitious now
Come, King Apollo, our defence.   And all
Ye gods, that o'er the works of war preside,
I now invoke ; thee, Mercury, my avenger,
Revered by heralds, that from thee derive
Their high employ ; you heroes, to the war
That sent us, friendly now receive our troops,
The relics of the spear.   Imperial walls,
Mansion of kings, ye seats revered ; ye gods,
That to the golden sun before these gates
Present your honour'd forms ; if e'er of old
Those eyes with favour have beheld the king,
Receive him now, after this length of time,
With glory ; for he comes, and with him brings
To you, and all, a light that cheers this gloom :
Then greet him well ; such honour is his meed,
The mighty king, that with the mace of Jove
Th' avenger, wherewith he subdues the earth,
Hath levell'd with the dust the towers of Troy ;
Their altars are o'erturn'd, their sacred shrines,
And all the race destroy'd.   This iron yoke
Fix'd on the neck of Troy, victorious comes

The great Atrides, of all mortal men
Worthy of highest honours. Paris now,
And the perfidious state, shall boast no more
His proud deeds unrevenged : stript of his spoils,
The debt of justice for his thefts, his rapines,
Paid amply, o'er his father's house he spreads
With twofold loss the wide-involving ruin."

SYMMONS.

" Ho ho ! my native and paternal soil !
Ho ho ! my country, and the sweet approach
Of Argive land ! in ten long years return'd,
I stand upon thee gladly, O my country !
And save this one of many a shipwreck'd hope.
O much I fear'd I ne'er should see thy shores,
Nor when I died, be gather'd to thy lap.
Now Earth, all hail ! all hail, thou sun of light !
And Jove, this realm's great paramount ! and thou,
O King of Pytho, hurling from thy bow
Thy shafts no more against us ; full enough
We felt thy ire by sad Scamander's banks :
Now be our saviour, and our lord of games,
O King Apollo ! and I call ye all,
Ye Gods of Festivals, and thee, my patron,
Sweet Herald God ! whom heralds most adore ;
And ye, the worshipp'd Heroes of old times,
Who sent your armed sons to battle forth ;
Receive what now remains of us, the gleanings
Of hostile spears. O palace of our kings !
Dear roofs, and venerated judgment-seats !
And ye, sun-facing images of gods !
Now, now, if ever, beam with joyful eyes
Upon your king returning ;—lo ! he comes,
King Agamemnon, bringing now at last
A light in darkness, and a general shine
On you, on all the people, on all those
Who throng around. But greet him, greet him well
(Such honour is the mighty conqueror's meed),
Who, arm'd with vengeance and the mace of Jove,
Unloosed the stony, massy girths of Troy.
Ay, now Jove's spade has finish'd its dread work,
And made a mound of all that mighty field ;
Altars and fanes in unknown ruins lie,
And without seed lies all the blasted land.

Thus comes Atrides from the siege of Troy,
Which 'neath his yoke has bent her turrets high.
O happy, glorious, honourable man,
Deserving praise of men, far, far beyond
What any worthy of this age can claim.
The vaunts of Troy and Paris are no more,
Boasting the arm of Justice could not reach them ;
But it has spann'd them with a hand as large
As their offendings : the convicted thief
Has lost his main prize, and the ravisher
Has with his beauteous fair one lost himself,
And bared his father's house to the dire edge
Of naked ruin ; and old Priam's sons
Have with their blood his double forfeits paid."

Potter excellent—Symmons admirable.—The Chorus thus
accosts the eloquent Herald,—

" Herald of the Argives from the host, all health,
    And joy be with thee ! "

Herald,—

.   " Take me to ye, gods,
    I ne'er can live to greater joy than this !
    Meanwhile, where is Clytemnestra ? "

Symmons has rightly put into the mouth of the Chorus the
above words, which Potter, merely to oppose Heath, whom
he hated almost as bitterly as Gifford did Monk Mason and
Coxeter, assigns to Clytemnestra. " Potter," quoth Symmons,
" was to that critic what the elephant is said to be to the
rhinoceros." Symmons tells us—and we tell you—to observe,
that Clytemnestra, during this whole scene, being now fully
apprised of the taking of Troy, and of the approaching return
of her husband, and finding herself brought by events to the
eve of what she had long meditated, is apart, wrapt in
gloomy meditations, and gaining time to collect herself. In
the mean time, the dialogue goes on between the Herald and
the Chorus, which is very artfully conducted by the Poet,
and rendered intentionally obscure; the Chorus appearing
fearful of being overheard or understood by Clytemnestra, in
their covert complaints of her and Ægisthus during their
regency, under which it is insinuated, that it would have
been a crime to have expressed great regret at the absence

of Agamemnon. The Herald's part is also very characteristic; his curiosity is momentarily raised by the insinuations
of the Chorus; but on their declining to be immediately
explicit, buoyant with the joy of the moment, he forgets them
and their complaints, and returns to the narrative of his adventures. For that narrative we have no room—but it is the best
in poetry of the sufferings of campaigning—and contains a
glorious description of a bivouac.

The Unity of Action—and no action can be simpler—is
preserved in this play; but there seems to be a violation of
the Unity of Time. For what but a miracle could have
brought the Herald home so soon, supposing the exhibition
of the beacons to have taken place immediately on the taking
of Troy? But the truth is, as Mr Symmons says and shows,
that the Greek poets did not observe the minor Unities of
Time and Place so scrupulously as the French. Sophocles
presents in his *Trachiniæ* a more glaring example, in the
mission of Hyllus and his return (a distance of a hundred and
twenty Italian miles), which took place during the acting of
a hundred lines. In the *Eumenides*, Æschylus opens the
play at Delphi, and ends it at Athens. Aristotle, as Twining
properly remarks, does not lay down the Unity of Time *as a
rule;* but says that Tragedy endeavours to circumscribe the
period of its action to one revolution of the sun.

But Mr Symmons observes that, strictly speaking, the
Unity of Time is not violated in this play. How so? Why,
Æschylus the Bold has hazarded a miracle *off the stage,* artifi-
cially or clandestinely concealed from the attention of the
spectators; but everything *on the stage* proceeds rapidly and
consecutively in the space of a day, and nothing *there* occurs
to mark any greater lapse of time. The passions, the feelings
of the audience, under the influence of so great a Poet, could
admit of no marked delay, no interval; all their faculties
being wound up, and hurrying on to the horrid catastrophe.
Potter, too, writes with the same fine feeling of the truth.
" Æschylus," he says, " was as sensible as any of his critics
could be of the impropriety of making Agamemnon appear at
Argos the day after Troy was taken; but his plan required it—
and it is so finely executed, that he must be a critic *minorum
gentium* who objects to it. The whole narrative of the
Herald is calculated to soften this impropriety; a tempest

separates the royal ship from the Fleet; some god preserves
it, and Fortune, the deliverer, guides it into the harbour;
everything is as rapid and impetuous as the genius of
Æschylus, and the expression is so carefully guarded, that
no hint is given of the vessel's being at sea more than
one night." Müller, we are happy to see, though a German, also applauds all this daring, and says vigorously,
that Æschylus "fieri jussit." He ordered it so, and it was
right.

Clytemnestra, who had been apart during the previous
conversation between the Herald and the Chorus, now approaches, and addresses the Herald in a long hypocritical
speech—of which the hypocrisy, "the only evil thing that
walks unseen," is perfect. She sends a message to her
Lord.

> " Go bear this message to my noble lord :
>   ' Come quickly to thy city, much-loved Prince.
>   Come to thy consort true, whom thou wilt find
>   Such as thou left'st, a watch-dog on thy hearth,
>   Good, gentle, kind to thee, but to thy foes
>   A bitter enemy ; alike in all things ;
>   *One who has kept the print upon thy seals*
>   *For years unbroken and inviolate;*
>   *From all but thee a stranger still to pleasure,*
>   *And by the breath of evil fame unsullied*
>   *As the pure metal from the dyer's art.'* "

Lichas, in the *Trachiniæ*, bears the same message from
Deianira to Hercules. But Mr Symmons finely points out
the difference between the simplicity of her innocence, and
the artfulness of the other's guilt. Deianira, innocent and
attached, says nothing of her innocence or her attachment ;
but Clytemnestra, guilty, loudly professes both one and the
other.

The Herald then gives that most eloquent description of
storm and shipwreck alluded to by Potter, and the Chorus—
Clytemnestra having entered the palace—again takes up
the strain, almost as doleful as before, but containing one
passage of consummate beauty, of which we give Mr Symmons's translation. It is a description of Helen, the Destroyer of Ships—or of Helandros, the Destroyer of Men—
or of Heleptolis, the Destroyer of Cities.

" When first she came to Ilion's towers,
O what a glorious sight, I ween, was there !
The tranquil beauty of the gorgeous queen
Hung soft as breathless summer on her cheeks,
Where on the damask sweet the glowing Zephyr slept ;
And like an idol beaming from its shrine,
So, o'er the floating gold around her thrown
Her peerless face did shine ;
And though sweet softness hung upon their lids,
Yet her young eyes still wounded where they look'd.
She breathed an incense like Love's perfumed flower,
Blushing in sweetness ; so she seem'd in hue,
And pained mortal eyes with her transcendent view :
E'en so to Paris' bed the lovely Helen came.
But dark Erinnys, in the nuptial hour,
Rose in the midst of all that bridal pomp,
   Seated midst the feasting throng,
   Amidst the revelry and song ;
   Erinnys, led by Xenius Jove,
   Into the halls of Priam's sons,
   Erinnys of the mournful bower,
Where youthful brides weep sad in midnight hour."

But why tarries Agamemnon ? Where linger the wheels
of his chariot ? He comes—he comes—and with him the
captive Cassandra. The Chorus thus hails the king.—

   " O king ! O sacker of Troy, town divine !
   Spring from Atreus' godlike line,
   How shall I speak thee ? How admire ?" &c.

Agamemnon, before making any reply to their greeting, says
he must first salute Argos, and the indigenous Gods of the
Land. Having done so, how like a Warrior-King he speaks
of war !

   " Ye may now see the captive city far
   In smoke discernible : its embers burn.
   The hurricane of Ate scarce is spent :
   The ashes pale laid on their fever'd bed,
   Together with the dying city die,
   And gather up their latest breath to blow
   Clouds of rich freightage to the vasty skies !
   For this we are your debtors, mighty gods,

And we must pay you with a mindful heart,
And celebration of recording rites,
For our great hunters' toils with cunning hand
Laid to our hearts' content, and haughty Troy
(All for a woman lost) razed to the ground ;
Bearing the Argive dragon when the Horse
Yean'd in the city its terrific birth,
Who bounding burst, with helm and high-toss'd shield
Brandish'd in air, horrific on the night,
The Pleiads setting in their paly spheres ;
And the fierce lion made a bound in air,
And high o'er tower and temple rampant came,
And with red jaws lick'd up the blood of kings."

The King of Men then moralises and philosophises to the
Chorus in a style worthy of him, and then looking at his
palace, says,—

" But now straight entrance to the house I'll make,
There to pour out the gladness of my soul
Before the hearths unto my household gods,
Who gave me conduct to far distant climes,
And now return me to their sacred domes ;
And may firm victory abide for aye,
Since hitherto my steps she has attended."

And now Clytemnestra comes forth from the palace—and
how doth she meet her lord ?

" She-wolf of Greece, with unrelentless fangs,
That tearest the bowels of thy mangled mate !"

How dost thou hide thy murderous intents in that deep and
high-swelling bosom, on which lay last night the head of
Ægisthus ? That learned wiseacre, Is. Casaub., dares to say—
" Congressus primus Clytemnestræ et Agamemnonis. Hæc
tota pars friget. Æschylus *inscite;* Seneca evitavit hæc."
And afterwards he saith — " Hic proimum Clytemnestra
Agamemnonem, quam frigide, quam prolixe !" Poor gentleman ! he prefers Seneca to Æschylus ! Æschylus, in the
opinion of Is. Casaub. wrote here ignorantly—with no knowledge of human nature ! The address of Clytemnestra is
cold and frigid. So it is—and why ? Because her heart was
hot with its own hell—and therefore, to prevent the very
flames from bursting out of her mouth, she first compressed

her lips into frigidity—and then, when she felt that she had the flames safely smothered for a while, she became prolix—and then she ventured stealthily upon affectionateness of manner—and then at last she hailed the doomed Hero with the honeyed words of connubial love and delight, adoration and reverence. And Is. Casaub. said, " Æschylus *inscite!*" But Potter, who was a fine fellow, knew better, and his words are worthy of being recorded in Maga. " According to the simplicity of ancient manners," quoth this excellent and eloquent clergyman, " Clytemnestra should have waited to receive her husband in the house; but her affected fondness led her to disregard decorum. Nothing can be conceived more artful than her speech; but that shows that her heart had little (no) share in it; her pretended sufferings [she asserts she had thrice tried to hang herself, but always unfortunately got cut down.—C. N.] during his absence, are touched with great delicacy and tenderness; but had they been real, she would not have stopped him with the querulous recital; the joy for his return, had she felt that joy, would have broke out first; this is deferred to the latter part of her address; then, indeed, she has amassed every image expressive of emotion; but her solicitude to assemble these, leads her beyond nature, which expresses her strong passions in broken sentences, and with a nervous brevity, not with the cold formality of a set harangue. Her last words are another instance of the double sense which expresses reverence to her husband, but intends the bloody design with which her soul was agitated."

Thus far Potter, who had a soul to understand Æschylus, though hardly a pen equal to translate him; but Mr Symmons has,—and what can be nobler, in his version, than the concluding part of Clytemnestra's address?

> —— " Meantime
> The gushing fountains, whence so many tears
> . Chasing each other trickled on my cheeks,
> Are quite run out, and left without a drop;
> And these sad eyes, which so late took their rest,
> Are stain'd with blemish by late watching hours,
> Weeping for thee by the pale midnight lamp,
> That burnt unheeded by me. In my dreams
> I lay, my couch beset with visions sad,

And saw thee oft in melancholy woe !
More than the waking Time could show, I saw
A thousand dreary congregated shapes,
And started oft, the short-lived slumber fled,
Scared by the night-fly's solitary buzz :
But now my soul, so late o'ercharged with woe,
Which had all this to bear, is now the soul
Of one who has not known what mourning is,
And now would fain address him thus, e'en thus :
This is the dog who guards the wattled fold ;
This is the mainsheet which the sails and yards
Of some tall ship bears bravely to the winds ;
This is the pillar whose long shaft from earth
Touches the architrave of some high house ;
A child who is the apple of the eye
To the fond father who has none but him ;
Ken of the speck of some fair-lying land,
Seen by pale seamen well-nigh lost to hope :
A fair day, sweetest after tempest showers ;
A fountain fresh, with crystal running clear,
To the parch'd traveller who thirsts for drink :
So in each shift of sad necessity
'Tis sweet to be deliver'd hard beset.
Thus my fond heart, with speeches such as these,
Pays to his worthiness what she thinks due :
Let no one grudge me the sweet pleasure now,
But think upon the sorrows I have borne.
But now, O thou most precious to my eyes !
Light from thy car : but soft ; step not on earth,
Lay not thy foot, O king ! Troy's overturner,
On the bare ground. Why dally ye, my women,
Who have't in charge, by my command, to lay
The field with tapestry whereon he walks ?
Quick strew it, cover it ; let all the road
Be like a purple pavement to the house.
That Dikè to his house may lead him on
As the unhoped-for comer should be led :
My care, that sleeps not, shall do all the rest :
Do all that duty at my hand requires,
If Gods will hear me, and the Fates allow."

The king replies with much tenderness, calling Clytemnestra

" Daughter of Leda ! guardian of my house !
Well hast thou spoken, as a true wife should ; "—

but he tries to dissuade her from her fond intention of strewing his path with purple garments—pageantries these fit only
for the gods. Well saith Potter, that Agamemnon appears
here in the most amiable light—he knows his dignity, and is
not insensible to the fame which attends him as the conqueror
of Asia ; but he shows that manly firmness of mind, and that
becoming moderation which distinguishes the sober state of
the King of Argos from the barbaric pride of an Asiatic
monarch. The part which he has to act is indeed short ; but
it gives us a picture of the highest military glory and of true
regal virtue, and shows us that, as a man, he was modest,
gentle, and humane.

> " A being, as I am, but of to-day,
> To walk in such high state bedizen'd out
> With flaunting purples, studiously devised
> With quaint embroidery, beneath my feet,—
> Not without fears and terrors could I do it.
> According to a man's height, not a god's,
> Take measure of the duty thou wouldst pay me.
> Though not on purple rests she her bare feet,
> Nor yet with cloth-of-gold is cover'd o'er,
> Fame is heard far and wide —so loud she cries.
> To be possess'd of that clear soul within
> That thinks no folly, but is wise and meek,
> Is the most precious jewel God can give :
> And blazon not the happiness of man
> Till he has ended life, still ever blest
> In that sweet state which, fixèd to the end,
> Stands like a constant summer all his days.
> Let me speed thus hereafter in all things
> As well as up to now, my soul will be
> Full of a happy confidence serene."

But Clytemnestra will not be dissuaded from her fond purpose
of strewing the ground with purple garments for his feet,
walking, after that ten years' absence, into his palace—and
the King, relenting, at last gives his consent. He calls on
" some one " to " take off the pride of sandals from his feet "
—" the thralls of the haughty treading," lest the " grudge of
some god's eye throw its long cast upon him,"—and then,
showing Cassandra, requests the Queen to be kind to her ; for
that " God beholds the gentle ruler governing with mildness

his subject slaves." He then declares that he is ready so to walk into the Palace as she wishes :—

> "I will unto the mansions of the house
> Move, footing it on purples as I go."

Then exclaims Clytemnestra,—

> "Who'll quench that sea, which gives us plenteous store
> Of beaming purples from her azure caves,
> Eternal dyer of the blood-red robes,
> That sparkle o'er the silver's paly shine ?
> Thy house, O King, has plenteous store of these ; ·
> 'Tis no poor house, blest be the gracious gods !
> These gorgeous robes were dust beneath my feet,
> When deep in domes oracular I pray'd,
> Kiss'd the pale shrines, and pour'd forth many a vow
> To give the gods all I could give, in barter
> Of their kind grace to save a life so dear !
> The root is living, and the laurel thrives,
> And makes a sweet walk for us under shade,
> When the hot dog-star rages in the skies.
> The lord is come ! the household hearth burns bright,
> And merrily the winter days we pass.
> And now the pale grapes turn to luscious wine,
> The vintage comes, Jove treads the purple vat ;
> We joy beneath the noontide air imbrown'd,
> Stretch'd in cool zephyrs under bower and hall,
> And sweetly live ! Our lord he is at home !
> A man in prime, frequenting his glad halls.
> Jove ! Jove ! thou perfect and perfecting one,
> Perfect my prayers, and whatsoe'er to do
> Thou hast in hand, to do it be thy care."

All this is very dreadful—nor do we hesitate to say, equal to anything in Shakespeare. In translating Æschylus, Symmons has here "quitted himself like Samson."

How characteristic and sublime this last speech of Clytemnestra ! With all the pomp, profusion, and prodigality of a Queen, has she lavished cost upon cost unappreciable, on the pageant that leads her victim into the house of murder ; and with what a frenzied eloquence of exulting joy does she pour over it intenser splendour ! She bathes and steeps it all in the poetry of blood. When she calls the sea

> "Eternal dyer of the blood-red robes,"

you feel on what her imagination is running,—the tunic in which her husband is about to be helplessly involved in the bath, empurpled then as the garments on which, to gratify her, he now sets unwillingly his princely feet. She pours a brighter light, because never before was her heart so elate, upon the household hearth, than ever she saw it shining with ere she meditated murder.

"The lord is come ! the household hearth burns bright ! "

And then how she revels, seemingly in a holy joy, over the holiest images of domestic bliss ! She would have said to her husband, "there's blood upon thy face ! " She would have touched it with her lips, licked it with her tongue, an antepast of her revenge. Believe all that welcoming sincere, and she seems an angel. Know that 'tis all deceitful, and she is worse than the wickedest of the Demons. How religious ! How impious ! How blasphemous !

> "Jove ! Jove ! thou perfect and perfecting one,
> Perfect my prayers, and whatsoe'er to do
> Thou hast in hand, to do it be thy care."

Turn from Æschylus to Shakespeare, from Agamemnon to Macbeth. When King Duncan is about to enter the Castle in which he is murdered, what says he ?

> "This Castle hath a pleasant seat ; the air
> Nimbly and sweetly recommends itself
> Unto our gentle senses.
> *Banquo.* This guest of summer,
> The temple-haunting martlet, does approve,
> By his loved mansionry, that the heaven's breath
> Smells wooingly here ; no jutty, frieze, buttress,
> Nor coigne of vantage, but this bird hath made
> His pendent bed and procreant cradle : where they
> Most breed and haunt, I have observed, the air
> Is delicate."

And how does Lady Macbeth receive her king ?—she who some short hour before had said,

> " Come ! thick night,
> And pall thee in the dunnest smoke of hell !
> That my keen knife see not the wound it makes !"

Why, she receives her king as a lady should, with bland aspect

and a gentle voice, but *over-courteously*, mark ye that, for the
wife of a Highland Thane.

> " All our service
> In every point twice done, and then done double,
> Were poor and single business, to contend
> Against those honours deep and broad wherewith
> Your majesty loads our house : for those of old,
> And the late dignities heap'd up to them,
> We rest your hermits."

'Tis not so bad, perhaps, to murder one's king as one's husband. But both are bad, very bad ; and then such hypocrisy
is unpardonable !

People will write about what they do not understand—
perhaps they are doing so now ; but we hope the best. The
ingenious reviewer of Schlegel on the Drama, in the *Edinburgh Review* (the number is an old one, and the reviewer,
we believe, was Mr Hazlitt), endeavours, after Schlegel, to
state the essential distinction between the peculiar spirit of
the modern or *romantic* style of art, and the antique or classical. All he can make out is this—that the moderns employ
a power of illustration which the ancients did not, in comparing the *object* to other things, and suggesting other ideas of
beauty or love than those which seem to be naturally inherent
in it. And he explains his meaning by reference to Shakespeare's description of soldiers going to battle,—" All plumed
like estriches, like eagles new-bathed, wanton as goats, wild
as young bulls." " That," he says, "is too bold, figurative,
and profuse of dazzling images, for the mild equable tone of
classical poetry, which never loses sight of the object in the
illustration. The ideas of the ancients were too exact and
definite, too much attached to the material form or vehicle in
which they were conveyed, to admit of those rapid combina-
tions, those unrestrained flights of fancy, which, glancing from
earth to heaven, unite the most opposite extremes, and draw
the happiest illustrations from things the most remote."
Alas! for the futility of philosophical criticism, when the
philosopher and critic happens to be utterly ignorant of the
life and soul of the subject-matter on which he philosophises !
There is no glancing from earth to heaven in that passage of
Shakespeare. The images are closely connected with each
other, and with the earth—estriches and eagles—goats and

bulls. But let the reader look back on Clytemnestra's first speech of welcome to Agamemnon, and to her speech on his agreeing to walk over the purple path to the palace—and then consider with himself on the knowledge or ignorance, the wisdom or folly, of saying that the ancients "never lost sight of the object in the illustration;" and that to do so would not be consistent with the "mild equable tone of classical poetry"!!!

Agamemnon is now within the palace which he will never again leave alive, and the Chorus renews his wailings—more woeful, the nearer they come to the catastrophe. Portents keep flitting before his eyes, and then again he recovers courage, and chants a less lugubrious strain. He labours, says Mr Symmons, under a forced and involuntary inspiration. In his character of man, and with reference merely to his human faculties, he is described as totally unconscious and unsuspicious of a plot, not only then, but even subsequently, when the catastrophe is presented more to his eyes; but in his character of prophet, and actuated by a sudden inspiration, he, throughout one passage in this Ode, darkly adumbrates the death of Agamemnon. He sings,—

> "Many a time the gallant Argosie,
> That bears man's destiny with outspread sails,
> In full career before the prosperous gales,
> Strikes on a hidden rock,
> And founders with a hideous shock!"

That image is perhaps but the suggestion of a melancholy fancy, brooding over the instability of human affairs. But having been led to this point by an involuntary train of reflections, here, says Mr Symmons, very finely, "here, as it were, he scents the blood; he catches, as it were, a glimpse behind the curtain, when all of a sudden it drops, and leaves him in darkness, amidst the embers of his expiring inspiration." Thus,—

> "But O! upon the earth when once is shed
> Black deadly blood of man,
> Who will call up the black blood from the ground—
> With moving incantation's charm?
> Check'd not Jove himself the man,
> The mighty leech, who knew so well the art
> To raise the silent dead?

> I pause ! some fate from Heaven forbids
> The fate within me utter more,
> Else had my heart outran my tongue,
> And pour'd the torrent o'er.
> Silence and darkness close upon my soul,
> She roars within, immured,
> And in the melancholy gloom
> Of dying embers fades away ! "

But where, all this time, has been Cassandra? Sitting mute and motionless in her chariot, before the palace. Agamemnon and his train have all entered within the gates, all but the Trojan Princess and Prophetess. But Clytemnestra having got her prime victim into her clutches, now seizes upon the captive. She comes out to order in Cassandra, with words of unkindness and insult, that harrow up one's soul. " Come forth out of that wain, nor be too overweening —too high-stomached for thy lot. What! she hears me not —the language she is mistress of is strange—and like the swallow's, a barbarian talk. Nay, I have no time to dally with her. Cannot she at least speak with inarticulate barbarian hand?" Still Cassandra utters not a word. The Chorus, always kind, tries to soothe her into speech ; but she remains stone-still and stone-mute. Her looks are waxing wild. For the Chorus says, " That stranger maid, the manner of her bearing is, as it were, of a wild beast's newly caught! "— " Why, yes," cries Clytemnestra, savagely ; " why, sure she looks as if she would rave — she who comes among us from a new-sacked city with all its horrors fresh upon her soul ! She champs, and knows not yet how to bear the bridle; but soon shall her bloody mettle be foamed away. But no longer will I submit to such dishonouring ; thus casting away words upon *Her!*" and Clytemnestra re-enters the palace.

Then comes the Scene of Scenes—the Inspiration of Inspirations—the Immortal Prophetic Ravings of Cassandra. We remember dear old Henry Mackenzie once descanting to us with his mild volubility on the prodigious power the Poets of our modern ages possessed in describing the workings of disordered intellect—a power which, he said, was unknown to the ancients. He had forgotten all the Three Greek Tragedians ; but we ventured to read off-hand—translating as we went—the madness of Cassandra. The old man was astonished, and confessed that it was equal to anything in Shakespeare—to Lear!

"O woe, woe, woe! O Earth! O Gods! Apollo! Apollo!"

So raves she for a while, the Chorus catching the contagion, and wailing in dismal harmony with the Prophetess. Symmons has here all the spirit of Æschylus.

CASSANDRA.

"Ha! ha! that dismal and abhorred house!
The good gods hate its dark and conscious walls!
It knows of kinsmen by their kinsmen slain,
And many a horrid death-rope swung!
A house, where men like beasts are slain!
The floor is all in blood!

CHORUS.

The stranger seems sharp-scented like a hound,
And searches as for bodies she would find!

CASSANDRA.

These are my witnesses! I follow them!
Phantoms of children! terribly they weep!
Their throats cut! and the supper that I see
Of roast flesh smoking, that their father eats!

CHORUS.

We heard, O prophetess, of thy great name;
Ay—but we want no prophets in this house.

CASSANDRA.

Alas! ye gods, what is she thinking on?
And what is this that looks so young and fresh?
Mighty, mighty is the load
She is unravelling in these dark halls!
A foul deed for her dear friends plotteth she,
Too sore to bear, and waxing past all cure!
Where's succour? fled far off! Where's help? it stands at bay!

CHORUS.

What means she now? 'twas lately Atreus' feast;
'Tis an old story, and the city's talk.

CASSANDRA.

Alas! ah wretch, ah! what art thou about?
A man's in the bath—beside him there stands
One wrapping him round—the bathing-clothes drop,
Like shrouds they appear to me, dabbled in blood!

O for to see what stands there at the end !
Yet 'twill be quick—'tis now upon the stroke !
A hand is stretch'd out, and another, too !
As though it were a-grasping—look, look, look !

CHORUS.

'Tis yet all dark to me : by riddles posed,
I find no way in these blind oracles.

CASSANDRA.

Ha, ha ! Alas, alas ! What's that ?
Is that hell's dragnet that I see ?
Dragnet ! or woman ! she, the very she
Who slept beside thee in the midnight bower,
Wife and murd'ress ! Howl, dark quires !
　　Howl in timbrel'd anthems dark
　　For Atreus' deadly line,
　　And the stony shower of blood.

CHORUS.

Ye gods ! what vengeance of a Fury's this
Thou bidd'st take up her clarion in these halls ?
　　As I heard thy doleful word,
　　Chased is my merry sprite,
　　And trickling up my heart has run
　　The blood-drop changed to saffron hue ;
　　Which from the spear-fallen man
　　Drops apace upon the ground,
　　Flitting together with the rays
　　Of the setting sun of life.

CASSANDRA.

Ha, ha ! see there ! see there !
Keep the bull from the heifer, drive, drive her away !
The bull is enchafed and hoodwink'd, and roars ;
His black branching horns have receivèd the death-stab !
He sprawls, and falls headlong ! he lies in the bath,
Beside the great smouldering cauldron that burns :
The cauldron burns,—it has a deadly blue ! "

In many a lovely lay Cassandra then laments her lost
delights—when like a nightingale she used to sing in her
native groves—and interweaves magnificent pictures of the
destruction of Troy. All holy feasts, sacrifice, and blood of
kine, when her father kept festival in his old bowers, all unavailing ! Nought availed the sacrifice gorged with the blood

of the rich meadow-feeders, to save the sacred city! "She passed through the storm of passion and suffering, even as I now shall pour out soon my warm blood upon the earth!" "Hush! hush!" sings the Chorus—"'Tis some God who hath put that bad sprite into thy mind—with the power of a demon, and with strong heavy spells, making death-bearing outcries and horrible moans! I am confounded—and know not what may be the end." Cassandra cries, "But thou'lt know it soon! No longer like a bride veils the God his visage! The oracle peeps through the mistiness, driving the clouds eastwards. Blow! blow! ye winds! for soon he will come! he will come! rolling his woes upon the beach of storms! soon out of the troubled deep will he stir up huger far, and dashing in daylight a wave against the eastern cliff!"

> " I shall have no more
> To teach you in enigmas; I'll speak plain.
> And be ye witness whilst I, snuffing blood,
> Run on the footsteps of things done of old.
> Pale phantoms brood within yon guarded towers,
> And ne'er do vanish from the spectred halls ;
> Screams are heard nightly, and a dismal din
> Of strange, terrific, and unearthly quires,
> Singing in horrid, full harmonic chord !
> Like what they sing of! nothing good I ween !
> And there are those, who bide within the house,
> Right hard to drive such inmates out of doors,
> For, blood of mortal man since they have drank,
> Their riot more unquenchable does grow ;
> The Masque of Sisters! the Erinnyes drear !
> They are all seated in the rooms above,
> Chanting how Atè came into the house
> In the beginning : gloomily they look !
> Each sings the lay in catches round, each has
> Foam on her lips, and gnashes grim her teeth,
> Where heavily the incestuous brother sleeps,
> Stretch'd in pale slumber on the haunted bed.
> Ha ! do the shafts fly upright at the mark ?
> Fly the shafts right, or has the yew-bow miss'd ?
> Methinks the wild beast in the covert's hit ;
> Or rave I, dreaming of prophetic lies,
> Like some poor minstrel knocking at the doors ?
> Come, bear thou witness, out with it on oath,
> That I know well the old sins of this house !"

" Who gave thee," asks the Chorus, " the prophetic power ? "
"Apollo !   Apollo ! he was the champion who vehemently
breathed upon me the breath of love and pleasing fire : I said
it should be, but I spoke him false—and for my transgression
none believed my words."

" O ! O ! hu ! hu ! alas !

The pains again have seized me ! my brain turns !
Hark to the alarum and prophetic cries !
The dizziness of horror swims my head !
D'ye see those yonder, sitting on the towers ?
Like dreams their figures !   Blood-red is their hair !
Like young ones murder'd by some kinsman false ;
Horrible shadows ! with hands full of flesh !
Their bowels and their entrails they hold up,
Their own flesh. O most execrable dish !
They hold it ; out of it their father ate !
But in revenge of them there's one who plots,
A certain homebred, crouching, coward lion ;
Upon his lair the rolling lion turns,
And keeps house close, until the coming of
My master !—said I master ?   Out ! alas !
I am a slave, and I must bear the yoke.
King of the ships, and sacker of great Troy,
Thou know'st not what a hateful bitch's tongue,
Glozing and fawning, sleek-faced all the while,
Will do! like Atè stealing in the dark !
Out on such daring ! female will turn slayer
And kill the male !   What name to call her ?   Snake,
Horrible monster, crested amphisbæna,
Or some dire Scylla dwelling amid rocks,
Engulfing seamen in her howling caves !
The raving of Hell's mother fires her cheeks,
And, like a pitiless Mars, her nostrils breathe
To all around her war and trumpet's rage.
O what a shout was there ! it tore the skies
As in the battle when the tide rolls back !
'Twas the great championess—how fierce, how fell !
No, 'tis all joy, and welcome home, sweet lord,
The war is o'er, the merry feast's begun.
Well, well, ye don't believe me—'tis all one.
For why ! what will be, will be ; time will come ;
Ye will be there, and pity me, and say,
' She was indeed too true a prophetess.'

CHORUS.

The Thyestean feast of children's flesh!
I know it, and I shudder! Fear is on me,
Hearing it nothing liken'd at or sketch'd,
The very truth ; but for those other things,
I heard! and fall'n out from the course I run.

CASSANDRA.

I say thou shalt see Agamemnon's death!

CHORUS.

Hush, hush, unhappy one, lie still thy tongue!"

" What MAN?" asks the Chorus, " What man such execrable
deed designs?" "Of murder are their thoughts?" "I
heard strange things, strange rumours!—yet the name of a
murderer I heard not!" "And yet I know the Greek tongue
—ay, I could speak!"

" O what a mighty fire comes rolling on me!
Help! help! Lycean Apollo! Ah me! ah me!
She there, that two-legg'd lioness! lying with
A wolf, the highbred lion being away,
Will kill me! woeful creature that I am!
And like one busy mixing poison up,
She'll fill me such a cup too in her ire!
She cries out, whetting all the while a sword
'Gainst him, 'tis me, and for my bringing here
That such a forfeit must be paid with death!
O why then keep this mockery on my head ?
Off with ye, laurels, necklaces, and wands!
The crown of the prophetic maiden's gone!
[*Tearing her robes.*
Away, away! die ye ere yet I die!
I will requite your blessings, thus, thus, thus!
Find out some other maiden, dight her rich,
Ay, dight her rich in miseries like me!
And lo! Apollo! himself! tearing off
My vest oracular! Oh! cruel god!
Thou hast beheld me, e'en in these thy robes,
Scoff'd at when I was with my kinsmen dear,
And made my enemies' most piteous despite,
And many a bad name had I for thy sake ;
A Cybele's madwoman, beggar priestess,
Despised, unheeded, beggar'd and in hunger ;
And yet I bore it all for thy sweet sake.

And now to fill thy cup of vengeance up,
Prophet, thou hast undone thy prophetess !
And led me to these passages of death !
A block stands for the altar of my sire ;
It waits for me, upon its edge to die,
Stagger'd with blows—in hot red spouting blood !
Oh ! oh ! but the great gods will hear my cries
Shrilling for vengeance through the vaulted roofs !
The gods will venge us when we're dead and cold.
Another gallant at death-deeds will come !
Who's at the gates ?—a young man, fair and tall,[1]
A stranger, by his garb, from foreign parts ;
Or one who long since has been exiled here :
A stripling, murderer of his mother's breast !
Brave youth, avenger of his father's death !
He'll come to build the high-wrought architrave,
Surmounting all the horrors of the dome.
I say, the Gods have sworn that he shall come.
His father's corse (his crest lies on the ground)
Rises, and towers before him on the road !
What ! mourning still ? what ! still my eyes in tears ?
And here, too, weeping on a foreign land ?
I, who have seen high-tower'd Ilion's town
Fall, as it fell ; whilst they who dwelt therein
Are, as they are ! before high-judging Heaven !
I'll go and do it ! I'll be bold to die !--
I have a word with ye, ye gates of Hell !
                    [*To the gates of the palace as she is about to enter.*
I pray ye, let me have a mortal stroke,
That without struggling, all this body's blood
Pouring out plenteously, in gentle stream
Of easy dying, I may close my eyes !"

" O woeful creature," sings the Chorus—" woeful, too, and wise ! O maid ! thou hast been wandering far and wide ! But if in earnest thou dost know thy fate, why like a heifer, goaded by a god, why fearless dost thou walk to the altar ?"—" Foh ! foh ! foh !" " What means foh ! foh ! Some loathing at thy heart ?"—" The house breathes scents of murderous dropping blood !" " How so ? 'tis smell of burning sacrifice !"—" Like is the vapour as from out a tomb !" " A dismal character thou givest this house !"—" Well ! well ! I'll enter, carrying with me all my shrieks ! I'll enter ! E'en in these horrid domes I'll wail aloud myself and Agamemnon. Life, farewell ! I've had

[1] Orestes.

enough of *thee!* But remember me! A dying woman speaks!
For maid one day shall die wife! man for man! for that ill-
starred husband!"

> "Once more! once more! oh let my voice be heard!
> I love to sing the dirges of the dead,
> My own death-knell, myself my death-knell ring!
> The sun rides high, but soon will set for me;
> O sun! I pray to thee by thy last light,
> And unto those who will me honour do,
> Upon my hateful murderers wreak the blood
> Of the poor slave they murder in her chains,
> A helpless, easy, unresisting victim!
> O mortal, mortal state! and what art thou?
> E'en in thy glory comes the changing shade,
> And makes thee like a vision glide away!
> And then misfortune takes the moisten'd sponge,
> And clean effaces all the picture out!"

Cassandra enters the palace, and the Chorus, confounded and
lost in awe, moralises over the dangerous glories of high estate.
"The gods," they say, "have blessed the arms of our king!
The gods have given him the city of Priam. Home has he
returned with celestial honours. But what if now he is to
rue the blood of olden times, and dying to pay forfeit to the
dead! Oh! who of mortals, as he hears this story told, would
wish not that his own horoscope might be beneath a low
and harmless star!"

> "*Agamemnon (within).*
> O! O! WITHIN THERE! O! STABB'D TO DEATH!
> *First Chorus.*
> HIST! SOME ONE CRIES! I HEARD A VOICE CRY STABB'D!
> *Agamemnon.*
> O! O! AGAIN! ANOTHER BLOW! O! O!
> *Second Chorus.*
> 'TIS THE KING'S VOICE! YE GODS! THE DEED IS DOING!
> *Third Chorus.*
> HARK! LET US QUICKLY COUNCIL WHAT TO DO!
> *Fourth Chorus.*
> LET'S RAISE THE TOWN, AND CRY THROUGH ALL THE STREETS,
> HELP! HELP! AND SUCCOUR TO THE PALACE-GATES!"

Who had murdered the King of Men?—who? Why—who
could it with any propriety have been but the Queen of

Women?   'Twas fitting that none but Clytemnestra should murder Agamemnon.   He was her own husband—she alone had a right to show him into the bath, with her own hands to put the tunic tenderly over his shoulders, and to enclose his heroic arms within its inextricable folds, and then to smite him on the forehead with her two-edged axe — once and again—till down he fell, as Homer says, somewhere in the Odyssey, like an ox at the stall.   There was no one who dared, at the instigation of Cassandra, to keep the heifer from the bull.   She gored him to death, and then filled all the byre with her lowings and her bellowings, till echoes shook all the stalls, and the floor ran with blood.   You would not surely have had the cowardly Ægisthus to slay his sovereign?   He was a dolt —she was a demon.   " Fierce as ten furies, terrible as hell." she strode out of the bath, forth from the palace—and, lo ! she comes with the bloody axe over her shoulders, and proclaims the deed to the Chorus,. that they, like ballad-singers, may chant it over Argos.   Lo ! she comes ! she is here—and hush ! for she is about to speak.

——— " These hands have struck the blow !
'Tis like the deeds that have been done of yore !
Past ! and my feet are now upon the spot !
And so I did it, and I'll not deny it,
That fly he could not, nor himself defend !
A net without an outlet, as it were
A drag for fishes, round about I staked,
An evil garment ! yet all richly wrought !
I smote him twice : after two groans his limbs
Sunk under him, and then upon the ground
I clove at him again with a third blow,
To quit my vow to Hades under ground,
Warden of dead men in the pale blue lake !
Thus falling, his own life he renders up,
Sighing and sobbing such a mighty gush,
Which spouted from his streaming wounds amain,
That he cast on me the black bloody drops,
In that black dew rejoicing, as the seeds
Joy at the coming of the heaven-sent shower
Raining upon them, in the blowing hour,
When the sweet blossoms glow with purple birth.
This being e'en so, ye prime of Argive men,
Rejoice ye, if rejoicing be your mood.
I am so full of joy, that if 'twere seemly

To pour libations on a corpse, I would do it ;
And just it were—ay, most exceeding just.
With such accursed potions he who here
Has fill'd a chalice, drinks it off himself !

CHORUS.

Amazement ! that a woman should thus speak !
What horrid boldness ! o'er her husband's corse !

CLYTEMNESTRA.

Ye try me like a woman weak in mind.
My heart shakes not, my tongue proclaims the deed.
And thou, or praise, or blame me, as thou wilt,
'Tis one to me. He there is Agamemnon,
My spouse—a corpse ! this right hand did the work,
A righteous handicraftsman ! Even so !

CHORUS.

What evil thing, O woman ! hast thou ate,
Eatable, nursed upon earth's venom'd lap,
Or potable, from out the hoary sea,
That thou hast put this sacrifice to burn
Amidst the curses of the tongues of men !
Thou hast cast him from thee, thou hast cut him off,
Thou'lt be cast off thyself !
A mighty hate unto thy country's men !

CLYTEMNESTRA.

Now ye do doom me from this city flight
And hatred, and to have the tongues of men
In curses on me ; but to this man then,
No, not one word in pity didst thou speak,
Who thought no more his tender child to spare
Than a young lamb from fleecy pastures torn
From out the midst of his unnumber'd sheep,
His child, and mine ! the dearest of my womb !
When he her blood a drear enchantment pour'd
To lull the howlings of the Thracian blast !
Wasn't that a man to drive out from the gates
To expiate pollutions ? But to me,
Sitting in audience of my deeds, thou art
A harsh judge ! But I say this unto thee !
Threaten away, for I too am prepared
In the like manner—rule me, if thou canst
Get by thy hand the mastery—rule me then—
But if the contrary be the doom of God,
I'll teach ye lessons for greybeards to learn."

Then follows a dreadful colloquy between Clytemnestra and the Chorus. Her soul is up in the clouds—his soul is down in the dust. She yells like an eagle, he sobs like a pigeon—she growls like a lion, he groans like a stricken deer—what careth the Fury for the idle imprecations of a silly old man ?   He tells her,

> "Thy soul is maddening yet
> As on the gore-drops fresh and wet !
> A drop upon thy eyes does show
> Of unavenged blood !
> The time will come, when, left alone,
> Thou'lt wring thy hands, and vainly moan
> Thy friends away ! Thy murderers by,
> Thou wilt pay blow for blow !"

What hath she to say in answer to that ?   Quails she, in her pride of place, already with remorse ?   Sees she already the snaky sister ?   Shudders she at the avenging phantom of her own son—Orestes doomed to shed in expiation his own mother's blood ?   You shall hear.   She calls on the Chorus to listen to her defence.

CLYTEMNESTRA.

> " And thou shalt hear my just and solemn oath !
> By the full vengeance taken for my child,
> By Atè and Erinnys, at whose shrines
> I've slain this man, a bloody sacrifice,
> I think not in the House of Fear to walk.
> Whilst on my hearth Ægisthus burneth fire,
> As he is wont, his heart still true to mine :
> For he's my boldness, and no little shield.
> Low lies the man who did me deadly wrong ;
> Low lies the minion of Troy's fair Chryseïs :
> And she his captive, and his soothsayer,
> His paramour, his lovely prophetess,
> She whom he trusted, true to him in bed,
> And, on the naval galleys as she rode,
> Not unrequited, what these two have done !
> For he e'en so ; and she most like a swan
> Kept singing still her last song in the world,
> A deadly, wailing, melancholy strain :
> Now on the earth she lies, stretch'd out in blood,
> And her dishevell'd tresses sweep the ground :
> Cold sweats of death sit on her marble face ;
> His love ! his beauty ! 'Twas to me he brought
> This piece of daintiness."

The drama is done—well done, we think; but there remains a dreadful dialogue yet between the Queen and the Chorus. Mr Symmons has made poetry of it—but we venture to hope that the spirit that breathes through it (the want of the divine music of the Greek versification is a sad one), may be given better in very literal prose. Let us try—sometimes at a loss.

CHORUS.

Alas! alas! O that some fate, not agonising nor couch-confining, with speed might come,—bringing upon us the endless sleep! Since now the most benignant Guardian of the State has been overpowered, and endured the last extremity from the hands of his own wife! For by his own wife hath he been murdered! Oh law-violating Helen! Who singly having destroyed many heroes innumerable lives at Troy, hast now cropped as a flower the life of the noblest of them all—the high-honoured Agamemnon, by an inexpiable, an unwashed murder!

CLYTEMNESTRA.

Do not thou, we beseech thee, overwhelmed by these things, pray for the lot of death! Neither turn thou thy wrath, we beseech thee, against Helen—because she was, as thou sayest, a man-exterminator —because singly she slew, forsooth, the lives of the Grecian heroes— because she, so sayest thou, hath caused an incomprehensible distress! Why blame, why be thus wrathful with Helen?

CHORUS.

Oh Deity! who pressest heavily upon this house, and the two descendants of Tantalus, and who confirmest in women a heart-gnawing strength, equal to that of men! But see—see like a hateful raven, lawlessly placing herself on the body, and hear how she glories hymning a strain.

CLYTEMNESTRA.

Why—now thou hast rectified the judgment of thy mouth, by naming the Family Demon! the Demon of the House! For from this source the blood-licking lust is nourished in its bowels, and before that the former affliction had ceased, lo! a new blood-shedding!

CHORUS.

Assuredly thou referrest to a Demon in this house mighty and heavy in his wrath! Alas, alas, a grievous evil of destructive and insatiable fortune!—Alas, alas, by means of Jupiter, the Cause of all, the Worker of all! For what is brought about for mortals without Jupiter? Which of these things is not God-ordained? Alas, alas, O

King! O King! How shall I weep for thee! What can I say out
of a woeful heart! Thou liest in the meshes of this spider, breathing
out thy life by an unholy death! Alas, me—me! subdued by a
treacherous destiny, there thou liest on this servile couch, by means
of a two-edged weapon brandished in the hand.

CLYTEMNESTRA.

Thou assertest that this deed is mine. But do not affirm . . . . . .
that I am the wife of Agamemnon! The ancient grim Fury of Atreus,
that stern banqueter, impersonating the wife of him that lies dead,
she hath punished him—sacrificing over the young a full-grown victim!

CHORUS.

But that you are sackless of this murder who shall testify? How?
How? The Fury, indeed, sprung from his father may have been a
fellow-helper! Black Discord constrains them by the kindred afflux
of blood ; whither also advancing, Black Discord shall give them over
to an offspring-devouring horror. Alas, alas, O King, O King!

CLYTEMNESTRA.

Methinks that he met with a death not unbecoming a freeman.
He did not, indeed, inflict mischief on this house in a guileful manner—no, not he; but then my fair Branch sprung from him—my
much-wept Iphigenia—having used her unworthily—why, let him
not, now that he has received a worthy recompense, vaunt exultingly !
Let him not exult, having expiated, by a sword-inflicted death, the
deed which he was the first to do—the sacrifice of my Iphigenia !

CHORUS.

I am at a loss—being deprived of judgment—how I shall turn my
kindly cares—for this house is falling around me into ruin. But I
dread—I dread the house-shaking, blood-covered rattling of the
tempest ! For the sprinkling drop by drop ceases ; and Fate, for
some other matter of vengeance, is sharpening retribution on other
whetstones !

SEMICHORUS.

Alas! Earth! Earth ! Oh that thou hadst received me, before I
had looked upon this Man, now occupying the earth-lying couch of
the silver-sided bath! Who shall bury him ? Who lament him ?
Wilt thou dare to do this, having slain thy own husband ?
Wilt thou dare to bewail his spirit, and for a dreadful deed unjustly
to perform an ungrateful service ? Ungrateful to the murdered !
Alas! alas! Who, pouring out with tears a funeral eulogium on
the godlike man, shall mourn in truthfulness of soul ?

CLYTEMNESTRA.

It suits *you* not to speak of this concern! By *our* hand he fell-—
he died. And we will bury him—not with family-lamentations—
but Iphigenia, his daughter, shall cordially, as she ought, meet her
father at the swift-flowing Ferry of Sorrows, and folding him in her
arms, shall kiss her father! Ha! ha!

CHORUS.

This reproach springs from a former reproach ; but all is mystery.
She—Iphigenia—cuts him off who cut her off—the Slayer *drees* his
weird. But it remains that she, the other Perpetrator, should suffer
in Jove's destined time. For who could expel from the house this
devoted family? Are they not all glued and fastened to one another,
and to calamity?

CLYTEMNESTRA.

The Divine Decree hath justly fallen on this Man. Look at him !
My wish, then, is to frame a Covenant with the Demon of the Plis-
thenidæ ; and though difficult to be borne, yet to bear all these
things! As to what remains, let the Demon depart and afflict
another family with self-inflicted death. Provided I have but a
small portion of the possessions, it is quite enough for me—having
driven from the house mutual-murdering madnesses!

Ægisthus now appears for the first time, and it seems to
have been the aim of Æschylus to make him as contemptible
as was consistent with the laws of the drama. He vindicates
the murder, on the score of the horrid conduct of Agamemnon's father Atreus to his (Ægisthus') father Thyestes—the
old story of the stewed children. He therefore calls himself
" righteous executioner."

> "I have my wrongs too, like my wretched sire,
>   For I was with him when he took to flight,
>   And all his children follow'd at his back,
>   Thirteen in number. I, the youngest, was
>   Then in my swaddling-clothes, a child in arms,
>   Not conscious of the horrors of that day ;
>   But I grew up, and Dikè rear'd my head,
>   And brought me home : though exiled, I was near.
>   Revolving curiously each means of death,
>   And all the phantoms of the assassin's soul ;
>   And I have gall'd him : now, if it is my fate,
>   Why, let me die : I cannot fall disgraced.
>   Now I have seen him wrapt in Dikè's toils."

The Chorus, however, cannot stomach this argument—which might perhaps have availed a nobler man—and they threaten him with an evil end.

> "Sure as thou livest, I say, thou shalt not 'scape
> The volleys of the people, stony showers,
> And their just curses, hurled at thy head!"

The Chorus then upbraids him with having had the villany to plot, without the courage with his own hand to perpetrate, the murder. But there Ægisthus has him on the hip—for he cries vauntingly,—

> " Why, you dull fool ! 'twas stratagem and guile !
> And who so fit as Woman for the plot ?
> 'Twould have marr'd all had I but shown my face ;
> I must have been suspected as his foe,
> His ancient, old, hereditary foe.
> But now 'tis done, and I am at my ease !
> I'll take his treasures, and I'll mount his throne."

He then, after the fashion of usurpers, threatens to scourge, imprison, and kill all who are disobedient, and especially the Chorus. But the Chorus is not to be intimidated in the discharge of his duty, and keeps satirising the coward to such a pitch of virulence, threatening to call in armed people to kill the cowardly murderer of the king, that but for the interposition of Clytemnestra, we suspect the old gentleman would have bit the dust. Clytemnestra is now the most merciful of murderesses, and glides purring round about her prey like a satiated tigress. How sweet!

> " Stay, stay, *dearest Ægisthus !* stay thy hands !
> Let's not do further harm. Behold, here lies
> A wretched harvest which we have to reap!
> We have had enough of woe ! *Let's not be bloody !*
> But go, old men ! repair unto your homes
> Before aught happens ! 'Twas the Time and Fate
> That made us act e'en so as we have acted :
> But with the deed sufficient has been done !
> And we are plunged, alas ! full deep in woe,
> Struck by the demon in his horrid rage."

The Chorus takes the hint, and departs—muttering something about—Orestes.

CLYTEMNESTRA (*to Ægisthus.*)

' Think nought of these vain barkings : Sin and I
Will take the rule, the sceptre, and the might,
And order all things in this house aright."

[*Exeunt Omnes.*

The drama, then, ends well—*happily*—and some persons
may object to it on that score, who wish always " to assert
eternal Providence, and justify the ways of God to man."
But in the first place, remember that it is a Greek tragedy,
and what Milton says of Fate. Æschylus lived before the
Christian era some hundred years, and the wisest men held
then strange doctrines about Jove.

But, secondly, though the last words that fall from the lips
of Clymnestra are,

" And order all things in this house aright,"

we have our own doubts about her being able to accomplish
her household plans. We question if she were perfectly
happy that night in the arms of her paramour. Who knows
but that she walked about the palace in her sleep, wringing,
as if washing her hands, like another great sinner, and muttering, " Out, damned spot ! " Sleep has a very sensitive conscience. Somnus is as good as a Chorus, and the moment an
atrocious criminal shuts his or her eyes, the inner kingdom
undergoes a reform, which certainly is revolution. You are
wrong, then, in saying, that the tragedy ended happily—for
Clytemnestra—hanged herself !

Hanged herself ! Shocking ! But 'tis not mentioned in
my Lemprière. Well, then, she did not hang herself ; but a
beautiful young man, almost a boy, a mere lad, cut her throat,
and haggled her body into pieces. Her own Son ! and that
was retribution. An eye for an eye—a tooth for a tooth—
blood for blood. 'Tis a law as old as the hills—and often has
the fulfilment of the law made the hills blush red, without
the aid of the setting sun. Rivers of gore have run down
their sides, and all the trees round about been like purple
beeches, from the spray of such ghastly waterfalls. Yes ! as
one of our own dramatists says,

" The element of water moistens the earth,
But blood flies upwards, and bedews the heavens ! "

What think ye was really the character of Clytemnestra ?

Did her hatred of her husband originate in the sacrifice of Iphigenia? Perhaps. No mother can endure to see her daughter
killed "like a kid," by her own father, even on the altar. But
we fear that her hatred of her husband grew out of her love for
her paramour—not the reverse process. The adulteress longed
to be a murderess. The two characters are kindred and congenial—and walk hand in hand. Besides, ten years is a long
absence—and many are the trials and temptations of a lone
" widow-woman." Ægisthus was probably the finest man-
animal in Argos—nay, in all Greece. And know you the
full force of —— infatuation? Then—are you a miserable
man or woman—and beware !

But all this throws but faint light on the darkness of the
mystery of that guilt. The secret to be told is the constitution of Clytemnestra's own soul. Thoughts that entered there
changed their colour. Some waxed wondrous pale, and others
grew fiery red—some were mute and sullen, others hissed like
serpents—and some roared like very thunder, rolling all round
the horizon with multiplying echoes, and then dying on the
far distance like an earthquake.

But whatever was the constitution of her soul, her conduct
was magnanimous. It showed her soul was—large. It could
hold a prodigious sum of wickedness. It was like one of the
Cauldrons of the Bullers of Buchan. They, you know, are
not only always black, but always boiling ; and the reason is,
that day and night the abysses are disturbed by the sea. The
sea will not let them rest in peace—but fills them, whether
they will or no, with perpetual foam—everlasting breakers—
an eternal surf. In the calmest day, the lull itself is dreadful ; yet is the place not without its beauty, and all the world
confesses that it is sublime.

This is impressive, you say, but vague. Ay—vague enough
—dim and dismal—and so is Sin. But we beg leave to say
something more definite. Issuing from her Palace, to give
orders that the whole city should be set ablaze with sacrificial
fires, Clytemnestra looked every inch a Queen. Her figure
dilated almost to gigantic height—yet still "grace was in
all her steps." Her face was fierce but fair—bold but bright
—for was she not the sister of Helen ? Stately stood she, as
Juno's self, and glorious exceedingly were the white wavings
of her arms, as she described the " Fires that drew their line-

age from Mount Ida;" the Poetess of the Burning Beacons.
Never was sovereign so bid hail as Agamemnon, on his
return to Argos, by her whose words flowed richer than the
purple robes she bade be strewed beneath the victorious feet
of her lord the king. As she followed him into the palace,
she was—was she not, a magnificent Erinnys? See her with
haughty head encircled with scorn and fire, frowning fear and
fright upon the soul of Cassandra, then awakened to the
doom of death! Imagine the Fury with uplifted axe—and
then, with brain-beaten forehead, her victim falling, a Groan,
at her feet beside the Bloody Bath. Won't you believe her
own word? See her then sprinkling herself with her husband's blood, as with the dewdrops of the sunny morning.
Then down on your knees before her, as red from the sacrifice
she issues forth exultingly into the light of day, before her
own palace—for now it is her own, in the heart of·her own
Argos—for now she is indeed a Queen, in presence of the
Chorus, who, you know, are the representatives of Humanity
—with the dim axe cresting her crown, and justifying the
deed, with her "I did it!"—and then say if she be not a
more glorious being far than mortal eyes have beheld before
or since—and that but one being ever lived on earth who
might have personated the fateful Phantom,—who else but—
nay, do not start at "the change that comes o'er the spirit of
my dream"—who else but SARAH SIDDONS?

And have we not a single word to say for Cassandra? Not
one. Yet methinks there is one yet alive who might once
have well personated the raving Prophetess. Beautiful must
have looked the captive Princess, in her car, mute and motionless as a statue, during all that kind but cruel colloquy
between Clytemnestra, Agamemnon, and the Chorus, that
determined the fate of the King, and of her his bosom-slave,
by the fate of war. Yet, though Agamemnon enjoyed what
was refused to Apollo, in soul Cassandra was still a virgin.
But when Apollo overshadowed her, and her soul awoke to all
those sights of blood, then fell down from its holy fillet all
that bright length of sun-loved hair, and shrouded her fragile
form in the mystery of madness, dishevelled in harmony with
the music that wailed from her inspired lips! Never was
madness so disastrous and so divine as hers—Poetess, Priestess, and Prophetess—raging and raving with the God. And

when in the act of flinging away all her secret adornments, that they might not be profaned by the gushing of her own blood, how piteously must she have implored the Chorus only for their compassion! And when turning to take one last look of the Day, of the Sun-God, who had turned towards her with passion, and was shining now on her dying day, who would have resembled the delirious victim on the threshold of the Palace of Blood—who but she who was so beauteous as Juliet, on the Balcony and in the Tomb—who but THE O'NEILL ?

Agamemnon we saw but for a shortest hour—a glorious tree doomed to fall in a moment axe-stricken by the woods-woman, with all its shade and sunshine, leaving a gap in the sky. Never saw we but one man who looked on the stage like the "King of Men." Well would the Grecian regal robes have become his majestic form,—well would that noble face—though haply 'twas more of the "Antique Roman's" than the Greek's—have shed its mild and monarchical light over Queen, Cassandra, Chorus—all Argos ! Who might have adumbrated Agamemnon the Sovereign Shadow—who but—KEMBLE ?

Who, the Chorus? There have been persons who thought the Chorus a blot on the Greek Drama ! ! They would have washed it out—or cut out the piece—and left a hole in the veil. Others have called it an encumbrance—a drag. It is precisely such an encumbrance as a man's soul is to his body. But let us not allude to fools. The Chorus in the *Agamemnon* is a noble character. He keeps to the affair in hand, as if he were himself the chief actor ; yet he is never too forward—and on the wished-for opening of his lips you hear " the still sad music of humanity ! " Who shall be the Chorus ? We must have fifteen elderly gentlemen. Let Oxford, Cambridge, The Silent Sister, Edinburgh, Aberdeen—each send Three Professors—and then let Christopher North be appointed THE CHORAGUS OF THE CHORAGI. But alas ! Kemble sleeps—The Siddons " has stooped her anointed head as low as death ; " The O'Neill " in the blaze of her fame," fell down into private life, and in among all its obscure virtues ; so, how now, alas ! shall we ever be able to *get up* the *Agamemnon ?*

Let it remain, then, for ever, an unacted Drama. But what forbids that it be acted—on that private stage which every man may behold nightly, free of all expense—in the Theatre of his own Imagination? There is the glorious Greek—there is the no less glorious English. Look at the words—and 'tis as into a magic mirror. The curtain is drawn up—and lo! Siddons as Clytemnestra! O'Neill as Cassandra! Kemble as Agamemnon!—and Christopher North as Choragus of Choragi! Hear him!

CHRISTOPHER NORTH AS CHORAGUS OF CHORAGI.

But Justice sheds her peerless ray
In low-roof'd sheds of humble swain,
And gilds the smoky cots where low-bred virtue dwells:
    But with averted eyes
    The Maiden Goddess flies,
The gorgeous Halls of State, sprinkled with gold,
Where filthy-handed Mammon dwells;
She will not praise what men adore,
Wealth sicklied with false pallid ore,
Though drest in pomp of haughty power,
But still leads all things on, and looks to the last hour.

END OF VOL. VIII.

PRINTED BY WILLIAM BLACKWOOD AND SONS, EDINBURGH.

MESSRS BLACKWOOD & SONS'

PUBLICATIONS.

SECOND EDITION.

Narrative of the Earl of Elgin's Mission to China and Japan.

By LAURENCE OLIPHANT,
Private Secretary to Lord Elgin.

Illustrated with numerous Engravings in Chromo - Lithography, Maps, and Engravings on Wood, from Original Drawings and Photographs.

In Two Volumes Octavo, price £2, 2s.

St Stephen's: A Poem.

Originally published in *Blackwood's Magazine.*

This Poem is intended to give succinct Sketches of our principal Parliamentary Orators, commencing with the origin of Parliamentary Oratory (in the Civil Wars), and closing with the late Sir Robert Peel.

Foolscap Octavo, price 5s.

Conquest and Colonisation in North Africa;

Being the substance of a Series of Letters from Algeria published in the *Times*, and now by permission collected. With INTRODUCTION and SUPPLEMENT, containing the most recent French and other Information on Morocco.

By GEORGE WINGROVE COOKE,
Author of " China in 1857-1858."

Crown Octavo, with a Map, price 5s.

Fleets and Navies.

By Captain CHARLES HAMLEY, R.M.

Originally published in *Blackwood's Magazine.*

Crown Octavo.

Complete Library Edition of Sir Edward Bulwer Lytton's Novels.

In Volumes of a convenient and handsome form. Printed from a large read-able type. Published monthly, price 5s. per Volume. Vols. I. to V. are published.

" It is of the handiest of sizes ; the paper is good ; and the type, which seems to be new, is very clear and beautiful. There are no pictures. The whole charm of the presentment of the volume consists in its handiness, and the tempting clearness and beauty of the type, which almost converts into a pleasure the mere act of following the printer's lines, and leaves the author's mind free to exert its unobstructed force upon the reader."—*Examiner.*

" Nothing could be better as to size, type, paper, and general getting up. The Bulwer Novels will range on the same shelf with the Scott Novels ; and appearing, as these two series will do, together, and in a mode tempting readers, old and young, to go through them once again for pleasure and profit, will inevitably lead to comparison of the genius, the invention, the worldly knowledge, and artistic skill of the great Scottish and English writers."—*Athenæum.*

New General Atlas.
Keith Johnston's Royal Atlas of Modern Geography.

Part V., now published, contains—

AUSTRIAN EMPIRE, Western Sheet, comprising Austria Proper, the Tyrol, Bohemia, Venetia, &c.

AUSTRIAN EMPIRE, Eastern Sheet— Hungary, Galicia, Transylvania, the Servian Woiwodschafts, and the Banat of Temes, Slavonia, and the Military Frontier.

NEW SOUTH WALES, SOUTH AUSTRALIA, & VICTORIA.

OCEANIA, WESTERN AUSTRALIA, TASMANIA, & NEW ZEALAND.

WEST INDIA ISLANDS & CENTRAL AMERICA.

This Atlas will be completed in Ten Parts, price 10s. 6d. each, and will form a handsome portable Volume, size 20×13½ inches, consisting of a series of 48 original and authentic Maps, constructed by ALEX. KEITH JOHNSTON, F.R.G.S., Author of the "Physical Atlas," &c., and beautifully engraved and coloured in the finest style by W. & A. K. JOHNSTON, with a Special Index to each Map.

A Cruise in Japanese Waters.

By Captain SHERARD OSBORN, C.B.,

Author of " Leaves from an Arctic Journal," " Quedah," &c.

A New Edition. Crown Octavo, price 5s.

" The fascination of this strange country was undoubtedly great, for it is transferred to every page of Captain Osborn's narrative."—*The Times.*

" One of the most charming little books that for many a day we have had the good fortune to peruse."—*Literary Gazette.*

" One lays down the book with an irresistible desire to pack up all one has and start at once for Japan."—*Evening Herald.*

" In reading many pages of this book we almost feel that the action of the events is proceeding before us. . . . . . There is not a dull or uninteresting line in the book."—*Morning Herald*

Lays of the Scottish Cavaliers, and other Poems.

By W. EDMONDSTOUNE AYTOUN, D.C.L.,
Professor of Rhetoric and Belles-Lettres in the University of Edinburgh.

Twelfth Edition, price 7s. 6d.

"Mr Aytoun's *Lays* are truly beautiful, and are perfect poems of their class, pregnant with fire, with patriotic ardour, with loyal zeal, with exquisite pathos, with noble passion. Who can hear the opening lines descriptive of Edinburgh after the great battle of Flodden, and not feel that the minstrel's soul has caught the genuine inspiration?"—*Morning Post.*

Bothwell: A Dramatic Poem.

By the same Author.

Third Edition, price 7s. 6d.

The Ballads of Scotland.

Edited by Professor AYTOUN.

Second Edition. Two Volumes, price 12s.

"No country can boast of a richer collection of Ballads than Scotland, and no Editor for these Ballads could be found more accomplished than Professor Aytoun. He has sent forth two beautiful volumes which range with *Percy's Reliques*—which, for completeness and accuracy, leave little to be desired—which must henceforth be considered as the standard edition of the Scottish Ballads, and which we commend as a model to any among ourselves who may think of doing like service to the English Ballads."—*The Times.*

Firmilian: or, The Student of Badajoz.

A SPASMODIC TRAGEDY.

Price 6s.

"Without doubt, whether we regard it as a satire or as a complete drama, *Firmilian* is one of the most finished poems of the day. Unity is preserved, and the intensity of the 'spasmodic' energy thrown into the narrative carries the reader through every page, while the graces of poetic fancy, and the touches of deep thought scattered throughout, challenge comparison with selections from the most modern poems."—*Liverpool Albion.*

The Book of Ballads.

Edited by BON GAULTIER.

Fifth Edition, with numerous Illustrations by DOYLE, LEECH, and CROWQUILL.

Gilt edges, price 8s. 6d.

Poems and Ballads of Goethe.

Translated by Professor AYTOUN and THEODORE MARTIN.

Second Edition, price 6s.

"There is no doubt that these are the best translations of Goethe's marvellously-cut gems which have yet been published."—*The Times.*

The Poems of Felicia Hemans.

Complete in One Volume, Royal Octavo, with portrait by Finden, price 21s.

ANOTHER EDITION, with MEMOIR by her SISTER, Seven Vols., Foolscap, 35s.

ANOTHER EDITION, in Six Vols., cloth, gilt edges, 24s.

"Of no modern writer can it be affirmed with less hesitation, that she has become an English classic; nor, until human nature becomes very different from what it now is, can we imagine the least probability that the music of her lays will cease to soothe the ear, or the beauty of her sentiment to charm the gentle heart."

The following Works of Mrs HEMANS are sold separately, bound in cloth, gilt edges, price 4s. each :—

RECORDS OF WOMAN.
FOREST SANCTUARY.
SONGS OF THE AFFECTIONS.
DRAMATIC WORKS.
TALES AND HISTORIC SCENES.
MORAL AND RELIGIOUS POEMS.

The Course of Time : A Poem.

By ROBERT POLLOK, A.M.

An Illustrated Edition, in Square Octavo, bound in cloth, richly gilt, £1, 1s.

"There has been no modern poem in the English language, of the class to which the 'Course of Time' belongs, since Milton wrote, that can be compared to it. In the present instance the artistic talents of Messrs FOSTER, CLAYTON, TENNIEL, EVANS, DALZIEL, GREEN, and WOODS, have been employed in giving expression to the sublimity of the language, by equally exquisite illustrations, all of which are of the highest class."—*Bell's Messenger.*

ANOTHER EDITION, being the Twenty-second, in Foolscap Octavo, price 7s. 6d.

The Poetical Works of D. M. Moir (Delta).

Including "Domestic Verses," and Life by THOMAS AIRD, and a Portrait. Two Volumes, Foolscap Octavo, price 14s.

Works of Professor Wilson.

Edited by his SON-IN-LAW, Professor FERRIER.

In Twelve Vols., Crown Octavo, price £3, 12s.

The following are sold separately :—

NOCTES AMBROSIANÆ. Four Vols. 24s.
ESSAYS, CRITICAL AND IMAGINATIVE. Four Vols. 24s.
RECREATIONS OF CHRISTOPHER NORTH. Two Vols. 12s.
TALES. One Vol. 6s.
POEMS. One Vol. 6s.

Works of Samuel Warren, D.C.L.

Uniform Edition, Five Vols., price 24s.

The following are sold separately :—

DIARY OF A PHYSICIAN. 5s. 6d.
TEN THOUSAND A YEAR. Two Vols. 9s.
NOW AND THEN. 2s. 6d.
MISCELLANIES. 5s.

Works of Thomas M'Crie, D.D.

Edited by his SON, Professor M'CRIE.

Uniform Edition, in Four Vols., Crown Octavo, price 24s.

The following are sold separately, viz.—

LIFE OF JOHN KNOX. 6s.
LIFE OF ANDREW MELVILLE. 6s.
HISTORY OF THE REFORMATION IN ITALY. 4s.
HISTORY OF THE REFORMATION IN SPAIN. 3s. 6d.
REVIEW OF "TALES OF MY LANDLORD," AND SERMONS. 6s.

Curran and his Contemporaries.

By CHARLES PHILLIPS, Esq., A.B.

A New Edition, Crown Octavo, price 7s. 6d.

"Certainly one of the most extraordinary pieces of biography ever produced. . . . No library should be without it."—*Lord Brougham.*
"Never, perhaps, was there a more curious collection of portraits crowded before into the same canvass."—*Times.*

Life of John, Duke of Marlborough.

WITH SOME ACCOUNT OF HIS CONTEMPORARIES.

By Sir ARCHIBALD ALISON, Bart., D.C.L.

Third Edition, Two Vols., Octavo, Portrait and Maps, 30s.

Tales from "Blackwood."

Publishing in Monthly Numbers, price 6d., and in Volumes Quarterly, price
1s. 6d., bound in cloth.

The Volumes published contain—

VOL. I.   The Glenmutchkin Railway.—Vanderdecken's Message Home.—The Floating
Beacon.—Colonna the Painter.—Napoleon.—A Legend of Gibraltar.—The Iron Shroud.

VOL. II.   Lazaro's Legacy.—A Story without a Tail.—Faustus and Queen Elizabeth.
—How I became a Yeoman.—Devereux Hall.—The Metempsychosis.—College Theatricals.

VOL. III.   A Reading Party in the Long Vacation.—Father Tom and the Pope.—La
Petite Madelaine.—Bob Burke's Duel with Ensign Brady.—The Headsman : A Tale of
Doom.—The Wearyful Woman.

VOL. IV.   How I stood for the Dreepdaily Burghs. — First and Last. — The Duke's
Dilemma : A Chronicle of Nieseustein.—The Old Gentleman's Teetotum.—"Woe to us
when we lose the Watery Wall."—My College Friends : Charles Russell, the Gentleman
Commoner.—The Magic Lay of the One-Horse Chay.

VOL. V.   Adventures in Texas.—How we got Possession of the Tuileries.—Captain
Paton's Lament.—The Village Doctor.—A Singular Letter from Southern Africa.

VOL. VI.   My Friend the Dutchman.—My College Friends—No. II. : Horace Leicester.
—The Emerald Studs. — My College Friends — No. III. : Mr W. Wellington Hurst.—
Christine : A Dutch Story.—The Man in the Bell.

VOL. VII.   My English Acquaintance.—The Murderer's Last Night. — Narration of
Certain Uncommon Things that did formerly happen to Me, Herbert Willis, B.D.—The
Wags.—The Wet Wooing : A Narrative of '98.—Ben-na-Groich.

VOL. VIII.   The Surveyor's Tale. By Professor Aytonn.—The Forrest-Race Romance.
—Di Vasari : A Tale of Florence.—Sigismund Fatello.—The Boxes.

Adam Bede.

By GEORGE ELIOT.

Seventh Edition.   Two Vols., Foolscap Octavo, price 12s.

Scenes of Clerical Life.

THE SAD FORTUNES OF AMOS BARTON—MR GILFIL'S LOVE STORY—
JANET'S REPENTANCE.

By GEORGE ELIOT.

Second Edition.   Two Vols., Foolscap Octavo, price 12s.

The Mill on the Floss.

By GEORGE ELIOT,
Author of "Scenes of Clerical Life," and "Adam Bede."

In Three Volumes, price £1, 11s. 6d.

Salmon-Casts and Stray Shots :

BEING FLY-LEAVES FROM THE NOTE-BOOK OF JOHN COLQUHOUN,
Author of the "Moor and the Loch," &c.

Second Edition, Foolscap, 5s.

What will he do with it?

By PISISTRATUS CAXTON.

Originally published in *Blackwood's Magazine*.

Four Volumes, Post Octavo, price £2, 2s.

Lady Lee's Widowhood.

By Lieut.-Col. E. B. HAMLEY.

Third Edition. With Engravings. Crown Octavo, price 6s.

"A quiet humour—an easy, graceful style—a deep though confident knowledge of human nature in its better and more degrading aspects—a delicate and exquisite appreciation of womanly character—an admirable faculty of description, and great tact—are the qualities that command the reader's interest and respect from beginning to end."— *The Times.*

The Athelings; or, The Three Gifts.

By Mrs OLIPHANT.

Three Volumes, Post Octavo, price £1, 11s. 6d.

"It is quite charming. The beginning is perfect, and may rank with any picture of an interior that we know. In *The Athelings* Mrs Oliphant exercises with the greatest success her talent for picture-painting. There is not a stroke or a shade too much or too little. A sweeter story than *The Athelings*, or one more beautifully written, we have not seen for many a long day."—*Globe.*

Zaidee: A Romance.

By the same Author.

Three Volumes, Post Octavo, price £1, 11s. 6d.

Katie Stewart: A True Story.

By the same Author.

Second Edition, Foolscap, price 6s.

The Quiet Heart.

By the same Author.

Second Edition, Post Octavo, price 10s. 6d.

Cheap Editions of Popular Works.

LIGHTS AND SHADOWS OF SCOTTISH LIFE. Foolscap 8vo, 3s. cloth.

THE TRIALS OF MARGARET LYNDSAY. By the Author of "Lights and Shadows of Scottish Life." Foolscap 8vo, 3s. cloth.

THE FORESTERS. By the Author of "Lights and Shadows of Scottish Life." Foolscap 8vo, 3s. cloth.

TOM CRINGLE'S LOG. Complete in One Volume, Foolscap 8vo, 4s. cloth.

THE CRUISE OF THE MIDGE. By the Author of "Tom Cringle's Log." In One Volume, Foolscap 8vo, 4s. cloth.

THE LIFE OF MANSIE WAUCH, TAILOR IN DALKEITH. Foolscap 8vo, 3s. cloth.

THE SUBALTERN. By the Author of "The Chelsea Pensioners." Foolscap 8vo, 3s. cloth.

PENINSULAR SCENES AND SKETCHES. By the Author of "The Student of Salamanca." Foolscap 8vo, 3s. cloth.

NIGHTS AT MESS, SIR FRIZZLE PUMPKIN, AND OTHER TALES. Fcap 8vo, 3s. cloth.

THE YOUTH AND MANHOOD OF CYRIL THORNTON. By the Author of "Men and Manners in America." Foolscap 8vo, 4s. cloth.

VALERIUS: A ROMAN STORY. Foolscap 8vo, 3s. cloth.

REGINALD DALTON. By the Author of "Valerius." Foolscap 8vo, 4s. cloth.

SOME PASSAGES IN THE LIFE OF ADAM BLAIR, AND HISTORY OF MATTHEW WALD. By the Author of "Valerius." Foolscap 8vo, 4s. cloth.

ANNALS OF THE PARISH, AND AYRSHIRE LEGATEES. By John Galt. Foolscap 8vo, 4s. cloth.

SIR ANDREW WYLIE. By John Galt. Foolscap 8vo, 4s. cloth.

THE PROVOST, AND OTHER TALES. By John Galt. Foolscap 8vo, 4s. cloth.

THE ENTAIL. By John Galt. Foolscap 8vo, 4s. cloth.

LIFE IN THE FAR WEST. By G. F. Ruxton. A New Edition. Fcap 8vo, 4s. cl.

The Sketcher.

By the Rev. JOHN EAGLES, A.M., Oxon.

Originally published in *Blackwood's Magazine*.

In Post Octavo, price 10s. 6d.

"There is an earnest and vigorous thought about them, a genial and healthy tone of feeling, and a flowing and frequently eloquent style of language, that make this book one of the most pleasant companions that you can take with you, if you are bound for the woodland or pastoral scenery of rural England, especially if you go to study the picturesque, whether as an observer or as an artist."

Essays.

By the Rev. JOHN EAGLES, A.M., Oxon.

Originally published in *Blackwood's Magazine*.

Post Octavo, 10s. 6d.

Contents—

Church Music, and other Parochials—Medical Attendance, and other Parochials—A few Hours at Hampton Court—Grandfathers and Grandchildren—Sitting for a Portrait—Are there not great Boasters among us?—Temperance and Teetotal Societies—Thackeray's Lectures : Swift—The Crystal Palace—Civilisation : the Census—The Beggar's Legacy.

Thorndale : or, The Conflict of Opinions.

By WILLIAM SMITH,

Author of " A Discourse on Ethics," &c.

A New Edition, Crown Octavo, price 10s. 6d.

" More literary gems could be picked from this than almost any recent volume we know. It is a repository of select thoughts—the fruit of much reflection, much reading, and many years."—*Scotsman.*

" It is long since we have met with a more remarkable or worthy book. Mr Smith is always thoughtful and suggestive. He has been entirely successful in carrying out his wish to produce a volume, in reading which, a thoughtful man will often pause with his finger between the leaves, and muse upon what he has read. We judge that the book must have been written slowly, and at intervals, from its affluence of beautiful thought. No mind could have turned off such material with the equable flow of a stream. We know few works in which there may be found so many fine thoughts, light-bringing illustrations, and happy turns of expression, to invite the reader's pencil."—*Fraser's Magazine.*

Lectures on Metaphysics.

By Sir WILLIAM HAMILTON, Bart.

Edited by the Rev. H. L. MANSEL, B.D., and JOHN VEITCH, A.M.

In Two Vols., Octavo, price 24s.

Institutes of Metaphysic :

THE THEORY OF KNOWING AND BEING.

By JAMES F. FERRIER, A.B., Oxon.,

Professor of Moral Philosophy and Political Economy, St Andrews.

Second Edition, Crown Octavo, 10s. 6d.

Diversities of Faults in Christian Believers.

By the Very Rev. E. B. RAMSAY, M.A., F.R.S.E.,
Dean of the Diocese of Edinburgh.

In Foolscap Octavo, price 4s. 6d.

Diversities of Christian Character.

Illustrated in the Lives of the Four great Apostles.

By the same Author.

Uniform with the above, price 4s. 6d.

Religion in Common Life:

A Sermon preached in Crathie Church, October 14, 1855, before Her
Majesty the Queen and Prince Albert. Published by Her Majesty's
Command.

By the Rev. JOHN CAIRD, D.D.

Bound in cloth, 8d. Cheap Edition, 3d.

Sermons.

By the Rev. JOHN CAIRD, D.D.,
Minister of West Park Church, Glasgow.

In Post Octavo, price 7s. 6d.

Prayers for Social and Family Worship.

Prepared by a Committee of the General Assembly of the Church of
Scotland, and specially designed for the use of Soldiers, Sailors,
Colonists, Sojourners in India, and other Persons, at Home or
Abroad, who are deprived of the Ordinary Services of a Christian
Ministry. Published by Authority of the Committee.

In Crown Octavo, bound in cloth, price 4s.

Prayers for Social and Family Worship.

Being a Cheap Edition of the above.

Price 1s. 6d.

Theism:

THE WITNESS OF REASON AND NATURE TO AN ALL-WISE AND
BENEFICENT CREATOR.—(BURNETT PRIZE TREATISE.)

By the Rev. J. TULLOCH, D.D.,
Principal, and Primarius Professor of Theology, St Mary's College,
St Andrews.

Crown Octavo, 10s. 6d.

Lives of the Queens of Scotland,

AND ENGLISH PRINCESSES CONNECTED WITH THE REGAL SUCCESSION.

By AGNES STRICKLAND.

With Portraits and Historical Vignettes. Complete in Eight Vols., price £4, 4s.

History of Europe,

FROM THE COMMENCEMENT OF THE FRENCH REVOLUTION TO THE BATTLE OF WATERLOO.

By Sir ARCHIBALD ALISON, Bart., D.C.L.

A New Edition of the Library Edition is in the Press.
Crown Octavo Edition, 20 vols., price £6.
People's Edition, 12 vols., double cols., £2, 8s. ; and Index Vol., 3s.

The History of Europe,

FROM THE FALL OF NAPOLEON TO THE ACCESSION OF LOUIS NAPOLEON.

By Sir ARCHIBALD ALISON, Bart., D.C.L.

Complete in Nine Vols., price £6, 7s. 6d.   Uniform with the Library Edition of the Author's "History of Europe, from the Commencement of the French Revolution."

Atlas to Alison's History of Europe;

Containing 109 Maps and Plans of Countries, Battles, Sieges, and Sea-Fights. Constructed by A. KEITH JOHNSTON, F.R.S.E. With Vocabulary of Military and Marine Terms.

Library Edition, £3, 3s. ; People's Edition, £1, 11s. 6d.

History of Greece under Foreign Domination.

By GEORGE FINLAY, LL.D., Athens.

Five Volumes Octavo—viz. :

Greece under the Romans. B.C. 146 to A.D. 717. A Historical View of the condition of the Greek Nation from its Conquest by the Romans until the Extinction of the Roman Power in the East. Second Edition, 16s.

History of the Byzantine Empire. A.D. 716 to 1204 ; and of the Greek Empire of Nicæa and Constantinople, A.D. 1204 to 1453. Two Volumes, £1, 7s. 6d.

Mediæval Greece and Trebizond. The History of Greece, from its Conquest by the Crusaders to its Conquest by the Turks, A.D. 1204 to 1566 ; and History of the Empire of Trebizond, A.D. 1204 to 1461. Price 12s.

Greece under Othoman and Venetian Domination. A.D. 1453 to 1821. Price 10s. 6d.

"His book is worthy to take its place among the remarkable works on Greek history, which form one of the chief glories of English scholarship. The history of Greece is but half told without it."—*London Guardian.*

"His work is therefore learned and profound. It throws a flood of light upon an important though obscure portion of Grecian history. . . . In the essential requisites of fidelity, accuracy, and learning, Mr Finlay bears a favourable comparison with any historical writer of our day."—*North American Review.*

The Eighteen Christian Centuries.

By the Rev. JAMES WHITE.

Third Edition, with Analytical Table of Contents, and a Copious Index. Post Octavo, price 7s. 6d.

" He goes to work upon the only true principle, and produces a picture that at once satisfies truth, arrests the memory, and fills the imagination. When they (Index and Analytical Contents) are supplied, it will be difficult to lay hands on any book of the kind more useful and more entertaining."—*Times*, Review of first edition.

" At once the most picturesque and the most informing volume on Modern History to which the general reader could be referred."—*Nonconformist*.

" His faculty for distinguishing the wheat from the chaff, and of rejecting the useless rubbish, while leaving no stray grain unsifted, makes the 'Eighteen Christian Centuries' an invaluable manual alike to the old and young reader."—*Globe*.

" Mr White comes to the assistance of those who would know something of the history of the Eighteen Christian Centuries ; and those who want to know still more than he gives them, will find that he has perfected a plan which catches the attention, and fixes the distinctive feature of each century in the memory."—*Wesleyan Times*.

History of France,

FROM THE EARLIEST PERIOD TO THE YEAR 1848.

By the Rev. JAMES WHITE,
Author of the " Eighteen Christian Centuries."

Post Octavo, price 9s.

" Mr White's 'History of France,' in a single volume of some 600 pages, contains every leading incident worth the telling, and abounds in word-painting whereof a paragraph has often as much active life in it as one of those inch-square etchings of the great Callot, in which may be clearly seen whole armies contending in bloody arbitrament, and as many incidents of battle as may be gazed at in the miles of canvass in the military picture-galleries at Versailles."—*Athenæum*.

" An excellent and comprehensive compendium of French history, quite above the standard of a school-book, and particularly well adapted for the libraries of literary institutions."—*National Review*.

" We have in this volume the history of France told rapidly and distinctly by a narrator who has fancy and judgment to assist him in seizing rightly and presenting in the most effective manner both the main incidents of his tale and the main principles involved in them. Mr White is, in our time, the only writer of short histories, or summaries of history, that may be read for pleasure as well as instruction, that are not less true for being told in an effective way, and that give equal pleasure to the cultivated and to the uncultivated reader."—*Examiner*.

Leaders of the Reformation:

LUTHER, CALVIN, LATIMER, AND KNOX.

By the Rev. JOHN TULLOCH, D.D.,
Principal, and Primarius Professor of Theology, St Mary's College, St Andrews.

Crown Octavo, price 5s.

" We are not acquainted with any work in which so much solid information upon the leading aspects of the great Reformation is presented in so well-packed and pleasing a form."—*Witness*.

" The idea was excellent, and most ably has it been executed. Each Essay is a lesson in sound thinking as well as in good writing. The deliberate perusal of the volume will be an exercise for which all, whether young or old, will be the better. The book is erudite, and throughout marked by great independence of thought. We very highly prize the publication."—*British Standard*.

" We cannot but congratulate both Dr Tulloch and the university of which he is so prominent a member on this evidence of returning life in Presbyterian thought It seems as though the chains of an outgrown Puritanism were at last falling from the limbs of Scotch theology. There is a width of sympathy and a power of writing in this little volume which fills us with great expectation. We trust that Dr Tulloch will consider it as being merely the basis of a more complete and erudite inquiry."—*Literary Gazette*.

" The style is admirable in force and in pathos, and the book one to be altogether recommended, both for the merits of those of whom it treats, and for that which the writer unconsciously reveals of his own character."—*Globe*.

The Chemistry of Common Life.

By Professor JOHNSTON.

A New Edition, Edited by G. H. LEWES.

Illustrated with numerous Engravings. In Two Vols., Foolscap, price 11s. 6d.

The Physiology of Common Life.

By GEORGE H. LEWES.

Illustrated with numerous Engravings. Two Vols., 12s.

Contents— Hunger and Thirst.—Food and Drink.—Digestion and Indigestion.—The Structure and Uses of the Blood.—The Circulation.—Respiration and Suffocation.—Why we are Warm, and how we keep so.—Feeling and Thinking.—The Mind and the Brain.—Our Senses and Sensations.—Sleep and Dreams.—The Qualities we Inherit from our Parents.—Life and Death.

Sea-Side Studies.

By GEORGE HENRY LEWES,
Author of "Physiology of Common Life," &c.

Second Edition, Illustrated with Engravings, price 6s. 6d.

The Physical Atlas of Natural Phenomena.

By ALEX. KEITH JOHNSTON, F.R.S.E., &c.,
Geographer to the Queen for Scotland.

A New and Enlarged Edition, consisting of 35 Folio Plates, 27 smaller ones, printed in Colours, with 135 pages of Letterpress, and Index.

Imperial Folio, half-bound morocco, £12, 12s.

Atlas of Astronomy.

A complete Series of Illustrations of the Heavenly Bodies, drawn with the greatest care from Original and Authentic Documents, and printed in Colours by Alex. Keith Johnston.

Edited by J. R. HIND.

Imperial Quarto, half-bound morocco, 21s.

The Geology of Pennsylvania.

A Government Survey; with a General View of the GEOLOGY OF THE UNITED STATES, Essays on the Coal-Formation and its Fossils, and a Description of the Coal-Fields of North America and Great Britain.

By Professor HENRY DARWIN ROGERS, F.R.S., F.G.S., Professor of Natural History in the University of Glasgow.

With Seven large Maps, and numerous Illustrations engraved on Copper and on Wood. In Three Volumes, Royal Quarto, £8, 8s.

Introductory Text-Book of Geology.

By DAVID PAGE, F.G.S.

Third Edition, with Engravings. In Crown Octavo, price 1s. 6d.

" It has not been often our good fortune to examine a text-book on science of which we could express an opinion so entirely favourable as we are enabled to do of Mr Page's little work."—*Athenæum.*

Advanced Text-Book of Geology,

DESCRIPTIVE AND INDUSTRIAL.

By DAVID PAGE, F.G.S.

Second Edition, enlarged, with numerous Engravings, 6s.

"An admirable book on Geology. It is from no invidious desire to underrate other works—it is the simple expression of justice, which causes us to assign to Mr Page's *Advanced Text-Book* the very first place among geological works addressed to students, at least among those which have come before us. We have read every word of it, with care and with delight, never hesitating as to its meaning, never detecting the omission of anything needful in a popular and succinct exposition of a rich and varied subject."— *Leader.*

" It is therefore with unfeigned pleasure that we record our appreciation of his *Advanced Text-Book of Geology.* We have carefully read this truly satisfactory book, and do not hesitate to say that it is an excellent compendium of the great facts of Geology, and written in a truthful and philosophic spirit."— *Edinburgh Philosophical Journal.*

"We know of no introduction containing a larger amount of information in the same space, and which we could more cordially recommend to the geological student."—*Athenæum.*

Handbook of Geological Terms and Geology.

By DAVID PAGE, F.G.S.

In Crown Octavo, price 6s.

" 'To the student, miner, engineer, architect, agriculturist, and others, who may have occasion to deal with geological facts, and yet who might not be inclined to turn up half a dozen volumes, or go through a course of geological readings for an explanation of the term in question,' Mr Page has carried out his object with the most complete success. His book amply fulfils the promise contained in its title, constituting a handbook not only of geological terms but of the science of geology. It will not only be absolutely indispensable to the student, but will be invaluable as a complete and handy book of reference even to the advanced geologist."—*Literary Gazette.*

" There is no more earnest living practical worker in geology than Mr David Page. To his excellent *Introductory Text-Book of Geology* and his *Advanced Text-Book of Geology, Descriptive and Industrial,* he has now added an admirable system of geological terms, with ample and clearly written explanatory notices, such as all geological observers, whether they are able professors and distinguished lecturers, or mere inquirers upon the threshold of the science, must find to be of the highest value."—*Practical Mechanics' Journal*

" But Mr Page's work is very much more than simply a translation of the language of Geology into plain English; it is a Dictionary, in which not only the meaning of the words is given, but also a clear and concise account of all that is most remarkable and worth knowing in the objects which the words are designed to express. In doing this he has chiefly kept in view the requirements of the general reader, but at the same time adding such details as will render the volume an acceptable Handbook to the student and professed geologist."—*The Press.*

The Book of the Farm.

By HENRY STEPHENS, F.R.S.E.

A New Edition.   In Two Volumes, large Octavo, with upwards of 600 Engravings, price £3, half-bound.

"The best practical book I have ever met with."—*Professor Johnston.*
"One of the completest works on agriculture of which our literature can boast."—*Agricultural Gazette.*

Book of Farm Implements and Machines.

By JAMES SLIGHT and R. SCOTT BURN.

Edited by HENRY STEPHENS, F.R.S.E.

Illustrated with 876 Engravings.   One large Volume, uniform with the "Book of the Farm," price £2, 2s.

"The author has omitted, most judiciously, those machines not now used, and he has confined himself to those in actual operation, thereby rendering a great service to the agricultural mind, which is liable to confusion in cases of much complication. Some of the machines described are commended, and deserve the commendation; others, on the contrary, are condemned, and it would seem with equal justice : but the character of all is stated distinctly. . . . . Full, complete, and perfect in all its parts ; honestly compiled, and skilfully illustrated with numerous and valuable engravings and diagrams, it is not saying too much to state that there is no parallel to this important work in any country of Europe, and that its value to the agriculturist is almost incalculable."—*Observer.*

The Book of the Garden.

By CHARLES M'INTOSH.

In Two large Volumes, Royal Octavo, published separately.

VOL. I.—On the Formation of Gardens—Construction, Heating, and Ventilation of Fruit and Plant-Houses, Pits, Frames, and other Garden Structures, with Practical Details. Illustrated by 1073 Engravings, pp. 776.   Price £2, 10s.
VOL. II.—PRACTICAL GARDENING contains: Directions for the Culture of the Kitchen Garden, the Hardy-Fruit Garden, the Forcing Garden, and Flower Garden, including Fruit and Plant Houses, with Select Lists of Vegetables, Fruits, and Plants. Pp. 868, with 279 Engravings.   Price £1, 17s. 6d.

The Year-Book of Agricultural Facts.

Edited by R. SCOTT BURN.

In Foolscap Octavo, price 5s.

A Handy Book on Property Law.

By LORD ST LEONARDS.

A New Edition, enlarged, with Index, Crown Octavo, price 3s. 6d.

" Less than 200 pages serve to arm us with the ordinary precautions to which we should attend in selling, buying, mortgaging, leasing, settling, and devising estates.   We are informed of our relations to our property, to our wives and children, and of our liabilities as trustees or executors, in a little book for the million, a book which the author tenders to the *profanum vulgus* as even capable of ' beguiling a few hours in a railway carriage.'" —*The Times.*

Works of Professor J. F. W. Johnston.

A Catechism of Agricultural Chemistry and Geology. 1s.

Elements of Agricultural Chemistry and Geology. 6s. 6d.

Instructions for the Analysis of Soils, Minerals, Manures, &c. 3s.

On the Use of Lime in Agriculture. 6s.

Experimental Agriculture. 8s.

Notes on North America—
AGRICULTURAL, ECONOMICAL, AND SOCIAL.
Two Volumes, Post Octavo, 21s.

Rural Economy of England, Scotland, and Ireland.

By LEONCE DE LAVERGNE.

Translated from the French. With Notes by a Scottish Farmer.

Octavo, price 12s.

The Architecture of the Farm.

A SERIES OF DESIGNS FOR FARM HOUSES, FARM STEADINGS, FACTORS' HOUSES, AND COTTAGES.

By JOHN STARFORTH, Architect.

Sixty-two Engravings. Medium Quarto, price £2, 2s.

Catechism of Practical Agriculture.

By HENRY STEPHENS, F.R.S.E.,
Author of the "Book of the Farm."

With Numerous Engravings on Wood, price 1s.

Stable Economy.

A TREATISE ON THE MANAGEMENT OF HORSES.

By JOHN STEWART, V.S.

Sixth Edition, Foolscap, price 6s. 6d.

Handbook of the Mechanical Arts

CONCERNED IN THE CONSTRUCTION AND ARRANGEMENT OF DWELLINGS AND OTHER BUILDINGS;

Including Carpentry, Smith-work, Iron-framing, Brick-making, Columns, Cements, Well-sinking, Enclosing of Land, Road-making, &c.

BY ROBERT SCOTT BURN,
One of the Authors of the "Book of Farm Implements and Machines."

Crown Octavo, Illustrated with 504 Engravings on Wood, price 6s. 6d.

IN THE PRESS.

———◆———

In Two Volumes, price 24s.,

LECTURES ON LOGIC.
By SIR WILLIAM HAMILTON, Bart.
Edited by the Rev. H. L. MANSEL, B.D.,
and JOHN VEITCH, A.M.

LECTURES ON THE HISTORY OF THE CHURCH OF SCOTLAND.
By the Late Rev. JOHN LEE, D.D., LL.D.,
Principal of the University of Edinburgh.

In Two Volumes, Octavo.

THE BOOK OF FARM BUILDINGS:
THEIR ARRANGEMENT AND CONSTRUCTION.
By HENRY STEPHENS, F.R.S.E., & R. SCOTT BURN.
In large Octavo, with numerous Engravings.

A Third Edition, enlarged, of

THE FORESTER.
A PRACTICAL TREATISE ON THE FORMATION OF PLANTATIONS, THE
PLANTING, REARING, AND MANAGEMENT OF FOREST TREES, ETC.
By JAMES BROWN,
Wood-Manager, Grantown, Strathspey.

AN INQUIRY INTO THE NATURE AND CAUSE OF THE PREVAILING DISEASE AND PRESENT CONDITION OF THE LARCH PLANTATIONS IN GREAT BRITAIN.
By CHARLES M'INTOSH,
Associate of the Linnæan Society, &c. &c.